THE TRILOGY: KATHRYN'S BEACH HIGH TIDE STORM SURGE

NADINE LAMAN

Arizona USA

THE TRILOGY:
KATHRYN'S BEACH, HIGH TIDE, STORM SURGE

25th Anniversary Edition

Copyright © February 05, 2025 by NADINE LAMAN
All Rights Reserved. Copyrights enforced.

First Edition.

ALL RIGHTS RESERVED BY THE AUTHOR. No part of this book may be reproduced or transmitted in any format or by any means, including scanning into a data base or use by Artificial Intelligence (in part or in full), without written permission of the author – with an actual ink signature, NOT a digital signature. Rights use requested are logged by the author. Purchasers of this book do not purchase any rights of use other than to read for their own enjoyment and cannot assign any rights. NO ONE may scan this book in full or in part. For permission to use requests: Nadine@CactusRainPublishing.com.

This is a work of fiction. Names, characters, places, and incidents are fictitious or are used fictitiously. Any perceived resemblance to actual persons, living or dead, business establishments, events, or locales is false. A few family and friends wanted cameo roles in this adventure or to name characters, they have read and given approval of those items. This work was written completely by a human.

Proofreader: Anita Beery
Cover Design by Nadine Laman
Cover Photo Seal Beach, California, USA, by Nadine Laman

ISBN 978-1-947646-14-8

Published by Cactus Rain Publishing, LLC, San Tan Valley, Arizona, USA
Published February 14, 2025
Originally Printed in the United States of America

~ Dedication ~

To Charley Lawrence Laman
and our sons,
Sean Russell James Laman,
Maitiu Ioseph Lawrence Laman,
Tomas Andrew Lambert Laman

~~~

To my mentors:
Dr. Lois Johnson, Ilene Shrimplin Wood,
Jeannine Garsee, Janice Laman Zitek,
Judith McKee, and Ellen Lyon.

~~~

In affectionate memory of:
Julia Marquis, Governor Joan Finney,
Jean M. Flynn, G. Irene Unruh,
Irene Watson, and Karen Stewart.

~~~

A humble "thank you" to
Gladys Knight and Rhonda Holman,
two women who inspired me
and touched my heart and soul.

~~~

To Ann Zimmerman
for permission to use her lyrics.

~~~

To those who have profoundly come into my life,
you know who you are.
~~~

Kathryn's Beach

It isn't how long one lives,
it is how wide that really matters.

~ CHAPTER 1 ~

Enigma

"And you?" he asks. "What about you?"

"Oh, I don't know. Someone called me an enigma once."

Quickly, I pour a highball, hoping to appear disinterested in the conversation.

He stirs on his barstool, turning to look directly at me and squints his small middle-aged eyes through the bar's dim light.

"Enigma?" he queries with a tone of renewed curiosity.

Smoke from his cigarette curls above his head, then floats lazily into the light hanging from the ceiling. Carelessly he flicks his ashes in the direction of the ashtray. He doesn't notice or doesn't care that the ashes miss their mark and fall on the bar. It's a lazy kind of evening with no real purpose, like most of the nights before it and those in the foreseeable future.

The smoke works its way toward the light a second time. I watch it as I wonder why I have given him such a truthful answer. Silently, I admonish myself for letting my guard slip with this man who ordinarily wouldn't be an intellectual match for me.

"Yeah." I smile with a slight laugh to cover my previously mistaken honesty. "I had to look it up, then still wasn't sure it was a compliment."

I laugh again, take a step back, adding some distance between us. Moving away from him is only a symbolic gesture, but I make it anyway. It's a reminder to keep my wits about me. It seems I need reminders more often these days, and even then, he slipped by my defenses. Before I noticed, we were into the wrong conversation.

To escape further, I plunge the last two dirty beer glasses, one in each hand, up and down on the glass brushes at the bottom of the sink. The activity and renewed frothy beer-scented suds tranquilize my mind.

He watches me work as he swirls the last of the drink in his glass. "Well, was it?" He shoots back the question with a serious tone. While drinking most of the amber liquid in one large swallow, he eyes me for an answer.

As I take another step back my heel catches on the rubber mat. Why am I so clumsy? Once, long ago, I was a model of confidence in and out of the courtroom, but not now.

On the floor near the sink a stowaway lime wedge catches my attention. Thankfully, to cover my clumsiness with the mat, I scoop up the exiled garnish and smoothly deposit it in the trash bin.

Still not sure of the answer, I wipe the counter, weighing the best reply. I need an answer that isn't too serious and certainly not too revealing. Quickly, I sort through possible responses while continuing my distancing act. Think, think, I pressure myself. Turning away, I wipe the back bar with a bar towel. I don't want to get engaged in a personal conversation with him, or anyone else.

Slowly turning, I say in a matter-of-fact tone, “Yes. Yes, it was a compliment.”

Briefly, I look straight into his eyes, then attend to wiping the beer taps one more time.

A lie? No, it’s true. It is a compliment, but it wasn't meant to be when it was said.

Shrugging off the memory, I continue to work. As I wash the last of the bar utensils, my thoughts hurl me back in time. I remember the moment I was called an enigma. I remember being hurt by the tone of the word. I remember feeling my face grow hot and my eyes water with the sting of the insult. I was younger then and had hoped to please, though now, I wonder why conforming had been so important.

He finishes the last half-swallow of his drink and sets the glass on the bar with the tenor of finality. The sound hangs in the thick air. He stirs, hesitates, then slides off his barstool. He pulls out three or four wadded bills from the front pocket of his jeans, sorts through them, then tosses a crumpled bill next to his empty glass.

“Catch you later,” he says.

Glancing toward the door, then back to me, he slips on his coat and ball cap with a seed company logo on it. After a final adjustment of his cap to secure it against the wind, he opens the door and goes out.

Dropping my towel on the bar, I hurry to lock the door behind him. Finally! I draw a deep breath and sigh with relief to be alone.

This is an odd little town. It’s stuck in the time of post-WWII days. Very little has changed and isn’t likely to change any time soon. To look at it, the town is charming. Ancient oak and elm trees line the sidewalks with their branches touching above the street to create a green, shady archway.

Autumn blazes with color, then blows into piles behind the shed. In the winter everything has a covering of snow that shimmers in the sunlight. Spring comes, goes, then comes again to stay, but is gone all too soon to be replaced by summer’s waves of heat. Then the cycle repeats to mark yet another year’s passing like the rings inside a tree, and we become a year older.

There are stately stone mansions that were built after the Civil War by those who came to town with carpetbags full of money. Most of the other houses are white wooden structures with black-trimmed windows and a modest porch, all remnants of the railroad town it was originally. The railroad and the interstate highway bypassed the town two generations ago. A tree grows through the window of the abandoned train station as a reminder that those days will never return.

The town is picture-postcard pretty. But the people aren't pretty. Life has been especially hard for them through the years of the Dust Bowl and the droughts. It shows on their faces and in their walk. Farming isn't easy, but they love it. When the winter wheat sprouts, everyone drives slower simply to admire the wonder of it and hope for a good covering of snow.

The only other thing they love is gossip. These people live for gossip as if an addiction. They accept it as they accept thunderstorms and tornadoes. They know its sting, but seek a fix every chance they get. Like every other addiction, it cuts deep into relationships and scars them for all time.

Moving to a small, rural town is a careful, dangerous dance. Soon after my arrival, I observed firsthand gossip's sting. The townspeople usually didn't keep the facts straight even when they did know the truth. In time, I made the extra effort to remain uninteresting. They could, and would (and often did) say what they wanted to say about me, an outsider.

Even years later outsiders are still only outsiders. They can never be elevated to the status of being one of the locals; they are never quite allowed to belong in this place. Besides gossip there isn't much entertainment in this town of 1,523 people—gossip is about all they have.

Despite the summer heat, they congregate on the bleachers down at the ballpark, gossiping while watching the games or on front porches along the railing, the steps, and the porch swing—gossiping.

In the winter the people gather in Rex's Diner on Main Street for breakfast, and here, Ruthie's Bar, later in the day to talk about each other, about the absent locals, and especially about the outsiders.

Occasionally the gossip is innocent, but usually it's just plain mean. Sometimes it seems the meaner, the better. The face of the informant lights up with a surge of power they hold over the listeners. It's a fleeting moment until their face hardens with the spirit of their hurtful words. Then their audience tries to outdo them with their own moment in the spotlight.

Expertly, I have managed to keep my private life private. I stay out of political arguments. There is little discussion of religion since there are only two churches in town. I never mentioned that I am Catholic because everyone here is either Baptist or Methodist. I drive to the next county to attend Mass.

Just last Easter a bunch of Methodists became Baptists overnight when the Methodist Bishop sent a woman minister into their midst. As it turns out, she is a nice person—but no matter, they will run her out of town before next Easter.

My best defense became turning the conversation away from me and on to farming. They didn't know where I was from, but they knew I needed educated on farming. I could write a book about what I have heard from my side of the bar. It would be a bestseller, with the gossip.

With an approving nod I compliment myself that I have escaped once more. Luckily, I timed my response to his question just right, avoiding a conversation about me.

"Besides," I say aloud, "bartenders listen to people talk about their lives, not the other way around."

I shake my head, thinking about this place. It's becoming more difficult to maintain my reclusive lifestyle. I long for friendships and maybe even a romance. Real relationships elude me, leaving the re-emerging desires for intimate connections unanswered.

Of all the choices of places to go, I am not certain why I came here. At the time, where didn't matter. I came to escape from life, my life. Like the corporate executives who started cottage industries in Vermont to escape their rat race, I am taking a break from the real world.

On rare instances, I admit being amused by my introduction to rural living. There is a strange wholesomeness about rural America. Nevertheless, this is an odd refuge, an unlikely choice considering who I once was and who these people are. My observations of how they treat each other only prove that we have nothing in common and I don't belong here. I'm becoming lonely—terribly, terribly lonely.

Straightening the barstools and restocking the liquor, I'm deep in thought about what I left behind in Los Angeles: my work, my friends and family, my beach, and my comfortable life. Memories play like a movie trailer in my mind. The scenes hook me and I want more. I want to experience the story and escape into it, buttered popcorn and all.

Despite the overwhelming flood of emotions churning inside me, I return to the nightly ritual of closing the bar. After removing his ashtray and wiping the ring of ashes left on the counter, all that remains is to close the cash register tape and count the money.

Tonight my mind won't allow idle thoughts; it continues to demand an awakening of memories I abandoned five years ago. I had driven aimlessly for days. When I arrived here, I simply couldn't go any farther. I was emotionally exhausted. By the time I stopped driving, I was a shell of my former self.

Suddenly, five years seems like a long time. I am urgently restless. Why have I stayed so long?

"Okay, Katey. It's time to go home," I say aloud, as I adjust the thermostat for the night, and walk around the room shutting off the lights. Standing by the door, ready to shut off the last light, I look back at the buzzing neon beer advertisements dimly lighting the pool table. Decisively I admit, "It is time to go back to the world where I belong; back to my real life."

Securing the door, the deadbolt clicks sluggishly from the cold. Slipping the key in my pocket, I pull up my coat collar, and tighten the scarf around my neck and across my face to keep the cutting cold from taking my breath away and burning my skin. My gloves barely make a difference. The cold sneaks up my sleeve before I can put my hands in my pockets.

With the wind chill below zero again tonight, I feel tired of winter. The ambient temperature has not been above freezing for more than three weeks, and the wind chill makes it all the more inhospitable. A blast of night-wind cuts through my scarf with a stinging that burns my cheeks. It makes me eager to get home, to my real home in L.A.

After snowing all day, the previously shoveled sidewalk is covered with six inches of new snow. The bar is only two blocks from my apartment and it is easier to walk than to drive in this weather, especially after the ice storm we had yesterday.

Tonight's walk home is different. For five years my routine has never varied. I have had no plan to my days except to work at the bar. But now my mind is planning the trip home. It's strangely refreshing to plan something meaningful, especially like being where I belong.

I begin to carefully ascend the icy incline toward my apartment. The street I live on is up the first block of the hill, then right for half a block, and walk up the alley. It is a slow ascent. My steps are unreliable when the unanchored snow gives way from the ice beneath it. Racing thoughts deep inside me add to the difficulty to concentrate. Inching up the incline, I grab for the metal railing along the sidewalk.

Pausing at the corner I turn and look down the street behind me. The snow goes over my shoes and sticks to the top of my socks. Distracted for a minute by the wet cold soaking my ankles as the warmth of my body melts the snow, I shake the snow from my shoes —wishing I had taken my bigger boots to work this afternoon. It's a mute thought now.

Looking into the night, there is an eerie quiet. Even the wind isn't making the sounds one would expect. I look back at the bar at the foot of the hill, down on Main Street. It looks alone in the cold dark—if a building can look any particular way.

"Lonely buildings? I have lost all sense of reality. Reality, Katey! Reality? Now there is a concept foreign to my life."

With that, I resume inching the slope toward my apartment. The fat snowflakes fall lazily from the dark heaven. Stopping midway across the street, I look around in the crisp night air. The Christmas-movie snow reflects the moonlight, making it easy to see well, while increasing the sharp contrast between the snow and the night shadows.

Considering my feelings toward the meanness of these gossiping people, it is still a pretty town. My glance settles on an old house someone is restoring to the Grand Old Victorian era. It has dentil and gingerbread trim. It's painted like a paint store advertisement. Painted Ladies are what they call the bright mix of contrasting colors. It looks out of place next to the plain white houses up and down the street. As with many of the things here, it is all a façade.

It is obvious by the architecture (littlebalconies outside of each bedroom's window) this house was originally a bordello. I surprise myself when I laugh out loud. It is so quiet this time of night that my laugh echoes against the buildings along the empty street. It embarrasses me that I have made such a noise.

Stepping up the curb to the sidewalk, I grasp the railing to steady my step. The incline is steeper on this side of the street. My knit glove sticks to the frosty metal handrail.

"It's cold out here, quit being so smug and go home," I admonish myself under my breath and begin to walk more deliberately. Pay attention, Katey, or you will roll down this icy hill.

My focus doesn't last. It would be quite a sight when they chisel me out of the ice at the bottom of the hill. I laugh again visualizing the American Gothic people cutting me out of a block of frozen snow and ice. Wait, no! They would leave me, discussing my situation, but not wanting to get involved.

Despite the pity I feel toward these people and their petty ways, they do amuse me. The few of us who are outsiders probably amuse them with our other-world ways.

"Katey, you're talking to yourself entirely too much." The realization startles me. "Oh, Katey!" I sigh. "Go home!"

I carefully walk up the ice-crusted wooden stairs to my two-room apartment above the garage. In an effort to regain control of them, I begin to organize my thoughts. Go to bed. Tomorrow, start packing.

Heaped with blankets, I lay listening to the snowflakes, now frozen into ice crystals, softly pelting against the window. It feels good to make a decision. In reality, I haven't put much thought into the decision to go home, though now I grasp it firmly. I desperately own it.

There is no escape from the daunting presence of the memories. What do I hope to gain by going home? I don't know. But, then again, there is nothing to gain by staying here.

The rafters creak when the wind gusts. The steady sound of the wind driving the sleet against the window eventually lulls me to sleep.

~~~

In the morning, I lay in bed listening to the sound of ice cracking and falling through the frozen tree limbs, crashing to the hard ground below. Obviously, the sun has been up for hours, for the ice on the higher limbs of the trees to begin to melt. There is no real hurry to get out of bed, so I snuggle deeper under the blankets and listen to the winter sounds until I am fully awake. Slowly I realize I had the best night's sleep I have had for a very long time. No nightmares.

The next few days my mind is remembering more and more about the home I left, thoughts that I haven't had for years. I miss the pleasant weather, the familiar freeways, my friends, and the comforting sense of belonging—at the beach and with my family.

The bar provides a constant supply of boxes. Selectively, I watch for good ones to take home. The few cooking pans I have go into the thrift store box along with other less-used kitchen items. I didn't bring many things with me when I came, only what I tossed into my car. Perhaps I brought too much emotional baggage. But I will deal with that later.

The only thing left for me to do before I leave is work through the holidays while Ruthie visits her grandchildren in St. Louis. I have no holiday plans, so I'll wait to go home in January.

The patrons' activities at the bar never change from day-to-day. But Ruthie takes on an alternate personality during the holidays. Beginning before Thanksgiving, each time she leaves the bar to run an errand, she returns with her arms full of bags of Christmas decorations.

Even though Ruthie does this every year, it never ceases to amaze me. Her decorations multiply exponentially. They're everywhere, from the oddly shaped Santa on the inside of the front door that erupts into an off-pitch electronic version of eight different Christmas songs every time the door opens to the plastic snowman lights hanging precariously from the light fixture above the pool table.

I have never known any one person to own so many Christmas lights. She has the usual blinking lights, chasing lights, icicle lights, in addition to red chili pepper lights, tiny angel lights, and plastic reindeer lights that insist on hanging upside down no matter what Ruthie does to right them. Lights are strung on the juke box, the walls, around the beer glass shelves, the pool cue rack, the restroom doors, and beyond. By Christmas the bar looks like the Las Vegas Strip. She even found a battery-operated blinking bow tie for me to wear on New Year's Eve. Oh, lovely.

Amidst the chaos of Ruthie's all-out eclectic version of Christmas decorating, my packing goes quickly and effortlessly. Most of the things
~~~

I acquired during my time here land in the thrift store boxes. There are only a few boxes to ship home to my cousin Ilene. Shortly, I can give away my winter clothes.

I hate winter.

~~~

After New Year's Day I ship my boxes to California, purchase an airline ticket home, and arrange to sell my car with the delivery date set for the morning I leave. Perhaps for a little post-holiday cash I can convince someone to take me to the airport in Lincoln. Everything is settled. Soon I will be on my way home. I've been here entirely too long.

As usual, it takes the whole first week and a half of January to get Ruthie's lights down and packed in boxes. When Raymond came into the bar Ruthie talked him into helping move the boxes to the attic. While he was in the mood to be helpful, I asked him to if he would give me a ride to the airport. Actually, it took more cash than talk to get the ride, but there is no shuttle service out here—so I pay up.

Finally, the day to leave arrives. As a traveling companion, Raymond isn't the best choice. His conversation is anything but stimulating. In addition to the periods of silence from my driver, he has the radio tuned to the monotone AM station's farm report.

The news of hog futures and wheat prices fade into the background noise of my mind while I think of the life waiting in L.A.

The five-hour car ride to the airport seems to last for days. We get behind a slow-moving farm vehicle with a huge round bale of alfalfa completely filling the bed of the truck. We can't see around nor go around him since the two-lane road has only three ruts in the hard-packed snow.

For months the snow plows have piled the snow at the sides of the road until the endless mound on either side is above the top of our pickup cab. In essence, we are driving 35 mph through a topless white tunnel, staring at the butt-end of a bale of alfalfa. At the "T" in the road, the truck ahead turns right while we skid left toward the next one-horse town, then eventually to the interstate leading to Lincoln.

~~~

In contrast to the road trip, the airline seat caresses me. There are no farm reports to be heard, and for that I am thankful. I have never felt more relieved than I feel now. Committed. Ready.

After the usual delays, the air rushes out the little spout above my head, the engine sounds accelerate, followed by a backwards lurch as the tow vehicle begins to push the plane from the gate. Taxi, another wait, then the rush down the runway pavement, incremented by expansion joints, and the anticipated leap into the sky. With it, my spirit leaps.

It isn't long before we are flying west over the Platte River. This is where the cranes nest? I didn't get around to seeing the annual migration. But now I am on my own migration, I whisper to myself, as I look out of the oval window at the wide river basin below. Just like the birds, I am driven by instinct to go home.

As the plane makes its final approach to the new Denver airport, the dim silhouette of the city appears far in the distance and the snow-covered mountains rise in the west beyond the city. The snow is falling thicker as we approach the ground. The sun's descent behind the Rockies is beautiful. A few hours past those mountains and I will be home. There is only a short delay scheduled as we change planes for the next leg of the journey.

Unfortunately, just as we prepare to board our connecting flight to Los Angeles, we are told it's canceled. The planes can't de-ice fast enough to get airborne. As a matter of fact, the snow plows can't keep up with the windblown snowdrifts across the runways—the airport is now closed.

"What! Closed?" I ask the person beside me in line to make sure I understood correctly.

Several other travelers with a deer-in-the-headlights stare nod affirmatively to my question.

The information seems true. Flights in or out of the Denver airport are canceled. Furthermore, all of the hotels near the airport have been full for hours, reports an airline spokesperson. It hardly seems worth the long bus trip to Denver for a short night's stay.

Some stranded travelers are visibly frustrated, and a few spew their anger at the gate staff. Certainly, it must be true, the staff caused the storm as part of a conspiracy against the passengers. I smile to myself at the thought of such reasoning.

Like many of the other passengers, I decide to stay in the terminal and sleep across several seats near the gate until we can get airborne.

~~~

In the morning, as the terminal comes to life, I wake with an airline blanket covering me. Someone must have come during the night and laid one over each of us.

Sitting up, I look around wondering if the person who had been so thoughtful is still nearby. No one seems to be watching us for a sign of appreciation for the deed. It leaves me with an uneasy feeling—I don't like being in debt. Not to anyone. Not ever.

Watching people come and go, I sit at the gate for a long time thinking about going home. These past five years my world has been narrow and solitary. It's a defense mechanism, no doubt, but in L.A. all of that will have to change.
~~~

Maybe the layover in Denver has been good. In the airport the transition back to L.A. doesn't seem as easy as it did in the empty bar. I needed this time.

My thoughts overwhelm me. I feel frustrated. A sense of panic rushes over me and I begin to wish for the security of a plan—a definite, concrete plan. I desperately wish for a traveling companion to tell me everything will be all right.

Grandmother's words come to the forefront of my thoughts. In the way only grandmothers can, mine would smile, tilt her head and say, "If wishes were horses, beggars would ride; if turnips were watches, I'd have one by my side..."

Irish women of her vintage were on a first-name basis with hardship. The memory of her words is enough to stop my whining. I straighten in my chair, searching for new resolve.

The wind and snow subsided during the night, allowing the snow plows to liberate the runways. In a language distinctive to airport public address systems, a voice not meant for such purposes announces our plane is ready for departure.

"My plane," I whisper while joining the line forming at the jetway entrance. Despite any uncertainty about going home, I am relieved to be on my way. I vow never to leave again. I am tired of being an outsider, especially with no hope of acceptance.

As the plane lifts from the runway and climbs, it lurches in response to turbulent weather above us. Another winter storm is brewing over the Rockies. The land disappears below, and I am glad to see the snow and ice go out of sight.

We jerk in our seats with each bout of turbulence. There's a loud, sudden thud, then metallic crash from the galley as a soda can hits the floor and rolls against the cabinet. Startled outbursts and excited half-whispers from passengers follow the decidedly abrupt "bump in the road" as the plane lifts straight up.

A terrified baby cries, followed by whimpering, then sucking sounds. A young female voice from behind me hums softly, soothingly. Soon the sucking sound becomes more rhythmic and less desperate. Within minutes the baby takes a deep breath and begins to breathe as if it is asleep.

~~~

I don't mind the storm. I am determined to ignore the pain from my body jerking against the seat belt across my lap. This is nothing compared to what I have been through. I can take turbulence.

Rising into the clouds, the sky disappears from view. Glued to the window, I stare at the wings, watching the pattern the moisture makes as it rushes over them. It's good to see moisture rather than ice on the
~~~

wings, but I am not sure I would care about ice as long as we continue to fly west.

The plane breaks through to the top of the clouds where the sun is bright above us. To crowd out the chill of winter, I lean toward the window and soak in every ray of sunlight.

By the time our plane reaches L.A. I am beginning to thaw. But there is still a deeper chill in my bones.

~~~
~~~

~ CHAPTER 2 ~

Home, Sweet Home

Among the crowd waiting for our luggage at LAX, reality is a lot different from my imagining of how this would play out once the plane landed. I don't know what I was thinking, but my plan only went as far as getting here. Beyond that, well, I simply couldn't imagine beyond that.

None of the luggage inching down the conveyor looks familiar. Is this some kind of hidden camera joke? Next time I'll have to remember that everyone has black luggage and put a strap or something on mine. But there will be no next time. No point in it, is there? With my luggage in tow, I make the customary pilgrimage to the rental car counter.

With unexpected certainty, I pull into the traffic and decide to stop by my old office. It isn't exactly on the way home, but most of my friends are there. They are part of the importance of coming home.

Heading downtown, the mass of humanity on the freeway catches me off guard. I am glad to see the rushing, reckless traffic, but I am dangerously out of practice driving in it.

Driving someone else's car doesn't help, but at least I know my way around the area. Soon the familiar surroundings inspire my confidence and I accelerate into the fast lane. This is going to be easy, I decide, as I realize the speed with which I eased back into city traffic.

~~~

Outside the towering building, I pause to get the feel of being home. I think about my friends and wonder how many of them still work here. Maybe it is a mistake to come. I hope not. Standing in front of the door is a bad time to second-guess my decision.

With the draw of a deep breath, I pull open the heavy glass door. The comfort of familiar surroundings wraps its arms around me as I walk back into my former life. It is almost as if I am returning from a day at court rather than having been away for five years.

Things look much as I remember, typical government office decor. It is funny how something like this makes me feel good to be back. I breathe easier.

After the routine security check, the lobby receptionist waves me to her desk. She greets me enthusiastically, dispelling more of my doubts about the visit. Reaching for the phone, she winks, and motions me toward the stairs. "I'll tell them you're coming."

My step gains confidence as I start up the stairs to the inner sanctuary. In the time it takes to walk the three flights, I nearly delude
~~~

myself into thinking the last five years were a bad dream and I am coming back to the office from an investigation.

At the top of the stairs I recognize three police officers in the corridor that joins our buildings, police department and welfare department. Seeing them completes my delusion that I haven't been away long.

It feels good not to be an outsider, even though it has only been slightly over two hours since the plane landed at LAX. Coming home was long overdue. I was foolish to leave, and more foolish to remain away.

The corridor opens into the large room that is the heart of the work area. The least inconsequential thing brings comforting memories of the time I spent in this room, first as a student, then as the resident expert.

I scan the room, enjoying the solace of familiarity. Groups of desks are crowded around the perimeter. The desks are situated in sets of two, facing each other to optimize the space. My old desk is among those perpendicular to the coveted wall of large, arched windows, molded with wide, dark 1920s woodwork.

Most of the people I worked with are still here. Former colleagues congregate around me. Ever so slowly, I notice how different everyone seems. It is more than their new hairstyles and five years' worth of aging. The reality of how long I have been gone creeps into my thoughts. I wonder how they see me after all this time. How much have I changed in their eyes?

In a brief time, everyone filters back to their desks. It feels awkward with no desk of my own. I should have left before the last person walked away. I wish for a dignified means of escape. It would be perfect timing if Keith walked through the corridor from the police station. I'd exit in the pretense of a conversation. Keith is the detective who was my counterpart from the other building. He was my mentor, my partner.

Unfortunately, Keith doesn't come to rescue me from the awkwardness of standing alone while everyone else is engaged in work. Still, I glance in the direction of the hallway with the hope he will come, he always had before.

Feeling lost, I look around one more time for the missing co-worker I most wanted to see. Her desk next to mine, the one that was mine, is empty. I look at our space for a minute. Disappointed with her absence, I turn toward the door to leave.

Barely catching my peripheral vision, Maggie enters at the back of the room. She stops at the coffee machine, notices me, and raises a cup in my direction as if she half expected me to be here.

Relieved to see her, I walk toward her and whisper excitedly, "Coffee?"

She pours a cup for each of us and we slip down the back stairs to our old spot on the patio at a table away from everyone where we can talk privately.

After the leafless dreariness of a Midwest winter, it's good to see green plants. The sun is soft in the winter sky. A slight breeze moves the branches of the palm trees. Just like the old days, I'm content sipping the industrial-strength coffee with Maggie.

It's good to see her. It's entirely my fault that we haven't kept in touch. Under the influence of the coffee aroma, I study her.

We met in undergraduate school, then attended grad school together. We became closer when a forced transfer brought her to our department because her department never fully recovered from Reaganomics' cuts decades before.

We reconnected our college friendship once we were working in the same department. Our paths had paralleled so many times that it was either our destiny or just plain luck that we became close friends. It was this friendship that proved priceless to me five years ago as we worked on what became my last child abuse investigation.

It's comfortable to sit in our spot, together again, after my self-imposed exile. Maggie looks really good. Her shoulder-length dark hair is in a new and very flattering style that suits her quite well. I hope I look good too, though that might be expecting too much after the overnight stop in the Denver airport.

Putting down my cup, I study her again, watching for the Maggie I knew. There! I see something familiar in her eyes. Her green eyes can go from ornery to intelligent with the tilt of her head.

It's reassuring to see my old friend again. Taking another sip of coffee, I think about our shared history. Quietly, I reminisce fondly about this place and these people, my friends. The memories are calming. Relaxed, tentative music begins to meander in my mind, soothing the five years of forced silence.

"It wasn't your fault, Kate." Maggie jumps right into the conversation.

Startled, I look up for an indication of her intent. Five years doesn't mean anything to her. Damn! She's good.

Maggie doesn't mention my abrupt departure or my sudden reappearance. She looks at me intensely as she speaks, pausing only slightly to catch a breath between sentences—leaving no chance for a response from me.

"It was a clean investigation." Maggie continues confidently, "I reread the case file. We chipped in and ordered the transcript of the trial, even Karen."

"Maybe so—" my voice trails off, still not processing that Karen had contributed.

The entire case springs to the forefront of my memory with the bitter taste of day-old coffee.

"It was all there, Kate. No one could have done better," she says in a soft, reassuring voice that echoes within me.

She's taken aim and shot right to the heart of things. I can't sidestep her volley. Court transcripts aren't cheap. Maggie hasn't given me time to process that Karen, a keen fiscal manager, had ordered it.

I'm obligated to the conversation now. There is no getting out of it.

I set my cup down and wrap my fingers around it for the warmth it provides.

"But it didn't save her," I counter.

"It was Judge Jones' ruling that was in error, not anything you did or didn't do." Her tone dares me to disagree.

"He didn't see it. He let that sick bastard go!"

My voice betrays me with its mixed tone of anger and hurt. I feel the flood of emotions rushing over me and I'm not ready to deal with the memories. Struggling to process what she is saying and wrestling with my emotions is getting the best of me.

Maggie pushes straight on.

"The night before the murder trial, Judge Jones was dead."

"Dead?" I whisper, stunned. I lean forward at the shock of it, resting my arms against the edge of the table to brace myself. I had wished him dead when he sent her home to her abuser, essentially ruling a death sentence for the little girl in my case. I didn't mean it, not literally anyway.

I don't know if it is intentional or not, but Maggie is moving too fast. I had hoped to ease back into my L.A. life, not be tossed into the deep without warning.

"He shot himself in chambers," she continues with the matter-of-fact tone of someone who has seen too much violence for her age.

"Keith said, it looked like he was reading the grand jury indictment on the murder charges against the perp in your case. Maybe he saw the horrible thing he did. Maybe he knew it would come out in the murder trial." She finally pauses. The silence hangs in the thick city air.

It's all very complicated. I don't believe for one minute he admitted his culpability—even to himself. He might have feared that I would testify, and he should have, if he didn't. I am an excellent witness. The words of my testimony would have pointed at him with benign contempt and delivered him at the feet of Lady Justice.

The only flaw in that scheme is no one knew where I was. Even if they did, the subpoena wouldn't reach that distance. They could ask, but not compel me to return. If he was afraid of me, he killed himself for nothing.

My coffee tastes bitter.

Maggie stops playing with the last of the undissolved sugar at the bottom of her cup, "And Kate, Judge Jones wrote a letter to you."

She sets her cup down and looks at me, seeming to search for an indication to the letter's content.

There are no clues for her to discover. I can't imagine why he would write to me. Maybe later I will be amused, wondering if Maggie thought there had been some sort of scandalous relationship between the Judge and me. But for now I am just as surprised about the letter as she must have been when it arrived.

Looking directly into my eyes, she continues a little softer, "Keith brought the letter by the office, hoping I knew where you were."

I make no response. She isn't going to guilt information out of me. If she wants to know about the last five years, she will have to ask outright.

But she doesn't ask. "We didn't open it. Keith said the suicide note was all the police needed."

I cock my head to the side, studying her, listening.

Maggie looks at her cup again as if trying to coax more coffee to appear. "I have it at home. We thought you should be the first to read it."

First? I catch her meaning and make a mental note she expects the letter to be shared with her. "Why would he write to me? It doesn't make sense."

Maggie looks straight into my eyes—I can't escape her gaze. I am trying to put it together as fast as she is handing out the information. I can't keep up with her. Struggling deep in thought, I realize she is saying something about dinner at her apartment.

"Oh, thanks. I can't tonight," I lie. Actually, dinner sounds good, but I am not up to more of her direct ways, at least not today.

I should have kept in touch with Maggie while I was gone, but it is too late to change that now. I'll just have to sort things out the best I can.

"Then come, and pick up the letter." Maggie can still read when I have reached my limit. "We'll have dinner some other time." She reaches for our cups, saying something about time to call it a day, then smiles.

At last this conversation is over. Knowing Maggie, I am sure this is only a temporary reprieve. When she has something to say, she will wait for her moment, then say it perfectly timed. There is never a permanent escape from her.

Maybe it had been a mistake to come to the office. No. No, it is good to see Maggie and the others. At one time Maggie, Keith, and I had been quite the team. No one in the state came near our record of closed cases or favorable court dispositions. We made sure the facts were clear and correct before we submitted the case to Karen to be sent to the District Attorney's office.

I have missed Maggie. Seeing her again is a significant part of why I came home. I was correct, I had to come here first. No other way would have felt right.

I would have liked to have seen Karen. It will be harder to come back the next time. In the end, my instincts have served me well. I had to come here before I can think about anything else.

When I reach the stairs to leave, Karen is coming up them. I quietly study her as she comes closer. She has lost about ten pounds and her hair color is a little different. Karen looks good. She is taller than I, with beautiful hazel eyes, an engaging smile, and short, dark brown hair.

There is something solid about her. She was always very classy, charming, and bright. I never wanted to be friends with Karen, I was perfectly happy with the distance afforded by our roles within the department, nothing more.

It surprises me that Karen chipped in for the transcript. It has nothing to do with money, but seems different from how I remember her.

As Karen nears the top of the stairs, she looks up. When she sees me, she smiles.

"Into my office, Kathryn," Karen says without breaking stride as she walks past me—not looking back.

Some things don't change. I smile, thinking about how natural it is to be summoned to her office.

It is good to be home.

Out of instinct I almost reply, "Yes, ma'am," as I follow her. I spent more than my share of time being reprimanded in this office. At least this time she won't lecture me to move a case along before I'm satisfied I have all of the facts. This time, she isn't my boss. This time—

"Yes, ma'am," I say for the pure enjoyment of it just as Karen shuts the wooden door. The latch, sluggish, causes the frosted glass to rattle in the dried-out putty.

She sets her briefcase and armload of files on her desk.

I stand back and wait near the door, perhaps poised for escape, then ease toward the chair in front of her desk.

Karen is always in command of her environment. It has been a long time since I felt a sense of command over my world. Life seems uncertain ever since that horrible last case. I've been lost a long time. I don't know what the rules are anymore. Someone changed them, and I didn't get the memo.

She startles me when she turns and gives me a motherly hug. It seems to fit the moment, though it wasn't her usual way. Neither of us is the hugging type—certainly not with each other.

Ours was an antagonistic relationship, to put it nicely. I was the problem employee. I never crossed the line in the process, but I wasn't afraid to come toe-to-toe with it. I questioned everything. I wanted to see all sides of the case. Most of all I didn't want to follow along mindlessly with the masses. Doing what everyone else did was the worst reason to do anything. I never bowed to pressure to close a case prematurely, not that she would have asked. But others did, and she'd hear about my mouthy reply. Usually they'd fail to mention their role in the exchange.

Until five years ago, social work was my life. I lived and breathed social work. Almost nothing else mattered, nothing except my family and the beach. I was good at my job, very good, in fact. However, I was unconventional, and that resulted in many summons to Karen's office.

Only my skill kept me from being transferred out of the department, or worse. Most of the time the results paid off and I was given absolution for my transgressions.

That was a long time ago. The hug feels good on my weary shoulders. I hope to remember this unprecedented moment, and the brief feeling of a sense of security.

"Kathryn, how are you?" she asks in a warm maternal tone unfamiliar to me. She continues before I can answer the first question. "Are you ready to get back to work?"

I can't help being amused. Is it me or are these people behaving strangely about my return?

Apparently I was more surprised with the decision to come home than they are with my arrival. I press my lips together just enough to conceal the grin that I'd rather not explain.

In the past I irreverently referred to Karen as a "Mother Superior." She was always commanding and unwavering in her opinions, only yielding to irrefutable empirical evidence. After the headaches I gave her, Karen is brave to invite me back to the department.

"I'm not sure." I hadn't expected her reception or the offer of a job. I'm not sure what I expected, but this certainly isn't it.

"Maggie told me about Judge Jones' letter," she says as she looks up from sorting her papers. She still sounds maternal, though she is busy unpacking her briefcase.

Again with the letter? The letter is nearly five years old. How could it possibly matter now?

When I think I have people figured out, they rewrite their script, and it's a whole new scene. Maybe I still have jet lag. It seems that, that—I don't know how it seems. It's confusing.

"When you are ready to read it, if you like, you can call me." She looks up and smiles, "We hated to see you leave." Without missing an opportunity, she says softly, "Kathryn, we couldn't all run away. Now that you're back we need to finish this."

Something is different now. Her ultimatums are not annoying me the way they did when she was my supervisor. I know she is right. She was always right.

"All right," I acquiesce, a bit unsure of entering into an agreement with her. Karen takes a business card from the card holder on her desk, writes on the back, then hands it to me.

She has written her personal phone number. It's a bit odd, but odd seems to be today's theme.

In the moment it takes for me to glance at the card and slip it into my jacket pocket, she starts packing the reports she is taking home to read over the weekend.

I know her weekend habit. I have seen her on the beach reading reports a million times. I went to the beach to get away from work and to clear my mind. It seemed she went there to get work done. We had nothing in common, not how cases should be managed or how to spend time on the beach.

In retrospect, she is probably a better social worker than I had given her credit. I don't know much about her, only that she left her private practice as a child psychologist in San Francisco to take the governor's appointment to head our troubled department with the mandate to straighten it out.

I know she has a master's degree in social work, as well as a Ph.D. in psychology. Somewhere I heard she graduated with honors, I don't remember the context of the conversation.

When Karen came on board with the department it was rumored that she had received numerous prestigious awards in both fields. If they exist, they are not on display in her office. It occurs to me now that other than her excessive work habits, I really don't know her after all the years of working for her.

~~~
~~~

~ CHAPTER 3 ~

Lullaby Litany

Speeding along the freeway after leaving the office, I come alive in the fast pace of the traffic. Moving across the lanes, it feels good to be unleashed again after all the time away from the city.

I love it here. I feel less confined surrounded by millions of strangers in the second largest city in the country than in a small town in the wide-open plains.

"These are my kind of trees, my gray-hazy skies, my buildings," I announce aloud, chanting to myself as the freeway loops. One last time, I look back toward the towering buildings glistening in the late afternoon sun, for a final glimpse before the interchange that sends me speeding south toward the beach.

"I love the Pacific." The litany suddenly stops.

Why was it that I left? I desperately ask myself. What did I think I could find somewhere else that I couldn't find here? And worse yet, why did I stay away so long?

The questions continue, even though I really don't want to know the answers, especially after the intensity of the visit to the office. My mind doesn't care what I want. My thoughts continue to taunt me. "What had I been thinking?" I say aloud.

That is just it. Five years ago there had been too many things to think about—all of them competing for attention. The torrents of emotion were overwhelming after years of child abuse investigations. I couldn't take it any longer. I couldn't reconcile the senseless death of an innocent child simply because the system didn't work as it should.

There was more to the emotions than a case of burnout that sent me running from the place I love. That last case was one too many. It focused all humanities' ugliness on one small child, a child I could not save.

It frightened me when I couldn't make the system work as it was meant to work. For the first time, being a good social worker was not good enough. A child died a horrible death. If my skills weren't enough, I didn't know what to do for the next child that was sure to come. The system was a lie. It was a horrible lie. I was hopelessly powerless. I left. It was that simple.

~~~

My thoughts ricochet back and forth between the past and the present. I am lost in thought when the sign for the off-ramp leading to
~~~

Maggie's condo catches my sight. Mindlessly, out of habit, I ease onto the ramp.

At the first traffic light I realize what I have done. "Katey, I guess you are going to pick up that letter whether you planned to do it tonight or not."

I can see in some ways being back in L.A. is going to be easy. I am being swept along by instinct even after all the time away.

Reality strikes in waves washing over me. Obviously, that case is still on Karen and Maggie's minds too. Karen is right. Our lives can't move forward until we move past that horrible death. Me running away trapped part of each of us in a fragmented past. We have to see this to the end, whatever that might be. It is my hope we each find peace, and that my little client found a better place than this world was for the short time she was here. Sigh.

The air is heavy to breathe. Guilt and feelings of responsibility for failing to save that little girl begin choking me into overwhelming restlessness. The tightness in my chest forces me to gasp for air. No inhaler, no source of oxygen can cure this. I break my thoughts away from the case and my emotions. I struggle to think benign thoughts.

Amazed, I wonder how long my friends would have waited for me to come back before someone opened the judge's letter. If I never came back would they have eventually opened it? I try to focus on that thought to block out the more demanding thought, thoughts that really matter. It's a draining struggle, but, for the time being, I am winning.

~~~

When she opens the door, Maggie must sense I'm not ready to continue our earlier conversation. At least not on the terms she exacts. She hands me the manila envelope, then politely guides me to the door and out into the early evening light.

Back in the rental car, I open the envelope only to see another smaller, sealed envelope inside. It isn't worth playing his game. I shudder and toss both envelopes onto the passenger seat.

As I accelerate down the on-ramp of the 405 freeway, I can see the traffic thinning to a fluid flow toward Orange County and beyond. Rush hour has passed, a definite indication that it is time to find lodging for the night.

I wonder whether instinct will find me a place to sleep. "No time to worry about dead judges." I'm talking to myself too much.

Out of sheer desperation, my mind recalls an inn near the ocean. The owners were in their late fifties, as I remember. We saw each other on the beach during the tourists' off-season, when they had the time to enjoy the ocean. We never spoke at length, but acknowledged each other—as beach people do—with a smile and a nod while walking on
~~~

the beach. "They might have a room. And it's close to the beach," I whisper with relief for an easy answer.

With new confidence I continue south, moving parallel to the coast. As I approach the exit that leads to Pacific Coast Highway, the ocean smell begins to soothe my frayed emotions. Highway One: One—the beginning. I am coming back to the beginning. Is this instinct or is that just how things have to be, some law of physics, the natural order of things? I have the strangest sense of security here, near where I lived when I last felt vital, whole.

~~~

The sounds of the seagulls and smells of the ocean bring a wave of comfort. Waiting for a few minutes before going inside, I want, maybe need, to inhale every moment of this safe feeling before it passes. It's a sweet, secure, comforting mother's-milk feeling. It's like a towel, still warm from the dryer, after coming inside from a sudden and unexpected downpour. My eyes close and everything slows to a pleasant quiet for the first time since I arrived home this afternoon.

Even after I am absolutely certain the calm has passed and is not returning, I sit completely still. The nagging questions in my head are silent. My doubts and uncertainties are quiet. I could be content to sit here all night if there was a promise the comfort would linger.

I glance at the Ocean Shores Inn sign above the 1940s-style building and decide to chance stirring, with the hope that I have the strength to dare to move.

Once inside the office, I am struck with the decor that hasn't been updated since the 1960s. The woman behind the counter has her face tilted downward, writing a letter on tie-dye-designed stationary. Her blonde hair is long, mid-back long, with bangs covering her eyebrows. Pink, orange, and lime green plastic bangles rest on her wrist. She is wearing a peasant blouse and love beads, and, I suspect, her usual peasant skirt and leather sandals, as she did in the past.

"May I help you?" the woman asks without looking up.

"Yes. Do you have a room?" I ask, fairly confident there is at least one available this time of year. There were only two cars in the parking lot. How busy could they be?

"How many people?"

"One," I reply, slightly curious whether she will recognize me when she finally looks up.

"Fill out the registration form. There's a pen on the counter."

She hasn't aged as much as I expected. She still looks about the age I thought she was five years ago.

Finally she looks at me when I put the pen down and hand the small clipboard and attached registration form toward her.
~~~

For a moment she looks as though she is trying to figure where she has seen me. I can almost see her straining to place me somewhere within her daily routine. Maybe a store clerk, a bank teller? What the heck, I'll save her the trouble of guessing.

"Hi. I used to see you walking the beach when I lived here."

She smiles with one of those sure-I-remember-now smiles and gives me a room key. I haul my luggage to the room. The decor is 1960s too. It isn't a retro decorating trick, it's original.

The ocean isn't visible from the window, but it doesn't matter. I plan to spend my first morning home on the beach, my beach. Since I won't be in this room more than a week or two, the view can wait until I have a place of my own.

I'm tired from the travel and the intensity of the day. I don't know what I had expected, but the reality was more than I wanted. A couple pieces of fruit and the mint from the pillow is all I eat before I fall into bed too tired to be hungry. Home.

~~~

Reluctantly waking to the sounds of the surf muffled through the walls of my room, I turn over to go back to sleep. The dream of the ocean is too good to waste by getting up. After a moment more my mind realizes that it isn't a dream. I am in California.

It is perfect to wake up at home. In a very short while I'm out of bed, pulling on jeans and a hooded sweatshirt, and out the door to the beach. The bakery down the street provides me with a muffin and two cups of coffee to go: One for now, the other for right after "now."

My pace increases as I near the water's edge. It is an unseasonably cool Saturday morning. It could have been a blizzard and still I would have come to the beach today. My beach. Kathryn's Beach.

Winter is the best time of year to spend on the beach. Only real beach people are out on a day like this. A few surfers and kids with boogie boards are dressed in wet suits and booties. The water is always cold. It's the ocean currents swirling down from the Aleutians that make the California Pacific so cold.

I have never quite trusted the Pacific since she nearly swept me out to sea when I was seven. I was caught in the undertow at Morro Bay, a place famous for such dangers. It is a memory vivid in my mind.

The beach has always been a comforting, healing place for me, especially during the long gray winter. I hope to find the beach healing and nurturing again today. God knows I need it.

The earthy smell of the water, the dampness in the air, the sand, all of it, is consoling. And the sounds: wave sounds, crashing on the beach before rushing out to collide into the next incoming wave; bird sounds, operatic, excited screeching of distant birds pursuing fishing boats as
~~~

they chug out to sea, and those nearby; and boat sounds, motors, signal horns and an occasional human voice carried across the water. The beach delights my senses, much as the sight of a lover would. I have been away far too long.

An innate urge to feel the sand beneath my shoes pushes me to walk a half mile along the shore, just out of reach of the cool, gritty spray. The ocean-water smell begins to clear my head.

Even before the sun comes fully, I find a place in the dry sand to rest out of reach of the incoming spray. I had expected walking would keep the chill away, but I had walked too slowly to feel the effect of exercise. The breeze coming off the water is chilly, but I shiver for a different reason.

The waves crash onto the breakwater to the left, farther down the beach. Dampness awakens me to the core in a way that I have not been awake for the last five years.

Perhaps later, I will walk to the jetty for a second helping of this treat. Aware that I am tired, but not necessarily from the walk, I begin to feel a sense of focus awaken as I sit quietly, running my fingers through the silky dry sand. This awakening feels similar to the clarity I felt when I decided to come home.

It was an oddly decisive moment in the bar that resulted in a clear decision to return to L.A. Today, born out of my defenseless fatigue, I'm aware of its emerging again. I welcome the sensation of renewed awareness, while I watch the waves break and rush forward into tan froth on the wet sand not far away.

Mimicking the receding waves, the awareness slips back into the deep waters of my consciousness. Closing my eyes to shut out everything, except for the sounds and smells of the beach, I try to hold on to the retreating feeling of well-being.

Despite my best effort to capture and internalize it, the feeling fades completely. I wonder what will come to fill the void, and hope it isn't tormented memories.

After the clarity is gone, I release my barrette, shake my head, unleashing my long auburn hair to fly wildly free in the morning breeze. Perhaps removing the barrette is symbolic, but now isn't the time to analyze my behavior. I am free.

The rising sun reveals a greenish cast to the water and the glitter in the wet sand. I lean back on my elbows to take it all in. My lungs respond with a deep, slow breath, a breath that brings a sigh of relief as it leaves. The essence of safety remains as an undefined melody in my mind. It's a timid score, but it is growing stronger.

Seagulls screech, claiming ownership of the morsels left behind by the retreating tide. The sandpipers play a hurried game of tag with the tan foam at the waves' edge as it advances and retreats. The endless sound of the waves coming and going, and the occasional sound of a boat motor revving to pull away from the pier are familiar and comfortable sounds. The surf soothes my thoughts into idleness.

The last of the commercial fishing boats begin to come in with their morning catch. They pass into the channel leading to port. The boats are near enough to see the swarm of seagulls following them to the wharf beyond my view.

It is a relief to sit and enjoy the knowledge that I am where I belong. The familiarity of the sights, sounds, and smells wrap around me in a maternal embrace. There seems to be nothing in the world except this corner of the Earth. I belong here. Comfort wraps its arms around me and holds me securely.

The day drifts by on the unpeopled January beach. I imagine the weather deliberately turned cool, so I can have the beach to myself. It's a harmless fantasy.

The mindless musing doesn't hold my attention. My mind begins to sift through Maggie's unexpected information from yesterday. It reminds me of a jigsaw puzzle without a picture on the box, maybe one without a box. A few pieces fit together here and there. But I can't tell what to make of it. Something does not feel quite right about the Judge's letter.

Hunger moves me to the present. I've been too preoccupied to think of eating. Now the sun has crested and is beginning to make its descent. It must be 2:00 or 3:00 o'clock, judging by the sun's westward placement.

Walking back to my room, I stop to purchase a fish taco and vanilla shake from a beachfront restaurant. Pulling a chair from across the room, I sit with my feet propped on the bed and my drink set within reach on the TV stand. After dinner and a shower, contentedly I crawl onto the bed on this, my first full day home. The last thing I remember as I drift off to sleep is thinking it is good to be here.

~~~

Early Sunday morning, I return to watch the water, to feel the sand between my fingers as I rake through the soft grains and bits of shell, and feel the ocean breeze in my hair. My beach bag is laden with an ample supply of steaming coffee, the complimentary Sunday paper, and a beach blanket on loan from the Inn. It is a bit unbelievable that I am home and about to spend a second day on the beach.

I watch the horizon for the sunrise, and the water's edge for the next wave, alternating my gaze between the two. A satisfied sigh slips from my lips, followed by a smile. A genuine smile, not the bartender variety.

"Listen to the calm rhythm of the waves, Katey." I lean back on my blanket, shut my eyes, and reach to touch the sand with my fingertips.
~~~

Until now I hadn't realized the full impact of being away. The morning slips by under the influence of caffeine and the intoxicating setting.

With my container of coffee empty, I turn my attention to the Sunday paper. Reality in the form of caffeine surges through my veins motivating me to look for a job, an apartment, and a car of my own, but not necessarily in that order.

I love the freedom of having my own car—it's an L.A. thing—but shopping for a vehicle is of little interest to me. Knowing this, I promise myself to return the rental car by the end of the week. Deadline or goal? It doesn't matter, it's a start.

For employment. It seems peculiar that Karen offered me a job in the department that I abandoned without notice five years ago. On the other hand, the fact is that I am very good at my job. It takes a certain breed of social worker to do child abuse investigations day in and day out, and to do them well. Child Protective Services doesn't exactly have social workers fighting for the positions, for obvious reasons.

Now that I think of it, the job offer is quite practical from her standpoint. If Karen rehires me, she saves training time needed to get a social worker ready to carry a full caseload. Also, she knows what I can do, and I know how to deliver what she expects. It might work.

The only thing is that the nature of the work is physically and emotionally demanding. Unfortunately, society requires that someone does it and, until five years ago, I was one of the social workers who did.

When I was a student, a career in Child Protection was the last thing I wanted. At the beginning of my junior year, I was assigned to the department for the mandatory internship. I was told to do necessary non-social work tasks that bogged down the real social workers' schedules. For the department, my internship was purely a staff utilization decision.

The attitude in the department was unbearable, worse toward students. I was determined to complete the internship even if it killed me. The next year wasn't any better until Karen arrived at midterm, and students were given useful experience. After graduation I was eligible for a real social work position. Consequently, I have worked in Child Protection since then. (The job at the bar doesn't count.)

Outside of CPS, I'm not sure what else I could do or would want to do. On the other hand, what I am most uncertain about is not whether I want to return to Child Protection, but if I can handle it again. It was all-consuming. It consumed my energy. It consumed my soul.

Unfortunately, today's classifieds don't offer employment in my field. Fortunately, there are more strategic ways to find employment than the want ads. I'll worry about employment after I find a place to live.

Systematically, I scan the real estate ads for a feel of the real-world prices with hopes of a beach house to sublet. Actually, what I want is my old apartment back. I wonder if there are any apartments available in my former complex. Is that an attempt to recreate the past? The familiarity draws me, but I am concerned about the danger of picking up where I left off. I know that sounds like approach-avoidance, and it probably is. The urge to follow my instincts is strong.

The questions about what course to take for an apartment and employment, in addition to all of the trivial details of living, continue to dominate my thoughts the rest of the afternoon. Am I trying to recreate the life I left, the life that I couldn't live? Or have I come back to release the past, setting each of us free, so we can allow that thread of time to intertwine with the present? Why exactly did I run away, and what is driving me now?

The beach sounds and smells recede into the background of my thoughts. I am restless. The waves of questions catch me off guard. The answers don't follow. Only the questions fill my mind. I can think of nothing else as I walk along the beach back to my room.

I can't say what I had for dinner or exactly when sleep overtook my thoughts. It was a hard sleep, a deadman sleep.

~~~
~~~

~ CHAPTER 4 ~

Sweet Dreams

Restlessness enters my dreams. There is someone in my room. I can't tell if the presence is a danger, but I feel alerted to run.

"Kate? Kate. Kate! Wake up!" Maggie shakes me—saving me from the certain peril looming in my sleep.

My eyes aren't willing to open, but I can smell the coffee she brought. Slowly, I awake from the unconsciousness of the night. Finally, but only slightly, I open my eyes. I am groggy, but not so much that I don't remember I am back in California. At least, that isn't a dream.

"Good morning, sleepyhead," Maggie teases cheerfully.

I smile and pull myself up on one elbow. It is good to see her. I have missed her more than I realized.

"Sleepyhead? Aren't you late for work?" I tease back with an invented serious expression.

"It's a holiday. I'm not on call," she replies in a mischievous tone. She hands me a Styrofoam cup—tempting me to complete wakefulness with the steaming brew.

"Holiday?" I ask, and inhale the steam rising from the cup.

"Martin Luther King," she says, concentrating on removing the plastic lid from her coffee without getting burned.

I hadn't kept track of the date. Of course, it's Monday and mid-January. There is no particular reason to be mindful of the actual date until I am employed.

"Thank you," I say before taking a sip. I pause, savoring its taste. "It's good to see you," I add warmly, still amazed at her ability to figure out where I'm staying, but not willing to ask her.

After all, she had the weekend to find me. I know I would have been able to track her down, as well. The two of us had the most investigative experience in the department and the best professional records in the state. Things are back to normal.

"And what do you have planned for your holiday?" I ask, wondering what sleight-handed adventure she has in mind.

"Besides bribing the housekeeper to let me in here?" She grins before taking a full drink. "I thought we'd go apartment hunting," Maggie replies without hesitation. "I'll drive, if," she smiles widely, "if you can get dressed before noon."

"You know I'm a night owl." I fire back a grin, throw back the covers, crawl out of bed, and begin searching through my suitcase selecting something to wear. Besides, it is nowhere near noon. I have plenty of time.

"It's because of the nightmares, Kate. You aren't fooling me." Maggie becomes serious, but smiles when I wheel around to look at her.

The only way Maggie could know about the nightmares is if she has them too. She isn't going to trick me into an admission of what neither of us want to confess. Ignoring where she is taking the conversation, I move back to safer ground.

"So the plan is?" I ask, looking for my other shoe.

"I thought we would go by your old apartment and see if they have any apartments available, then go from there." Maggie pauses for a drink before resuming, "Unless you'd rather not."

My apartment? I quietly mouth her words, glancing at my friend through the doorway of the dressing area, to see if I can detect whether or not she is serious.

I lean against the vanity to tie my shoes, but really I am absorbing the reassurance that Maggie thinks there is nothing terribly wrong with moving back into my old neighborhood. I worry about things like the sanity of returning to my past. Nevertheless, there is a certain security in being back in my old neighborhood. I'm glad Maggie came.

I brush my teeth and wash my face. I have no intention of arguing the case about whether there is sanity involved in any of this. Certainly, I'm not going to mention concerns regarding sanity to Maggie, of all people.

~~~

With noticeable confidence, Maggie steers into the freeway traffic. Meanwhile, I settle back and enjoy her company. We chat about nothing, the way people do when they can't find the words to say what needs to be said. Or can't find the courage to say them.

My former apartment and one a floor below are available. They just finished painting both. I can have the pick between them and move in immediately. It takes only a moment's hesitation, I choose the lower-level apartment. It seems right to have a new view of the Pacific this time around.

Maggie approves the choice, though she doesn't say why. I don't ask. I know better than to ask Maggie for a rationale when she doesn't volunteer one. Besides, I don't care what she thinks. I'm home. Nothing else matters.

~~~

The next weekend, Maggie, her brother, Frank, and a couple of his friends help to move my things out of storage, and into my apartment.

After the guys leave, Maggie stays to help set up the kitchen, which begins with making a pot of freshly ground coffee. We look through the boxes to find the coffee cups. There are a few detours along the way, but we find the cups by the time the coffee sputters to a stop.

The truth is, we move to the sofa to catch up with each other and never really get back to unpacking.

The next day, Frank helps me find a suitable used car. Suitable to me means a 5-speed, something with a tight suspension for corners, and a sweet clutch for getting through the gears when the traffic will allow it. Frank's primary task is to check the mechanical integrity. I have been known to blow a head gasket or two in the past, but never a clutch. I don't really speed, but I do get to the speed limit quite efficiently —keep the RPMs up. Having my own vehicle liberates me.

After a quick walk on the beach, I unpack until I am tired of it. Then I shop for towels and accent pillows for the sofa. It's a relaxing activity. Additional items will come once I get a paycheck coming again.

Maggie returns the next weekend to help me finish the unpacking. Of course, there is a certain amount of good-natured ribbing that goes along with her assistance. She jokes about my collection of movie sound tracks. Each time the CD changes she moans. I applaud her dramatics, but she is quite bad at acting. I taunt her to guess which movie the songs are from, at least she is good at that.

With the unpacking nearly finished, I start settling into a routine. Piece by piece, I am constructing a life again. My hair is cut short and styled. It takes a few weeks to complete enough continuing education hours to get my license current. I rework my résumé. Things are falling into place.

My cousin Nick meets me at the pier for some catch-up time. We are only two months apart in age, so we have always been close. Before I left, we would get together for lunch on the pier, then head to the ballpark. Our all-time favorite activity was to attend Dodgers' games when they were in town. He doesn't seem to mind that I left without saying a word. Unlike my friends, he asks if I want to talk about why I left and my return.

After brief consideration, I tell him, "Not now. Thanks for asking. Maybe some other time."

He understands my confession that I am not sure I can put it into words just yet.

After lunch we take our time walking up the pier toward town, stopping to look over the railing at the water below.

"You still surf?" I ask, curious whether he still enters surfing contests, and amazed at his bravery since he can't swim. It would seem that he would have learned by now. I wouldn't take that kind of risk.

"I'm back to making custom bats. I'm making practice bats for the Dodgers." He raises his eyebrows in emphasis.

"Thank God it's not the Angels!" I tease.

"Yeah, how 'bout them Dodgers! Lookin' good," he jokes playfully and nods his head.

"It must be the bats."

"Must be." He smiles sheepishly.

We stop again to lean on the guardrail overlooking the waves breaking below. Spending the day with Nick reminds me of how much I have missed him.

~~~

The search for employment continues, but only half-heartedly. I still haven't decided about Karen's offer to return to the department. Getting the job would be easy. Doing the job, with no end of little victims in sight, is never easy.

I haven't worked up the energy to face Karen, and make the hard decision about child abuse investigations. Perhaps it is because I can't envision myself doing anything else, even though I desperately need to do something else.

In the meantime, I am getting back into shape walking the beach twice a day. Walking in the soft, dry sand nearly killed my calf muscles the first few days. My muscles still ache terribly, but my head is beginning to clear and the distant winter's chill inside of me is thawing.

Occasionally, I experience a sense of clarity, but most of the time I am operating on instinct. So far it serves me well.

~~~

Many of my old neighbors still live in the apartments. Mr. Goldstein, who reminds me of an older version of Ben Kingsley, stops in every couple of days to check my progress with the last of the unpacking.

It seems like it's taking forever to unpack, but I haven't seen this stuff for five years. The hours slip by as I get lost in old photo albums. I hardly remember the person in the pictures of me. She looks strong, confident, and alive. I gently touch the image with my fingertips while tears well in my eyes at the loss of that person.

While I make lunch for us, Mr. Goldstein inquires about the pile of photos I've left out. Solely to satisfy his curiosity, I invite him to the sofa after we eat and look through the photos.

These are the photos I laid aside to look through a second time: photos from my childhood at the beach with my parents; old black-and-white photos of my parents before I was born; photos of me with my first bike, wavy hair flowing behind; prom photos; graduation; Mother and her friend, Amelia; Mother and her sisters and brothers; but none of Father's family.

Mr. Goldstein listens to the narratives and studies each photo in depth. He asks thoughtful questions. I freely answer them. While he is learning about me, I am rediscovering myself.

Thinking about it now, I realize I have been afraid that I would never find myself again. Maybe that is why I stayed away for so long. Maybe that is why I left in the first place. In the end, being lost among strangers was far worse than facing my lost self on home ground.

The afternoon drifts on lazily. Before Mr. Goldstein leaves for his rest, he offers unsolicited advice about the arrangement of my framed movie posters and helps me hang the biggest ones. The chair isn't quite rightly placed in the room. He tests it several times before he is satisfied with its final location. The view of the ocean has to be perfect. The more he visits, the more I discover that I want him in my life in a way that no one else seems to fit.

I watch Mr. Goldstein climb the stairs to his apartment. His wife died while I was away. I would have liked to have seen her again. The two of them were inseparable. I can't imagine him living alone.

He is frail without a companion. It is obvious he hasn't been very active, and he probably doesn't eat right, either. For the most part, he seems to do all right. I'm sorry I had not kept in touch with them. I've made a lot of mistakes.

Throughout my career, being the quintessential social worker was my identity. In the end I couldn't accept failure or separate my career from me as a person. Failure was personal, an unacceptable weakness. I couldn't take any more tragedy, especially murder—a preventable murder. So I left it all. I see now in doing so, I left everything that defined me.

Trying to figure out things alone was another horrible failure. Coming home was my only option to be alive again. At last I can admit I need people to complete my life in a way that being alone left it incomplete. Yet, I need to become comfortable with myself before I can allow anyone to see my vulnerabilities. I have not mastered that quite yet. But there is hope.

There are fleeting moments when I feel focused and determined, moments when it's more than innate instinct driving me. Unfortunately, the focus comes and leaves on its own volition. It encourages me that I am allowing Mr. Goldstein inside the perimeter of my defenses, a widening of my inner circle.

Mr. Goldstein returns unexpectedly as I am preparing to leave for my evening walk on the beach. He wants to walk too. I accept his desire for companionship and acknowledge my need for the same.

Since he doesn't have athletic shoes, he is wearing his everyday street shoes. With his shoulders back and his chest swelled, he looks proud in his new warm-up outfit, complete with price tag still dangling from his armpit. With a quick snip, the price tag is removed and we are officially walking buddies.

On this first walk, Mr. Goldstein makes it across the street and to the edge of the sand. Technically, we are on the beach, but at least a hundred yards from the last high tide mark. It is obvious this is as far as we are walking today.

He's frail from age and limited activity. Now that we are in the sand, I am not sure he can make it back across the street on his own. Apparently, neither is he. He slides his arm desperately around my waist, while I slip mine around his back to steady him. I hope this is enough support for his weak, spindly legs. The urgency in his grasp doesn't boost my confidence in this endeavor. It seems the spirit is willing, but the flesh is weak.

He has an odd quick-step gait that is hard to match. His pace throws me slightly off balance, causing us to be even more out of step with each other. We stop to rest several times before we make it home where we are safe.

I think we were both scared he wouldn't make it back, but neither of us mention it. We breathe a sigh of relief when I finally ease him into a chair to rest before going upstairs to his apartment.

~~~

Mr. Goldstein becomes stronger as the days pass. We walk a little farther each time. By the end of two weeks he is walking to the water's edge with ease and has bought shoes better suited to the task.

During our walks, we begin to talk about things people with a two-generation age difference talk about with each other. They are comfortable, non-intrusive conversations. Still, a deeper warmth is developing between us. I love the easy way we laugh together. It is always preceded by a slow grin on Mr. Goldstein's lips, and a twinkle in his eyes.

Today's conversation is more personal. Without warning, he talks about losing his babies in the war. He confides, in detail, how frightening the death camps were for Mrs. Goldstein and for him, and the others. Without hesitation he describes the things they did to survive and to help each other to survive. His honesty makes listening to the details of his experiences difficult. I don't interrupt.

He seems extraordinarily accepting of the people around him who responded differently to the same situation, even if becoming lackeys when survival required it. He makes no excuse for their behavior, nor passes judgment on them.

"Those were terrible days, Katerina. No one could be blamed how they survived the camp." He confides in a soft steady voice that some
~~~

gave in to their fears and ended it all. There was little to account for why any of them lived through it.

There is nothing I can say in response to what he tells me. No comment is worthy of this story. Nothing, nothing justifies the death camps. Nothing can be said to heal what he went through. I don't understand this kind of hate, nor how so many people found it acceptable. I wonder whether any of those people later had regrets for what they did to people, including children.

We walk in silence for a long time. Suddenly he stops, looks at the evening sky, then he looks at me in an intense moment. All he says is, "We should go now," and turns for home. And that is that. We go.

~~~

The following day Mr. Goldstein returns for what has become our daily ritual: an evening walk on the beach. Since California is the only place Mr. Goldstein has lived in the U.S., he asks questions about life on the prairie.

I tell of the combines cutting wide swaths around the wheat field until it circles down to the final pass of the equipment.

"There is haze in the air from the machines churning out the chaff to remove the grain from the heads of the plants."

I explain that only the most essential activities occur during harvest. It was always a race with the weather and crop prices. Nothing else mattered until the wheat was in, until harvest was finished.

Twelve-year-old children, women, and old men drove two-ton grain trucks. Some trucks were so old they looked like a parade of vintage vehicles creeping down Main Street. Some farmers had several matching new grain trucks that were bought on the gamble it would be a good crop this year.

I describe the long lines of trucks at the elevator waiting to weigh and dump their load of grain. I tell him how the drivers got out of their trucks to stand under shade trees along the road, waiting for their turn at the scales and worrying about their grain's moisture content. Sometimes two or three drivers would gather near the lead truck, visiting with each other while watching the activities across the yard at the Double Circle Co-Op elevator until it was their turn.

Mr. Goldstein listens to my stories with interest and has many questions.

During those first few weeks home, Maggie and I see each other every few days. I suspect her of helping me readjust to city life as if I am a stray in need of adoption.

Sometimes Maggie and I get together for lunch with several of the staff from work. There has always been a standing lunch invitation at the office. At times, I almost imagine being part of the team again.
~~~

Most often Maggie and I eat alone in one of the sandwich shops we frequented when we worked together. Maggie can be so frustrating with her direct ways. Yesterday, for example, she took advantage of the privacy to talk seriously. She smoothly eased the conversation into making her point.

"Kate, you are a one-woman world. You haven't always been that way. You think instinct brought you home. I think it was courage. It's easier to run away and keep running than to come home and face something you consider a failure. I think you have courage," Maggie spoke softly, hauntingly.

Why in the world did I confide my feelings to her? I admit, she makes me think about things, especially things I am avoiding. But I don't have to admit it to her—only to myself.

~~~

Today when I come to the office looking for Maggie for an impromptu lunch date, Karen is with the receptionist. I was preoccupied with having lunch that it catches me by surprise to see her. She looks pleasantly surprised to see me, which still seems odd.

"Hello, Kathryn. Do you have a minute?"

This might seem strange, but I'm sure she said, "Into my office, Kathryn!" Though I know that she didn't, I fight the temptation to respond with my usual, "Yes, ma'am," as we walk toward the elevator to her office.

Once inside, Karen shuts the door and the glass window in it rattles.

I smile to myself.

Karen goes straight to her desk to unload her cargo. I watch her dispatch her briefcase and the armload of case files. It occurs to me that she wants my answer about the position. I don't think I can handle the horrors the investigations reveal, then repeat them in court under the strong objections of the defense attorney. I can't risk having another client murdered because I can't make the system work as it should. I miss my work and my friends, but I don't think I can do this again—at least not yet.

Karen seems to detect my thoughts. It makes me uneasy to be transparent in her gaze. She occupies her attention with shuffling the stacks of files on her desk to make room for more. But I can tell she is thinking in the background of the activity.

After a minute of awkward silence Karen looks up and asks, "How have you been, Kathryn?" in that new-to-me motherly tone she has acquired.

"I've been unpacking and working on my résumé." I catch the implications of saying "résumé."
~~~

Karen looks at me intensely. To my surprise, she seems to understand my offhand reply, though I haven't really answered her question.

"You've decided to leave Child Protection."

"Yes. Yes, I guess that I have." She makes me realize working on my résumé indicates I am headed elsewhere in social work. I haven't made much progress. However, if I was returning to the department, I wouldn't need a résumé. They have my HR file. I am moving on.

"I just returned from a meeting with the director of a new program. It's a program for homeless families. You might like it. It'll be a change of pace for you." Karen adds after a brief pause, "As of an hour ago she was still hiring staff."

By her expression, it's obvious Karen is providing me with an alternative to working in her department again. I see through her manipulation, but I let it pass. She must think it is a good agency or she wouldn't have mentioned the job.

Karen writes down a phone number and a name, "Sister Elizabeth," on the back of one of her business cards and hands it to me. We pause.

Obviously, we are both reminded of the last time she gave me her business card with her home phone number.

The pause makes me uncomfortable. I look away from her gaze, busying myself with putting the card in my purse.

Karen hesitates a minute, then returns to arranging papers from her briefcase into piles on her desk, but she stops again.

"I was waiting for you to call," she says as she studies me.

I feel terrible. "I'm sorry. I hadn't realized I wasn't coming back to the department until now." I am embarrassed that I have been thoughtless about her need to fill the position.

Maggie told me that Karen had placed me on extended leave of absence. Of course, she hadn't kept my slot open for five years. It just worked out that she has a social work position coming open soon. However, the workload demands that she get the position filled as soon as possible. I feel very selfish for not giving her an answer sooner.

"I know," she says in an understanding tone. "But I'm referring to the Judge's letter," she says softly.

Karen speaks in a hurt tone, one I have never heard her use before. "I would like to know what the man who tore apart my department had to say." Quickly she tempers her tone, her anger isn't directed at me. Karen turns toward me and continues in a softer voice. "If you need to talk about the murder, I'm available."

"I haven't opened his letter, but—" I take one of her cards from the card holder on her desk, and write my address and phone number on the back. "It is Friday. We can order Chinese takeout and open the letter, if you don't have other plans."

"As it turns out, I don't have plans, and I will bring dinner."

Karen picks up the phone as I leave her office.

This seems a little too easy. Is she calling to cancel her plans or is she really free tonight? And the letter, who cares about the damn letter? It won't change anything. It can't bring back that little girl. It won't bring back the last five years or my career.

"I hate him and his stupid letter!" I say under my breath, repulsed with the memory of Judge Jones.

Before leaving the building, I slip to Maggie's desk to use her phone and call Sister Elizabeth. Sister asks me to email my résumé to her and sets an interview appointment for Monday morning. I'm being biased with my surprise about her use of email. This computerized nun intrigues me. Even better, I have a job interview—as easy as that.

~~~

Red enameled chopsticks laid across my mother's hand-painted Chinese dishes are the perfect accents to Mother's black-and-yellow muslin tablecloth. On second thought I add a fork to Karen's place.

The table setting is simple, but ideal for Chinese takeout. The shades are raised, revealing the evening sun glistening on the waves across the street.

Standing back to inspect the room one last time before my guest arrives, I nod approval. I am pleased with my apartment. It's comfortable and cosmopolitan—an absolute contrast to my sparse two rooms above the garage just months ago.

My plan is to eat first, then open the letter from Judge Jones—a simple, but efficient agenda.

By the time Karen appears at the door the tea is brewed and the air filled with its aroma. She comments that I live close to her beach. I smile about her sense of ownership of *my* beach.

We are nimble with our chopsticks, which is something newly discovered that we have in common. To my relief, dinner moves along nicely. The food and conversation are a comfortable fit.

It occurs to me now that when I worked for Karen we never had a conversation that wasn't work related. After all the years at odds with her, I am slowly realizing Karen is a warm and interesting person.

We finish eating just about the time the sun sizzled into the Pacific and the residential lights came on. Glancing at the letter on the coffee table where it has been for the past six weeks, I wonder what the "almighty" Judge Jones had to say. I haven't given the letter as much thought as everyone else seems to have. Honestly, I didn't care for Judge Jones then, and I don't care for him now that he's dead. A letter
~~~

from him seems inconsequential after what he did in his courtroom. I'm sorry he committed suicide, but I don't miss him. The man was an arrogant ass, and he flexed his power too irresponsibly for my taste. I found it hard to even respect the robe with him in it.

Something is odd about him writing to me. How can I give much credence when Maggie and Karen weren't curious enough to open it for nearly five years, so why bother with it at all? What could it possibly say that would make any difference?

Was he going to try to explain his ruling? Was he apologizing for letting that deranged man continue to sexually abuse his daughter —leading to her murder? Perhaps he blamed me? No, Maggie said the transcript disputed his ruling. None of it matters. Nothing he wrote will bring the little girl back from the dead.

Karen moves our tea to the living room, then comes to help finish clearing the table.

"Before you open the letter, let's talk," she requests as we move back to the sofa when we finish. "Kathryn, whatever is in the letter, it's collateral to the main issue."

Apparently getting together to read the letter was an excuse to pin me down and make me face that case. It is true the Judge's letter is only a small part of a bigger picture, certainly less important than the children. Even less important than us.

However, after the first year passed without knowing where I was, I would have opened it or tossed it in the trash had I been them. Truthfully, I would have tossed it in the trash when it arrived. It wasn't important to the police, and it wouldn't have been important to me. It still isn't.

A letter from Judge Jones doesn't make sense, and it is likely a moot issue after all of this time has passed. I am slightly disappointed that we aren't opening the letter—only because I would like to be done with it and put it with the garbage bin and have it hauled away.

Her hazel eyes are unable to hide the pain reflected in her tone of voice. There is a sense of urgency about Karen that I hadn't expected. Maybe she thinks there will not be another opportunity to resolve the past, maybe she thinks that I will slip away again. We were never friends, and having dinner together once doesn't mean we will become friends. "Now" may be all we have. In many ways, all we ever have is "this moment."

I'd rather not have a conversation about the past. Nevertheless, I follow her lead. This pending conversation seems important to her. I suspect it is only a temporary truce between us. We'll see what happens after I've been home for a while. That will be the real test whether things will be different or not.

“Everyone was angry when Judge Jones made that horrid ruling.” Her voice is clear and controlled. “It was always hard to get a good ruling out of his court.” She pauses briefly. “I was angry too,” Karen confesses more softly than before, making direct eye contact as she speaks.

Her near-whisper catches my attention. I study her and sit more upright. She is direct. It is definitely similar to Maggie’s approach the day I returned. The way she sits forward hints there is an underlying emotion that is still unclear to me.

Karen continues, unaware that I am trying to listen beyond her words. “I knew for a long time that Judge Jones set serious abusers free on petty technicalities, and it was destroying my staff’s credibility with other judges.”

She pauses for a thoughtful sip of her tea. “Not to mention the children,” she almost whispers breathlessly. “He betrayed their trust. I don’t know how the man slept at night.”

The thought of what Judge Jones did to the children, to us, and eventually to himself—his actions make us both shudder. We look at each other but say nothing, only sip our tea in silence for a minute or two. My mind adds Karen’s words to the memories I possess.

Five years ago I hadn't thought about the rest of the staff. There wasn’t a bigger picture in my perception, there was just one small, vulnerable child.

In the end, I took his ruling as a personal defeat. I hated not being able to protect that little girl. I hated feeling helpless. I hadn't seen that it was more than my case. It was our case.

“I didn't know—” my words are lost.

“Kathryn, I was wrong.”

“What?” I whisper. Stunned, I meet her gaze without retreat.

This time her eyes don’t betray her, she has gained control over them. Looking past the coffee table between us and directly at me, she continues, “You had a solid case. I wanted you and Keith to prevail for both departments' sake. I wanted this to be the case that beat Judge Jones. You both did everything right. I want you to understand that what happened in court was not your fault.”

Keith and I were the lead investigators on the case. Keith was a seasoned police detective. Kevin, a younger officer, was assisting him. Maggie had been assigned to work with me. Ordinarily, there wasn't the staff allocation to double-team the case assignments. I had thought it odd, but didn’t question it.

Now I understand why Karen read the file daily. Back then I interpreted her involvement as excessive supervision, nearing micro-management. In reality, she was making sure we could avoid any legal technicalities that would give cause to Judge Jones' dismissal of the case. At the very least, she was maneuvering for a request to the District Attorney to file an appeal.

"Is that why you ordered the transcript?" I ask, now knowing she was preparing for an appeal.

"You know?"

"Maggie told me."

"I could have taken the money out of the budget, but we needed to own it with our own money. This work is difficult enough without judges undermining the system. That case killed a part of everyone involved in it." Then she nearly whispers, "It murdered the little girl."

Karen falls silent.

When she stirs again her voice is more measured. "Keith and I went over every detail of the transcript. I hired a criminal lawyer to review a redacted copy for procedural flaws."

With ease she makes the transition to invoke her motherly tone, "Kathryn, there were no problems with the evidence or the testimony. The 'problem' was Judge Jones."

Clearly, Karen is offering me absolution, that was her agenda for this evening. Her face shows the stress of her job. If only we had known five years ago what we know now, things might have been different.

Emotion wells up inside me as I watch her remember the past. I feel ashamed that I left the way that I had. I have not earned her absolution.

Karen interrupts my regret when she begins to tell what transpired after I left. "Everyone had the opportunity to read the transcript, and almost everyone did. We wanted, no, we needed answers to our questions about Judge Jones' unconscionable rulings." She hesitates, then nearly whispers again, "But there was nothing there. There was nothing we could have done differently then or changed for the next time."

She catches me off guard. The breath I had been holding now slips free, "Nothing?" I lean forward in my chair, slightly closing the distance between us. "There was nothing there?"

Still, I feel there should have been a way to protect my client. There must have been something extra I could have done to protect her from her father and Judge Jones.

The image of her little sweet face, when the Judge made his ruling, flashes in my mind. She was barely old enough to read, but she knew exactly what he had done to her.

Judge Jones sat perched on his bench in his pompous self-righteous smugness. Everyone else in the courtroom was completely stunned. The court reporter's hands hovered over her machine, shaking, and horror showed on her face. The silent slumped bodies of the attorneys standing behind their tables with their heads hung down were an eerie sight.

I can hear her little girl voice plead with the Judge, then each of us. But I was the one she called by name, pleading with me to save her. I wanted to kidnap her and run far away.

The memory is vivid. I feel my throat tighten and my eyes burn with tears threatening. The images are raw even after all of this time has passed. It's as if it happened yesterday.

When I close my eyes at night I still hear her horrifying scream echo throughout the marble and granite courtroom. I see her eyes plead with each of us as she looks around the room from one face to the next. She calls my name. Then it begins again, the scream, the horrifying scream that left a deafening silence when it finally ended. I wake yelling, "Run! Run away!" That was the last day I saw her.

It was less than a week when she was found dead. Homicide notified Keith when her name brought up a red flag in the system. Keith came to tell Karen what had happened. Karen called me to her office.

I thought it was just one more of the seemingly million times I was to be summoned to her office. I expected to be fired for something. Karen and I seemed to be in constant conflict over how to handle my cases. En route to her office I wondered what I had done this time.

Keith was there when I entered Karen's office. I halted. They both looked pale. I was filled with an unimaginable rage when Karen told me my client was dead. I looked at Karen as if it was somehow her fault that I had failed to save the little girl.

When I could finally speak I told her I needed time off. Without waiting for her reply, I slammed the door, hoping that annoying glass would shatter.

It didn't break, but I nearly did. Grief and anger consumed me in the days that followed her funeral. I wandered the beach until I was tired enough to sleep, hoping it would be without hearing her screams just as I am hearing them now.

A shudder travels through my body in response to the memories, forcing me back into the present. I look up to see Karen's face pale. She looks like she is reliving all of it too.

"I am so sorry," I repent for my role in all of this.

She ignores my apology. "I had grad students review our court cases for the twelve months prior to yours." She takes a long breath. "The results showed we had no convictions in Judge Jones' court, none. Our next worse record was Judge Lawrence's court. There we had a 68-percent conviction rate." She pauses to sigh.

"Judge Jones had been dead almost a month by the time we had the stats compiled and verified, and the report written. I know he was aware we were checking out court files from the Clerk of the Court. He had to figure out what we were doing." Her voice sounds like she thinks that it might be her fault he killed himself or that she, too, thought she had missed something pivotal in the little girl's case.

"I don't think that had anything to do with his suicide," I assure her the best a strong person can be reassured.

I remember fuming for days, then alternating between self-pity and horrifying anger. I was angry with Judge Jones and the justice system. Justice? That wasn't justice. I couldn't find a way to deal with it. Thinking about it repulsed me, but I could think of nothing else. I had to leave.

I hadn't given Karen time to react the afternoon I walked into her office and tossed my keys and pager on her desk. I had to get away from all of the craziness, the dysfunctional people, and the dysfunctional system.

Karen tried to maneuver her department around Judge Jones. She depended on this case to give her the leverage to serve him notice that justice would prevail. Now I know I had been wrong about everything. None of it had been about me. While I ran away, Karen and Keith stayed and did a retrospective investigation of the system. They didn't run.

"Homicide threw its resources into the investigation. In two months the murder case went to the grand jury."

She looks up and catches my gaze, "Within a week after the grand jury issued an indictment, Judge Jones shot himself." Karen's voice is strong and unemotional. "Eventually our stats convinced the DA's office to request a judicial review of Judge Jones' cases—many of his rulings have been overturned."

"Oh, good." I wonder, but don't ask, about the ones he dismissed. They can't be retried because of double jeopardy.

"Yes. It was a lot of work, but I think it was worth it." She looks past me as she speaks. "The mistrials were retried de novo." She looks tired.

"I didn't know—" I am still apologizing. It must have been difficult retrying my cases without me on the stand. My throat tightens, making it difficult to breathe normally. Inside me is a profound sense of sadness.

I should have been here to help sort through this mess. It was my case. Besides, I am very good at statistics. I tutored it all through college. Karen could have used my help.

"We didn't know where you were," she says in an unaccusing voice.

"I was tending bar in a little town in Nebraska."

Karen laughs, "NEBRASKA?" Her laughter breaks the solemn mood hanging over us.

~~~
~~~

The hours pass unnoticed as we move through the shared memories. We need to sort through this ourselves, before we can deliver any sense of resolution to the other people involved in this tragic case.

Perhaps everything can't be resolved in one night, but there seems to be a sense of urgency in Karen to resolve as much as possible. She uses her skills to get us through the tough spots. She knows no one can be their own patient, and most of the time she is only a mere mortal like me.

Hours ago we traded our tea for coffee. Through the window the sky is showing signs of sunrise. By the sound of the surf it is already high tide.

When I return with another pot of reality, Karen is still amused at the thought of me in Nebraska.

Relentlessly Karen continues, "You'll be pleased to know we took a conviction on the murder trial," she says triumphantly. "We couldn't get a repeat sex offender status on him because Judge Jones had dismissed the felony case." She doesn't have any anger in her words, which surprises me.

I am still struggling with the memories—not just this case, but all the bad cases. Though none of the other bad cases compares with this last case.

"Since you were unavailable to testify, but were under oath on the transcript from Judge Jones' case, Judge Lawrence allowed your testimony into the record in the murder trial as motive for murder."

Karen deliberately makes eye contact, holds a beat, then continues, "With the coroner's report of sexual abuse prior to her death, we had murder while committing a felony."

"Murder One?" I nearly breathed the words, unable to say them out loud.

First degree murder usually is reduced. Plea bargaining is a reality of the justice system we have come to expect, if not accept. I can't believe the system actually worked full tilt.

Karen smiles with my appreciation of their accomplishment. We had won a battle, if not the war.

I look at the cup in my hand to avoid the clumsy moment of truce between us. My gaze strays to catch sight of the unopened letter on the coffee table. I look up to see Karen looking at the envelope too. We look at each other briefly.

Karen is correct, the letter is collateral to the "blood and guts" of who we are and the work we do. What we do is real. Judge Jones' robe was a façade for a man who made a mockery of the system and the ideals of justice. The envelope doesn't hold any power over us.

The sound of the surf is restlessly calling me to the beach. We have relived enough of the past for one night. I know that I can't take any more. Karen looks depleted and doesn't attempt to hide it behind her usual commanding composure. It would take too much effort to hide her emotional exhaustion—or maybe she doesn't feel it's necessary to keep up her guard any longer.

Along with the emerging resolution of the past, I sense the development of a new understanding between us. Karen is probably tired of our battle. I know I am. Maybe the problem had been me all along, but I feel our conflictive relationship is evolving into a more agreeable posture. At least, I hope so.

Dawn is showing fully in the bit of sky visible through the window. It's safe to go on the beach now without stepping on a jellyfish or a piece of debris that washed up during high tide. I am ready for a walk. I need to stretch my legs and clear my head, and get some distance from the memories.

In unspoken agreement we look toward the door and the waiting beach beyond it. This moment of common thought is a refreshing change.

It is decidedly awkward once it's apparent we are officially no longer at odds with each. We will have to adopt new roles in the absence of our old ones. It might not be easy. Certainly it will prove interesting, considering the personalities involved, if nothing else.

Giving in to the beckoning of the surf, Karen suggests a walk before she leaves. I don't need coaxing. There is a consolation that only the beach brings. It has been a long night and the sea air will be a refreshing change.

Karen pulls on the oversized sweatshirt I offer to guard against the morning's chilly mist and we're out the door.

The loud calls of the seagulls dull the further intrusion of memories from the past. Everything is washed new with the ever-changing tide. It's the constant renewal of the surf that I seek this morning.

Karen and I walk along the shore we both think of as "our" beach. We talk only a little before we slip into silence.

Karen seems different from how I remember her. When I worked for her, I didn't think of Karen as a person touched by the same things that haunted her staff. She always seemed to be in control of the intense emotions that raged out of control within us, especially in me. She seemed peaceful and calculated.

I had no idea she shared our humanity. I'm sorry that I hadn't taken the time to notice before now. Me running for five years accomplished nothing. I have wasted all that time being emotionally numb in Nebraska.

Now, I have a second chance to actually see Karen and the other people I had taken for granted. This time I will not make the same mistakes. I am beginning to understand myself a little better in the process. Yet the anger and hurt remain buried inside of me, seeking an exit.

It took the entire night for Karen to relate the saga that unfolded after I left. I have nothing to contribute, although it seems to have been enough to allow her to talk. Maybe receiving was exchange enough for now.

For me the total emotional dynamics of this work, and that case in particular, haven't been resolved. I know one day I will need to let go of all of my thoughts and emotions, even the anger, related to "that" case. I have not found the key to such a release. At least I have information that may come into place at the right time to help me heal and be whole again.

It was good Karen and I spent this time together, but I will have to find my own healing. Now would be a good time for a wave of clarity to wash over me. I like the feeling of confidence I have when things come into focus.

The clarity doesn't come. When I have tried to coax the feeling before, it would not be forced. I can control it no more than I can control the tide. I will have to be patient with it and with myself.

Karen and I walk quietly along the morning beach—our silent thoughts drifting out to sea with the waves.

~~~
~~~

~ CHAPTER 5 ~

Letter, Letter, Who Gets The Letter?

Immersed in our private thoughts, Karen and I walk for a mile and a half along the deserted beach. The bird calls and the sounds of the surf blend into a symphony in the background of my thoughts. The caffeine in my system is slowly being replaced with the awareness of hunger.

Breaking the silence I ask her, "Could I interest you in breakfast?"

Karen looks around as if I awakened her from her thoughts. "I should get home."

"I make a great omelet," I coax. "We can invite Maggie and open the letter," I add more incentive.

I'm tired, but more interested in breakfast than sleep. There is the constant threat of nightmares that make me think twice before sleeping. It's not only this one bad case that I dream about, but it is the one responsible for most of the nightmares.

That little girl would be eleven now, if Judge Jones had left her removed from her abuser and in a safe home. Not only did he dismiss the criminal case, he dismissed the Child Protection case. I keep thinking there must have been something I missed that would have prevented the system from failing her.

Karen changes her mind. "Okay, you talked me into it. I didn't bring my phone, did you?"

"No. I don't bring my phone to the beach."

"Let's walk to the pier and use the pay phone." She turns back toward the pier.

~~~

Luckily, Maggie-the-early-riser is still home. I tease her, "I will serve my 'world-famous omelet' and unveil Judge Jones' letter—if you can get here by noon." It is nowhere near noon, but I couldn't resist repeating her words from before.

She laughs and accepts the challenge. By the time Karen and I return from the beach, Maggie is leisurely waiting on my patio looking smug that she arrived first, though she couldn't have waited long.

Maggie and Karen slice mushrooms, bell peppers, dice onions to be sautéed, and grate the cheeses. I add secret ingredients to the egg mixture. The omelets cooperate and are perfect.

We eat on the patio, casually visiting in the slight morning breeze. I begin to realize why Maggie seemed comfortable to dive into the conversation my first day back.
~~~

It must have been therapeutic for her to go through the department's internal investigation, rather than run away as I did. Certainly processing small increments of this nightmare is easier, and saner, than being bombarded with everything at once, as I have been since I returned.

As I listen to Karen and Maggie visit, it's obvious Karen has not healed completely, though she hides it well. I am convinced leaving when I did, the way that I did, made things worse for her. It is almost as if Karen cannot, or will not, allow herself to put this aside until all of her staff has been "accounted for."

It was necessary that I return, not just for me, but because I am one of Karen's unaccounted-for factors in her nightmare. It seems that Judge Jones' letter is another, albeit minor, unanswered question. I suspect Karen cannot find closure until everything is finished and put away in neat stacks. It's difficult to gauge how many items remain on Karen's list of unfinished business regarding that case.

~~~

When I return to the patio with more orange juice, I bring Judge Jones' letter with me. Maggie and Karen are engaged in conversation and fail to notice the letter until I refill their glasses and set down the juice container.

There is a sudden serious curiosity in both of them. They watch intensely as I slip my unused butter knife inside the flap of the envelope, then hand the opened envelope to Karen.

She and Maggie stir to sit up straighter in their chairs. Karen clears her throat. While she unfolds the handwritten letter on the court's stationery, Maggie and I settle back in our chairs to listen. My focus turns to the waves across the street while I look past Karen, listening as she reads:

"Dear Kathryn." Karen stops, looks intensely at me.

Her abrupt halt pulls my attention back to her. There is almost a discernable moment of silent pause in the morning sounds that had surrounded us only moments ago.

Karen and Maggie look at me questioningly.

I understand the question, but shrug unknowingly, wide-eyed because I don't have an answer.

> Dear Kathryn,
> Don't judge me. Tell my daughter
> I'm sorry.
> Wm. Jones
~~~

Karen settles back in her chair to begin again.

"That's it? He didn't tell us anything!" I snap, allowing my anger to finally surface. I am filled with disappointment that he didn't mention regret for his hand in the little girl's horrible death. He owed me that. He owed all of us that much. They have been waiting all this time for what? For nothing.

"Why did he bother?" The betraying tone of my voice is filled with pain and anger that is impossible to disguise.

Karen and Maggie look directly at me. Judging by the look of disappointment in their eyes, they seem to share my sentiment about the letter. They say nothing to confirm my assumption.

After a couple of minutes, Maggie becomes alert as she shifts straighter in her chair.

"Read it again, Karen."

Maggie loves a mystery. She often focused on an obscure detail that didn't quite fit together. She pulled at it until the whole case unraveled, then sorted through the pieces looking for the truth with single-minded devotion. She was relentless, even sometimes to the annoyance of those around her.

Karen becomes interested and picks up the letter from the table where it had been discarded.

She reads again, "Dear Kathryn."

"Stop!" Maggie turns directly toward me and studies me.

"Why the familiarity?"

"I don't know. We were never on a first-name basis," I defend my honor.

"Symbolism then?" Karen inquires.

I reply with a shrug. Honestly, I have no idea.

We toss around several possible explanations.

"A desire for a personal relationship?" Maggie suggests.

She deserves the sour-milk face I make in response to such a comment. The whole concept of a relationship with Judge Jones is repulsive. There was something about that man that made my skin crawl.

"Certainly NOT!"

"Did he hear other judges call you 'Kathryn'?" Karen asks.

"No. Never. I kept a professional distance with the court." Just to make myself completely clear I add, "None of the judges called me Kathryn. Give me some credit. I knew better than to let that get started."

"Lack of professional respect, or was it just his emotional state at the time he wrote this?" Karen submits.

"I don't know. He was a jerk!" That is the nicest thing I can say about him. I'm unable to articulate my thoughts any better than that.

Karen looks back at the letter and reads, "Don't judge me." She looks up.

"What does he mean, 'don't judge me'?" I am annoyed with him for writing a letter that said nothing. "This is dumb. Certainly not worth the time we are spending on it." But they aren't finished.

"Could there have been a conflict of interest?" Karen asks.

Maggie looks at Karen, and asks, "Then why didn't he recuse himself?"

"Maybe he didn't have a legitimate conflict." Karen sounds suspicious. Maggie and I are alerted by her tone, but we say nothing, waiting for her to continue.

Karen's eyes look thoughtful. She looks back to the paper and reads, "Tell my daughter, I am sorry."

"Sorry for what, the suicide?" Clearly, I am not getting whatever secret message he tried to convey. I have forgotten the secret handshake, and I seem to have left my decoder ring in my other jacket. If he was going to be cryptic, he should have sent the letter to someone who would understand it.

"Kathryn, do you know his daughter?"

"No. No, Karen, I don't think so." I slowly shake my head, searching my mind for a clue to his thinking. Nothing rings a bell. Sending the letter to me makes absolutely no sense at all.

"Sure? Maybe, you know his daughter and that was a conflict of interest," Karen questions.

"I have no idea who she could be," I repeat.

"Then why ask you to tell his daughter?" Maggie is looking at me as she asks, hoping to trigger some recognition of his daughter among my acquaintances. "Maybe he thought you knew her."

"He shouldn't have heard any of my cases, if he thought that was true."

"This just doesn't make sense. Something is not right with this." Karen states the obvious. She has a serious, pensive look.

"Why didn't he mail the letter to his daughter? Why play this silly game, and why with me?"

"Maybe he didn't know where she was?" Maggie says.

"Neither do I!" I regret my tone. I'm not angry with them. But, this is ridiculous.

"This is getting us nowhere," Maggie admits.

Karen is watching both of us try to decipher his message.

"I agree. After my interview on Monday, I'll stop by the courthouse and see what I can find out about Judge Jones' daughter," I offer a small penance for my anger.

Maggie asks, "Was her name is in his obituary?"

"No, I don't think so," Karen rejoins the conversation. "As I remember, I thought the obituary sounded like it was written by someone who didn't know him intimately. Besides, the daughter wouldn't be new information if we had seen it in the obituary."

Maggie glances at Karen and nods in agreement. "True, you have a good point."

"I don't understand why he didn't send it to you, Karen. You're the department head. It would make more sense to expect you to give it to me. Why would he put it in an envelope addressed in care of Keith?"

"I don't know," Karen replies. "You two worked as a team, almost exclusively. Did he think Keith knew where you were?"

It hadn't occurred to me to say anything to Keith about leaving. Our relationship ended when I walked out of the department for the last time. I worked with him exclusively, but he worked with many people in the department. What difference would it make to him if he didn't see me again?

"Judge Jones may not have known you were gone. No one knew you were in Nebraska."

"Nebraska?" Maggie laughs heartily and looks at me amazed. "Really, Kate, how could you?"

Maggie stares straight into my eyes until I look away. Without another word about Nebraska, she resumes speculating about the letter. "Why did he sen it to Keith?"

"Maybe Keith knows his daughter," Karen offers.

"Even if he does, that brings us back to why write the letter to me?" I toss the original question back into the conversation.

Karen looks thoughtful, but doesn't respond. She is usually quick in seeing through these things. "May I take this, and show it to Keith?" Karen asks, holding up the letter, waving it slightly.

"Sure, go ahead. I don't want that thing." I re-fold my napkin and scoot my chair back from the table slightly. "This whole silly game with Judge Jones annoys me." I say it as if there was the slightest chance they didn't clearly get the message already.

"I have to get some sleep." Karen stands and begins to collect the dishes. She has had enough mental gymnastics about the letter for now. Or maybe she is onto something that she isn't ready to share with us.

"Leave the dishes, I'll get them," I say. Maggie and I stand. "I'll let you know what I find out Monday," I add while walking to their cars.

I am tired of Judge Jones. I can't even think about that ridiculous letter right now. I don't expect much to come of it after all this time. Besides, the man is dead. We aren't likely to learn the meaning of the letter. I doubt it really matters in the long run.

My mind resumes the questions as I start the dishwasher. My thoughts ramble while I change my clothes for sleep and brush my teeth. Obviously, people don't decide to shoot themselves out of the blue. Apparently he had been a disturbed man for a long time. It only became obvious how disturbed he was when he fired the gun into his mouth.

Karen answered some questions; however, the cryptic letter raised others. I detest him intruding on my life from his grave. I crawl into bed. I am furious with him all over again.

"Ooh, I hate him," I whisper as I turn over and settle into my pillow.

The rest of the morning and most of the afternoon are lost to restless sleep. The Judge came into my dreams. I wake covered with sweat, my heart is racing, and my bed looks like I have wrestled the devil. Those damn nightmares. The recurring high-pitched blood-curdling scream from the dead little girl is the worst of all. Now Judge Jones is making his debut in my dreams. Is there no escaping them or him?

In the hours after I wake, I don't accomplish anything. The shower doesn't revive me. My mind wanders and I can't stay focused on any task. I start to empty the dishwasher, but have to come back to it three times before I actually finish putting the dishes away. Coffee doesn't taste good. I sit, get up, sit, wander to the window, and sit again. I've tried all the chairs and none are comfortable. I would read, but I can't concentrate and only flip through the pages of a magazine. I'm tired, but I wouldn't nap for anything, not even a million dollars. I have had enough nightmares for today—enough for the rest of my life.

Finally, I force myself into a semblance of routine and stand in front of the open refrigerator with the intention of preparing dinner. Nothing looks good to me. But I'm not really sure I actually looked at the food. I'd go out to eat, but I don't have the energy. If I sit long enough, dinnertime will pass and I won't have to bother with it—at least, not officially.

"I need to shake this, this mood," I whisper to no one. I need time to get on with life after the little girl's scream over and over again in my sleep.

Settling back on the sofa, I pull my feet up on the coffee table and sigh. My eyes roam to my favorite movie poster hanging on the adjacent wall. I stare at the poster, feeling myself being drawn into the scene. It isn't long before the harsh, real world drifts away and music begins to play in my mind. I squint my eyes to focus all of my soul on the music and the mood of the scene. "Play it again, Sam," I whisper.

The Moroccan movie in my memory is interrupted by the distinctive tap at the door. Mr. Goldstein arrives for our daily walk along the beach.

It takes a second to realize what stopped the music, and another second to come to my senses and answer the door. I don't mind the interruption. It's Mr. Goldstein. I get my walking shoes and ease into the comfort of walking along the beach with him.

Maybe it's Mr. Goldstein's personality or his life experience, I don't know which, but he was the first to reveal a deeper level of himself during our walks. He talked about the death camps while I talked of wheat harvest. However, this evening I am beyond talking about the weather and crops.

If my father had been alive I might have discussed with him my frustration about the letter. In Dad's absence, Mr. Goldstein is becoming a fatherly mentor to me. I feel safe and secure with him. Because of that easiness, I enjoy an unexpected freedom in his company. I always look forward to our evening walks, especially today's.

I would never tell Mr. Goldstein, or anyone, the nightmarish details of my work, even if confidentiality wasn't an issue. No, I want his perspective on the hidden dynamics of the Judge's letter.

In the beginning I thought Mr. Goldstein simply wanted to have someone around so he could venture safely farther into the world. Now, I think it is more than that. I think he is looking for companionship, as am I.

Mr. Goldstein seems willing to take our friendship wherever it leads. We both need the exercise. We both need the inter-generational friendship. And today I need to verbalize my thoughts without fear of rejection, and yet have someone I respect stop me when I veer off course.

Whatever is developing between us, it works well because, unlike a real parent, I don't have to struggle for independence from Mr. Goldstein. I can confide in him in a way unlike anyone else I have known. And he willingly, thoughtfully, guides me. There is no tangible explanation for what is special between us, but we have connected. Right now a sense of connectedness is what I crave most.

To have this conversation, this relationship, with Mr. Goldstein, I am willing to dispense my self-preserving defenses and admit that I am clueless. I am willing to divulge my private thoughts and fears about my reaction to the letter.

Mr. Goldstein listens expertly, wisely. My thoughts are disjointed and fragmented. I talk in circles with no direction. I bare my heart to him.

He asks no questions. He simply allows me to talk until I have no more to say, then asks, "What do you think the letter means?"

I consider the questions we had when the letter was opened. I look out at the waves, then confess, "I don't know what it means. That's the problem. I don't know how much credence to give the letter or Judge Jones, considering he committed suicide right after writing it."

I'm used to figuring things out, but can't get enough distance from my feelings about the case or Judge Jones to see the letter objectively. My defenses are completely down, which seems to be what Mr. Goldstein was waiting for.

He remembers the Judge's suicide—it was in the news. Mr. Goldstein smiles, "Katerina, maybe he just wants you and the detective to find his daughter and give her the letter."

"Maybe so," I say, "but what do I tell her?"

"Just what he wrote. Tell her 'he is sorry.' She will know what he meant."

He speaks in a soothing voice. Mr. Goldstein looks at me like he can see into my thoughts and know whether I am still making things more complicated than they need to be. He seems pleased with himself that he understands and I do not. I think that is the beauty of age. It certainly is its privilege.

"You're right. I don't have to understand the letter." I finally understand what he is telling me. He has a refreshing way of simplifying things. Eventually, I hope to learn to do the same.

Mr. Goldstein smiles again and his eyes twinkle.

We have nearly completed our walk. By the time we return home I have decided to put more energy into finding the missing daughter than I had earlier intended.

Maybe Keith can run her driver's license and find her address—if he knows her name and she still lives in California. I am not sure what he can do if she lives out of state. If that's the case, I'll just have to take the risk of raising questions by going to the courthouse to track her down.

~~~

The upcoming job interview moves into the center of my thoughts. The anticipation of it excites me more than I had expected. True to my investigative nature, I decide to research the agency for information in preparation for the interview. With a cup of coffee in hand, I begin. Several online searches come up empty. With more coffee I try different search parameters.

I don't find any information about St. Mark's homeless program. Even the online newspaper archives reveal nothing about it. Apparently, it is too new to have hit the press. Maybe the media hasn't considered it newsworthy. After all, the homeless don't have money to purchase newspapers or advertise in them, so why cover their news, if it doesn't generate revenue? Who else would care?

There are a few articles about St. Mark's Convent that shed light on this potential employer. It has been a long time since I have interviewed
~~~

for a real job, bartending doesn't count. I am probably over-preparing, but it satisfies an indescribable need in me, so I continue the research.

Saint Mark's is a descendant of one of the original California mission communities. They come from a group of Franciscan nuns brought here just before California became a state. The sisters celebrated their 150th anniversary a few years ago. They're a relatively young community of nuns, considering the age of the Catholic Church and religious communities.

The article indicates the convent had been quite large at one time, but it is now down to forty-six nuns. It has been eight years since their last novice made final vows. Their community is in decline. I wonder what that means.

A decline isn't entirely surprising, since many religious communities experienced a decline after Vatican II, but it is worth keeping in mind when I meet with Sister Elizabeth. Their decline could be the result of something unrelated to the changes from Rome. It could be the result of internal problems. I don't want to work somewhere dysfunctional. The information in the article is facts and figures, nothing I can grasp for security.

I'd rather not walk blindly into this situation. On the other hand, how dangerous can forty-six nuns be anyway? After all, it is not like I have to take the job if it doesn't seem right. At the very least it will be interviewing practice.

If I can't find something else, I can work for Karen. I try to keep everything in perspective, but I remind myself that I want a little more out of life than I had expected from it before. I want somewhere I can be myself without being consumed by those around me.

~~~

Monday arrives. I am awake and stirring uncharacteristically early. The interview is scheduled after the morning rush hour, so I have time to savor my coffee before I make my way downtown.

As I drive into the heart of the city, my mind is a whirl with last-minute questions and prepping. Before long I am standing in front of the convent. It is a large, old building with a Spanish influence in its architecture.

One nice thing is that it's located only four blocks from the office where Maggie and I had worked. That will be convenient for having quick lunches with her. I give the nuns extra points for their location.

I pause for a moment or two at the large double front door of the convent. It doesn't seem right to walk into a convent as though it were a place of business, but there is no doorbell. I use the heavy black metal ring-shaped knocker on the weathered wooden door. I take a breath and straighten myself as the knocker hits the strike plate.
~~~

A sister in a traditional brown habit appears at the door. She looks to be in her mid-forties, slim, cheerful, and holy. Very holy.

She says politely, “Good morning, I am Sister Theresa.”

I tell her who I am and why I have come.

She nods awareness of my appointment and says softly, “Follow me, Kathryn.”

After she closes the door, her hands briefly go to her side and disappear as the long sleeves fall over them. I notice with interest as she clasps her hands together in front of her stomach, where her hands remain completely covered in the sleeves of the rough brown fabric. Her slim face is the only part of her humanity in the open.

She says nothing more. Abruptly, she turns her back to me and walks swiftly through the quiet halls. It strikes me as funny, but I contain my humor from erupting into a nervous laugh.

I begin to question my choice of attire as I follow her. I didn’t know they still wore the habit or I might not have worn slacks. The newspaper articles didn’t mention the habit and there were no photos included with it. It’s too late to worry about that now. I hurry to catch up with Sister Theresa.

I steal glimpses of the convent decor as we pass through the halls. It is stark. I feel out of place here. Several large statues, set in alcoves in the walls, loom over us. The delicate statues are beautifully hand-painted. Their faces are serene. As I look into their eyes, I feel their calming influence on my nervousness. I take a deep breath.

Sister Theresa continues to walk silently and swiftly through the hallways. Suddenly she stops before an open door, turns toward the opening, steps past the threshold, genuflects, backs out, then hurriedly continues down the hall.

When I arrive at the doorway, I see a dimly lit chapel. No one is inside, but there is a red candle burning near the altar and the faint smell of lingering incense. It seems strange that incense was used at a weekday Mass. I do what she did and hurry to catch up without letting my shoes make too much noise on the tile floor. It is difficult to walk fast and maintain the look of confidence I want to portray.

Sister Theresa shows me into a waiting room and smiles slightly before quietly disappearing. I sit up straight on the old no-frills leather sofa, waiting uncomfortably.

In about ten minutes, right on time for the appointment, another sister dressed in a brown habit enters. She moves with the same commanding confidence and grace as Sister Theresa, maybe even more. I automatically stand because of the respect she commands.

“Hello, Kathryn. I’m Sister Elizabeth,” says the mid-fifty-ish woman. I am just guessing her age, because all I can see is her face peeking out of the headpiece. A white hand appears from her sleeve as she offers a businesslike handshake.

Protocol. I will have to learn the convent protocol. “Sister, it’s nice to meet you.”

“I understand you worked for Karen Craig,” she says as she leads me into the inner office. “Tell me about that, if you would.”

She sits behind her large desk, motioning me to sit in the chair across from it.

There isn’t time to acclimate to the environment. I begin the textbook description.

“Our department was responsible for investigating suspected child abuse. We worked with the police department on sexual abuse cases, then the district attorney's office—if a case went to court.”

I relax speaking about a subject I know well. “I worked exclusively on sexual abuse cases.” I make the transition from talking about the department to speaking of my role there. I have never told anyone the exact work I did as a social worker. Talking about it feels awkward and yet comfortable.

With her hair tucked under her veil and the habit disguising any taste in fashion she might have, I can’t get a sense of her personality. Her face—even her eyes—don’t yield information about her as an individual. Consequently, I have to answer her questions blind of external clues about the best way to present myself or how well I am doing in the interview. Since she doesn’t give me verbal feedback, I am left to follow my instincts.

“And your co-workers?”

A smile fills my face and I feel my eyes dance. “We were a good team, Sister. We worked extremely well together,” which I believe with all of my heart, and say it with passion.

“What was your relationship to your supervisor?” She looks straight at me with each question, with the knowing look only a nun has.

This is not the time to confess how often we butted heads. “Dr. Craig gave us direction when we needed it, and room to work when we didn’t.” I am surprised by my answer. “She has confidence in her staff. We—we were an incredible team.”

Overall I am proud of my answers. However, I am beginning to wonder if I will regret not taking my old job back while I can.

“Then, why aren't you working there?”

“I am ready for a change from CPS. Dr. Craig suggested I apply here.” I hope she is satisfied with my answer. Now I am unsure why I’m not back at my old job. As a matter of fact, my old job paid more than twice what this job offers—plus benefits. Worse work, though.

Sometimes money isn't the deciding factor in the choices we make. This is one of those times. I want more than money from my next job. I want a life.

In an open file folder on her desk, she has the résumé and copy of my diploma I had emailed to her. There are a couple of other papers. Perhaps they are letters of reference, but I don't know for sure, and I can't imagine how she has them in two days. One thing for certain, I didn't give them to her.

Without obviously staring, all I can do is glance intermittently at the papers, hoping to figure out what they are. There are newspaper clippings sticking out from under the other papers, but I can't see enough to determine which they are.

"I see there is a five-year gap in your résumé," she says.

I'm busted. I hope she doesn't back me into a corner, forcing me to mention the bar. I'm not ashamed of being a bartender, I just don't want to talk about Nebraska and the events of my self-imposed exile, or recent return to L.A.

"Yes, Sister, I was out of state during that time, so I omitted it," I say smoothly. I will probably never mention the bar to anyone—except Karen and Maggie.

To my amazement, Sister Elizabeth lets it slip by without asking additional questions. A slight relaxing smile comes over me as I think about my hidden "wild" past.

Sister Elizabeth looks at my résumé for another pausing moment, then looks over her reading glasses at me.

I would feel better if she would smile or something to give me a clue about how this interview is proceeding. In the absence of indicators, disappointment creeps over me. I brace for the inevitable.

Unexpectedly, she continues, "Do you know anything about homelessness, being hungry, or alone with no one to help?"

I understand the sense of the hopelessness she is describing, but the perfect words don't come to explain the concept in terms of human reality. I'm doomed. I simply answer, "Yes."

She begins to provide a quick overview of her program. She must have decided to hire me. Otherwise, she could have ended the interview. Why else is she telling me about the program? I must have the job. I listen carefully to her review—just in case I am correct in assessing her behavior.

Sister Elizabeth's face lights up and her eyes dance. "This is a pilot project. It is designed for families who have been homeless less than two years." She pauses for a minute before revealing her hope for the future when she adds, "Then we will expand the program to people with less chance for success."

There are several innovative social work aspects in their program. And she wants staff who are creative, diligent, and committed to get the program off to a good start.

No, not committable, committed. I nervously joke to myself in this foreign environment that is making me feel like I am trespassing.

“Kathryn, can you start tomorrow morning at 9:00?” Sister Elizabeth asks as she stands up from behind her huge old desk, obviously concluding the interview. Does she know I’m not working?

“Yes, ma’am.” I stutter, “I, ah, yes, Sister.” I feel my cheeks blush. I wish they hadn’t betrayed me, but I will survive.

“Dress casually, and we will review the program and your duties.”

That will be a nice change of pace—something between business suits for court and blinking bow ties at Ruthie’s Bar.

Unaware of my inattentive thoughts, she smiles warmly before directing me back to the main hallway. She stops and looks at me squarely. “And, Kathryn, you don't have to genuflect at the chapel, if you are not Catholic. It's acceptable to walk past the doors.”

Did nothing escape her? I wonder how she knew I had genuflected at the chapel—maybe it was just a lucky guess.

Walking beside Sister Elizabeth through the halls to the front of the building, I am aware that she behaves in a motherly manner reminiscent of Karen’s new manner.

Sister Elizabeth genuflects expertly despite the yards of brown fabric that balloon on the floor as she kneels. She smiles at me, then turns back in the direction of her office, leaving me on my own to find the way out.

I do genuflect at the chapel doors. I am glad to have a job, and it won't hurt to show that I'm thankful.

Sister Theresa joins me near the front door and conducts me out into the waiting California sunshine.

~~~

Inside the main entrance of the courthouse, I wait for the arrival of an emotional avalanche from returning to the setting of my nightmares. Nothing happens. Nothing? Certainly, not the response I expected.

Either I am in denial or stronger than I think. Could it be I really don’t feel anything in this place? For five years I have felt broken. Was it all a lie?

The routine security check hardly interrupts my thoughts. I pause in the middle of the foyer, still waiting for the emotions that should have come. To buy time to adjust, I choose the stairs over the elevator.

It concerns me that I feel nothing, although it is convenient not to deal with rampant emotions right now. I have no plan to return to the courtroom we were in that day—that’s too risky.
~~~

The place to start my query is the Clerk of the Court's office on the third floor. If anyone knows anything, Agnes will. She has been the Clerk since the courthouse opened a hundred or more years ago. Well, maybe not quite that long, but almost. All I have to do is get her talking, then move her on topic.

After several unrelated stories, Agnes finally comes up with a gem—Judge Jones' law clerk, Sam Jackson, now works for Judge Lawrence.

One of the criminal lawyers, who is filing documents in the Clerk's Office, overhears the conversation and says, "I saw Sam in the law library about fifteen minutes ago. He looked like he planned to be there for a while."

"Thanks." Well, that was easy enough.

Since I have no idea what the guy looks like, I hope Mr. Jackson has stayed put. As it turns out, it was a useless concern. There is only one person in the library.

He and his laptop are surrounded with stacks of law books and a legal pad on the table. He is typing at a fast clip, and he doesn't look up from his work when I enter. Finally he stops typing and flips through a fat file of papers.

"Mr. Jackson?" I ask, approaching his table, ready to extend a handshake if he responds affirmatively.

"Yes?" He looks up and smiles a broad smile. He is a handsome Black man, appearing to be about my age—maybe a little older. He wears thick-lens glasses and a very engaging smile. There is a sense of approachability about him, though he is dressed in a tailored suit that looks strictly business.

"Hello, I'm Kathryn. I am looking for Judge Jones' daughter."

"I don't know anything about Judge Jones' family. I only clerked for him a few months before he killed himself." He is soft-spoken with a deep, rich voice.

"I see. Well, thanks for your time." I smile and turn to leave.

"Wait. I do remember something. I think Judge Jones' wife died years ago, but now that I think about it, he did have a picture of a young woman on his credenza."

It isn't much to go on. Oh well, it was a long shot anyway.

"It is probably still around here somewhere. No one claimed his personal belongings after he died, that is, those not taken by Homicide."

His comment reminds me that suicide is just another form of murder. That old case is a collection of one damaged life after another. I feel terribly sad about the whole ordeal.

"I'll make some inquiries. Give me a number where I can reach you, Kathryn. I'll call, if I find the picture."

I wish he knew more. This will have to do for now.

Agnes left for lunch. I know several other people who worked in the courthouse. I spend a little time visiting the offices in search of someone who might be helpful.

Unfortunately, after an hour, I don't find anyone I know well enough to ask directly about the Judge's daughter. I'm sure there were rumors about Karen's investigation, and I don't want to raise suspicions. No one mentions Judge Jones or his death, so I'm unable to maneuver the conversation to get what I want. It was probably a dumb idea anyway.

~~~

As planned, I meet Maggie for lunch and tell her about my new job. Maggie, like any good friend, is pleased I am still employable in my field.

"Will you adjust to a job without tips?"

There is no resisting a laugh at her wit, even if it is at my expense. Tips aren't the issue. We both understand that the bar brought no nightmares. She must appreciate why I needed a job like that. In this moment of pause, I feel deep appreciation for Maggie's friendship and for Karen's lead on the new job.

"Before I head back to Orange County, I'm going to thank Karen for the job information."

"Have a nice trip. She's in Sacramento all week for a conference." Maggie laughs.

~~~

Even though I haven't learned anything about the Judge's daughter, I have accomplished quite a bit for one day. Time to go home and start reconnecting the rest of the pieces of my life. Until I had the basics—a car, job, and an apartment—I didn't feel ready to reconnect with my extended family.

There are twenty-seven first cousins in my family, so it is not terribly unusual to lose track of one of us from time to time. I am certainly not the first or likely to be the last to disappear for a while, then return. I tend to be one of the less colorful members of this family. I guess running away for five years is my turn to fly in the face of convention. My world is steadily expanding now that I'm home again. Once I reconnect with my family, my world will expand exponentially.

I begin with a call to my cousin Ilene. We decide to meet at Laguna Beach on Saturday morning. Her schedule only allows a little over an hour, but it will be enough time to touch base. Baby steps.

~~~

Mr. Goldstein comes after dinner and we go for our walk. I've lost focus on the physical exercise and look forward to our talks. Hollow conversation is a thing of the past. Instead we speak of feelings, dreams, and hopes.
~~~

He is genuinely happy I managed to get the job. I am pleased too. It was easy, wasn't it? Things are moving along effortlessly, taking on a life of their own—or rather, giving me a new life.

Mr. Goldstein asks numerous questions about the homeless program. He is very knowledgeable about the homeless issues. It's his passionate cause. I promise to tell him more tomorrow.

The day's activities have energized me. I make a new pot of coffee and settle in with my computer. The online newspaper archives produce the Judge's obituary.

Karen is correct. There isn't much to it. There is no mention of a daughter. It does mention his wife preceded him in death, but doesn't list her name. I have no idea how long she has been dead. I know it is absurd, but I put the name "Jones" into the obituary search and hope that the daughter would be mentioned in Mrs. Jones' obituary. As expected, the archives pull up an unmanageable amount of obituaries for people named "Jones."

I begin to mark off names that are obviously male names. I wish I had asked for her first name while I was at the courthouse, but it hadn't occurred to me then.

Starting at the top, I skim each obituary listed looking for one mentioning a spouse named William Jones. I had hoped to have a lucky break and find Mrs. Jones' obituary quickly. It doesn't work that way. I get through the list as far as the letter "H." That's enough for tonight.

Standing before the closet, I prepare for my first day at my new job. I select a blue blouse, black slacks that I think look casual enough, and a pair of flats. I set two alarm clocks out of reach of my bed, so I won't shut them off. I feel excitedly ready for tomorrow morning.

Lying in bed, working through the morning routine in my mind, I decide to take the mass transit to avoid any unexpected delays on the freeway. It has been five years since I drove that route during morning rush hour. I won't be late the first day at my new job.

I'm not leaving anything to chance, so I get up and check the transit schedule on the internet. Finally, I crawl back into bed. The activity of the day settles on me. At last, I am tired enough to fall asleep.

~~~
~~~

~ CHAPTER 6 ~

Nun Other Than...

The morning transit takes less time than I expected. I decide to wait at the bus stop a block from St. Mark's, so I won't be too early for my first day at work. There is nothing worse than appearing too eager.

Finally, as nine o' clock approaches, I walk down the street to the convent. Like last time, Sister Theresa greets me at the door. She is not hurried today. Instead, she directs a tour of the old school and convent, at least, the public areas of the convent.

The Catholic grade school is still in operation, but three years ago the high school merged with a larger school in a better neighborhood. The nuns converted the old high school building into living quarters: one classroom for each anticipated homeless family. Sister Theresa identifies the other rooms by their new use rather than the former function, even though she acknowledges that some remodeling still needs to be completed.

The cafeteria is now the common dining room. The families will eat in a communal fashion, much like the sisters do in the adjacent convent. There is a playroom for the children and a community room for relaxing.

"One of our sisters and a local artist painted a mural around the walls of the playroom," she beams.

I stop in awe just inside the playroom door. Amazingly, it isn't overwhelming to have the mural from floor to ceiling on all four walls. It's detailed, but not too busy. All in all, it's calming. I feel its effect just standing here, though my eyes are eagerly moving from one surprisingly delightful detail to the next.

To the left of the door and around the nearby corner is a country scene with a cottage and a variety of domesticated animals and squirrels that ventured near the dwelling. Midway along the wall the terrain rises slightly to gentle rolling hills covered with wild flowers. A paved road emerges from the far side of the hills and turns the corner onto the next wall.

The road quickly grows into a freeway system with bridges over a barge-filled river in the forefront of a city, which includes a collection of tall smokestacks belonging to a factory. Towering apartment buildings glow with the setting sun. The buildings blend into silhouettes with light-filled windows as the painted sky fades to darkness, except for the moon and stars in the heavens. The cityscape takes nearly the entire wall opposite the door.

Beyond the city, nearing the third corner of the room, the ground rises to a high meadow at the edge of a forest which begins on the third wall. The forest grows dense with hardwood trees that reach to the ceiling, blocking most of the painted light to the forest floor and a small overgrown footpath. Tiny shimmering rays of sunlight filter through the forest canopy to illuminate deer, bears, and other indigenous adult animals in the distance, keeping watch over their youngsters in the forefront—within reach if a child wishes to touch them.

Moving along the wall, the forest thins and a stream gives way at a steep drop. The rising sun glistens through the mist of a waterfall cascading down the corner of the room and splashing into a freshwater pool with brightly colored trout, frogs, and dragonflies. At the far edge of the lake, the water rushes to the sea and the waves splash with a pair of dolphins. Farther back, a California gray whale spews a waterspout while another breaches into the water. Beneath the surface, a whale calf is visible swimming at an adult's side.

On the fourth wall the waves rush onto the shore where there is a wonderfully intricate sandcastle. Beyond the grassy sand-dune beach, a desert materializes. It is full of cacti, Joshua trees, horny toads, a burro, and a scorpion with its tail turned up. The sand grows green and golden with California poppies that end at the door. The entire picture connects together, and I love it!

Sister Theresa says they will have a story hour as she points to the overstuffed pillows and beanbag chairs. The beanbags were selected because of the cradling effect of them—perfect for little ones who need to be cradled, but don't want to be handled.

My eyes go around the room a second time looking at the details. There are butterflies, seagulls, hummingbirds, soaring eagles, and a cactus wren—all in the appropriate habitat.

I assume there are no people in the mural because the children are encouraged to place themselves into the settings, stimulating their imagination. No explanation about the missing people is offered, and I don't venture to ask. The idea and the art are brilliant.

Inconsistent, inadequate education, and housing erodes the homeless children's confidence, social skills, and emotional security. Sister Theresa says they have a place for craft projects to facilitate communication among the children and the supervising adults. They have group activities planned and are always looking for others. They have a whole forest's worth of stuffed animals for the children to cuddle.

Sister Elizabeth and her staff thought through the entire program. The children will attend the parish school, tuition free, and there will be after-school tutoring to catch them up academically while helping them with their current homework.

Sister Theresa moves the tour along. Two sisters are near storage closets in the school's auditorium, organizing musical instruments.

Sister Theresa introduces Sister Mary Veronica, the grade school music teacher, and Sister Marie. Sister Mary Veronica slightly nods her head in my direction in response to the introduction. She looks older, well past retirement age, but full of energy. I can only imagine the kind of music she teaches.

We had an old teacher like her when I was in grade school. We sang "Salve Regina" and "Ave Maria" until our Latin was perfect. Unfortunately, she was so particular about diction that those were the only two songs we sang the entire year, but we sang them beautifully.

Not to be left out of the action, Sister Mary Veronica explains her plan to make musical instruments available to the families. "Maybe we can have jam sessions!" She admits to secretly hoping, "Maybe I will be asked to give music lessons."

Jam sessions? I think to myself how things are rarely as they appear. Sister Mary Veronica smiles at me as if she can read my thoughts. I am sure that she can't really read minds—can she?

Sister Theresa turns to me to explain, "The new residents will need a form of expressing what they have been through, and words don't always come easily. Music may become their voice for a while, maybe for the rest of their lives."

Sister Mary Veronica adds excitedly, "We can start a choir!"

These two nuns act like children scheming a wild adventure. Their enthusiasm is contagious. A smile rises to my lips and I realize I am happy to be here in this place, and to be a part of this wonderful scheme to help people. I love it. I simply love it.

Gesturing her hand toward the other nun, Sister Theresa continues, "Sister Marie teaches mathematics—she also studied dance all her life and wants to teach dance to the children."

Sister Marie smiles sweetly and nods agreement with Sister Theresa. "I would love to teach ballet, but they will like jazz or tap better."

Tap? Tap is noisy. The image of this woman in a habit teaching dance flashes into my mind. How is she going to teach isolation exercises for jazz to the children? They won't be able to see the incremental movements under her habit.

"Dance is a physical activity, but more importantly it will free their little spirits. They can benefit from something setting them free of the weight of life's reality, while giving them the success of mastering the steps." Sister Marie lectures her opinion in a math teacher matter-of-fact way. "Performing arts are esteem builders. Besides, everyone should learn to dance."

Looking at Sister Marie's young face and bright eyes, she must be the one in the newspaper article who made final vows eight years ago. I think the kids will like her. For a nun she seems pretty cool, but I still can't imagine her in a leotard leading a rag-tag dance troop across the gymnasium floor.

We progress in the direction of Sister Elizabeth's office. Sister Theresa deposits me at the door, as she had yesterday, and points me to a leather sofa. Then she announces our arrival to "Mother Elizabeth."

What? Mother? She caught me off guard. I don't know what I expected. They do wear habits, so it makes sense they still use the formal title Mother for their leader. With increased interest I think how now I can see what a real Mother Superior is like and see if Karen's nickname fits her.

The unexpectedness of this new job is definitely a refreshing change from child abuse investigations. Working in this place promises to be mentally stimulating, plus the program has creative social work elements that satisfy me.

An abrupt noise interrupts my thoughts when Mother Elizabeth shuts the drawer of her desk. She stands up and moves a wooden chair she was using as a credenza back to its place in front of her desk.

I don't mean to watch her, but the sound caught my attention. I am embarrassed when our eyes meet in an awkward moment. I look away.

To the left of where I am seated on the leather sofa, I see into a conference room that I hadn't noticed yesterday. People are beginning to congregate in the meeting room via a door from the hallway. Mother Elizabeth comes from her office and motions for me to follow her through the door to join the group.

Apparently, I am the last person hired. Everyone else seems to know where to go and appears comfortable with their surroundings. Inside the conference room on the table near the door there are stacks of folders along with other materials arranged in neat piles, ready to be disseminated.

After we have filed through the line to pick up our folders, we sit on one side of the dining-room-style tables surrounded by straight-back wooden chairs, so we are all facing Mother Elizabeth. I glance at my new co-workers at the table I join, and smile at any who makes eye contact with me. I look around to see if I know anyone. I know this, I'm in a good place.

Mother Elizabeth begins immediately after the last person takes his seat. There is so much new information to absorb that previewing the entire staff will have to wait until later. For now I stick to scribbling notes as Mother gives a précis of the handouts. I can work with anyone for the good of my clients, so the staff are secondary to my mission.

It has been a long time since I have had a new area of study. (Bartending doesn't count.) I take copious notes. My attentiveness is based on my desire to understand so completely that the knowledge will be second nature to me by the time the clients arrive. It is stimulating to hear new information in my field. I feel alive.

Mother Elizabeth reviews the program with us, her secular staff, explaining that whatever it takes to help these yet-to-arrive clients get back on their feet, is what will be done. At the end of an hour, Mother Elizabeth announces, "You have the rest of the week to learn the information in the packets. You will be paid for forty hours of work this week. Take the material home—study it. Come on Monday ready to work." She dismisses us, and that is that.

There are no questions from her new workers. What she expects of us is clear. Apparently she has determined we are capable of the task. Just like in Catholic school, we line up in an orderly fashion and file out the door past Mother Elizabeth.

~~~

The week passes quickly. Reviewing the material from work is an all-consuming task. The days are spent devouring the material and internalizing it. I do nothing else during these days except walk on the beach and study. The hours blend with each other. I lose track of time. I eat when I am hungry. I sleep when I am tired. The rules of night and day become meaningless.

I enjoy the freedom from the constraints of time and external schedules. It is an interesting experience, one that I want to explore further when I have more time. For now, I focus on the assigned task.

Reading about the reality of the situation of these yet-unknown-to-us homeless families makes me cry. It overwhelms me to think about the kindness of these nuns who are opening their home and resources to strangers.

Mother Elizabeth's material reminds me why I switched majors to social work during the first year of college. The sisters' project seems to have real potential to make a difference for the people they will serve. The prospect of making a difference sparks a renewed enthusiasm for my chosen life's work. Finally, slowly, I am regaining my focus of who I am as a social worker. I had wanted to make a difference. Perhaps it's possible to do that at St. Mark's in a larger way than I could by doing child abuse investigations.

Mother Elizabeth maintains absolute control of the program. No one can vandalize this program like Judge Jones did to our cases ensnared in the judicial system. I don't think anyone with any common sense will try to sabotage her plans. This woman runs a household full of nuns; she is not someone to mess with. We are as safe from the craziness of
~~~

the system as anyone in this business can be, something I desperately crave.

At last I reach the final information packet. It contains the referral criteria. The grant the nuns wrote specified traditional families—father, mother, and children. That, and limiting the length of time of homelessness to two years or less, is clearly designed to help the program succeed. Mother Elizabeth impresses me with her insight to anticipate unexpected problems before admitting people at greater risk of failure; people who will need more support and resources that will need to be developed to meet their critical needs. Hopefully, that will improve the families' chances for a sustainable success, as well as renew funding for another three years of the program.

In addition to everything else, I like the name she gave the program, "Spirit of Hope." As I learn the material, I find myself caught up in the spirit of hope that the program emanates.

~~~

Mr. Goldstein continues to come for his evening walk during my study week. Now that he is physically stronger he has started attending the Senior Center on a regular basis. Sometimes while we are out for our walk he tells stories about the goings on at the Center, especially about the older women. (As if he is so young.) In truth, he is enjoying the company of the women his age. He does seem younger than before he started getting regular exercise. The companionship and fresh air probably helps too.

We talk endlessly during our walks. Our hands are animated, and we nod in agreement or disagreement. This week he is especially interested in the material I am studying. It helps me internalize the information more easily to discuss it with him.

Mr. Goldstein makes a curious sound when he hears the program's name, thinks it over, then indicates his approval. Of course he likes the name. Who wouldn't like "Spirit of Hope"? His unpretentious response amuses me so much that I have to fight back a laugh and the urge to hug him. I don't think he would mind either, but it doesn't seem to fit the mood of our conversation.

I managed to return to California late enough in the winter to miss the worst beach storms that come in November. As the days pass, the winter skies are beginning to show signs of the approaching spring. The beach doesn't seem as cold and desolate as when I first came home, yet the tourists are still months away. It is a peaceful winter-beach. With Mr. Goldstein's help, it is a place of refuge.

About mid-week Maggie stops by to check on my progress with Mother Elizabeth's homework assignment. For "graduation" she offers
~~~

dinner at her place—Friday night. "Besides," she tells me, "Dave" her long-time live-in partner "thinks you are a figment of my imagination." She laughs as she tosses her head back in her usual mischievous manner.

"Dave," I whisper. "It will be good to see him again." I smile and I accept her invitation for a good meal and conversation among old friends.

The days continue to blur together. Wisely, Maggie calls Friday afternoon to remind me of the graduation dinner in a few hours. In the course of our conversation she mentions that Dave invited a friend from the law office where he works. I am beginning to get suspicious, but since I am already committed to the evening, I still plan to attend. After all, I can claim fatigue and leave early if the evening turns disastrous.

Dave greets me at the door with a kiss on the cheek and a hug. He is a full partner in a large law firm downtown. He and Maggie became an item during Dave's last year in law school, when she was a freshman. They have been together ever since. Surely they must have discussed marriage at some point, but never married. Whatever their arrangement is, it works nicely for them.

~~~

Joseph McLean, Dave's friend, arrives shortly after me. Joseph is heart-stopping handsome. He has beautiful dark eyes with the blackest lashes to match his wavy black hair. There are laugh lines around his mouth and eyes. He is quick to laugh, flashing his bright white teeth. Joseph is charming, and he knows it.

I catch myself staring at him several times in the first few minutes after he arrives. This is embarrassing, but I don't stop admiring him. He has an Irish accent. I love to hear him talk and see him flash his big, easy smile.

Maggie makes an excuse for me to help her in the kitchen where she gives me Joseph's condensed biography.

"Joseph is spelled I-O-S-E-P-H, but pronounced 'Joseph.' He is thirty-seven, a successful criminal lawyer, AND never married. At least not yet," Maggie says with a disturbing amount of delight as she grins at me. Eros has nothing on her. No doubt she is hiding Cupid's arrows behind her back as we speak. Yikes!

Dinner is relaxing. The men don't occupy the conversation with discussions of their conquests in the courtroom. Dave allows Maggie to shift the conversation to discussing my new job. As I explain the new program at St. Mark's, they seem genuinely interested in the homeless.

Dave and Joseph ask many insightful questions about the legal needs of our clients. I agree legal services probably are needed by some, but unfortunately it is unlikely there is money in the budget for it,
~~~

and I'm not sure even the filing fees would be manageable. There probably isn't much hope for these two to add to their client base at Spirit of Hope.

Dave offers pro bono work. Joseph says he can swing a case or two to clear some old offenses, then flashes a toothy grin. The guys talk about asking the bankruptcy attorneys to send a paralegal or two to Mother Elizabeth to see if any of the clients need a bankruptcy to get a fresh start.

Their generosity catches me by surprise. It suits the altruistic social worker in me. They both draw business cards out of their pocket business card holders as if it is a contest to be first-draw in a poorly scripted Western showdown.

For Joseph's benefit Maggie tries unsuccessfully to divert the conversation back to me. I resist her efforts to take it to a personal level, and she gives me a disapproving look. I don't care, she can disapprove all she likes. On the other hand, I want more information about him.

Much to Maggie's distress, I am spared the problem of things getting personal. We continue discussing the program and the likely needs of the clientele.

Eventually other safe topics of interest make their way into our conversation. Regardless of the topic, I like listening to Joseph's thick accent. Verging on being obsessive, I ask him as many questions as I can to keep him talking. I try not to seem too mesmerized by him, but I doubt anyone is fooled. Needless to say, there is no need to attempt an early escape.

~~~

Driving home, I wonder what Joseph thinks of me and if I will see him again. Maybe Maggie and Dave can be persuaded to arrange another dinner party in the near future. I can only hope.

My thoughts are still occupied with Joseph when I reach my apartment. I need to refocus. Though it is not entirely the wisest thing to do alone at this hour, I walk to the empty beach and listen to the waves come to shore.

I think about how pleasant it was to see Maggie. When I left California I didn't say goodbye to her, which makes no sense. Strangely, she still has not asked me why I did not contact her during the five years away. She hasn't pushed discussing any of the old issues from work since the reading of the judge's letter with Karen.

I am glad not to continue either conversation. Perhaps now that we are working at different agencies our friendship will continue in new and different ways.

The longer I sit on the beach, the more sentimentality washes over me. I think about Maggie and Dave and what a treasure their friendship
~~~

is to me. I think about Joseph. The mysteriousness of him intrigues me. And Mr. Goldstein, an unexpected welcomed friendship bundles all into coming home.

I have missed California and all the nuances of life it holds for me. Contentedly, I sit soaking in the experience of the beach, smelling the sandy saltwater scents, and listening to the sound of the crashing waves as the tide comes in. My mind settles softly into the rhythm the waves play in my thoughts.

As the tide rises, the mist of the breaking waves reaches out to touch me from the darkness. Behind me on the lifeguard station, the handless clock confirms time is truly standing still. I look up at the moon in the black night sky and think, if this was a movie, they would be playing the good music right about now.

~~~

In the morning, my cousin Ilene and I meet at Laguna Beach. She is standing on the beach looking out at the ocean as I approach. She looks just as I remember her. The greeting is always the same whether we saw each other last week or five years ago. She greets me with a hug as if I am her little sister. This warm and genuine affection is the hallmark of our family. I reciprocate. In this family any other behavior would be alien to our nature.

We have only an hour to visit before her tennis date. Ilene tells me she is a grandmother now. I tell her about my job. We make plans to get together for lunch at her new house when we can really catch up with each other. We move the boxes I had shipped from Nebraska out of her car and into mine. She asks if I want to talk about going away. I know there isn't time to get into that conversation, so I decline.

~~~

Monday morning Mother Elizabeth appears with shopping lists. She divides us into two groups. One group is assigned to descend upon the local merchants in a never-before-seen swarm. She dispatches the first group of staff out into the world of commerce, two-by-two, to purchase shampoo, bath towels, hairbrushes, laundry detergent, and everything from aftershave to nail polish. She gives specific instructions to her shoppers: "Get the good stuff, the bright cheery colors, the fluffy towels."

She turns her attention to the remaining group. Mother Elizabeth assigns the non-shopper group to sort through the sizable stacks of applications under the watchful supervision of Sister Theresa. I am assigned to this group. We are to stack the applications in piles based only on the initial screening criteria, families and length of time of homelessness, nothing else.

I know several of the social workers among the staff. We've met at professional conferences. We never actually worked together, but all of the staff have excellent reputations in the social work community. It is rumored the others with essential specialties are equally as good as the social workers. We are the quintessential staff. We can do more than basic paper-sorting tasks.

Mother Elizabeth is counting on us to make this program work despite the odds. I wish she would trust her judgment in hiring us and let us jump in and use our talents and training. However, she is specific with her instructions. Perhaps eventually she will trust us with more responsibility once we have proven ourselves to her. For now she alone has taken on the task of deciding who will be admitted to Spirit of Hope and who is refused. Maybe she is being cautious. I hope she isn't one who tends to micro-manage projects.

At our coffee break two staff members report they heard that Mother Elizabeth requested the referring agencies not to tell the families they refer. In that small way, if they are not selected, she can protect them from one more disappointment. She can't take them all in, not yet, anyway. But I bet she finds a way to increase the number of people she can get off the streets.

As I triage the applications, I have to admit that I am beginning to respect Mother Elizabeth for not asking anyone else to make the hard decision of who will be turned away. I had only thought of the screening as who would be accepted, not those rejected. That must weigh heavily on a person—even a nun who has God's benediction.

We silently continue our screening duties. Whatever their opinion is, none of the staff mention their thoughts. After failing to be acutely aware of the struggles of my co-workers at CPS, I intentionally make the effort to be astute regarding what is going on around me at this job. It is a fresh start with a new program, and I plan to pay attention.

As I reach for another referral from the stack I see Mother Elizabeth rubbing the back of her neck. When she looks up and sees me watching her, a strange look comes over her face.

Quickly, I look at the papers in front of me, but I am not really reading them. I am still thinking about Mother Elizabeth's fatigue. Perhaps she is a little embarrassed with being caught as a mere mortal that gets stiff muscles like the rest of us. Though I shouldn't, I look back at her—squarely at her.

Mother Elizabeth removes her reading glasses, but leaves her hand suspended at half-mast. Her eyebrows move slightly, and it is hard to tell how much they would have moved if the forehead piece to her veil hadn't restrained the movement. It seems like a long pause. Finally, she lays her glasses on the table and addresses me from where she sits.

"Kathryn, you are an expert on children, aren't you?"

"Mother, I don't have children," I answer, noting the nearby co-workers are listening to the conversation without looking up.

"No, but you know about children, don't you?" She tips her hand to the answer she expects.

"Yes, Mother Elizabeth, I do." I understand her directive.

"Then, come with me," Mother Elizabeth says as she stands to leave.

As I rise, I look to my co-workers for a clue, a hint, about what Mother has in mind. A few of them are now looking up from their work. Their expressions make it obvious that none of them know what she is up to, either.

I follow her out of the room and down the hall. Unlike Sister Theresa, Mother Elizabeth waits for me to catch up and walk beside her. She doesn't talk en route. She genuflects at the chapel doorway. I do the same. As we walk to her office, this reminds me of Karen summoning me. She takes a checkbook and a small wallet from her desk drawer. She removes a set of keys from one of the hooks on the inside of the coat closet door. I follow her out the back door to the garages, slide in the front passenger seat of the vehicle, and secure the seat belt.

Mother Elizabeth drives carefully through the narrow alley and pulls into the traffic. Silently looking directly forward, I sit motionless in the front seat, insuring I don't distract her from her attention to driving.

This ride reminds me of the other time I rode in a vehicle with a nun at the wheel. In first grade one of the sisters drove me to the hospital to be with my mother after my parents had been in an auto accident.

I remember Sister instructing harshly, "Sit quiet," while she concentrated on driving. She seemed uneasy and nervously hesitant with the traffic. Thinking about it now I wonder whether she even had a driver's license. Some didn't back then.

During that entire trip I clutched the strap of my book bag until my knuckles were tight, while staring at my oxfords dangling above the floorboard. My father died later that afternoon. I haven't been in a car with a nun since then.

Mother Elizabeth begins to speak casually. It takes a moment for me to leave that memory of long ago and mean old Sister Dominic. The sound of her voice comes through the memory, relaxing me into the conversation.

Mother Elizabeth has never given me a reason to distrust her. It was the unknown element in her request that made me uneasy. Eventually I will to adapt to her expectation of blind obedience without responding with uneasiness. After all, how threatening can a nun be?

Mother Elizabeth expertly turns the car across three lanes of oncoming traffic and into the parking lot of the shopping center. Curiosity crowds the other thoughts from my mind. I forget my concerns about riding with a nun or being summoned to blind obedience. Why are we going to the mall? What is her mission?

Inside the store, our task turns out to be shopping for children's sheets and blankets. Well, this is easy enough.

In my previous job I learned the children's modern heroes. It was one of the tools of my trade. Children are not going to tell their deepest secrets to someone who doesn't know the name of the character pictured on their shirt or the doll tucked under their arm.

It is purely a matter of credibility to know their heroes. There is no such thing as winging it with kids. Either you know what you're talking about or you don't. Instinctively they know too much to ever be fooled by phony credentials. Some social workers try it, but it never works—not in a million years. Working in children's services requires advanced studies in the children's section of the bookstore, hours of children's television, and browsing toy store aisles to know the neighborhood where kids live and play.

Mother Elizabeth and I cruise the linen aisle looking at the displays. All of the characters on the packages are familiar to me. I differentiate for Mother which characters are the good guys and keep her from purchasing those with a questionable reputation, even if they look cute. Mother Elizabeth appears to enjoy purchasing children's bedding for a change of pace. It was thoughtful of her to even think of children's sheets, considering she has never had children.

After shopping, Mother stops at the soda fountain at the food court. She whispers, "They make the best vanilla colas here."

It intrigues me to have an unexpected moment off the clock with her. After Karen's honesty about the emotional and physical strain of being in charge, I had been concerned when I noticed Mother Elizabeth assumed all of the weight of the program for herself.

It is a relief to realize that she monitors her own barometer. She paces herself, obviously something I need to learn after my experience five years ago. "All or nothing" is too stressful of a way to conduct work or life.

As we enjoy our drink, we visit about the Dodgers upcoming season —she is quite the fan. A fashionably dressed woman walks past us, moving our conversation to fashion—somewhat surprising me, considering what Mother Elizabeth wears. I remind myself she hasn't always been a nun, but it's hard to imagine. She is very much a nun, even with a cherry-vanilla cola in her hand, and fashion or baseball in her words.

Mother Elizabeth turns her attention to the people carefully selecting plants from a potted plant display. She remarks she loves to garden without removing her gaze from the plants. She moves to the display and carefully examines the specimens, but purchases none of them. That is not the purpose of this trip. She is very disciplined.

Watching her, I recall seeing the usual convent vegetable garden while on tour with Sister Theresa. Of course, there are flower gardens around the outdoors grottos. She speaks fondly, though briefly, about her own private garden.

In my mind's eye I can imagine Mother Elizabeth outside, alone in her own garden, recalibrating her self-monitoring systems. The idea seems to fit with the character of this woman I am becoming acquainted with today. I wonder who she turns to when gardening isn't enough? God? Yes, probably.

When we return to the convent we put away our new treasures until they are needed. She wants them left in the packages so the children know they have new sheets, and to select their own. There will be hand-me-downs later, but she wants as many new items as the program can afford in the beginning.

While we work side by side, her thoughtfulness for the children continues to amaze me. Most people, especially virgin nuns, would not have thought of special linen for the children. I have come to believe she has a detailed plan for everything. I admire her tenderness and her gentle ways.

~~~

Throughout the week Mother Elizabeth takes other staff on errands. No doubt she is getting to know each of us away from the convent environment. It is rumored that each of the staff was recommended to Mother Elizabeth by people she knows. Equal opportunity employment doesn't seem as important to her as a hand-picked team to help the people who will soon come through the front door of St. Mark's convent, school, and now, home for the homeless.

Mother Elizabeth applied for grants from private foundations. Thanks to her savvy ideas, there is no danger this program will be one of those giving the appearance of helping, but in reality just creating employment for otherwise unemployable staff. Those programs are only smoke and mirrors—they alleviate nothing for the people in need. Spirit of Hope is real, and I desperately need to be part of something real.

These nuns touch something in the core of my being. Most real social workers, as Maggie and I call our breed, chant the prayer, "God save us from the do-gooders." It looks as though Mother Elizabeth knows the same prayer. Or maybe God has heard our prayers.

~~~

The next Monday morning when the staff arrive, we encounter a group of men, women, and squirming, clutching children in the foyer of St. Mark's Convent. Small groups of homeless families continue to arrive in bunches every few minutes. There is a sense of uncertainty and excitement that grows with the increasing population.

Sister Theresa is at her usual post by the door warmly greeting each arriving person and directing them down the hall to the left toward the school.

Stationed strategically along the way, sisters are posted at the intersections in the hallway like brown-robed traffic cops keeping everyone from getting lost in the catacomb corridors connecting the buildings.

The disbelieving newcomers walk hesitantly through the hallway, suspiciously examining their surroundings. It is as if they are taking in every inch of the place in wonderment. After all, the convent is spotless, as one would expect. There are no rodents, nor drunks in the doorways to step over. The homeless families are understandably unsure of the validity of their surroundings and the program they have heard so little about—only enough to get them here. Too good to be true? I think not.

It doesn't take clients long to learn that the worst thing to do is believe too eagerly that the do-gooders will actually do good. I don't blame anyone for being skeptical. There are far too few real professionals to offset the havoc the ne'er-do-wells cause before they skip off merrily to yet another worthy cause. Those do-gooders only help the deserving poor.

I'm not sure who that is—I haven't seen anyone who deserves a life of profound poverty.

Now it is Mother Elizabeth's task to convince them, within a short period of time, to commit to Spirit of Hope project for a minimum of one year, and that she and her band of sisters are worthy of their trust. The request to trust strangers to help them, one more time, is a big request. She'll have to be patient.

The families move slowly toward the school auditorium under the protective guidance of the nuns. Meanwhile, Sister Theresa instructs the staff to go to the convent dining room and wait at the ready to assist with registration as soon as Mother Elizabeth finishes her presentation.

It is no surprise we find the application forms in neat stacks on each table. We spread through the room to allow comfortable space for everyone to register. Privacy is a luxury the poor can't afford. Space is the best we can offer them.

During our orientation, Mother Elizabeth made it perfectly clear she didn't intend to spend time holding our hands through each detail that was to follow, though I worried about micro-managing. She has been true to her word. Quickly, I review the registration form and prepare for the families' arrival. Other staff members are doing the same. There is no doubt in anyone's mind that Mother Elizabeth expects us to think on our feet once the families arrive. That day is at hand.

The form is straightforward enough—not too prying. I anticipate no real problems with registration. We wait quietly at our posts, patiently watching for signs of approaching families. We know this is it—the moment when life surges into Spirit of Hope and it becomes real.

~~~

It is an hour before the meeting concludes and families begin to congregate at the tables in the dining room. They stay huddled in family groups, some children are straining at the hand holding on to them, others are clinging tightly to a parent's clothing. Sister Theresa directs each family toward a table, while we motion them in our direction if they hesitate along the way. The room fills with people sounds and chairs scooting toward table sounds.

A few minutes after the families' arrival, Sister Bridget appears in the doorway, announcing she has paper and colors in the adjacent room for children who want to draw while their parents fill out the forms. Sister Bridget is the robust art teacher on loan from St. Mark's grade school next door. She is large, and I imagine, from a child's perspective, scary.

The children hesitate, crouching in their seats near their parents, while some are peeking over the chair back to keep an eye on Sister Bridget. Some of the older children look like they are sizing her up in a streetwise manner, not sure if she should be trusted. A few younger children look as if they want to go, yet aren't sure if they should leave their parent's side. Their eyes say, "Maybe this is a trick."

A little wisp of a thing, with unruly, curly blonde hair and big, dark eyes is kneeling in her chair with her hands on the top of the backrest, studying the nun. She whispers something to her mother. She makes the first move to join Sister Bridget once she decides Sister is worthy of the risk. The little girl walks up to the towering, round nun, and takes hold of her hand. Almost immediately there are whispers to parents and the scraping sound of chairs as most of the other children move to follow the mismatched pair out of the room.

Within minutes Mother Elizabeth walks in and heads for the table where I am sitting with my family. "Kathryn, please help Sister Bridget with the children," she says as she sits down next to me, taking my place with the parents.

Mother Elizabeth is confident and commanding, without being intimidating. Obediently, I follow the children out of the room. After all, I am the resident expert on children, am I not?
~~~

Twenty families accept Mother Elizabeth's invitation to commit to Spirit of Hope for a year. I easily calculate forty adults. However, the number of children is significantly greater. Each family must have three or four children, occasionally more. Most of the children are under the age of ten.

It doesn't take long to figure out that Mother Elizabeth selected families with the most kids in order to get the largest number of children off the street and into school as soon as she possibly can. That must be why she chose to do the admission screening herself.

Sister Bridget and I are outnumbered, even if one of us in the room is a nun. Seemingly unaware of this mathematical fact, Sister Bridget already has all of the children seated with colors in hand. For the most part, they are quietly coloring. She's amazing.

We move around the room visiting with the children, helping where needed. The little artists are strained, reserved, and withdrawn. There is not the usual chatter and giggling that accompanies a room FULL of children. The kids steal sideways glances to watch the jolly, round nun, the other children, and me. They are careful not to let their eyes meet Sister's or mine as they sneak peeks of us. I am careful not to let them know I'm watching too.

As soon as registration finishes, the cafeteria ladies appear, announcing they have milk and homemade cookies, fresh from the oven, in the grade school cafeteria. The children pause—it has been a long time since they had cookies, never mind fresh cookies.

They exchange stealthy glances with each other to confirm what they heard is true. Their bond with each other is beginning with a mutual admiration of sweets.

Sister Bridget and I exchange glances, as well. All of us pause for a minute as the information sinks in and the children look like they are beginning to believe—at least in the cookies.

After the parents collect their children in anticipation of the welcomed snack, Sister Bridget and I are left alone to collect the art supplies. Sister is an outgoing, cheerful person, full of excitement about Spirit of Hope. She confides that the sisters have been developing the Spirit of Hope project for four years.

"The planning was difficult. We were impatient and wanted to begin helping people immediately, but Mother Elizabeth kept reminding us that we must be truly prepared." Her expression dulls slightly as she looks at the door. "The little darlings weren't sure about the cookies, were they? They're in for a treat."

As she speaks, Sister Bridget's hands move about in an animated fashion that I haven't seen in the nuns until now. Her face bursts into a hearty smile as she loses her sisterly composure and giggles with open delight. "I can't believe our families are finally here!" Sister Bridget squeals with excitement. For a brief moment I think she is going to grab me by the shoulders and shake me, but she doesn't.

When she notices her behavior, she immediately regains her sisterly composure, retracting her hands into her sleeves. To ease the awkwardness of the moment for her, I capitalize on her enthusiasm for the final reality of Spirit of Hope, the admission of the homeless families. It is obvious she loves children and is a natural at working with them.

"Sister, the children will love the playroom." I smile at her, and we resume picking up the art supplies and depositing them into the box on the table. I take the risk of being wrong and guess she is the one responsible for the mural. "The mural you painted is beautiful. I love it!"

She stops working and smiles back. "Thank you. I had help." She smiles to herself as she busies herself with full focus on the task.

That ends the unrestrained interaction. We never again mention the sadness surrounding the children's uncertainty of the cookies or her response to the long-awaited arrival of the families. I do understand her excitement. It feels good to be a part of something that is really going to make a difference in their lives.

We finish putting away the art supplies in the grade school cabinet, then join the others in the cafeteria. I'm having coffee.

Sister Bridget heads directly to the cookie trays. Our arrival coincides with preparations to show the families to their new homes. We take a minute to have a cookie, then she returns to class and I catch up to the rear of the tour. There is no indication how they decided which family gets which room. Most likely it is random, but no one says. I relax, realizing none of the decisions are on my shoulders.

At the end of the tour, Mother Elizabeth asks the men to return to the gymnasium—she needs their help to assemble the cribs that arrived yesterday afternoon.

There is a slight laugh from the men as she admits the sisters don't have any experience in such things.

It is obvious the sisters can easily master assembling the cribs, blindfolded. I don't believe anyone here really thinks the nuns need help. These are not helpless women by any stretch of the imagination. Mother Elizabeth is thoughtful to give the men an immediate physical task—one with rapid, measurable success.

Each family is assigned a staff person for the week, beginning with the family we registered. The nuns and staff help our families move their belongings in and get settled. We make beds, do laundry, and bathe children while the parents unpack their meager possessions. I have no idea where all of the hot water comes from, but, surprisingly, there is an ample supply.

Mother Elizabeth had previously arranged with Sister Barbara, the elementary school principal, for the school children to have a picnic lunch in order to make the school cafeteria available for our families, the staff, and the good sisters on the occasion of this our first meal together. After today, the nuns will resume eating in the convent dining room, and the staff—well, I'm not sure where we will eat.

Each family huddles together at a table, though there is ample room to spread out. As it should be, the staff and sisters are last in the food line. It seems a little awkward. I don't want to intrude. It is more my nature to not push my clients into a forced affiliation. I like to ease into the client-social worker relationship.

Sister Bridget returns and sits at the table with her little curly-haired friend and family. The woman I was to register makes eye contact. That is good enough for me, and I ask if I may join her family. Everyone scoots down a bit and I take the movement as an invitation.

Lunch is quiet, barely more than introductions. The woman's name is Monica. The children talk to each other in Spanish. I don't let on that I understand that the youngest boy thinks I am pretty. The children giggle. Monica is uncomfortable that her children are speaking about me in Spanish. She shoots them a quieting parental look. I act like I don't notice and continue eating. The dad teases the youngster about our romance in English until he squirms, grins with a first grader missing-tooth smile, then giggles.

All of the families are hungry for home-cooked food, and lunch is over quickly. The cafeteria ladies are standing at their post, announcing how inconvenient leftovers are. A big man named Race gets up and goes through the line again.

The cafeteria ladies beam. He smiles back and takes an additional helping of food. His wife and others follow the big man's example. The children aren't shy about the cookies. There is not one crumb of food left when the meal is finished. It is spiritual to watch hungry people eat until they are satisfied. The cafeteria ladies are visibly pleased to have their meal appreciated more than school children appreciate them.

After lunch one of the staff, Rhoda, walks around with a large box of individually wrapped toothbrushes. Pete, previously an elementary teacher, hands out donated boxes of toothpaste. Rhoda has a permanent marker in her hand, in case siblings want the same color toothbrush. Otherwise we refrain from marking their belongings. Marking them is too institutionalized. Like everyday life, the families will have to keep track of their things the old fashioned way—just like the rest of us.

The day passes quickly. Our families are getting settled. They seem tired from the burden of life, though they are free with their expressions of appreciation for the smallest thing done for them, and sometimes for nothing in particular.

Generally speaking, this is a day job. The sisters will be available, if needed, when the staff is gone. The parents will retain their positions as heads of their household, and the nuns will only be on call.

When five o'clock arrives and the staff gather at Sister Theresa's desk to sign out, the sisters begin moving in the direction of the chapel.

It was a good day.

As I reach for the door to leave, I hear the sound of female voices chanting, signaling the beginning of Evening Prayers.

Pausing to listen for a moment, I feel a sense of satisfaction with our first day at Spirit of Hope. I feel a sense of hopefulness again, like when I was a wide-eyed, young social worker.

~~~
~~~

~ CHAPTER 7 ~

Go Forth and—and What?

By the time I arrive home, fatigue outweighs my hunger. I am content with my new job. One thing for sure, I will wear more comfortable shoes tomorrow—ones equal to the adobe tile floor. The sisters wear black shoes with thick rubber soles. While leather soles may look better, the more practical shoes are a wiser choice.

Relaxing with a cup of coffee and my feet resting on the coffee table, I think about Spirit of Hope and everyone involved in the project. If I am tired, I can only imagine how the parents feel. They had a big day, the beginning of a new life. Hmm, a new life. I drift off to sleep sitting on the sofa.

It's dark when the phone awakens me. It takes a disoriented minute to realize it is Karen's voice on the phone. I have been so distracted with Spirit of Hope, that I forgot to call to thank her for the reference she gave Mother Elizabeth on my behalf.

I give her a brief review of the last three weeks. Karen is pleased to hear I am happy with the change in direction of my career. I remember to tell her I met Sam Jackson, but he didn't know anything helpful about the Judge's daughter. With my new work, I forgot to finish looking through the obituaries, but I told her what I had accomplished thus far.

Eventually, I notice the correlation between her telephone call and the first day of clients at work. Ah, it was probably just a coincidence. I pause long enough for her to understand it is her turn to speak.

"You will never believe this. I just returned to the office and found a note from Keith. He learned Judge Jones' wife's name was Kathryn!" she says with an excited voice.

I sit up straight and put my feet on the floor. "How does she spell it?" I ask suspiciously.

"K-A-T-H-R-Y-N," Karen adds a dramatic flair to her voice.

"That is too weird," I whisper. "What did Maggie say?"

"I don't know if Keith told her or not. She was gone by the time I came back to the office."

"So do you think the letter was really to me or, or to her? To his Kathryn?" I ask barely audibly, as a spooky feeling shoots up the center of my back, giving me a shiver.

Karen offers no insight into my question. She is intrigued with the name issue too. We talk for at least a half hour about the new development in our mystery.

Now I am fully awake. I pop something quick for dinner in the microwave and make a pot of coffee. While my dinner is cooking, I hunt for the obituary list I printed earlier.

Driven, I scan the list while I eat. I hadn't looked ahead while I was searching the obituaries. I wonder if I had previously seen the various spellings of "Kathryn Jones" if I would have thought to try them all to find Mrs. Judge Jones and skipped the name-by-name search.

In minutes I am online in the newspaper archives. There she is. There is "Kathryn Jones, wife of Judge William Jones." Kathryn's obituary lists a couple of siblings that may be helpful—if they can be found—AND a daughter, LINDA.

"Ah, Linda, we have been looking for you," I whisper while the printer produces a copy of the obituary. I email the link to Maggie at work, knowing she will forward it to Karen and Keith, since I don't remember their email addresses from before and haven't thought to ask for them.

Despite my satisfaction with Linda's discovery, I am furious all over again that the Judge invaded our lives with his absurd letter. He should have sent it to his daughter. If he was going to kill himself, why didn't he make a clean break with the living? Why couldn't he just go away and leave us alone? Hasn't he stolen enough life-spirit from us with his inept rulings?

In my heart, I have no doubt Judge Jones killed that little girl as surely as if it had been his hand on the knife stabbing her ninety-six times. She had died long before the stabbing to her still, lifeless body stopped—that shows how demented the guy was.

Her father must have been out of his mind when he killed her. Maybe she threatened to tell on him again. Only he knows what happened. It wasn't the fault of drugs, as his tox screen was negative. It was him, all him.

I shudder violently with the thought of her needless demon-ridden death, while my mind remembers the vivid crime scene photos of the beaten and stabbed bloody body of the defenseless little girl with blood matted in her curls.

We all knew he was sicker than most. That's why the Judge's ruling was so unbelievable. Eventually, in one way or another, death reached out and touched each of us, literally or spiritually.

Kathryn Jones' obituary is lying on the coffee table, but I decide not to pick it up again. I plan to be careful with my new life and not spend time on anything that could become consuming, then consume me.

I sit for a long time sipping my coffee on the patio while listening to the sound of the waves from across the street. It is good to be home where I am not an outsider.

With a change of location, back to the sofa, Joseph comes into my thoughts. But every thought of him is pure speculation, fantasy, daydreams. Every ounce of my being tells me I should not entertain this fantasy. It was only a chance meeting. It has been two weeks, and nothing seems to have come of it. I cannot dare to indulge in such thoughts. I need reality, a sane reality.

My thoughts turn from fantasy lovers back to my present life. I seek to remember how Maggie's friendship had grown out of a simple working relationship. There is this new Karen that I do not understand. And, of course, there is Mr. Goldstein—my dear, dear Mr. Goldstein.

Mr. Goldstein is the only male in my life with whom I spend significant amounts of time. From him I learn about overcoming the difficult, impossible moments in life. As he continues to tell me dreadful details of his confinement in the death camp, I am more and more amazed with humanity's resilience.

As I look up, lost in thought while pressing my tired body into the back of the sofa, my gaze catches the clock on the wall. Suddenly I am aware of the time—in a few hours I have to get ready for work. Almost with a jerk, I am on my feet and shutting off the lights. In no time, I am in bed and asleep.

~~~

Morning seems to arrive only minutes after I close my eyes. Pushing myself to get ready for the day, I move reluctantly through my routine. I feel a little wobbly this morning after last night's encounter with the haunting memories of the crime scene. There is no time for indulging my wounds from the past now. I have other duties—other people need my undivided attention.

I manage to miss the bus. To get to work on time I have to drive aggressively. The families are up and around by the time the staff arrive. They look more rested today than yesterday, but their eyes are still dull and their expressions reveal their continued disbelief in the longevity of their good fortune. I suspect the dullness is due, in part, to poor nutrition, but largely to living in unending hopelessness on the streets and in their cars. Even the children, though scrubbed and combed, look dull.

Understandably, their recovery will be slow in the beginning. First, they have to learn to trust in us to truly help them. Then the adults will have to give their children a sense of security again.

Resilience. Hope. Security. All of these come from the human spirit, and they are not things easily taught, nor replenished. We have to be more than a dry-dock along their journey. In the beginning, I suppose that is what we are, but we will have to transform into a harbor pilot and guide them on their way again.
~~~

Trust is a slow process. Self-sustaining trust is fragile and elusive. More than usual, today I fully appreciate the reality of wobbly feelings that come and go with a will of their own.

Strength of character demands facing those weak moments squarely. Oddly, we seem to manage to have the strength we need when it is needed the most.

Our homeless people will find their strength to begin again, as it is human nature. Thank God, it is even possible.

Perhaps, I am feeling philosophical because of vivid memories of the bloody photos. Regardless of my life's complexities, work has its own demands. We are to assess clothing needs and to get everyone a new outfit to start rebuilding their lives.

The nuns are sharp negotiators and have made deals with their usual vendors, and others who are seeking to gain the convent and school's business through this back door. Some of the benefactors are "good Catholics" who attended St. Mark's school. To generalize this scenario, the nuns use one motivation—Guilt!

At any rate, each staff person is given a list of merchants who have agreed to provide for our needs at cost or below, and the store representatives to contact for smooth facilitation of the transactions.

Without expression, my family goes through the motion of assessing their clothing needs. It is glaringly obvious they don't have much. What they do have is too small or too ragged to count as clothing.

Lunch is slightly early, so we can get a running start with our shopping trip. We are given an envelope of cash and Sister Theresa tells us to "go forth" with our families. She hands a set of convent keys to each of the staff who do not have an adequate size vehicle.

My family is polite but reserved as they climb into the cream-colored van with a St. Christopher medallion hanging from the rearview mirror. Keeping in mind the shopping trip with Mother Elizabeth, I take a detour to a shop in the neighborhood and treat us to ice cream with my own money. I am careful to protect the identity of the source of the finances for the ice cream, so it doesn't seem like charity.

It takes coaxing to get the parents to have more than a single scoop of vanilla ice cream.

"At least sprinkles?"

These people strike me as too unassuming and polite to reach out and grab life. It's not a criticism—I do understand. We will have to start small and work toward believing they deserve more than vanilla when they really want something more exotic.

The young daughter slips free of the constraint and asks her mother if she might have strawberry sauce on her ice cream. Her mother looks at her, then at me. I smile and tilt my head in a "Why not?" way. After a considering pause, she approves.

The little girl squeals with delight. It wouldn't ordinarily have been my choice, but I order strawberry sauce on my ice cream too. It is as if a dam broke and we all indulge in various toppings on our vanilla ice cream. The laughter that might ordinarily accompany a moment like this —is silent. I watch Monica with her family and love her immediately. She is a good mom.

With ice cream treats in hand, we walk to the shaded picnic area. There we examine our shopping list while we eat. Choosing the stores from the merchant list, we plan our attack on the world of commerce. I ask what style of clothes they like in an effort to plant the idea that they have choices, something that has been lost to them in their homeless state along with everything they owned.

The parents go through the motion of complying with my requests without being an inconvenience to anyone. Not to be stopped so early in my mission, I turn my focus on my previous ally, the little girl, and her three brothers who willingly engage in the conversation. After the experience with the ice cream, the children are quite adamant about what they want to purchase. They are not visibly excited, but decisive nonetheless.

Returning the question to the more reserved parents, they comment that "anything would be fine" with them. Conversely, I reply they might as well have something they like. Hesitantly, the man suggests that he needs clothes for job interviews. We talk about what type of job he wants, so we can decide what will be the best attire for his interviews. Gradually they relax—slightly. I only wish I could have figured out a way to facilitate an even more relaxed atmosphere for them.

At the store the parents are stoic until the children and I begin voting on the parents' clothes with thumbs up or down, and make faces when necessary to further cast our vote on the items they select. I admit it, I am the instigator of this spectacle, but it worked to make shopping less awkward for the parents. They stand a little taller when they see themselves in the mirror wearing our final, best pick of outfits in our budget.

Before long the parents are enjoying our outing almost as much as the children. They seem to get a flicker of hope for the moment, but I know it is not self-sustaining, not yet anyway. It is a good start—something for them to build on as they work their way through the Spirit of Hope program.

While we are in the check-out line at the service desk, I slip the money to the father to pay for the items himself. His eyes meet mine, but overall he is agreeable with the covert money exchange. I plan to have him give Sister Theresa the sales receipt and change. The rationale is that it takes me out of the middle of this transaction and keeps him in the position of head of his household.

~~~

Back at the van, he seems surprised when I refuse the change and receipt. Gently I push his hand back. "You give it to Sister Theresa when we get home." I figure exchanging trust has to start with one of us. His eyes understand, but he says nothing as he pockets the money.

We arrive back at the convent with plenty of time to admire the purchases they made before carefully putting dad's interview clothes on hangers until needed. The children want to wear something new, now—right now.

The husband sits back, lovingly watching his wife and children with their first new clothes in a very long time. It is almost a spiritual experience. I watch them too.

Our eyes meet. We don't speak. He must sense that I understand his pleasure. He makes no indication with his unchanged facial expression. When he looks back at his family, I quietly slip out of the room to leave them alone.

In the hallway, little Shasta, Sister Bridget's newest best friend, can be heard insisting on wearing her new white sandals with the pink "diamonds" with her pink shorts outfit. Her mother adds pink barrettes to keep her curly strands of hair out of her face. Shasta dances around their room trying to go up on her toes like a ballerina in her sandals with the pink diamonds.

Watching Shasta dance is a "Spirit of Hope" moment that will be repeated many times in the days ahead.

Mother Elizabeth must have been notified that her first dispatches had returned home, probably by the watchful Sister Theresa at the front desk. Mother locates me in the hallway and invites me to her office.

As we walk together I wonder why it is that I often find myself being summoned to the boss' office. This is reminiscent of working for Karen, only more pleasant.

~~~

One family left their three youngest children with relatives while they migrated to California to find work. Work didn't come. They haven't seen their children for over a year. With that one piece of information, I know exactly why she accepted that family into the program.

"We contacted each airline in person until we found one willing to fly the children to be united with their parents—at no expense."

I am only slightly surprised. Who among us can refuse a nun in full traditional habit when she needs help to reunite children with their parents? Surely, I don't know anyone that brave.

Mother Elizabeth asks me to take Sister Theresa to LAX on my way home. On my way home? It is obvious Mother Elizabeth needs only twenty-four hours to request and receive miracles.

Of course, I agree to take Sister to LAX, since Mother Elizabeth already seems to assume I have. Besides, it's an opportunity to get to know Sister Theresa a little better, on my turf, or at least off hers.

Sister Theresa is near the front door ready to depart for Detroit to escort the children back to their parents. The children have never flown before, and even if they had, Mother Elizabeth would never consider allowing them to travel alone. Sister Theresa will leave today and return with the children tomorrow. She'll spend the night with the local nuns who meet her at the airport. Someone will pick them up in a convent van when they return.

During our road trip, Sister Theresa is pleasant when I speak to her. She briefly answers my questions, but she doesn't initiate any conversation of her own. Maybe she has the trip on her mind. Nonetheless, I am disappointed with her silence. I amuse myself with the thought that she is probably desperately conversing with Saint Christopher, the patron saint of travelers about traveling with three children.

As I drive through the heavy traffic on the way to LAX, I glance at her from time to time. She is tall and thin. She has laugh lines around her mouth and bright dark brown eyes that hint at the person behind the holy exterior.

When I drop her off at the airport I say, "Have a good trip."

She bends down to look in the open car window and smiles broadly. "Thank you, I will—I love to fly!"

With that, she turns and quickly disappears into the terminal with a small black travel bag in her hand and her full-length veil blowing behind her. I hadn't expected her response and laugh at the thought that she is happier to fly than to ride in a car. She is probably skipping down the concourse, for all I know.

~~~

After taking Sister to the airport, I take advantage of the early release from work. First, I'll catch up with my cousin, Ilene, via email, then go for a walk on the beach before the sun sets and it gets chilly.

Just as I am about to log off the internet, an email from Maggie arrives. She is coming over tonight after dinner to work on our "missing Linda" project. I am glad to see Maggie, but a little annoyed with the intrusion of the past when the present is much more pleasant.

Now that we have a lead on the Judge's daughter, I feel the urgency is gone. My new job is more interesting than dedicating time to the past, a past that is not at all enticing to me. I hope Maggie doesn't want to go
~~~

at this with too much enthusiasm tonight. I don't need a second full-time job. I am enjoying discovering who I am now, or maybe who I have always been. The interruption from the past interferes with the present.

The work at the convent is refreshing, but I intend to enjoy being in California again. For one thing, I want to spend time going on walks on the beach with Mr. Goldstein. Luckily, there is time for a walk before Maggie is scheduled to arrive.

~~~

For a week now Mr. Goldstein, who is developing friendships with several females at the Senior Center, has been giddy. I am curious to learn more about this new adventure in his life.

Mr. Goldstein comes for our walk right on cue. He doesn't say much about specific friends at the Senior Center. They had taken a short trip to the Huntington Library today. It is hard to tell what he liked best, the art or the one-of-a-kind rare books. He really loved the gardens, especially the desert garden.

He had never seen so many different varieties of desert plants before, and was pleased some of the cacti were in bloom. It is delightful to see the world through his eyes. It is amazing how quickly our walk is done and he is heading up the stairs to his home.

There is barely enough time for a cup of coffee before Maggie arrives. I enjoy reconnecting with Maggie. However, I have waited five years to deal with the past, so I am in no hurry for it to become an all-consuming activity. I would rather spend time visiting—casually visiting.

Unfortunately, as it turns out, Maggie wants to do more. She indicates Keith said that with a name like "Jones," he needs a middle name before he runs Linda through the system to get her current address on her driver's license.

At Maggie's insistence, we search the online newspaper archives for articles about school activities, awards, anything that might indicate which school Linda attended. Almost two hours pass before we discover Linda had received several awards in debate and always did well in tennis. One article lists her high school in the valley. The school does not have past yearbooks posted online. Finally, Maggie is content to sit and relax. For this I am more grateful than she will ever know.

We have eased back to the level where we had left our friendship and perhaps beyond where it was five years ago. I am beginning to feel less guilty about not keeping in contact while I was away, now that I realize our friendship transcends time and location.

Better than I, Maggie seems to understand why I left. I admit I had been too self-centered in thinking, "It was about me," especially the failings at work. We leave it at that, sparing me from divulging the details of my emotions then and now.
~~~

We are both older and wiser. Soon I will be thirty and she is thirty-four. We are enlightened—and proud of it.

Somehow, Maggie has learned to find a little distance from the emotions of her cases. It's probably her "advanced age," I laugh to myself, since she is only a couple of years older than I.

While we talk, I have become lulled into a sense of contentment with our friendship. I tell Maggie about the trip to the airport with Sister Theresa. I relate how difficult—no, impossible it was to draw Sister Theresa out and meet the person hiding inside her shielding habit.

Maggie begins in a serious tone of voice, "Kate, you have an impenetrable 'shield' around you too."

I tilt my head in surprise. I study her eyes, trying hard to read her thoughts, while fearing where she is taking this conversation. I shouldn't have bothered guessing where her comment was leading. She is about to tell me what is on her mind, whether I want her to or not.

She looks at me long and hard. "The problem is your protective shield is much larger than usual, larger than everyone else's." She does not smile. "Your defense mechanisms set off too many alarms when anyone gets close to you."

"Maybe in the past that was true," I begin my defense, "but no more than—"

"With you, Kate, it's a one-way street." She barely takes a breath, leaving no time to interrupt again. "You are there for others, but won't allow others to reciprocate." Her voice is confident.

"My personal problems are mine to—" I start to agree in a revealing, but justifying tone.

Maggie interrupts, "Don't misunderstand. You're a wonderful friend and exceptional social worker. When people are around you, they open up the deep recesses of their life to you." Maggie softens her tone and continues, "Instinctively they feel your strength."

I look at her, then look away. What can I say to that? Of course I'm strong. My strength is one of the things that makes me good at my job. I deliberately set out to be strong. I consciously work at it. How can that possibly be bad?

Maggie leans forward, reaches across the table, and touches my wrist.

I fight the urge to pull back my hand. I decide not to confirm her comments with such an action. She can think what she wants, she does anyway. There is no point in proving her point.

"You are too self-sufficient, Kate." She lets go of me, but continues to speak—even more softly this time. "You only allow glimpses of who you are and your struggles," she says, then she leans back in her chair again. "When things get to be too much, you pull away from everyone."

At last, Maggie finally smiles compassionately. She adds with a slight laugh, "I understand running to the beach on occasion—but Nebraska?"

I may deserve the Nebraska wisecrack, but I take advantage of her pause, "Maggie, what can anyone really do?"

She draws a slow, deep breath before she speaks. "Listen, care. The same things you do for us."

"I need to process things for myself. I have to understand—" I counter her comment.

"Maybe, but not alone." Maggie continues to look at me more intensely than I like. "This isn't about me being hurt because you keep part of you out of our friendship, this is about you hurting—alone."

"But—" I protest, then comply with her silencing glance.

It is obvious that we have opposing opinions on the subject, but I expect more understanding from her than that. She knows the horrible things we saw and heard in the worst of the child abuse cases. She knows the details don't always come out in court because we aren't asked the right questions on the witness stand. Some things are too bad to tell anyone. She knows. We have to keep it to ourselves.

In the end, the most we can do is write about them in our case notes and try to leave them there. Sometimes the cases haunt our dreams for years. She knows that too. I feel trapped, and it must show on my face.

Maggie gives me the don't-argue-with-me look as she pushes on. "You aren't the only one who has nightmares over this job," Maggie confesses for the first time, leaning forward again. "I just want you to know that Karen, Keith, and I understand." She tries to be consoling. "Sexual abuse cases are the worst. You don't have to do this alone. You never did."

This time I can't help moving my arm out of her reach as a precaution in the event she attempts to go for my wrist again. I appreciate her friendship and her words, but I can't do this right now.

She knows my parents are dead, but I am not alone. I have a close-knit extended family. Even though I don't have siblings, I have a lot of cousins. They fill any gaps that might exist.

"Kate, please don't leave us out again, if things get to be too much for you." With that, Maggie concludes her lecture.

So much for my relaxing evening. This bonding thing Maggie is doing isn't what I am in the mood for tonight. I go to make more coffee in an effort to permanently disrupt the conversation.

Maggie follows me to the kitchen, telling me how Karen holds the entire system to a higher level of responsibility than before, and everything is not on the department now. I guess this is in some sort of response to what happened to me. I don't know.

When I reach for a new coffee filter, I nearly trip over her. I express appreciation that things have changed for the better. Yet, I am thankful to be out of Child Protection and into the Spirit of Hope project.

She waves off the offer of a refill of coffee. Shamelessly, I am glad that it's getting late and Maggie is talking about going home. This conversation has become exhausting.

Just as she is leaving, Maggie turns back and says, "Oh, by the way, Joseph asked me for your phone number." Her eyes have a dangerous twinkle.

Maggie always knew how to get my attention. The evening might have played out differently if she had mentioned it when she arrived. It pleases me that Joseph wants to call me.

I smile and whisper, "Give it to him."

~~~

Long after Maggie drove away, I stood on the patio looking toward the ocean. I need the beach after the intensity of the evening's conversation. The rhythm of the waves always seems to calibrate my soul in a way nothing else can. It is too late and too chilly to go to the beach tonight.

I turn and go inside. Mostly I just want to go to bed, sleep, and get up to my new job in the morning. There is no point in living in the past or a daydream future involving Joseph.

~~~

~ CHAPTER 8 ~

Romance? Are You Kidding?

More than I want to admit, I think about Joseph. I remember the sound of his laugh that came so effortlessly during dinner. The essence of his smile and dark eyes still lingers. What is taking him so long to call me? Has he changed his mind about wanting my phone number?

When I don't hear from Joseph by the end of the week. I get his number from Maggie with the intent to leave a message on his voicemail Uncharacteristically, I decide to take the initiative. After considering several messages, I decide to leave only my name and phone number. He's a lawyer—he should be able to figure out the rest for himself.

At first I don't wander far from my phone, except for work and walks with Mr. Goldstein. Finally, as the days pass, I decide staying by the phone is silly, especially since the answering machine is always on.

I am glad no one knows I have behaved so pathetically. Apparently Joseph isn't worth pursuing. I refuse to call him a second time. I am not desperate. There will be others who come along in time. No rush.

~~~

The week passes. I venture out to sit on the moonlit beach most evenings. I sit in silence for hours after the sun blazes into the ocean, until the damp cold or the beach patrol drive me inside.

When I am on the beach, time drifts away. I sit and think of nothing more than the sound of the waves coming to shore.

Several weeks after Maggie's visit, I'm on the beach, remembering the bitter Nebraska winters in contrast to the agreeable California weather. It makes me thankful I will have no more cold winters in my life. Those days are gone for good.

"Never again!" I say, as thoughts of the below zero temperatures make me shiver. The sound of the waves and the hum of my thoughts block out everything else.

"What did you say?" asks a male voice from behind me.

I jump at the unexpected human response. He repeats the question as he moves to where I can see him. It's Joseph!

"So this is Kathryn's Beach?" He smiles.

It has been nearly a month since Maggie asked permission to give my number to him. My surprise quickly fades into curiosity at how he found me. He says it was the message on my answering machine saying I was either ignoring the phone or on the beach.
~~~

Joseph had telephoned Maggie to find out the location of the alleged beach. And now he is here beside me. Instantly I forget, or forgive, that he has taken his sweet time in calling. A visit is less awkward than a phone call would have been anyway.

I take a deep breath to calm my giddy heart. I'm more excited to see him than I'm ready to admit. I'm acutely aware of his presence. I can smell his aftershave and hear his breathing.

Sitting near me on my blanket in the sand, Joseph takes a deep breath. Clumsily, we silently watch the moon reflecting on the waves for a while. Then we speak at the same time about the scene we are watching. After a nervous laugh, we start again and ease into talking about general things at first, things that don't really matter.

Joseph says when he was fifteen, he left the fighting in Dublin to come to a boarding school in the U.S. He is excited about going home for the holidays this year. He talks fondly of his homeland, his family, and his friends. Listening to his accent makes everything he says sound romantic.

He intrigues me when he speaks Gaelic. I love the soft sound of it. His bright white teeth flash in the moonlight when he smiles, and he smiles easily. He is kind, almost gentle, in his way of talking about life. I like him. I really like him. Beyond that, well, one can always hope. Love doesn't come easily for me. But this time seems different.

The spray from the rising tide makes us get up to move toward higher ground. Once we're up, we decide to go to my apartment for freshly brewed coffee to warm away the dampness.

To my surprise, Joseph welcomes the coffee despite the hour. Maggie found it unusual that I drink coffee every night before going to bed. Joseph doesn't seem to mind. There is another thing to like about him, he likes coffee as much as I do.

The stereo provides background music, so that the pauses in conversation won't be obvious or awkward. It may be nothing, but I take it as a good omen that the first song we hear is Ella Fitzgerald and Louis Armstrong's Summertime—my favorite jazz song. I savor the moment listening to the brassy sounds.

Eventually it is time for Joseph to leave. I want him to stay, but I am too tired to stay up much longer to entertain my guest. Of course, staying the night is out of the question. We have barely met. No, I do not want him to stay and complicate my life in that way. Besides, I do hope this is more than a physical attraction.

After Joseph leaves, I lounge on the sofa with my feet on the edge of the coffee table finishing my cup of coffee. I am incredibly tired, but my mind is not quite ready for sleep. I stay up a little while to savor the evening. I haven't felt this attracted to anyone in a long time. I know to be cautious, but I am beyond the warning. I smile a faraway smile as I think about him on my beach. Summertime dances through my mind.

The freeze inside me is melting. It was, no doubt, a defense mechanism to ward off the horrors of work. Somehow it had crept into every aspect of my life. But it didn't keep away the nightmares. No, be honest, Katey, the freeze is more than that. It started long before then.

I was six years old when my father died, and I began to guard against abandonment. I cannot count the times I allowed myself to fortify against intimacy. I didn't want to feel the devastating feeling of loss ever again. I don't want to feel that kind of vulnerability, either.

Why this seeming disarmament toward Joseph? I felt a change occurring in the last weeks I was away, more so since I returned home. I longed for friendships, and maybe even a romance while still at Ruthie's Bar. There was not a chance of a romance for me in Nebraska, not since I was an outsider. And now this handsome, intelligent, intriguing man is melting my heart. I shut my eyes to remember his smile, his voice, his aftershave.

~~~

The ringing phone wakes me. The sun is bright and the clock on the wall reveals I am lucky that it is Saturday or I would have been late to work.

"Do you have plans for this morning?" Karen asks, wanting to come by in an hour.

My bed is still made since I fell asleep on the sofa. I calculate that I can be presentable within an hour. "Sure, a visit will be nice."

Quickly, I make a pot of coffee and take a shower. By the time Karen arrives I look like I have been up for hours. She wouldn't have cared, but I want to put some distance from my reputation as a night owl. The realization of a deliberate change in my attitude is curious, but exploring it will have to wait.

~~~

"Good morning, Kathryn. Guess what Maggie found out—" Karen stops suddenly. "Kathryn?" Her voice spreads to a wide-eyed whisper, "Tell me all about him. Leave nothing out."

By my widening smile at hearing her words, there is no hiding that she has read me well. Karen wants to know about this mystery man. I find her interest in me personally very different from how I remember her.

"His name is Joseph," I begin. "All I can say is my heart is way ahead of where our relationship is." I confide in a whisper, "I think his heart might be there too."

Karen smiles a warm, knowing smile. It feels awkward. We move away from talking about my feelings toward Joseph.

She looks out the patio door at the ocean across the street. "Did you know I grew up two blocks from here?"

So this is her beach. It is no wonder she often found her way here to read documents from work. That explains why she gravitates to the other side of the pier when given the choice.

"No, I didn't know."

"If you want to go for a walk, I'll show you which house it is." She offers an excuse to walk on the beach.

After we pass the pier, we walk up to the street and view the house.

"My parents are away visiting my brother and his wife. Sometimes I house-sit and bring paperwork to read at the beach."

I smile because I have seen her working on the beach.

We walk back, soaking in the ambiance of the shore. It is a different world from being inland. It's odd how humans adapt to a specific environment and aren't quite at home anywhere else.

It isn't until later that I realize Karen never told me what Maggie found out. Joseph must have been such a shock that she forgot about Maggie.

The previous night with Joseph is still intriguingly running through my thoughts. My life is transforming in ways I had not anticipated. The memory of the Judge's letter is so remote I have all but dismissed it. I have someone new and more pleasant to think about—I have Joseph to fill my idle-time thoughts.

~~~

Life has a way of settling into a comfortable rhythm. Work is demanding because of the premeditated, deliberate way Mother Elizabeth expects us to think and perform. At the same time, it is invigorating to be openly creative and to work with an energetic staff, not to mention the tireless good sisters. Our families are beginning to respond to Spirit of Hope.

The children are laughing, maybe not as often as regular children laugh, but they are laughing. The expressions on the faces of the parents are beginning to relax. Their eyes look less scared now that they are not living from moment-to-moment with their little ones' hunger on their mind. To that extent and more, the program is showing signs of success.

Mother Elizabeth knows someone who knows someone at a plush Hollywood salon. Several of the hair-magicians-of-the-elite are coming to the convent this week to donate haircuts. It's a good idea. Everyone feels better when they look in the mirror and see someone attractive looking back at them.

Our clients will begin to see themselves differently as each piece of the program integrates their survival skills with successful experiences.
~~~

With enough positive experiences, they will become strong again. Then they will interview for jobs with more confidence.

One of the sisters posts a haircut sign-up list on the bulletin board in the family room. Also, there is a notice of dates when trips to a dentist and health screening teams, all volunteers, of course, will be available.

Mother Elizabeth is taking care of the basics before approaching the issue of employment. However, she is not forcing any of these free services on our families. They have to take the initiative to set their own appointments and make their own decisions about the services they want or need.

Sister Theresa has posted a list of repairs needed around the property. This household of single women intends to keep the men busy and feeling useful until they find jobs. I am pleased to see they will not be left to sit idle, as they are given the opportunity to "work for food" so this doesn't feel like charity.

Even though working for food is not required, the projects provide finished results that are concrete and observable. It's obvious the sisters intend to rebuild the adults' self-esteem before sending them out into the world of work. Feeling useful is a good place to start. They are given many opportunities to re-establish their roles as adults and parents within this safe closed society. It will only be a matter of time before they will be encouraged to expand their roles into the outside world while living safely at Saint Mark's Spirit of Hope.

~~~

Maggie found Linda's middle name, but we run into one dead end after another. Has Linda left the state or married? We have no trail to follow.

As our schedules allow, we canvass Linda's high school classmates. We follow leads, only to end with nothing helpful. Linda hasn't maintained contact with anyone from her school days. She doesn't attend class reunions. The last two invitations were returned as undeliverable, so the reunion committee has taken her off of their mailing list.

We find no newspaper archives of a wedding announcement for Linda Jones. Maggie jokes that maybe Linda became a nun. Karen and Keith don't laugh. I catch my laugh, but it comes out as an odd faint sound. Unfortunately, they heard the sound, which causes the three of them to laugh at me. It breaks the tenseness of our duty to find Linda—a duty imposed upon us by her dead father. Damn him!

There is no help from Linda's mother's siblings. One of her aunts has advanced Alzheimer's disease and is in a nursing home. Another has died. The third has had no contact since Linda's high school graduation.
~~~

To my relief, we unanimously decide to put Linda on the back burner of our lives. Until she surfaces, we will have to wait for inspiration about where to search next. I mind the decision the least of us. The others are more reluctant to give up on Linda, but I am ready to spend my time in ways not related to Judge Jones.

The warm spring weather brings tourists to the beach. I still find time to have the beach to myself by varying my walking schedule to very early or very late—yes, early. All the people in my life are woven into a nice package. This is the least stressful and out-of-control I can remember my life in a very long time. I enjoy the peacefulness of these days.

~~~

Mr. Goldstein is more mentally alert from the stimulation at the Senior Center, and I like to think our friendship helps too. He is looking and acting younger.

He and his friend, Karl, go to Spirit of Hope to read stories to the children every Sunday afternoon. The reports are that the children love the voices Mr. Goldstein uses for each character while reading. I imagine him reading, then chuckling to himself.

Karen and I have become closer than I would have ever thought possible. Maggie and I make sure we find time to get together once a week to shop, lunch, visit, and sometimes to do things with Dave and Joseph. My life is a nice, tidy package. I couldn't be happier than I am right now.

Joseph and I have been seeing each other almost weekly for over a month. We have exercised restraint in our physical attraction to each other. I suppose that we both want this to last longer than the heat of passion.

On Memorial Weekend we drive the short distance to Malibu to visit the remodeled J. Paul Getty Villa, which has recently re-opened. The Villa is beautiful. The gardens are in bloom and the grounds are inviting.

What I will remember most about today is the walk up the seemingly hundred or so steps beside the Greek reflecting pools, under columns, and around statues of gods and goddesses. At the top of the steps, turning back to the west, we can see the blue Pacific stretch peacefully to the horizon and blend seamlessly with the sky. The breeze from the ocean cools us as we stand in silence holding hands at the top of the hillside paradise.

Later, Joseph wants to drive to Griffith Park Observatory to gaze at the night sky. No doubt it is an excuse to make the day last longer. We pick out the few constellations we know. I don't know that many and I am suspicious of some of the ones Joseph mentions. The dragon and Athena constellation can't be right. I know for certain that he is making
~~~

up the leprechaun one. We laugh about it, and for a moment, when we look at each other, I think he is going to kiss me. He smiles warmly, then seems to change his mind about a kiss. We have kissed before, so I am not sure why not now. Even though I would have welcomed the kiss, it is still a romantic evening without it. The day has taken on the air of ancient Greece—her mythology was visible in statue form at the Villa and now in the night sky.

Joseph leans his head near mine while directing my vision toward yet another stellar cluster. As he does, he puts his left arm around my shoulder and pulls me toward him slightly while pointing his outstretched right arm toward the heavens.

My heart begins pounding as soon as Joseph touches me and pulls me closer to him. There is a stir of excitement inside me. Yet I want to be sure not to make more out of his action than is really there. I want the memories for the future, in the event this relationship doesn't develop further than what it is now. I want to savor every moment. As I lean into his touch, my heartbeat reaches a crescendo.

~~~

It has been a wonderful day. As I make a pot of coffee, I can tell Joseph doesn't want to leave. I want him to stay too. I put on some music. Joseph offers his hand for a dance. We dance slowly in the small space between the sofa and the dining area of my apartment. Joseph is a wonderful dancer. In his arms I feel like I am floating on air. With his gentle touch, a stir of desire wells inside me. I close my eyes and melt into his arms. He smells good, and his hand on the small of my back feels good. He leans down and kisses my cheek near my ear in a snugly way that gives me chills. I stretch up to reach his mouth with a kiss. Our selection of music is perfect. Everything is perfect.

It is getting late as we move toward the door. Hesitantly, he goes out into the night air. He turns back to me and puts his arm around my waist, gently pulling me toward him. I stretch up to put my arms around his neck as he leans down to kiss me goodnight. The stir inside me longs for him to stay—my resolve weakens. I say nothing as I watch him go away into the night. The taste of his kiss is still on my lips.

~~~

~ CHAPTER 9 ~

The Obvious Truth

One Saturday a month, Karen provides therapeutic group activities for the children at St. Mark's. On one of our beach walks, she reports her little "patients" are a refreshing diversion from a steady diet of abused children. It also allows her back in the therapist chair and away from administrative duties.

Silently, I agree with Karen. I have had enough of child abuse cases for a lifetime, maybe two lifetimes. Children are amazingly resilient, but adults who work with abused children have to develop ways to deal with the intense emotions silently directed toward abusers. Personally, I am delighted to be away from child abuse investigations. Spirit of Hope is brings out the best in each of us.

~~~

Mother Elizabeth has a talent for rounding up free services for our families. No one in their right mind would get in the way of Mother Elizabeth and her little army of nuns when they are on a mission.

It wouldn't surprise me that she is aware her volunteers and benefactors benefit as much from giving as the recipients benefit from receiving. It's that mutual give and take that gives meaning to what we do and who we are.

This is certainly true of Mr. Goldstein and me. I hadn't expected any depth to our relationship when I began including him in my walks. Now I look forward to seeing him more than he can know. I couldn't have imagined what richness he would bring to my life. It doesn't seem the same when he is gone on overnight excursions with his Senior Center friends, as he is today.

~~~

On a solitary walk along the beach, I stop to watch an artist drawing sketches of seagulls with the surf spewing into the air near them. I have seen her at the beach on and off over the years, but have never officially met her. Her work on display at the library is quite good. Something about the way she captures the water and the beach impresses upon me that she has an understanding with the beach others cannot hope to have. She must have grown up here. There is no other explanation for her ability to get it right like she does.

I stand a slight distance away and I watch her work. Just as I am about to move on, she speaks, apparently aware of my presence all along.

"Are you an artist?" she asks without looking away from her canvas.

"Oh, no! No. I'm not." I gasp with surprise at the question. "But I do admire your work." I move closer to look at her painting.

She smiles in response to the compliment. "Are you from here?" she asks. She had been looking back and forth from the water to the painting while she spoke, but now she looks at me for the first time.

"I grew up in Huntington Beach." I motion over my shoulder in the direction of Huntington Beach. "But I moved here years ago. Are you from here?"

"All my life," she laughs.

"I've seen your work at the library. I love how you make the feathers on the seagulls ripple in the breeze."

She smiles again as she dabs grayish-white paint on the water's edge.

It is amazing to watch her work.

"I own the art gallery on Main Street."

"I've been there. It's a nice shop."

"Do you work downtown?"

"No, in L.A. at Saint Mark's program for homeless families."

She smiles. "I helped Sister Bridget paint the mural for the playroom."

"Ahhh, it's wonderful."

"You know Sister Elizabeth Craig, then?" She stops painting for a moment, putting her brush at rest, then turns directly toward me.

"Yes, I know her," I reply as I realize for the first time that Karen and Mother Elizabeth have the same last name. I don't think of nuns as having last names. Their first name is always "Sister" and another name or two—but no last name. That's not exactly true about their first name being "Sister." It is only their title, but the part about rarely using their last name is true.

I am becoming suspicious, very suspicious, about Karen and Mother Elizabeth's shared last name—and how I came to be employed at Spirit of Hope. It was easy to get the job.

The conversation goes on a few more minutes. The artist attended grade school with Elizabeth and knew her younger sister, Karen. That confirms my suspicions the shared names between the two are not a coincidence.

Walking along the beach toward home I am still amazed, Mother Elizabeth is Karen's Sister-sister. Wow! Imagine having your sister turn out to be a nun.

This new information explains a lot. Things seem to fit together, especially the thing about organizing papers into neat piles that both Karen and Mother Elizabeth do. When she asked me to take Sister to the airport "on my way home," it explains why Mother Elizabeth did not ask where I live.

At the time I thought she just assumed I would want to do it in the way nuns do not expect anyone to say, "No." Or Mother Elizabeth could have looked through the staff addresses and found that the airport was nearly on my way home. Who knows?

There may be no connection to any of it, but it sure seems connected. Of course that is how she obtained a first-rate child psychologist to volunteer with the Spirit of Hope children. And my employment? Did Karen pull strings with her Sister-sister? That explains the file full of papers on Mother Elizabeth's desk at my interview.

I hope that I landed the job on my own merit. I guess it doesn't really matter. Things are working out in my life much to my satisfaction. This is an interesting twist of events, yet it makes no difference in the overall scheme of things.

Thinking about my long-awaited contentment with life makes me think of Linda Jones. I had forgotten about her after we ran into one dead end after another. Now I have a sense of needing to find her. The instinct is only a guess that something is wrong, but I think I should do what I can to see if I can help her. Now that I know running away doesn't cure the pain, I know it won't for her either.

Judge Jones, for whatever reason, asked me to tell her he was sorry. Mr. Goldstein rightly said I need to do that. If I can help her, then I should. I believe delivering the letter is part of the healing process for all of us touched by her father. In this, the choice is not mine to make. I must find her. After that, what she does with the letter and its message is part of her life's journey. The problem is I have no idea where to search next.

~~~

Much to my old-fashioned Irish luck, Linda attends her first class reunion ever. It is the fifteenth reunion. Maybe it is just one of those nice round numbers that compelled her to attend. Or maybe it is her time to come home. Whatever the reason, she came to the reunion on the three-day 4th of July weekend.

One of her school friends, Melissa, kept Keith's business card from when he asked her about Linda. She notified Keith that she had permission to give him Linda's address. "Linda went home, suddenly, after the first day of the reunion," Melissa adds.

This seems a little too easy to me, but maybe Linda is ready to be found. Maybe she doesn't know she has been lost. Maybe it is no different than me returning from Nebraska without warning. It is just time to get on with life, a better life.
~~~

On Monday, Maggie, Keith, Karen, and I meet for lunch to discuss Linda. It is just like the old days when I worked with them. Keith tells us that Linda lives in the Bay Area. She is married to Todd Whitmore.

"Todd Whitmore?" I asked surprised. "Todd Whitmore whose father is Governor Whitmore and his mother is actress Angela Whitmore? That Todd Whitmore?" We must have missed the wedding in the newspaper archives.

"Yes, that's the one," Keith answers.

The first family aside, we all agree we should make contact, face-to-face contact, to put the letter directly in her hand as soon as possible. Keith is unavailable for an out-of-town trip anytime soon, as he is under a subpoena for a lengthy jury trial starting next week.

Before anyone can say anything else, Maggie "suggests" that I go—alone.

"Oh, I don't know about me going." My voice fails to disguise my uncertainty. "What do you think he might have been sorry about?" I ask the same tired question again.

"It could have been any one of a hundred things," Maggie answers. "Whatever it is, you can do this, Kate. I know you can."

Karen helps more than Maggie. "The obvious thing is the suicide, but it is hard to tell what was on his mind when he wrote that letter of yours." Karen is staffing this like it is an active case—and maybe it still is, at least, for us.

"No, it's not *my* letter."

Keith says nothing. His silence does not mean he isn't paying attention to our conversation. He's astute. I was fortunate to have been assigned to work with him. Keith taught me more about child abuse investigations than any of the graduate classes I took.

"Suppose it is the suicide, what does Kate do?" Maggie asks as an atonement for volunteering me for the trip.

Karen briefs the interventions on the most likely scenarios as I listen with urgency. I don't like going into this blind. If the letter triggers a crisis situation, I will have to handle it until I can get help. Since I haven't done crisis intervention for a while, going solo makes me uneasy. Not to mention, I will be in a city where I don't have professional contacts or favors to call in. These guys are only a phone call away, but isn't the same thing.

I wish Karen would go in my place. She is clearly the best qualified to handle any reaction Linda might have to the letter. The boxed-in feeling of this ordeal makes me uncomfortable. Once again, I have Judge Jones to thank for bringing this unwanted disruption into my life.

Maggie reaffirms her belief that I am the one—the only one—to make the trip. The truth is we all know that I have to do this. Maybe it's because the Judge sent the letter to me. I know I must make the trip north, alone, whether I want to go or not. We all want this finished. Clearly, this is mine to end.

It is amazing how often really intelligent people can pool their energy and come up with a terrifically lame idea. We decide I should wait to call Linda until I am in San Francisco. It never occurs to us that she might not be home when I arrive. All I am concerned with is the possibility of a copycat suicide from this unknown woman. There is no way for me to anticipate how she will react to the letter from her father.

It is decided. I fly to San Francisco tomorrow after work and deliver the letter. I am reasonably confident that I didn't get to vote on this timetable.

Maggie says, "You're going before you have time to back out."

I think she is kidding, but I am more than a little annoyed they are pushing me so hard. Before I can protest formally, Maggie is on her cell phone making my flight reservations with her mom, a travel agent.

She says, "You will leave on the first flight after work tomorrow."

Not that I am a good sport, but I pull my credit card out of my wallet and hand it to her to pay for the ticket. They bought the transcript. They waited patiently for me to return and open the letter. The least I can do is pay for the flight to San Francisco.

~~~

The time passes quickly at work. Soon I am pulling into the parking garage at LAX. I spend the flight to the Bay Area reviewing Karen's advice regarding hypothetical responses to my arrival and the letter from Judge Jones, now five years old. I desperately try not to forget anything Karen said.

When the runway appears beneath the plane, I settle down, check my apprehension, and clear my thoughts. Even after all the years spent away from investigations, instinctively the clear, focused discipline returns . I welcome the familiar feeling of confidence as I walk into this unknown situation.

I hail a taxi at the San Francisco airport. The driver drives up and down the hills and across a bridge. Clearly, I have no idea where I am. On previous trips to the Bay Area I hadn't paid much attention to our wanderings, since I was with people who knew the lay of the land. It is probably best for Linda this way, but I would feel better if I was on home turf.

When the taxi pulls onto her street, I make the call to Linda's house from my cell phone. She's home and willing to see me after I explain my connection to Detective Knight.

Linda cannot possibly know about the letter, since Keith and I didn't mention it to Melissa. I can't help thinking Linda isn't prepared for the
~~~

visit she is about to have. I feel sorry for her, but the truth is she wouldn't have had any more warning if her father had mailed the letter directly to her.

The taxi comes to a stop across from Linda's house. There is the usual damp chill in the air, but no fog. At the top of the steps of the stylish, historical Bay Area-style building, the door opens almost as soon as my finger leaves the doorbell. The first thing I notice is that Linda is attractive and dressed nicely. She has a sophisticated air of upper class about her demeanor. There is a sense of grace about her.

The room is tastefully decorated and shows the residents are well-traveled and well-educated. There is an unmistakable sense of old money in the Whitmore furnishings.

Linda brings coffee in a polished silver serving set, reminding me this is a formal visit. Protocol. There are rules of etiquette to follow, but I am not sure they will fit the occasion for very long.

She offers coffee and I am relieved to have it. She pours herself a cup and sits on the sofa with me. After explaining who I am and how I came to be at her door, I remove the letter from my purse and hand it to her.

As Linda accepts the letter from me she asks, "Why did my father send this to you?"

"We have no idea why. My cases usually weren't docketed in his court." I offer the last information as proof I truly didn't know her father.

"We?" she questions, looking up from the letter in her hands.

I explain the letter went to Keith, to Karen, then Maggie, and finally to me. "The delay is because I moved out of state for five years. I didn't know the letter existed."

Linda still doesn't understand why her father sent the letter to me, since he knew where she was. They spoke on the phone and went out for dinner when he came to San Francisco.

Frankly, I admit I don't understand either. I mention the name similarity with her mother's. She looks a little sad when I say her mother's name, but she quickly regains her composure. Linda thought over the name similarity for what seemed longer than it probably was. Finally she agrees, "It is one possible explanation, but who knows? He wasn't well."

Considering his state of mind at the time, he could have meant anything when he wrote it. I won't go into that detail unless she asks. We leave the topic of why me and move on. His motive is apparently to be left unsolved. It probably doesn't matter now anyway.

"I wish my husband was here," she says softly. She shifts her position and leans forward as she looks at the letter in her hands. "Todd is in Paris for another week."

I suggest she can wait and read it with her husband when he returns, but Linda insists that it isn't necessary to wait. She is resigned to go forward.

As she fingers the letter she whispers pleasantly, "Thank you for bringing this to me."

Linda is proper, she could have easily convinced an observer that she was about to read my favorite omelet recipe. I am ashamed that I didn't eagerly make the trip.

Linda unfolds the letter and silently reads it. On the outward appearance she looks perfectly calm. I know better. I don't understand the message, but I know the letter must be heaped in emotion. Especially considering that her father wrote to her as one of his last actions before committing suicide.

When Linda finishes reading the page, she glances toward me. Her eyes begin to fill with tears. Incredibly, she keeps the tears from spilling over and down her cheeks. She looks deeply hurt. I want to comfort her, but manage to check my desire. My sixth sense tells me it is not the time to intervene.

"Thank you," she says in a nearly clear voice.

"Do you know what it means?"

She nods affirmatively. She understands. She looks at me again, but this time a tear slips loose and trickles down her face. Another tear follows closely behind the first one. She makes no attempt to hide her tears. Simply, silence lingers.

I know not to touch her. A touch could rally her strength to hold back everything waging war to break free. What I have learned in doing investigations was "Questions result in answers; well-timed questions produce information." It is premature to ask Linda questions. It is premature to touch her.

Following my instincts I say softly, "Linda, no more secrets."

Linda looks at the letter for what seems like five minutes, though it couldn't have been more than one. Her hands shake slightly, so slightly that it is barely apparent and could easily have been missed by someone not watching for her reaction.

She looks straight through the letter and the floor. She begins to slowly relate the time after her mother died as feeling alone in "confused darkness." Her father threw himself into work. She was raised primarily by domestic help. Linda pauses and looks at me to see if I understand.

Yes, I understand. Even though I was only six years old, I remember what it was like after my father died. A child losing a parent can't be described to someone who has never been through it. They can guess what it's like. They may even think they understand, but they can't possibly comprehend the loss.

I nod my head, just slightly, to indicate that I understand. The feelings of abandonment are strong, even when the person leaves because of a terminal illness. Suicide has to be worse.

She takes a deep breath and slowly, softly begins her real story of her father's sexual advances. I offer an encouraging, yet slight nod when she chooses to look at me, but I say nothing. I won't disturb the moment for her. She is not only telling about what happened. In her mind she is going back in time and reliving the moments and emotions attached to the memory.

It would be easy to touch her hand or say something to ease her pain, and bring her back to the present. I have heard this story before and it would be so easy not to hear it again. It would be easy to stop her and protect myself under the disguise of consoling her. I do nothing, except listen attentively. I am back in the role of child abuse social worker, even though she is not my client.

Linda continues to relate the graphic details of her father's behavior, her feelings of desperation and shame, and her struggles to survive each day.

Her eyes dim as she relives the experiences in her memory and every fiber of her being, except her voice, moving far away from her living room to the child she once was—a sex slave with no mother to save her.

I feel myself slip into her story. I know there is more to it than words can express. There are things about sexual abuse that elude expression in words. Years of experience and training taught me to recognize the feelings that defy language—I listen for the clinical markers in her words. Sadly, I find them. She is speaking from personal experience—no doubt about it—she didn't make this up.

I believed her from the beginning. There is a sense of truth in the telling of it, but now I have clinical verification. A person can't make up this story, in this way, and get the feel of it right. She is telling the truth.

"It escalated into confusing and frightening sexual involvement," she continues in the matter-of-fact, numb way incest victims relay what had happened to them. "I had nowhere to turn; he was a prominent man—I was alone." Her voice wavers with the weight of the memories. She allows her voice to reflect the circumstances she is relating—it is a knife piercing my chest.

Linda draws a deep breath that has a little quiver in it. She tells about the day she approached the school counselor under the guise she wanted to talk about her mother's death. The counselor had been flirting with the vice principal when Linda came into her office. She was disinterested in listening to Linda's pain. After that reception, Linda didn't bother revealing her real problem to the counselor—her father's incest. Until now she had told no one. She had buried it so deeply that she had blocked the memory.

Each time I heard this story it was the same, and yet distinctly different. The story is told to a very few people, if ever told at all. It still lives on inside of her.

I dreaded cases that were covered by the media, reports which were insensitive and poorly done. On one of my longest days at work, I heard three of these stories' first telling. How does a person deal with that? I can't explain the emotions I feel stirring in me as Linda relates what happened to her.

Linda's face has an out-of-place smile as she continues, "You know what is funny about that?"

I shake my head. "No, what's funny?"

Her smile disappears, "When I went to the class reunion this summer, that same counselor came to our table and started talking to me like we were friends."

I hear the hurt in her trembling whisper.

"She was trying to impress Todd. It never occurred to her how gravely she had let me down the day I went to talk with her. The incest continued for three more years—the counselor could have ended it, if she had only listened and intervened. But she wasn't interested."

Linda's tears well up in her eyes again. "I couldn't take it any longer. I desperately wanted someone to make him stop. It had taken weeks to gather the courage to talk to her about him. And she couldn't be bothered. Three more years—" Tears fill her eyes and roll down her cheeks. She wraps her arms around herself as her body begins to sob.

Now it's time. I reach my hand around her shoulder and ease her into my arms. It's a few seconds more before I feel her weight relax onto me and her sobbing increase. She has let go. It is all coming out. She is no longer quiet. I can hear the pain in her voice as she cries for help.

The counselor's original lancing blow was eighteen years ago. Damn fool. I'm angrily aware that the pain this woman caused Linda again this summer is still a fresh wound.

I know full well the system, as well as the professionals, were capable of letting her down, even if she had told anyone what was happening. It would have been a media nightmare if the story broke. It is unfortunate the system doesn't always work correctly, especially when a prominent person is the offender. Society doesn't want to hear that persons in a position of public trust have violated that trust, especially when it has been violated in this way.

Several hours pass as Linda talks about her feelings of guilt and responsibility for the situation occurring at home. The confusion she felt compounded her need to keep the secret and emotionally withdraw.

In her case, the outward over-achievement in academics and extracurricular activities was her smoke screen to keep the secret hidden from others. Linda worked hard to convince everyone, including herself, that everything was fine, couldn't be better.

Eventually, Linda confronted her father. There was no scene, no admission of guilt, or responsibility—nothing. Linda says she went into therapy after she was in college at Stanford. Even though the therapy helped her to intellectually cope with her mother's death, she had buried the memories of her father's abuse by then. Until the reunion this summer, those memories had not resurfaced.

Linda thinks the letter is about the sexual abuse. At least the second part of the letter. She isn't sure of the meaning of the rest. Another tear rolls down her face. She gently wipes it with a tissue from her pocket.

I hope the letter is enough to help her begin to process the relationship with her father and the unresolved emotions she carries with her. I hope it will act like a long overdue admission of his guilt. I hope she will be able to accept that what happened was not, and could never have been, her fault.

Tears build up inside me, but I don't tell her about her father letting the alleged perpetrators walk. I realize if he had admitted they were guilty, he would have had to face his own guilt. I am beginning to understand what happened in court.

Finally, I realize why he sent the letter to me. I had testified flawlessly in that last case. At least, I testified well enough for him to know that I understood sexual abuse. We had hammered home the point that it was a parent's duty to protect his child, not rape her. I made it impossible for him to ignore what he had done to Linda.

Still, he didn't understand soon enough. He let that sick bastard go rape and murder his little daughter. It took the death of my little client for Judge Jones to finally realize what he had done to his own daughter and what he was doing through his power as a judge.

Apparently he chose me to be with Linda when she read the letter, otherwise he could have mailed it directly to her. If he had sent the letter to Karen, she might have assigned it to someone else to handle since I was gone. By sending the letter to Keith, my former partner, Judge Jones must have figured the letter would somehow get to me. It had nothing to do with his wife's name and mine being the same. It had to do with me. He was sending the quintessential social worker by special delivery.

His apology, though simple, seems to be a starting place for the healing to begin. Now maybe she can put the abuse in perspective and get much-needed help.

She looks up again to meet my eyes with hers. "It is good you came, Kathryn."

I smile warmly at Linda and touch her hand. Yes, it was worth the inconvenience the letter caused to deliver it. After everything that has happened, she deserves the special effort of this trip. Finally, her father did one small, correct thing when he wrote the letter and sent it in care of Keith.

Linda and I talk for another hour. I encourage her to make an appointment for therapy and suggest a few things to look for in her selection of a therapist.

I say things I can say at this juncture to reinforce that it was not her fault that this horrible thing happened to her. I want to make sure she really is coping well enough to be left alone tonight. I ask that she consider spending the night with friends or having a friend stay with her.

She says thanks, but she will be fine. I think she will be fine, but it won't happen overnight.

Before I leave, I tell her I am sorry this happened to her and assure her again it was not her fault that it did. I admit that after the incident with the school counselor, it made sense to think the next person would let her down. I want her to know she deserves many apologies—from her father, from the counselor, and from me as a representative of a horribly flawed system within our society.

I give her Karen's business card, since I don't have any of my own. On the back, I add my number and encourage her to call either of us—at any time. It's important for her to know this time someone "official" is listening and there are people she can turn to who will listen and believe her. I am listening, Karen will listen, and her therapist will listen. The expression in her eyes moves me when I tell her she is not alone with her secret any longer.

~~~

Just before leaving, I ask Linda's permission to tell Karen, Maggie, and Keith the meaning of the letter.

She has a faraway look for a moment, then quietly agrees. The secret has lost its power over her life. Maybe it has lost its power over all of us. I hope so. I need to believe this will soon be finished.

During the taxi ride to the airport I think about Linda. I own the guilt for the system. Hopefully, she will find a qualified therapist. This isn't over for her yet. Even the letter will take time to resolve. I whisper a brief prayer she will get the help she needs to do more than survive what her father did to her. I hope she can begin to thrive—not just make it through the day.

The usual airport bustle has quieted. There aren't many people at the gate waiting for the last flight to L.A. I am glad to have time alone to
~~~

think about the lives the Judge touched. It's sad his crime was the very thing allowing others to continue to perpetuate their crimes. He must have been in full-blown denial to be capable of what he did. There can be no other explanation, other than he was sick and didn't get help.

A shudder goes through me at the thought of how Judge Jones' own crime lead to the brutal death of the sweet little girl in my last case for CPS. I wonder if he saw the police photos of her little dead body. I hope so. I hope they gave him nightmares—the really bad ones, ones that woke him up in a sweaty panic. It's mean, I know, but I'm angry.

I'm not sure that Karen will tell the staff the real reason why their cases failed in Judge Jones' court. He sentenced himself to death. What would be the point of saying anything now? Nothing can bring back the little girl.

~~~

At LAX Maggie is standing with the few people meeting the flight as I come down the stairs from the gates. She explains she is here, "In the event I have to pick up the pieces after your meeting with Linda."

I reassure her, I am fine.

Maggie looks at me intensely, wanting answers. I signal to wait until we're outside, so our conversation won't be overheard. In the parking garage, I tell her everything. We stand leaning against my car in silence for a long while. I wait for Maggie to make the first move.

"It is good he apologized, that's the first step for her."

My tone is more critical than hers and my thoughts aren't as well contained.

"Sure, it's important to her recovery. Linda must fully internalize the knowledge that the responsibility was not hers and he finally had remorse for what he did to her. But it is not enough, not nearly enough. How do we stop these rapists? These, these bastards who rape kids?"

Maggie shakes her head and offers to drive. Dave must have dropped her off at the terminal. I'm glad that I had taught her to drive a stick shift. Willingly, I hand her the car keys. I am spent.

I am justifiably angry that we let people do this to children. Rape is sick. I always saw the children. I had never seen an adult still living with all the pain and damage. The longevity of the abuse disturbs me.

Once inside the car Maggie confides, "I'm relieved he admitted his guilt, though he could have thought of several better ways to do it."

"It would have been better if he had done it sooner or started with grief therapy and worked into discussing his physical feelings for his daughter. Especially if he had gone for help and never raped her in the first place." I can only speculate why he didn't get help. It could have simply been his pride that caused so much harm to so many, beginning with Linda. "But you're right. I had to find Linda."
~~~

The intimate details of Linda's story play over again in my mind. My mind's eye constructs an image from Linda's words and the expression on her face as she spoke them. It is like the old days; my mind is preparing to write case notes, a court report, and eventually testify. But this time none of that will be necessary. So why can't I turn off the instinct?

The distraction of arriving home is a welcomed relief from our discussion and my thoughts. I cannot think about Judge Jones any longer. I am too drained to fight the anger those thoughts bring.

~~~

Maggie has Karen's mothering look on her face. It makes me feel uneasy as I fumble with the door key. I know she is up to something.

"Kate, do you think," Maggie begins, her eyes widening with her words, "well, I was wondering if your testimony finally made Judge Jones grasp what he had done to Linda?"

"I doubt it. Linda confronted him years before that." I appreciate her gesture to give me credit. I'm not willing to admit I agree with her assessment. Though I think the case is what led him to commit suicide, I do not want credit for any part of it. I want to finally be done with Judge Jones. I don't want to say aloud that I may have played a role in his death.

Maggie sets her jaw and looks at me as if she is debating whether to argue with me or let it ride.

"He didn't admit it before. Why would an unrelated case make him repent, especially considering his ruling?" I ask, hoping she has an answer. It's unkind, but I hope he suffered over the death of my little client.

Tossing my jacket on the sofa, I head straight to make coffee and breakfast. Not to be distracted, Maggie waves off the offer of toast.

"Kate, ask Karen to let you read the transcript—you were good, very good, practically perfect."

"Oh, Maggie, don't say that. I don't want the guilt of contributing to Judge Jones' suicide because of my testimony," I plead. I am too tired—emotionally and physically—to keep from being honest with her.

Until now I haven't told anyone that the moment I heard about his suicide I did fear my testimony made him realize what he had done. That I pushed him into a corner and over the edge when his error was confirmed by the bloody pictures and the grand jury. I didn't know he was a "perp," but he had to see his responsibility in the little girl's death.

"No, Kate. When you hold up a mirror, you aren't responsible for what the other person sees in it. All of the guilt is Judge Jones'. Eventually, even he knew it."

She reaches to touch my wrist as she speaks.
~~~

I don't want to be touched. I escape to interrupt the coffee and fill our cups under the drip. I know she isn't going to let me walk away from the past just yet. But I want to run from it. I don't want to think about this anymore.

We talk for a long while, interspersed with silence. Whether I want to or not, we have to process our thoughts. She insists on it. At least that is something we do well together—staff cases. But this isn't a case, this intimately involves us and I can't be objective about my anger.

In retrospect, there had been a few signs of an abuser in the Judge's behavior. He flexed his power to keep his secret hidden. We know we couldn't have been expected to notice the clues with such limited contact with him, but still I think we should have—at least I should have seen it.

Even if we had suspicions, the statutes do not provide for witch hunts. Without someone outside our agency reporting him, an investigation wouldn't have been initiated solely on hunches.

Eventually, with enough coffee in my system, I collect my thoughts and order them to respond in the manner a seasoned professional should. We are attempting to give each other a sense of absolution through our conversation. I'm not sure it's really working. We express feeling ignorant and inadequate for letting him deceive us. We were supposed to be better than that, smarter than that. I was supposed to be smarter. I was supposed to be the expert.

~~~

By the time we finish the pot of coffee, I am able to drag myself to the shower. I am more emotionally drained than tired. It is a good kind of tired to be rid of Judge Jones' secret. But still I wish I had never heard of him.

I stand in the shower hoping the warm spray will wash away the years of pain caused by the Judge's horrible secret and corresponding rulings. I think about the pain of the last five years of isolation. I am overwhelmed by the senseless waste of the little girl's life; Linda's stolen innocence; the anguish Karen, Maggie, and the department staff went through; and the pain that I carried with me. I lean against the cool, wet tiles, sobbing quietly as the water pours over me.

I don't know how long I stood in the shower before I slid down in a heap and rested my head on my arm on the edge of the tub.

I think of the years I spent numbed in Nebraska. I think of what Judge Jones stole from me. As inconsequential as my pain is to the pain Linda felt, I am still overcome with it, and I sob uncontrollably as the warm water showers down upon me.

Finally, there are no more tears. I put a cool cloth over my eyes, hoping it will erase the redness from them before I face Maggie again.
~~~

When I emerge from my private refuge, I find Maggie has moved to the patio. I refill my coffee cup and join her. If she does notice I have been crying, she says nothing. Apparently she realizes now is not the time to probe my fragile feelings.

I wonder about her inner response to resolving the Judge's letter. I think about consoling Maggie, though she shows no signs of needing my counsel. I think about my duty to her as the lead staff on this case. But I know, at this moment, I am not really able to deal with her emotions in addition to mine.

She doesn't seem to need my strength. It is a good thing, since I don't feel strong. Maybe I'm not a very good friend right now, but I barely have enough strength to hold myself together, there isn't enough of me for any more than that.

"Dave and I left my car here last night. Listen, You look tired. Get some sleep. I'll pick you up in a couple of hours."

"Sure? Okay," I answer.

"I'll go with you to tell Karen—partners to the end," she adds.

"Yes, to the end."

It is strange to say out loud that this nightmare is ended. The feelings of completion have not come with the spoken words. "Partners to the end." I was never really alone, if I had only realized it. Nebraska was an unnecessary detour to get to this point.

~~~

Wrapped in my robe, I crawl into bed and marvel at the mess Judge Jones made of life. We know Karen and Keith will be eager to hear about my trip. Undoubtedly, they will be distracted from work until they hear the outcome of meeting Linda. The last few hours of waiting must have been harder than all the previous years.

It is finally time to end this. Maggie and I go together to find Karen and Keith and put an end to the Judge's legacy for all of us. It has been a long road to San Francisco.

When we walk through the doors, Karen is in the reception area leaning over the receptionist's shoulder. They both are looking intensely at the computer monitor. Karen looks up as we approach the desk. Of course, she knows why we are here. She seems to be trying to read our expressions, so that she will be prepared for what we have to say.

Before we can speak, Karen directs us, "Let's go to my office."

Once inside her office Karen telephones Keith to see if he is able to join us. He is on his way to court in a case where there was a change in venue, so Karen leaves a message on his voicemail for him to call when he comes back.

Maggie listens while I tell Karen the Judge's secret. Karen suddenly puts her hand over her mouth to ensure her self-control as she catches
~~~

her breath before she can gasp. Her other hand has gone to her stomach. This is that sickening that she could vomit.

She checks her emotions almost immediately. I think in that brief instance, she is thinking the same thing I thought: How could we have missed this? We should have seen it—somehow. It's hard to watch her go through what Maggie and I have just gone through.

I choose not to respond to her initial reaction. Karen will verbalize it when she is ready—or deal with it privately on her own terms. I continue to describe Linda's reaction to my visit and to her father's apology.

The three of us process the information in the familiarity of established procedure. This time we do it for us. There is nothing we can do about Judge Jones. He made sure of it with one simple bullet.

When she hears the school counselor's role in Linda's silence, Karen slowly shakes her head in response.

"Something has to be done about this. Those people are our first line of defense in saving these kids and stopping this madness." The look on her face makes tears well in my eyes.

At last Karen's frustration shows. "How could we have been so blind?" She isn't assigning blame, but maybe assuming it.

"We saw him in a limited setting. We couldn't have known," Maggie counters Karen's assumption of guilt. She takes a step closer, softly touching Karen's shoulder as an invitation to be held. Karen pivots into Maggie's arms.

"Karen, it wasn't your fault," I insist, nearly reaching to touch her—but I catch myself. Touchy-feely stuff is Maggie's department, not mine.

When it is all said and done, we have to be careful how we deal with our guilt. This won't be over if we don't find absolution.

Before we leave her office, Karen calls Linda. She says what I had said last night, only with a more expert twist to it. Karen ends the conversation by reiterating, "I am sorry he raped you. I am sorry you had no safe place to go." Karen's tone of voice is warm and healing as she continues, "Linda, you didn't deserve what happened to you. It wasn't your fault. You did nothing wrong. You didn't cause this to happen to you."

She suggests to Linda, "If you don't have a therapist in mind, I will give you the name of two who are good. Use my name when you call for an appointment." Karen listens to the phone quietly then says, "Maybe it will help bring closure for you."

In a way, Karen is healing all of us as she reaches out to Linda. We desperately need to know we have done everything we can for her. Maybe Linda will be able to move beyond being a survivor—beyond going through the motions of getting through the day, and really thrive.

With all of this behind me, I am ready for sleep. It was a short night. However, for now, I have to get to work.

~~~

It isn't a particularly busy day, but I am "dragging-butt" tired. My duties do not occupy me enough to keep me energized. I can't wait for a nap as soon as I return home. Hopefully there will be no more nightmares of the little girl. Maybe now she can rest in peace. Maybe we all can find peace.

By the end of work I am less interested in a nap. I am craving time on my beach. The waves will be full of surfers. I don't mind the surfers. At most they leave their packs where they can see them from the water. There is an unwritten code among the beach people: No one bothers a surfer's backpack left unattended.

The next thing to consider is whether I want to bother with the tourists or to drive to another, more secluded beach. No, I am too tired to drive the 405 again this time of day, or to deal with stoplights if I hop over to PCH.

To be alone, I can walk to the end of the pier and have no one between me and the ocean. I can get lost in the swirling water near the pylons. Or I can walk the beach a safe distance from the masses, or even dare to walk silently among them.

When I arrive home, I change clothes and walk to the beach. I stand at the water's edge just beyond the reach of the breaking waves. The fine misty spray blesses me (in a Catholic sort of way) and bathes away the grime of Judge Jones' memory. With each crescendo of the waves, I take a step back from the incoming tide.

And so it goes, a series of waves blessing me with the Pacific's "holy water," while the rising tide slowly pushes me back into the real world with every step backward, on and on, until the tide pushes me to the mark left on the beach from the previous high tide.

The spray nudges me like a mother gently prodding a child to move toward the classroom door on the first day of school or in the wings nudging her hesitant offspring on stage for the first piano recital. The waves push me to go home and sleep—it will be all right.

~~~

~ CHAPTER 10 ~

Comfort Returns

The August sun bakes the sand. It is too hot to walk shoeless on the beach, unless at the water's edge. The beach is filled with tourists taking the last days of summer to play in the ocean. Standing ankle deep in the water, I watch the children play in the waves. For some unexplainable reason I don't mind sharing the beach with the crowd of strangers, not that I could keep them away if I wanted. But I notice the change in my attitude.

My life is sufficiently settled to stop the nightmares now that Judge Jones is truly dead. I haven't forgotten any of the cases that gave me nightmares, but they do not haunt me like they have for years. I am beginning to get perspective on who was really at fault for these horrible cases slipping through the court. It was not us—it was not me. It was the abusers, the perps, and Judge Jones.

Things seem to lull into a comfortable routine again. Work is a joy, especially now that the Judge no longer interferes in my life from the grave.

Several of the Spirit of Hope men have found work, maybe not as CEOs of profit-sharing corporations, but it's steady work with the possibility of some advancement. For the families and staff, there is an air of hope surrounding their employment.

When someone finds work the Sisters throw an employment party complete with all of the festivities, and the ceremonious presentation of a new lunch box to take to their new job. Some people wouldn't get excited about a new lunch box, but to these men it is a trophy of what they have endured—and endured successfully. Even though they had every justification to think life was a stacked deck, they took the risk to come to Spirit of Hope, and it paid dividends.

The program at St. Mark's is providing more and more services. Volunteers are appearing miraculously when a need is identified. Mother Elizabeth never ceases to amaze me with her resourcefulness, her inner strength, and her compassion. She possesses a spirit of hope and she shares it just by being herself. The woman is contagious.

Most of all, I like to watch her with the families, especially with the children. This morning she was in the family room sitting on the floor surrounded by children. The skirt of her habit was gathered in balloon-like mounds close to her, and she was demonstrating the finer points of playing jacks. The whole affair was quite a sight to see. Mother held the children spellbound. She is amazingly good at jacks and already has some of the kids able to do their "twosies." I leave unnoticed.

I long to find the sense of peace I see in Mother Elizabeth. The past has been put to rest, but I have not found peace with it, even though it ceases to haunt my sleeping. Each passing day seems to help a little. But a sense of harmony is still lacking. Nonetheless, I cannot find reason to complain.

There is a certain amount of pride connected to the fact that Spirit of Hope is the envy of all the social work directors in the city. It shows in the way the staff say where they work when we are at conferences. I feel it when I speak about Spirit of Hope. Even the pious nuns show an un-nun-like pride in the program and the success it is demonstrating.

To make good times even better, we are going to have a baby! The older sisters are busy crocheting, knitting, and sewing everything imaginable for the new baby. Mother Elizabeth thinks it is a good sign, "A sign from God," she said, to have a new life come during the first year of the program. I agree with her.

Sister Clare, one of the oldest and most reserved nuns, takes a special interest in the coming baby. Ever since the news of the baby, it is rare to see her without her yarn and knitting needles busily working, even while she fills in at the switchboard for Sister Theresa.

I like watching the interaction between Karen and her Sister-sister, Mother Elizabeth, as they discuss Spirit of Hope and the people who are the object of our hope. Karen advises Mother Elizabeth's staff how to involve all of the children in preparations for the new little life, especially since the baby is already getting a lot of attention and still months away. She also reminds us not to forget the adults' needs in our excitement.

It is important to keep in mind that everyone has needs for support. Even those around us who appear to be strong—everyone needs to recharge their inner strength. Consequently, we must ensure our own needs are addressed in healthy ways, so we do not drain those around us with our whining or neediness.

Karen warns, "Life isn't a competition to see how much we can GET from each other. The trick is how much can we reach inside and pull from ourselves for others, and ourselves. In the end, the competition is only within us."

Mother Elizabeth adds, "Saint Francis said, 'Grant that I may not so much seek to be consoled as to console.'"

"Exactly," Karen confirms.

Karen and Mother Elizabeth's comments have a ring of truth about them. I take them to mean more than the conversation about the clients' needs and the coming of a baby. I take them to be larger than this place and this time.

Since my trip to San Francisco, I spend every minute I can on the beach. Mr. Goldstein is busy more often than not these days, but he joins me for walks when his schedule allows. Maggie joins me sometimes. It seems that she is also healing more completely since we understand the intricacies of the case. Joseph has been consumed most of the summer with a major criminal case. Almost nightly, I see him in sound bites on the local news ignoring the reporters as he exits the courthouse. I would like to see him in person, but, in a way, I need this time to allow the conversion that is occurring within me, as I continue to heal from the emotional trauma that drove me to Nebraska.

~~~

This weekend my mind is flooded with old images that finally fit together. Things that hadn't made sense are becoming clear to me. I have been acquitted of contributing to the little girl's death. It is as if some sort of transition is occurring within me. I just have to let it run its course and embrace the person I am becoming. Absolution is sweet.

As I walk along the beach, Karen waves for me to join her in her usual spot on the sand, the place where she often sits to read reports. She is talking with another woman. As I approach them I am surprised to see the woman with Karen is Mother Elizabeth. The possibility of meeting Mother Elizabeth on the beach has never occurred to me. They both have a good laugh at my expense when they figure out the confusion going through my mind.

I make them both admit the Lakers T-shirt, slacks, and sandals are quite different from the brown habit and veil Mother Elizabeth usually wears. They confess Mother borrowed the clothes from Karen. They fit fine, but the look isn't quite right. I smile at them. After all, who am I to decide the look isn't right? I find myself studying her hair. I don't know what I expected. Mother Elizabeth's hair is nearly the same color as Karen's, only cut shorter. It is a nice cut, though very different from having her head completely covered by a veil.

Her white arms and feet seem out of place on the beach where everyone else has some degree of brown to their skin. Mother Elizabeth reaches for the bottle of sunscreen in Karen's beach bag. She casually applies another layer of lotion to her arms and offers the bottle to me.

I have on sunscreen, but allow her to squirt a bit into my palm. It was a caring gesture, and I have tried to allow more of them after what Maggie said about me keeping people at a distance. It is difficult to be less self-reliant, though in the past self-reliance didn't work well, either.

Mother is at ease on the beach. I struggle to remember that she wasn't always a nun. I try not to laugh. After all, I was more out of place in Nebraska.
~~~

Accepting their invitation, I join these two sisters. At first, as I listen to them banter back and forth to get the rhythm of the conversation, something gives me the sense that they had been having a sister-to-sister, heart-to-heart talk about a more serious topic before I arrived. They move the conversation to memories of sitting in this spot as children, then to the present. Mother gets up and walks to the water's edge. She removes her sandals and gets her feet wet. Karen and I watch her enjoy the waves, sandals in hand, full of abandon. I relax into the moment.

Karen says she met Linda the last time she was in San Francisco. She thinks Linda is going to be fine, better than fine. The cryptic letter was the admission she needed. First she was a victim, but when she told her story, she became a survivor. She is no longer a survivor. She is whatever is beyond that. I have never heard a word that suits going beyond surviving. Perhaps it is a higher plane of thriving. I like to think of it as a living symphony. All I know is surviving isn't quite enough, even though sometimes that is the best we have. We seek thriving for ourselves and our clients.

Mother Elizabeth returns with a handful of shells to take home to the children. She smiles contentedly. I get terribly sentimental about having these two women in my life, but I don't mention it. If Maggie were here, it would be perfect.

The sun, the beach, and the company get the best of us. We discuss how good life is going for each of us. Karen mentions that life is an enigma.

Her comment makes me think about how I used to call her "Mother Superior," and claim she must have been a nun in a previous life, when in reality it is her sister who is the nun. Still, I bet Karen was a nun in another life. Without considering my audience, I mindlessly ask, "Do you believe in reincarnation?"

I'm not sure the Church approves of such talk. I wish I hadn't asked about reincarnation without thinking about my audience and checking the question until some other time with some other person.

Typically, Karen asks back, "Why do you ask?"

Smiling, I say, "Oh, I don't know, no particular reason, I have always wondered." There is no way I am going to admit to them what I had been thinking about her previous life.

Mother Elizabeth studies me a minute, then answers, "I don't really know, Kathryn, but I plan to get my money's worth out of each day in the event I only get one shot at life."

We laugh. Obviously, she isn't being theological. The thought of this panhandling nun getting her "money's worth" is hilarious. For her, most things in life are free. Who among us can refuse any of her charitable requests? Not even God, I think. Besides, for people like her there is probably an express route to heaven when they die—no toll, of course.

~~~

After an hour of visiting, I leave Karen and Mother Elizabeth and walk down the beach, past the pier to my favorite spot. I sit watching the waves break while thinking about the importance of the beach in my life. I think about Maggie, Karen, Mr. Goldstein, Joseph, and now Mother Elizabeth on my beach. We grew up near the ocean. We know her moods, and as much as anyone can, we understand them. The beach is the place we go throughout the ebb and flow of our lives.

It seems strange how easily Joseph accepts my beach, especially since his world is very different from mine. He doesn't share the attachment, but he accepts it. On the evenings when he takes time out from his trial preparation to come over, he usually finds me sitting, watching the Pacific, or walking along the beach. There is something about the sand and the ocean that enhances the mood required for authentic conversation.

Watching the water rise and fall mesmerizes me. I watch the gulls hover on the breeze then land to peck at shells, accessing the meal inside with the usual amount of bickering over ownership of the food.

A smile comes over my face when I see Joseph approaching. Right on cue. I draw a deep breath as he sits down in the sand beside me. The way he settles close, I feel confident he feels the same toward me, but our feelings are the one thing we haven't discussed. I can't believe he still gives me chills when he is near me. And, oh, when we kiss, I melt in his arms.

~~~

Life goes on comfortably through October. Things are much better than I could have hoped they would be. The summer is gone, and with it the tourists. As winter approaches the beach seems peaceful. I am more satisfied with life than I remember ever being before. This year I am not dreading winter. Maggie and I spent a weekend on Catalina Island without the guys, for girl time. Good friends, good work, and good, good times with Joseph—what else is there?

~~~

Joseph is still a mystery in my life. After all these months I think of him, on and off, during most of my waking hours. I thought infatuation might have burned out with the departing of the summer sun. Yet he remains my knight in shining armor.

Our relationship is becoming more romantic. We are no longer casually dating. He is more than someone to fill an empty space in my life. It has nothing to do with hormones or the infamous biological clock driving me to connect with someone. I adore him as a person and want
~~~

to be near him for its own merit. Together, I feel richer than I am alone. I am happier because he came into my life. I am beginning to entertain the notion of actually being in love. I love his laugh. I love—him!

The best thing, though, is the smile that erupts on his face when I walk into the room unexpectedly. I have noticed that smile more than once. Not only do I think I love him, I feel loved.

Thanksgiving is coming in a few weeks. Emily, my cousin, has mailed out the family newsletter telling who is planning to attend Thanksgiving dinner and the latest news we have submitted for her to share with everyone. After I read each article about trips taken, new additions to the family, and the usual updates about everyone, their spouses and children, and sometimes their grandchildren, I study the photos of the people I haven't seen since my return. Everyone looks much as I would expect. It is comforting to know that no matter how my life spins out of control, these people are a constant.

My family always has Thanksgiving dinner together—my vast, extended family. I consider taking Joseph to meet my family. I have never taken a boyfriend to meet them before. But Joseph is special in a way no one else has been. I want to share them with him.

My family will notice this change in my behavior and understand the implications of bringing Joseph to dinner. I have discussed him at length with my cousin Ilene. Her knowing grin when she meets him is sure to confirm anyone's suspicions.

My mother's family is a little difficult to describe. The sense of belonging and acceptance is something I have never felt anywhere else. I never think about having a paternal family.

The Stewart family resemblances are strong. It's comfortable to look up and see familiar faces across the table laughing and telling stories, heavily embellished stories. I see Grandmother's smile and Grandfather's mischievous eyes in the faces around me. Without a doubt, that connectedness has sustained all of us through many difficult life experiences.

Long before I was born, Thanksgiving dinner was moved to the local park, because It takes three large turkeys to feed everyone. I have twenty-seven first cousins. Together they have sixty-three children, so far, in addition to aunts, uncles, and everyone's spouses. There isn't room for all of us at any of our homes. Why rent a hall? Nothing beats a day at the park. After all, it is a long-standing tradition. No one with any sensibilities would break a tradition that holds such bonding power.

With a group this size, we have a grand time. When one of us goes our own way for a while, as we occasionally do, we are always welcomed home with no questions asked. This family is an accepting group. This will be my year to prove that.

I know they will like Joseph, simply because I love him. That alone will be good enough for them.

Should I tell Joseph this is no ordinary family dinner, or will that scare him away? Before the first round of horseshoes is finished, I'm sure he will feel at home. I know it will be fine, but how can he know that? How can I explain it? What we have as a family isn't that common these days. Joseph will just have to come and see for himself.

I make a quick phone call to Maggie. "Maggie, the newsletter is here," I say dramatically.

"Oh! I'll be right there!" She laughs.

"Actually, I was thinking about lunch."

Maggie practically reads the entire newsletter out loud while I prepare our meal. She studies the photos and asks questions to reacquaint herself with everyone since she saw them last.

"I love your family. I actually considered going to the park the first year you were gone just to see if you would show up," she says, not intending to invoke the guilt that suddenly surges through me.

"Sorry! I didn't come back!" I joke, not admitting how I feel.

"Well, I am glad you finally did!"

"Me too," I admit softly.

During lunch I broach the topic of taking Joseph to the family dinner this year. In the typical girlfriend style, Maggie comes to my rescue with her definite opinion.

"Take him. He'll love it—and them. But don't tell him how big your family is, you might scare him. It scared Dave at first. After all, this is no ordinary family dinner."

"Okay." I laugh. I can't imagine anyone being scared of my family. It's not like we are part of the Irish Mafia or anything.

"I wouldn't know how to begin to explain your family to him anyway. He will just have to go and see for himself." She laughs warmly. "It will be fine, Kate," she says with a reassuring pat on my hand.

Maggie is right. I'm complicating things with unnecessary worry. Okay then, it's decided. I will let him experience the moments as they unfold.

I wish Maggie and Dave could come. My family would be happy to see her again. But they have plans to spend Thanksgiving at Lake Tahoe. They are flying up with friends for a long weekend of skiing. Sounds fun, but cold. It's not my kind of holiday.

Maggie and I vow to get together soon after she returns to L.A. I promise to tell her how Joseph reacts to the day. The last thing Maggie says to me is, "Let your family work their magic on him. And don't worry—it will be fine." We hug goodbye. "Tell your family 'Hello' for me."

"I will. Plan on coming next year."

I smile, thinking about bringing him with me. It would be so easy to imagine a life with him as part of my family. But I dare not entertain those thoughts, since neither of us has said "I love you" out loud.

The next time Joseph and I are walking along the beach I ask, "Do you have plans for Thanksgiving?"

"No, no, I don't," he says thoughtfully. "Do you want to make some?" he asks, turning his head in my direction.

I smile. "Sure, I have an idea, but let me surprise you."

~~~

Thanksgiving morning the picnic basket is packed and waiting by the door when Joseph arrives. I hope I don't have a ridiculous grin on my face. But I am excited enough to grin like the cat that ate the canary.

"What do you have here?" he makes a joking grimace as he lifts the basket up and down a couple of times before putting it back in its place. "It feels like enough food to feed an army," he comments as he gives me a hello kiss.

Little does he know — "One never knows how much food we'll need. Maybe we will be stuck on the freeway all morning and need a snack," I tease back with a laugh, and I stop him just as he is reaching for something to sample from the basket.

He laughs as he turns to the door, giving me a dramatic, cavalier wave to go out first. We stop abruptly. We almost forgot the picnic basket. He picks up the basket and carries it to the car, mumbling about being hungry as he pretends to attempt a peek inside again.

As we drive to the park I begin to feel a little guilty that I had not been forthcoming with Joseph about the size of my family. Giving in to guilt, I tell him, "My family might be a little larger than the average family."

He nods as he says, "Yes, Catholic."

I have forgotten he is an Irish Protestant. After all, he rarely mentions the fighting in Ireland that brought him to the States after his grandmother insisted on sending him to a boarding school. His mother gave in to her mother-in-law's insistence to send him out of harm's way and keep him from joining the fight.

He doesn't seem to mind that I am Catholic. Joseph makes such a funny face along with his comment about Catholics that I let out an uncommonly loud giggle. I am surprised by the sound, but it eases my apprehension.

It is, true to California style, a wonderful day. The weather is perfect. We arrive at the park early, before most of the crowd. The usual hugs and kisses ensue, then the introductions.

Arriving early allows Joseph to meet people in small groups as the family begins to congregate. Each new arrival deposits food at the food
~~~

table, then greets everyone. Volleyball and horseshoe games are getting underway and someone invites Joseph to join in. He does. The little kids love him and hang on his every word.

Old family stories are retold to pass them on to the next generation, with new exaggerations added. We laugh, hug, and look at photos of family members living around the world. Most of us, though, make the annual migration home for Thanksgiving dinner to renew our bond.

After lunch, visiting takes center stage. I usually table-hop. After I see how comfortable Joseph is, I relax and enjoy visiting on my own.

We pose for photos, then the games begin again. Out of the corner of my eye, I notice two aunts sitting at a table visiting. It looks like—yes, they are discussing Joseph. I know how these women think. My aunts and uncles moved in to fill the gaps in my life caused by my parents' death. These two are grinning with a look of approval regarding Joseph, nodding their heads affirmatively as they watch him play horseshoes. I smile back when they notice I am watching them.

Growing up, there were too many of us to ever get away with anything mischievous. The women in this family are experts regarding the antics of massive numbers of children. They can tell what any one of us is up to, just by looking at us. I know they can tell I love Joseph. It pleases me they approve of him.

The day passes too quickly. It seems, as it does every year, no one wants to be the first to leave. We stand near the parking area for one last dose of family before we reluctantly depart.

Joseph says he genuinely enjoyed the day. Most people don't like going to their own family gatherings, much less someone else's family functions. I'm happy he had a good time.

I can't wait to get home and give Maggie a quick phone call. Actually, I can't wait for her to get back to town for a very long talk. I can't wait to tell my best friend everything, absolutely everything. Things are perfect. Who could have imagined a few years ago that my life would be so perfect now? I have come a long way this year.

Joseph doesn't stay long after he helps me unpack the picnic basket and put things away. He is tired from all of the fun. I understand. Besides, I am ready for a solitary walk on the beach after the big meal, but more importantly I want to call Maggie and tell her about Joseph's approval rating.

After Joseph leaves I look for the Tahoe number that Maggie left. It is late and I can't think where I put it. I decide to have a cup of coffee and savor the day. I'll find the number in a minute. Knowing Maggie, she will call me to find out how it went once she gets a minute. I smile, pleased with the way things are going for me this first year home.

~~~
~~~

~ CHAPTER 11 ~

Consumed by Fog

Sitting down was a mistake. I don't feel like going for a walk tonight. In a little over an hour, just as I am thinking about getting ready for bed, I hear frantic knocking at my door. Someone, not Mr. Goldstein.

I ask who it is through the locked door.

"It is Joseph!" says the voice from the other side.

Joseph nearly runs over me when I open the door. He glances at my television as he brushes past me without a word of explanation. His behavior makes no sense. I rarely watch television unless Joseph is in the news or an old movie is playing that isn't on DVD yet. Why would he expect the TV to be on tonight? Joseph heads straight for the remote and turns on the set.

By the look on his face I can tell something is wrong, terribly wrong. Just as he begins to search the channels, the phone rings. I move for the phone while watching Joseph's peculiar behavior.

Karen is calling. Karen and I may have stayed up all night, one time, discussing a mysterious letter from a dead judge. However, she does not call me late at night, not ever. It seems strange when she asks if I am alone. What does that matter?

Suspicions run through my mind when she asks to speak with Joseph after she learns he has just arrived. This is very uncharacteristic of her—of them. I have a horrible feeling about Joseph and Karen's odd behavior.

Joseph takes the phone. I try not to eavesdrop. Yet, I can't help but move closer to him while he is speaking with Karen.

"Yes, I heard it too," Joseph is saying to Karen. "That's why I came—to be with Katey."

I can only hear one side of the conversation, so I am still in the dark regarding this sudden spin of activity in my home.

"No, I don't think she does," he continues, quickly glancing at me as he speaks, then flashing a hurried half smile when our eyes meet. He gives me the phone and returns his attention to the television set.

"Hello, Karen. What's up?" I ask hesitantly as I walk to the window to mindlessly look across the street in the direction of the ocean while we talk.

"Sit down, Kathryn. I wish I could be there with you, dear." Karen's voice is serious and strained. "This may be nothing, but I wanted to tell you before you heard it on the news."

Automatically, I turn to look in the direction of the television. Joseph is still searching the channels.

"A news report just came on, Kathryn. A small plane went down near Tahoe this morning," she says.

I gasp as I sit down. Stunned. Frozen. Barely breathing.

"They aren't releasing names." She takes a deep breath. "The 'weather' came in without warning. Have you heard from Maggie?" I can hear the urgency in her voice.

"No, not yet." I cradle the phone to my shoulder while looking through my purse for the paper with Maggie's Tahoe phone number on it. "I am expecting a call, since I haven't called her. Actually, I thought it might be her calling now."

Karen's voice is not her usual capable, confident tone. Joseph has finally settled on the edge of a chair. I watch him glued to the TV while I listen to Karen. She is deeply worried about Maggie, and Joseph is worried about Dave. Neither have come right out and said they think Maggie and Dave were on the plane that went down, but it doesn't take a rocket scientist to tell they do.

I wrap my arms around myself for comfort. I catch the look on Joseph's face and hear Karen's tone of sadness. I realize I have to be the strong one this time. Acknowledging my feelings is a luxury right now. I don't have time to think about me. Karen and Joseph need me. Well, maybe it isn't me they need, but I am the one here.

"It could be another plane. When Maggie and Dave hear about it, they will know we are worried and call one of us," I fumble for words. "If they did go down, it doesn't mean they were killed." As soon as I say it, I wish I hadn't. Of course they could be dead.

Karen gasps, then finishes our conversation quickly.

My words haven't come out as comforting as I had hoped. I am upset and embarrassed for saying something stupid.

We can only wait for information that will give us a clue to who is in the missing plane. It is easy to worry. Surely it's not their plane that went down. There must have been others going to Tahoe for the extended weekend to feed their ski addiction. No, it's probably not them. Probably not.

Joseph finds a local station running the television news report. The reporter says, "...due to the severity of the sudden storm, the search planes couldn't get airborne..." It's a blizzard more than a snowstorm.

Each report we catch says much the same thing. I know we aren't likely to hear anything before morning, unless Maggie calls to tell us it wasn't their plane. There is nothing to do but wait. It is late now. In the morning we can call her brother Frank to see if he heard from his sister or Dave. It will be a long night for us.

Joseph wants to stay the night. We have never spent the night together, intimately, even though we have shared many late nights talking on the beach. I offer him my bed since I am just as comfortable sleeping on the sofa—as I do more nights than I am willing to admit.

This night is not a restful night. I toss and turn. I fling the sofa pillows onto the floor. A strange dream comes into my tormented sleep.

I awake with a start, covered in sweat. When I fall back to sleep the dream begins again in the tunnel and runs its course exactly as the first time. I can't say how many times the dream occurs. Each time I am more and more restless.

When I awake between dream cycles, I can hear Joseph in my bed making restless sounds. I could go to him and offer comfort, but I know what might follow would be for all the wrong reasons. So I restlessly stay on the sofa.

~~~

In the morning the newscast says the weather has cleared enough to get the rescue underway. I feel relieved, but only a little. They don't say where the downed flight originated. They don't mention whether the plane locator beacon is sending signals. What kind of news report is this? I wish for more information, but the reports are sketchy. I need to satisfy my investigative nature, but they offer no relief. I have to wait.

On the outside chance Maggie and Dave stayed home, I call their apartment. Joseph shoots a look in my direction like I am wasting my time. No one answers the phone. I suppose it was a waste of time to call, but I had to give it a try. In my heart I know it is unlikely they had only stepped out. I suspect they have gone on their trip as planned.

Finally, I find the Tahoe phone number Maggie gave me. It was on the kitchen counter and Joseph had set the picnic basket on it. If the basket hadn't been in my way, it might have sat there all day before I moved it. Before I tell Joseph that I have found the phone number to the ski lodge, I take my cell phone out on the patio when he is in the bathroom. The call doesn't go through. The phone lines must be down due to the storm or jammed with calls. I don't know which, as there was only a phone company recording on the line. The point is that I can't get through.

I try her cell phone, thinking that it won't matter if the lines are down if I call her cell. I try Maggie's cell phone, then Dave's. I try the Tahoe number again. Nothing works, and my anxiety rises with each attempt.

~~~

Karen and I call each other every couple of hours. We keep the calls brief. We are afraid to tie up our phones, but we need to hear each other's voice. I try not to say anything I have not thoroughly thought through, like before. One major brainless remark is enough to keep me aware of how vulnerable we all are. I call Frank, but he doesn't answer. We have to wait. That is the hard part—waiting.

My instincts tell me to run to my beach for comfort. But I only look at it from my window—afraid to leave the phone. The hours tick by slowly. I wish Karen was here, rather than home alone.

Karen is divorced. She has lived alone for four years now. Her children are away at college back East somewhere. This isn't a good time to be alone, even if she is used to it. I am glad for Joseph's company.

The local station runs the news briefs too seldom. It doesn't seem right that the regular programming is on, but apparently there is nothing new for them to report about the downed plane. The day ticks along slowly.

Joseph and I have trouble finding enthusiasm for meals or conversation. We sit around stunned. We pace. We take deep breaths. We fear the worst. There is no hope of hiding our fear from each other, but we don't mention it so it can't become real.

~~~

Later in the afternoon Karen calls to say Mother Elizabeth came over to be with her for a while. I feel only the slightest relief in that knowledge. We are each still alone with our thoughts.

I hope, if it is Maggie and Dave's plane, that they were able to put on their ski clothes and stay warm. I don't know if they had skis or planned to rent them. If they have skis with them, maybe at least one of them can ski out for help, although I know it is unlikely no one was hurt when the plane went down. At the very least the plane would have hit trees in the descent.

I am immobilized. I feel powerless. I desperately try to think of something that will console us—something to grasp and hold. Maybe the pilot had been able to land on one of the small, remote landing strips up there, somewhere, even an abandoned one. It isn't likely to have a tower, and if the plane was damaged—or even if not—they couldn't take off again with the snow on the runway. But they could be safely on the ground waiting to be found. My mind torments me as it races through possible scenarios. Realistically, I know these are not plausible options, though this time I keep my thoughts to myself.

Joseph goes home for clean clothes. He had a choice of either going home or wrapping up in a sheet while I do his laundry. My robe will not fit him. Besides, when he saw it, he declined to wear it—quite emphatically. I'm restless with him gone. It shouldn't take this long for him to get back. I'm more restless as each minute advances.

As evening approaches in L.A., it is already dark in the mountains. The news reports the search has been suspended for the night. I am
~~~

uncontrollably worried about them. The whole incident makes me extremely sad, and panic fills my insides.

I cannot stand that it has been forty-eight hours without a walk on my beach to find some sort of consolation. Yet I can't leave. I urge the phone to ring, but it won't comply with my wishes. I even try to bargain with God. There is no indication that worked, either.

We are grasping at anything that might tell us Maggie, Dave, and their friends have arrived safely in Tahoe.

While he was gone, Joseph checked his machine at home and his voicemail at the office. There were no messages.

Karen calls, but she has heard nothing.

I call Frank, but he is still not home.

We have nothing to go on.

The long periods of silence are thick. It is obvious our minds are racing. Out of desperation, I say that people have been known to survive for several days in a downed plane

Joseph looks at me, horrified—probably wishing he hadn't returned. It would be safer for him at his house without me and my mouth.

Instantly I wish I had kept my thoughts to myself. But it is said, and I can't take it back. I didn't learn from my first spoken blunder yesterday. I really feel incapable of getting through this successfully. I have no idea of a plan, but I would pay any ransom to have one.

~~~

Morning arrives after another restless night's sleep. It is Saturday of what seems to be the longest Thanksgiving weekend of my life. We poke at our breakfast with our forks. We hardly speak. The fog is in, covering both the view of my beach and our moods.

The news reports another winter storm in the mountains near Tahoe, hampering the search efforts further. There is little chance of a rescue today. Until the plane is located, it's dangerous to send rescuers into the forest. The area is too vast to search from the ground.

The day ticks by slowly. Night comes again and brings with it another tormented sleep.

~~~

Sunday morning arrives. A thick fog still covers everything. We can't see the patio beyond the window. The television reporter excitedly reports clear skies in the mountains. We look out the window at the fog. We look at each other in disbelief and amazement that the mountain weather has cleared. We become alert and hopeful that the search will produce our friends. By now we believe it is their plane or we would have heard from them, but we don't acknowledge our beliefs aloud.

Reporters from affiliate stations are in Tahoe reporting live from in front of a crackling fireplace or outside of the lodge to show the amount of snow mounded by the doorway. Their voices are excited, but they have nothing new to report. The plane has been down since Thursday morning, and that is not good. Not good at all.

~~~

Karen comes in the afternoon. She couldn't stand the isolation any longer. Mother Elizabeth had been only able to stay a few hours, and that seems like months ago. It took her over two hours to make the twenty-minute trip to my apartment. The fog has not lifted. She took surface roads to avoid the dangers of the freeway in the poor visibility. She is obviously a wreck from the trip and probably wished she had stayed home. She looks as if she hasn't slept since Thursday. I can't think of words to comfort her, but being together is better than being alone. Maybe words of comfort will eventually come.

It's Sunday afternoon when the news reports the emergency locator beacon has been faintly detected south-southwest of Tahoe in a steep isolated canyon. By late afternoon the reporters indicate the officials are fairly sure they have located where the plane went down. The plane is buried in snow, but they have a fix on the beacon, and trees have recently been knocked down where the plane should be. They aren't seeing any evidence of a fire or explosion. The news is only partly reassuring.

Rescuers are having trouble getting a ground crew into the canyon, because earlier winter storms had already made the trails impassable. The record snowfall coupled with the steep terrain, and the extremely dense forest is making them scurry for a rescue plan. The underbrush is too dense for snowmobiles. Parachuting into the ravine is impossible because of the dense trees and gusty canyon winds.

A reporter announces that San Francisco's U.S. Coast Guard sent a Dolphin helicopter and crew to provide additional support. "The four-person rescue team will be lowered by a cable apparatus from the Coast Guard chopper, similar to a rescue at sea, since the only access is from above. They are hoping to get into the canyon as close to the crash site as they can, then snowshoe to the plane."

The report continues that the Coast Guard will have to air-evacuate the people up from the surface, but first they will have to be moved to the pick-up area. The window of opportunity to get everyone off the ground is small. Of course, there are no rolling waves to contend with, but the rotor wash will whip the snow off the trees, decreasing visibility for the workers in the air and on the ground.

Another television station says the rescue is not going well because of the velocity of the wind gusts, not to mention the fact that by the time the sun falls behind the mountain, it will already be dark on the ground in the canyon below.
~~~

None of the stations have reports about the passengers. We have to wait. The news crews can't get near the crash site, so they still report from Tahoe, limiting their information, which is often replaced with speculation. We can't tell the bits of truth from media fiction.

My imagination and emotions run out of control with the information we have and the parts that are missing. For the most part we cling to silence. I fear I will say something moronic out of the dullness of desperation.

I have given up bargaining with God. Karen, Joseph, and I are exhausted from the emotional intensity of waiting, and it shows on our faces. They rely on me for meals. I don't have the strength to do any more than sandwiches and snacks. It doesn't matter—we aren't hungry.

Karen laments she needs to get to the beach. It's welcome news to me. There is an unexplainable bond between us and the Pacific. The beach is the comfort of coming home. The closer we are to it the better, especially today.

I urge Karen to follow her instincts and come walk on the beach with me. Joseph supports my efforts and encourages her. He volunteers to stay by the phone. She gives in after only a tenuous protest. I think she knows we are right about the walk.

I am not sure any of us have the strength we are going to need. There is no way I am emotionally ready to give up on Maggie being found alive. She is the best part of me.

Our friendship developed deeply from seeing things that cannot be shared with people outside the circle of investigators. Maybe it isn't that as much as the haunting nightmares that came from the work we do, the unspeakable horror we share. At any rate, there is something private we share that others cannot know, and we rarely mention, but it bonds us together.

Karen and I pick our way to the street corner marked with only the stop light's alternating glowing red ball above our head in the fog. We inch across the sand, listening to the sound of the breakers to judge our distance from the ocean. Karen and I walk carefully in the murkiness. We stay close, not wanting to become separated in the fog. I have never seen fog this dense so late in the day in this part of California. It should have burned off hours ago, but the sun did not shine today.

In a strange way, the fog shrouds us from the outside world. Unable to see the waves before they hit the beach, we are occasionally showered unexpectedly with spray when they break, even though we hear them coming.

We pause for a moment, standing silently, listening to the waves, occasionally feeling the mist thrown toward us by the backwash. The rhythmical sound is like a mother's voice to her infant child in the dark.

We are standing near to each other. I can see Karen slightly tip her face downward. When she lifts her head tears roll down her face. I can't see them, but I see her hand move to wipe them away.

I take a step closer.

She takes an audible deep breath and begins to walk in the direction of the pier. There is nothing to do, but silently walk with her. I can't imagine how to console her. When she is ready to share whatever thoughts she chooses to share, I can only hope the necessary words come.

We are nearly at the pier when she finally whispers, "I am not sure I am ready for this."

Her whispered comment begins a reckoning of our reality. With it, I realize Karen hasn't resolved the past. Her voice tells the burden of her responsibilities and all of the pain and loss that comes with it: Our murdered child, my leaving, the Judge, and a million other cases and staff problems that I know nothing about.

More than any of us, Karen must have blamed herself for the murdered child. After all, she was the senior staff member involved, and, as supervisor, the buck stopped with her. The retrospective reviews, the second-guessing—none of it has helped ease her burden of guilt or the raw emotions left behind.

People outside CPS can't possibly understand. Sometimes it is just one person standing between a child and an abuser until the system begins to work, if it works at all.

Multiply my caseload by all of the staff's cases, and the budget, and the legislature, and the public—and the court. All of this has been harder on her than I realized, harder than she allowed us to see. She isn't ready to lose another staff person. Unlike losing me, this time is forever. Unfortunately, that looks like how it will turn out.

"I am not sure there is a way to be ready for this," I answer.

She turns toward me, close enough to see her face in the thick fog. Tears are rolling down her cheeks in a steady trail. She is not sobbing, but she is no longer able to hold back the tears. Maybe it is just time and she has no choice.

Without thought of my own comfort level, I reach for her hand. Karen silently squeezes my hand in response. Maybe she is looking for an excuse to let go of her strong exterior and quit warring with her vulnerable side. I intend for my touch to be that invitation.

Slowly she talks about feeling she let her staff down by allowing us to think it is our sole responsibility to save the children in our cases.

Karen hesitates for a moment, slightly tightens her hold on my hand and says, "I never told Maggie what I should have." Karen's voice trembles and goes silent.

"You can tell me. I'm here," I say softly.

Karen lets out a breath that becomes a sigh. She begins. She discusses at great length her horror about the murdered child in my last case. The sound of her voice weeps. She speaks quietly of other murdered children that slipped through the cracks in the system. Just like Maggie and I felt, Karen still feels she should have seen what was going on with Judge Jones and others—the cops, social workers, mandatory reporters—anyone who left gaps in the system. She has forgotten none of the children who died in this social war. Not one.

People who choose this profession are not the type of people who turn off the responsibilities at the end of the day. There is a decisive innate sense of responsibility attached to advocating for those who cannot advocate for themselves. There's a sense of guardianship involved in this type of social work. We have a deep-running responsibility to do what is right while residing in a corner of society that has gone all wrong. To think otherwise would be a lie.

She knows her staff were sent into harm's way. She worries she pushed us too much, that she didn't notice in time when we were in trouble, that she couldn't do enough to heal us.

I am not sure what to say or if I should say anything. If I accidentally invalidate her feelings, the conversation is over. Who knows when she will be ready or able to let go of her self-imposed guilt again—if ever?

There is no doubt our emotions are on the edge, a raw edge. There is nothing I can do to fix the plane crash. I don't know what to say to ease her guilt about what we go through at work.

If the system is going to work, it will have to be accountable. We can only do so much on our own. But the changes that are occurring now are too late for a horrifyingly large number of children. We are human, so this appalling sickness in society wounds us deeply.

All that I can say is, "I'm here."

Karen clears her throat and says, almost in a desperate whisper, "There are so many things I need to tell Maggie." Her voice breaks, she turns toward me, grabbing my arm above the elbow and holding on desperately tight.

"Now I may never see her again. I may never get to tell her I was wrong about so many things, about our duty, the cases, the system—about everything. Oh, God! Why did I wait so long?" Karen is pleading with her Creator for a second chance with Maggie.

She is quietly sobbing.

I wish I could tell her honestly that she would have that chance. By now, I don't even think God can give it to her. The best I can do is to gently place my hand on hers. I feel her lean toward me in response to the touch.

"Maggie knew, we all knew. It's all right."

Karen begins crying softly audibly now. I don't know what more she wanted to say, but she is unable to speak. Her shoulders start shaking violently. She sinks down to the sand, her face in her hands—uncontrollably sobbing, louder now.

I sink to the sand beside her. The knees of my jeans quickly soak through as I kneel near her in the damp sand with my arm around her shoulder. I want to say something—the right something—but I have no idea what else to say.

I don't think absolution is enough for Karen today. She needs more.

Children's Services social workers are a different breed of social worker than all of the rest. Not necessarily better—just different. As alone as we sometimes feel, we are a family, a unit, a community (not unlike the nuns), and we hurt terribly when one of us is in trouble. Maggie is in trouble. So is Karen. I whisper a prayer for wisdom.

I don't know if my prayer has been answered or not, but I have to intervene. I gently pull her against my shoulder.

"Maggie already knows," I say because I think it is true. "She knows—we all know. It is all right. We are alright, Karen," I say and gently I move her hair out of her eyes and ease my arms tighter around her.

She melts into my arms, sobbing uncontrollably, unashamed. From somewhere I gain the strength to hold her and comfort her. Not the physical strength to support her weight, but the inner strength to shoulder some of the weight she has been carrying on our behalf.

I speak for all of us in the department. On some level, even when the case blew up in our faces, we knew none of it was her fault. I probably should say the things I had been taught are the things to be said, but I have to go beyond the mechanics of this. No one, not even she, could have predicted the outcome or prevented Judge Jones' rulings, especially considering what we know now. I doubt we could have made a difference in time to save the little girl, even if we knew about the Judge then.

The nature of the system leaves social workers powerless. We know others are relying on us, which adds to the weight of the situation. We fight to overcome the immobilizing force. Most of the time we succeed. We never forget the times we don't.

I continue to follow my heart as I console Karen. I talk softly about everything I know to be Maggie's true feelings and beliefs, about all of the things Maggie would want me to tell Karen on her behalf. Daring to take it one step further, I apologize for my behavior, absolving her of everything. Karen could not have prevented what happened to me, nor was it her responsibility to do so. We need to carry our own weight.

She did nothing wrong. She had omitted nothing that would have made a difference. None of this, not the murdered child, or the Judge, is her fault. If only she could understand that we don't blame her for what went wrong, especially Maggie. Maggie admired her.

If anything, Karen strengthened us. She gave us the training needed to improve our skills and save more children than ever before. We are better professionals and better people because she came into our lives. No, she is not at fault. I do not blame her. Maggie does not blame her. No one blames her, and she must not blame herself for anything that has happened.

Karen's sobbing continues. There are years of weight on her shoulders, years for her to reconcile—to heal. Her strength and position within the welfare system had isolated her to keep all of the problems to herself. I knew she lived alone, but I had mistakenly thought Keith shared some of the weight, supervisor-to-supervisor. Apparently that was not the case.

Even the strong need a place where they can rest from being strong. When I worked for her, I didn't realize a friendship between us could be possible. None of that matters now. Or maybe everything matters. Maggie loves her—we all do.

Karen stops crying and sits quietly. Then she gets up, spent—almost in a daze—and starts walking back toward my apartment. Even in the obscurity of the fog it is clear that she is emotionally exhausted. I catch up and hold her weight as I did with Mr. Goldstein, with my arm around her shoulder. I can only hope this walk has helped her begin the healing process, the process she guided her staff to find, but hadn't found herself.

As soon as we open the door and see Joseph's face we know he has heard something, and that it is not good news. They have called off the rescue due to the darkness and the bitter cold. But that makes no sense. They were arriving at the crash site when we went to the beach, and it was expected to take hours to fly them to the hospital and go back for the rescuers.

My imagination is uncontrollably running amuck, I say nothing.

"The news reports said there are no survivors from the plane crash," Joseph says softly. "Everyone was killed instantly when the plane crashed into the mountain."

He has tears in his eyes as he speaks. His voice is filled with overwhelming grief, though he gives a failed attempt to hide it behind a weak smile.

"Have they released the names yet?" I ask cautiously as I move Karen and myself to be near him.

They don't have to release the names. We have a feeling that Maggie and Dave were on that plane. They aren't coming home. We will never see them again. I will never hear Maggie's laugh as she torments me about something she thinks I am totally wrong about, then offers coffee to make peace so I will forgive her.

"No, they are in the process of contacting the families now," Joseph replies, still trying to be strong for us all.

Karen says, "Maggie carried her department I.D. in her wallet. Maybe the rescue workers will call the department if someone sees the card."

She calls the social worker on call to see if there have been any calls about Maggie. But there has been no call. Karen is frantically in denial. "Good, no calls. It might not be them," she tells us.

She knows it's them, but isn't ready to admit it.

Desperately searching for hope, Karen calls her voicemail to check for messages, and her home answering machine. There is no reason there will be a call at either of these message centers, but she had to try anyway.

Karen looks at the floor as she listens to her messages. When she finishes, she looks at us. Her eyes are hollow with disappointment. There is no message from Maggie. It doesn't matter if the authorities call or not. We know.

We huddle together trying to hear from the phone receiver as I call Frank, Maggie's brother. His wife answers the phone. She says Frank has just hung up from talking with the rescue command center. He is on the way to his parents' house in Monrovia to tell them about Maggie and Dave. Elda, Frank's wife, confirms our worst fears. It had been Maggie and Dave's plane that crashed. Now it's official.

My chest tightens, I can't breathe. My heart is pounding in my ears now that the words have been spoken. I gather my manners and ask if there is anything we can do. Elda declines the offer. Before I hang up the phone, I offer our condolences.

With my comments, the horrible truth is confirmed for Karen and Joseph. They've moved even closer together as they listen to my side of the phone conversation. Now they are holding on to each others' hand like they will die if they let go.

Slowly I sit down in the chair by the phone. Joseph and I just stare at each other like zombies. His eyes that were full of pain minutes ago are blank, now that we know for certain that our friends are dead.

Karen moves her other hand to Joseph's arm, as if holding his hand isn't enough to keep her on her feet. Joseph puts his free arm around her shoulder, and, rotating her toward him, he pulls her close to him with both arms holding her secure.

She is sobbing quietly into his chest. When her sobbing subsides momentarily, Joseph steers her to the sofa and eases her down. She complies with his assistance without a hint of strength of her own.

We can't speak. Words are nowhere to be found. Our throats are tight. The tears roll down our faces. We sob with the desire to cry out in sorrow, but not the strength to do so.

I move to sit on the other side of Karen. She begins to shiver, partly from the damp, but mostly from the loss of Maggie. I put one arm around her shoulder and reach across in front of her to hold onto Joseph's leg just above his knee.

Joseph reaches out and touches my hand softly, then firmly. The three of us sit there and sob nearly inaudibly, huddled together on the sofa—hanging on to each other.

I don't know how long we sat crying. The fog shuts out the rest of the world beyond the windows. We are horribly alone. There is no Hollywood movie music to go with this moment. Our world is silently empty.

~~~
~~~

~ CHAPTER 12 ~

Requiem

There is no denying that I miss Maggie terribly. Sometimes I actually physically ache on the inside. We had a bond that occurs only once every now and again. Maybe, just maybe, only once in a lifetime.

We knew things too. With one glance across our desks, we knew how each other's cases were going by the look in our revealing eyes. Even after I had been away, we still had that connection.

I shut my eyes, reliving a montage of memories involving Maggie. I can hear her laugh, but I can't recall an image of her face. During the five years in Nebraska I remembered every detail about Maggie's look. Now I can't see her in my memory, and it scares me.

I bolt up and begin pulling boxes out of the closet, dumping their contents on the floor and rifling through them for a photo of Maggie. "No, not that box," over and over again until I find the box from college. Leaving the mess on the floor, I seize the photos of Maggie and collapse on the sofa. I study her image carefully. I can't believe she is gone. My fingertips touch her image softly.

It was reckless for them to fly in such a small plane, in the mountains, in the winter. What had they been thinking? I don't dare allow myself to be angry with her—but if they had survived the crash, I would have given her a severe scolding.

~~~

Because Maggie and Dave have so many mutual friends, both families agree their funerals should be combined. As I think about the upcoming funerals, I imagine the attendance will be enormous. There would be two families in addition to twice the friends. All of the publicity about the crash will bring people out of the woodwork, including the media-grabbing politicians. I saw what happened at the funerals for the others in the plane; it was awful. I can't begin to imagine this production.

Until now I have made it a point-of-rule to avoid funerals. There was something about seeing my father in the casket that I could never quite shake from my memory. I would not have gone to my mother's funeral if there had been any way to avoid it. There was no avoiding it. I went. Likewise, I will attend Maggie and Dave's funeral. But I will attend no others, no others.

~~~

I plan to wear a black dress, the one Maggie helped me select for some function that is far removed from my memory now. Maggie really liked the dress, and it looks good with my mother's pearls. I am as ready as I can be for this cultural requirement.

Karen, Keith, Joseph, and I ride together. None of us have the strength to go alone. Karen and I are in the back. I reach for her hand on the seat between us. Staring out the car window, I don't remember much about the drive to Monrovia. Everything seems a blur until we walk through the church doors and it hits me in the face. It's real.

The funeral begins. Keith and Joseph aren't Catholic, so they sit through the ceremony rather than genuflect and kneel as the Catholics do. Karen and I stand, sit, kneel, and recite the congregational responses. It is a very nice Mass. Father gave a nice homily. That is what they always say after a funeral, "Father gave a nice homily."

Maggie and I had conversations about the predictability of Mass. It calmed us after our work in a very unpredictable world. Maybe in a way it shielded us—for an hour—from the evil contra-culture that was forced upon us by its very existence.

Still, seeing their caskets side by side with matching ornate palls draped over them is not at all comforting to me. Who says funerals are to comfort the survivors? My knees are aching from the kneeler. The incense fills the air, making me dizzy and sick to my stomach with its thick, sweet smell. My chest hurts from missing Maggie, and I can hardly breathe because of the empty stabbing pain of her loss.

After the graveside service we walk aimlessly to the car. It is hard to say goodbye to Maggie and Dave. We are a mess. We ride in silence as Joseph drives Karen and Keith back to their cars. Then he drives to his office where I left my car. He said he isn't going to stay longer than it takes to look through his messages. He doesn't feel like working.

Maggie would have been pleased with her Mass. The singing from behind us, in the choir loft, sounded like angels from heaven. I turn the radio on, then turn it off again, and drive myself home in silence. Even my mind is empty, aching.

Karen said she might come by later. I don't really expect to see her. It is going to be an unproductive day. There isn't energy for even the most mundane tasks. After I change into something comfortable I sit on the sofa with my feet on the coffee table and a cup of coffee in my hand.

About the time I finish my first cup Karen is at my door. She waves off the offer of coffee, but I go for a refill. She stands just inside the door like a zombie until I return from the kitchen and gesture her to a chair. She makes no attempt to remove her coat when she sits down. Karen is pale and expressionless as she watches me drink.

"Father gave a nice homily," I comment.

She nods her head slightly in agreement.

"The music was nice, too."

"Let's go to the beach," Karen says and rises.

Quickly I set down my cup, grab a coat and keys, and catch up with Karen, who is already out the door.

~~~

The ocean is rough from a tropical winter storm coming from the west coast of Mexico. The waves pound the beach with a thunderous booming that resounds in my chest. It is like a war zone and the coast is being bombarded with thousands of rounds. The ocean beats the Earth angrily, just the way I want to drop to my knees and pound my fists into the sand, full of grief.

For the longest time we say nothing, there isn't much to say. We smile an uneasy smile from time to time, but words don't come. Eventually, she tells me Linda followed the story about the downed plane in the media, as did most everyone else in the state. Because of Karen's contact, Linda asked if the lost social worker was one of hers.

"Linda and Todd made a sizable contribution to a statewide child abuse prevention coalition in Maggie and Dave's names."

"That's very thoughtful," I comment. "How is Linda?"

"Linda is doing as well as one might expect. It has only been a few months, and she still struggles. She did start therapy, and that's good," Karen answers quickly.

They must have had quite a conversation. It really doesn't surprise me that Karen would have kept in touch with Linda.

"Todd and his parents have been supportive of her. Linda has testified to the State Legislature about child abuse prevention and treatment funding." Karen smiles for the first time I've seen since before Thanksgiving. "The governor appointed Linda to the coalition's board."

It seems a little soon for Linda to be doing these things when she has personal wounds that need healing, but I reserve comment. It is nice to know our efforts to find Linda paid dividends by involving her and her celebrity in-laws in child abuse prevention efforts.

Karen shows me the "thank you" note she is sending to Linda and Todd. Maggie would approve of the donation—at least that is what Karen wrote. More importantly, Karen sincerely communicated deeply felt appreciation for Linda and Todd's thoughtfulness.

My fingertips run over the ivory-colored embossed card like it's a connection with Maggie. I stop when I notice Karen watching me. She says nothing when I return the card to her trembling hand, but I watch her fingers follow the same path as mine had. Everything, even the slightest things, connect us to Maggie, and to each other.

~~~

Joseph, Karen, and I help each other through the grieving process as best as we can—but life and work get in our way sometimes. There's a piece of the process we have to do on our own. I have done very little to reconcile her death in my mind. I don't really know where to begin, and I am not sure I want to whisk away the emotions tied to Maggie. I don't want the grief, but I want everything else. Is that possible?

Maggie and Dave are buried beside each other. In the weeks that follow their funeral I often stop by Rose Hills Cemetery on my way home from work to spend time with Maggie. I believe the essence of Maggie is not in the grave, but I sit and talk with her anyway. And, I wander to the beach as often as possible.

Slowly, very slowly, I am coming to accept the reality of the plane crash. Death is a part of life and we are not necessarily expected to comprehend it. I am glad for our years of friendship. These last eleven months have been very special. In some ways I am glad I went away, so when I returned we stopped taking our friendship for granted. Now I am glad we put so much effort into these last few months. She is a permanent ingredient to the wholeness of my being.

~~~

Several weeks after the funeral Frank brings two boxes to me. Maggie had kept a diary since she was in junior high school. Frank says he knows she never intended for him to read them, but he couldn't bring himself to throw them away.

After discussing it with his parents, they agree he should give them to me. He says he feels certain Maggie would approve of the idea. He shoves the boxes toward me rather abruptly.

I'm humbled with the thought, though it seems like an intrusion into her privacy.

Sensing my hesitation as I accept one of the boxes into my arms, Frank asks, "Did Maggie ever punch you?"

"What?" I reply as I struggle to readjust my hold on the box. "No, of course not," I say with a puzzled tone as I set the box on the table.

Frank sets his box on top of the other one.

"The first time I teased Maggie that I was going to read her diaries she punched me." He grins slightly with the memory. "She punched me so hard that I knew better than to ever think about reading them again."

Frank reaches into the box on top, handing me one of the diaries.

"Thank you, Frank. I will take good care of them for her," I say taking the book from his trembling hand.

He begins to cry.

I hold him tight with my arms around his shoulders and Maggie's diary clasped in my hands behind his back. My eyes and heart are begging to cry, but I insist they wait until Frank leaves.

Many times since Frank gave me Maggie's diaries I sit and hold one of them tightly to my chest. Holding her diary feels like a link to her. Her
~~~

family was thoughtful to give them to me, and it brings tears to my eyes every time I think of it. I hope Maggie would have approved, somehow I think she might.

Eventually I find the courage to open her diary. When I see her familiar handwriting, I am not sure if I should or can read her entries. I snap the book shut and lay it on the coffee table. I stare at it from a safe distance, and I sip my coffee.

After a long painful silence within me, I set my cup down and pick up the diary. I open it again, then quickly shut it. I clasp my hands around the diary, lean my head down on the book with my chin resting on its edge, and shut my eyes. My chest hurts from missing Maggie. My eyes are begging to cry.

After a few minutes, I take a deep breath, then open her diary again. Deliberately, I turn to the entry of the day I returned to L.A. I wondered what Maggie thought of the day that I stopped by the office unannounced. She never really commented about my abrupt return. Maggie simply wrote,

Kate has come home. I am glad.

I sit staring at the page for some time, trying to imagine that day from her perspective. I had expected her to write more than that. I become lost in the moment of it and time passes more easily. I read the entry again.

In the evenings while I wait for Mr. Goldstein to arrive for our walk, I begin to venture to other places in her diary—looking for insights into my friend. Some days Maggie wrote a great deal. Other days she didn't make an entry at all. I begin to read her diary at length when I miss her the most.

She wrote fondly of Karen. I consider sharing those entries with Karen as part of her peace-finding process. For now, Karen is keeping busy with her new diversion, the California Child Abuse Prevention Coalition (Cal-CAP). Linda submitted Karen's name to her father-in-law, the governor, for appointment to the Cal-CAP Board. Regardless of the nobility of her diversion, Karen will eventually have to return her attention to the loss of Maggie and finish grieving.

~~~

To shake up my life even more, Joseph is going home for a couple of months over the holidays. The timing for his trip is incredibly lousy. He asks me to go with him, but work will not allow me to go right now, even for a short visit. Besides, I don't feel up to meeting a lot of new people in an unknown country. Joseph offers to change his plans, but I urge him to go home and see his family. After all, the ticket was bought
~~~

months ago. Somehow life has to continue. We should stick to our plans and move forward.

Moreover, after losing his best friend, the trip will comfort him in ways I cannot. He needs Ireland. It is his beach, his place of solace and healing.

Luckily for me, Joseph's flight is scheduled at a time when I can take him to the airport. At least we have that much.

While we wait for his flight and after Joseph exchanges his U.S. dollars, we go to the duty-free shop for gifts for his family. Finally, he disappears from sight as he boards the plane. I watch the runway long after his plane enters the sky and vanishes.

Leaving LAX I brave the torrents of traffic, I instinctually make my way home, too numb with loneliness to mind the wait as the traffic stalls to a standstill on the 405 heading south.

When I arrive home I am painfully aware of the void caused by watching Joseph leave. I sit down to write an email to him. It takes several drafts to get past a sappy-sounding message. It isn't perfect, but I want some sort of connection with him.

The email helped, but is not enough. I take Maggie's diary with me to sit in the sand and listen to the ocean sounds on the deserted winter beach.

My dearest Diary; There are moments in life beyond words, beyond emotion. Only the silence around me fills my breath, and gives me life. For lingering moments, everything stands still, as if frozen in time. There is no violence or laughter, only silence beyond the sounds of my breathing. I shut my eyes, not wanting to disturb the moment and hurl myself crashing into the world again. My soul desires peace and quiet, without thoughts disturbing it.

Karen and I see very little of each other in the weeks that follow the funeral. I planned to spend time with her, but found myself spending time alone. I make several failed attempts to finish my Christmas shopping, but I lack the initiative to maneuver the masses. I decide the only solution is to survive this holiday duty as best I can. Sending Christmas cards will have to wait until next year. I just need time to get up to speed again. Shopping and everything else will eventually get done.

I look forward to walks with Mr. Goldstein when his social calendar will allow the time. To think less than a year ago he had trouble walking across the street and down the beach to the water. Now he has a social calendar.

Mr. Goldstein deliberately directs our conversation to Maggie. At first I resist the discussions, but they are healing once I trust him.

Many nights I sit for hours, feet propped up, drinking coffee and reading Maggie's diaries. Sometimes I read only one entry, then re-read it several times. Sometimes I read a month's worth. Most of the time I pick up the book and read where it falls open.

I am learning so much about the depth and breadth of my friend. I am learning some things about myself, too, as I read Maggie's insights into the complexities of life.

Tonight I leaf randomly through the pages of Maggie's diary—reading whatever catches my eye.

....Life is good, not necessarily easy, but good.

Yes. Rather simplistic, though, I hope that it is true. I need it to be true. I hope Maggie knew what she was talking about when she wrote this. I want something to hold on to that will make me feel secure, even for a minute, to see me through this time of mourning.

My dearest Diary: Sometimes I wonder if there is a better way to make life decisions; is there some simple formula to seeking clarity? Is there a guideline to one's destiny—optimal destiny?

Are we—am I—close to being all that I can be? Is this all there is or are there other depths of who we are—yet undiscovered?

Staring at the page as I run my fingertips across the handwriting, I understand the quest, and crave a sense of clarity for myself. I wish Maggie and I had more time to have these discussions when she was alive. I am envious of her diary for knowing her so well.

My dearest Diary: It is days like this that I understand the true value of friends. Friendship is an amazing thing. No one can tolerate too many needy people in their life. But the give and take in real friendship occurring over the years is a wonderfully fulfilling experience. Hurry home, Kate.

"Maggie, I'm sorry I left without a word. I am sorry I wasn't a better friend," I whisper to her diary, wishing for a reply. Sometimes it is almost as if she does reply.

I am not sure if I feel better or worse. I think about our friendship, the many cases at work that flung us into a dark and evil world, a world we fought to keep from totally eradicating our humanity. I know what she meant about needy people and about friendship, true meaningful friendship. I understand her entries in a way that I think no one else can. I really miss her, but feel blessed for the time we had together.

Often Maggie's diary does not elaborate on the external things that occurred to bring her insight—only the results.

My dearest Diary: Lately I have been reminded of both the frailty and strength of the human spirit. What exactly constitutes the human spirit? "Choice." I think that we "choose" to be strong, we "choose" to succeed, we "choose" to triumph over the adversities of life. Even on our own, alone, we choose how to face life on our terms: in an honorable fashion or to whimper and whine, feeling sorry for ourselves every time there is a bump in the road.

The simple truth is others can't fill that "place" within that allows—no, compels us—to continue forward on our personal sojourn. I believe each of us possesses the power to face adversity with dignity—to stand alone and walk through the tempest, and emerge—perhaps wounded—but not broken. Clearly, the choice is ours to make.

After months of agonizing entries about the dead child, the graphic police photos that showed only a glimpse of the horror the child went through, and the horrible guilt of not being able to stop the murderer from abusing again, there was a long silence in her diaries.

Since I was the primary on the case, I hadn't realized Maggie felt the same guilt as I felt about being unable to protect the little girl. The difference between us was that my silence was from a distance which lasted five years.

A few months later, without saying what happened to her or inside of her, Maggie finally wrote again.

My dearest Diary: Please believe it was not my intention to neglect you. My apologies. I have discovered something about myself –I am very strong through adversity, though not as good with 'good' times. Things are going well now, but I find myself tentative in trusting that things are, indeed, well.

I suppose I don't want to be blindsided again by my childlike trust in the goodness of life. I will strive to relax and learn to trust in God during good times, as I do in tough times. Though I suppose it is easy to trust in God when there is nowhere else to turn.

Somehow Maggie found peace. Did it have something to do with God or something to do with her? I wish she had written the details of her recovery, leaving a map for me to follow.

Maggie and I never mentioned our personal spirituality. I wish now that we had. The next entry was written a week later.

My dearest Diary: We are laughing again at work. I see the creative side in each of us starting to emerge from the dark night. We must consume it and be willing to be consumed by it.

Though I don't know what prompted her comments, I find them strangely enlightening and comforting. They give me hope.

I tell myself I will read one more entry tonight, then go to bed. My inner spirit is in need of consoling words.

My dearest Diary: It isn't how long one lives, it is how wide that really matters.

Right on cue, Maggie's words are exactly on point, as if she was here to deliver them herself. I want to believe Maggie's life was not cut short, that it was as long as it was meant to be. Her words make it seem a little less like her future had been robbed.

In time I will reconcile Maggie's death. After all, I have managed all of the other deaths in my life.

With that I lay her diary on the coffee table and go to bed. Tomorrow is another day, and I am too tired to contemplate the wisdom of the universe any further tonight.

~~~
~~~

~ CHAPTER 13 ~

The Celebration of Miracles

The good sisters are planning a Christmas pageant with the Spirit of Hope families. I love Christmastime, but I haven't been able to get into the mood since the little girl was murdered. I thought this first Christmas home would be different, but it is even more difficult with Maggie gone. I am barely able to get my shopping done, and that was only because Ilene pushed me to get it done or I might have missed it all together.

Hopefully, the activities at Spirit of Hope will provide a suitable diversion from my grief. Sister Clare let it slip that she is praying for "our" baby to arrive in time to play the starring role in the Christmas pageant. True to what I have come to expect, I, too, believe our baby will be born in time for Christmas, not only because that is the due date, but because the nuns want it that way.

I am beginning to think even God, with His infinite wisdom, thinks twice before refusing these sisters anything they request. If He did refuse them even the slightest of their desires, I see no evidence of it. It seems there is a steady flow of well-timed miracles around here.

Sister Clare is frequently heard going to the chapel. Because of her limp there is a distinctive clicking sound from her dangling rosary, swaying on her belt as she walks. Whenever I see—or hear—her heading in the direction of chapel, I can't help smiling. I think to myself, though I would never admit it out loud, "Look out, God, Sister Clare is looking for you."

The Christmas program is scheduled for two days before Christmas. In the meantime, children, their parents, and nuns are singing Christmas songs under their breath while they are busy with their daily routine. That is, all except Sister Mary Veronica, the music teacher, who believes one should "PRO-JECT" their voice at all times. And she does. Luckily, Sister Mary Veronica has a beautifully trained voice. It echoes throughout the building and down the hallways, adding to the Christmas feeling in the air.

The staff is willingly recruited as stagehands. Those who can sew are persuaded to bring their sewing machines and are pressed into service making costumes.

Others are delegated to Sister Bridget's work detail. She is busy making the scenery and is convinced anyone can paint under her watchful direction. To my surprise, she is quite handy with power tools and seems to have an endless supply of lumber.

All of the staff is expected to scavenge for props. Looking at the prop list, one would think this is a Broadway production.

I send Joseph a Christmas card and later another email. He never answered the first one, but I miss his toothy smile and twinkling eyes. The email doesn't return as undeliverable, so I have hope that he will respond this time. I am eager for any contact from him. Maybe I will hear from him at Christmas.

The other man in my life, Mr. Goldstein, has invited me to celebrate Hanukkah with him. While we are on our walks he helps me prepare by teaching me the prayers and responses for the celebration. I give my sincerest effort to the process because the goal is important to Mr. Goldstein, and to me.

He is a patient teacher and I am an eager student, even after it is painfully apparent that I am not necessarily adept at learning Hebrew. I want to at least memorize the prayer that seems to be his favorite or the most important to our celebration. He accepts my pronunciation attempts, if they are reasonably correct. I believe it pleases him that his young Irish-Catholic friend wants to make the effort.

It pleases me to be included in his celebration. We are family, now. Little does Mr. Goldstein know that I have become desperate and have the neighborhood rabbi helping me. It requires a group effort for me to be ready in time, but I am committed to do my part. Granted, it will take a miracle.

Whenever possible I walk along the beach listening to the tape of Hebrew prayers Rabbi Karol made for me. I repeat the words over and over, struggling to master them. All I can do is give my best effort, the rest is up to God, providing Sister Clare allows Him time for projects other than "her" baby.

Before long my footsteps in the sand are matching the rhythm of the waves and the sound of the prayers in my earphones.

Baruch atah Adonai
Eloheinu melech ha-olam
Asher kideshanu b'mitzvotav
Vitzivanu
L'hadlik ner shel Chanukkah
(Praised are You,
Our God, Ruler of the universe...)

I am pleased the words are beginning to sound familiar and I'm beginning to master the pronunciation. I am immensely pleased with the gift of sharing I can give Mr. Goldstein, the gift he has given to me countless times.

In the evenings I to curl up on the sofa with coffee and Maggie's diaries. With the hopefulness of the season, I scan the diaries' pages with a willingness to learn more—more about Maggie, more about me in the process, and more about the human condition in general.

I find I have gravitated to reading only from the diaries covering the five years I was away. Sometimes I include that last, highly visible investigation Maggie and I did together up to my return to California, nearly a year ago.

For some reason I can't bring myself to read the entries from this year, except the entry of the day I returned. I have some catching up to do before I read this year's pages. I recognize that I fear reading her last entry. For now, instinct is guiding me to read her entries of the lost past.

Maggie's mood fluctuated during the end of the investigation. I know, in retrospect, that my mood did too. As it became increasingly clear in court that Judge Jones was biased in his denial or acceptance of motions, evidence, and testimony, especially my testimony, she writes:

My dearest Diary: I am grieving the wasted years. Damn them all, and damn my stupidity!

Maggie continues to write through the nights and days of darkness until she writes herself into the light. Within weeks, her writing indicates she began again to reconcile her pain in intermittent intervals. I wish for her sense of clarity and ability to look within myself and within life. I wish I had better insight during those days. I wish that I had been stronger.

Her writing amazes me. I cling to it. There seems to be something there for me in each entry, even if I don't see it the first time I read it. I need her and she is here from beyond the grave.

My dearest Diary: Flashes of insight come unexpectedly, at random moments, but, in truth, I think there is always "insight" dimly looming in the shadow of our consciousness. I feel unsophisticated when I'm betrayed, yet betrayal may be the greatest teacher. I think there are many distractions in life and the hardest thing any of us does is see the big picture, then focus on the narrow bit that is our path to travel. When we try to catch it all and hold it all, we lose our balance and struggle to right ourselves and stay on track. It is letting go of the distractions that frees us to be who we are in our innermost being.

I have an unquenchable desire to read Maggie's diaries. On the weekends I take them to the beach and sit reading. I almost think the light of day helps me understand her writings more than anything else, though coffee and the beach help too.

But it is at night her words are most able to speak to my spirit. Even though her resolution of the guilt we silently shared was a fleeting remedy, I would have learned that reality sooner if I had read her entries in the order they were written. For now, I am committed to my method of reading randomly and seeing how her writing touches me at the moment.

My thoughts take me back in time to before I threw my keys on Karen's desk. I can remember the frustration of those last days in the department. I can identify with Maggie's thoughts the first few days after we learned of the little girl's death.

At the time, and for years later, I shared similar feelings of uncontrollable hopelessness and inexplicable feelings of despair. Maggie found the strength to be honest about those feelings. Perhaps in time I will, too.

> *My dearest Diary: ...As for myself, I dream up projects and goals to give myself a sense of purpose—but I don't really feel it. I am just trying to survive for now and hope there is a future, and that it is far better than this.*

Even now I fight the memories of those days when Maggie and I struggled to make sense of things. While I was tossing my keys on Karen's desk, Maggie found a brief moment of clarity. I am thankful Maggie decided to write something specific this time.

> *My dearest Diary: Dave says I am too circumspect. That is why things bother me so deeply. ...I have been attempting to pray more and think less.*

As I try to make sense of my confused and yet unresolved emotions from the past and the loss of Maggie, I find my mood beginning to pace Maggie's secret thoughts in her diary.

> *My dearest Diary: There seem to be several new insights on the horizon, though they are still unfocused. In addition to whatever reflections those insights spawn, I still must remain motivated to stay the course. There is the lure of intoxication in enjoying the emergence of "peace." But it has been slow in coming and long overdue. The drunkenness should not take too much of my time, yet I want to pause and appreciate my new birth. After all, I have suffered the wait. And, oh, it has been such a long and lonely wait.*

I'm sorry that my actions left both of us alone with our pain and guilt. At least she had her diary and Dave. For a while she must have expected to hear from me. My remorse is useless.

I desperately want to mimic what she did to heal, if there is any possible way to do so. I wish she wrote more of the internal workings of her thoughts, not just the outcome of them. I know, though, there are no easy answers.

It was nearly three years after I went to Nebraska when Maggie finally wrote:

> *My dearest Diary: I have come to the end of some sort of self-imposed penance. With a certain amount of contentment, I find no burning emotions to express. Though not everything is as I would hope, I cannot bring myself to be dissatisfied with life.*

I frantically search preceding entries for what brought Maggie's absolution. I want the same for myself. But there is no key to unlock the secrets. I have only the slightest hope that I will find the inner peace she found.

> *My dearest Diary: It is comical how different life looks in the light of day. We expend a great deal of energy getting things physically in order—then, to avoid inner boredom, we crave the spontaneity of the moment, though we are afraid to risk the uncertainty it holds.*

In life, spontaneity cannot come from chaos. There must be some sort of order about the workings of the universe for life to make sense. I hate it when I feel the unresolved turmoil running rampant inside of me. I thought I was making progress until Maggie died. That grief has stirred everything inside me into a whirlwind.

The coffee tastes particularly good tonight, so I make another half pot. I sit for a while sipping it, and I hold her diary on my lap—closed. I am not thinking anything in particular, simply holding my link to Maggie.

After a while, I lean forward and slide the diary onto the coffee table in front of me. It isn't the end of the book, but I feel finished with it. Perhaps I am beginning to understand. I decide to put away all of Maggie's diaries. For now I must move on with my own life. I must find my own absolution.

~~~

My full attention turns to Mr. Goldstein and our Hanukkah celebration. As I prepare for this celebration, I review in my mind as many of the details as I can remember from my research. I continue to practice the prayers in Hebrew.

The first day of Hanukkah arrives. It takes me awhile to go through my closet to select just the right outfit to wear. With a selection in each hand, I position myself before the mirror and alternate the choices in front of me to see which seems right. I decide I don't like either of them, toss them on the foot of my bed, and start the process all over again. I settle on a nice navy-blue suit—Maggie always said navy is one of my good colors.
~~~

It might be a little early to get dressed, but this is one time there is no such thing as being fashionably late. Since the celebration must begin at sunset, I have checked the paper for the predicted time for today and have paced myself accordingly.

I ring Mr. Goldstein's doorbell, grinning with excitement and holding his gift. I try unsuccessfully to calm myself, but when Mr. Goldstein answers the door my grin explodes.

Mr. Goldstein attempts to be more formal—or maybe it is reverent, but I can see the excitement in his eyes. He is dressed for the occasion and looks handsome in his emeritus suit. He smiles warmly as he holds out his hand and says, "Katerina, please come in, come in."

Unsure of exactly what to do, I hand him the gift wrapped in blue-and-silver paper. As I enter his apartment I smell the wonderful aroma of the potato pancakes he made.

"I used Sylvia's recipe," he says, glancing at her photograph then back, "We always cooked together for Hanukkah."

I smile warmly and say, "I miss her too."

Before I arrived he had cleared the little table by the window and covered it with a beautifully hand-decorated cloth. I can't help running my fingertips over the raised threads of the embroidery design.

Mr. Goldstein moves the menorah and the shamash from a side table and notices that I am admiring the stitching on the tablecloth. He touches the threads and says, "Sylvia stitched this during her long recovery in hospital after we were liberated from the camp. Everything we had was taken. We didn't know where our families were or if they were alive." His eyes redden.

He pauses to regain his composure then begins again. "She said, 'Abraham, it is a miracle we are alive. We will celebrate the miracle of Hanukkah with a new tablecloth this year. It is a new beginning,' and she kept stitching without saying another word about our imprisonment," he says, then falls silent.

We move close together near the table to watch out the window for the last of the setting sun to disappear into the Pacific across the street. Then Mr. Goldstein begins. His voice is rich and clear.

Baruch atah Adonai
Eloheinu melech ha-olam
Asher kideshanu b'mitzvotav
Vitzivanu
L'hadlik ner shel Chanukkah...

For all of us—in uniquely private ways—it has been a year of transitions, a year of loss, a year of healing, and of struggling to find inner strength.

Thus began our celebration of eight days of light and of the miracles in our lives.

After spending the evening with Mr. Goldstein, it seems a natural transition to sit on my sofa with my feet propped on the coffee table and reflect on the evening—and the events of the past year. "Life is good; not necessarily easy, but good," Maggie wrote. I smile.

I miss Maggie, but she is gone and isn't coming back. I need to concentrate on the people who are here. Karen has taken up the torch of the California Child Abuse Prevention Coalition and moving it into a viable force in Southern California, as it is up north. She is so driven in her commitment that I sometimes wonder if it is a release of her expertise and energy—or a consuming diversion from dealing with Maggie's death.

Karen's department is scheduled to host the Coalition's December roaming meeting. Karen has invited Linda to stay an additional day after the meeting and attend the Spirit of Hope Christmas Pageant.

Since Linda's public disclosure of her abusive childhood, she has become the Governor's ambassador of California's children. He calls the coalition "guardians of our children."

Savvy politicians and marketing firms have adopted the Governor's battle cry, "for our children." The solution to every debate about violence, drugs, hate crimes, homelessness, abuse, and even the ongoing energy crisis comes down to doing what is "right for our children."

It's not that I disagree with these issues, it's that as a society we have a long way to go to protect our children. It is everyone's duty to care and intervene. I believe when we take care of the tiniest members of our world, all of us will be better people, and richer for having made the effort to keep our children safe.

It is obvious Karen is proud of her sister, Mother Elizabeth, and her contribution to alleviating the homeless situation. Karen wrote articles about Spirit of Hope for social work and child psychology journals and a feature for the Sunday newspaper insert.

Because of those articles, even the media has taken notice of Spirit of Hope. Saint Mark's switchboard is inundated with calls begging to make referrals or for interviews with Mother Elizabeth, and on occasion to make donations of Christmas gifts for the families. A decorated tree arrived yesterday, to the children's delight.

Governor Whitmore is encouraged with the possibility of a real plan to help California's homeless families. He and Mother Elizabeth have become close allies. Mother Elizabeth made it clear in her public comments that she hopes the governor will find funds for duplicating Spirit of Hope in other cities in the state.

I suspect it is more than coincidence that Karen wants to introduce Linda to Mother Elizabeth. As for Linda, she fills her life with her role as "the children's ambassador." Karen reports Linda enthusiastically accepted her invitation to the Christmas pageant.

December 21st, right on schedule, the "Spirit of Hope" baby arrives. She is beautiful, with big eyes and blushing cheeks. Her parents name her Clare Elizabeth, for obvious reasons. Words are inadequate to describe Sister Clare's reaction to the baby and her name. Little Clare's birth gives all of us at Spirit of Hope a renewed sense of hope.

Watching Sister Clare hold baby Clare might be described as a spiritual experience. Sister Clare chuckles under her breath when baby Clare squints and squirms before making new-baby sounds as she snuggles and settles for a nap in the nun's arms.

Little Clare had perfectly timed her arrival. She came home from the hospital in time for dress rehearsal, not that she needs to rehearse being the most beautiful baby in the universe.

Later, one of the other children asked if she was the new Baby Jesus. Only a child would accept Jesus as a boy or a girl.

Little Clare's parents are cast as Mary and Joseph. Father Herber is the narrator, and his rich, deep voice is perfect. The homeless choir opens the program with Handel's "Hallelujah." It is marvelously professional sounding.

Little Clare Elizabeth stretches, as if on cue, reaching a tiny hand out of her blanket so everyone can see that she is a real baby. When she moves, the congregation catches their breath. The sound of the audience caught off guard takes advantage of the marvelous acoustics in the church, sending chills through me—and probably others, too.

Mother Elizabeth's eyes fill to the brim with tears during the opening moments of the Christmas pageant. The tears stay in their place. Her face is beaming with excitement and pride. She looks as serene and holy as the statues in the alcoves in the hallways. I feel as if even I have been deeply transformed.

Karen is sitting next to me. I glance in her direction to see if she has seen her Sister-sister's response. Karen is looking in Mother Elizabeth's direction and smiling. Apparently Karen has seen her too.

Linda and her husband are sitting on the other side of Karen. They seem lost in the drama of the play. This night puts the rest of the year into its proper perspective, at least for the moment.

Life is good; not always easy, but good.

Karen's daughters are home from college, so, of course, I don't plan to see her today. I could go to Spirit of Hope and watch everyone open the gifts that one of the Indian casinos donated, but instead I spend time at "Vinney's" (Saint Vincent de Paul) Mission helping serve Christmas dinner to other homeless people.

After lunch I walk along the beach with Mr. Goldstein. Since he is Jewish, there is no risk of intruding on his Christmas plans.

The ocean is strangely still. The sky and the water are the same tint of gold as the sand. I have never seen anything like it. There are no waves. The water looks like a calm lake. Both Mr. Goldstein and I are surprised by the silence of the ocean. We walk to the pier to look down on the water and see its stillness from above.

The pier anchors the beach. That is where everything begins and ends, that is where the high and low tide is posted, that is where the Beach Patrol has their base station. And that is where I sometimes go to the Ruby's Diner at the end of the pier to eat and look out on the ocean without obstructions to the view.

There are no warnings posted to stay out of the water for any of the usual reasons, such as high bacteria count or an abundance of various water creatures that bite or sting. There are no waves, even small ones, breaking on the pier pylons. For that matter, there aren't any swells in the water that I can detect from our vantage point.

Mr. Goldstein remarks about the calm, peaceful feeling of the nearly deserted beach. We keep looking at the mirror-smooth water, then at each other in amazement, and back to the water.

All of the action is stopped. It is the strangest real-life thing I've ever seen. Mr. Goldstein agrees. It seems so silent without the sound of the waves crashing on the beach and against each other in the backwash.

For the first time, I notice the absence of the seagull sounds. I look around for the birds, but they are nowhere in sight. Even the sandpipers are gone. That probably means something. Maybe a tropical storm is coming, but I haven't heard of any typhoons in the Pacific during the previous week. Even so, it has never been like this before a storm.

"Wait here, I'm going home and get my camera," I tell Mr. Goldstein.

He nods in agreement. It is as if he is left to guard this mysterious mood, so that it won't slip away while I am gone.

Sometimes photos don't capture what we see with our eyes. This time I was lucky. The photos show nearly exactly what we saw. I had double prints developed. Mr. Goldstein tilts his head to get near his stack of photos at the correct angle for his bifocals. I study my copies. We comment on things in the pictures. It's amazing that we were there to experience such a phenomenon—a still ocean. I think it was a miracle or a sign of some sort.

~~~
~~~

~ CHAPTER 14 ~

A New Beginning

Joseph is still in Ireland. I think of him often, but I haven't heard from him. I won't admit it to anyone, but I am terribly hurt that he didn't at least send a Christmas card.

I consider hopping on a plane to spend New Year's Eve with him, but I decide to stay in L.A. I don't want to intrude on his visit home during the holidays.

Early in the afternoon, when it is New Year's Eve on his side of the globe, I think of him. With my freshly brewed cup of coffee I toast him and the New Year at what I believe to be precisely midnight in Ireland. Even having my feelings hurt doesn't keep him out of my thoughts. I am hopelessly in love with him.

Instead of a trip to Ireland, Karen and I plan to spend New Year's Eve together. Her girls are with their father for the second half of their holiday from the university.

Mr. Goldstein is at the Senior Center with his friends, although he thinks the party will use New York time and end early, so "those old people can be in bed by 9:00." He is so funny.

Our party isn't glamorous. We bring in the new year with carry-out Chinese food. The meal reminds me of our first dinner together after I returned home. It is almost as if the year has come full circle.

I can't help laughing when I read my fortune. "Now they tell me," I say as I hand the slip of paper to Karen.

She smiles when she reads it, but doesn't seem to see the same humor in it that I did.

Simplicity of character is the natural result of profound thought.

"I guess the paradox just struck me funny," I lamely explain, but don't say it is the paradox with my life that is funny.

This year has been difficult in so many ways, but all of the details are left unsaid. I was on the right track when I allowed myself to be led home by instinct.

When will I learn not to try so hard to avoid the things about the past that caused me to question my self-worth, my abilities, and my emotions? I really must learn to trust my emotions—to trust me.

Maybe, just maybe, everything will find its own equilibrium if I don't fight it or push it forward before its time. Maybe there is a natural order to the universe. Sometimes I wonder what made me want to get my life back on track. Whatever it was, this has been quite a year. Though most of it was good, I would have to say I hope the new year will be less exciting. I'm ready for some peace and contentment, and maybe, for a while, a little less growth. Whether or not I have the answers doesn't seem to matter as much as it once did.

My thoughts return to the casual conversation at hand, as it always does on New Year's Eve, to what we did last New Year's Eve.

Karen reports she spent a quiet evening at home last year. However, the year before she attended an elegant party.

"I was tending bar in Nebraska," I say with a tongue-in-cheek grin.

Karen laughs.

But the words mean so much more to me than "tending bar." I came home.

I return her laugh with a smile. There is only one thing to do to make the coming year complete—we bundle up and walk to the beach.

The night is clear. The moon seems brighter than usual. The rushing waves are somewhat calm with a rhythm of serenity. We turn toward Karen's favorite place on the beach, reminding me of the day Mother Elizabeth was there, too, and the day we learned Maggie was dead.

"Do you believe there is an afterlife?" I ask, more seriously than before.

"Yes. I think I do, Katey. Do you?" she says thoughtfully, seriously.

"Yes," I agree willingly. "If not, then I will miss our beach, I will miss you, and I will miss me," I say, realizing it is true. I really do (finally) feel that way about myself again after all of these years of exile.

I have come a long way to think of myself in affectionate enough terms to miss me. Finally, I am beginning to find my own sense of peace. It seems we really are all going to be okay.

Karen nods in agreement, then smiles. "Life is full of contrasts, of paradox, like your fortune cookie."

"It isn't how long we live, it is how wide that really matters." I softly speak Maggie's words to our mutual friend.

The clock at the church chimes twelve strikes, indicating midnight. A new beginning.

"Happy New Year, Katey!" Karen says as she lifts her coffee.

"Yes, Happy New Year!" I laugh and I raise my coffee to join the toast.

~~~
~~~

HIGH TIDE

Chase after life with the drive
of an eight-year-old
chasing an ice cream truck.

~ CHAPTER 1 ~

LAX: The Gateway of My Life

"Katey, when does Joseph get back?" Karen asks softly just at the moment I lean close to refill her coffee cup.

Straightening up I answer smartly, seriously, "Nineteen days, eleven hours, and twenty-two minutes!"

"Really!" She looks at me intensely. Obviously Karen hadn't expected such a precise answer.

"No," I admit casually, moving away to deposit the coffee pot on its burner. "It was a wild guess."

The sincerity of the moment she attempted is rapidly replaced by my widening grin. Turning to face her gaze, my laughter explodes. "I made it up." It takes a minute to settle down enough to give her a respectable answer. "He comes in on the 23rd—late. I'll have to check to be certain of the exact time." Smiling, I restrain an abbreviated laugh seeking its freedom.

Karen isn't usually gullible. It seems a bit odd that she didn't realize I was joking, but I shake it off.

"I was just wondering." She picks up her cup for a careful sip of the steaming brew. She hesitates thoughtfully. "You haven't talked about him lately—" Her voice falls away in an obvious invitation for me to fill in the gaps of the conversation.

I study her. For a second I mistrust that she isn't more probing with her questions since she said she was "wondering." She may be older than I, but I am wise to her tricks to coax information out of me. Not today, my friend. Not today. I am not falling for the long-pause-while-I-take-a-drink trick.

"Oh, I—I was busy with the holidays." I offer a lame answer as a diversion from the topic. I can tell by the look on her face she isn't buying my story. Without additional incentive, I confess, "Actually, I haven't heard from him."

Karen tilts her head slightly, studying me for a brief moment. She managed to get past me that the original question was a prelude to the later one. She says nothing, simply letting the hush fill the room until the silence closes its fingers around me.

That does it. That does it! I confess the rest as if I was being interrogated by rebels. "I tell myself that I didn't expect to hear from him since he hadn't been back to Ireland for a few years." Cradling my warm cup I whisper, "But that isn't really true."

"No letter, Christmas card, or phone call?" Karen gently clarifies.

I shake my head to each item on her list. “No, not even an email,” I add softly. Hopefully, the full degree of agony I feel doesn’t show in my face. It doesn’t matter, I have betrayed myself by telling her the truth.

The truth is I don't understand why there has been no outward sign Joseph has thought of me, even once, in the month he has been in Ireland. Surely he has. Yes, of course he thinks of me.

Karen looks up from her cup, meeting my gaze while shaking her head slightly in disbelief. She offers a reassuring smile before another sip of coffee. I fully expected a comment, but am relieved there is none.

I smile sheepishly to keep my thoughts hidden from her. This time I take advantage of her pause and change the topic.

“Since the rain finally stopped, do you want to go to the beach?” I ask, knowing she rarely refuses an invitation to the beach when she is in such close proximity.

Within minutes we have crossed the street and the rain-soaked sand to the water’s edge. The air is thickly moist and smells of the fishy sea. We pause looking toward the horizon—comfortable to be alone with our thoughts, but near each other and the ocean.

Ah, life is good, I tell myself. Readjusting to stand straighter, I face windward to search the soul of the Pacific.

The sounds of the seagulls’ cry and the waves crashing on the sand surround us. We are close enough to the water to feel the spray from the waves. In unspoken agreement we turn to walk toward the estuary at the far end of the beach toward Long Beach’s marina.

The afternoon’s post-rainstorm beach, with its fantasy-like mood, impedes thoughts of the neglectful Joseph McLean. He is being thoughtlessly cruel, and I can't think of a worthy excuse for his behavior.

Recognizing my anger is driven by the hurt I feel doesn’t belay its fermenting. In this high-tech world, Ireland isn’t that far from California by any number of electronic means. He could contact me. He has all of the gadgets, the tech-toys. He lives and breathes in a world full of the latest communication devices all the lawyers use. It’s a fact, he strives to be the first in the firm to have the newest contraption, as if it is somehow a proof of manhood. No, I can’t think about him.

Though we walk pensively, we quickly arrive at the estuary. The San Gabriel River is running high from the rain’s runoff. Trash flows into the ocean when the rains come. Still there are no warnings posted on the beach. The rain has caused no bacterial hazard. We are safe. It’s too bad there isn’t a patrol to post warning signs for dangerous things in everyday life, jobs, relationships, important decisions. I’d clutch the warnings in exchange for feeling safe from the hurt of my real world.

Karen and I watch the river dump into the cold ocean. Surfers dubbed this place Ray Bay because stingrays like the warm river water.

There are many hidden dangers lurking in the beast-filled waters. Yet Karen watches the mingling waters, speaking fondly of the ocean, her moods, and the healing properties of being on her beach.

Karen's words regarding healing may be an invitation to resume the conversation about Joseph, but I let them fall to the sand. I am not strong enough to admit more than I already have. I cannot talk of my dreams and fears regarding Joseph.

She is right, though, when she said, "The rhythm of the waves and the call of the seagulls blend into a tonic that heals the disquieting things in our lives." I wish for such a salvation. I'd wear it around my neck on a chain like a holy metal.

January might not be the tourist's idea of when to be on the beach, but growing up at the beach teaches the value of a year-round commitment, not just for the summer months. The winter sky may gray the mood for some people. It's like the moods we go through in longstanding relationships. The gray skies are simply part of the package.

~~~
~~~

~ CHAPTER 2 ~

Homecoming

After Karen leaves, I curl up with a blanket on the sofa to watch a Katharine Hepburn and Spencer Tracy movie marathon. Easily I draw a correlation between their constant war of wills and the inconsistencies in Joseph's behavior. Kate and Spencer always end in each other's arms. Surely it will be our fate as well.

The sun blazes into the horizon and sizzles into the sea. It's hushed outside now. The winds that rushed inland this morning with the rain have died down. I sit on my patio, feet perched against the side of the railing. The coffee is warm against the cold, moist evening air. Clouds are blocking the moonlight, obscuring the ocean. It is the perfect setting to become reflective while mindlessly listening to the ocean sounds in the dark.

It has been nearly a year since I returned home and Maggie helped me reconstruct a life more meaningful than tending bar in a small Nebraska town, away from my family and friends, away from my beach. Beyond that, it is a life more meaningful than I had before I ran away to a five-year, self-imposed exile.

I'm not sure whose idea it was for Dave to invite Joseph to the dinner party. Obviously, Maggie and Dave were both involved in the scheme to introduce us. They intended for us to become a couple, and we did. Because of them I learned that even I am capable of falling in love. It's true, I'm hopelessly in love, regardless of how brainless he can be or how angry I am with him at the moment.

The last time I saw Joseph was in December when I drove him to LAX for his flight to Ireland. I expend a great deal of effort to convince myself that I hadn't expected to hear from him. Secretly it isn't true. I had hoped he would write, but I know how fast time passes when away from L.A. Besides, he's a guy. He may think to bring back a gift, but not to write or call. My emotions are disquietingly fluid. It doesn't really matter now, everything will be all right once he comes home.

~~~

I've hardly slept the last two nights. Mother Elizabeth gave me off work tomorrow, but not without asking for a reason. Reluctantly I told her I was picking up a friend at the airport tonight. When she clarified, "Boyfriend?" I admitted the truth. Lying to Mother Elizabeth is never a viable option.

With the luxury of a weekday off, I plan to spend every moment of it with Joseph. I want to hear his voice, to soak in every detail of his visit
~~~

to Ireland, and watch his eyes dance at the telling of it all. I miss him more than I am willing to admit, even to myself.

The late-night traffic is light, allowing me to arrive at LAX early. Eagerly, I make my way to the concourse and his gate where a group of people are congregating at a bank of monitors listing flights.

The intensity of their interest causes me to look closely at more than Joseph's flight. In a mass, but not too close to each other, collectively our faces are turned upward to the screens above eye level. Studying the display, I watch as more and more of the flights from the east are listing "delayed." Delayed flights are rapidly changing to "canceled."

Blinking slowly, I cannot believe what I see. I look again. It is hard to think the weather is that bad back East, when it is so pleasant here.

Portions of the crowd moan each time the word "canceled" appears. A few people drift away from the group and dejectedly move back down the concourse.

In a matter of minutes "delayed" appears on Joseph's flight. I should have expected it, but somehow it seemed that his flight would be spared the fate of the others. I understand what the others must have felt. It's like a magic trick; you know what you saw—but surely it can't be real.

None of the gate staff has information about the anticipated length of the delays. We stand around not entirely sure of what to do next. We behave like a restless herd. Do we make eye contact with each other, or not? Do we strike up a conversation, or not? Unsure, we smile awkwardly at each other.

A large man is cranky with everyone, especially the young man standing at the desk. He intrudes on my spirit as he belittles the attendant as if he is responsible for the weather. I walk down the concourse to pace away the time and escape the cranky man. Every few feet, I thieve glances at each bank of monitors to keep a vigil—hoping to guard against Joseph's flight becoming canceled, not that I really have such powers.

It is after midnight when Joseph's flight arrives. I step through the small group of people, still waiting to clearly see him. The arriving travelers look tired after the long flight from New York. I watch for the first glimpse of Joseph.

Finally the stream of passengers stops coming through the door. It takes a moment for me to comprehend everyone is off of the plane.

There is no Joseph. What? I still watch the gate in case his bag dumped when he took it from the overhead bin, or some other unlikely thing happened to delay him. When the flight attendants depart, I move to intercept one and ask if anyone is left on the plane.

She looks tired, but says in a friendly voice, "All of the passengers have left, ma'am."

"Thank you." I smile weakly, dazed with this unexpected turn of events and not sure what to do next. The gate attendant has left his desk. On the monitor there is another delayed New York flight. The later one is the last scheduled for the night. Could it be that Joseph volunteered to give up his seat if his flight was overbooked and waited for the second flight? I decide to wait.

I am sure he expects to call for a ride when he arrives on the wrong flight or maybe he planned to take a taxi at the curb and not call me until morning. It will be fun to surprise him.

I have missed Joseph more tonight than I have the while he was abroad. I wish the monitor would indicate how delayed the flight will be. Eventually, I avoid the screen and look out the windows at the ground crew activity in the lights near the plane that just arrived. Even that mindless activity lacks solace.

In an hour, the gate attendant reappears and announces the NY flight is arriving in fifteen minutes. A muffled stir moves through the few people waiting.

The passengers come wearily through the gate. It must have been a turbulent flight. Craning to see Joseph come into view, I wait. Again the passengers quit coming and there is no Joseph. Tears threaten.

The breath rushes out of my chest. I can't believe it. This can't be true. I'm tired and my mind can't think straight. My stomach aches. Perhaps I will collapse into a chair, unmoving, defeated by fatigue, loss of hope, and anguish beyond belief that he hasn't returned and he didn't bother to tell me he wasn't coming back.

Tears fill my eyes. One escapes. Turning from the others, I briskly wipe it away. I wait for the rest of the tears to subside, at least until I can make my way out of this place.

I begin to doubt our relationship again. Maybe he isn't ever coming back. Maybe he hadn't intended to return. I feel betrayed by Joseph, by me, and by my half-witted emotions. I'm numb inside. I try to smile since I am in public, but I probably don't fool anyone. I doubt they notice. Why should they care?

I walk back down the concourse in a daze. People with bulging carry-on luggage come from another gate and overtake me. One woman mutters, "Excuse me," when she bumps me hard with her bag while she tries to squeeze between another person and me.

Of course, Joseph is coming back. I am just tired. He's probably still in New York. Surely there is a simple explanation and no reason to be alarmed. Attempts to reassure myself that I am being silly are fruitless. I feel abandoned.

Riding down the escalator, I feel like a zombie. Despite attempts to console myself, I feel profoundly sad. There is some sort of stir behind me, but I don't bother to turn to see what it is. What's the point? I don't care. I just want to go home and go to bed. I don't even feel like going to the beach. I am glad I don't have to work tomorrow. I don't think I could force myself to go. I feel completely empty.

~~~

"Katey!" a voice shouts from several feet above me on the escalator. The voice has a distinctly thick Irish accent.

It's Joseph! I wheel around. Life surges back into me. My smile is uncontainable and my eyes mist with tears of joy. I feel like running up the escalator, but I freeze in astonishment. Is it true? Is it really him?

The few people standing between us move aside to let him pass. He repositions the strap to his laptop case on his shoulder as he hurries down to meet me. He barely mumbles, "Excuse me. Thank you," and nods gratitude, as he weaves past the people between us.

He grabs me and delivers a passionate kiss. I melt into his arms in relief. If this was a movie, the other travelers would applaud or someone would sing. But, it's real. It's all real.

I don't notice stepping off the escalator when it reaches the bottom. In my imagination, we are center stage with a single spotlight on us, swirling in each other's arms to the score's crescendo. There is nothing else in the world except us. This is as real as it gets.

"Ooh, Katey! I have missed you!" Joseph tosses his head back and laughs a hearty, toothy laugh.

We pause for a moment at arms' length looking at each other. Unable to contain my excitement, I give him a delighted hug and kiss.

Weary passengers file past us and turn toward the luggage area. We watch them push through the glass doors to the carousels that are beginning to belch forth luggage. We reconnect for an encore kiss.

I turn, expecting to follow the other passengers. I'm more than ready to collect his belongings and take him away from LAX, so he can never leave me again.

He pulls me toward him and laughs. "My luggage won't catch up with me until tomorrow at the earliest."

Hesitating to understand what he said, I look up at his face. It makes no sense, but I don't care. I don't care. Gently, I nudge him to move toward the exit leading to the parking garage across the street.

"Tell me everything!" I insist as we move away from the activity. "I want to hear all about Ireland."

"The trip back was the most exciting part!" Joseph laughs again.

I can't imagine that is true. "I want to hear every detail," I say and slip my hand in the crook of his elbow. We push through the glass doors and out into the California night. Being near him more than makes up for the wait.
~~~

"There was a nor'easter stalled over the Atlantic seaboard," he begins in a storytelling voice.

I let go of his arm and move a step sideways to get the full effect of his adventure. His arms and hands are animated. His eyes dance and his smile flickers on and off like a blinking Christmas light.

"They diverted us to Canada for refueling, then to Chicago where I caught a flight to L.A."

"Chicago?!" I never thought about a diversion.

"Yes, Chicago. I never made it to LaGuardia." He adds a hardy laugh and squeezes my hand in excitement. Suddenly, he looks at me seriously, somewhat startling me.

"Did you know it is snowing at O'Hare?" He impishly grins because snow at O'Hare Airport is like sunshine at Sky Harbor in Phoenix. It's January, of course it's snowing in Chicago. Something would be seriously wrong, if it wasn't snowing in the Windy City.

I give him a playful shove for being so ornery. It feels wonderful being with him again. I am a little embarrassed for having let my imagination run wild when he was not on either of the New York flights.

Clearly, I am not going to tell him about my doubts; besides, they no longer matter. He is home, that is all that's important.

Since it's late and my apartment is closer than his place in the foothills, we decide to drive to my place at the beach. Joseph eases out of the parking garage, into the traffic, and heads south on the 405. There is almost no traffic on the freeway, at least in comparison to daytime traffic.

Settling back in my seat, I listen to the caramel sound of his voice as he tells me about his trip, his family, and the shenanigans they did while he was visiting his homeland.

~~~
~~~

~ CHAPTER 3 ~

Eire! It's Eire!

The sun is up. I awake to the smell of steaming coffee within reach on the nightstand. It reminds me of when Maggie woke me with coffee the day she helped me to find an apartment and get on with life again after coming home.

Rolling over, I touch the empty pillow beside me, thinking about Joseph. Slowly, the sounds and smells of cooking in the kitchen come into my awareness. It takes a second to get oriented and remember Joseph is back in L.A. and with me.

In no time, I'm in my robe, with cup in hand, venturing to the kitchen to watch him prepare breakfast. It is nearly perfect having Joseph here when I wake.

He is dressed and fully awake. I had forgotten about the eight-hour time difference between California and Ireland; his internal clock must still be on Gaelic time.

This is the first real chance to study him since he arrived. In all honesty, the two months in Ireland have been good for him. He looks rested, but different from how I remember him.

I take a deep, satisfied breath and smile. When he notices me watching him, he ceremoniously pulls out a chair and smiles his toothy smile.

Graciously, I allow him to seat me at the table. Our eyes meet as he positions himself across from me. I almost pinch myself to make sure this isn't a dream and he is really home.

He reaches across the table, taking my hand as I set down my cup. His touch sends thrills through me. Two months is a long time to be apart. Joseph's departure had come too soon after Maggie and Dave's funeral.

"Katey, I've missed you," he says softly.

"I missed—" I begin to reciprocate the endearment and lean toward him, but Joseph interrupts.

"I'm going to Eire and I want you to come with me," he blurts out, then looks flustered, which is uncharacteristic for him.

"Eire?" I ask, not remembering it as one of our usual places to go. Does he really want to go out and do something his first day back?

"Ireland! Ireland! Come with me, Katey." The intensity of his voice rises considerably.

His impatient response baffles me. He is usually composed and confident, not awkward like now.

Sure, I know Eire and Ireland are the same place. I just hadn't expected him to talk of going back to Ireland his first day back here.

"You're going back?" I can barely whisper the question.

"Yes. Come with me."

What? Ireland? I study his eyes without an answer to his intent. My mind races in circles. Panic comes over me at the thought of Joseph leaving again. He just returned. He can't leave.

My insides are jittering. What is he asking? A trip to see Ireland? Something more? Me to leave my life behind and move to Ireland? In addition to everything else that would make a move complicated, I'm not ready to move away from my beach, it anchors my life.

On the other hand I have an urge to say, "YES! Yes, I will go with you!" without knowing anything more. I want to be with him. I don't care if we're on Mars, if we are together.

I need more time. Please God, rewind everything back to the way it was last summer when Maggie was here, and Joseph and I were falling in love, not now when he is talking of going away.

The thought of impetuously going with him to this mysterious island of his is a bit romantic, and I am an incurable romantic. Is this a prelude to a marriage proposal?

Should I blindly say, "Yes," or slow down?

My spirit sighs. I'd hoped this year would be calm after last year. Joseph is complicating it in ways I had not anticipated. Still, something isn't adding up here.

I look at him for a hint of what he means. I don't want to ask, "Are you proposing?" I don't want him to think I didn't get it. If he isn't, I don't want to be the one to bring up marriage.

Besides, I have never thought of myself as married. I had always hoped to enter the Benedictine Priory. My mother's dying from breast cancer when I was in high school confused my plans to be a nun. I don't know what I thought the end result of loving him would be. I hadn't really thought that far ahead. Maybe this is a test to see if I like Ireland.

It seems like several minutes have passed, but it's probably only seconds that all of this has been racing through my mind. Joseph is sipping his coffee. I smile slowly, imagining he had rehearsed a better speech than blurting it out the way he did.

"Katey?" Joseph smiles at me.

I focus on the laugh lines around his mouth. Dreamily I look into his eyes, but they aren't dancing. It takes me aback when I realize he is still waiting for an answer.

"What?" I clear my throat. "What are you asking?"

"I am asking you to come to Ireland with me." His accent is crisp and so is his tone.

"Joseph, I don't understand." My frustration is manifested in my responding tone.

"Kathryn!" Joseph retaliates impatiently.

"Joseph," I say softly. "We're both tired." I speak calmly this time to exercise some semblance of maturity. Clearly, I will have to risk the embarrassment of being wrong about his intentions in order to clarify his question. "Joseph, are you asking me to visit Ireland or move there?"

A frustrated breath slips from my tight chest. I'm disappointed in my failure to ask the real question on my mind, *Are you proposing marriage*? Which, by the way, you weren't romantic, if that is what you are doing. Be clear. Regrettably, I settle with the question I managed to ask. Though I failed to realize the absence of the offering of a ring.

"I've missed you. I want to be with you, Katey," he says sincerely.

I hesitate to press him further. He had the perfect opportunity to clearly ask me to marry him, and didn't take it. I can't quite make the leap to just say, "Yes," whether or not it is a proposal. "Joseph, I need a little time to answer." What does "I want to be with you" mean to him, because it is certainly unclear to me.

"Okay, Katey! Okay!" Joseph snaps, obviously annoyed. "It will take me a couple of months to close my office and sell my house. Can you decide by then?" he asks in a cutting tone.

"Yes." I keep my reply short, not wishing to accelerate the volatility of the moment. His abrupt change of attitude and the mixed message of missing me (but no contact), his tone, and the vague request is confusing.

Joseph scoots his chair away from the table, obviously invoking the universal lawyer-language that the conversation is concluded.

"I need to get home. My bags should arrive this morning. I want to get to the office, so I can hit the door running on Monday." He puts his hands on his knees with an air of finality, then stands. It's obvious his schedule is not negotiable.

Quite clearly, I get the message.

"I'll get dressed and give you a ride," I say, getting up from the table. Our breakfast is cold, forgotten. Besides, I'm no longer hungry.

Joseph snaps back a little softer, "No, I've called a taxi. It should be here soon."

Feelings of disappointment well up inside me. I am hurt that he hadn't planned to spend today together. I had expected to be together today and this weekend. I had assumed he would want that too.

My disappointment is interrupted by the honking of the arriving taxi. Was he going to get up and walk out if I had agreed to go with him? Well, either way, he is leaving now, and I don't like the way we are leaving things.

Joseph grabs his laptop and coat and heads for the door. "Goodbye, Kathryn."

"Joseph, I'm glad you're home," I say softly.

He smiles and nods in acknowledgment, then goes out. No hug. No kiss. He is gone.

After the taxi drives away, I turn from the window in a daze. I feel a profound void. The winter sky outside contributes to my disappointment. He said, *Kathryn*, not *Katey*. That is not a good sign.

I wander to the sofa and sit with my feet against the edge of the coffee table, mindlessly holding my coffee cup for its warmth. What just happened?

"God, I hate feeling like this," I remark out loud to the empty apartment. Setting down the cup, I pull one of the sofa pillows to my chest, holding it tightly. I am determined not to cry. Clinging to the pillow helps to hold back the tears, but just barely.

I work my neck and shoulders a little to shake off the stiffness, and settle back on the sofa with another cup of hot brew. But none of it helps my sad mood.

Perhaps a shower will help. "I'll be okay; I just had the wind knocked out of me, that's all," I console myself. "I'm okay, I'm—"

The shower feels good, but the sadness lingers. The coffee left on the vanity has the bitter taste of abandonment. I dump it down the sink in disgust. The shrill whine of the blow-dryer numbs my mind. I nod to my mirror image and say, "You'll be all right." My reflection makes a failed attempt at a reassuring smile.

Obviously, I am indulging my hurt feelings.

"Oh, Katey! Make the best of your day off. Go forth and be productive," I say in an effort to jump-start my momentum.

Determined, if not truly inspired by my pep talk, I look for a task to fill my day. In anticipation of Joseph's return, the apartment was clean.

"Well, so much for cleaning," I say when I finish clearing the breakfast dishes and the uneaten food from the table. The bed is made. There are no other menial tasks to perform to occupy my time.

Standing at the window with a new cup of coffee, I watch the waves break on the beach across the street. A walk on the beach? Finally, I have a reason to get out of the house.

~~~

I am glad the Pacific is so cold that it attracts only real beach-people during the winter months. If I am going to feel alone, I might as well be alone on the beach as anywhere else.

This time yesterday I was filled with excited anticipation to see Joseph. Could my doubts at the airport have foreshadowed his homecoming? Ah, I don't know. That's a bit too literary for me.
~~~

Usually the cool, misty ocean air clears my mind like nothing else can. However, today there is no clarity for me. My disappointment in Joseph's homecoming hangs over me like a dense fog. Restlessness washes over me as I seek the beach's consolation in vain.

A shell gleaming in the wet sand draws me nearer the foamy ribbon marking the water's edge. I move closer to the tan froth that runs up the beach with each wave and pick up the semi-buried shell.

"Damn him!" I tell the shell for lack of anyone else to tell. "I have waited too long to fall in love for it to be like this," I whisper to the defenseless shell as I turn it over in my sandy fingers and lightly close them around it. I am so disappointed. "Damn him!"

In a way, alone on the beach the little shell personifies my own sense of abandonment and defenselessness in the wake of Joseph's disturbing mood. My fingers bend upward, sliding the shell to my palm, again securing my grip on the nickel-sized prize. It's as if I am clinging to it to provide everything I need right now: security, comfort, sanity.

A silhouette walking in the distance catches my attention. The approaching figure looks like Karen, though it is unlikely she would be walking the beach on a Thursday when she should be at work. It must be someone who walks like her.

Slipping the shell safely in my jacket pocket and increasing my stride to close the distance between us, I see it is Karen. In all of the years I have known her, I have not known her to take a day off work. For a moment I have to think to be sure it is not really Saturday.

No, it's Thursday, I conclude, confirming reality.

Karen is looking at the distant ocean as she strolls along the beach. It seems to startle her a bit when I speak as I approach.

"Well! Hello, Katey!" Karen's voice indicates her surprise.

It strikes me funny that in our professional roles she still calls me "Kathryn," even though she is no longer my boss. But on the beach she began to call me "Katey" after Maggie died.

"Out for a winty walk?" I ask.

"I come to the beach on the 25th every month, just to have a day away from the madness."

She studies my expression for a hint of recognition of the date last November when we learned Maggie was dead.

Yes, I know the significance of the date. That was a terribly long weekend for all of us; Karen, Joseph, and me. I understand the need to take the time away from the insanity and spend time on the beach. But today is January 24th. I decide not to mention the discrepancy.

"Are you all right?"

"Yes," she lies. "You?"

"Fine. Never better," I lie back.

We walk in the direction I came from, pausing uncomfortably long when we get to where to cross the beach to my apartment.

"Coffee?"

"That would be nice."

Karen glances around the room, depositing her jacket over the back of the sofa. She has a curious look on her face.

"Wasn't Joseph supposed to arrive last night?" She follows me into the kitchen.

"He came, but he was eager to get settled," I half explain and hand her a cup of coffee.

She seems to accept my answer without question. I hope so, but that was a little too easy. Most likely she is too polite to embarrass me with more questions.

The truth is I am embarrassed that Joseph and I did not have a romantic homecoming weekend, especially after he had been away for two months.

"Lunch?" I ask, noticing the time. I begin to set out the food from the refrigerator that I had planned to serve Joseph for lunch.

When I turn around, I see her studying the food on the counter.

"Katey, it has been quite a year since your return, hasn't it?" she asks, then takes a sip of her coffee to weave pauses into the conversation. She's keen to remember something as trivial as the time of year I returned to California.

"Yes, quite a year," I agree. Remembering why Karen had been on the beach in the first place I ask, "Do you want to talk about Maggie?"

Her eyes squint.

"I'm okay with Maggie. Do you want to talk about Joseph?" She answers with a question, reawakening in me the pain and confusion about Joseph.

I look at her for a moment, processing her question and my option of answers. But if I talk about Joseph, I have to admit aloud that his homecoming hadn't been what I had hoped. On the other hand, I could use insight into Joseph's invitation. It is too soon, too fresh, too—

I smile, take a deep breath, and bargain, "Thanks, maybe later. Rain check?"

Karen smiles knowingly. "Sure, rain check."

It doesn't take long for our small talk to dissolve into silence. Maybe I should talk about Joseph. For certain, this morning did not go as planned.

It doesn't matter, I missed my opportunity. Karen is ready to head home. She has to go to Sacramento tomorrow for a meeting with the governor. Now, I understand why she was on the beach today rather than tomorrow. We promise to catch up with each other next week.

My empty apartment is deathly silent, except the click of the latch when the door closes. I pour another cup of coffee, then wander to the sofa to enjoy the comforting warmth of the drink. As I pull my feet up, maneuvering them to rest on the coffee table, I see Maggie's diary laying where it was left the last time I was reading it.

When Maggie's brother brought her diaries to me after she died, I felt awkward about having them. Once I realized how much I needed her, even if it was only to hold a relic or see her handwriting, I slowly eased into reading them. Her entries have consoled and counseled me for two months. Now I can't imagine being without them, especially since she is gone.

Without looking, I pick a page at random.

...The funny thing about insight is, at the moment it comes, I feel enlightened. However, now it occurs to me that this insight—each insight—is not the pinnacle of wisdom, but only one step among many along life's journey...

After reading Maggie's diary for a while, my coffee tastes better than the previous cup. I return to the first entry. "Insight, hmm." Another sip of coffee. "Insight?"

Maggie knew much more about life than I do. How did she? She was only four years older than I. If it was not age, what then? Was it writing her diary that helped her sort her thoughts and examine them more objectively, or at least get them out of her system so they could percolate safely?

Maybe I need a release valve like that. How does one start a diary? I look through both boxes of books for Maggie's first diary, but I can't find it. I am grasping at straws, but at this point in the day I am willing to entertain just about any idea to restore my lost sense of well-being.

In the absence of her first diary, I wonder how I would start a diary. Dear Diary, seems rather pedestrian. Should I start with some sort of introduction in the first entry? That seems awkward, utilitarian. Just start writing? Who knows? I am clueless.

~~~

Mr. Goldstein arrives for our evening walk on the beach, rescuing me from the intimidating idea of writing my most intimate thoughts in a book.

"Mr. Goldstein, come in. I'll grab my jacket."

I enjoy the comfort of our daily routine of walking on the beach, especially today. I have known Mr. Goldstein for years, but I would have
~~~

never dreamed we would become more than neighbors and rely on each other for inter-generational companionship.

Closing the door behind us, I wonder what he knows about diaries.

~~~
~~~

~ CHAPTER 4 ~

Answering to a Higher Power ~ Shasta

Morning comes all too early. If I had been thinking ahead, I would have asked Mother Elizabeth for two days off. Perhaps it was intuition that we would not spend time together, so I only asked for Thursday. Still it would have been nice to be off work until Monday.

It didn't work that way, so I get out of my car and head for the convent door. I'm determined to act enthusiastic, hoping to eventually feel the same as my actions. Before I open the heavy wooden door, I take a deep breath, straighten myself, and prepare to face the day.

Right on cue, little Shasta is waiting inside. She is a cute little thing with big brown eyes and unruly, curly blonde hair, the kind that is slightly frizzy in soft little wisps around her face. She is shy, as are many of the other formerly homeless children at Spirit of Hope, though less shy in comparison.

I stoop to her level, while brushing a wisp of hair from her eyes. "Hello, little one."

"Where were you yesterday?" she quizzes me with her hand on her hip for added emphasis of my impending demise.

"I met a friend at the airport."

"You should have told me you were going to be gone! I was late for school waiting for you." Shasta scolds me with a pout forming around her mouth, making sure I understand that it is my fault she was late.

"Yes, ma'am! You are absolutely right," I agree, as I look into her sweet face. "I'm sorry, pumpkin." I honestly apologize. It had been foolish to trade a date with her for one with Joseph. I feel guilty.

I hand her my appointment book to carry, as she does every morning, while I sign in at the front desk. Hand in hand we walk to the back hall where I hang my jacket and set my lunch box on the shelf above the coat hooks. The shelf is the convent version of a locker. It is assumed our belongings are as safe here in the open as surfers' packs are on the beach. Both seem to be true.

Turning and kneeling at Shasta's level, I reassure her. "It won't happen again, Shasta. I promise to tell you first, if I take another day off."

"Well." She pauses, tilts her head. "I forgive you." She pronounces her forgiveness with the seriousness of a confessor. "It was boring around here anyway. You didn't miss nothing."

I wonder if I would have been forgiven so easily if I had missed something.

"It's getting late. Be on your way to school." I put my hands on her shoulders, and turn her around to face the door. "You'd better scoot!"

She looks back over her shoulder with a big grin. "I know a shortcut!" She giggles a little squeal and disappears.

Shasta is wrong. I had missed something yesterday. I had missed her and everyone else at Spirit of Hope. I had been wrong to wish I had asked for today off. This job has given me back my passion for social work. It has reminded me why I went to social work school in the first place. Working with our homeless families and the nuns who share their home with them has enkindled a spirit of hope in me.

On Fridays we prepare our once-homeless families to be on their own for the weekend and to finish any remaining tasks on this week's staff assignment list. It's an easy day. I work ahead of the schedule to have most things done by Thursday in the event of an unplanned disaster. Usually there are no disasters.

Mother Elizabeth appears from around the corner behind me. Without looking, I know who is coming. The nuns, in theory, are identical. Even so, there are distinct differences in the sound of the rosary beads gently clicking, as they sway on their belt clip because each nun walks with a unique rhythm; thanks to their rosary, it is an audible rhythm.

"Kathryn." Mother Elizabeth catches up with me. "Did you drive or take the bus today?"

"Drove, Mother."

"Good. Would you run this over to Sally's?" She asks in such a way there can be only one answer. "Commander Jenkins left it here yesterday; I suspect he is lost without his vade mecum." She hands an appointment book toward me.

"Yes, I will be glad to take it to him."

In all honesty, I am not quite ready to settle down and concentrate on work just yet. I don't mind running errands for Mother Elizabeth—especially today.

~~~

The traffic is thinning to a manageable flow, since most people coming downtown are at work now. The sun is peeking through the haze, making everything look brighter after the rains that come in January. The traffic sounds and the people sounds that come from a massive number of people in a small space drift in through one open window and out the other.

A car pulls away from the curb in time to free a prime parking spot near Sally's front door. There are street people, the homeless, milling around on the sidewalk. A couple of them look in my direction as I feed the meter, but generally they don't seem to notice me. I suspect they
~~~

have scavenged the alleys for aluminum cans to sell, then came to the Salvation Army Mission for breakfast.

A man devouring the last bite of toast brushes past me as I walk through the door. A younger man at the counter, not a street person, greets me. He studies me. Obviously, I am out of place.

"Can I help you with something?" the young man asks in an are-you-lost way of asking.

"I have Commander Jenkins' appointment book," I say, knowing I have said the magic words to allow me to enter the inner sanctuary.

"Just need you to sign in." He nudges a clipboard.

Compliantly, I take the pen tied to the clipboard and sign.

He spins the clipboard around. "McKenzie, hmmm?"

"Yes, but not *that* McKenzie!" I laugh.

He smiles and waves me to proceed to the office area.

Commander Jenkins is visibly glad to have his little book back in his possession. Had he been Catholic, I might have been canonized on the spot. I am, at least, his newest hero.

I feel good about the day so far. Yet, I can't shake the hurt from Joseph's odd behavior. Even when I'm not intentionally thinking about him, a gnawing ache sneaks up on me unexpectedly. Truly, I do not understand what is going on between us. Despite what I said to Karen, I know his behavior has to be more than fatigue from his flight. Something about him is different. Have I simply been blinded by love and not seen this side of him? Did something happen to him in Ireland? I have no answers. I'll have to wait for him to give them to me.

Sister Theresa looks up when I come through the convent front door. A sentinel, she monitors the comings and goings in a receptionist sort of way. Other times she seems to be second in command of the convent, if there is such a thing as an assistant Mother Superior. Sister Theresa is quiet, but I have decided it doesn't necessarily indicate she is shy. As the saying goes, "Still water runs deep."

"Hello, Kathryn." Sister Theresa greets me as usual, but she doesn't stop there. "Is everything all right?"

"Delivered to its owner." I dismiss her question, and sign back in—first name only. We don't use last names here.

Sister Theresa leaves her desk and steps closer to speak in a hushed voice: "No, no, I mean about your gentleman friend."

I swear, are there no secrets around these nuns? Mother Elizabeth must have told her about Joseph's homecoming. I had to tell Mother I was picking up my boyfriend at the airport before she would give me the day off. Mother Elizabeth would settle for nothing short of the whole truth. Being secretive with her makes things worse. Her curiosity is not something to toy with.

Looking Sister Theresa in the eye, I say, “He is fine. Just tired from his trip. Jet lag—you know.” That much is vaguely true, so at least I escape the fires of hell by not actually lying to her. It’s a double whammy to lie to a nun, isn't it?

Sister Theresa nods in knowing agreement, though I doubt she has flown abroad. Maybe she believes me or at least understands it is not a topic for further discussion. It’s personal.

I don’t want to elaborate on the Joseph topic to anyone, at least not yet, and especially not to anyone at work. My answer was a bit misleading, but really, Sister Theresa and I don’t know each other well enough to discuss my personal life. Besides, I am still trying to convince myself there is a little truth to what I told her.

Our formerly homeless families are requiring less attention and reassurance from the staff. This day, as most days, moves along effortlessly without anything out of the ordinary intruding on my nearly perfect world.

Shasta comes to find me after school. My case notes, Weekly Summary Report, and Needs Assessments have been updated, so I take the time to pay back some of the attention she missed yesterday.

“What did you study in school today?”

“We studied the explorers that came to California,” she says in a disappointed tone.

“Explorers?” I ask with piqued interest. “Why don’t you be the guide and we can explore your shortcut?” I deliberately demonstrate that I had paid attention to what she said this morning.

The convent has had many additions over its 160 years, not all of them with an eye for future additions or aesthetics. Even I have noticed places where the outside of the convent structure doesn't quite fit the floor plan inside. Unlike a child, I have not indulged my explorer instincts. It appears Shasta has taken full advantage of hers.

“Well okay, but you can’t tell no one else,” she insists with deadly certainty.

“Deal!” I agree and offer her a pinkie-promise as a sign of my sincerity.

Quickly, Shasta hunkers down and tiptoes down the hall in the direction of the alcove where the staff hang their coats.

I follow behind her a slight distance.

She stops abruptly and turns toward me. “You gotta get down!” she harshly whispers the command, motioning me lower with her hand.

“Of course,” I whisper. “And that would be because of—”

Shasta stands up straight, hands on her hips, seemingly annoyed with my adult ignorance. “Because of the bears! Haven’t you seen the California flag?” Her voice is full of indignation and disappointment.

Quickly, I stoop down. I've seen the flag. I know enough to hide from bears. My mamma didn't raise no fool!

We tiptoe near the wall as if in step to Henry Mancini's "Pink Panther." Rushing to stand flat against the wall next to a statue of Saint Ann, Shasta motions for me to do likewise.

I don't even want to think about what we look like sneaking around the hallways of the convent. I can just imagine what would happen if Mother Elizabeth came around the corner.

We tiptoe in tandem past the saint and down the hall, then slip in an alcove behind the statue of Saint Ursula.

Shasta pushes on the wall behind Ursula.

I look back to make sure we weren't seen. However, I am sure our names would have been sounded had any one of the sisters noticed us.

A faint click earns my undivided attention. To my surprise, Shasta pushes open the panel to a hidden passageway. It's an interior hallway, but there is sunlight coming through narrow horizontal windows high in the walls.

"Wow! How did you find this?" I whisper my amazement, as Shasta shuts the secret door behind us.

"I'm a kid!" She beams.

Of course! I think sarcastically. That explains it! I simply smile and nod understanding.

Shasta leads hastily to a door with a small window. "Lift me up," she requests. "I wanna see inside."

No wonder she agreed to show me the secret passage without protest; she has an agenda of her own. I marvel at how long she must have wanted to see in the window. Before I agree to help her look, I peek through the window to see if there is something she shouldn't see beyond the door. It looks safe enough for a child's eyes.

"Come here, little one. Ah, you grew while I was away!" I say as I lift her to peer through the window.

Shasta giggles at the thought she grew so much in one day. Growing is a big thing to a first grader. She slides her arm around my neck, and leans closer to the door to see through it.

When she leans, she throws off my center of balance, forcing me to lean against the door jam to balance her weight.

Together, we look through the glass at an open-air courtyard garden fully in bloom around a larger-than-life-size gray statue. Although the statue is facing away, from the look of it, it's a statue of Saint Francis of Assisi, the patron saint of these Franciscan nuns. There is a marble bench in front of the statue.

Shasta nudges me. We both catch a glimpse of a brown-robed nun move from the bench. My instincts scream, Run!

The back of the nun comes into full view as she walks away from us, toward another door. It's Mother Elizabeth! Run!

Shasta wiggles to get down and away from the window.

We seem to share the urgent need to escape. Even though we were never told it was a restricted area, it's clear it is not intended to be public. Guilt sets in. I feel I crossed the line by being in the secret passageway, especially after my earlier thoughts about privacy and Sister Theresa. I should have turned back as soon as Shasta showed me the hidden door.

We hurry out the hidden doorway, past the statues, past the coat hooks, and out the door to the playground. Breathless, we burst into an excited, nervous laugh.

"It is bea-u-u-ti-ful!" Shasta squeals, dances in circles, then comes to squeeze my arm—hard.

Guilt is weighing on me, bringing back all my Catholic grade school instincts. I must find Mother Elizabeth and confess.

"Yes. It's a lovely garden, but I think we were intruding on Mother's prayer time."

Shasta freezes. Her eyes diminish to a squint. Her hands go to her hips. She looks at me steady, considering what I said, possibly wondering if she is in trouble.

"I think that, without meaning to, we intruded on Mother Elizabeth's privacy. And the way this works is I am the adult, so I am responsible."

"What are you doing?" Shasta demands, grabbing for my arm to stop me where I stand.

"I did something wrong, at least it feels wrong, so I have to make it right."

"Nobody caught us," she pleads her opposing opinion. She hesitates, but follows reluctantly, not ready to relinquish her stand in the conversation.

"Still—" I start, but Shasta interrupts.

"We didn't mean to do nothing wrong."

"I think I should apologize to Mother. You don't have to come with me."

I fully expect Shasta to leave, but she stays by my side. As we turn the corner, we both halt suddenly when we see Mother in her office. Shasta still has time to escape, but my little partner in crime stays with me to the bitter end.

Outside Mother's office, I straighten my blouse, push my hair into place, then knock lightly on the open door.

"Mother Elizabeth, may I speak with you?"

Mother looks up from her stack of papers, sliding her reading glasses down her nose far enough to comfortably look over them at us.

"Certainly, Kathryn. Have a seat," Mother invites, as she waves us toward the chairs opposite her desk.

Shasta holds back, hiding behind me. I nearly trip over her when I get my feet tangled in hers as I step around the chair to sit down. Shasta tightens her grip on my hand. She is clearly visible now. We stand awkwardly for a moment glancing at Mother Elizabeth, then I sit.

I begin. "Mother, I came to apologize. I, I intruded on your privacy."

Mother Elizabeth thoughtfully removes her glasses the rest of the way, slowly laying them toward the desktop, but still holding them. She gazes intently at Shasta, then at me.

Quickly I add, "I brought a 'friend' with me." I nod toward Shasta. I feel like I'm in the principal's office and the same age as Shasta.

Shasta loosens her grip slightly to reposition her hand. It is enough for me to pull free. I guide her around the arm of the chair to give her the opportunity to sit beside me. Instead, she stands next to me—planted. She would have done well in the seventies singing protest songs: "I shall not be, I shall not be moved." She is firmly entrenched.

It is an awkward moment with Mother looking at us, receptive to whatever it is we are up to this time.

Finally Shasta relaxes enough to settle down on the edge of my chair. She lets out a little breath.

"I intruded on you while you were in the garden. I am truly sorry," I say softly.

"Thank you. I forgive you—and your friend." Mother Elizabeth's gaze moves between Shasta and me. "Now come with me." She leaves her glasses on her papers and walks out, clearly expecting us to follow.

We look at each other quizzically, then hurry to catch up just behind Mother in the corridor.

I lean down to Shasta and whisper, "See, it's all right."

She puts her finger over her mouth and shakes her head. "No, shhh!"

She gives me a look to put me in my place and dares me to transgress again. The matter isn't closed, and I am not to talk about it until it is finished.

Mother Elizabeth leads us to a door opposite the front door of the convent. She holds the door open for us to follow. Shasta and I peer inside, then enter.

My curiosity is piqued. I have passed this door many times a day, and thought it was another exterior door, perhaps an unofficial fire exit. It looks like an exterior door. All this time and no one mentioned anything about it leading to a garden.

"This is my garden," Mother says, quickly surveying her plot of Earth with the eyes of a parent looking at her child. She nods at the statue.

"Saint Francis, of course." She turns, "My roses." She smiles gesturing in their direction.

It is a rare moment to see Mother Superior relaxed. I had forgotten she had told me she loved to garden. At the time, I was new to the job and had many other things to remember. I had assumed she meant vegetables, something practical.

"Shasta, dear, come smell them." Mother reaches to gently tilt a petal-laden stem toward Shasta.

I nudge Shasta forward.

Shasta beams, deeply inhaling the rose's sweet aroma, then looking up at the nun with a smile.

This multidimensional holy nun is quite a woman, happily gardening, delighting in this child's wonderment, running a house full of nuns, and a homeless shelter. Why does it take so long to get to know people, to really know them?

I can't begin to speculate about what makes people tick. It seems as though everyone is predictable and rational; then one day, without warning, everything is turned upside down and they aren't who I thought they were. It isn't all bad, these rare unpretentious moments with Mother Elizabeth and Shasta are worth the wait. But why have the wait at all?

After our tour of Mother's garden, I leave the two of them to conspire. In a few minutes Shasta skips past me (no running allowed indoors) and off to play with the other children.

Mother Elizabeth quietly catches up with me (no running) and slyly motions for me to come with her. It really isn't that I was frequently summoned to the principal's office as a child, but I always get an uneasy feeling when I am summoned by my boss. What could it be now?

Mother Elizabeth is smiling as she whispers, "I want to show you something really cool."

"*Really cool*, Mother Elizabeth?" As I walk beside her, I honestly want to stop and study her a minute, but of course, I don't. *"Really cool?"*

Mother Elizabeth leads the way down the corridor behind Saint Ursula to the secret passageway, the same one Shasta and I had taken just a little bit ago.

I'm not sure if I should confess that I already know about this or not. Maybe she figured it out when I apologized since she hadn't seen us intrude. There is the pinky-promise to uphold. I volunteer no information, hoping that this doesn't count as a sin of omission.

"The other end of this hall opens to a doorway at the grade school, behind a statue of Saint Dominic," she says.

We duck into the secret hallway and shut the door behind Saint Ursula. "We put in the front door to the garden about twenty-five years ago," she says with a proud smile. "This is the old entry." She nods toward the garden through the window Shasta had found.

Mother Elizabeth was probably praying when we saw her. I think prayer is a private affair, something one shouldn't intrude upon. I still feel awful, but she doesn't seem concerned.

"When the school was first built, this statue of St. Francis and the garden was between the school and convent. The additions eventually enclosed the garden as the buildings grew together." Her tone indicates an endearing fondness for her home and her chosen life.

Mother Elizabeth leads into the garden and around to the bench in front of Saint Francis. Her affection for her patron is sweet. I study her silhouette as she looks lovingly into the saint's face, but speaks to me, "I was praying for you."

"For me? You, you were praying for me?" I query in a whisper equivalent to being in church. I cannot describe the tenderness of the moment. It is as if I have been touched at my core by simple holiness, by the realization that I'm not alone and the confusion surrounding Joseph will diminish. I don't feel compelled to offer her a hug or even to say anything more, rather to let the moment live simply as it is.

Maybe Karen told her. Or Sister Theresa said something to Mother Elizabeth about my boyfriend. I really thought I had sidestepped her inquiry—maybe not.

"There was something in your eyes when I saw you this morning." Mother Elizabeth's voice is soft, nun-like. She answered as if she heard my thoughts.

My gaze meets hers. There must have been a strange look on my face, a wrinkled brow, my eyes—something.

A laugh escapes from Mother Elizabeth. One hand goes to her mouth. Then as quickly as it left, her composure returns, unashamed.

I was beginning to feel smug, thinking that she was predictable. Well, not today. Perhaps not ever.

"Don't be so amazed, Kathryn. It doesn't take a rocket scientist to tell yesterday did not meet your expectations," Mother says softly, woman-to-woman, not boss-to-employee, not nun-to-civilian. "There is no shame in being human."

I am relieved that it was deductive reasoning, not Sister Theresa or Karen, who brought her to a dead-on conclusion. I would have been disappointed had either tattled, as strange as that may sound. Relieved she doesn't read minds, but feeling wholly transparent, I confess, "No, it was not as I hoped."

"I fully expected you to call and ask for today off."

She says no more about my "gentleman friend."

Neither do I.

On the way home I stop by the bookstore to purchase a diary. I had not realized how personal the selection of a diary is. I'm still not sure about the mechanics of writing in one, but Maggie's diary seems to have held healing powers for her, and now for me. At this point, I am willing to try anything—even to the extent of confiding my inner thoughts, questions, doubts, and hopes to a book of blank pages. I looked at all of the choices, touched their cover material, and selected one. Be it a talisman or a savior, I have a diary of my own.

~~~

After dinner, I sit on the sofa holding my new acquisition. My fingers slide across the spine and over the top, feeling the smooth cool cover of the book. Perhaps, if I hold it long enough, I'll be inspired to write, preferably something profound.

I think about the lesson I intended to teach Shasta about making things right when you do something wrong, even if it was unintentional. That doesn't seem to inspire any lofty thoughts worthy of inscription. I look around the room. I shut my eyes and take a few deep breaths. Nothing comes to me.

I relocate across the street to sit on the beach. No inspiration here either, not even with the magnificent sunset. This is harder than I thought. I am sure I'm making it too mechanical, giving too much thought, as usual.

~~~

~ CHAPTER 5 ~

In Concert!

The days wind on in a mundane way. Overall they have been good, but I remain haunted by Joseph's cool mood and cryptic invitation to Ireland. It is probably a moot question. He hasn't made any effort to contact me since he walked out of my apartment more than two weeks ago. I had hoped he would call. But, he has not.

The man isn't known for his communication skills, especially when he is wrapped up in his own little world. I shouldn't be surprised. Rather than surprised, I'm disappointed.

Clearly he was not proposing marriage. I recognize now, he had no ring and didn't mention the M-word. Besides, he doesn't seem driven to spend time with me. That's the part that bothers me the most.

I feel foolish for thinking we were in love. The sad thing is, I am in love with him. When I think of the past year I am overwhelmed with a desire to run to him, forgive him, and spend every minute of the day with him. Then, like a wave crashing over me at high tide, I shudder with the cold reality that he doesn't seem to share my desire.

My mood vacillates from hurt to angry, angry to confused, and then to hurt again. Sometimes I am disappointed with Joseph, sometimes with myself. I replay his return over in my mind, wondering if I could have done something, anything, differently—and, would it have made a difference? It wears on my spirit and my confidence. It wears on the whole of me.

Though I would deny it if confronted, I have stayed home in the evenings more than usual, hoping he would call. When he doesn't call, I am embarrassed that I waited by the phone. All the more, I am determined not to call him. I will not chase after him. Pride, what a dangerous flaw! The complexities of love, are they really necessary?

It should be a relief that he didn't propose marriage, now that I am uncertain about our relationship. Besides, I'm not sure marriage is what I want right now. And Ireland—oh, that is a long way from my beach, much farther than Nebraska ever was.

My emotions have raw edges. Feeling vulnerable is toxic. With all of this boiling inside of me, I reach for a dose of consolation and healing from Maggie's diary. I have become dependent on her writings to combat my recurring feelings of aloneness. I miss her terribly.

Dearest Diary, Being superhuman is what's expected of me. At least it seems it is. So, why not go with it? That's what's required of me, or at least what we have all come to believe (myself included). Superhuman—kind of has a nice ring to it, doesn't it? Life's easier for everyone if I'm superhuman, isn't it?

...It is easier to be strong. Others feel more secure when I am strong. Where's the advantage to feeling ordinarily human?

Everything else becomes larger than life, if I am not larger than life. Where's the percentage in that? "Be strong," then is my motto for today. The only problem is I don't feel strong.

I don't feel strong either, Maggie. Sometimes I think going to Ireland with Joseph is certainly better than the alternative of staying here without him. On second thought, his insensitivity makes me so exasperated that I don't want to go anywhere with him. If he walked through the door right this minute, I would tell him so.

I am as restless as the ocean with a winter storm brewing off the coast. My emotions are as enormous as the swells that come with it. My heart is gray—stormy, winter-sky gray.

How could I have been so wrong about Joseph and me? Is there an "us" in there somewhere?

~~~

With perfect timing, Mr. Goldstein appears for our nightly walk. His presence is enough to remind me how connected I am to this place. I need the stability of being here. I'm not really alone. I belong here.

"I haven't seen your gentleman friend lately." With a glance, Mr. Goldstein unpretentiously indicates the topic of today's walk as we cross the sand to the water's edge.

I start to tell him the line about Joseph being tired or busy, but our relationship is beyond that, so I tell the truth. "I don't know what is going on with him. He is distant, and abrupt. I don't know what to think."

Mr. Goldstein walks in silence for a minute, looking out at the waves coming to shore.

I look past him to the waves, hoping to see what he sees, to find the solace and wisdom he finds.

"Katerina, has your Joseph always been this way, maybe a little?"

I begin to say "No," but upon consideration I admit, though it is exaggerated now, he has been this way from the beginning. I thought it was subtle cultural differences between us. But he did take forever to call me after Maggie gave him my phone number. I always interpreted his behavior by American norms or ignored their implications all together.

"My dear Mr. Goldstein, you are absolutely right!"

Mr. Goldstein smiles a knowing smile.

I savor the look of him.
~~~

We continue our walk and examine the topic from every side—circling, discussing, pondering. He understands me better than I understand myself. Quite possibly, he accepts me as I am better than I do. Luckily, he doesn't really expect an answer. His goal is to make me think. He knows his question will linger in my thoughts and eventually find their own truth, the whole truth. He does not need to say more.

~~~

Long after Mr. Goldstein has gone home, I sit with my feet on the coffee table, relaxing with a cup of coffee while reflecting on his questions and the insights that prompted them. I know that I seek conformity, though it is not my first nature. I have always tried to yield to what I think are society's expectations of me: to be tolerant, evaluative, and considerate. Maybe it's time to abandon all things conventional, and look only at the naked truth. What is the truth of our relationship? Not what I want, or think, or even hope. What is it really?

If Maggie was here she would push beyond Mr. Goldstein's questions. She would demand answers, allowing no time to delude myself with romantic notions. She would leave me bloody and beaten. Just when I could take no more, she would demand more until I knew the truth—and admitted it.

~~~

The ringing phone interrupts my struggle to understand myself and Joseph.

"Hello," I answer, hoping to hear Joseph's voice.

"Hello Katey. Linda sent four comp tickets to the 'Have-A-Heart' concert."

"Have-A-Heart concert?" I'm barely making the transition from whom I expected to hear to who actually is on the phone. I pause to catch up with the conversation.

"At the Hollywood Bowl on Valentine's Day, the California Child Abuse Prevention Coalition is sponsoring a charity concert." Karen seems surprised I haven't heard about it. "It's been in the papers and on the radio." She is polite, but her voice indicates she seems to think I am "out of the loop."

"CAL-CAP, oh. I didn't think the Bowl was open this time of year," I respond, eager to demonstrate that I am not totally unaware of the world around me and I do know the coalition by its acronym.

"It will be fun. Bundle up. Come with me." Karen is too enthusiastic to be turned down. "They're going to have some big names there...and, and that singer whose CDs you play...the one you like from Kansas. What's her name?" Karen has leverage and plans to use it.

"Ann Zimmerman," I answer. I would have gone to the benefit anyway, but now I am more interested.

“Katey, two tickets!” Karen tempts.

“Sure, sounds good!” I throw in enthusiasm out of politeness.

We arrange to meet for lunch tomorrow so I can pick up my tickets.

I wonder who Karen will take to the concert—Mother Elizabeth, her Sister-sister? Ordinarily Maggie and I would go together to a benefit. Should I give in and invite Joseph? I am hopeless. I still want to believe that things will be good with us again. I back down on my pledge to let him make the first move to contact me.

~~~

Waiting for Karen, I see note cards are for sale at the cashier counter. I get one and write to Joseph. I have second thoughts about enclosing one of the tickets, and hurriedly seal the envelope before Karen arrives. It’s odd that I don’t trust Joseph to not waste the ticket. That should be telling.

Quickly, I drop the invitation in my purse just as Karen comes through the door. She hesitates, locating me, then walks toward me. I am embarrassed that I have acquiesced so easily when it comes to Joseph. Luckily for me, Karen can’t read minds.

~~~

Armed with my CD player and one of Ann Zimmerman’s CDs, I head to the beach. I know better than to let the invitation sit long enough for me to change my mind or, should I say, come to my senses? On the way to the beach the invitation is dropped into the corner mailbox. It’s gone, done deal.

The moist air is cold and uninviting. Catalina Island across the channel has disappeared in the fog. The bad weather has cleared nearly everyone else off of the beach, leaving the seagulls and me to a solitary walk. The sounds of the surf subside into the background of my awareness when the guitar intro to “Absolute Zero” begins. Ann’s voice is driven and clear. She means business with this song, a song that fits perfectly with the night and my mood.

♪♪Absolute zero, colder than ice.
Coldest cold that cold can be,
to be precise.

♪♪Ultimate coldness on the
absolute scale.
At this cruel point even the molecules fail...

♪♪Absolute zero, frozen in time.
No warmth, no heartbeat, no rhythm or rhyme.
No motion, no sympathy, no loving embrace.
Just what I see when I look in your face...

© Ann Zimmerman

Tears stream down my cheeks. I have a horrible feeling things will never be the same between us. He's shut me out of whatever is going on with him. Part of me wants to help him. The other part of me is so disappointed in him that I can't possibly imagine our relationship surviving this mood of his. Yet, I can't easily afford the loss of him, the loss of us. Not now, no more losses for now.

A beach patrol's Jeep slows as it approaches. I wish to be left alone and give them a friendly wave. Recognizing me as a local, they wave back and continue on, disappearing into the fog in the distance. I listen to the waves and seek their consolation, but I know in my heart I have to find peace within before the contented sound of the waves can wash over me.

The thick mist packed the sand, making it feel hard and uninviting through my shoes. My calves tighten with the cold and the walking. Turning toward home, "Absolute Zero" sings in my earbuds again.

It's too bad I dropped the invitation in the mailbox. I am sure now that it was a mistake. It is too late to have second thoughts about inviting him. Nonetheless, I have them—third thoughts, too. At least Ann has a description for Joseph— "Absolute Zero, coldest cold that cold can be..."

Coffee brews while I take a shower. Wrapped in my robe, thick socks to warm my frigid feet, and my coffee in hand, I settle down on the sofa with my new diary. I put my feet on the edge of the coffee table. I think for a minute, adjust my feet, and think, Dear Diary, but I write:

> *Dearest Maggie, I'm letting those around me set the tempo of my mood. I know better than that. I can do better. I deserve better. I need to trust my instincts of who I am. Lately, I have misplaced that trust, but I am determined to find it again. Only, I wish it wasn't so hard.*

With that I close the book and lean back on the sofa. Finally, I have written my first entry—no explanation, no detail of the situation, just the rawness of it.

It's a small accomplishment in comparison to the many difficult things I did as a child abuse investigator. It is an accomplishment nonetheless: something I need, so I can feel that my life isn't spinning completely out of control.

A sip of coffee, a deep breath, and I reaffirm the decision to attend the concert, with or without Joseph. I feel liberated making a decision not based on what someone else does.

Maybe I was wrong to think I could operate on instinct when I came back to California. In truth, I have to admit I lost my way long before Maggie died. I have to "own" my own destiny and my own spirit.

The small act of deciding to get on with my life has given me a slight sense of who I am again. It is tentative, and I know it is. It seems to me that it should have taken more than writing in my diary, and more than deciding to attend the concert. The constant gut ache I have felt since Joseph's return subsides to a barely detectable dull pain. I will survive this, too.

~~~

It has been nearly a week since I sent the note to Joseph. He's had time to receive it and respond, at least by phone. He hasn't made the effort. Regardless, he should have called by now if he planned to spend Valentine's Day together.

I give my tickets to Mother Elizabeth and Sister Theresa. The sisters can sit with Karen. I want, or maybe need, space of my own, so I purchase a single ticket for myself. It's a good cause; I don't mind spending the money for a ticket.

I am surprised I don't feel worse about his silence. Maybe I'm accepting his mood as my reality. It isn't like I have a choice.

~~~

With my stadium blanket and thermos of coffee by the door, I pull on my coat to leave just as the doorbell rings.

"Joseph!" I whisper.

My betraying heart beats quicker. In an instant I am forgiving all the pain and confusion. The constant dull gut ache turns to excited butterflies. I take a deep breath just before flinging open the door with open-arm anticipation.

A gangly florist-delivery kid presents me with a box of long-stemmed roses accompanied by a big grin. The grin alone is worth the generous tip. Quickly, I put the flowers in water, set the crystal vase on the table, and leave for the concert. At least Joseph didn't forget Valentine's Day entirely.

~~~

There is an amazing number of people who came to the Hollywood Bowl on a cold Thursday night. The brisk Santa Ana wind cuts through the open amphitheater.

Nebraska taught me what winter cold was—below zero wind chill for days on end. I managed that, I can manage this. I pull my gloves out of my pockets where they have been since the last time I wore this coat in Nebraska over a year ago, and wrap the wool scarf more securely around my neck. This is nothing.

There is an infectious excitement in the crowd. Perhaps, it is the act of doing something as wild as an outdoor concert in the middle of the winter—to do a good deed. It is, after all, for a good cause. Whatever it is, soon I am infected too.
~~~

The lively music begins abruptly when the master of ceremonies comes out in a tuxedo, looking very Hollywood. It feels good to be home and to have a feeling of belonging.

The performers come and go. There is a group singing Rat Pack songs convincingly well. The artists are singing better than their usual best tonight because it is a gift to abused children. Raising awareness is nearly as good as raising money. This is doing both.

Haunting statistics appear on the screens on either side of the stage. Too bad they can't show the photos of the things I've seen: the battered bodies, the broken spirits, the images that haunt my dreams, the nightmares that keep me from going to bed any sooner that I absolutely must. The donations would more than triple, if people saw what I have seen.

Ann Zimmerman appears on stage just before intermission. Not that I have missed Nebraska, but I feel a connectedness of having met Ann before. It's like a friend from the dark days of my self-imposed exile has stepped out into the light of the stage, merging my time in Nebraska with my real life in California.

Ann sings several of my favorite songs, including, of course, "Absolute Zero." I lean back in my seat, shut my eyes, and softly sing along with each of them.

After intermission comes an endless list of A-list performers. Some say a few words before they before they sing, others don't. Either way, this is an incredible "feel-good" evening.

~~~

When I flip on the light switch, the roses on the table are the first thing I see. Still beaming with the energy from the concert, I touch the button on the CD player. "Absolute Zero" fills the air. I pause at the eeriness of the coincidence.

Without forethought, I pull one of the roses from its vase and sing into it like a velvety microphone. Stage-strutting around the room.

♪♪Absolute Zero...no loving embrace...♪♪ I sing to the movie posters on the wall, then return to the vase to sing the chorus to the audience of roses. I am as passionate with my concert as anyone. I put everything I have into singing, without regard for the hour or my neighbors. I feel better, silly maybe, but better. A little worse for the wear, the long-stem microphone is returned to the vase.

In my haste to leave, I didn't glance at the card. Now, I study it. It is a nice gesture, but perhaps an afterthought on his part. His note simply says, "Happy Valentine's Day," and it isn't his handwriting.

At least he remembered, I'll give him that much. The evening and my own private concert with the roses dispersed the malice I felt. It's a
~~~

relief to release my pent-up feelings, something I never did well enough when I was a child abuse investigator.

The coffee tastes better than it has for days. I pull my feet up to the coffee table, and reach for my new companion, my diary.

> *Dearest Maggie, Despite the resistance to acknowledge my confusion, anger, and hurt-owning those emotions seems to have taken away their power to dictate subsequent responses in me. Strangely, for the first time in weeks, I feel confidence and inner strength returning, perhaps even a sense of peace. I need to trust myself more.*

It would seem this was indeed a benefit concert. My spirit has benefited from the evening. It's good Karen invited me to attend. I enjoy the absence of feeling wobbly. The gut ache retreats for the first time in what feels like ages. Perhaps tonight I can sleep.

~~~

When I call Karen to thank her for telling me about the concert, she seems confused because Mother Elizabeth and Sister Theresa used the tickets she gave me. Maybe I should have warned her, but it didn't occur to me then. I explain I was going solo and gave the two tickets to the nuns since they travel in pairs. I laugh freely at the Catholic joke, even though it isn't necessarily true these days.

Karen laughs. "I'll tell Mother Elizabeth you said that!"

I'm not scared. After all, she laughed too. That makes her a sister in the sin. Ready to be serious, I begin with the second reason I called.

"Karen, I want to bounce something off of you when you have time." Without expecting to spill my guts, I admit, "Joseph asked me to go to Ireland with him...he's leaving...for good, I think." I sweeten the deal: "I will throw in Chinese takeout for lunch."

"I was going to say 'No,' until you mentioned Chinese food." She follows her answer with another mischievous laugh.

I pick up our food while Karen traverses the freeways. She arrives just as I'm unpacking the little white takeout boxes. I offer her a plate and chopsticks.

Karen takes the chopsticks, but declines the plate. "It is nice out. Let's go to the beach and eat." She smiles, knowing I cannot resist the suggestion. I grab my beach blanket and we are out the door.

The sun is warm. The sand is manicured. They drag something behind a tractor that churns the sand, leaving it soft and silky-smooth. It may be that there is some ecological benefit to the procedure besides collecting trash and debris; all I know is, it looks fresh and welcoming. Previous high tide lines are erased, along with the footprints of all of the
~~~

people who came before us. What's left of today is the most recent high tide mark and our footprints.

Karen and I position ourselves out of reach of the spray from the incoming tide. We poke at the contents of the cartons with our chopsticks. A few seagulls stand watch, ready to take anything we leave behind or toss in their direction.

Karen begins, "So, what is this about going to Ireland?"

"I'm not sure what he's asking. I don't necessarily sense he is working up to a marriage proposal."

Rather than ask twenty questions like most people do, Karen repositions herself for a more direct view of me, but continues working her chopsticks.

"Okay. Tell me your thoughts," she says, picking at a bean sprout, then looking at me intently once she captures the morsel.

"The invitation is flattering. I have no ideas what he is asking me, but he is leaving." I pause to take another bite. "I think the timing is off for me, and forcing things never works." I study her eyes for a clue to her perception of my thoughts. It's an awkward moment. Quickly, I poke at my food again.

Karen says nothing. She gives me a go-on-with-it silence.

"I think he should get settled before I visit." The sound of my tentative voice distresses me.

Taking another bite, Karen offers a listening nod.

"Besides, I can't get away right now." I am not being honest. I hate being so vulnerable. I look directly at her. "No, the truth is, he didn't say visit, and moving with him doesn't feel right either."

"No, I suppose not," she agrees. "You have to live the life you believe, or you will come to believe the life you live." She smiles with her clever play on words—the exact ones Father Herber used at Mass last week.

I tilt my head and let her words marinate for a while. "My morals may be a moot issue. I haven't seen Joseph since the day he returned."

There, I said it.

I take a deep breath, "He sent roses on Valentine's Day. They arrived just as I was leaving for the concert. I expect to see him before he leaves." Anyone can pick up the phone and order flowers to be delivered. He didn't do anything all that special. My appetite wanes.

For a fleeting moment, Karen's brow wrinkles. "I thought you two were becoming 'close' before he left?"

"So did I." My eyes water with the admission. "Truthfully, his behavior devastated me. I don't understand it. He's different now." I feel my cheeks grow hot with embarrassment as I speak. Ordinarily, I would hold back a confession like that.

"Different, how?" Karen sets aside her dinner, focusing her full attention on my words. The seagulls notice and take a hurried step forward, but abruptly stop when she waves them away.

I take another sobering breath. I pause to find the words to describe his behavior, but fail. "He hasn't spent *any* time with me, not even a phone call."

Hurt is beginning to sound in my voice. My throat tightens. If I say any more, I'll probably cry. Not just about Joseph, but about all the losses: the loss of the idea of romance in my life; Maggie; my parents; my career; five years lost in Nebraska; and, ultimately, losing my way in life in the process of it all.

"Perhaps you're right to wait. The timing doesn't seem right, does it?" Karen confirms my thoughts. She reaches to briefly touch my hand and says softly, "You will know when to go. Trust yourself."

I nod and force a smile.

Karen is right. It is a matter of timing, as much as anything else. I take a deep breath, it wavers, I let it go. "I need this place—at least for now. I can't leave yet. There's things I must do, things I can only do here."

"What things?"

I resist the urge to poke at my food with my chopsticks as a diversion. Slowly, I begin, searching for the words to explain my confused feelings.

"When Judge Jones ruled contrary to the facts of the case—I, I lost my innocence, my belief in the system. I mean, until then I thought if I did my job well, the system would work as it should."

Karen listens with a slight nod of understanding.

"I worked hard to be a good social worker." I stop because my eyes are filling with tears and my voice follows suit.

"You did nothing wrong. The fault was with Judge Jones. You *are* a good social worker. You are the quintessential social worker."

"Thank you. But when the little girl died, I became so angry, I was consumed with anger." I look straight at her again. "I am so sorry. I shouldn't have taken my anger out on you."

"No, no you didn't—even if you think you did. I understood you weren't angry with me." Karen pronounces a much-needed absolution. I almost feel that I should make the sign of the cross or something.

"I have been wobbly inside since then. The murder scene photos haunt me. I lost my confidence in me, in the system, in everything I believed in." I whisper, "Even my faith in God."

Karen smiles. "If God can withstand the Spanish Inquisition and priests who can't keep their zipper shut—and I think He can—then, He can weather a test of your faith. He hasn't gone anywhere."

It's a Catholic thing, who else would mention the Spanish Inquisition? I know what she means and it isn't that I am insignificant. It's that—

She interrupts my thoughts, "As for you, 'you' haven't gone anywhere either. You'll find yourself again. You can see beyond the ordinary." She smiles an older, wiser, knowing smile.

"Because of everything else that has happened, it's harder to get a feel for what is going on with Joseph. It is like I've lost my ability to read people, to assess and understand."

"Stay at the beach as long as it takes. You have everything you need. You don't need to do anything more to be worthy of love," she adds, knowing thoughts that I can't express.

Her words and the sound of the waves have silenced my mind. I close my eyes to focus my thoughts and get control of my anxiety, something I perfected when I was a child abuse investigator. At least, I like to think that I perfected it.

The idea of me being worthy of love, despite evidence to the contrary, lingers. It gives me pause. I feel like crying. For a moment, I almost believe I will get my instincts, focus, and confidence back again.

Karen moves the conversation to safer ground to allow me an escape, if I want one.

But I bring it back. I think aloud more than talk to her. "I think I will leave my options open with Joseph, delay the trip for now, without burning any bridges."

"Always a wise choice to keep the bridges. That way you don't have to swim the river." Then Karen resumes her meal.

"Yes," I agree thoughtfully.

I hope to wade through Joseph's cryptic invitation, my churning emotions of self-discovery and forgiveness for being solely human when life demands so much more. No one likes to feel out of control, but reaching out and grabbing control is another thing entirely.

"Perhaps I am afraid I will lose him." I risk the honesty. "In the final analysis he either loves me or not, regardless of my decision."

"Love complicates life, doesn't it?" Karen adds.

Her tone sounds personal. I don't think her comment has as much to do with me, as it does with her. I know she divorced almost four years ago while I was in Nebraska. I missed that part of her life. Her comment sounds philosophical, but I suspect that's only a ruse. There is more than philosophy in her eyes. I wonder what her comment really means.

My legs are beginning to ache from the way I am sitting, and from the damp sand. I reposition myself, becoming aware again of the breaking waves. Most of my food is gone. I offer the leftovers to the watchful seagulls. They become noisy with excitement.

Karen rouses from her silence. We collect the blanket and put our trash in the barrel on the way back to my apartment. For the first time I can remember in my life, I didn't read my fortune or eat the cookie. I need something more. I need the present, not the past, and not a future that may very well turn out to be fiction.

Karen hadn't given me advice, but her company made me feel less alone. It made me hunger for the confidence I once had.

After Karen leaves, I sit on the sofa, drinking coffee and thinking about the complexities of life. Karen's gift of a much-needed absolution marinates in my thoughts. I reach for my diary.

> *Dear Maggie, There's freedom in not needing to have answers to every question. Sometimes it's enough to be open to the natural unfolding of life, unforced, un-tampered with, bravely. I don't feel the least bit "superhuman," and maybe it isn't necessary that I do.*

My thoughts consider the life I have and how far I've come. Because of my mother's fatal struggle with breast cancer, leaving me alone, I poured myself into my studies. Not quite alone, it was the revolving door at my house. Someone in my mother's extended family managed to drop by daily, as if they had concocted a schedule of visits among themselves. I finished high school at an accelerated rate. I remember how falsely confident I was when I entered college at sixteen.

I knew my aunts and uncles and older cousins were checking on me. Frankly, I liked their visits. They came to help me move when I sold my childhood home for a more practical apartment. I didn't have time to maintain the upkeep on a house and attend college. Besides, it seemed time to have a place sans the memories of losing both parents.

Back then, I didn't know enough to be intimidated by the university setting. I was numb with youth and artificial strength from hanging tough during Mom's last days. With nothing else to fill my life, both sessions of summer school became a matter of routine. I lived on my trust fund allowance. All of my monthly expenses were paid by my trustee. It was an uncomplicated time—not at all like now.

By eighteen, I had earned enough college credits for my professor to recommend me for an intern position with the Child Protection Unit. It wasn't the internship of my choice, but I knew at my age I had to take what was offered. In the pecking order, I was definitely at the bottom.

My job was mostly slave labor for the real social workers. It wasn't pleasant. I vowed when I became a social worker, I wouldn't behave as they had toward me.

My silence during the internship paid off. I typed their reports and did their filing. Both activities gave me access to the files full of the real inner workings of social work. By running errands and acting as their document courier, I began to make contacts of my own in the field. The contacts proved to be one of my most valuable tools in later years, besides my education.

Most of my family attended my graduation. Their support in my accomplishment touched me deeply.

By the time there was a real social work position open in the department, I had passed the entrance exam and was accepted in graduate school. Karen's predecessor hired me when her first choice for the position took a better job in the private sector. Regardless of being the second choice, I had a real social work position, and my life began.

With little else to distract me, I threw myself into work and school. There was no time for romance. It wasn't something I missed. Perhaps, because my father was killed in an accident when I was six years old and I grew up with a woman who had no romance in her life, I expected none in my own.

Hard work paid meager dividends until the governor sent Karen to clean up our department. We were in desperate need of Karen's guiding hand. Because of her, the department staff began to thrive. Finally, I had a job worth having.

Little did I know then she would direct me to my next job worth having, Spirit of Hope, and that she would absolve me of the guilt and anger that robbed me of my life for the five years I was in Nebraska.

~~~
~~~

~ CHAPTER 6 ~

Shamelessly in Love, Again

After work there is a message from Joseph on my answering machine. For a moment, I think he is a coward to call when he is certain I am at work. But the sound of his accent cuts through my resolve. In reality, he probably gave no thought one way or the other to the time of day.

It takes no effort whatsoever to immediately return his call. I am shameless in my delight to hear his voice—his soft, manly accent melts like milk chocolate. He offers what I take as a peace offering, dinner at my favorite R&B restaurant in Hollywood. How can I possibly resist?

We set the dinner date for tomorrow night. Ah, I take a deep breath, ready to forgive all of his transgressions, imagined or real.

~~~

Work is the farthest thing from my mind. However, little Shasta's morning greeting pulls me back to reality. Before I know it, I am humming to myself immersed in working with my family-of-the-week.

Monica has a job interview on Friday. She is jittery with hope. Her husband has been working for two months, and she is understandably nervous and excited about finding a job. They are one step farther from being homeless, one step closer to being members of society again. She wants my opinion on what to wear or, at least, my company while she decides.

"You'll watch the children while I go?" she verifies for the millionth time.

"Yes, definitely. I have a new book to read to them, then we'll play on the swing." I offer proof I am prepared to keep my word.

"Should we do another practice interview?"

"Oh, no! You're ready. You'll do just fine—I guarantee it. You could conduct the interview!" I laugh.

She contributes an excited, nervous giggle.

"If I find work we can get a place of our own that much sooner." Monica jabbers a mile a minute, full of excitement and hope for the future.

"I'm sure you will find something." I encourage her optimism while keeping open that there is something out there, if not this job.

Her confidence is slowly rising to the occasion at hand. "What do you think? How does this look?" she asks, turning around like a model, only more hesitant.

"Yes, I like this one better than the other," I agree. "Something is missing though."
~~~

"What? What! These are my two best outfits." Her voice is worried.

"The dress is fine. It's just—" I start to say, but Monica interrupts.

"What? Just what?" she demands.

"The dress is perfect. How are you going to wear your hair?" I pinpoint the problem, her hair.

She pulls her dark brown, wavy hair stylishly away from her face. "Something like this. Will this work?" Her voice is uncertain.

"Beautifully!" I remove the jewel-colored scarf from around my neck and tie her hair back while she holds it. "There! Just needed a touch of color." I stand back, so she can look in the mirror.

She smiles.

So do I.

"See how the rich colors look against your hair? You're beautiful!" I turn her shoulders perpendicular to the mirror, so she can have a better view. In fact, she is beautiful. Wisps of her hair frame her face in a way that smooths some of the hardship she has endured.

She smiles as she turns back and forth to examine every view in the mirror. The colors in the scarf are attractive. And the cool khaki color of her dress is a nice contrast with her warm Latin-brown skin.

I wish all of our families' problems could be solved this easily.

Monica touches the scarf, hesitates, then removes it and hands it toward me.

Gently, I close her fingers around the scarf and push her hand back. "No, you keep it. It's a gift—for luck," I whisper.

Monica hesitates again.

Sensing she might feel it is charity I say, "Really, it's for luck. Something borrowed, something blue. Something-something—"

"That's for weddings." She laughs.

"It's for luck, and luck is luck, right?"

"Gracias," she says softly, as she carefully fingers the silk scarf.

Sometimes it isn't the big things that work so right and feel so good. Social work is about helping individuals traverse through society in a socially effective manner. The goals are theirs, as well as the effort. We are simply trained, resourceful facilitators.

At the CPS Unit, there was a great deal of stress for the social workers who were to facilitate behavioral changes and teach new, appropriate social skills, i.e., not abusing children. In some ways, I was lucky to only have to confirm the problem, not mend the wounded or work with the abuser. But the Spirit of Hope people have easier problems. They are less damaged, more focused on reaching their goal. A silk scarf is nearly magical.

I wish I knew real magic for the homeless. Sometimes they made poor choices that led them into homelessness. Just as often, they were the victims of economics, and didn't have the education or resources to weather the storm. Often they had little or no warning of plant layoffs. They found themselves suddenly unemployed with inadequate resources at their disposal, an unresponsive society with ineffective leadership not committed to help people who can no longer contribute toward their political aspirations. Then, it was downhill from there.

Everyone knows that the Food Stamp program was designed by the Department of Agriculture to stimulate the farm economy. Feeding people is only a by-product. It's still true today. The program doesn't allow for laundry soap, toothpaste, deodorant, shampoo and other items needed to be presentable for job interviews or to stay healthy. It would have provided those items, if the poor were the program's primary interest. It would, if we really cared.

A silk scarf is powerful magic. Monica looks one last time at her image in the mirror. It's too bad the system wasn't designed to spare her from what she has endured. Once her family had no address, many social entitlements were no longer available to them. Before long, their self-esteem was so deficient, it wouldn't matter whether they had clean clothes or not, they couldn't possibly land a job worth having.

Spirit of Hope is changing that reality for a dozen families at a time, and I am glad to be a small part of the process. More and more, the homeless families take up residence in my heart. I am privileged to know Monica, Shasta, and the others.

The hours pass quickly. On the way home, I remember my date. I had become accustomed to Joseph not being around, so I forgot he had quietly slipped back into my life. I feel as excited as on our first date. Maybe, even more. I have missed his sense of humor, thick-accented voice, ready smile, and easy laugh. It won't be long now.

Coffee brews while I shower. The edges of the mirror are still misty after shooting my blow-dryer at the center to clear the condensation. I stand in front of the clear spot, framed by the softer edges, listening to the music from the radio. By the second cup of coffee, I have made my selection of what to wear, dried my hair, and am well under way with my makeup.

During the drive to Hollywood, Joseph says he managed to sell his house in one week. Most of his cases at work have been closed by the simple matter of meeting with his clients, then filing a Motion to Withdraw. To make it seem even more like an omen that he should go, the bulk of his clients elected to transfer to someone within the firm.

Dinner goes well. It's like we're back in time when our relationship was new. He wants to see me again on Friday. I crave to be near him at any cost. Without hesitation I accept wholeheartedly. I'm shameless in my forgiveness of his neglect.

The next two weeks Joseph and I spend every free moment together. Effortlessly I am remembering why I fell in love with him. He has an easy way about him. He is charming, witty, and more attentive than usual. We spend quite a bit of time walking the beach or sitting, watching the sun sizzle into the horizon. I feel like royalty, the Queen of Hearts. And when he touches me...

Joseph never mentions his return. I never mention my decision to stay here, at least until he is settled in Ireland. He never asks for my answer. Which is fine, since I still don't clearly understand what he was asking. I am perfectly happy to ignore it. Life is perfect. No point in rocking the boat.

~~~

One evening as we sit on the beach enjoying the sounds of the ocean, there is a fairy-tale feeling to the fog coming across the water. It has already engulfed Catalina Island and is heading toward the mainland. The gulls are settling down. Most of the people on the beach have gone. Joseph and I plan to walk out on the pier and have dinner at Ruby's Diner, but we haven't made it that far yet.

"Katey," Joseph says in his thick Irish accent, pausing to look out at the water.

I don't care what he is going to say next. The way he says my name sends shivers through my body. All he needs is a one-word vocabulary, as long as that word is "Katey."

He leans toward me and his mouth finds mine. My eyes close and I am swept away to some other world, a world far removed from the world I know all too intimately as a social worker. He leans down on his elbow, pulling me down to the sand beside him, kissing.

"Shall we skip dinner?" he whispers between kisses.

My body says "Yes," but my mind comes out of the fog.

"Joseph, we need to talk," I say softly, returning his last kiss gently at the corner of his mouth.

"Haven't we talked enough?" He responds, pulling my body closer to his.

All I can think of is, *You must be delusional. No, we haven't talked. You have ignored me for more weeks than I can count.* Who the hell does he think he is? He was doing fine until that comment. Damn him.

The damp sand and the awareness that we have only spent the last two weeks together since January keeps reality painfully near my consciousness. I have to ignore my body and heart, and listen to my head.

The last two weeks have been delightful, making it easy to disregard the reality since his return, but not quite enough. Carefully, I pull away from him. I'm a responsible person by nature, despite my best
~~~

efforts to be otherwise. His thoughtless words have brought back the memory of the first day he returned. We were having a good time until then. Unfortunately, now I am firmly back in reality. Damn him.

"Joseph, we need to talk about Ireland. I think it is best if you go and get settled before I come." I push on with what I want to say, or rather, what needs to be said before I lose my willpower and give in to his lingering touch. "I think that would be best."

He pulls away. He fires at me, "I object," completely breaking any hope of regaining the romantic mood.

We move farther apart as I sit up.

"Overruled," I interrupt his impatient tone with one of my own. He might as well know that I can hold my own—if he wants to engage a battle, fine. Fine!

I don't know what his Irish women are like, but he has met his match in me. I'm Scots-Irish and Welsh, and have the instinct of three ethnicities on my side. Besides, I'm NOT intimidated by lawyers. He can save his lawyer lingo for someone else. I refuse to foolishly dismiss the pain I endured by his moodiness. I have commitments at Spirit of Hope that I can't walk away from on a whim. I have responsibilities to myself.

"I'm not abandoning everything to go," I say softly, but firmly.

He lets out a deep breath as he rolls over on his back. After a minute, he sits up. "I know, Katey. I know," he says, looking toward the sound of the incoming waves.

"You know?" I ask. His defenseless tone softens mine as well.

"You have not talked about coming with me."

I feel betrayed by his comment. How dare him! After all, he was the one who didn't contact me for a month after his return, and only barely on Valentine's Day. I'm not sure the flowers on Valentine's Day count. He never responded to my invitation to the concert. He hasn't talked about his trip, the places he'd show me and the people I'd meet, his friends and family. Frankly, we hadn't talked about us at all.

Whatever the Irish celebration of Valentine's Day is, he has been in the States enough years to know what it means to American women. The roses were nice, very nice as a matter of fact, but they were insufficient for the circumstances. I would have preferred his company. What an arrogant ass he is!

These two weeks of questioning my decision to stay here are suddenly washed over with waves of our reality. He hasn't even seen that his aloofness is what convinced me to wait and go later. I let out a deep breath. I am not going to fight with him over something he clearly doesn't understand. Lawyers!

"Joseph, you need to get settled first. I will come this summer for a visit." I turn to watch the waves.

"A visit?" he questions my choice of words.

"Well, what did you expect?" I challenge cautiously.

"Well, ah—"

"Let's go eat before we are robbed of this evening." I stand up. I've rescued him. That was his chance to clarify that he meant marriage, and he didn't take it. Whatever else was in his invitation to Ireland, marriage was not part of it. He's offering nothing and expecting me to give up everything.

The way Joseph brushes the sand off his jeans, I can tell he is smoldering. As long as he keeps his anger in check, I can keep my disappointment under control, too. With luck, we can finish the evening on civil terms.

I know he will be leaving soon. I don't want what we once had—the love of my life, however short lived it seems to be—to end with fighting. I say nothing more about Ireland.

We walk to the pier and out to the diner for dinner above the restless waves. I hardly notice the pair rollerblade past us in the mist, the worn planks on the pier deck, or the fishermen along the railing for an evening catch. I am in the oddest state of numbness. I've never felt this way before.

Apparently Joseph decided to check his attitude at the door. We ease into a booth by the windows and a safer topic of conversation.

I think it is an okay, but not spectacular, end to the day.

~~~
~~~

~ CHAPTER 7 ~

Lawyers and Their Ability to Complicate My Life

Inevitably the day comes when Joseph announces he is leaving on March 17th. He doesn't mention about me not going. On the other hand, he doesn't restate his invitation either. Maybe he senses my desire not to engage in a fight about it during our last days together, and silently agrees.

More than Joseph can imagine, I understand his drive to go home. It's like my consuming drive to come home from Nebraska. I'm still not ready to leave again. Hopefully, I will recognize when it is time to leave; then again, perhaps I will never leave. But I do understand how the mythological sirens taunt, "Go home."

Maggie was a large part of my adjustment to returning home. As much as I would like to help Joseph adjust, it doesn't seem right for either of us. Certainly, I am not the one with the answers he is seeking. It is only a slim likelihood things would be any different between us in Ireland than they are here at the moment.

My thoughts of Joseph are fond today. I do wish my emotions would make up their mind, and stay one way or the other. I am staying here. I am definitely staying in California.

I may weaken my resolve when I see him leave and decide to go with him. As a preparatory move, I set an appointment with Mr. Bradford, the trustee of my trust account. He is a lawyer who was a classmate and close friend of my father's in high school or college, I am not sure which.

Ever since I completed graduate school, not counting bartending, I have had an income of my own, and lived within my budget. Because I didn't need the trust money, Mr. Bradford has been reinvesting my allowance, and I suspect he has done well for me. My own investing in the stock market has done all right, so I expect better than that from someone who actually knows what he is doing. There should be plenty of mad money available for a trip to Ireland and living expenses for a couple of weeks or longer this summer, if I can't bear to let him leave without me.

~~~

Crystal looks up from her computer when I come into Mr. Bradford's office. "Hello, Miss McKenzie. Go in, he's waiting for you."

"Thank you." I never have to wait to see him. Either he is very organized and on time for his appointments, or he doesn't have much of a law practice. Who knows?
~~~

The balding lawyer seated at a huge mahogany desk looks up from the documents he is reading "Come in, Katey."

His office is in an old bank building. This part looks as if it could have been the bank president's office. There are many obligatory law books, statutes, and treatises filling the shelves, overflowing to every horizontal surface within his reach. A statue of Lady Justice stands on a side table, where she had been moved some time ago to make way for more books.

"Katey, how are you? Have a seat, have a seat."

"I'm well, thank you."

The woodwork of his desk is magnificently crafted. I long to touch it, a trait from my father's architectural genes. He couldn't keep his hands off of a fine piece of wood.

"I see you have returned to paradise. Nebraska too cold? What is it that warrants a visit, Katey?"

A fat legal file with my name in bold type on the tab lays on the middle of his desk:

Kathryn Keavy McKenzie

Keavy is Gaelic for Grace. It's obvious that my parents reached back in our family for names. Our roots are deep, but reach across the Atlantic.

It should make sense to Mr. Bradford that I would want to go see the old country. I'll use that as my pitch.

He looks up briefly while I talk. Otherwise, he reads through my file.

"Is everything all right, Kate?"

"I need funds for a trip to Ireland...a couple of weeks' worth or...more."

Mr. Bradford frowns. He doesn't seem pleased about funds request. He isn't very subtle on the matter. But he is a different sort of person, not that any lawyer is normal like the rest of us.

I tell myself that at the end of the day, it is my money. I know I will win this one, so I wait patiently, and smile sweetly each time Mr. Bradford looks up.

It isn't really necessary for me to make the trip to sign documents for the funds. I just thought I could plead my case better in person. I have been careful not to mention Joseph. Hopefully, he doesn't notice something is missing from my story about taking the trip. I state my intentions fairly well, but all the while I feel as if I am asking for an extension to my curfew.

Not finding the document he wants, he disappears. The file room is the former walk-in bank vault. He roots around in there a minute and returns with an additional fat file. I am surprised how quickly he returns. I can see into the vault from my side of his desk. Frankly, it doesn't look all that organized. I don't know how he finds anything.

Still watching this eccentric man who had been my father's friend —wait! Something catches my attention. When he opened the second file, a small manila envelope fell out. Something gold and shiny peeked out the edge of the envelope's unsealed flap.

"What is that?" I ask, pointing in the direction of the envelope, file, and his desktop clutter.

"What is what?" he asks, looking away from the document with his glasses poised near the end of his large nose.

"In that envelope," I say, rising and pointing more strongly.

He scans the disorganized pile in front of him, sifting through the papers while inadvertently sliding them over the envelope.

"There! You just covered it with those documents!" I lean over his desk, reaching toward the mound of papers. Just as I touch the stack, he waves off my reconnaissance. I sit on the edge of my chair ready to re-engage my efforts.

He gives in and uncovers the envelope, tilts it, dumps the contents on the desk, then looks straight at me.

"Ah, sit down, Katey. I suppose it's time for this." He struggles to pick up the delicate chain with his stubby man-size fingers. After three clumsy attempts, he picks up the tiny gold heart, then captures its trailing gold chain with his other hand. He seems satisfied that he has achieved his objective and proudly dangles the necklace toward me.

"The day he signed your trust papers right after you were born, your father left this to hold for you."

I extend a decidedly dainty hand, accentuating all the more the size of his hand. Carefully, I open the heart-shaped locket with my fingernail, revealing the photos inside. The faces are tiny, but I recognize immediately that they are my parents.

"He said it belonged to his mother and gave it to you."

Without giving Mr. Bradford a chance to retrieve it, I fasten the chain around my neck, and settle the heart in its place near my heart. Though I don't expect it, there is no reason to tempt him to take it back by examining it now. I will study it once I get it safely home.

Rather than attempt to reclaim the locket, he offers a ring. "This is your father's wedding ring. Your mother gave it to me before she died."

I slip the ring on my finger. It feels cool and heavy. I feel my eyes burning with mounting tears and blink slowly. Luckily, the tears remain in their place, but my eyelashes are wet.

I plan to keep the ring, too. I'll have it sized and wear it as a reminder of who I am in context of my family legacy. I look at Mr. Bradford with a sense of thankfulness that he was my parents' friend.

"This is your mother's ring. Your father gave it to your mother after she told him you were 'on the way.'" He hands me the second, much smaller ring full of diamonds.

I slip the ring on my left ring finger. It is a perfect fit. The tiny diamonds sparkle like stars. That's it. I can't hold back the tears.

It is obvious that my tears make Mr. Bradford uncomfortable. He seems uncertain about what to do with them. He fumbles with a tissue box and nearly launches it at me in his hurried, awkward attempt to offer assistance.

I startle with the threat of the projectile, even if it is a harmless tissue box. "Thank you. Thank you, Mr. Bradford." I wipe my tears and dab the end of my nose.

After a few minutes, I collect my wits about me and request another appointment to finish at a later date. He decides to transfer the money and save me a return trip. I have more than enough to think about, and want to think alone, which seems to suit Mr. Bradford just fine.

~~~

On the drive home, I take Father's ring to the jeweler for sizing. They clean and check Mother's ring while I wait. I hate leaving Father's ring with them, but I ignore the feelings. At least I have the locket and Mom's ring to keep with me.

Out in the sunlight, Mother's ring sparkles as I wiggle my fingers and admire it in the sunlight. It actually feels comfortable on my finger, not at all foreign.

The thoughtfulness of the jewelry threatens to overcome my composure again. I wonder when Mr. Bradford would have given them to me if they hadn't fallen out of the file? I bet he had forgotten they were there. Well, who cares, they're mine now. And I love them.

For the balance of the trip home, I can't keep my fingers off the tiny gold heart around my neck. By second nature, my hand keeps reaching to touch it. Its metal is cool and a nice size to fiddle with between my finger and thumb. My breath is slow and shallow. I feel peaceful. The usual freeway traffic doesn't bother me, I'm driving my little treasures home. The heart locket has a design etched on it that I feel with my fingernail. I can't wait to get home and examine my gifts further.

~~~

Quickly, I exit the car and pursue the sanctuary of my apartment. Tossing my jacket on the sofa, I reach to unclasp the necklace. As I do, I see the blinking light on my answering machine. I look away, planning to ignore it, but years at the CPS unit taught me to immediately answer my messages. Maggie might be on-call and need help, I think automatically. The instant I touch the button, I remember Maggie is dead. It is too late, the machine gives forth its message.

"Katey. It's Joseph. Call me back and I'll take you to dinner."

The machine beeps, and resets for the next call. I stand still, thinking, barely breathing. I love Joseph, but I need to be alone tonight. I don't want to risk fighting with him. He is high maintenance lately. My fingers rise to my lips, as I think about the message, then they slip down to find the little locket again. No, tonight is mine.

In a heartbeat, I grab my jacket and keys, and head out the door to the beach. From my front step, I see the ocean is calm this afternoon. I hesitate, wanting seclusion where I cannot be found. My beach is the obvious place for anyone, especially Joseph, to find me. I turn and walk toward my car.

I ease through the gears and settle into fifth gear in the flow of the traffic. Almost from instinct, I drive north to Leo Carrillo Beach where my mother took me as a child. She called it "Father's beach."

"Father's beach," I say softly. This migratory drive to revisit Father's beach, where I will be alone with my thoughts, is comforting. As the beach comes into view from Pacific Coast Highway, I feel emotion wash over me. "Father's beach."

The parking lot is on the opposite side of PCH from the beach. There is a walkway beneath the highway to access the ocean. The sound of the waves breaking on the rocks is not to be taken for granted by the dullness of familiarity. It brings a sharpness to my senses with water and noisy birds perching on the rocks in the ocean, screeching when the waves hit and disturb them.

At the edge of the beach, I pause to watch the water rush toward me and crash over the boulders. Father's beach is rugged in contrast to mine, perhaps more manly. The waves break a second time, launching foamy white spray into the air, raining down onto the sand in front of me, making a dollop sound I haven't heard in years.

Old memories return. Like a child preparing to run inside a swinging jump rope, I judge the rhythm of the water flow, so I can pass the rock formation that runs its fingers into the Pacific. Moving closer, I pose to run when the next wave goes out. Just when the water begins receding, I run like my life depends on getting past before the next incoming wave arrives.

On the other side of the boulders, out of the water's reach, I turn back and laugh at the waves just as they break and a light spray rains down on me. I remember running through that pass holding Mother's hand when I was a child. She always turned and laughed too. When Father was here he carried me on his shoulder out of the water's reach.

Turning away from the ocean, I walk to the rocky cliff ahead, carefully searching for the hidden entry of the cave that opens onto the next beach. The opening is obscured by an outcropping of rock.

The passage in the cave is damp. It fills completely with water at high tide, blocking a retreat to safety. There are barnacles low on the cave wall near a tide pool. Not nearly as agile over the wet rock floor as when I was a child escaping pirates, I occasionally reach out to touch the moist wall to steady myself. Carefully making my way through the cave, I am surprised by the fishy smell I don't remember from before.

As soon as I clear the cave, Mother's favorite rock formation is in view. We would sit sunning like a couple of seals on the large, flat rock, watching the kelp floating on the swells while talking about Father. Here is the place I seek to savor my parents' memory.

There are several pelicans sitting on boulders farther out in the water. They seem to be soaking up the last of the sun's rays for the day. What a life! Certainly, they must have their problems, but spending the entire day at the beach every day can't be bad. They are entertaining to watch when waves splash over their rock, disturbing them. They stand, act indignant, then settle back where they were before the wave came.

Father's beach is beautiful. Memories of this place with my mother and father are sweet. I miss Father. I miss what might have been if that police car had not run into my parents' car while in pursuit of someone else. I imagine what it would have been like to have a father. He would have been here while my mother received chemotherapy, and when she died. I miss him. I miss them both.

I examine the finger that will soon wear Father's ring. I nod approval of the gifts they left for me. Memories sail me away.

I can't afford to forget to watch the stealthily rising water, or the tide will cut off my exit. This isn't a good place to swim for shore because the force of the waves pound a swimmer into the rocks like a puppet. More importantly, I don't want to get the pictures wet in my new locket.

Forty-five minutes is all the time the incoming tide allows for my retreat, but it's enough. Waves begin to reach midway up the rock where I am sitting, forcing me to leave my perch between wave crests, wade to the beach, and disappear through the cave. The water level has risen enough that when the waves recede completely, about four inches of water remain on the floor, obscuring the best places to step.

The water at the passage around the protruding Jump Rope Rock is knee-deep at best. I miscalculate the increase in frequency of the incoming waves. Midway past the wall of rocks, a wave catches me squarely. I grab for my necklace to protect it. The wave is chest high, the force causes me to nearly lose my footing and get slammed against the rocks.

When the wave breaks on me, foam and spray leap above my head, showering ocean water down upon me. The Pacific is cold anytime of year, but especially in early March. It takes my breath away, and I gasp in some of the spray. I am startled and chilled to the bone.

My shoes are soaked and full of wet, abrasive sand. They rub against the tender skin on my heels every step back toward the parking lot. As soon as I start my car, I flip the heat on high and slip off my shoes, before pulling my feet inside the car.

The heat is beginning to come through the vent, and I wiggle my toes in the direction of the warm blast of air. There is something invigorating about ocean water teeming with life, microscopic and otherwise, that surges life into me with its touch.

No more daydreaming about what might have been; what's real is what counts.

The CD player accepts the disk from my fingers and devours it. I'm in the mood for some sassy jazz. I slip through the gears, watching the miles fade behind me in the rearview mirror as the sax intro plays.

~~~

After I shed my wet clothes, shower, and put on my robe, I examine my locket again. It is dainty and the etched flower is delicate. The photos are small black-and-white photos that are slightly faded, but they are clearly emotion-filled for me. I am relieved they didn't get wet. That was pure luck. From now on, I'll take it off when I go to the beach.

The light is flashing on the answering machine again; I comply with its summons while crunching raw carrot sticks and waiting for my microwave dinner.

It is Joseph again. I return his call, but wave off an opportunity to spend time with him tonight. After his apparent disinterest for weeks, I don't feel compelled to chase after him on demand just because he waltzed back into my life whistling a sweet tune. I am content sitting on the sofa with my feet on the coffee table, listening to music, and eating my TV dinner, minus the television.

It has been a long time since I felt this content. Not that I am always miserable, but content isn't exactly the word I would use to describe my general feelings either. Nonetheless, it feels good to find a bit of peace and to have it come so easy.

~~~

The two diaries, Maggie's and mine, lay near my feet. Should I write in mine or read from Maggie's? A classic dilemma, give or take? Perhaps a bit of both.

I set down my plate and hold my diary and pen, poised and ready for inspiration to strike like a bolt of lightning from the atmosphere. Nothing happens. I wait, ready. No, nothing.

I pick up Maggie's diary, holding it against my chest, hoping osmosis will pour inspiration through me and into my pen. Still, I can think of nothing worth writing that will capture today and its essence.

I allow Maggie's diary to fall open. Even though I have read it through several times, I am pleased to see the entry of the day I returned to California from my self-imposed exile in Nebraska.
She writes:

Kate has come home. I am glad.

"Short and sweet, that's Maggie!" I say aloud. It seems so natural that I named my diary "Maggie." Reading her diary feels like a conduit to communicate with her beyond the grave. I find that connection comforting. I am hoping that naming my diary after her helps make the connection even more real for me.

Quickly, before the moment slips away and eludes me again, I write in my diary:

Dearest Maggie, I have come home!

For me, it isn't the physical homecoming Maggie wrote of; it is the realization that I am deeply connected to this place, this life. I'll try to explain it to Joseph, with the hope that he will understand. Be brave, my love, the truth can't possibly be fatal. You will survive. I reach for the phone to call him.

Joseph must have gone out; at least, he doesn't answer his phone. Rather than pursue him on his cell phone, I'll catch him another time.

Relieved he wasn't home, I head to bed. As I walk past my dresser, I see the new jewelry and can't resist handling the locket one more time before I crawl contentedly between the covers.

~~~
~~~

~ CHAPTER 8 ~

Computers, Baseball, and Lawyers
~ as American as Apple Pie

It was a good day at work. I ease into the traffic and get smoothly though the gears. Relaxing my hands on the steering wheel, I wiggle my fingers, moving Mother's ring back and forth in the ray of light coming through the windshield. I smile. I don't feel as lost and alone any longer.

The other things I have of my parents are sentimental reminders of our life together, but none are as personal as this jewelry. I like having something I can carry with me through my days and nights.

~~~

Finally home, after I quickly change out of my work clothes and into beach clothes, I run up the stairs to Mr. Goldstein's apartment. He is scheduled to return today from a Senior Center trip. I can't wait to tell him about the jewelry.

Mr. Goldstein opens the door with his usual greeting, "Katerina! Come in, come in," he says, motioning me inside. He was unpacking, but is delighted with the interruption and invitation to the beach.

While I wait for him to change his shoes, I remember the first time we went to the beach a year ago. He barely made it across the street and to the edge of the sand before he played out. I nearly had to carry him home. Now, we are walking two miles, one mile in each direction. Imagine that!

Perfectly in stride, we walk down the stairs and head for the beach. Before I tell Mr. Goldstein about the jewelry, I ask about his trip. I have learned that life isn't all about me; I can wait.

"San Diego was good." But he wants to talk about one of the ladies he met on the excursion.

I smile at the possibility of his budding romance.

"Mrs. Levy told me about finding her children." He stops walking and looks me in the eyes, searching for words to express the fullness of his thoughts. "She found two of her children and her brother from the prison camp through the computer." He glances out to the ocean then back at me, as he begins to explain further and to walk again.

The death camp memories are extraordinarily emotional for him. He nearly always wipes a tear and catches his breath whenever he speaks of losing his young children.

"She gave me a name with www on it," he says as he removes a folded slip of paper from his shirt pocket. He stops walking and turns, while handing me the paper: "Katerina, you help me?"
~~~

I take the paper from his eager hand and unfold it. It is a flyer about a website that searches for Holocaust victims and reunites them with family members. I look at him. He is eagerly waiting for my response. Oh, my dear Mr. Goldstein! He must have nearly got out and pushed the bus home with this information in his possession.

"Yes, I can find this on the internet." I smile warmly.

"Good!" He immediately takes my arm and steers me back in the direction of our apartment building. Our walk is concluded for today. His eager, quick steps make it awkward to keep pace with him in the sand. His excitement causes a giggle to rise in my chest, but I don't make a sound, considering the subject.

Once inside my apartment, I toss my jacket over the back of a chair. Mr. Goldstein does the same with his before I can take it from him to hang it in the closet. I power up the computer and a pot of coffee. Mr. Goldstein quickly drags a chair next to mine in front of the computer. He sits, leans forward, his eyes fixed on the monitor going through its start-up regime.

With two cups of coffee in hand, I slip beside him in front of the computer. He sets his coffee aside, uninterested in it. He watches the monitor intensely while I type the web address into the browser. Mr. Goldstein doesn't budge. His gaze is eagerly fixed on the screen.

I explain the home page to him as I look over the basics of the site. It is as he said, a site claiming to reunite persons dispersed because of the Nazi annihilation more than fifty years ago. The sign-up screen asks for extended family names and last known locations in the 1940s. Obviously, they need that information to search their database and to add to it.

The questions make me skeptical. While I print each screen, I explain my reservations to spew forth personal information without knowing about the people responsible for the site. It could be a ruse by a hate group.

Mr. Goldstein fails to disguise his disappointment, but his interest is piqued when I hand him the stack of papers and give him the assignment of completing the information by hand. That will give him a sense of moving forward with his project and give me time to check the website with Keith.

As gently as possible, I explain my intention. "You know better than I, you must be careful about telling people where your European family might be."

"Yes, yes. I know this is true." He looks at the pages, still warm from the laser printer.

"Keith and I worked together for years. I guarantee he is the best detective in California. We can count on him." I smile reassuringly at

Mr. Goldstein and touch his hand for emphasis. "I wouldn't want anything to happen to you or your family."

Mr. Goldstein studies my eyes. His eyes soften, he smiles, and nods agreement.

"Fill out these forms, then we will get them entered on the website as soon as Keith says it's safe."

~~~

Keith arrives at his office just as I phone him. After working together, I know he arrives early. He agrees to have the website checked. He suggests we meet for lunch at a sandwich shop near the police station, so he can tell me what he finds out. It surprises me that he can get the information that quickly, but I trust him to be thorough.

~~~

Maggie and I ate lunch here regularly. She loved their gazpacho. Sometimes Keith would join us. I haven't been there since she died. I haven't seen Keith since her funeral. This is an opportunity for us to connect again. We may not be ready for the reminder that she is gone. I will know shortly.

Our relationship was strictly professional, seasoned with years of joint child abuse investigations in our logs. It also included Maggie.

As far as running into each other socially, we weren't friends, just partners. I don't know much about his personal life. I know he is married with kids. We never found the time for personal discussions. I don't even know how many children he has. Ours wasn't the kind of work that mixed business with pleasure. Child abuse doesn't mix with anything.

My friendship with Maggie was different. We were friends in college, so there was more to base our friendship on than work. We had shared a history.

Keith and I arrive at the same time. He looks good. I am sorry I haven't contacted him since the funeral. No doubt he feels Maggie's loss too, since she was my replacement when I left the department for Nebraska.

We order lunch at the counter, then find a table. I stay away from Maggie's gazpacho to avoid the memories. Keith orders, "The usual," whatever that is. I'll know when it arrives.

"The website checks out to be what you thought. But, you never know. It's better to be safe than sorry, Maggie." He says, "The hate crimes division likes to check out these sites just as a precaution. This one is well known. It's okay."

I catch my breath the minute he calls me "Maggie." I don't think he realized what he just said. I tune back into what he is saying in time to catch that Mr. Goldstein should get a post office box to use on the website as an added precaution.

"Thank you. That is good news. I don't know how I would have told Mr. Goldstein that the website was not legitimate. With his wife and children gone, he doesn't have any family. I know he must feel alone, even with his Senior Center friends and me to keep him entertained." I never let on I noticed Keith's slip of the tongue.

~~~

Mr. Goldstein must have been watching for me to come home from work. He is at my door before I have the key in the lock.

Once inside, I tell him the website is legitimate, turn on the computer, and fix coffee. Mr. Goldstein is delighted, but not surprised. He has a strange ability to hope in the goodness of life, even after all he has witnessed. He half drags, half carries a chair to the computer, watching as it goes through its start-up.

Mr. Goldstein isn't interested in distractions. He waves off the offer of a cup of coffee. I set my cup aside to cool a bit while I set up a new email address for this project. He selects his wife's name, Nadia, a Slavic name meaning "Hope."

"I thought her name was Sylvia."

"Nadia," he rolls the name off his tongue with a smooth accent. "Sylvia was her American name."

I smile. "Nadia. It's a perfect name."

He hands me the completed pages from last night. Reviewing the sheets as I transfer the information to the website, I notice his full name: Josef Abram Goldstein. Another Joseph in my life.

"Josef?" I look at him to try the fit of the name. I have always called him "Mister."

"Abraham, that is my American name," he says matter-of-factly, pointing to his homework sheet.

A satisfying wave comes over me as I settle in to respond to his desire to be connected with his lost family. I type in the names of the siblings, nieces and nephews, uncles and aunts, of both him and his wife for the website questionnaire. He knows some of them are dead, but the site requested every name for cross-matching purposes. I explain what Keith said about getting a post office box, and he likes the idea. He'll go tomorrow and get one. Now all we have to do is wait.

Mr. Goldstein watches while I print a copy of the entry for him to keep, more likely to show his friends at the Senior Center, or at least his friend Karl. He startles in his chair when I click the "send" button and everything disappears from the screen. A "Thank you" for the inquiry screen appears with a confirmation that his information will be processed as quickly as possible. I print that too. We'll add his mailing address when they need it.
~~~

With that done he pronounces it "Good" and puts away his chair. Before he goes out the door, he turns and looks back and says, "Thank you, Katerina." He looks at the monitor again. The screen saver has come up and is scrolling through beach pictures. He nods to himself and leaves.

~~~

In a strange way, resolution, even a disappointing resolution, is better than indefinite turmoil. There seems to be no meeting of the minds between Joseph and me. For the most part, I try not to think of him, except for when we are together. Beyond that moment, I cannot think about what is or what might have been. Whether it is denial or avoidance, I am not attempting to explain my behavior about him.

When I am alone, there will be plenty of time for figuring out what went wrong. I am leaving to take Joseph to LAX for his flight to Ireland. None of that complicated stuff seems to matter while I am saying goodbye.

Much to my surprise, when I arrive to pick him up, he greets me with a passionate kiss. He awakens my body and my heart to what we once had. I realize how much I have missed that.

During the drive to the airport we laugh at the silliest things. Joseph's face is relaxed and his eyes dance. I drink his voice, his accent, his easy way. We have had so few memorable moments lately that I want to remember this moment as the embodiment of our relationship. This time together must last in my memory until I see him again.

The wait for his flight passes quickly. First, we go to the gift shop where I purchase a bright yellow-orange sweatshirt with Los Angeles written in black letters on it for him to wear in Ireland. He loves it. This is the first day I can do nothing wrong since he returned two months ago. What timing.

"Well, Katey, I'll see you this summer!" Joseph says with uncontrollable excitement.

"Yes. Yes, this summer," I repeat softly and offer a smile.

Joseph's flight is announced. He bends down, puts his arms around me, pulls me close to kiss again. I close my eyes, melt in his arms, and kiss back.

"You have my email address," I whisper as he releases me.

"Aaah, Katey, I do love you," Joseph says as he moves to board his plane. He looks back one last time. With that, he is out of sight.

I move to the window with hopes of one more glimpse of him. Systematically, I scan the small portholes in the body of the plane. People moving about in the plane are visible, but none are unmistakably Joseph. I don't know what difference one more glimpse of him would
~~~

make, but I strain to get one anyway. Finally he appears in one of the window seats and waves. I smile and return his wave, thrilled he made the effort for one last goodbye.

~~~

I check my email shortly after arriving home. I don't want to see if there are any messages on the Nadia email address. I fear this website will take Mr. Goldstein away from me. It seems since I have come home, one person after another has left, and they aren't coming back.

Mr. Goldstein and Karen are my only friends left. I don't want to lose him, even though there is no reason to believe that this website will take him away.

I move to the computer and find a reply in the Nadia account. A wave of sadness washes over me, joining the void caused by Joseph's departure. I take a deep breath and pretend to strengthen my resolve, as I always have in the past.

The email turns out to be an acknowledgment of Mr. Goldstein's initial contact. I print it, and take it upstairs to him. He is gone, but his cleaning lady is just leaving, so she lets me leave it on his table for him to see when he gets home.

Coming back down the stairs, my steps quicken in response to my sense of urgency to get to the beach. I dash inside to change my shoes and head out again, eager to get to the beach. Once I am close enough to feel the cool spray on my face, I take a deep breath. All I know is that the beach provides me with more comfort than anything else.

I walk aimlessly for a while, then sit on the sand to watch the swells. The seagulls are particularly chatty today. Their noise drowns out everything beyond the beach. I lean back on my elbows to listen until my breathing begins to match the rhythm of the breaking waves. An inner calm emerges on the horizon of my consciousness. I feel a sense of clarity. Not wanting to disturb the feeling, I stay perfectly still and drink in the sense of peace like it is an oasis in the desert.

There may be some sort of message in the fact that peace returned when Joseph left. I hadn't realized, until now, exactly how much chaos he brought into my life. I want a long drink of that peace.

My diary awaits my homecoming. It draws me to it. I am beyond the self-consciousness of being honest and the risk of vulnerability at being exposed in the future if someone reads it.

Dearest Maggie, Sometimes it's the small things, grouped together, that knock the wind out of me. Sometimes it feels as though only one thing sustains my energy – my time at the beach – a kiss – a moment in time. It's the "movie moments" of life that fill my memories for the times when I'm alone. I can almost feel Joseph's embrace, if I can silence everything else...
~~~

From now on, I will always remember St. Patrick's Day as the day Joseph went back to Ireland. What a cruel joke that is. I can almost hear him say, "Eire, Katey, it's Eire!" Am I a fool to let him go? Why are relationships so complicated? And, why can't I understand them?

Tomorrow promises to come faster than I can sleep. But, I want to hold today for as long as I can. I want to remember Joseph's agreeable mood. I want to remember the moments of clarity at the beach. I lie on my pillow, savoring the moment until I drift off to sleep.

~~~

This is my week to work with Race. What timing! Race isn't his real name, but that is what he wants to be called. Nonetheless, his name isn't the problem. The problem is his attitude. He is volatile.

His wife, Lana, is a dull person—dull hair, dull eyes, dull everything. They have two children who seem like the other children at Spirit of Hope. But Race is, in a word, distinctive.

Race is a big guy, tall and wide. He isn't fat—more of a combination of a football player, a lumberjack, and a steelworker. If I was homeless, I would befriend someone like Race. No one would dare bother me. It isn't so much that he is mean, as he is coarse, with an unpredictable, hair-trigger temper.

Mother Elizabeth and Shasta like him. By the end of a week of working with him, I always feel drained. Then, I put him out of my mind completely until the next time I am assigned to work with his family.

Mother Elizabeth's aversion to an institutional atmosphere means we didn't do Social Histories on our families. We only learn the part of each person's story they elect to tell. It is a trust issue. We get what we earn, nothing more.

I know part of Race and Lana's behavior is born out of the hurt and fear from homelessness. Most of the time, I keep that realization in the front of my mind when I work with them. It makes patience come easier.

Race has no formal computer training. As we work together to compose his résumé, I notice he has a natural ability to understand the possibilities of computers. I can teach him to run almost any program, but he wants more. Race's appetite for information is insatiable. He wants to know how to write programs, and he wants to open the computer to see its insides.

Cautiously, I persuade him not to take the computer apart without Mother Elizabeth's permission, especially since it is the only one we have. He wisely declines to ask her.

"Race, I'll be right back." I look at him straight in the eyes. "Please, don't take the computer apart while I'm gone."

He looks at me slightly unamused. "I'll spell-check my cover letter while you're gone. Will that make you happy?" he snaps in reply.
~~~

"Yes, that makes me happy," I say as matter-of-factly as possible, not wanting to push teasing him too far.

I depart in search of Mother Elizabeth. It seems to me, even though Race is looking for manual labor, he might be a natural at something involving computers, which is worth bringing to Mother Elizabeth's attention.

Mother Elizabeth and I hook up outside her office. She is interested in this new facet of Race.

"Find out if he's interested in going to school, then we can check to see what is available." As she speaks, Mother writes the words, "trade schools" on a notepad she keeps in her top desk drawer.

Mother Elizabeth looks up, pulls down her reading glasses in her usual manner, and says, "Good work, Kathryn, I have been looking for a way to reach him."

I smile at her, a little embarrassed with her praise since I haven't really earned it.

Walking back to Race, I am pleased a new opportunity might be opening for him. I have every confidence that Mother Elizabeth will find a way to make computer training a reality.

Race is printing his cover letter when I return. He looks proud, not like other people look proud, but a Race-proud.

"Race, how does it look?" I ask, as I slip into the seat next to his, careful not to lean into his space. He has come a long way to trust me, and I don't want to spoil it.

Unceremoniously, he hands me the page for inspection. When he does something unguarded like this, he almost reminds me of a child full of innocence and hope.

I read over the letter. "Looks good to me! I'd hire you," I say and I hand it back to him. "All we need to do is finish your résumé, then you can insert addresses in your letter. Let's plan to mail the first batch by the end of the week, okay?" I try to be encouraging.

"Okay," Race says in a deep monotone voice.

"I was wondering if you would be interested in going to school to learn about computers?" I take advantage of the day's progress and his interest in the computer.

Race shoves his chair back and jumps up. The chair tips over with a brassy crash. "No! I don't want to go to school to learn computers!" he shouts and leans toward me in an intimidating way.

It works. I feel threatened.

He shoves his papers off the table and onto the floor, and leaves without looking back.

My instincts tell me to let him go. I pick up his papers and put them in his folder. Obviously, I have struck a nerve with him. Maybe it is a good thing. Eventually, we will have to go forward from here, but for today, we are definitely finished.

Since we don't have desks or offices of our own for storing papers, I take his papers to Mother Elizabeth's office.

"Will you keep these for me?" I ignore her inquisitive look.

"Kathryn?" Mother inquires.

"We've had enough fun for today. If you don't mind, I will help with playground duty." I make haste to leave before she corners me. I don't want to tell her what happened yet; she was so excited about Race.

I am not sure that we really need playground duty. Kids play in neighborhoods all the time without a supervising adult. I think it is just a habit for these nuns. Someone must take playground duty, it's in the teacher rule book somewhere.

Just as I reach for the door to go out, I hear someone call my name. It's Monica. I turn back to see what she needs.

"Kathryn, I have a job!" Monica blurts out, as she grabs my hand in a two-fisted clasp combined with an excited handshake.

"Monica, great!" I turn the handshake into a hug.

"It must have been my lucky scarf," she says wryly, fingering the scarf in her hair.

"Yes, I'm sure that's it." I grin back. "When do you start? I want every detail!"

"I'll tell you all about it later," she says over her shoulder, and she is gone to share her news with everyone else.

That moment with Monica put a positive spin on all of our efforts. I turn to go outside to play with the children who are laughing and hollering on the playground. Each day they get a little louder, a little braver, a little more like other children.

Paul is leaning against a tree, supervising the playground activities. It is a nice day to be outside. I join him in the shade.

"Hi, Paul. I'm done for the day, if you want to be relieved from playground duty."

"Thanks, Kathryn. I was thinking I may have to give some batting lessons to that bunch over there." He nods toward a group of pathetic ballplayers.

"Want some help?"

"Sure, they need all the help they can get." He laughs.

We walk toward the ballplayers. Two or three of the older boys are trying to arrange a game, but they have a lot of raw talent on the field. One of the boys throws the ball in the dirt, disgusted, but checks his half-spoken cuss word when he sees Paul and me approaching the group.

"What's up, Ronnie?" Paul asks the boy who threw the ball.

"Ah, it ain't no use. Girls can't hit worth a darn," Ronnie answers honestly.

That's news to me, but who am I to question an eleven-year-old expert on girls?

Paul turns to me with a cheeky grin and a smirk in his voice. "Can you hit?"

"Think so. Can you pitch?" I field his question and take up the bat by the makeshift home plate.

The kids gather around to see if girls can hit. The pressure is on to uphold the honor of my gender.

"Paul is going to need fielders," I say, and I give the bat a few easy warm-up swings, then point the tip toward the outfield to show them where to go.

The children take field positions in more or less the right place with some impromptu positions, as well.

"Want a couple of practice pitches?" I call to Paul, knowing that I need them too.

Paul is in average shape, just about like me. Neither of us can be classified as athletes, but we aren't couch potatoes either.

Paul winds up and throws one over the plate. I evaluate it for his idea of a strike zone, and hope it is somewhere near mine. He throws another one just as good as the first.

The catcher yells, "Plllaaaay baaallll," as he throws it back.

"Bat-ter up!" Paul calls with a smirking grin. He squirms his shoulders and begins his windup.

"No fancy stuff, Paul, I'm not a kid anymore," I taunt him and smile.

"Ready, slugger?"

The kids laugh.

Holding the bat in my left hand, I make the sign of the cross with my right hand. "God, pleeeaassse, don't let me strike out!" I say just loud enough for my fans to hear my prayer.

The catcher falls over laughing at my petition, which is nothing like the nuns' prayers, thus causing a game delay.

"Give me a break. I haven't even swung yet!" I fake insult, and extend a hand to help him up, playing up the moment for the fun of it.

The kids laugh loudly, infectiously.

I make the sign of the cross again, lift my bat, take my stance, and check my elbow position. I nod to Paul. "Let's see what you got!"

Before the kids can laugh again, Paul pitches a sweet strike right where I like them.

Crack! My bat makes solid contact. The ball is headed for orbit, well at least past the infield, toward the oddly placed multiple centerfield players.

Paul jumps for the ball as it whizzes past the makeshift pitcher's mound. I'm not sure, but I think he let the ball get by him on purpose.

No one fields the ball, not the girls or the boys. We all stand there in amazement, including me.

"Well that settles it. Girls can hit!" Paul announces.

The ballplayers applaud. Someone tags me out once they retrieve the ball. I forgot to run to first base. I also forgot to find out what was first base in this misshaped ball diamond.

I hadn't noticed that Mother Elizabeth joined the spectators. "Nice one, Kathryn," she says, as she approaches.

Shasta cuts through Mother's path, and reaches me first. "You did good, Kathryn!" she bursts in amazement and pride, patting my hand.

Mother grins. "You have a phone call." She takes the bat from me and hands it to Shasta.

One of the kids yells, "Hey, ya wanna play tomorrow?"

"If I can, I will," I call over my shoulder, as I walk back inside with Mother Elizabeth.

"Here Kathryn, use my office phone; it's closer."

"Thanks, Mother Elizabeth."

"Hello. This is Kathryn McKenzie."

"Katey, Mr. Bradford here. Your Grandfather McKenzie would like to meet you," says the voice in the phone—all in one breath.

"What?" I question, as I slowly sit in Mother Elizabeth's chair.

"Do you want to meet your grandfather?"

"Well, yes. I guess so. Why? I mean, why?" I can't think of anything else to say, and I am absolutely certain I am not making sense.

"All right. I'll set up a meeting, then get back to you." He hangs up the phone without another word.

Lawyers! I think they are communication-challenged. I sit for a moment, and shake my head in a muted manner. As I hang up the phone, I realize I am in Mother Elizabeth's chair. Startled and clumsy, I struggle to get up.

Mother holds the back of the chair steady to help me get free.

"Is everything all right?" she inquires.

"Oh yes, I think so." I brush off her question.

"Kathryn?" Mother Elizabeth insists.

From the tone in her voice, it is obvious she expects more, but there really is no more.

"It was just my lawyer. Everything is fine."

"Lawyer?"

Now I've done it. I have piqued her curiosity. "My parents are dead, and he was my father's friend. He tries to keep track of me, that's all. I have to check in with him once in a while or he will track me down."

I leave her office before she can ask follow-up questions. Later, it occurs to me that I am probably the only staff member with a lawyer on retainer.

~~~

Thank God, it's finally five o'clock. I grab my jacket and make a beeline to sign out at the front desk.

It's been a long day. I check with Mr. Goldstein about a walk, but he's not home. I go solo. The water doesn't seem as gray as it has been lately. I'm not sure that the ocean really changes its color in spring. It's probably the change in Earth's relationship to the sunlight coming through the atmosphere as spring comes, a change that enhances the appearance of the water's color. I don't care about the explanation. I'll take it. It fits the day.

There is a seagull with an injured wing who, sometimes, follows me along the beach. It must be an old injury, since he seems strong when he flies. The only problem is that he is reckless in flight, and even worse with his landings. I have to watch out for him.

He has never actually flown into me, but he flies directly toward me, then veers off just before landing. It makes me duck needlessly. I am sure the whole scene is comical to view, especially my role in it, but he does manage to safely land near me.

After months of these aerobatic landings, he doesn't make me flinch as much when he approaches, providing I know he's around. Otherwise, he startles me with his wild flapping as he flies by before his abrupt touchdown.

For no particular reason I like him. It is like having a pet for the afternoon, a very independent pet. I christen him "Livingston."

I like Livingston's company. He seems content to walk in silence. Periodically, he will stop to pick at a snack deposited in his path by a wave. Then, he flies to catch up with me. I admire his persistence, his resilience. Besides that, Livingston seems happy in spite of the difficulties his old injury brings.

I sit to watch the incoming waves. Livingston joins me, standing a couple of yards away. There we stay, both staring out at the ocean. Every once in a while, I glance at him, then he glances at me. For a seagull, he is very quiet. I wonder what he is thinking. Maybe, seagulls don't think about anything besides their next meal. I like to think Livingston is more esoteric than the average seagull.

My mind wanders to thinking about Mr. Bradford's phone call.

"Strange about my grandfather, isn't it?" I ask Livingston. He cocks his head, but makes no other acknowledgment of me. I only stay for an hour or so, but Livingston stays with me the entire time.

~~~

~ CHAPTER 9 ~

Are Things Really This Complicated?

The kitchen fills with the smell of coffee beans grinding. Soon the colored brew begins to drip through the filter and sizzle onto the bottom of the glass pot. Unable to wait longer, I remove the pot and slip my waiting cup under the drip.

With coffee in hand, I walk to the sofa, pull my feet up to the coffee table, and lean my head back as far as I can stretch. I'm tired. My shoulder muscles are tightening from my earlier home-run hit. If it didn't require getting up, I might consider drinking something stronger than coffee tonight.

~~~

The phone rings. It's Mr. Bradford again. I can't imagine a lawyer working late for something like this.

"Kathryn, your grandfather wants to meet with you on the first, at one o'clock by the fountain in the park."

"Which park?"

"I'll have Crystal get back to you with directions."

"Wait!" I don't want him to hang up abruptly again. "I want to know what is going on," I interrupt him.

"Let's meet. Crystal can set up a time for you when she calls with directions." With that he concludes the conversation.

I look at the phone receiver for a moment before hanging up. Lawyers! I transfer the information from my notes to my appointment book. "April first, 1:00 PM."

"April first? April Fool's Day!" My brow wrinkles. I wonder if this is a joke. Mr. Bradford doesn't seem to have a sense of humor. Then again, when it comes to lawyers, those are the dangerous kind. I laugh, and refill my cup.

Walking back from the kitchen, I decide to check the email. Nadia brings forth a response to Mr. Goldstein's search.

I catch my breath while I read that they have located a niece in Austria.

I don't know why this scares me like it does. The only thing I can figure is it's fear of abandonment. Now that I realize a possible explanation for my uneasiness, I should be able to overcome it. Right?

Of course, Mr. Goldstein comes right down when I call him. The email asks if he wants to exchange addresses.

"Yes! Yes!" He eagerly leans in close, speaking to the monitor. He is so cute. I love him!
~~~

I click "yes." A screen pops up requesting his address. He stands up and pulls out his wallet, excitedly searching. He lays a piece of paper on the desk and flattens out the folds.

I'm pleased with him for following Keith's advice about having a post office box address. I click "print," then "enter," and send the information on its way. Another click to instruct the computer to alert me when there is a response, and it is done.

We move to the sofa. I bring a bottle of wine and two glasses. Regardless of my fears of losing him, I love Mr. Goldstein. Seeing his beaming face is more than enough reason to toast his good fortune.

By ten o'clock, there has been no alert. He has glanced at the monitor so many times over the course of the evening that he must have all of the photos on the screen saver memorized. Mr. Goldstein is growing restless. He looks tired in spite of his excitement.

"You know, it is the middle of the night over there. We might not hear from them until morning."

"Yes, I go now." He stands to leave, but looks longingly toward the screen saver moving from one photo of our beach to the next.

"I'll check it in the morning before I go to work. If they send something, I will bring it to you," I reassure him, as I take his cap from the table by the door and hand it to him.

He smiles. "You are a good person, Katerina."

"Thank you," I say softly and smile.

My aching shoulders from my "at bat" this afternoon are restating their presence. I pull on them with my hand, attempting to massage away the pain. Not willing to succumb to such a simple cure, the muscles tighten. I take an aspirin and a hot shower in search of relief.

The warm water feels good as it pulses on my shoulders. The sound it makes splashing on the tile lulls my mind.

Comfortably wrapped in my robe on the sofa, I quote Maggie: "Life is good, not necessarily easy, but good." I hum along with Ann Zimmerman's song, "Kiss on the Mouth." Life is good.

~~~

The computer awakens me from my comfort with its beeping alert. In the Nadia email there is a response with a postal address. A picture of a fifty-year-old-looking woman appears. The background and her dress are definitely European. I print everything, including the photo for Mr. Goldstein. Without reading it, I slip it into a manila envelope, along with a note to call me when he gets up in the morning. I assume he, like the rest of the world, starts the day much earlier than I ever hope to—and, unlike me, he is already in bed, so I don't call him.

The night air is chilly on my wet hair as I climb the stairs. As I expected, the lights are off in his apartment. There isn't a way to secure
~~~

the envelope in his doorjamb, so he will find it in the morning. I run back down the stairs to get tape. Finally, with enough tape, the envelope is secured to the outside of his window. Surely he will see it when he opens the drapes in the morning.

It's late, and Race and I have work to do tomorrow. I settle into bed, and fall asleep almost the moment my cheek touches the pillow.

~~~

I delay leaving for work as long as I can, waiting for Mr. Goldstein to find his note and call me. Finally, I can't wait any longer. The day is overcast, but I welcome the impending rain as I drive the freeway.

As usual, Shasta delivers her morning briefing before I send her off to school and go my own way. Mother Elizabeth is busy with a project of her own, so I quietly reach across her desk for Race's file. Her office is one of the few places that can be locked, though she probably doesn't lock it. The résumé isn't a big secret, but I feel responsible for it until it is returned to its owner. Distracted, she misses a perfect opportunity to shanghai me and ask questions about yesterday.

Race isn't a person to push, so I go to the computer to wait for him. He will find me on his own schedule, or not come at all. In the meantime, I check the internet in search of batting information for Paul to share with the kids.

While several swing diagrams are printing, Race appears. He looks at the page on the monitor and says, "Trying out for the Angels this year?"

"No, Dodgers. Do you think I have a chance?"

"Not a chance in hell," he says dryly.

Had it been anyone else, I might have teased back one more time, but I only laugh and agree, "You're probably right."

"Listen, I'm sorry about yesterday." He slowly shifts his weight back and forth between his feet as he apologizes.

"It's all right." I dare to broach the topic again. "You really seem to be a natural at the computer, Race."

I scoot my chair over to make room for him, but don't dare say any more about school.

Race adjusts his chair in front of the keyboard, but turns to face me. He takes a breath and whispers earnestly, "I never finished high school; I can't go to college."

Hmm, "college?" We were thinking trade school. Well, well, I think that I am going to take advantage of this open door. I look around to ensure we won't be overheard by anyone, especially any of the nuns, lean toward him slightly, and lower my voice.

"I wouldn't worry about it. High school was a waste of time for me too. I was putting in time to get my ticket punched. College was the real
~~~

education." I lean closer and whisper quieter, "You can take a class to test out of high school. Do you want to do that?"

"How's that work?" he whispers back.

We probably look like we are up to something. He looks around, watching for anyone who might walk in and catch us whispering like we are in grammar school.

"We could check it out."

"No, *you* check it out, and tell me." Race is adamant. With that he resumes working where he left off yesterday.

~~~

Paul and I meet with the kids for batting practice after school. When it is their turn "at bat," each of the kids makes the sign of the cross, as I had yesterday, but with inconsistent results. They aren't all Catholic, so some of them use their left hand or make the cross backwards, but I don't think that is responsible for their inability to get a solid hit. And, I don't bother to correct their form regarding religious displays.

Quite by accident we have discovered something cohesive to work on as a community—baseball. We can sneak in all kinds of social skills under the guise of the game. The feeling of spring and the agreeable weather work in our favor.

When he thought I wasn't listening I heard Paul tell them that if I can bat, so can they, or maybe he didn't care if I heard him.

The children glance in my direction and give a hearty laugh at my expense in response to his logic. I play along with his joke, though his sense of humor may be lacking. I wonder if my bat-making cousin would come and talk with the kids about how bats are made? The kids would think it was cool he makes bats for the Dodgers.

~~~

No doubt, Mr. Goldstein will be watching for me to come home, so we can check his email. As soon as the day is finished, I beat a path for the sign-out sheet. On the way home from work, I call him to say I am on my way home. I don't know how he made it through the day after he found the photo in his envelope. He is waiting at my door by the time I arrive. He's my hero.

"Katerina!" Immediately he corrects himself. "Kathryn, Kathryn, they sent me a picture," he says, excitedly pulling it out of the envelope.

"Great! I have an idea. Come with me. You can tell me all about her on the way to the beach," I say, and grab the digital camera.

"What are you doing? What is that?"

I smile broadly. "It's a camera that makes pictures the computer understands, then we can send them a picture of you!"

With appreciating eyes and loving smile, he takes the small silver camera from my open hand and looks it over carefully.

"Yes, yes. Good. We will send a picture through your computer." He begins to politely crowd me out the door.

We end up with eight good shots. One photo outside our apartment building, and seven of him on the beach. With our heads leaning toward each other, he scrolls through the photos with my help. When he is satisfied, he points the camera at me and takes a picture. He is so eager to try new things, to adapt to life, to drink it all. We get our photo shoot completed well before the sun sets.

Back at my apartment I ask, "Will you turn on the computer while I start my coffee? And, do you want tea or coffee tonight?"

"No, no tea. No coffee," he answers, while he fiddles with the computer to turn it on, adjusts the angle of the monitor, and moves his chair into position next to mine.

Before the coffee is finished brewing, we have our photos on the screen and are looking at them. I switch from my laser printer to the color inkjet. Just for fun, I print the picture he took of me and hand it to him. He is obviously impressed. What the heck? I print a copy of each of the pictures for him, using photo paper to make it all the better.

He has such a gentle way about him. "Katerina, you are good friend," he says while studying the photos and comparing them to the ones on the screen.

He is so sincere. What a sweetheart! "Have you decided which picture to send to—" I realize that I don't know who was in the photo he received.

"Yes. Send this one." He holds up the photo of choice for me to examine.

It's a pleasant diversion that Mr. Goldstein is as excited as a child going to Disneyland for the first time. When I pull up his email, and open the photo of the woman, he leans in close to the monitor, and studies the color picture. My laser printer hadn't done it justice, so I print a new one on the color printer with photo paper. He tilts the photo under the desk lamp and studies it. He leans back with a satisfied, faraway look.

Seeing Mr. Goldstein study the picture of a lost family member displaces my fear of losing him. Perhaps meeting Grandfather is a parallel experience for me, giving me greater appreciation of Mr. Goldstein's situation. Only Mr. Goldstein's loss is much greater than my loss of someone I never knew.

Finally, he speaks. "She is my wife's niece, I can see the resemblance to her mother."

I sit silently, letting him drink in the moment. It is an honor to observe him. I study his face for the memory of him. It is probably only a matter of time before I will need those memories, because if we are successful, he will join his family.

Mr. Goldstein begins again. He still has a faraway look in his eyes. His voice is soft and emotion-filled.

"It was early in the war, before your country entered," he begins. "My wife's younger sister and husband came to live with us. Her husband was killed in the street by a German soldier shortly after that," his voice wavers. He pauses, slightly. "A few days earlier, we had just learned that she was going to have a child," he whispers.

Our eyes meet. His memories are horrible to hear. I can't imagine what it is for him to relive them.

He continues, "She was at the market getting potatoes for Hanukkah when the Germans took us. We never saw her again."

He pauses. "We asked whenever there were new prisoners, but no one knew of her."

Mr. Goldstein sits in silence for a long time.

There is nothing I can say that would be adequate to the moment. The only thing to do is to be present without disturbing him. I sit motionlessly, holding my coffee cup without being tempted by the brew.

After a while, he stirs in his chair. "What we do next?"

"You should respond to her message," I say, while setting down my cup and moving my hands to the keyboard.

Mr. Goldstein goes to the table by the door, and picks up the manila envelope I had taped to his window. As he returns to his chair, he pulls out the papers. It is then I notice that the message is not in English.

Pulling up his chair and sitting down, he places the papers in front of me on the desk. His finger moves across the page, following the lines of print.

"She says her mother is alive and well. Living in the same town." He scans the message further, then laughs. "She says her son is running the computer for her." He stops to smile at me like I'm an adopted child.

He smiles. "She has a son, our family has survived."

"Yes," I agree, putting my hand on his arm.

He smiles and resumes scanning the message.

"She has another son and twin daughters, but they live in other cities." He smiles again—a pleased smile.

He probably read and reread the message many times today. I like the way he chose to share it with me. A wave of appreciation for our friendship comes over me. I feel overwhelming fondness for him.

"Well, I suggest you tell them about you."

"Yes." He scoots his chair closer to the desk, touching the front of it with his knees, and leans in toward the computer. He is ready to communicate—his whole being is ready.

Most of his life has been spent preserving the culture that was all but stolen from him in the death camp. Mr. Goldstein hasn't moved into the computer age. He is not afraid of it, he simply takes it in stride—like he takes everything else. He leans into the monitor when he is ready to communicate. Mr. Goldstein's willingness to embrace life fully, after all he has witnessed of its worst side, is an inspiring testament to his faith.

Pushing my chair back and swiveling to face him, I offer a suggestion: "Write your message on paper, then I will type it for you and the computer will translate it, unless you think they speak English, then you can just dictate it to me and I will type it as you speak."

"I should write back in German for now. I can ask what other languages they speak." He takes the paper and writes quickly, pauses, and writes some more. Then he hands the paper to me. His eyes seem to ask for my confirmation.

I nod acknowledgment in response while I check that I can distinguish all of the letters.

Years of writing reports taught me to type like the wind. In less time than he has taken to write the note, I have it typed. "You'd better check for spelling errors before we send it," I suggest.

Again he leans toward the monitor, and adjusts his glasses. He tilts his head back slightly to read through the lower portion of his bifocals. He is nodding his head affirmatively, as he reads under his breath. When he finishes, he smiles and pronounces, "It is good."

I move the curser to highlight the "print" button to make him a copy of his message. "Here, push this button," I say, pointing to the enter button on the keyboard and where to press on the mouse.

He pushes the button with confidence, and grins with his first computer contact.

He gathers all of his papers. "There, now I go." He turns around at the door. "You tape the message on my window again?"

"Yes, I will, I promise."

After Mr. Goldstein leaves, I decide to email Joseph. It doesn't flow well. Following several deletions and restarts, I settle on telling him that I am planning to come to Ireland in June or July, and want to know if he has a preference regarding when I come.

It is my way of dealing with his silence—though, he didn't write last time he was away—so, I shouldn't expect it now. I am terribly hurt that I seem to be so unimportant to him.

I know, however, Lady Justice is a jealous mistress. I hope that is all that it is.

~~~
~~~

~ CHAPTER 10 ~

April Fools, Grandfather!—I'm Catholic

The last Friday of the month, Mother Elizabeth lets me off work a few hours early, so I can meet with Mr. Bradford.

"Katey, all I can tell you is that your grandfather contacted me and said that he wanted to meet you." Mr. Bradford is evasive.

I don't know why I even bother to talk with him. I never feel like we communicate effectively. To my relief, he doesn't mention my trip to Ireland. He has moved on to this next item, Grandfather McKenzie.

"Why now? Why haven't we met before this?" I ask a specific question, hoping for a specific answer.

"As I recall, it had to do with your father marrying a Catholic. Your grandfather hates Catholics and makes no bones about it." Mr. Bradford actually answers my question!

"Well then, he'll love me! I'm Catholic," I say as mischievously as possible. It does seem odd that the man who would have nothing to do with my parents and me, has kept in contact with Mr. Bradford, Father's friend.

The meeting with Mr. Bradford was unnecessary, since he doesn't have any new information to share with me.

On the weekend, I decide to test Crystal's directions by driving to the park. It is near the foothills where I haven't been before. When I arrive, I walk around and get the lay of the land. I sit by the fountain. The fountain's soft bubbling sound fades as my mind begins to wander. It seems strange that Grandfather would choose this place to meet.

When I leave, I drive around the nearby neighborhoods wondering if one of the houses is his. Nothing looks familiar. If I had been to his house as a child, I don't remember it. Why in the world is he contacting me after all of these years? Meeting now seems rather pointless, both my parents are gone. Surely he knows that there can be no going back to have a relationship with my father now.

Grandfather could have enjoyed those few years with his son. He might have even liked my mother, if he had known her. Poor old man, he can never have the time he wasted. Maybe he has recognized his error and wants to salvage what he can with the one remaining member of Father's family, me. "What a sad travesty."

~~~

When I ask Mother Elizabeth for the day off on Monday, April first, I tell her it's personal business. Much to my surprise, she doesn't question further. This time I remember to forewarn Shasta that I will be
~~~

away from work and promise to return with a new supply of coloring books. All is set to meet this grandfather of mine.

~~~

April Fool's Day; I hope I am not a fool for agreeing to this meeting. I savor my first cup of coffee, pondering that question. I add a holy medal around my neck.

I timed the trip to the park. However, out of caution, I add twenty minutes to ensure I arrive before Grandfather. That way, I won't be walking into the situation: I will be the situation.

The weather is nice, as it should be here in paradise. With the windows down, and the music cranked up, I go smoothly through the gears. I feel confident and pleased. Whatever comes of this meeting, I am actually excited to meet Grandfather and put a face with the idea of having a paternal relative. I take it as a good omen that the traffic is light, so I can drive unencumbered.

The park is nearly deserted. Apparently recently cleaned, the fountain bubbles pleasantly, inviting my fingers to dabble in the water. It is colder than it looks, but it feels fresh—like a fountain should. Maybe there is extra magic to the first coin in the fountain after it has been cleaned. Even if not, I pull out a shiny penny from my purse, turn my back, close my eyes and take a deep breath. Plop!

"For luck, Kathryn?" a voice in front of me asks.

I open my eyes to see an old man in a wheelchair being pushed by a younger Black man.

"Grandfather?" I query to the wheelchair-bound man.

He doesn't look like, nor unlike, my father. I don't feel related, but not like a stranger either. He seems vaguely familiar. I extend my hand.

"Pleased to meet you, sir."

He extends his hand. It is a businesslike shake, maybe a bit warmer, but I still don't feel any overwhelming connection to him as our skin touches.

"Kathryn," is all that he says.

I look up at the attendant. He looks to be in his fifties. He is huge, a former football-player type. He smiles slightly, his eyes are warm and friendly. Oddly, I feel connected to him.

Noticing me look up at the man behind his wheelchair, Grandfather says, "This is James, my driver." He waves toward the man behind him without looking in his direction.

Grandfather is a dismissive old fart.

James and I shake hands and exchange smiles. He has a strong, but kind handshake. I pause a moment to take note of the exchange. He is the kind of person easy to like upon first meeting, without needing to know him further.
~~~

"Take me to the bench, James," Grandfather interrupts the moment demandingly, seemingly unaware there is a moment outside of himself.

"Yes, sir," James responds respectfully and pushes the chair with Grandfather through the grass to the bench.

I walk beside the chair. No thoughts in particular, just walking and waiting to see what Grandfather initiates.

"Do you play?" Grandfather asks, as his fingers lightly tap the wooden box on his lap. There is an inlaid checker square on top, surrounded with carving and other marquetry designs. It looks old and opulent. He handles it like it is a treasure.

"Yes," I say, not entirely certain of the game he has in mind, but sure that I am able.

James takes the box, positioning it between Grandfather and me. Grandfather opens the lid, and begins to remove chess pieces.

"Black or white?"

"Black, always black," I say without thinking that he might have preferred black.

The pieces are heavy and smooth. I think the black are mahogany. The white men are a lighter wood, not oak, maybe something exotic. Nothing I recognize. I like the feel of them, as I set my men in place on the board.

James locks the chair brakes, and retires to a nearby bench to watch.

The game begins.

"Your move," Grandfather says with an impatient look of "get on with it, girl."

Apparently, this is not meant to be a leisurely game. I ease into the competition looking for hints of his strategy. His moves indicate he is a serious player. He seems to have no intention of holding back. Then, I will not hold back out of politeness.

I lose my queen's bishop.

The game moves on.

There is no conversation. "Your move," is all Grandfather says. Maybe it is part of his strategy to rush me. I take his rook. He takes more of my men, and my pawns fall mercilessly.

I move. "Check."

He stops dead! His hands retreat to his lap. "That is your father's move," he says. "Enough of the game. You are Kathryn McKenzie!" With a slight grin, he waves toward James and the game board is removed.

It is all a little odd. I hadn't expected a game of chess to test my parentage. Goodness, there are DNA tests for that. How can a chess move prove anything?

Grandfather settles his hands together in his lap. "Tell me about yourself. Are you married?"

"No."

"Dating?"

"Sometimes."

"Children?" He seems to have a litany.

I stop the rhythm of the questions with a pause. "No," I say with a sound of boundary-setting finality.

He leans back in his chair slightly and studies me.

"You must look like your mother."

"I look like me." I'm beginning to enjoy our volley back and forth.

He grins. "Yes, I suppose so."

Grandfather twists in his chair to view James. Without exchanging words, James gets up and releases the brakes on the chair. From behind Grandfather's chair, James flashes a big smile that lasts only a second and is gone.

I smile in response.

"Shall we meet again?" Grandfather asks in a business-sounding way.

"Yes, I would like that." Finding a small spiral tablet in my purse, I write down my home phone number. "But let's not meet during work hours next time."

He nods an acknowledgment and we part company.

Well, well, well. That was interesting. Had it been a job interview, I would have been offered the position. I feel good about the way the meeting went with Grandfather. In a way, we may be alike. I don't like the way he treats James, but they seem to have worked out their relationship long ago. I like the old guy, but his social skills need some work. No, it isn't a project I'm taking on, except to try to establish boundaries on my terms.

On the way home, I fiddle with Mother's ring on my finger. I think my parents would have approved of how the meeting with Grandfather turned out.

It was a good use of the day, and there is plenty of afternoon left to spend on the beach. Maybe Mr. Goldstein will go for an early walk. Maybe we'll see Livingston. Lately, Livingston seems to be somewhere on the beach or around the pier almost every time I go for a walk.

Mr. Goldstein sees the similarity in him finding his niece and me meeting Grandfather. I thought he would. It is a strange parallel, though. I think he has the better deal.

We check his email, but there is nothing yet.

After returning from the beach and eating dinner, I sit with my feet resting on the coffee table, drinking coffee. It's been a good day. Even though I was a little anxious about meeting Grandfather, it was not as bad as it might have been. After thirty-some-odd years, I wonder why the sudden interest in knowing me? It would have meant more to my parents had the old man accepted their marriage.

Mother's family has more than compensated for the lack of Father's family. They have taught me the true nature of family. It's a gift that little else can match. Although, I do like the new connection with the other half of my family. I feel strangely balanced having two families; though I don't know my second family yet. Whatever comes of this meeting, today has been a good day.

The coffee tastes so good that I can't help smiling. A few more sips, I read my last entry, then write:

> *Dearest Maggie, I'm beginning to understand fragments of my life. (At this rate, I will need to live several hundred years to figure everything out; if I could only last that long!)*
>
> *Perhaps my decision not to go with Joseph is a means to avoid my vulnerabilities? Or is it a newfound strength?*
>
> *And Father's family, where does Grandfather fit into my life? For that matter, where do I fit into his life? Or do I?*

I wonder about the chess game. Maybe it was a family-coded test and the reason Father made sure he taught me his special move. We played chess nearly every day. It was more significant than I knew. It is kind of fun that our family has this secret code.

~~~

In the morning there is another reply for Nadia. It's raining, so I put the paper into a large plastic bag to keep it dry until Mr. Goldstein finds it. As I leave for work, I tape the bag with the printed copy of the new email to his window.

I'm in the mood to stay home and enjoy the rain, watch a movie or read a book. I don't really feel like driving or working.

By the time I ease into the traffic, the rain is coming down in sheets and pooling on the freeway. There is a restlessness in my mood that seems to be shared by the mass of hurried drivers. For the first time since I returned to California, I feel crowded by the traffic.

~~~

Sister Clare is at the switchboard when I arrive for work. I wonder if Sister Theresa is ill; she is always at her post in the office early in the morning. Sister Clare says nothing when I sign in, she briefly looks up from her knitting then resumes working the needles.

Little Shasta catches me in the hallway, as usual, and walks with me to hang up my jacket.

"Hello, Shasta. Where is everyone?"

"They're in the auditorium. Go there."

"Okay, I will! Have a good day at school."

We part company. I watch to see she isn't taking the shortcut to school, then I head to the auditorium. She walks with purpose and turns the corner.

There is a beehive of activity everywhere in the room. One of the sisters is pushing a large dust mop over the floor. A nun is following her with a whirling floor buffer machine. Paul is pulling racks of chairs out from under the stage, causing an obnoxious sound distinctive to moving metal folding chairs on a metal rack. Sister Theresa seems in charge of this operation. That explains why she isn't in the office.

She looks past me toward the door. "Pete and Ben, will you move the piano to the center of the stage?"

From behind me I hear, "Yes, Sister," from each of them.

Mother Elizabeth is standing at the waist-high stage, using it as a table to fold papers.

"Good morning, Mother. May I help?"

"Good morning, Kathryn." Mother Elizabeth divides her stack of papers with me.

I watch her for a minute to see the way she wants it done. We are folding programs for Sister Veronica's music students' recital. This isn't for her school students. It's for the Spirit of Hope students. Apparently, she feels the time has come for a recital. It has been a year since Spirit of Hope opened its doors.

Scanning the list of performers as I fold the sheets, it appears quite a few of the clients have accepted her offer of music lessons. There is a nice mix of children and adults. As a matter of fact, as I look more closely, she has everyone living at Spirit of Hope involved in a catchall choir. Race is playing the sax in a jazz band. I didn't know Race played the sax. I love jazz.

Thankfulness replaces my restlessness. I should never grumble about coming to work. This job has been a gift to me; it has enriched my life beyond my expectations. It reminds me why I became a social worker, something I had forgotten, but desperately need to remember.

Our clients have grown and flourished at Spirit of Hope, and I am honored to be a small part of the process. What they shared of their hopes and dreams is far more than what we could ever give to them.

"More to the left. There, that's good. Straighten it up..." Sister Theresa directs her piano movers.

Mother Elizabeth folds her last sheet and turns to Sister Theresa. "This is going to be wonderful, Theresa."

Sister Theresa nods in pleased agreement.

I finish my last sheet and join Paul's little crew to help set up the remaining chairs. We make quick work of the task.

Mother Elizabeth and Sister Theresa are standing near the empty chair racks. Paul and Pete slide the racks back under the stage, while Ben and I shut the doors behind them.

"There, that will give Veronica two weeks before the recital to rehearse with the chairs out. Get Clare to help address the invitation envelopes," Mother is saying to Sister Theresa.

I have never heard them speak of each other without using the title, "Sister." It seems more personal and warm than the usual formal interaction. I am beginning to suspect there is a dimension to them that I haven't noticed before.

The rain keeps everyone inside, but it doesn't seem gloomy. We have accomplished quite a bit on our list of their goals, as well as set up for the recital and hung posters the children drew.

~~~

On the drive home, the traffic seems more tame than this morning. My thoughts are preoccupied with the experiences at work. It has been a good day. There is something satisfying about doing a good day's work, even more so when it is done for the benefit of someone outside of ourselves.

There's a knock on the door, just as I finish putting away the last of my dinner dishes. Bursting with excitement and an armful of papers, the quiet, gentle Mr. Goldstein nearly flings himself at me when I open the door.

"Help me? I need help, Katerina," he demands excitedly, as he spreads the papers across the table.

"What is all this?"

"The email said I come visit my niece," he says in a tone suggesting I should have already known what was going on.

"Visit them in Austria?" I knew this would happen. I can feel my heart not wanting him to leave—not even for a visit. After all, Joseph went home for a visit, only to return with news that he was moving back to Ireland. Maggie and Dave went to Tahoe for a ski weekend, and didn't come home alive. I am reluctant for anyone else to travel very far away from me. Mr. Goldstein is damn lucky I survive his Senior Center excursions. Visit! Absolutely not!

"Yes, Austria."

"Oh, Mr. Goldstein, I am happy for you." I squeeze his wrist softly. Our eyes meet in an exchange of genuine fondness.

Looking through the materials, it becomes obvious that they fall into two major categories: passport information and flight information. Goodness, he and the library ladies have been busy.
~~~

Mr. Goldstein watches, while I sort the material into piles. My assistance is not to imply that he is helpless. On the contrary, he is a very capable man. He had protected his wife during the war, then brought her to America where he provided well for her. He has been through hell and back, and quite successfully.

"Well, it seems to me that if we divide the tasks, we can get through this project in short order," I say, as I finish sorting. "If you don't have a preference, you take the passport pile and work on that, while I take the flight information."

"Yes, and we send my niece a message?"

I hadn't thought about it, but he's right, we should coordinate the trip with her. "You turn on the computer, and I will get the coffee."

Mr. Goldstein writes out the message. When he is satisfied it is correct, we send it.

"You want the most direct flight possible, right?"

Mr. Goldstein nods, his eyes are alight with excitement.

"Let's figure out how long it will take to get your passport current and what date you want to go, and I will start on the flight list."

~~~

With that Mr. Goldstein takes his assignment home. I am beginning to miss him already. All of these months of sharing walks on the beach and our thoughts on life have created a bond that our differences in age and culture only enrich.

The day requires a fresh coffee, movie soundtracks on the stereo, and a note in my diary.

Dearest Maggie, There have been plenty of difficult times to endure. I must remember that life brings with it many gifts. It seems easier to remember the hurt. Maybe it's a mechanism of survival – reminding us to not repeat harmful experiences. On the other hand, remembering those times may just be a comfortable habit.

Either way, sometimes the memories make me too cautious and rob me of fully experiencing the "good" in life. Life IS good, not necessarily easy, but good. I must take risks, even if those risks require that I let others go away from me.

Sometimes growth takes us from everything familiar and comfortable. Sometimes it brings us together in ways more intimate and meaningful. I think it is worth the risk.

I must let Mr. Goldstein go; be happy for him, as an expression of my love for him. He hasn't said anything about leaving, only a visit, but it is inevitable – even I can see it.
~~~

My ability to pour thoughts into my diary is wordy at best. I haven't quite mastered Maggie's power to clearly express nearly intangible thoughts.

The sound of the pounding surf is a loud distraction from my writing critique. A storm must be brewing in the Pacific. Thundering waves are so intense that they resonate in my chest each time one comes in and hits hard, high on the beach, and again when the backwash collides.

The sound carries for blocks in the thick night air. From the window, I watch people run quickly to see what is happening with the ocean. Surfers huddle on the beach with their wetsuits hanging at half mast on their trim bodies. They evaluate the quality of the waves with the precision of the Army Corps of Engineers. Soberly, they gesture the value of the waves, discuss, counter, and fidget, longing to be in the water. The few hopefuls who brought their boards head for the water for a test ride. Others stand by ready to help if this is as foolhardy as it looks to the rest of us. The test-dummies turn back to the safety of the shore.

Low-hung clouds darken. Hypnotizing lightning comes. It spiders across the dark clouds, driving most of the people from the beach. Strikes of lightning light up the beach long enough for me to see the surf is more violent than it was previously. Before long, everyone has left, even the shorebirds.

The sound of the rain beating on my window keeps me from being drawn to the beach to see the waves up close. The rain falls in sheets. Still I am driven outside. I stand on the patio, under my umbrella. The wind is coming inland, bringing with it the comforting smell of the ocean since I can't get there on my own. Usually the wind blows out to sea in the evenings and inland in the morning, but not tonight.

For a long time as I sip my coffee, I stand and watch each flickering lightning in the distant sky. The umbrella is only a ruse. The rain ignores any attempt to be shielded from it since it isn't falling straight down. High tide will be monstrous tonight. Finally, long after I come inside, the lightning moves up the shore and away.

~~~
~~~

~ CHAPTER 11 ~

The Recital

By morning, the storm has blown itself out and taken the rain with it. The sun is warm and gentle. Mother Elizabeth asks three staff persons, me included, to come to her garden and help remove the blossoms that have been damaged by the rain. Mother confidently expects the sun to bring out new flowers in time for Sister Veronica's recital, a week from Saturday.

We are instructed in the proper pruning technique. Mother Elizabeth is a very disciplined, but gentle teacher.

Dearest Maggie, Mother Elizabeth became immersed in her flowers to the point of becoming one with them, maybe even one with the universe or with God.

The experience of watching her touches my soul; it's the kind of spiritual experience I haven't had for a very long time.

After dinner, Mr. Goldstein produces his original passport and his naturalization papers, and I present a table of flight times for him to choose one. I'm able to accept the fact that he will be leaving soon. All I can do now is make the most of the time we have left.

Sometimes, it seems as if all the Earth is separating me from those I love, leaving me to my own little world on the shore. I will miss him as much as I missed my parents and Maggie when they died, but at least I will know he is alive and his prayers to find his missing family have been heard.

The week unfolds in the usual way things happen in my life. Mother Elizabeth has requested our vacation plans, so she can schedule around them. Joseph hasn't replied to my email, but a postcard that had been lost in the mail arrives. He wrote it on the plane to Ireland. He had my address correct, but not the zip code. Who knows where it has been all of this time. It still doesn't explain why he hasn't answered my email, unless I have his address incorrect, like he had my zip code. I really expected him to write and send his new address once he was settled. I think my expectations are reasonable, but they don't seem to fit him.

I have to make a decision sans his input, so I select two weeks in August, then email the dates to him. I know that it makes no sense to go, but I cannot not go. No one else wanted the same time off as I did, so I get my vacation time without a hitch.

~~~
~~~

Karen has been busy the last few months with her tasks related to the Child Abuse Prevention Coalition, in addition to her day job. I have deliberately stayed off the beach on Maggie's monthly anniversary, so Karen can have the time to herself. That's her ritual. Since I know about it, I won't intrude.

She delights me when she unexpectedly appears at my door. I welcome her company and the opportunity to discuss the trip to Ireland.

Karen guides me to the admission that one-sided, long-distance romances are inherently difficult. She's right, they are.

"Relationships, satisfying relationships, take a great deal of work by both parties involved. Factor in distance and it's even more difficult to pull off."

"Yes, I know you're right. But, it was something special—"

"Is it balanced, two-sided?" Karen is painfully direct.

There is no reason to admit what she already knows. Maggie would not be as kind as Karen, and tell me directly that I am a fool and be right about it. She would chastise me for giving him another thought after the way he behaved in January.

Karen studies my eyes. "You have to go, don't you?"

"Yes, I have to make sure."

"Then go, settle this one way or another."

There is no reason to discuss the psychology of my need to see this through after running away from the death of my little client, and staying away for five years. Going to Ireland makes about as much sense as running to Nebraska. The one difference is this time I am going away to understand what's going on, rather than to run from it.

Karen understands that I have to face my fear of losing him. Perhaps I will be pleasantly surprised, and silence is only his nature. After she leaves I make my flight reservations, even in the absence of a response from him.

~~~

Neither Grandfather nor Mr. Bradford have contacted me with further requests to meet, so I guess that may be all there is going to be of that. At least, I met the old man, and it feels like a missing piece has been found and added to my life. I can't help desiring more meetings, but I have no choice except to be realistic and get on with my routine.

I call Nick, to see if he wants to catch the Dodgers opening game, but he is out of town on work-related business. I should go alone or call another cousin or two, but I don't. A dose of baseball, especially the Dodgers opening game, would have been good for me, but I don't follow through with it. There will be other opening games.

In addition to the walks with Mr. Goldstein, I often go to the beach on my own. I haven't seen Livingston since the storm. I watch for him
~~~

and worry about him. I know in my heart he is resourceful. He survived whatever accident crippled him. He probably knew the storm was coming in ample time to seek shelter. Still, I watch for him.

I am not feeling sorry for myself when I say, I feel alone. It is a simple fact that everyone I know is busy or has moved along in their life in ways that I can't seem to master.

After nearly a year at Spirit of Hope, no one has to ask the staff to help with the recital. We all know what is expected of us. The staff is an extension of the Franciscan community of nuns. Occasionally, we have the ability to anticipate Mother Elizabeth's wishes. Before the list went on the bulletin board, we discussed the cookies we'll bring for the recital. The rumor is Sister Theresa is delighted the sign-up sheet was filled before noon.

Like the other staff members, I get ambitious and bake several dozen cookies and signed up to help serve them as well. It feels good to be part of something, especially something that is making a positive difference in people's lives. I am careful not to take for granted the feeling of belonging.

Sister Veronica's excitement has been contagious for the staff and volunteers. I do love recitals; the results are always so unpredictable, and the littlest child steals the show every time.

Mr. Goldstein and Karl, his friend from the Senior Center, ride with me. We arrive early, or so I thought. Apparently, the cafeteria ladies decided to pull rank on the rest of us. They have taken possession of the food duties, summarily dismissing the staff from the area as soon as they confiscate our baked goods. Undaunted, they stand their ground behind the refreshment table, and none of us dare challenge their authority.

When we originally set out the chairs, I thought Sister Theresa was optimistic in her estimation of the audience. But now I see that they may run out of seating. I choose a seat near the back so I can give up my chair quietly, if needed, for guests. Besides, I like the back of a room for the vantage point it gives me. I can see the center of activity, as well as the other observers—probably a behavior I developed in Nebraska behind the bar at Ruthie's.

Karen is accompanied by Linda and Todd. Linda looks more at peace than when I first met her last year. I suspect her work with the Child Abuse Prevention Coalition is therapeutic for her. It's probably the power to do something about child abuse that is healing her pain from the lack of power to stop her own abusing father. Therapy, a supportive husband and in-laws help.

Following close behind Linda and Todd are Todd's parents, Governor and Mrs. Angela Whitmore. Nothing had been said about the governor attending the recital, so everyone is surprised. There is an instantaneous stir in the room. Everyone recognizes the governor. It's even more obvious everyone recognizes his wife, Angela Whitmore, one of Hollywood's most talented and respected actresses. She has the grace of royalty.

Karen directs the governor and Angela to Mother Elizabeth, who promptly introduces them to Sister Veronica and the performers, one by one.

Everyone is gracious and allows the performers to have the spotlight. With a great deal of interest, I watch Shasta's reaction to being introduced to the famous couple. She is masterful. Shasta shakes hands, then promptly produces her program from behind her back for autographs from the celebrities. What a mind that child has. She is always a step ahead of everyone else. I can't wait until Monday morning to hear her thoughts about all of this.

It isn't listed on the program, but Governor Whitmore gives opening remarks. He pulls a folded paper from his inside jacket pocket and produces a brief, but moving speech about the value of the performing arts in our lives and the richness the arts bring to Californians, and the world.

The recital begins. It's obvious that many of the performers had only a few months of lessons. There are others that must have played for years. The choir is good. There are two solos: one by Lana, Race's dull wife. She sings like Gladys Knight, energetic, passionate. Her dull shell seems to fall away when she sings. She may be the best vocalist in the show. This is a pleasant and surprisingly new insight into Lana. I imagine it doesn't come easy for Lana to take this risk after what she has been through living on the streets for so long.

Of course, my favorite is Race and his jazz band. I know how volatile and vulnerable he can be. He transforms into a confident, serene person when he picks up his instrument and fits his lips to the reed of his sax. His rendition of the emotions is excellent.

There is nothing on this Earth that compares to music on a saxophone. The trumpet player appears at the rear of the auditorium and answers Race's notes, as they walk to the stage where Race is sashaying like a St. Louis musician. I love the sassy way the trumpet and sax play back and forth. Today couldn't be more perfect.

Following the recital, the reception is full of the electricity of people coming together and enjoying life. I am sure it is a day all of us will remember for the rest of our lives. Angela Whitmore congratulates each artist in such a way as not to upstage the local stars. There is a buzz in the air. The recital has done a great deal to boost the self-esteem of the Spirit of Hope families. All of the nuns are beaming with pride in their families, just as if their own children had been on stage, young and old alike. I close my eyes briefly to savor the tender emotions of the moment, and say a word of appreciation to God.

Just as I am about to leave with my gentlemen friends, there is a crashing sound of metal chairs being knocked over behind us. Turning toward the sound, I see Monica lying on the floor with a chair on top of her. She looks grayish-pale and lifeless. For a moment lingering in time, it is silent and still as if everyone in the room is holding their breath in unison. Oh God, Monica looks dead. We are frozen in our places, but our minds are racing. Everyone's eyes are panicked—then, we move quickly to her side.

Lyle, her husband, is instantly removing the fallen chair covering Monica, desperately calling her name over and over again. Rhoda lowers her cheek near Monica's mouth.

"She's breathing, call 911."

Rhoda, a Spirit of Hope staff member, attends to Monica, carefully easing Monica's twisted, limp body into a more comfortable position.

Mother Elizabeth kneels beside Rhoda, commanding, "Quick, call 911—someone call 911!" Mother gently brushes Monica's hair off her face, whispering, "Monica dear, Monica," over and over.

Several people already have their cell phones out and are dialing before anyone had to tell them. Rhoda was a medical social worker before working at Spirit of Hope, and sets the tone with her comfort in medical emergency situations.

When she asks for a damp towel, one of the cafeteria ladies disappears. In a moment she returns with a towel. Monica stirs slightly when Rhoda begins gently wiping her face with the towel, but she never opens her eyes.

Sister Theresa hurries down the hall in the direction of the front door. Other sisters are clearing the remaining chairs out of the way, moving us back, getting blankets, taking charge. Still kneeling beside Rhoda, Mother Elizabeth continues stroking Monica's hair and speaking softly to her.

Shortly, Sister Theresa returns, leading paramedics into the room. Immediately, they rush to attend to Monica, flipping open their emergency cases full of packaged medical supplies. Mother Elizabeth, Rhoda, and Lyle move back only as far as required. The rest of us stand a short distance away quietly watching, hoping, and bargaining with God.

Monica stirs when the paramedics put an oxygen mask on her face. After a rudimentary evaluation, they prepare to take Monica away.

Their children are crying and calling for their mommy. Lyle looks torn between Monica and the children. Lana, Race's wife, quickly moves forward and begins to help Lyle with the children. Her youngest, who is two years older than Lyle's oldest, takes the youngster by the hand, while Lana takes the twins and comforts them.

"Thank you, Lana. Thank you." Lyle kisses the children's heads and returns his attention to Monica.

One paramedic starts to argue with Monica's husband and Mother Elizabeth, who clearly plan to ride along. The two look at each other as if he's lost his senses. The paramedic decides not to take on the determined nun. Wise choice.

"Sister Theresa, take over here. I'll go help get Monica settled." She turns to walk away with Lyle.

I suspect she plans to intervene when the health insurance issue arises. They might as well admit Monica without a fuss, or they will wish they had.

There is a heavy silence after the ambulance leaves, and its siren fades away. Someone in the room, probably a nun, starts the Lord's Prayer. Everyone takes hold of the hand of the person next to them as the prayer continues,"...hallowed be Thy name..."

I take Mr. Goldstein's hand. Obviously, since he is Jewish, he doesn't say the prayer, but I feel that he is part of this assembly of strangers, nuns, homeless, and famous—all melded into one. He and Karl softly, quietly cantor their own prayer in Hebrew. I lean toward Mr. Goldstein slightly to hear the soothing sound of his rich male voice softly raised in prayer.

When we leave, the cafeteria ladies are putting away the remaining refreshments, the families are returning to their homes upstairs, and the nuns are entering the chapel for a vigil of Evening Prayers.

On the way home, I tune the radio to a classical station, and turn the volume low. I don't know what the conversation might have been if Monica hadn't collapsed, but we are silent as we travel the freeway.

Mr. Goldstein decides to stay and visit with Karl for a while. I go the rest of the way home alone. Monica, beautiful Monica—lying motionless on the floor—is imprinted on my mind. I can still hear her children crying and see her husband's worried eyes.

~~~

It isn't unusually cold on the beach, but I pull my jacket up around my neck. Monica's children's cries overlap in my mind with the screams of the little girl in my last child abuse court case. I feel cold.

It is late afternoon and Livingston is still not on the beach with the other seagulls. As I walk along the water's edge, I look out to sea on the chance that he is late flying back to shore. But I never see him.

It seems especially lonely on the beach today. Karen, Mr. Goldstein, Joseph, Maggie, Livingston, all of my beach friends are gone. Even God
~~~

is busy right now watching over Monica—as He should be. Karen is probably entertaining the Whitmore delegation, since she is the local coalition big wig. If there were other plans, I am sure they have been aborted with Mother Elizabeth occupied.

The cold finally drives me indoors. After a hot shower and a steaming cup of coffee, I settle on the sofa to write in my diary.

Maggie; I wish you were here. You seem to understand life's mysteries far better than I. If there is a way to understand the events of today, I would like to understand. I cannot begin to express how heavy my heart is now. The euphoria of the recital was short-lived. I'm worried about Monica. Things seem to work out in the end—though the middle is the hard part. This must be the middle.

Laying aside my diary and shifting my position on the sofa, I still visualize Monica lying motionless. "How can this happen?" I ask God, not really expecting an answer. I hope all of His attention is directed toward her. It doesn't feel like what's wrong with her is trivial.

~~~

It was a long night. Shasta appears on schedule, then quickly disappears for school. No one mentions Monica, but I am sure she is in everyone's thoughts. I am not assigned to Monica's family, but I catch myself watching for her husband, wanting to know how she is doing.

Monday morning shrouds everyone in a dim light at Spirit of Hope. We half-heartedly go about our duties, trying not to let go of the accomplishments of the recital. It is distinctively not business as usual today. Clearly there is awareness that Mother Elizabeth hasn't been here. The other nuns are doing her duties. I hadn't realized how much we depend on Mother Elizabeth to set the tone and to make us feel secure.

The staff isn't close like Maggie and I were. We don't spend off-duty time together; I don't even know everyone's last name, since we don't use last names. We come to work, spend the day absorbed in our homeless families, then go home. We work well together and that is enough.

We have a closeness with our clients without letting them become dependent on any one of us. At any rate, it shows on our faces that we are all worried about Monica. I worry as if we are lifelong friends.

My assigned family is on autopilot. I suspect they will be our first success story. Mom and dad are working and the children are in school. God knows we could use a success about now.
~~~

I'm sent to help in the office since Sister Theresa is pulling double duty in Mother Elizabeth's absence.

Mother Elizabeth suddenly rushes into the reception area. There is a nervous vulnerability about her. She fumbles with the pen at the sign-in sheet.

I'm out of her direct sight near the copy machine. I can clearly see her face is pale. There is a tremor in her hands and her voice. It bothers me deeply that she is so unsettled.

"Theresa, get my sister," Mother Elizabeth nearly begs.

"Yes, Mother," Sister Theresa says softly.

Being called, "Mother" seems to snap Mother Elizabeth back into her role as Mother Superior.

"Sister Theresa, I am fine." She pauses to clear her throat, then speaks calmly. "Please call Karen, ask her to come over, if possible. I will be in the garden." Mother Elizabeth smiles an unconvincing smile and stands tall and confident. But her confidence doesn't look real.

Maybe it was caring for my mother when she was dying, or losing Maggie suddenly, that makes me feel protective of the people around me. I have seen the weight of her responsibilities wear on Mother Elizabeth, but this is different. This is worse.

Since Karen disclosed how lonely it is at the top, I am more aware of the vulnerability of persons in positions of ultimate authority. A lesson I vividly remember now as I watch Mother Elizabeth struggle.

Maybe, I am concerned because I need Mother Elizabeth to be strong. Maybe, that is why I find it disturbing to see her as an ordinary human like the rest of us. I am inadequate for the custodial task, and not likely the one she would turn to, if she turns to anyone other than God. It's good she has Karen.

I move for a better view, near the table used for collating papers, and watch Mother Elizabeth leave. From just the right angle, I can see through the open door and observe her sitting on the garden bench.

Her shoulders slump when she sits down before the statue of St. Francis. Mother looks longingly up at his face. I can see her fingers frantically work the rosary that had been clipped to her belt.

Within minutes, Karen comes in the convent door, briefly pausing to look at Sister Theresa, who points toward the garden without exchanging words. Karen's movements are deliberate, calculated, smooth. At the garden doorway, she pauses, visibly takes a breath, then enters the courtyard garden.

Karen slides on the bench beside Mother Elizabeth. Karen gazes at St. Francis. Mother Elizabeth begins to speak, but looks at St. Francis. Karen listens. Finally, she touches Mother Elizabeth's hand, still busy with her beads.

Mother's fingers stop moving, then drop the strand of beads. She turns to Karen with tears streaming down her face. Karen puts her arms around her older sister and guides Mother Elizabeth's head to her shoulder with a caring hand. Mother's body shakes, as she sobs in Karen's arms.

I feel like I am intruding, even from this distance. Mother Elizabeth is in good hands. Now that she isn't alone, I don't need to watch over her. I felt the need to be a sentinel. When Sister Theresa moves, I realize she was doing the same as me.

The day goes on in a bland way. Mother Elizabeth and Karen are nowhere to be seen. Without any news about Monica, the staff reluctantly goes home at the end of the day, feeling incomplete.

~~~

Just before lunch on Tuesday, Mother Elizabeth has Sister Theresa summon the staff to the conference room. Sister is standing near and slightly behind Mother Elizabeth, in a Secret Service way. There is a protective and official attitude to Sister Theresa's stance.

Mother Elizabeth begins, "I am sure you all want to know the news regarding Monica's condition." Mother pauses only slightly, as we sit more alert in our chairs. The room is quiet.

"Monica is in the latter stage of AIDS." Mother scans each face in the room. "Her prognosis is not promising. Living in their car, along with poor nutrition, weakened her immune system enough for the disease to progress quickly. Of course, while homeless, she did not have medical care."

Mother doesn't pause long. The medical screening at Spirit of Hope was not intended to be comprehensive; it was only the basics of a free clinic. Monica said nothing about feeling tired because she was feeling better with the steady diet and relief from the stress of homelessness. So no one knew until it was too late.

"Monica and her family are staying here. Anyone who wishes to leave Spirit of Hope should remain seated to meet with Sister Theresa. The rest of you may go to lunch now." That's Mother Elizabeth's final statement on the matter. Immediately, she walks out and is gone.

The staff silently file out of the room. I don't feel like eating lunch. Many of us end up scattered around the playground. No one has their lunch with them, and no one left the building for lunch. We don't talk to each another.

I sit on the lawn, leaning against a tree. Never once do I consider Mother Elizabeth's option of leaving this job. Monica always has a smile. I like working with Monica and Lyle. They were my first family assignment. All of these months, she never once complained or mentioned feeling ill. Maybe she became used to not feeling well.
~~~

At precisely noon the church bells begin ringing their loud chime. I look around the yard. It's funny how we want to be near each other, but not too near during this time. Maybe the staff is closer to each other in an intangible way than I thought.

Some of the staff are looking up at the bell tower. Rhoda moves nearer Paul. They seem to be discussing the bell. Others are staring away; far away.

The bells ring a long time, longer than the usual hour strike at noon. I listen with an out-of-focus gaze, close my eyes, and lose myself in it. Paul interrupts my escape into the bells.

"Kathryn, what do the bells mean? Is Monica dead?" Paul asks with a panicked gasp.

Paul and many of the other staff are not, or appear not to be, Catholic. They don't understand the change in the bell. I become aware of how alarming the long-sounding bells must be for them, especially on the heels of the news about Monica.

"Oh, no. Paul, it's all right. The bells are ringing the Angelus. It's a prayer that is said at noon, midnight, and six in the morning and evening. The bells are a call to a special prayer. It doesn't mean Monica is dead, nothing like that."

"Angelus?" he echoes.

"I am not sure I remember all of the words, I can bring you a copy tomorrow, if you like."

It is not my nature to share my faith, or to attempt to convert others. But this isn't about organized religion. It is about a sense of unity. It is about explaining the cause of their anxiety.

~~~

After dinner I look through Mother's things for her prayer book. Once I find it, I sit on the floor leaning against my bed, reading in the dim light of evening.

Angelus

Leader: The Angel of the Lord declared unto Mary.

Response: And she conceived of the Holy Spirit...

The words of the prayer return to my memory. After a few readings, I fully remember it. I will be awake at the hours of the Angelus. In this small way, I can join with the sisters. I find the prayer on the internet and print it for Paul.

~~~

After my usual morning meeting with Shasta, I give Paul the Angelus.

He looks at the paper. "Thank you, Kathryn," he says, still reading the prayer.

Hurriedly, I add, "I'm not trying to influence your religious beliefs—I just thought—"

Paul interrupts, "No really, thank you." He smiles, as our eyes meet in an awkward moment.

"Well, I should get to work," I mumble.

The non-social-work staff is assigned to care for baby Clare Elizabeth and the other toddlers, while the nuns and social work staff join the adult clients in the auditorium. It is easy to guess that Mother Elizabeth is going to announce Monica's condition to our families and field their questions and emotions. Obviously, we're on standby for crisis intervention.

Mother Elizabeth and Sister Theresa enter the room and quickly walk to the microphone stand that remains from the recital. Sister Theresa does not stand with Mother Elizabeth, as she did yesterday; rather, she takes a seat in the front row.

Mother Elizabeth waits for a minute, looks at Sister Theresa, then begins:

"For nearly a year, we have shared in our life journey. In a way, we have become a family. We have even added a baby to our family." She briefly smiles a slight smile. "I know that everyone is concerned about Monica. It is understandable to worry. I wish that I had better news for you." She pauses to take a deep breath. "Several years ago, Monica worked as a lab technician in a hospital. She was accidentally pricked with a needle that had been used on a patient who later tested positive for the HIV virus."

There are gasping sounds throughout the audience. Mother continues without comment to the reaction.

"I don't need to tell you about the hardships of homelessness. As you can imagine, the fatigue, stress, and malnourishment made it difficult for Monica's body to fight the disease."

A man stands up abruptly, interrupting Mother. "What are you going to do about this?" he demands. His tone and his stance are hostile.

There is a different kind of hush in the room than from before.

"The doctors think Monica will be strong enough to come home soon." Mother Elizabeth stops speaking when the man interrupts her again.

"Home! Are you nuts! She isn't coming here, is she?" the man insists as he looks angrily at Mother Elizabeth then around the room for support of his position.

Sister Theresa shifts in her chair, but Mother gives her a quick, "Let it go" look.

In a soft, but sure voice Mother says, "I can understand that some of you are frightened. I don't have to tell you that there is a risk that any one of us may have contracted the virus. And there is a continued risk having Monica here, a risk that I feel is justified. This is her home. I will not turn her away, not now, not ever. Not when she needs us the most."

"Everyone has to be tested later today. Then, if any of you want to leave, you must make the decision by Friday."

The man's voice becomes loud and forceful. "Are you f–ing nuts? You can't keep her here!"

Race stands before the man can say another word. Race is the unofficial leader among the families. Not so much because he wants to be, but because he was so tough on the streets.

A hush falls.

"Mother Elizabeth." Race's voice booms. "My family's situation was hopeless when you took us in. You asked no questions, and made no demands. What you are doing for Monica, you would do for any one of us. My family and I are staying. We support you, Mother Elizabeth, and will stand by you."

Mother Elizabeth looks like she is about to tear up from Race's passionate endorsement of her decision.

It gives me a lump in my throat.

Race's voice softens a little as he continues to address her. "If there is a God, He must be very pleased with you, Mother Elizabeth, with all of your sisters." With that Race's dull wife stands beside him, slips her arm around his arm, united in purpose. Together, they both stand taller.

There's a hush in the room.

Mother Elizabeth softly clears her throat and simply replies, "Thank you, Race."

I have never heard Race speak like that. It makes me choke back tears. Around the room others slowly stand. When everyone is standing, the belligerent man grabs his wife's hand and pushes his way to the end of the row of people, and out of the room.

Mother motions to Sister Theresa to take over the meeting, then follows the departing couple. As Mother walks to the back of the room to leave, she makes eye contact and smiles at Race.

He looks her straight in the eye and slowly, loudly begins to applaud. The applause builds as others join until everyone is applauding her.

The look on her face speaks volumes. This display of respect from these homeless people to the Godly nun is more than I can bear. Soon we are all wiping tears, except Race, who stands tall and determined.

Sister Theresa blinks back tears as she takes to the stage. When the applause dies, she leans toward the microphone.

"Thank you for coming. We know you will have questions. There is an expert coming to talk with all of us and answer all of our questions before Monica comes home." With that Sister Theresa concludes the meeting and leaves. There really isn't much to say—Race said it all.

Mother Elizabeth must have thought she'd need the social workers for crisis intervention. I don't think she expected such support from her families. She never asks anything of them. They rose to the occasion with class and dignity. They know that standing with her on this is the right thing to do, the only thing to do. I am proud to know Race and Lana—to know all of them.

~~~

Monica's prognosis is the final emotional blow. It's one person too many to go away. Life has been full of intense emotions, and in Joseph's case, abandonment. In a matter of a few months, I have lost my best friend; the love of my life; gained a grandfather for a day, then lost him again; helped Mr. Goldstein find his family, a half a world away; and now Monica, who, in my mind, has become the personification of the Spirit of Hope, is leaving.

I have to pull myself together before Monica comes home on Friday. However, that seems impossible at the moment. I don't know what else to do but walk on the beach. It has been rainy, and no one is around. Even the seagulls have found shelter somewhere else. I would cry, if it would help fix the way I feel.

I want to find strength, so Monica can rely on me. She will need all of us now. Dying must be hard with three small children. I can't begin to imagine what Monica is experiencing.

There is always an outside chance of a miracle, especially with these nuns around. But the reality of the situation is bad. She's probably going to die.

The damp, salty air is heavy on my lungs. Still, I walk along the shore. I feel like I am drowning in the high tide of life. Finally, it is dark. I am hungry and cold. There is nowhere to go, but home. The day feels empty. I am too spent to write in my diary tonight.

~~~

Before Shasta can meet me at the door, Sister Theresa hands me a note, sending me on an errand. The family who left yesterday left some belongings. I am to take them to the shelter where they are living now. Yes, I have noticed that I run a lot of errands. I don't really mind.

After I check in with Shasta, I head out the door with my cargo. The traffic is its usual annoying self. It is a lot of bother just to take two boxes to the shelter. Left to me, I would have waited an hour and let the traffic clear a bit. However, the decision was not left to me. I acquiesce to Sister's will.

One of the homeless men outside the shelter helps me carry in the boxes. They aren't particularly heavy, they are just an awkward size to carry both of them at once. I don't see our former clients. It is probably just as well. They are entitled to their opinion, and in a way, I respect them for sticking to their convictions regardless of whether I share them.

When I emerge from the shelter, a parade is coming down the street. It is obvious my car is landlocked until the parade passes. I sigh with frustration, and lean against the building to wait for the freedom to leave. There is an old Black woman sitting on the sidewalk near where I am standing. She looks like she has been living on the street for quite a while.

She speaks. "Gir-lie, youz stuck e'er. Mite a'swell sat 'n enjoy da pra'ade," she says with a musical rhythm to her words. The spaces between her pauses fill with a soft, grunting sound deep in her throat, somewhat like a cross between the cooing of pigeons and the purring of an old, contented cat.

She looks at the parade passing before us, then speaks again. She seems to be speaking to me, and perhaps to herself. It's difficult to tell.

"I cr-i at pra'adez, ya know. I seez da colar gard, 'n my eyez wat'r up, 'n my throat gets tite." She massages her neck gently to make the point.

I'm caught in her mesmerizing calm, unpretentious realness.

"Ev'ry ones sittin' up right strait 'n proud on der float. It don't matt'r if'n it's a fan-cy float or plain 'un." She pauses to watch a float overflowing with squirming, giggling children.

A junior high band follows the float. They are slightly out of step, and occasionally a sour note squeaks loudly above the rest of the budding musicians' lively score.

"I cr-i when da ban pl-ays loud, soo-o loud youz can feel it 'n youz chest, rattlin' youz bonz." She touches her hand to her heart. "I'z clap to da muzic a-as hard as I'z can, 'n I smile real big 'cuz I'm hap-ie. Gir-lie, I'z soo-o hap-ie. Why, I think I would bust if'n—"

Something on the passing float catches her attention. She silently watches for a moment, then continues.

"I'd bust if'n some o' my hap'ness coudn't run down my face." She wipes a tear running down the side of her face.

With that, she turns toward me as if to see whether I understand.

I smile.

Her eyes study me for a long moment. When she is satisfied, she continues her final pronouncement.

"Chi-l-d, a pa'arde is good."

A tear pauses on her cheek before it follows the crease of a line in her face. Her eyes are rich with wisdom. It feels awkward to be in the presence of such Aristotelian logic. I look ahead to the end of the parade, listening to her cooing.

When the last float passes, I am surprised to be disappointed to see it end. The chance experience of the parade feels like a mother's arms around me, consoling me. The old woman is right about parades being good for the soul.

I turn to say something to her, I don't know what, "thank you" doesn't seem like enough. But she and her cart are gone. She disappeared into the crowd. Quickly I walk to the end of the block, look ahead to the next block, and around the corner, but I don't see her. Slowly, I return to my car. The experience has been an unexpected gift, and its mood lingers.

The traffic finally clears enough to get my car into the street. Down the block from the shelter is a small neighborhood church with paper flowers strung everywhere. There are Mexican flags, "Fiesta" banners, and signs with "Cinco de Mayo" on them. The church parking lot is full of tables and chairs, food booths, and a mariachi band playing on the gaily decorated stage.

The houses around the church are decorated with festive Christmas lights and Mexican flags. They are gearing up to celebrate all weekend. The aroma of the food drifts in my car window, convincing me to round the corner and park. I walk back to the food booths. The tostada booth has the longest line—a good indication of the quality of their product.

While I wait in line, I look around, hoping to see the parade lady with the intention of buying her a meal. She is nowhere to be found. There are tiny children dressed in traditional costumes dancing with the band now. I join the crowd gathered near the smaller stage and watch the dancers while I eat. The food exceeds my expectations.

~~~

Upon returning to Spirit of Hope, I quietly go about the tasks of helping anyone with anything, since my family is away until later this afternoon. Most of the duties I help with are menial tasks. It gives me time to savor the experience with the old woman on the street.

It isn't until the Angelus rings that I realize how quickly the morning has passed. For the first time since Monica's collapse, I feel like eating lunch, despite my midmorning tostada. It is good to be hungry again. It reminds me that I am alive and that life goes on, even during the hard times.

The afternoon is quiet. I cover playground duty with the children who are too young for school, but too old for naps.

~~~

Walking along the beach after dinner, I tell Mr. Goldstein about the experience of seeing the homeless bag lady's immersion into the simple experience of a parade. I hope the experience will guide my actions in the coming weeks and months of the final chapter of Monica's life.

Maggie wrote, "It isn't how long we live, it's how wide." Between Maggie's words and the old parade woman's wisdom in celebrating the moments in life, I hope I am guided well.

Mr. Goldstein takes the news about Monica's condition as only a man who experienced the Holocaust can take it. His eyes are thoughtful. He nods affirmatively.

"Listen to your heart, Katerina, you will know what to do for her. Just listen to your heart."

"I will," I whisper. "I will."

We walk to the edge of the water in silence. It is a comfortable silence. We savor our time together. Monica's critical condition reminds me to appreciate each moment I have with Mr. Goldstein. He is a gift. It is best not to take for granted that people will always be here.

Dearest Maggie, Life is about touching people in a gentle, quiet way. It is about making a difference and not getting caught.

~~~

Everyone turns out to meet the car when Monica arrives home. Race pushes through the assembly when Monica's husband struggles to help her out of the back seat. Effortlessly, Race picks up Monica in his muscular arms, carries her through the door, down the hallway, and into her home.

Monica looks in each person's eyes as she is carried past us. She smiles at each of her well-wishers. Monica looks healthier than before. That's reassuring. Her hair is pulled back with the silk scarf I gave her. I hadn't realized it meant quite that much to her. It was only a simple gesture born out of necessity—she needed it for her interview, and I have more.

All of us follow Race and Monica in a procession, like the parade-lady's parade. As gently as a butterfly landing on a flower, Race lays Monica on her bed. We leave her and her family alone to get settled.

~~~

~ CHAPTER 12 ~

Farewell

It has been a long and emotionally draining week. I don't expect the weekend to be much better since Mr. Goldstein is flying out of LAX on Sunday. Saturday is the only time we have left on the beach.

We have a lunch date. Mr. Goldstein is ordinarily a quiet man, but today he is more talkative than usual. Conversely, I am more pensive.

Sitting back, I absorb the essence of his company, fixing in my mind the way he savors his wine, the dance in his eyes when he speaks of his family, and the richness of his voice.

We make our way to the beach for one last walk. His stamina is such that he can walk the entire length of the beach now. This is not a walk to be cut short. I know full well this may be the last time we see each other. Once he returns to Europe he may not feel the need to leave again.

There are so many things I want to say to him. But the thoughts are unspeakable emotions within my heart. Instead of words, I reach for his hand to walk the beach holding hands for the first time since I have known him.

He seems to understand. He grasps my hand in recognition that we have shared a richness beyond words. We walk in silence, holding hands. I stop to pick up a pretty shell, brush off the wet sand, and give it to him without saying a word.

He smiles and gives a little nod toward me. He slips the shell into his pocket, and smiles again.

> *Dearest Maggie, I spent the weekend bidding farewell to Mr. Goldstein. I have a new love-hate relationship with LAX. It brought me home. But since then it has taken away so many people in my life. I think I will never take anyone to the airport again. It is too hard to say goodbye. The time we have among our friends is far too short.*

On top of everything else grievous, Mother Elizabeth assigned me to Monica's family this week. One staff person and one family left after the announcement of Monica's condition. Maybe the other homeless families are just being practical—they don't have anywhere better to go. I don't think that is really it at all.

Mother Elizabeth says nothing more about it. Monica stays. The rest of the sisters line up beside her like an army staying their ground—a brown-robed army. In the days that follow, my resolve is strengthened by the conviction of the formidable Franciscan women. Righteousness surrounds them. It fills the room when they enter, like some people ooze confidence.

The only person in the universe able to upstage the nuns, even Mother Elizabeth, is Monica. It seems everything she says should be written down, maybe even published someday as an inspirational book, or at least given to her children when they are older.

Monica makes it easy to work with her. We have a great deal of time to talk while her husband is at work and the children are in school. Some days she feels up to short walks in the hallway. Sometimes Race carries her outside where we sit in the shade and ponder the wisdom of the universe. Often we sit in silence watching the little kids play.

"God is subtle, but He is not malicious."

"Excuse me?"

"Albert Einstein: God is not malicious."

I am not sure what to say, so I say nothing. I simply nod with an agreeing smile.

Friday, I regret the week is ending. As I turn to leave Monica's room to go home, Monica has one last bit of wisdom to impart. Her words are not wasted on me. I bought another, smaller diary to write her sayings each evening, as best I can remember them by the time I get home.

"Good night, Monica, have a good weekend."

"Kathryn—"

I turn back and sit on her bed.

"God has given us many, many blessings—all of which are unearned." She smiles weakly.

Her words have the richness of the final line in an old classic movie. They permeate my being as I drive home and linger throughout the weekend. It seems the outside world is suspended in time somewhere, far away from reality.

When I do think about the real world again, I divide my thoughts quietly between Monica and the parade lady. There isn't much I can do for Monica. It is better that she has the time with her family.

~~~

I decide to drive the area around Sally's, Salvation Army Mission, looking for the parade lady. It doesn't take long to realize that driving slowly to look down alleys is difficult without a partner. I wish Maggie was here to help.

I can't explain why I want to find the parade lady. There is something about solitary people that connects with my own aloneness —her in particular. When I was vulnerable she touched me with her words in an unexplainable way. There is something that draws me to want to reach out to her.
~~~

Surely everyone in the neighborhood knows her. I go inside the "fiesta" church office to ask about the homeless Black woman with a cart. The secretary makes it clear that she isn't willing to expend any effort to help in my search.

She makes a remark resembling, "You see one homeless person, you've seen them all." I wonder if she learned that lovely attitude in Sunday School. I look around a bit and go home.

~~~

My next plan involves standing around outside of Sally's and asking the homeless people if they know her. A couple of industrious fellows panhandle, but most give me a wide berth, much the same as other people give them.

The person at the sign-in desk inside is new and doesn't know the parade lady. I would think this Black woman with bright eyes and Southern Appalachian speech pattern would be noticeable, but apparently she blends in with the blur of street people. I go home without a clue who the woman is or where to find her.

~~~

The next Saturday, as I walk through the park back to where I left my car in front of the fiesta church, a woman across the street catches my attention. The homeless people in the park take little notice of me running to the edge of the park to catch up with the woman.

When I reach the other side of the street, there is no trace of the woman or her cart. I search a side alley to no avail, then return to the closest park bench to watch for her to appear again. My Welsh grandmother used to tell stories of angels in disguise. I wonder if the stories are true. Is the parade lady an angel in disguise?

Just as I am about to leave to get a bite to eat, I see her again. Quickly, I walk parallel to her on my side of the street, being careful not to take my eyes off of her this time. When I catch up, I cross the street ahead of her. As she walks past where I am leaning against the wall of a building, I say, "I love a parade." It has the desired effect.

She stops and looks at me for a long minute.

I take advantage of her interest in me and say, "Parades are good."

She looks at me a little more intensely, then jerks her cart and turns to continue down the sidewalk. She starts humming to herself while moving slowly away.

"Wait!" I speak louder than necessary—startling us both.

She picks up her pace slightly, but noticeably leaning into her cart to push it faster.

"Parade Lady, wait!" I maneuver to walk beside her without alarming her further, but determined not to lose her this time. I have invested three weekends trying to locate her.

She continues moving, perhaps concerned with my persistence and proximity to her and her cart.

My first instinct is to reach for her cart to slow her down, but I catch myself before I make a move.

She may have detected my intention or just planned to confront me. Either way, she stops abruptly.

"What you want, girlie?"

"You told me about parades. I want to talk to you."

She looks me over, then looks in my face—slightly closer than I like. There's a long pause while she inspects my eyes. I hope for recognition.

"Humph." She dismisses my seemingly benign words. She leans in to the handle of her cart as if preparing to leave.

"Wait! I have to talk to you," I plead.

She stops again, turns slightly and looks disgusted with me. "What you want?" she demands again.

I don't really know what I want. I look down to quickly gather my thoughts, and see that she is wearing old shoes that are too small. She has her foot into the toe, but her heel has flattened down the back of the shoe and hangs over the back edge. I realize her shuffling gait is meant to keep her shoes on, like a little girl shuffling around the house in her mother's high heels.

Quickly, I point at her feet. "Your shoes, I want to get you new shoes," I recover nicely.

"Humph. You do, do you?" She doesn't buy my line.

"Yes, well, your feet must hurt. And I would like very much to buy you new shoes."

My desperation is apparent in my voice. Here I am, begging a bag lady to let me buy her shoes and I don't know why.

"Nothing fancy, mind you," she says, as she looks at the cross trainers on my feet.

"What size?" I ask, grateful of any means to connect with her. I understand about nothing fancy. They might be taken from her, and she might get hurt in the process—all for a pair of shoes.

"Bigger than yourn."

"What color?" I continue while I have her engaged.

"No matter," she answers, and adjusts her hand on her cart handle, restless to go.

"Where will I find you?" I sense she is concluding the conversation.

She stops again, and points to a park bench across the street where someone is covered with a newspaper for an afternoon nap. It is not cold out, so I can only guess the paper is to keep the bugs off of his face while he sleeps. "O'er there."

"Tomorrow at one?"

She is moving away. She nods her head, but doesn't turn around to look at me.

~~~

The next day before twelve-thirty, I return with four shoe boxes. I sit and wait on the designated bench, watching in each direction for the parade lady to appear. By two o'clock she still hasn't come. It doesn't occur to me that she doesn't have a watch. It's nearly three, and I am thinking of putting the shoes in my car and going to find a restroom, when she finally arrives. She parks her cart, and eyes me and the shoe boxes for a minute before she sits down at the other end of the bench.

I open the boxes and set them in their lids on the bench between us. "I didn't know what size," I remind her, as I hand her a pair of socks. The shoes are basic canvas shoes.

Rather than take the socks, she reaches past the tan pair, and the navy pair, and hesitates over the box with the red pair. She looks at me.

I nod for her to continue and extend my hand with the socks a little closer to her.

She takes the socks in one hand, the red shoes in the other hand, and sets about to put them on. She says nothing. The shoes are slightly too small. She stops working at putting them on. She looks at the navy shoes with a sideways glance, as if she is deciding whether to try another pair or keep the color she likes.

While she has been trying the shoes, I watch her face. Her hard life shows in her weathered skin, but I think she is younger than I had originally thought. She might even be about my mother's age.

She plops the red shoes back in their box and tries on the navy ones. She wiggles her ankle as she extends her foot off the ground to examine the fit. She seems satisfied with the feel of them, but looks back one more time at the red shoes.

"Take those. I'll bring red ones next Saturday, at one."

"All right," she answers, as she gets up to leave.

I am pleased that she accepted the gift. It makes no sense to me, but I felt indebted to her for something that defies explanation.

~~~

The next weekend I return with red shoes. She doesn't keep me waiting this time. The shoes fit and she seems pleased. I offer her the shoe boxes, but she pulls a crumpled paper sack from her cart and wraps them inside it.

"Why you doin' this?"

"I liked what you said about parades," I answer honestly.

She readies her cart to leave, but she turns back and says softly, "Thank you, girlie."

"You're welcome. Watch for me. I'll be back, not every week, but always at one o' clock."

She is gone. She walks off pushing her cart over the uneven grass, humming to herself. I don't know if she heard what I said or not. I come back several times at the appointed hour, but don't see her again. I wish I had asked her name.

~~~
~~~

~ CHAPTER 13 ~

A Little Thing Like Reality

May blends into June with not even a hint of the progression of time. Most of the time I am lost on the timeless beach. The hands missing on the clock at the lifeguard building legitimatizes losing track of time.

Besides, time is insignificant. It's meaningful relationships and experiences that matter. I appreciate that bit of truth in the absence of the people who have come to mean something extraordinary to me. I sit on the early-morning beach, just before the sun comes up, and the masses of summer tourists come and drive me temporarily away.

Around 6:00 a.m. I pick up my blanket and empty coffee container, when Karen comes beside me. She is casually shaking the sand out of her sandals as if it hasn't been well over a month since we have seen each other. To me, it felt much longer than that. I can't remember if she knows Mr. Goldstein found his family.

While Karen has been consumed with her duties with the Child Abuse Prevention Coalition, I have been managing Mr. Goldstein's absence, the missing parade lady, and absent Livingston. I know that Mr. Goldstein belongs with his family. Still, I miss him.

"You're out early today." I smile at Karen.

"The Legislature has finally taken their summer break."

"Lucky for all of us!"

She grins, "Sometimes, I have that same thought," she laughs. "But, don't tell anyone!" She becomes more serious. "We are making slow progress. No one wants to hear about child abuse, it is a little too ugly for their sensibilities."

"And, children don't vote."

"Exactly," she concedes.

"If they had any guts at all they would serve notice to child abusers that regardless of who they are, society will get them and stop them at all costs," I say, thinking about how select people escape criminal prosecution for raping children.

As we begin to walk, I sense she has become, I don't know, different. Perhaps she is only tired from juggling her massive day job with the trips to Sacramento to spend time lobbying with people who are, at the very least, one step removed from the reality the rest of the population shares.

Karen begins to slip free from the artificial Sacramento world, and slide back into the real world of L.A. Yes, even Hollywood has more of a grasp of reality than most politicians.

"How is Monica?"

"She is managing. She had good days and bad days." I don't know how else to put it.

My memory replays the last time I saw Karen. She was consoling her Sister-sister the day after Monica's collapse. It seems odd that she hasn't kept in touch with Mother Elizabeth after that—and informed of Monica's status. Surely, she has at least talked with Mother Elizabeth by phone since then, and is only being polite by asking about Monica.

"So, other than political encounters, what is new with you?" I fear we are losing touch with each other on a personal level. If nothing else, I've learned how valuable relationships are, and how fleeting they can be.

"This year the Governor's Award Dinner is in L.A. It is a bit stuffy, but the food is excellent. It is obligatory for me, but I thought I would invite you." She set me up for the con. Oooh, she's good.

I wonder about the tone of her voice. It's a strange mix of frankness and a slight plea to attend. I don't even consider my options, she has done so much for me and this is the first time I remember her asking anything in return.

"Sure, it sounds interesting."

"Good, bring a date," she slips in the hint.

"Well, Joseph is a bit unavailable."

"Bring someone else, it is good insurance."

"Insurance?"

"Let's just say it'll keep everyone on good behavior, including drunk politicians." She smiles a knowing smile that guarantees I won't pursue her meaning. It's best not to know the details.

"Look, he's back!" I deliberately change the subject, pointing to a flock of seagulls on the beach ahead of us. "See that one with the gimpy wing?" I point to a seagull on the fringes of the group. "I've named him Livingston."

We stand and watch Livingston interact with the flock. He doesn't bemoan the struggles of survival or the glaringly apparent lack of accommodation from the other gulls regarding his disability.

> *Maggie, It seems clearly that the ultimate test of character is adversity. Livingston is the perfect example for getting on with life, thinking less about the unimportant details – ourselves, others' opinions of us, and the pettiness of the things outside our realm of influence. He is a reminder there is a nobility in being who we are meant to be.*

A date? That will take careful consideration. I'd ask Paul from work. He is a nice guy and we both enjoy baseball. But I recently found out he is married, so he's off limits.

Roberto is new staff and considers himself to be the original Latin Lover, though there is nothing original about him. Despite Roberto's obnoxious behavior, he is a hard worker. I tolerate him only because he is a bright financial advisor to our clients.

Oh, I hate this. My life is not even remotely rich in male friends. Maybe, I can entice my cousin to accompany me. Nick is between girlfriends, maybe he has a free evening. I'd better be quick, since his calendar is not likely to remain free for long.

What to wear? I have a shimmery blue gown that Maggie and I found the last time we were out shopping. It will be perfect. It is ocean blue. That works, especially with my hair pulled up.

It will be fine, I can do this for Karen.

~~~

When Nick and I approach Karen's table, the look on her face convinces me that we should keep to our prearranged deal, and not reveal we are cousins.

Her date is a familiar face—Keith. Goodness, we are such risk-takers. The guys look handsome in their tuxedos. Karen is beautiful with her hair up and emerald-colored gown.

We exchange the usual pleasantries, then I look around the room. There are several celebrities and prominent political powerhouses. The orchestra is playing movie scores. Just as one would expect jazz in Kansas City, it's movie scores in Hollywood. It is a perfectly wonderful fantasy, including the fun of dressing for a formal evening. This is too enchanting to worry about a little thing like reality.

Linda and Todd arrive and join our table. Dinner comes and goes, as well as the political rhetoric directed to impress Governor Whitmore. He smiles periodically from the dignitary table, but doesn't seem to take it for more than it is. Smart man.

Todd is very attentive to Linda in a classy way. Nick is a good sport to come with me, but really, observing the closeness between Linda and Todd makes me miss Joseph.

Finally the governor is introduced. I catch Karen's eye, as I am about to sip my champagne. Slightly, I raise my glass and nod a silent toast to her (and the fact that we are getting through the speeches).

She nods in return.

Governor Whitmore invites his famous actress wife to assist him in presenting the awards. They begin with the people who are on the front line of charitable works, the ones who really make a difference in this world of ours.

The recipients exchange greetings with Angela Whitmore, the Darling of Hollywood. No doubt for the rest of their lives they will talk about meeting her.
~~~

We work our way through the politicians who have contributed in one way or another. The PR firms have been busy. It seems everyone in local politics receives an award for one thing or another. Even the governor's exchanged glance with his wife seems to indicate that the event's planners have overdone it.

"There's one more person to invite to the podium tonight. Most of you know her, my daughter-in-law, Linda Whitmore." The governor moves his hand invitingly in Linda's direction and initiates the audience's applause. He looks as if he could burst with pride. He hugs her.

Graciously, she takes her place beside him. The applause is hearty. Linda waits for the audience to silence, smiles regally, and begins her comments.

"For months, many people have labored to bring awareness of the severity of child abuse to our legislators and the citizens of California. No one wants to believe that we have this ugly problem. Survivors of abuse, of all ages, have bravely testified publicly regarding their personal and painful experiences."

The audience is silently fixed on Linda. There is no sound of dishes, or glasses clinking, or people moving.

"Each of these people deserves your recognition and appreciation. Some risked their careers, their relationships, and their privacy to publicly disclose their past." Linda looks around the room, and then continues.

"It isn't possible for each person to be with us tonight. So we chose one person to stand in the place of all. Combined with the testimony, this person singlehandedly researched, wrote, and lobbied the bill requiring school counselors to have annual training and certification on child abuse detection and reporting. This is the most specific and unique law to address the fight against child abuse in the country." Linda is interrupted by the roaring applause for the accomplishment.

"Please, ladies and gentlemen, meet Dr. Karen Craig!" Linda concludes by initiating the applause.

Keith pulls out Karen's chair. She stands and turns to him. Their eyes meet in an observable intimate exchange.

Nothing is said that would hint to the truth behind the bill, the inside story about when Linda tried to tell her school counselor that her dad, the Judge, was raping her. It had taken so much for Linda to reach out for help. When the counselor was more interested in flirting with the vice principal, Linda backed away. She had to endure three more years of her father's raping before she could go away to college and be free.

But she wasn't free, even though the rape had stopped. It takes more than that, much more to end the lingering effects.

Linda steps back to make room for Governor Whitmore to join Karen at the podium. The governor holds up the bill in the usual celebratory political style.

The audience applauds wildly.

Karen looks embarrassed with all of the attention. That might explain why there are no awards in her office, even though it is rumored that she has received numerous, prestigious awards throughout her career.

Governor Whitmore smiles proudly and reaches inside his jacket. His hand re-emerges holding a pen. He pauses, signs the document into law, and ceremoniously holds up the pen for everyone to see before giving it to Karen.

Karen speaks briefly about the work yet to be accomplished as the coalition continues to promote laws to decrease the child abuse rate in California.

I listen with increased interest as Karen outlines the coalition's plans. They have encouraged the Legislature to introduce the social and educational policy reforms intended to decrease child abuse among at-risk children, as well as proposed mandatory stiffened punishment guidelines for the courts to use for repeat abusers.

When Karen returns to her seat with her plaque and pen, Keith pulls out her chair. Their eyes meet briefly before she sits. There it is again, that "thing" between them. He is more than attentive. They have a bond, and it seems personal. It's not quite romantic, but more than a standard-issue working relationship.

Nothing else out of the ordinary, for this type of event, happens. Governor and Mrs. Whitmore dance the first dance before they leave. My good-sport cousin and I dance a few times before we call it a night, too. Karen and Keith stay with Linda and Todd while they finish the evening as guests of honor.

~~~

I place Mother's diamond necklace back in its case and remove the matching earrings, then prop my feet on the coffee table, and savor the experience. It has been quite a night.

Karen and Linda are probably still celebrating the accomplishment. My eyes close as the aroma of my freshly ground coffee vapors rise from my cup.

What is that thing between Keith and Karen? As his investigative partner, we never developed a relationship beyond a tight, professional one. I can't remember any hint of a relationship between Karen and Keith. I don't know much about his personal life, but I am pretty sure he is married.

~~~

The most poignant memory is the time Keith was in Karen's office when I was summoned and told about the little girl's death. Unless I missed something, all I remember is the unbelievable sense of disbelief that she was killed by her father. There was no indication of closeness between them. It didn't appear that they connected with each other in that horrible moment. No, we were each profoundly alone then. It was, in a personal sense, an individual experience for each of us.

Karen divorced while I was in Nebraska. She never talks about her marriage or divorce. Maggie didn't mention it, either. I haven't read all of her diaries, but so far she hasn't written anything that remotely resembles gossip. Her entries are more in the vein of her own questions and insights.

Another cup of coffee doesn't bring any brilliant insights to mind. Maybe they are at the beginning stages of something. I hope it works out for them. But isn't Keith married? Clearly, it is none of my business. End of discussion.

~~~

Thinking about Joseph and me makes me sad. Maybe it is only a temporary rough time with us, and we will find our way back into the romance again. If not, maybe we are at that in-between place, between what was and what is coming next. I guess I will know more when I see him in a few weeks. I miss having that intimacy that Todd and Linda have. I miss being in love and being loved.

I have no reason to complain. In three weeks, I'll be in Ireland with Joseph, and that is a happy prospect. But this morning, my coffee isn't comforting. Strangely, I don't feel up to driving in the traffic, or the confines of a bus full of strangers—but duty calls.

Determination sees me through work. Since a family went to the shelter, we easily absorb the extra duties of Monica's illness.

While I sign out for the day, I can hear the Gregorian chanting coming from the open door to the chapel. Pausing for a moment, I consider walking down the hallway to listen briefly to the nuns' Evening Prayer, then think better of it.

Mother Elizabeth comes into the reception area to leave papers on the desk. She moves quickly, not rushed, it's more like efficient. Mother Elizabeth is often late for prayers because of interruptions from the secular world.

"Kathryn, do you have time to join me?"

"Yes, of course, Mother," I reply, uncertain of where we are going.

She walks out of the reception area with her rosary rattling at her side. She stops at the chapel door, dips her finger in the Holy Water font, makes the sign of the cross, and quietly enters during a break in the prayers.
~~~

My instinct is to hesitate. I feel uncomfortable intruding during Evening Prayers. Mother Elizabeth continues walking down the center aisle to the front pew. The gap between us is widening, which will make me walk in alone if I hesitate any longer. I commit to follow her, genuflect, and slip in the pew beside her.

She joins in mid-prayer from memory, as her hand reaches for the prayer book and effortlessly turns to the correct page. Suddenly, in unison all of the sisters slip quietly to their kneeler and continue praying without missing a beat. They stand, bow, make the sign of the cross, and bow deeply—this time from the waist. Returning to their seats, the leader reads from the Bible. Then without warning, back to their knees, and they are silent. They are like a religious drill team. Everyone knows the routine perfectly.

I, on the other hand, do not know the routine or the prayers. I am hesitant; my movements are delayed. I focus on the crucifix hanging behind the altar, but can't help noticing some of the sisters glancing at me. They aren't sideways glances. They are full-blown, all-out looks. I feel their eyes on me even from behind me. It makes concentrating on the prayers all the more difficult. I try to follow along in the prayer book Mother Elizabeth is holding between us. I feel like I am intruding, and I wonder what she is doing inviting me to Evening Prayers.

At the same time, it is interesting to see this private part of their lives. There is a strange sense of holiness in the air. The rhythm of the chanting is soothing. Their voices are angelic-sounding. A song, closing prayer, and we are finished.

Sisters begin to silently file out the back of the chapel. I hear a couple sisters moving in the wrong direction, in our direction. Without hesitation, Mother Elizabeth kneels and closes her eyes.

Uncertain of what to do, I follow her lead. In a few minutes the chapel is silent. Mother stirs again. I follow her to the holy water font.

She places her hand on my elbow and says, "You know, the sisters will have their eye on you now!" She laughs a little too much for my comfort.

There is no way to avoid the confused look her laugh spawned on my face.

Mother laughs again and softly pats my shoulder. "Have a good evening, Kathryn," and she is gone.

Needless to say, this has been a strange day. The snapshot view into the private world of the nuns was a curious treat. The otherworldly sound of their voices doesn't feel real. Mother Elizabeth seemed to enjoy the thought that some of the sisters would think I was interested in joining the Order. Ha! That will be the day! Maybe she was just giving them something else to think about besides Monica. Who knows?

Ah, who cares what she is up to, as long as she doesn't convince me to be a nun. At least, it was diversion from painful thoughts about Monica and Joseph.

~~~

I brew a new pot of coffee while I think about when I was young. I was a timid child, but my mind played out movie after movie to appease that timidness. Of course, I was always the heroine. Those were really great times, better than an imaginary playmate. I relished those moments of grandeur, the savoring of the experience of life at its richest.

Despite my intentions, the evening is lost in thought and coffee. Easily, I slip back into my old night-owl habits, before I notice it is nearly four in the morning and I haven't been to bed yet. I don't take the time to write in my diary. Sleep has to come quick—and thick.

~~~

Things go along smoothly at work through the month of July. I spend several Sunday afternoons on the park bench hoping to see the parade lady, but she doesn't appear. After that, I spend most of my energy during my off-duty time on the beach, as when Mr. Goldstein and I went for our daily walks. My tolerance for the other people on my beach has moved to acceptance. Beyond the beauty and calm, I enjoy discovering the natural harmony.

There are fewer shells in direct relationship to the increase in children collecting them. I take special note of the sandcastles. They, too, increase in proportion to the increase in children. I must have walked past them last year, but I see them now.

The castles are unique to their builders. There are those that show an adult hand had taken over and rigidly formed the standard-issue castle. The most intriguing are the ones that have no hint of adult intervention. One that catches my eye has an airport with runways that end at a cliff. There are tiny grooves on the upward-sloping runways, remnants of the child playing here and their small left-behind airplane.

Farther along, there is a dainty castle adorned with sea shells; it is pretty, very artistic. There is another that someone has ruined. The stomp marks are hard and deep, it was subdued by violence. Children are little echos of the sounds of their society.

The one good thing about everyone in my life being otherwise occupied is that I am becoming more aware of the details of the beach. I am beginning to anticipate the tidal flow, to sense the distant storms of the Pacific long before they reach land, to see previously overlooked barnacle formations in discrete places on the pier pylons hidden by the tide. What seems a bit odd is that any of this should matter to me.

~~~
~~~

I have walked the entire five-mile length of the beach today and not seen Livingston. I hope he is all right. There is a seal floating on its back in the rising and falling swells. He is watching the activity on the beach from a safe distance. It is common to see or hear seals, otters, and sea lions farther up the coast in Monterey Bay, but I rarely see them from my beach. He disappears when an old man launches on a wind surfer in his direction.

The subtleties of life are slowly transforming something deep within me. A subtle appreciation for my own company is developing. I no longer chase moments of clarity that are fleeting. If they come, they come—if not, fine.

Perhaps, in part, the changes in me are the influence of the nuns. There is not a real word for it, maybe “essence” describes it. I am beginning to feel “older”—not the tired kind of old. It is more that I am growing, not necessarily aging.

~~~

Time passes quietly. Almost before I realize it, I am beginning to pack for my trip. At least my passport photo is better than the one on my driver’s license. That has to be a good omen.

Little Shasta has been well prepared for my pending absence. I brought an atlas and showed her where I am going. She loves the atlas, and is delighted when I tell her that she can keep it for me while I am away. I plan for her to keep it as her own, but if I tell her now, she may interpret it to mean I am not returning. First graders are smart.

Monica is spending a lot of time outside in the shade watching the children on the playground, and looking well. Her days are mixed, so I am delighted that she is having a good day. I promise to bring her something special from Ireland. Most of the time she is in her robe and has little use for scarves. But, I hope telling her I am bringing a gift will help her stay on Earth until my return.

Monica guesses the nature of my trip. She says my beaming grin gives me away whenever I speak of Ireland.

I doubt it. I wasn’t grinning that much. But there isn’t much point in keeping the usual client–social worker distance with Monica since she is rapidly dying. I will never admit it out loud, but I don’t think she will be here past Christmas.

I give Monica the abridged story of Joseph, leaving out auite a few details. By the time I finish, he is able to leap tall buildings with a single bound.

Monica laughs at my description of him. She agrees that the men in our lives become larger than life once we find their endearing characteristics.
~~~

Maggie, I think this time with Monica would be much easier if I could understand the necessity of her death. I do hope there really is a greater order to the universe and we are here for a specific purpose and at a specific time for that purpose.

~~~

Once again, I find myself at LAX. Before long they will give me my own parking space. Then again, I might decide to move to Ireland, and I won't need a space.

I am tired of telling everyone goodbye as they move on with life, while I stand still. Maybe, I am ready to move on. Maybe it is my time.

Finally on the plane, I sit beside a twenty-something woman, Gwen, also on her way to New York. She is excited about her first flight. We trade seats, so she can sit by the window. It seems to me that she should have a window seat on her maiden flight. The trip is her college graduation gift from her parents.

Before we have crossed the Rocky Mountains, I hear the overview of Gwen's life. It is probably her nerves talking. It doesn't seem long before I feel the drag as the plane prepares to land at LaGuardia, where I change planes.

On the plane to Ireland, I am surprised to see Gwen boarding. Perhaps, she hadn't told me everything after all. Midway over the Atlantic she convinces the man sitting next to me to trade places with her. It seems that I have a new best friend; at least Gwen seems to think of us as traveling buddies.

Since Joseph never answered my letter telling him my flight information, I don't expect him to meet me at the plane. I try not to think about how silly it is to fly 5,000 miles to see a man who doesn't respond to my letters. Okay, it is ridiculous. But I am ready for the diversion of the trip. I have to go. I simply have to get this settled for myself.

As I expected, Joseph is not here to meet me. Expected, yes; yet, I'm disappointed. He always said that he liked my independent nature. I suppose that it never occurs to him that I would like to feel important enough to him that he sees me as a person with feelings, in addition to my abilities. I hoped to be important enough to him that he would make the effort to meet the plane.

Gwen and I are staying at the same hotel, so when we emerge from the plane and Joseph isn't there, I ask if she would like to share a taxi. We ride in silence, both looking in wonder out our own window, absorbing every detail of our new surroundings as the taxi hurries us to our destination.

It's midafternoon. After we check into the hotel, Gwen suggests dinner together. Obviously, she doesn't have a plan any better than
~~~

mine. We are on a different meal schedule than the locals, so okay, we'll go to dinner. I'll catch Joseph when we get back to see if he wants to meet for a drink.

Gwen meets me downstairs in the lobby after we get our things to our rooms. We decide to walk two blocks to a little pub featured in one of the tourist brochures that Gwen picked up. It is fun walking around an unfamiliar city, experiencing the sights and sounds up close. We check out a few of the shops on the way to the pub. Being good tourists, we pick up gifts to take home and a few things for ourselves.

As we had hoped, the corner pub is full of old-world charm. I suspect that it isn't the normal Irish establishment, it seems that it is set up to meet the expectations of tourists. The place is absolutely perfect fun. Joseph can show me the real Ireland tomorrow. Tonight is girls' night out.

Gwen is understandably excited. It's too early in the day for a crowd. The television above the bar is tuned to the local news. I watch the unfamiliar pictures with casual interest, listening to their thick accent. A reporter is reviewing their candidates for an upcoming election.

Politics! Ugh. The first candidate is not appealing. The second one is more engaging. He has a believable quality about him. His stated concerns are like the ones that interest me. I wish I had caught his name. It might be interesting to follow his career to see if he is the person of conscience that he appears to be.

The event is over. As each candidate is announced again they wave and leave the stage. Suddenly, my interest piques. Joseph is running for office. Yes, I'm sure that it is Joseph on the screen next to the candidate that I like. No wonder he didn't meet me at the airport.

The camera zooms to Joseph as he waves to the audience. No wonder he was too busy to write to me. I am proud of him and about to point him out to Gwen when I see he is with a woman. "His new wife," the reporter announces.

I feel betrayed. My breath catches in my throat. My eyes water and threaten to cry. I am considering excusing myself and running out the door, but the server arrives with our dinner. My voice feels shaky as I try to seem casually curious and ask her about the man on the television. She looks, and says he returned from the United States to marry his childhood sweetheart. She giggles, and says something about "romantic," but I can't listen to the details.

On the screen, Joseph walks to the edge of the stage to leave. He had apparently given his speech before the two we caught. He turns, waves, and I am certain there is a wedding ring on his finger. It's true, he is married. I didn't hear anything else the server said. I don't need to know more. I am numb inside. No longer hungry, I pick at my food.

Dinner eventually passes. I tell Gwen I am going back to my room to rest, since my internal clock is still on Pacific time. She has plans to go on a guided tour tomorrow. I lie that I already have plans, and decline the invitation to join her.

"Maybe we'll run into each other at dinner tomorrow."

"Yes, maybe. Well, good night, Gwen," I say, feigning a smile as I leave the elevator at my floor, and numbly walk to my room.

I expect to cry once I am alone in my room, but I don't. Finally, I understand his mood when he came back to L.A. I bet he was trying to decide between her and me.

If they still meant something to each other after all of these years, I am glad that I didn't accept his invitation to come with him. I wish that he had been honest with me. I would have liked to have ended things between us with a sense of resolution, not in this hurtful way.

Did he ignore my email? What does it matter now? I don't understand why he didn't tell me. I have never known a lawyer to have a loss for words: loss of clarity, yes; words, no.

More than anything, I am stunned and ashamed. I don't know why I feel ashamed—I didn't do anything wrong. I toss and turn in the unfamiliar bed. The sleep that finally comes is tormented.

Breakfast doesn't interest me. I stay in bed. I sleep some, but mostly I lie looking at the ceiling as if I am waiting to wake up from this horrible dream or waiting to cry, I don't know which. Neither happens.

By late afternoon, I shower and go out for a newspaper and coffee. Mostly, I am driven by the need for coffee, but I do pick up a muffin of some sort. I was hungry even though I hadn't realized it.

When I return to the hotel, Gwen is waiting at the elevator to go to her room. She is full of excitement about the sights she saw on the bus trip. We make dinner plans. She promises to tell me all about her day. Luckily, she doesn't ask about mine. I have no words for today.

I do my best to be attentive to Gwen's tale of her tour. She shows me the pictures on her digital camera. I turn to my social work training and courtroom experience on the witness stand to control my raw emotions, so I can listen to Gwen's adventures. Gwen laments that she only has a week to see the entire country, which is more ambitious than I remember her original plan.

"I could stay twice that long, and it wouldn't be long enough!" She is in love with Ireland.

~~~

Sleep eludes me again. I am not sure why I bother, but I don't know what else to do. It was time for bed, so I went to bed.

In the morning, I take a taxi to the airport, and pay the fee to change my ticket and arrange for an early return trip home. I am drained.
~~~

Finally, I am able to sleep.

Late afternoon, Gwen calls and wakes me with another invitation for dinner. Again she fills the conversation with her travel experiences.

She asks about my plans.

"Something has come up. I have to return to the States."

"Oh, that's horrible!" She is honestly upset for me.

"I thought that you might want to trade airline tickets with me," I say, as I hand her a ticket I had made in her name while I was at the airport.

"My room is paid for two weeks. You might as well use it. I leave in the morning." The money she will save on her room should take care of her expense of staying longer than planned. I didn't have to do it that way, but I wanted the enjoyment of seeing her face when I told her.

Gwen knocks over my drink in her exuberance to hug me from across the table. "Katey! Thank you! Thank you, Katey!"

"You are welcome, Gwen. Enjoy your trip. It's a gift." I smile. It is the first time I really smile since learning Joseph is married.

"If you'll excuse me, I need to pack. Enjoy your stay," I say, as I get up to leave.

"Hey, wait! Here's my ticket," she says digging through her oversized bag.

Even though I have already purchased a ticket for another flight, I take hers, so the exchange doesn't feel like charity to her.

~~~
~~~

~ CHAPTER 14 ~

The Band Played On

Leaving the LAX parking garage, my eyes burn and fill with tears. I have not been allowed the luxury of crying while in Ireland, not even alone in my hotel room. The trip from Ireland to LAX was incredibly long—long and sad.

I hardly remember driving home. I take my bags inside, and set them on the bed. Looking at the bags full of unrealized hope brings a panic rushing over me. I turn around in a hurry to get out of the closed-in space. My hands reach out to the doorjam to struggle my way out of the room. My emotions are confused and I burst into the living room.

Obviously, Joseph was impossible in January in order to maintain his resolve to return to Ireland. Why on Earth did he ask me to go? Why didn't he just say he was going and end things like an adult? He was banking on me not going. Unless I am mistaken, when I took him to LAX he said he loved me and gave me no reason to doubt him. Anger washes over me. I pick up my keys and go out the door. Damn him!

~~~

I look in the direction of the beach, pause briefly, then hurry to my car. I feel like running. The radio comes on when the car starts. To drown out my thoughts, I feed it a CD, and turn the volume up before backing out. Quickly, I head for the freeway and despise the stoplights that delay me.

Finally on the on-ramp, I feel the car's torque transfer to the pavement. When my hand moves the shifter forward to third gear, I reach for the knob and add more volume to the stereo. Once I'm in the lane of my choice on the 405, I ease through the gears, keeping the rpm up. Gas—lots of gas—clutch, fourth gear. Fifth—more volume.

I slip into the back of a group of cars that are decidedly exceeding the speed limit. My eyes began to fill with tears again as the miles between L.A. and San Diego rapidly diminish.

I am terribly hurt and angry. I can't believe I didn't read Joseph better. My eyes burn. Words of contempt for him fill my mind. I would say them out loud, but he isn't worth the trip to the confessional. I am so disappointed. He hardly seems worth crying over. Someone else can cry over him as far as I'm concerned.

I touch the power buttons and the windows disappear. I shake my head and feel my hair fly wildly in the wind. The music swirls around me and out the windows. I breathe in the beat, and it slowly permeates my broken spirit with strength.
~~~

I ease back on the accelerator just enough to let the pack of cars slip away. I begin to breathe more easily. As I reposition taller in my seat, my hands respond by moving higher on the steering wheel. When my hands readjust, the sparkle of the diamonds on mother's ring catches my attention. Her words come into my thoughts: "Katey, you are your father's daughter." Which was a direct reference to his rebellion to conform to external pressure.

Glancing in the rearview mirror for my reflection, I look more like my mother's family, but there is the bit of me that isn't like them. I know from old photos of Father when he was younger that there is no denying that I am a McKenzie. In fact, I look a great deal like Father's younger sister. Grandfather might not have seen it, but I am Father's daughter.

As the 405 becomes the 5, hunger forces its way to my awareness. Slowing down, I pull off at the next exit, loop above the freeway and back down the opposite on-ramp toward home and a meal. My cousin who lives in Hawaii says, "Never order seafood if you can't see the surf." Good advice. There is a nice little restaurant near my apartment. I am going home to my world, and I'm treating myself to dinner out. How did I think, even briefly, that I could give up everything important to me and move to Ireland for that man?

All things considered, I am thankful to have a week and a half at home before I return to work. My head understands it is over, but my heart still hurts. My eyes seek his photograph on the stand whenever my mind is idle. I get up and toss it in the trash, frame and all, and take the whole thing out to the dumpster.

Tears frequently appear without warning. It's good no one knows I'm home. I am not fit for company. Withdrawal might be hell, but it is worth it. I am going to get Joseph out of my system.

For several days, I allow myself the luxury of living without a routine. I sleep when I want, sometimes on the sofa, sometimes in my bed. Instinct and convenience rule my nights and days. I'm glad that Maggie doesn't know what happened.

~~~

Eventually, on the third day I find my way to the beach. There I sit, watching the waves, surrounded by strangers and not caring about it one way or another. It's a free country.

"Katey?" a voice startles me. "Katey, are you all right?" Karen stoops beside me.

"Yes, I am fine," I say meekly, forcing a smile.

Karen sits in the sand along side me. She watches the waves, but says nothing more. Neither do I. We sit for twenty minutes, motionless. Well, what am I going to say? "Karen, have you heard, the man I love is married?" No, I am not ready to say that out loud.
~~~

The silence becomes heavy. Karen stirs and clears her throat. I set my jaw, not wanting to hear what she is going to say. I can feel my eyes squint behind my sunglasses, as I brace for her questions. Why did I come to the beach? It isn't a very private place. But Karen should be at work. Is this the 25th? I haven't paid attention to the date. After all, I am on vacation.

"Katey, I have something to tell you. I am afraid that it isn't pleasant news."

I hold my breath. I am not in the mood for this reality check. I realize exactly what she is going to say.

"Monica is dying," she says, even softer.

I breathe, then catch my breath and whisper. "Oh God, NO!"

"Mother Elizabeth didn't know you were home or she would have called you."

"I, I came home Tuesday morning." Reality check. My concerns seem inconsequential now.

She eases me to my feet. "We really need to go, if you are going to see Monica."

Compliantly, I walk with her back to my apartment. I wash my face, change my shoes, and pick up my bag. Karen takes the keys from my hand. "Come on, I'll drive."

She forgot that my car is a stick shift. Defiantly, the car jerks, killing the motor when Karen lets out the clutch too much while trying to back out. I pull it together enough to drive to where she parked her car. Relieved to give up the driver's seat, I melt into the passenger side.

"I hate to do this to you, but you are going to have to pull it together before we get there. You can fall apart when we get back, I promise." Karen's voice is compelling. Her calm tone is something I can hold on to and absorb.

I know she is correct. It is not time to be an emotional wreck. I don't want Monica to see me falling apart. I don't want anyone to see me this way. Hell, I don't want to be this way.

~~~

I feel wobbly inside, but begin to pull on a calm exterior—fake, but hopefully convincing.

I kneel beside Monica's bed, so that we will be at eye level with each other. She seems to recognize me. She is very weak, so weak in fact, that she is unable to speak.

I really don't know what to say. Becoming friends had been so easy. I hold her hand, and hum the Irish lullaby my mother sang to me when I was young.

Her breathing eases slightly.

~~~

I search through my purse for the scarf I purchased for her in Ireland. The silk feels rich in my fingers, as I ease it out of the tissue wrapping. Carefully, I drape it near her chin, gently tucking it in against her skin.

"Monica, thank you for being my friend," I whisper as I lean close.

There is no certainty that she heard me. I think, though, that she almost smiled. Leaning over her, I kiss her forehead, knowing this is our last time to be together.

"Sleep, little angel."

~~~

Karen and I fall into silence on the trip home. It seems that the number of stairs has tripled since I left to see Monica.

Karen makes coffee. I sit on the sofa, too drained to put my feet on the coffee table. Even the coffee doesn't smell good.

"Kathryn, I know that you don't feel like talking," she coaxes as she sits on the sofa beside me. "But that is exactly what we are going to do."

I take a deep breath. She is right, but I don't know where to start. I am terribly sad about Monica, but we knew she was dying. How am I going to say what is inside without falling apart? If that happens, will I ever get the pieces gathered up and put together again?

Our eyes meet. Karen's eyes are full of tears. Looking down at my coffee cup, I say softly, "Joseph is married."

I feel ashamed for my stupidity. Were the signs there all along, and I just missed them because I didn't want to see them? Was I only idle entertainment to him, and didn't notice it because I was preoccupied with falling in love?

"Joseph is married?"

"I feel deceived." My voice breaks, but I continue. "What a fool I am for falling in love when he wasn't in love with me."

Karen sits quietly listening as I pour out all of the hurt and betrayal I feel. There is no stopping it, even if I could try. My mouth pours from my heart, things that I am unaware of until I say them. I say nothing bad about the woman. It was Joseph, it was all Joseph.

My thoughts are unorganized. I am sure not everything I say makes sense to Karen. I jump back and forth throughout the entire relationship, or was it simply an affair. Joseph's apparent betrayal becomes linked to the emotions of all of the other losses and pain: My parents' deaths, Mr. Goldstein leaving, Linda's rape, Judge Jones' hand in my client's death, Nebraska, Maggie and Dave's deaths. "And, I can't find Livingston," I say.

I don't know if I am more angry with Joseph or me. How could he betray me like that? How could I have been so ignorant? My hand trembles as I take a drink of coffee, nearly spilling it.
~~~

She leans over enough to reach my hand to help as I set down the cup.

Karen listens as I spew forth hurt for over an hour.

"I know, Katey. I know," she says softly.

Her voice sounds like she does know. It catches my attention. I look in her eyes to be sure. They're full of tears.

I feel sad for her, hoping that we did not really share this experience. Surely, Karen meant the universal feelings that people have from time to time, borne out of fatigue or disappointment. I pray she doesn't mean the emotions I am experiencing from the culmination of many abandonments, lost loves, and foolish assumptions about relationships.

She leans forward, clears her throat, then bites her bottom lip in a thoughtful moment. Perhaps she is choosing her words carefully. After all, she is an award-winning psychologist. "Katey, my husband had an affair with Keith's wife."

I know it is the woman, not the psychologist, not the social worker, not the ex-boss, not even my friend who is talking. She doesn't expect anything from me.

I watch, listen, and remain silent. Besides, that is about all I can manage to do right now.

"Keith found them together. He must have suspected his wife, still, he was surprised it was Steve with her. We didn't do things together as couples, just an occasional government banquet—" She takes a breath. "Keith was the one who told me. I was working late, and he came to my office. I hadn't suspected anything was wrong in our marriage, so I was devastated when I found out about the affair."

Karen pauses again. "It was an ugly scene at our home that night. I don't know how things went at Keith's house. He and I have never discussed it."

Then she smiles a sad smile. "It took me a week to decide if there was anything worth salvaging. When I came home from work, Steve was gone."

I catch my gasp. I listen to her words and tone of voice, blending all of it with the Karen I know.

She continues. "I had the dispatcher locate Keith. When he returned my call, I told him Steve was gone. He went home and his wife was gone, too. I was ashamed that I hadn't known we had 'those' kind of problems. You would think I would know."

She straightens in her seat and takes a deep breath. "I never told anyone what happened, and I don't think Keith did either.

"About three months later, we were both served divorce papers at work. Well, then everyone knew about it."

What a hurtful thing to do to Keith and Karen, on top of everything else—serve the papers at work. She must have felt betrayed, questioned the validity of their relationship, wondering how much of it had been real.

They have three daughters. Yet, Steve wasn't faithful to his family. She has me beat. I look at her again with new eyes.

Karen finishes her coffee, goes to the kitchen, and returns with the pot to refill our cups one more time. Mine, she doesn't fill quite as much as hers this time.

That explains why Keith was attentive, maybe even protective of Karen at the governor's dinner. Also, it explains why I hadn't seen that closeness before I left for Nebraska. Maybe that was what was different about her when I returned. That can make a person stronger or destroy them altogether. She's my hero.

Karen takes a drink of coffee, then resumes her story. "Katey, the point of telling you about Steve is that you will get beyond Joseph, even if you never completely stop loving him."

"Yes, I'll try to remember." I wonder if she still loves Steve; even though, she would never trust him again if she had the opportunity. I study her choice of words, her expression, and hope to absorb it all.

"Just be patient with yourself, attend to your healing."

"Good advice. I'll do my best to follow it. Thank you."

We walk to her car and say goodnight. I consider hugging her, and don't remember whether I did or didn't.

~~~

I awaken in the night and write in my diary.

Dearest Maggie, Karen's disclosure was a kind touch to a hurting soul. I hope you knew about her divorce and found a way to help her when she needed a friend.

Life is a minute-by-minute journey. I'll try to remember that no matter how far I fall, I always land on my feet.

We dance the crazy dance between sanity and a life spinning out of control. In the end, I will get through this, though at the moment it doesn't feel like it.

It is nearly noon when Karen calls. As soon as I hear her voice, I have a sense of what happened.

"Kathryn, during the night, ah, Monica left us." Karen sounds tentative, like she is wondering if she should have delivered the news in person.

"Thank you," I say.
~~~

"I'm at St. Mark's. Mother Elizabeth called early this morning." Then she adds, "Everyone is fine here. How are you?"

"I am better. Do you know when the funeral is?"

"Maybe Monday, I'm not sure if the plans have been finalized yet." Someone in the background calls her name. "Listen, I have to go, but do you want to do dinner later?"

Of course I am available. "Dinner works, I'm flexible. Come when you can. And, and thanks for calling."

~~~

One more funeral to attend. For someone who swore never to attend another funeral, I end up attending far too many.

Funerals are not my best days. I have learned not to visit the casket. Not seeing them dead leaves better images of the person in my mind—older, richer memories. I don't want those memories clouded with a newer, less adequate, more haunting memory of them in a casket. No, funerals are not my best days. Luckily, the rest of the week is still vacation time. I can recover from the funeral.

~~~

Everything is out of whack. Young people are dying before their time. I don't understand anything about love. My insights and emotions don't serve me well. The strangest craving takes control of my diet. I begin to cook healthier meals.

I think about Mr. Goldstein building his stamina to walk the beach. In the morning, I begin to run along the beach and walk back. Not being a runner by nature, I am not very knowledgeable about it. First, thinking it will cushion my joints, I run in the soft sand that had been churned by the last of summer's tourists. The sand finds its way into my shoes and rubs against my skin, making blisters and hot spots. Maybe that is why I rarely see people run the beach.

~~~

The next day, I move down near the water at low tide. The sand is packed harder, it pounds my joints, but it is a less-hampered run. The calves of my legs complain. At any rate, it is the beginning of a new relationship with the beach. I am ready for something distinctively fresh and new in my life.

Sleep comes easier and sweeter. I know that it should be better, considering the more nutritional diet and increased exercise, but, restful sleep has always been a luxury for me. I haven't slept on the sofa since Monica's funeral. Strangely, life seems to be finding its own sense of equilibrium.

Physically, I am better. Emotionally, I am still mourning. The thing about death is that it isn't a personal rejection. On the other hand, I can find no argument not to take Joseph's lie personally—It feels personal.
~~~

At least when someone dies, it has a sense of "natural order" about it. When a plane crashes, it is expected that people die—sometimes not, but surviving is an unexpected outcome. A terminal disease, usually is terminal. Even when we don't like it, at least it follows the expected rules of life. What Joseph did is not natural, making it seem harder to reconcile. Wasn't any of it real to him? Of course, I feel like a fool. Then, anger follows.

~~~

Labor Day is a welcomed respite. With the starting of school we shift gears at work. It's a natural conversion to our schedule, which allows us to make other tweaks to the Spirit of Hope program. It seems that everyone welcomes the changes. Maybe we had fallen into a rut.

The first day after the holiday, Mother Elizabeth sends me on errands with Sister Theresa. Even after a year, I barely have a sense of who she is, apart from all of the other brown-robed nuns.

She always rides in silence. Most people visit with each other while riding around, it is almost protocol, but not Sister Theresa. I take to playing music softly to fill the void as we go about our chores. I play classical music, nothing happens. I play classical guitar, ragtime, swing, jazz, and even some ballads. I don't have any religious music. Still she is silent. I've never known anyone who didn't relax to music.

Out of desperation, I reach into the console between the seats, and select another CD. When I put it up to the steering wheel so I can use both hands to open the case, I see it is one of Ann Zimmerman's CDs. A grin comes over me: Okay Ann, work your magic!

Feeling a bit smug with my secret weapon, I slip the CD to the mouth of the player, and it inhales the plastic disk. The music starts and Sister Theresa stirs slightly. I see her glance in the direction of the CD player, perhaps recognizing songs from the Have-a-Heart concert. I wish Sister would say something. I'm dying to know what she is thinking.

Moving across the lanes, I slow for the off-ramp. I shift down to third gear to climb the incline of the ramp as the exiting traffic has quickly slowed. Sister looks at the shifter. An ambulance approaches and overtakes us from behind. It congests the traffic ahead even more than it was before.

It is apparent that the traffic has stalled to a stop farther ahead of us. I reach to the back seat for my book of city street maps as I pull away from the curb after the ambulance passes.

"Sister, find us another way around the accident."

Sister Theresa leafs through the pages of map sections to find our location. It isn't as easy as it sounds in a city this size, but she is going to have to jump in to it quickly.
~~~

In the absence of any direction from her, I turn right on a side street and move in the direction I think we should be going. It reminds me of the way rural people use right angle turns to cut across farm country around sections of pasture ground.

Come on, Sister, help me out here, I wish, as I slow to buy her additional time. I slip into first gear at the stop sign, and hesitate while I look each direction for a hint of the most promising direction. I decide to continue straight for now.

"Left, turn left here," Sister finally says at the next intersection.

"Thank you," I say and make the turn. In the rearview mirror, I see a line of cars turning left. "I hope they aren't following us," I comment, as I shift to second, waiting for more directions. I'm convinced that we are lost.

Sister ignores my comment. "Will you teach me to drive?"

"What?" I am surprised by her off-task remark.

"Will you teach me to drive your car?"

"You mean drive a standard transmission?"

"Yes, drive."

"You don't drive?" I don't mean to be indelicate, but I can't believe someone her age doesn't know how to drive.

"No. Will you teach me?"

God, she is relentless. "Sure, I guess. The first thing is to get the driver's handbook to study." Why ask me to teach her?

After my answer, Sister settles down and pays attention to the fact that I need her to navigate our route. The traffic is getting heavy, so her timing is perfect.

While she is doing whatever our mission is, I wait in the car, preoccupied with the idea of Sister Theresa learning to drive. It seems it would be best for her to learn to drive on one of the convent's cars. She wouldn't have to take one of the vans, just a car. I have seen a compact car in the garage that would be perfect for learning to drive, and I am sure it's an automatic.

Our errands take all day, chauffeuring her around from place to place. She disappears inside, and takes care of business without a word. When I take Sister Theresa home, she waits uncomfortably long before getting out of the car.

This is awkward. What do you say to someone who is so quiet?

"Kathryn."

"Yes?" Surprised, I turn toward her.

"Please don't tell anyone that I asked you to teach me to drive." Red flag! Red flag!

"All right, Sister."

She opens the car door and leaves without looking back.

Was that an implied pinky promise we just made? I wonder why she doesn't want anyone to know she wants me to teach to drive, or that she wants to learn to drive. Surely the nuns know she doesn't drive. Had the sisters tried to teach her before with disastrous results? As much as possible, I milk the mystery.

~~~

Things move along as usual at work. I go through the routine, but many times my heart isn't wholly in my work. When I work directly with clients, I put extra effort into pulling myself together to meet their needs, than when I am doing paperwork. I can't begin to imagine what they have been through. But I do admire their resilience.

I consider taking a night course to occupy my time, and even go so far as to get a course catalog and look through it. There's an American Cinema History class that looks interesting, but I decide to wait until I can put my heart into the experience, and really enjoy it.

Despite the danger of becoming bored or lonely, I decide to keep life simple, uncluttered, and healing. At times, it is tempting to rush the process of my recovery; but usually a hot shower, a walk on the beach, or an experiment in the kitchen (not always edible when finished) slows my anxiousness.

The band plays on, as I bravely dance life's tune. I'm not the first or the last to dance when I don't always feel like it. The important thing is to carry on publicly and sort things out privately.

Mr. Goldstein left a message on my phone, but forgot to leave his number. His voice sounds good. I send him an email and hope they think to check it.

Livingston has returned. I wonder where he goes when he is gone for so long. I suppose it doesn't really matter, as long as he always returns.

Here is another riddle: How is Sister Theresa going to learn to drive without anyone knowing? There seem to be no secrets in the convent. Is she just going to sneak out? The thought of her tiptoeing out under the cover of darkness makes me smile, not that I think she would really climb out the window, habit and all, but the image does come to mind.

While I am amused with the image of Sister Theresa climbing down the trellis from one of the small iron balconies outside the upstairs bedroom windows, I have another, more sobering thought: What if she told the other sisters she is recruiting me for the convent as her alibi? Not that I think she would lie, but she may not have corrected false assumptions. Oh, dear God!

~~~

~ CHAPTER 15 ~

Nothing Runs Like a Deere

Needless to say, I am leery when Sister Theresa announces that she has studied the handbook and is ready to take the written test for her learner's permit. I don't mean to, but I am sure that I look at her in horror. I didn't expect her to finish so quickly. Actually, I hoped she would be satisfied that I agreed and not pursue it just yet.

We set the date for the learner's permit test. I have no idea what she told Mother Elizabeth to get us both out of the convent for the afternoon. There's no reason to tempt fate and ask questions.

We stand in line for what seems like a very long time at the Driver's License Department. And by the way, a nun in full habit doesn't blend in very well with the average person in line. The other people obviously notice her. When we finally reach the attendant, Sister Theresa doesn't have any money with her. She thought the fee only applied to actual driver's licenses. Sister attempts to reason with the attendant, who is very nice not to laugh at her. It's a good thing that I came with her. I slip Sister a twenty-dollar bill, and she pays the fee.

While Sister takes the test, I realize if she passes it, I will be taking her driving.

Of course, she passes the test. She's a nun. She has a perfect score. I'm doomed!

With her permit in hand, Sister is beaming like a child leaving a toy store with that special toy. I shouldn't have, but when she shows me her photo, I glance at her birth date, she's 41. I look at her. Hmm, I guess that seems right. It's hard to tell a nun's age, and having their hair covered doesn't help.

While I have been preoccupied with her age, Sister has walked ahead of me to the driver's side of my car. Before I can react, she takes the car keys.

"Now, how does this work?" she asks while looking at the remote entry on my key chain.

"Careful Sister! You might set off the alarm."

"Ooh!" She squeals and returns the keys, holding them carefully by the tip of a key between her finger and thumb.

I laugh as I take the keys. "Go to the other side, Sister, we're not doing this here."

Not appearing to be disappointed, she eagerly gets in on her side of the car before I have my door shut. I am sure this whole exchange was caught on the security cameras, probably my license tag is now on a list somewhere. It's obvious that she plans to learn to drive in my car. How exactly did I get into this?

Not wanting to burst her bubble, I find a legitimate diversion for her.

"Sister, there is a manual in the glove box," I say, pointing to the latch in front of her. "Why don't you take it with you, and familiarize yourself with my car?"

She finds the folder with the manual in it and holds it up.

"Yes, that's it. Just take the manual out, and leave the other papers there."

She opens the book to the first page, and reads the table of contents. She reads each page in order, never once leafing through it to see what is coming next. Sister doesn't even notice that we are approaching the convent until I ask her to sign me out for the day, when she signs in.

It does occur to me that I have a knack for walking into situations destined for disaster. In all fairness to me, Sister Theresa hit me up for driving lessons while I was distracted by being lost in an unfamiliar part of L.A. That probably isn't much of an excuse, but it is all I have. I suppose I'm not as savvy as I like to think.

~~~

After revealing the details of her marriage's end, Karen hasn't come around much. It may be awkward for her or it may be that she is busy with the coalition duties.

Eventually, she does reappear, and we touch base again. We arrange to meet for dinner to catch up with each other. Quickly, I realize everything remains intact in our friendship. As I suspected, Karen had just been busy. She is still juggling work and the coalition tasks. We never mention Keith.

~~~

In a couple of days, Sister Theresa announces she is ready for her first driving lesson. She arranged for us to go Friday morning, so I suspect that Mother Elizabeth knows what we are doing. I choose not to mention it, just in case Mother isn't aware of our intended activity. We may have her permission, but I don't know if we have her blessing. I decide it is best for me not to know all of the details of this arrangement.

Friday morning turns out to be an excellent selection. The traffic is uncommonly light. Having had time to figure out a plan, I drive out to my uncle's horse farm. The private roads lined with rail fences seem to be a safe place for Sister Theresa to learn to use the clutch. Hopefully she won't use the fences as bumper-car guardrails.

~~~

We start Sister's first lesson in the large gravel yard by the hay barn. Carefully, I explain the mechanics of applying the gas and letting out
~~~

the clutch to start moving, and the timing of both activities. We switch seats.

Sister Theresa is beaming with confidence. She adjusts her mirrors, puts on her seat belt, checks the mirrors again, and starts the car as she has been instructed, with the clutch fully engaged.

As usual when first learning to drive a standard, she doesn't have the feel of the clutch. She sits straight and lets out the clutch. The car jerks to an abrupt stop. We jolt in our seats. She gives a nervous giggle while I tighten my grip on the armrest.

The next time we lurch forward about three feet before she lets the clutch all the way out in one swift move, killing the engine again with a harsh jerk. I reach for the dashboard in a defensive move. She has a bewildered look on her face. I wonder if she wishes she was in an automatic?

"Kathryn! This is harder than it looks!" she whispers in wide-eyed amazement.

"Everyone starts out rough, just give it a little more gas next time and let the clutch out smoothly. Go ahead. Give it another try."

This time, Sister gives it considerably more gas while letting the clutch out only midway, then fully—all at once.

Gravel and dirt fire out from behind us. In response, she grips the steering wheel in a death grip.

She makes rapid, short navigational corrections and counter corrections in her steering. We are off! Rocks are rifling into the barn and pelting the old pickup truck near it, leaving a cloud of dust behind us. She heads the car directly toward the John Deere parked in the corner of the alfalfa field.

The abruptness and Sister's absolute lack of control terrifies me. I am sure we are going to test the steadfastness of the tractor ahead. I'm not exaggerating, I fear for my life. In the worst way, I want to make the sign of the cross and make peace with my Creator. But there isn't time for that.

"LET UP ON THE GAS! LET UP on the G-AAA-S!" I say, as calmly as possible. "Look OUT for the TRACTOR!" I say, giving the steering wheel firm, helpful guidance with one hand and bracing for impact with the other.

We clear the John Deere with centimeters to spare, leaving tire indentations in the field as she plows through the soft soil.

Sister has both hands riveted to the steering wheel. Her eyes are WIDE with the adventure. To her amazement (and mine), she is driving!

"Eee-ase back on the gas! Slow down a bit, Sister."

Finally, she lets up the gas enough to move forward smoothly, under something nearly resembling controlled driving.

"How am I doing, Kathryn?" she asks, sitting tall, checking her mirrors, and clutching the steering wheel with determination and a proud grin.

Is that a trick question? "Fine. You're doing fine," I lie. It's only a venial sin. I have never seen anyone go quite that fast in first gear on gravel. It's a miracle she didn't flip us in the ditch as she exited the alfalfa field.

"Now what?" she asks, eager to take on the world.

"Just drive down the road. Stay between the fence rows," I instruct and begin to breathe again.

We drive straight for an eighth of a mile. I talk her through shifting to second gear, which is easier to do than starting from a dead stop. I am not willing to graduate to making right-angle turns yet. With the metal fences lining the road and her lack of respect for the word "slow," I wait until we are out of road before I brave turns.

I select a left turn, so that the road she is aiming for is on her side of the car, allowing her to see clearly where she is going. The engine falters as the rpm drop when she turns, but I am not ready to tell her about downshifting. New drivers use it too much and with the rpm too high rather than using the break. I seriously don't want to replace the transmission in the process of her learning to drive. I'll probably end up needing a new clutch and clutch cable before we're through.

After an hour of getting the feel of the clutch, I talk her onto a public dirt road. She needs to get comfortable going through the gears and making stops and turns before we get on the blacktop. I'm convinced the other nuns deliberately avoided this experience for good reason.

My heartbeat is still rapid and my anxiety high from the moment she first spewed the earth from under the wheels into the side of the barn. No doubt driving with Sister is far better than aerobic exercises—though, I wouldn't recommend it.

I was certain of dying when she attempted a demo derby with the John Deere. The tractor would have won, hands down.

Sister drives for two more hours. I doubt she would have had it any other way. Eventually, she is driving quite well, including shifting, stopping, and starting from a complete stop, though she sometimes skips the stops entirely. Sister Theresa has become so comfortable with driving that she begins to talk and laugh, not watching the driving as much as I would like.

I am intrigued with this new person. As soon as my heart rate returns to normal, I'll be fine. She is pleased as punch with her new skill. I, on the other hand, got "religion" a few hours ago.

I decide not to mention backing today, for obvious reasons. I don't want to see how fast my car can go in reverse. We'll come again, some other time, in a week or two, or maybe a month or two. We can cover reverse and parking then. I need more practice being a passenger before she drives in traffic.

Even though it is only three o'clock when we return to the convent, I am tired and ask Sister to sign me out for the day. One thing for sure, today I atoned for a huge number of previous transgressions. At this rate, I might actually get into heaven. I hope, though, it isn't anytime soon. Maybe we will get a family to replace the one that went to the shelter and I will be too busy to hold driving class.

~~~

It isn't until evening when I begin to relax that I realize how tense my shoulders had been while Sister was driving. The right one has a small bruise from the seat belt locking all the times we lurched forward—hard.

I admit that I share in Sister's satisfaction with her accomplishment, though the whole activity had its share of sheer terror, along with the activation of my inborn desire to survive the experience.

I call my uncle and confess the damage done to his barn and volunteer to come repair it. He noticed the tracks in his field, but I promise we won't be back and he forgives me. He admits to seeing the incident in progress and thought it was quite comical. His relentless teasing makes it hard to harbor remorse.

It is well worth driving with Sister to realize that life goes on, regardless of what happens. I admit that I have more respect for the possibilities ahead after fearing death when Sister was starting out in the barnyard.

~~~

Sister does learn to drive quite well with several more marathon-length lessons. We take plenty of freeway trips, but they are on the less congested freeways and never at rush hour.

Upon her insistence that she is ready, I take her for her driving test. By now, there is no point in suggesting she use a convent car, she earned the prize of taking her test in a five-speed Mustang.

When her turn arrives, I wait outside the driver's license building to see the examiner's face when the brown-robed nun leads him or her to my car. That would have been a perfect photo op.

Needless to say, she passes the driving test.

I would have taken her out to celebrate, but she is eager to show her license to the sisters. I still wonder if they had tried to teach her to drive at some previous time.

The children run to the playground fence as we round the corner and drive slowly in the school zone. Ronnie, my ballplayer, runs for the convent when he sees us. Apparently, Mother had been aware of where we were and Ronnie was her lookout to alert her to our arrival.

She rounded up everyone she could find to meet us. Sister Theresa has quite the welcoming party outside the convent door when she smoothly pulls up to the curb. It is touching how everyone comes to celebrate her accomplishment.

What they don't know is that she helped me put my hurt into perspective. Of course, I think of Joseph from time to time when something reminds me of our time together, but I no longer walk around wounded by what he did to me. I would have rather have had a swifter recovery, but I'll take what I have.

I have stopped looking for what I could have done differently. The truth is our relationship ended because of what Joseph did. Whatever I did wrong in the relationship had not permanently ended it. The responsibility was his. He ended it.

I have been given the gift of getting to know Sister Theresa a little better. Not that I think we will ever go out and do things like friends do, but we have a shared experience. The sharing has been enjoyable; well, at least after we got past the scary part.

~~~

On Monday morning, Saint Mark's nuns are a hum of activity. The Spirit of Hope staff and clients go about their usual routine. It is obvious something is happening in the convent side of the building. Deliveries are arriving at increasing intervals throughout the day. The nuns are as excited as children waiting for Christmas morning. The staff is becoming giddy, though we have no idea why.

On Tuesday, when Sister Theresa flips the page on the master calendar to October, it becomes apparent what is happening. Friday, October 4, is the Feast Day of Saint Francis of Assisi, the patron saint of these nuns. It is obvious that some sort of celebration is being planned, not an ordinary party, something big. I don't remember this kind of activity last year, so there must be something special about this year.

~~~

Things seem to fall into place easier this week. Two more people find work. Race begins studying for his GED. Sister Theresa is out driving a convent van. (Well, I'm not sure that is good.) Sister Clare says it's the special blessings of Saint Francis that everything is in harmony. Who knows? Whatever it is, I'll take it. It is better than the alternative.

Maggie, After a near-death experience with Sister Theresa at the wheel, I realize how numb I've been, except for the constant aching in my spirit. It seems a bit too human to have been so hurt. I realize how expansive the future is. I am going to enjoy the gifts of the present.

On Thursday something very odd happens. I am not attaching any religious significance to it, but, Mother Elizabeth stops me in the hallway and invites me to sit in the garden with her. I am the only single Catholic woman on the Spirit of Hope staff, and I sometimes wonder if the nuns have decided to systematically recruit me for the convent.

She's the boss. I accept her invitation. The weather is uncommonly perfect this week. Again, something Sister Clare attributes to Saint Francis. The bench is refreshingly cool in the building's shade. The fall-blooming flowers have sweetened the air with their aroma.

Mother Elizabeth makes the sign of the cross. I do likewise. She closes her eyes, and begins to silently pray her rosary, fingers busily working her beads. I sit motionless, enjoying the quiet. A bird flies down into the small courtyard, landing at the feet of the Saint Francis statue. It's probably a pigeon. I open my eyes. Odd, it is a seagull. Not that seagulls aren't seen inland, but I hadn't expected to see one in the convent courtyard. Then another seagull arrives. Then another, and another follows.

I am captivated with this unexpected sight. I estimate there are twenty-five to thirty seagulls quietly standing around the garden. Let's face it, seagulls aren't usually quiet birds. They are just standing here, not doing anything, just standing.

Another gull arrives. It is, it's Livingston! I don't know what to make of it. I keep looking around at the congregation of gulls. What is even more strange is that Mother Elizabeth doesn't seem to notice the birds' presence. Perhaps she is simply deep in prayer.

No one moves: not birds, not Mother Elizabeth, not me. The silence is beginning to feel awkward. Mother Elizabeth has one decca of beads on her Franciscan Crown before she is finished.

I control my desire to move. Her fingers move rhythmically over the beads. Her eyes are open now, fixed toward the sky. Her lips are moving slightly, as she breathes the prayers.

Maybe I should have prayed too. But I'm distracted. It seems to me that a number of things around here verge on other-worldliness. It is probably just this environment that skews my interpretation of things. Still—the seagulls?

Just as Mother Elizabeth finishes the next-to-the-last bead, the birds take flight and are gone—all, except Livingston. Livingston bird-walks over to me. He cranks his head, looks with a sideways glance, then takes flight. Weird, so weird. Is he an angel in disguise?

Mother Elizabeth stirs to a more wakeful state, makes the sign of the cross, finally finishing her prayers.

Quickly, I make the sign of the cross too.

"Well?" she says.

I don't know exactly to what she is referring, some holy thing or the seagulls? I smile, but remain silent.

"Aren't the seagulls amazing?"

"Yes, that is quite impressive, Mother," I answer, amazed with the oddness of it. Most people think seagulls are quite messy, and they are correct.

"This happens every October, and only when I am out here praying. It doesn't happen to the other sisters, we tested it," she divulges their curiosity. "Sister Clare noticed it first when I was a novice," she adds with a grin.

Whoa! I don't know exactly how old she is, but it was a very long time ago when she was a novice. I am not even going to think about it only happening to her!

Of course, I believe in God. We talk. Well, actually, I talk to Him. I have never heard Him say anything in particular back to me. However, for the most part, I only make comments on things that cause me to think about Him, or ask rhetorical questions, so I suppose there is no real reason for Him to say anything to me. But this bird-thing does seem almost spiritual. I am not going to venture an explanation, but I can see why she ended up Mother Superior—Sister Clare thinks she is blessed.

There is a glowing aftertaste to the experience. After my initial shock with Mother's comments, I begin to share her wonderment at what just happened. This is one of those once-in-a-lifetime things. Well, not for Mother Elizabeth, but it is for me, a civilian.

We are given our paychecks as we leave and told we needn't come in tomorrow. Too bad. I wanted to see what is happening at the Feast of Saint Francis. Someone said they were celebrating several Jubilees.

I catch Sister Theresa and ask what a Jubilee is. It's an anniversary of sorts. Several of the nuns are celebrating twenty-five, fifty, and one is celebrating seventy-five years as a Franciscan. I bet it is Sister Clare. Wow! That's impressive.

She said the formerly homeless families are independent enough to give the staff the day off. That way the staff won't feel awkward about the celebration. Besides, it is kind of a private party, I think.

That night I pray for the good sisters. I'm thankful to have them in my life. I know that I don't need to request anything on their behalf. They have everything their hearts desire.

~~~

Friday morning when I go to the bank, I find a Holy Card with my paycheck. Once in a while the sisters decide , by some means unknown to me, to put Holy Cards with our checks.

The gesture seems to be a gift rather than a recruitment tactic —unless I'm the only one getting them. Then, it's a problem.
~~~

This Holy Card has the Prayer of Saint Francis. Considering the day, I read the entire prayer out of respect for the good sisters.

Halfway through the first paragraph, I remember my father used to say the prayer from memory. I hadn't missed him for a long time, but I miss him now. I look at his ring on my finger, and touch it to be physically connected with him.

> *Lord make me an instrument of Thy peace; where there is hatred, let me sow love; where there is doubt, faith; where there is despair, hope; where there is darkness, light; and where there is sadness, joy.*
>
> *Grant that I may not so much seek to be consoled as to console, to be understood as to understand, to be loved as to love; for it is in giving that we receive, it is in pardoning that we are pardoned, and it is in dying that we are born to eternal life.*
>
> *St. Francis of Assisi*

~~~

Over the weekend, Karen delivers an invitation to Linda and Todd's masquerade party. It's an annual Halloween event. A coalition meeting in the Bay Area coincides with the party. That makes it convenient for Karen.

I can feel a frown working its way to my face. Quickly, I force it away. "That is very nice of her, but I don't really feel like taking a trip to San Francisco. Frankly, I have had all the traveling I need for a while."

"Maybe a trip is just what you need."

"I don't think so. Is this a 'couples' party?" I ask suspiciously. Since I'm not part of a couple, it's a good reason not to go.

"Not necessarily, Keith can escort both of us." She grins with a less-than-holy-look in her eyes.

She is teasing and I know it. "Ah, I think *you* and Keith should go, and I should stay here."

"You need to get out again. What about Andrew?"

"Andrew? Who's Andrew?"
~~~

"He is the new staff who replaced the one who left because of Monica. Mother Elizabeth says he is single."

"Oh, Drew. Yes, I can see it now, 'Andrew, you don't know me, I'm Kathryn the Crazy. Would you like to go with me to San Francisco to a party? Oh, it is just the governor's son and daughter-in-law, no big deal.' Yes, I can just imagine it!" I laugh at Karen's scheming.

"No really, Elizabeth says he is 'dreamy'—and that you would make a cute couple."

"Oh, she does?" I can't believe this conversation. And, Mother Elizabeth—for God's sake, she is a nun! *Dreamy?* Just what I need, a matchmaking nun. Dreamy?

"Yes, she does."

"Seriously, I think I'll stay here. But I will be sure to let you and your sister know when to play matchmaker." At least we've moved on from recruiting me to join the convent.

Karen starts to laugh at my comment about her and Mother Elizabeth. It isn't really that funny, but we laugh so hard that we are grabbing our sides, and gasping for air.

"Dreamy!" we repeat at the same time.

"Why in the world would I want a nun to play matchmaker? What does she know about this business? Nope, I don't think so."

We are undignified and we don't care. We catch our breath, begin to regain our composure, then look at each other, and bust into laughter again. By the time we are able to stop laughing, we both have mascara trailing down our cheeks from making our eyes water. Dreamy? Lord! Those women. No thank you. No.

~~~

> Dearest Maggie, The strangest things have been happening. You'd probably say that I deserve, at least, some of them. Sister Theresa suckered me into teaching her to drive MY car; Mother Elizabeth and Karen are playing matchmaker at some poor guy's expense; Mother Elizabeth attracts seagulls when she is in her garden praying, but only in October! My life seems so normal next to these people.

~~~

I didn't give in. Karen went to the party, and I'm sure Keith went with her. I am fond of both of them, and pleased that they are—whatever they are—for each other.

I am also proud that I held my ground on staying home. I am quite content to stand on my patio, bundled up, watching a winter storm raging toward the deserted beach across the street. Life is good, not necessarily easy, but good, as Maggie said.

~~~
~~~

Mr. Goldstein wrote. He is enjoying his family and plans to stay another two months in Austria. He'll spend Hanukkah with them. That will be good for him. I'm glad.

Even with a storm coming, I feel strangely calm about my unknown future. Somehow I feel that everything will be all right, not necessarily normal, but interesting nonetheless.

~~~

Mother Elizabeth scheduled a second round of HIV tests for all of us. As soon as our blood tests come back and we are all still negative for HIV, we'll get another family to replace the one who left. We will still have to periodically retest, Mother Elizabeth said so.

A new family just before the holidays will be perfect. They have no idea what a wonderful place they will call home. The nuns refer to everyone as a community, but I think of it more in terms of a family. One great big family, like mine.

Speaking of family, our Thanksgiving dinner at the park is coming up. No one seems to remember when the family dinner moved to the park. The best guess is that it is more than fifty years ago. Belonging is comfortable. No more Nebraskas in my future. And for the record, I am not becoming a nun either.

~~~

~ CHAPTER 16 ~

Everything Is Relative

It pleases me to hear from my paternal grandfather again, or at least to receive a message from him via Mr. Bradford. I kind of like the old guy, even though we have met only once. I wonder if he wants to spend time filling me in on the family stories. It is not uncommon to reminisce and pass on a sense of history, especially for someone Grandfather's age. I have such fond memories of my maternal grandparents, I would like to know about my other grandmother, too.

Grandfather said the weather is too cool to meet in the park. Arrangements are made for James, Grandfather's driver, to pick me up. I am perfectly capable of driving, if I had his address. Besides, I like having my own vehicle, so I can leave when I am ready to come home. However, Grandfather made the last visit short. It is likely he will not keep me longer than I want to stay. Actually, he will probably dismiss me sooner than I am ready.

~~~

James arrives at my door.

"James, please come in."

"Yes, ma'am." He hesitantly enters, scanning the room.

James is dressed casually, but acts formally as he stands by the door with cap in hand.

"Where is your bag, ma'am?"

"My bag?"

"Mr. McKenzie expects you for the weekend."

"Sorry, but I couldn't possibly stay that long," I reply softly. After all, the miscommunication isn't James' fault.

He sits in the nearest chair. "I'll wait," he says firmly.

Unfortunately, that struck a nerve. "No, I need to come home tonight. I'll drive myself. What's the address?"

"Very well, ma'am, I will bring you back tonight." James acquiesces, though I am not convinced that he has the authority to make such a promise.

"Thank you, James." I grab my jacket for later.

I anticipate the trip to be to a neighborhood near the park. Instead, James heads north on the 405 and slips over to the 10 at Santa Monica, and eventually to the Pacific Coast Highway.
~~~

I wait for James to say something, but he drives in silence. I'm being abducted. That sneaky old man! Just kidding—I hope.

"James, how long have you worked for my grandfather?" I decide to start a conversation.

"I was friends with your father since high school. A few years later, Mr. McKenzie hired me as his driver." James glances at me in the rearview mirror as he speaks.

Suddenly, I want to ask him all kinds of questions about my father. On second thought, I think I will wait until he brings me home, some of them might be answered by the visit or additional questions may arise.

We have been driving for at least an hour. I have no idea where we are. It's a little too remote for my comfort.

"Here we are, Miss McKenzie," James says, as he pulls into a gated drive and the gates slowly swing open.

Well, this isn't what I had expected. Is this some sort of place for old people? It seems a little large. The sign on the stone pillar reads "Pacific Estate." That definitely sounds like a place for old people. How did Grandfather think that I would spend the weekend here? It is a great view of the ocean, but—

A doorman meets the car at the bottom of the front steps. He reaches down his white-gloved hand to help me out of the car.

"Miss McKenzie," he says, as he takes my hand.

"Thank you," I say, charmed by the movie feel of this experience. I am grinning with the fun of it all.

Grandfather is waiting in his wheelchair just inside the door. Apparently, the chair is a full-time item, not just for outings, as I had wondered.

"Kathryn!" Grandfather reaches out both hands toward me, greeting me like I am a royal visitor.

I lean down and kiss his cheek, while he continues to hold my hands in his. He made a soft chuckling sound as my lips touch his face. I respond with a smile. It makes me remember the parade lady's cooing sounds.

Clearly this is not a place for old people. It is a place for rich people! I look at Grandfather closer. Goodness! Is my grandfather the rich Mr. McKenzie? After all of the years of telling people, I was not *that* McKenzie, I am *that* McKenzie!

Looking around the foyer, I'm surprised that I am not intimidated, but comfortable here. I smile when my eyes meet Grandfather's. He smiles warmly, too. A male attendant wheels Grandfather through the house (mansion) to the patio facing the side yard, which is an impressive English garden. There are several bouquets of freshly cut flowers placed around the patio and a smaller one on our table.

While Grandfather is being settled, I gaze at the manicured gardens spanning the east yard. The Estate is reminiscent of my visit to the Getty Villa.

"Missy, do you know who I am?" Grandfather asks, bringing my attention back to him.

This is a trick question, isn't it? I feel a little impish and reply soberly with feigned innocence, "My grandfather."

He grins. "Yes, I am Alistair McKenzie. Now, do you know who I am?"

"Yes."

"Well, what do you think?" He coaxes a more impressive answer.

I look around and move my hand in a scanning fashion. "Your home is lovely, Grandfather."

"Kathryn, I would like to get to know you," he responds to my warm tone.

I am pleased with his request. We visit through the afternoon. It is a get-to-know-you visit: relaxed, nothing too personal. I decide I like him, once we moved beyond his King of California façade. I am sure that he feels compelled to wear that role for most people, but my interest is the man who is my grandfather.

After all, his money doesn't change my life. He elected to disinherit my father before I was born. Why should I care if Grandfather has money or not? It just makes for a long drive to his house—ahem, mansion.

We have a wonderfully delicious dinner in the formal dining room, just the two of us seated perpendicular to each other at one end of a long dining table. At first, it seems like an unreal world, one with waiters attentively serving fabulous food on expensive-looking china. We have a waiter standing a slight distance behind each of us, ready to anticipate our every need. I feel he is going to reach out and butter my bread for me. At first it is awkward to talk with Grandfather with them there.

Grandfather doesn't seem the least bit concerned what they might hear. He asks many questions about me, my work, my friends. Wisely, he avoids politics and religion. We already know that we are religiously incompatible. As a social worker, I suspect that we have even less in common politically.

At the end of the meal, we are served a sinfully delicious dessert. It melts in my mouth in an extravagant sensation of flaky pastry with rich, creamy, chocolate sweetness. And, the coffee—it's wonderful. This must be heaven.

When we finish with dinner, Grandfather announces my departure.

"I understand you wish to return home tonight," he says in a businessman way.

"Yes, Grandfather, I must."

"Then, another time perhaps."

"I look forward to it."

Grandfather glances over his shoulder.

"Tell James that Kathryn is ready." Grandfather squirms to straighten himself in his chair.

I stand and kiss Grandfather on the cheek again.

"Thank you for dinner, Grandfather, and for the day," I whisper and squeeze his hand. I think we are warming up to each other.

On the way out of the dining room, I see a chair in the hallway where James must have been sitting, waiting. James leads me out the front door to a waiting golf cart. It seems like the trip might be a little long for a golf cart, but I keep my humor to myself, and climb onto the seat next to James.

We are off with a jerk. We go around the house quickly and north of the manicured grounds. A wind sock is blowing in the beam of a spotlight. Next to it is a helicopter, waiting, blades slowly beginning to rotate, wisping the air.

James ducks low, swiftly walking me to the cockpit. It becomes apparent that he is not going with me. I have missed my chance to ask him questions about my father.

We lift up and fly toward home at an angle parallel to the coast. Somewhere near Malibu, we fly out over the ocean. It is dark below. I watch the coastal lights on the left to keep my sense of direction straight.

Before long, the lights from the Port of Los Angeles come into view. Leaning, I look for the *Queen Mary* docked at Long Beach.

It becomes apparent that the pilot plans to land on the beach. I am quite sure that isn't allowed, short of an emergency. When the pilot uses the McKenzie name to clear his landing with someone over the radio and it is granted, I realize just how powerful Grandfather is.

I knew King McKenzie, as he is called, is rich, but this is a bit overdone, ostentatiousness. I hope no one sees me get out of the helicopter and walk to my apartment across the street. This show of wealth is embarrassing.

Dearest Maggie, You will never imagine this. I am the granddaughter of Alistair McKenzie! Who would have guessed? Despite what I have heard about him, I like the old guy. It is a shame that he didn't correct his mistake about my mother. I hope that I do not make such a grave mistake in my life—the kind that can never be undone.

~~~
~~~

After Saturday afternoon and evening with Grandfather, I am happy to have a day on the beach to reflect. I like having my other grandfather come into my life. It feels more balanced to know both sides of my family. But the beach landing bothers me. We are nothing alike.

Apparently, without knowing it existed, I had adopted my parents' attitude toward the family money. Since Father was disinherited, the money was more of an embarrassment, than anything else.

Still, Grandfather is family, and that counts for a lot more than wealth. I hope to see him again, and when it pleases him, he will no doubt summon me for another visit. Until then, I have a life of my own: a life separate from the King McKenzie's money.

~~~

At work, everyone's next round of HIV tests are negative, as I was sure they would be. We were tested twice, just to be sure, with more testing some months in the future. Our new homeless family is settling in well. They have the initial disbelief the others had when they arrived. Their reaction is a good reality check. The new family accents how far the first families have come in a year. Hopefully, the others will serve as a torch, showing what possibilities are ahead. The new ones seem to ease into the routine faster than last year, when everyone was new. Maybe because all of this was new for all of us, and now we have many things figured out.

Work is a pleasant diversion. I'm able to forget that my grandfather is not an ordinary grandfather. On the other hand, my real family will soon gather for Thanksgiving dinner in the park, a bit of tradition to recalibrate my world.

It will be good to see everyone. This is the family that sustained me all of my life. By every measure, they are richer than Grandfather in all the ways that matter. We have spent our entire lives sharing family times together: births, accomplishments, disappointments, deaths.

~~~

I sit on the sofa with my feet on the coffee table and a cup of coffee in my hand. Emily sent the annual newsletter. I pour over it, discovering who is planning to attend the dinner this year. Out of my twenty-seven first cousins, I am in the middle bunch. I can't wait to see everyone.

Rumor has it that our uncle who cooks the turkeys has estimated that we will need three turkeys again this year. That sounds about right. I settle back, thinking about the food and the fun last year.

Sadly, I remember also, it was the weekend that Maggie and Dave died when their plane crashed in the mountains on the way to ski in Tahoe. Sadness washes over me in a wave.

It is chilly outside this evening, but I decide to go for my customary run on the beach. The increase in my exercise habits has strengthened me. More than physically, I feel more inner strength. There is an emerging appreciation for me: me, the person with philosophies and hopes all my own.

With all of this thought of family and reminiscing of the things we do together and the bond we have, I think about the parade lady out on the street, alone. Who knows what her story is and why she is on the street, but the holidays are a terrible time to be alone. I want to help her in some way, in a way that will make a difference for her.

~~~

Abruptly, I decide to go look for her one more time. I know that she isn't likely to be found this time in the evening after all of the weekend afternoons that I have watched for her from the park bench where we met, and she never came. Now my old instincts that guided me well when I returned home are urging me to look for her tonight.

I know better than to tell anyone that I am going downtown alone at this hour. It isn't late by beach standards, but this is the beach; where she lives is a very different world, full of dangers I can't even imagine. I leave a note on my table about where I'm going and when I should be back. The only reason that anyone would find the note is if I don't come back, but leaving the note seems the responsible thing to do.

I top off the charge on my cell phone. I'm not sure of my intention as I drive to the area where I last saw her. First, I circle the block around the park, hoping to see her on the street.

There are a lot of people, street people, but I don't see her. I suspect she won't be one of the people who sleeps in a doorway. She probably has a more secure sleeping place; she seems very streetwise. I decide to try the park, since it doesn't seem late by street people time. If I don't find her shortly, I will try the shelters.

There are a lot of shadowy figures in the park. I hesitate a moment. A few people have made beds on the benches and the picnic tables. It is cool enough that most have newspapers spread over them. The "wealthy ones" have cardboard boxes covering them to keep their body heat in from the night chill.

I walk toward the park bench where we met. There is a small group of men sitting on the base of an equestrian statue near the bench. They have ragged coats, some have various hats, and all are smoking as they talk to each other. They give me no reason to be leery of them, but I give them a wide berth on my way to the intended destination.

One of the men facing my direction begins to watch me, or so I think, as I approach. "Hey, you. What are you doing here?"

My hand moves to my cell phone inside my pocket.

The others turn to look at me. After a look, some turn back uninterested. Two study me a bit longer. Obviously, I am a new face to
~~~

the neighborhood. Even dressed in my beach clothes, I am overdressed for my surroundings. It is unlikely that I wouldn't have stood out.

Well, do I run or take advantage of his inquiry? With counterfeit confidence, I approach the group.

"Hello, how are you guys tonight?"

"Fine," comes a female voice from the statue's shadow.

In the dark, I hadn't realized that one of the group was a woman. I strain to see if the parade lady is there too.

"You lost?" someone else asks.

"Shouldn't be down here," correctly comments a man.

No one moves to make room for me, so I stand at the edge of the group. "No, I'm not lost." I laugh a little, "I'm looking for someone." I direct my comment to the man who hailed me, thinking he is the group's spokesperson, although the group doesn't seem to need one.

"We're someone," someone answers.

Everyone else snickers.

"Yeah, we're someone," the woman repeats.

"Someone else, I'm looking for a specific person. Maybe you know her?" While they are quiet, but not necessarily interested, I begin to describe the parade lady: "She is a Black woman, about middle-aged, this tall, she pushes a cart—"

They're all uninterested. I can't tell if they know her or not. And I think that is exactly what they want. They are in control and all of us know it. Someone lights a cigarette and shakes out the match. The smoke comes my way. It reminds me of the two semesters in college that I was a smoker. I wasn't very good at it and eventually gave it up.

"A pack of cigarettes, if you find her," I negotiate.

"A carton for each of us?" the negotiations begin.

"No, a pack," I renegotiate.

"A pack then—for each of us," the leader guy agrees.

"All right." I agree to the terms we have set, even though I had intended a pack for them to split.

"In advance?" another asks.

"No, I don't think so!" I laugh.

They laugh, too. We have come to a meeting of the minds. I think they might be motivated to help now.

"What's she look like again?" a younger man requests.

I add to my earlier description the cooing sounds.

"That's Dana. Kansas, get Dana," the spokesman directs.

"Kansas" drops the stick he had been using to scratch in the dirt and leaves while the others resume talking.

"Get smokes. She'll be here," Mr. Spokesperson commands.

"What brand?"

Wouldn't you know they each smoked a different brand, or so they say. I drive to the convenience store I passed a few blocks back. The clerk looks at me uninterested as I read off the list of cigarettes.

One by one, he tosses the cigarettes carelessly toward the countertop. Most make their mark, but two fall onto the floor. Without apology, he picks them up and tosses them back on the counter.

Of course, the scanner doesn't work, so he puts in the prices by hand. The total for six packs of cigarettes came to fifty-two dollars and some change.

I know individual packs are more expensive than in a carton, but I think there was a sudden mark-up in the price when he saw the White chick who isn't from the neighborhood. When I hand him the money, he grins like he has pulled off the scam of the century. He has. Who cares? A private detective would have cost more than the inflated price of cigarettes and might not have worked so quickly.

"You need to check your math skills," I tell him to make sure he knows that I know about the mark-up.

~~~

Kansas and the parade lady aren't there when I arrive at the gathering with my cache of smokes. One guy reaches for the bag.

I wave him off and say, "No. Not until Dana arrives."

He pulls his hand back and slips it into his torn coat pocket.

"What you want with her anyway?"

"It's between us." I set boundaries again.

One of the guys shoots me a look, but says nothing.

Kansas appears rapidly pushing Dana's cart over the uneven grass. From the looks of the situation, Dana is as unhappy as a wet cat. She is following behind him, trying to reclaim possession of her cart. When she gets her cart back, she is going to have someone's head. This isn't the best way to make contact.

Dana catches up with Kansas and starts hitting him with her purse. The others intervene. One takes her cart, which starts her screeching. She turns her purse whipping on them.

Two others pull her away. Kansas scurries out of her reach. I'll have to use my crisis training to get her calmed down enough to talk to her now. I wonder why she has gotten under my skin. Why must I find her?

The group works as a unit to calm her and control the situation. They use none of the tactics I would have used. Actually, they are rather crude and abrupt with her, but to my surprise, they are quite effective.

"That lady wants to talk to you," one of the shadowy figures says and points at me.

Dana seems not to have noticed me until now. She leans forward, as if to see through the darkness, and peers at me.
~~~

"Give me my cart!" she snaps and jerks it free from the one holding on to it.

The spokesman looks at me. "Cigarettes."

I toss the paper bag with the cigarettes to him. They divvy up the contents, then resume what they were doing.

Not sure whether to approach Dana or not, I stand still.

Dana jerks her cart around as if to leave.

"Parade lady!" I say in a panic.

She stops.

"Please, don't go."

She jerks her cart around on the rough terrain to face me. She comes at me rather aggressively with the poor cart lurching as it crosses the sparse mounds of grass.

"What do you want?" she demands in a hushed voice.

Proper English? Well, isn't that a switch! Okay, let's see how this plays out.

"I don't know for sure what I want, but let me try to explain. What you said about the parade struck me. I had found out a friend was dying, and—" I look for a glimpse of understanding.

"So. People around here die all of the time," she says, not moved by my comment.

"I wanted to say, thank you, and—I don't know, do something for you. Something more than shoes," I say softly.

"What can *you* do for me? Can you get me a place to live?"

"Well, maybe I can. Can we find a place to sit and talk privately?"

She looks at me with a little more interest, but still distrust. She looks at a nearby bench.

"Here, get up. We need the bench!" Dana smacks hard at a man sleeping on the bench she wants to use.

He complains, but moves, mostly because she keeps poking and pushing him until he rolls off of the bench onto his hands and knees in the dirt. He slinks away grumbling, occasionally turning back to look at us. He grumbles some more.

"So, you think you can help me because you are grateful I helped you?" She is a bit snide in her tone.

I allow her the attitude. "I would like to try."

"Is your daddy rich or something?" She looks me up and down.

"No, actually my parents are dead. But I have a good-enough job," I answer bluntly.

"People die around here all the time," she repeats.

"Yes, I know they do. But you don't have to be one of them."

"So, you want to adopt me as your mother, since I made you feel good one time?" she condescends me.

"No, ma'am. I don't need a replacement mother. I just want to help. But if you don't think that's good enough or you question my motives, take your cart and walk away." I challenge her, so that we can stop playing this impossible game.

Dana looks at me hard, then sits up straight and seems to have decided she has more to gain out of this than I do.

"Okay, I need a place to stay out of the weather; winter is coming."

That is more like it. There is no reason to ask why she is out on the street or where she stays. If she tells me, fine. If not, fine.

"Do you know a place?" I ask, fairly certain that she must have something in mind.

"There is a place that rents rooms that aren't so bad."

"Okay, let's go."

She turns to the statue group and calls, "Kansas, come here, boy."

Kansas comes running. "Yes, Miss Dana?"

She holds out her hand to me and says, "Give me five dollars, girl."

I hand her the bill.

Kansas stops out of her arm's reach to avoid being hit again.

"Boy, you take my cart over to Hilda's and I'll give you five dollars. Five dollars, you hear?" she bargains with the underfed teen.

"You don't got no five dollars," he insists.

She shows him the money. Just as he is about to reach for it, she stuffs it down the front of her shirt and says, "You bring the cart, then you get the money."

Dana turns to me, "Where's your car, girl?"

Kansas grabs the cart and pushes it roughly, mumbling something that sounds like, "Crazy old woman. Where'd she get five dollars? Why, I otta—"

Dana and I get into my car. She navigates our trip, but keeps watch on Kansas and her cart. We arrive just as Kansas is crossing the street against the light. We wait for him in front of Hilda's.

"Five bucks, Miss Dana," he says, delivering her cart to her.

She nudges him over and grabs the cart handle.

He doesn't let go of it until he sees the color of her money.

"You don't let those whisky-drinking friends of yours know you have it, you hear? You get some good food. You're skin and bones, boy."

Kansas takes the bill and runs off.

At the old rooming house, Hilda doesn't take checks, but I have enough cash with me for six days. Dana and I prepare to wrestle her cart up the stairs. Dana is stronger, or more determined, than she looks. Hilda softens and gives Dana a ground-level room.

"If you want to go ahead and write a check for two weeks rent, You look good for it." She decided two weeks money was worth the risk.

Dana is delighted. At least, she is inside for the next three weeks. Now that she has an address, she might qualify for assistance. She easily agrees to another meeting to make more permanent housing arrangements and possibly some benefits like food stamps. I wonder if she has any family, but this isn't a good time to get that personal with her. I really pushed the limits tonight and better leave well enough alone.

I hand her a paper with my phone number. "Call me and we'll figure out things." I know she doesn't have a phone, but hope Hilda will let Dana use her phone to call me.

~~~

The approaching holidays brings out the family feeling in all of us. It's the one time during the year that people are likely to repair broken relationships. Conversely, if a family is going to have a parting of the ways, it is around the holidays or shortly after when disaster strikes.

An invitation to Pacific Estate is sent via Grandfather's usual, indirect fashion. I am summoned to Thanksgiving dinner.

I declined the invitation.

"Thank you, but I have plans."

I have other, long-standing plans with the family that has been a part of my life since birth. Even though my mother married the only Protestant in the family, they still loved her. The way they talk about my father, I can tell they loved him very much. It is obvious he became Catholic somewhere along the way. But I don't think it was required by Mother's family.

This family doesn't care about religious or ethnic differences, or degrees of wealth. Well, with religion, some of them can get preachy at times. With us, family is family. If you are going to marry into this family, be prepared to be a part of it in every way.

Poor Grandfather, he may have money, but he missed out on everything that matters. What is even worse, it was his choice.

Mr. Bradford calls again. A counteroffer is forthcoming. Grandfather will change his Thanksgiving dinner plans to Wednesday night, rather than Thursday noon, if I will reconsider the invitation.

Grandfather's acquiescence is completely unexpected. He certainly failed to live up to his reputation this time.

When I declined, I thought there was a possibility he would cut off all contact with me. I feel a slight sense of power that he still wants to see me despite the inability to control me.

For some unknown reason, he wants to get to know me. That pleases me, since I want to know him, but not at the cost of giving up time with my real family. Grandfather offers to send his helicopter to meet me at the John Wayne Airport after work. I accept. That is the only
~~~

way for me to get to the mansion from work in time for dinner. Besides, flying along the coastline was exciting. I loved the unusual perspective of the beaches.

~~~

The day before Thanksgiving, Sister Theresa summons me to the reception area. I have no idea what she wants, but I hope it isn't an errand that will keep me past three, when we are scheduled to leave.

Regardless, I will have to go.

"Yes, Sister Theresa?" I ask as I round the doorway.

Sister Theresa grins, nodding toward a dozen roses in a vase. Her eyes are fixed on me to catch my reaction to the flowers.

Just as I start reading the card, Mother Elizabeth enters. Sister Theresa motions toward the flowers. Mother lays her papers on the corner of Sister Theresa's desk and comes to the bouquet. She loves roses. Her fingers gently touch a velvety petal. Her eyes close and she smiles with the pure satisfaction of the aroma. Had Sister Theresa alerted her to the flowers' arrival, or is it simply good timing on Mother's part? Is it one of those convent mysteries that are always happening around here? Mother smells the roses again, and without looking away from the flowers says, "Your gentleman friend?"

As I hold the card to my chest, tears begin trailing down my cheeks.

"Yes, Mother," I admit, for the first time not caring about my pride or keeping my personal life personal.

Her hand reaches to my wrist, softly grasping it. She tilts her head and catches my gaze in hers. It is too revealing to look in her eyes for long. It makes me feel—don't know, it makes me feel—transparent? I close my eyes and more tears come. Immediately, I measure my breathing to a slow, deep rhythm, fighting an urge for staccato breaths.

The phone rings. Mother turns toward Sister Theresa to see if she is needed for the phone. Sister Theresa motions me to the side table phone and transfers the call from the switchboard.

Mother returns to the papers, giving instructions about them to Sister Theresa. She looks at me, then leaves.

I wipe my tears and take the call.

Karen says Joseph sent her roses, too. She is touched that Joseph remembered our shared loss. But for me, it is more than losing Maggie and Dave. I also lost Joseph.

She asks if I am okay with receiving them.

I lie, "He is being thoughtful." I think it was just a mechanical gesture, but I don't mention it, Karen is pleased with his kindness.

"Sister, let's leave them here, where everyone can enjoy them." I'm hoping to abandon them at the end of the day. She resists the idea, but since I don't have a desk for them, she is convinced to keep the flowers.
~~~

The roses have reminded me of more than Maggie and Dave's death. They remind me of last Valentine's Day, and beyond. Returning to work, I think about Joseph. I had promised myself that I would not, but it is a difficult promise to keep when he sends roses.

I round the corner, nearly colliding into Mother Elizabeth, who has apparently made a sudden U-turn. My hands raised to prevent the collision, land squarely on her chest with a thud, startling both of us and embarrassing me.

She stops abruptly, setting us nearly nose-to-nose. Without missing a beat Mother says what's on her mind.

"Kathryn, it is quiet around here. Why don't you go ahead and go home?" she states, more than asks. I am sure she remembers that Karen and I lost Maggie last Thanksgiving, and that the roses are an unexpected reminder of that loss.

"All right, thank you. Happy Thanksgiving!"

Sister Theresa notices that I have come to sign out for the day. I start to leave without the flowers, but she catches me before I escape.

"Take your roses, Kathryn," she insists without looking up from the work on her desk. These nuns are bossy.

I take them, but I don't know what to do with them. Their presence only entices me to think about Joseph. But it is easier to take the flowers than to make an issue out of leaving them. Sister Theresa expects to have her way. I let her win. There is no one on Earth who has won an argument with a nun—check the records on that.

With a little ingenuity, I figure a way to secure the roses with the seatbelt around the vase. My poor car. We sure get into strange situations. And I am quite sure none of them are of my making.

A car pulls next to me at the stoplight. A handsome male driver sees the roses in the passenger seat and smiles widely. I force a bit of cheeky smile in return. What the heck? Let him think it is romantic. Knowing Joseph sent roses to Karen makes it less romantic and more a simple gesture of thoughtfulness. That makes it easier.

I decide to take the exit to the cemetery where Maggie and Dave are buried. Sometimes sitting at her grave and talking to her feels almost like we are together again.

"Thank you for the diaries, Maggie," I whisper.

Words don't come easy today. Some things are beyond words. We always had a knack for sharing them in silence, a comfortable silence amid the haste and confusion around us.

"Oh Maggie, I miss you so much."

I place the roses in the flower cup between both graves on their shared headstone.

The helicopter is waiting at the airport when I arrive. Security stops me until the pilot motions that it is all right to let me pass. The McKenzie emblem and name on the side of the aircraft gives me an odd feeling.

I have to admit that it is a marvelous thrill to fly along the coast in this manner. The waves breaking on the sand, from this perspective, is an unusual treat, especially as we move up the coast and rocks begin to dot the beaches with waves crashing over them, spewing white foam into the air.

James is waiting with the golf cart when we arrive at the estate. We zip along the path to the front of the house as if this is an everyday occurrence; maybe it is for him. The white-gloved doorman escorts me into the library. As I enter, I feel the richness of the room: mahogany bookcases, books, paintings, sculptures, and leather furniture. It is difficult to remember that someone really lives here and it is not a movie set. My fingers explore the richness of the arm of the leather chair while I wait for Grandfather. How vastly different this is from Dana's world.

Conner, his male nurse, wheels Grandfather into the room, and sets the brakes on his wheelchair before leaving.

"Kathryn, my dear, thank you for coming," Grandfather says warmly.

"Grandfather," I acknowledge him, as I rise to give him a kiss on the cheek.

He beams with the greeting.

So do I.

"Thank you for rearranging your schedule. I'd made plans for tomorrow."

"Your mother's family?" he asks. "I should have known that you wouldn't have to be alone on the holiday."

I am not sure what he means by his comment, but I nod.

We visit in a grandfather to granddaughter comfortable way. I hadn't expected that we would hit it off so well. How can this be the same man who would have nothing to do with his son simply because he married a Catholic? Maybe developing a relationship with me is his attempt to atone for that long-ago decision. I don't know, but I want to be family, if that's possible.

"Dinner is served, sir."

"Thank you, Stanley."

He unlocks his wheelchair.

"May I help you, Grandfather?"

He nods and put his hands in his lap.

I smile to myself. The moments of life seem so fleeting, so temporary. I capture these moments in my memory for when they are gone. None of this seems real: Stanley, James, golf carts, white gloves, and helicopter rides.

The room is filled with the aroma of the real fire in the fireplace. The table is exquisitely set. Multiple glasses are at each setting, in addition to excessive flatware and china. I am not sure the purpose for each item. And I don't understand why there are five place settings.

The candles on the table flicker. The light from above brings the crystal to life. Floral arrangements lightly fill the air with a sweet scent mixed with the burly smell of burning wood.

After I am seated, one of the servers begins to carve the turkey. It looks so perfect that it almost doesn't look real. But I can smell that it is real. It delights my senses. My mouth begins to water in anticipation. The dinner rolls are homemade and still warm. The butter melts and disappears into the steaming bread. The wine is perfectly chilled. I have never tasted anything quite as good. My lips savor the touch of the cool liquid. I breathe deeply the satisfied, unbelievably wonderful sensual experiences into my memories. I can hear a musical score of my invention, crescendo in the background of my mind.

Grandfather interrupts my thoughts.

"Kathryn, what are your plans for your future?" he asks, almost demands.

My first instinct is to tell him it's none of his business. But I don't think he means to be so rough around the edges. In his business world of acquisitions and hostile takeovers, he is used to being direct, getting what he wants at all costs. He does not worry about human sensitivities. He probably doesn't worry about anything.

"Well, I love social work." I smile widely. "I can't imagine doing anything else."

"What about marriage?"

"Perhaps someday, but I'm happy with the way things are right now." I have no plans to deliberately complicate my life with another romance this soon.

Just as I had concluded that the three empty place settings at the table were symbolic in some way, three young people come in and sit down. Quietly and promptly, their turkey is served and wine poured.

Grandfather conducts the introductions like he is at a board of directors meeting.

"Kathryn, let me introduce Brooke, Timmy, and Danny, your cousins. Your aunt's children."

I smile and nod at each in turn. They don't seem at all interested in the introductions.

They do seem comfortable, even familiar with the dinner protocol. They know the staff by name. The staff knows them, but remains formal in their interaction with the trio. Obviously, their mother didn't marry a Catholic.

Their entrance concludes the dinner conversation. We eat in silence. There is a coolness in the room that the fireplace cannot warm.

Cousins? I had no idea that I had McKenzie cousins. Father had a younger sister, but no one ever mentioned I had cousins. I feel cheated out of growing up together. Maybe my parents didn't know about the cousins.

I steal glimpses of them. Occasionally, our eyes meet. I smile, but they do not reciprocate. Of the three of them, the young woman looks the most hardened. Her excessive Goth makeup and attire attribute to her hardened look. The older male, Danny, is shy and awkward. Timmy strikes me as a bit wild. He is conceited and arrogant, and it shows.

Danny appeals to my social worker side. The woman, though, will be the most difficult to approach. There is no reason to expect that I will need to approach any of them. I hope we will get to know each other and like each other, but it isn't required. And, they don't seem interested in me.

"So, dear cousin," Brooke says degradingly. "Are you here to claim your inheritance?"

Grandfather says nothing.

Timmy chuckles at my expense while he eats.

Danny shoots a worried look at me, but says nothing.

"No, I came to steal the turkey." She doesn't get a real answer. I already know that I don't get an inheritance. Maybe she doesn't know it. Maybe she is making a point to see if I know or to make sure I understand that I'm not one of them.

No worries, I realize being Catholic leaves me out of everything. Grandfather probably would rather burn his money and throw the ashes in the ocean than give money to a Catholic. Besides, I don't want or need his money. I do quite nicely with the trusts my parents left, my investments, and my own income. It isn't near enough to live in a place like this, but I don't want this lifestyle, so it works out just fine for me. Frankly, it is none of her business why I am here.

She says no more.

We eat in silence.

I wonder why they are having Thanksgiving dinner with Grandfather without their parents. They must come here often. They are at home with the surroundings and the staff.

Brooke lights a cigarette and tosses the match onto her dessert plate. The server slips a crystal ashtray beside her and removes the former makeshift one.

Grandfather has eaten in silence since the introductions. He takes his napkin from his lap, wipes his lips, and lays it beside his plate. He clears his throat. "It is good to have my family together."

Family? It seems a poor choice of words. Where is his daughter and her husband? I'd like to meet my aunt and uncle. The trio of cousins are seated with ample space between them. It is foreign to me that they are only close enough to manage to pass the serving dishes to each other; but they don't, the servers bring the food.

When our family has Thanksgiving dinner, we scrunch together to make room for one more person to slide onto the bench at the picnic table and join the conversation. We talk and laugh as we enjoy our meal and each other's company. At the park tomorrow will be a real family dinner. I have no idea what to call this, this gathering.

~~~

On Thanksgiving Day, I absorb the richness we share. We spent our entire lives connected together. It's comforting to be part of a family in the middle of five generations of tradition. As I watch my cousins' grandchildren play with each other, I remember playing with my cousins around the same big tree.

"Kate, where's that nice young man? The one you brought to dinner last year?" asks one of my aunts from behind me. I wheel to greet her and my uncle carrying their picnic basket and a small cooler.

My aunt is poised to hug me when I turn around into her arms. We both fully lean into the hug.

"It's good to see you," I say, while the hug squeezes to completion.

"Well, where is he?"

"Joseph? He went back to Ireland this year."

"He didn't take you with him? He seemed like such a nice young man."

"He is nice," I agree to avoid an awkward conversation.

Just as Auntie moves to the next greeting, my cousin Ilene catches me. We hug too, as with everyone before the day is over. We go through the conversation again about Joseph's absence. He must have really made an impression on them last year. Or maybe what they noticed is that I had finally brought a date to dinner to meet the family. I won't be repeating that again anytime soon.

Reading my expression, she executes another hug and whispers softly in my ear, "Katey, come walk with me."

"All right," I say as we turn and move away from the group. We casually pass the horseshoe pits, pausing to watch the games in progress. Then, we move on.

She begins the conversation in earnest, "Okay, talk to me. What's going on?"

Tears well up in my eyes because being here again where Joseph and I spent last Thanksgiving reminds me of what we had or could have had. And it reminds me how hurt I was to find out he was married.
~~~

"Actually, Joseph went home to Ireland and married his childhood sweetheart." My voice ends, unable to say more.

"He what!" Astonished, she whispers louder than we are talking. She abruptly stops walking, looks around to see if anyone heard her, then shoots me a questioning glance.

"The really hard part is that I found out when I went to visit him this summer." I turn to face her as I speak.

"Life has been hard for you, Katey. You deserve good things," she whispers warmly as she puts her arm around my shoulder and pulls me near for another hug.

At that moment I realize how much they have worried about me all of these years. Aunts and uncles have filled the gap, making my life complete. They shouldn't have worried. I want to find a way to tell them there is no need to worry about me now. Thanks to their contributions, I turned out just fine.

It's true. I am fine. I return the hug. "Don't worry. I am really fine. Really. More and more each day."

She smiles, holding me at arm's length. "I know you are."

We turn and walk to the picnic area where more family members have arrived.

Another cousin and uncle tell me they put flowers on my parents' graves while I was in Nebraska. For a moment, I am sad for my McKenzie family. They are missing the essence of family, and their money can't fix that.

"Thank you for taking care of them for me."

Someone starts a family story that begins a discussion about the shape of our ankle bones being unique. This begins a presenting of the ankles for inspection. It must be a dominate gene, since most of us have protruding ankle bones on one foot or the other, sometimes both. I adore the ease we have with each other.

Another family anecdote begins. Several relatives join us to hear the stories. The embellishing begins. What liars we are!

It has been a good day. It always is a good day with Mother's family, with my family.

~~~

After I put away the dishes from the park, I turn my attention to the rose I kept. Removing it from its vase, I smell the sweet scent and look closely at the velvet petals.

I smell it again with a lingering inhalation and look around the kitchen for an idea of what to do to preserve it. I rake through the junk drawer until I find my kitchen scissors. In one smooth movement, I snip off most of the stem, smell the rose one more time, then sandwich it in a homemade blotter. A dictionary and a few other large books on top,
~~~

and ta-da, a makeshift flower press. When it's flat, I will keep it in Maggie's last diary, which ended when they left for Tahoe to ski on Thanksgiving last year.

I'll send a "thank you" to Joseph on the wind. Nothing more.

Besides, in my heart I know that it would never have worked to live that far from my family and beach. I guess I have always known. But for a moment in time, what we had was a special addition to my life. It has been hard, and I wouldn't want another lost love anytime soon, but we did have something special for a few months, and we weren't alone when Maggie and Dave died.

I spend the rest of the weekend on the beach in memory of Maggie and Dave. Maggie enriched my life with her friendship, and this is my way to honor her life and death.

Dearest Maggie, I have missed you more than you can know or words can express.

~~~

Dana and I work on her living arrangement. I thought if she has family somewhere, I would spring for her airline ticket and a few clothes, so she could be with them for the holidays, or move in with them, near them, or something. But she has no family. I don't pry for more answers. I do not want to treat her like she is a client.

Whether or not it's true about her family, I help her make application for social service entitlements and promise to take her to her eligibility appointment. After I push her to have more than a room with a community bathroom down the hall, Dana tells me of an apartment for $150 a month with utilities included.

It can't be much for that price.

The intake worker starts to cop an attitude that I quickly nip in the bud. It isn't necessary for her to act so condescending. She tries to backtrack when I politely ask for her supervisor. It is too late to make amends with me. I tell her to apologize to Dana, and then I make her do the form again when she does a poor job the first time.

Dana, whose real name is ValDana, shoots me a horrible look when I tell the eligibility worker that the rent money is a loan; granted, a long-term loan, but it's not to be counted.

I can't resist giving her the lecture of how my tax dollars are funding her job and I still want her supervisor. I know it's a cheap shot, but I hate her attitude toward Dana, so I set her straight on what the rules are. Don't mess with me.

We get the situation amended, and I make it clear that I won't tolerate a repeat performance of that attitude toward Dana. The way the
~~~

worker keeps saying, “Miss McKenzie” makes me wonder if she thinks I’m *that* McKenzie. Little does she know, it’s in name only. The important thing is Dana doesn’t seem to care one way or another what my name is.

On the way home, Dana makes it very clear that she is not going to be in debt to me. Period. Not negotiable.

“Well, how about a trade?”

“Trade what?” She studies me, harshly critical.

“Let’s consider the first month’s rent payment for grief counseling,” I suggest, knowing she understands I am talking about her comments at the parade.

“Then, what?” She isn’t going to let me off the hook that easily. I don’t know why she is being so difficult, she is getting a good deal out of this.

“So, what else do you do?” I turn the tables on her.

“I was an intern fashion designer in L.A.’s garment district.” She doesn’t say how she became homeless, but that is a volatile industry, so I can imagine the scenario.

“Really!? Can you design something for me?” I ask, intrigued.

We strike a deal. I’ll purchase a sewing machine and fabric. She will make me something for the next time my date wears a tux. She agrees with a willing smile. So, she’s set. And so am I.

In exchange for paying her rent and a few expenses, she will design clothes for me. What a deal! If she uses the sewing machine to gain other income, it’s fine by me. The way I see it, I have the better part of this arrangement.

~~~

Race successfully completes his studies and passes his high school equivalency test, GED. At first he protests the suggestion of a graduation party. I know better than to push him, but the nuns don’t worry about such things. In a way, I understand his desire for privacy. I empathize with his embarrassment at not finishing high school.

Life is hard enough as it is, and we should celebrate the moments when we accomplish something we set out to do. Privately, I give him a gift of money and suggest that he take his family to dinner to celebrate on his own. The nuns want to host a community party. He will have it thrust upon him. He might as well not try to escape the party.

“Take the money.”

At first, he refuses. He laughs. “Do you really think that nun is going to leave me alone?”

“No, not really. You are a goner. Just go to dinner with your family and have a good time. You deserve it. Besides, it sets a good example for your kids that you finished high school.”
~~~

Race laughs again. It is a nice laugh.

I don't think I have ever heard him laugh before now. Hearing it makes me smile.

Needless to say, the nuns have their way. I think they appealed to his sense of duty to the others to let them show off his accomplishment. After all, he is an example now. He will have to learn to live with that responsibility.

Race seems to enjoy the party, once he sees how genuinely proud everyone is. Lana is beaming. Several times, I see them exchange knowing glances with each other. It is sweet to see this big guy so tender with his wife and children. Who would have guessed?

~~~

As Hanukkah approaches, I listen to the tapes Mr. Goldstein's Rabbi made for me last year. I don't have a menorah. I don't know how to make potato pancakes like Mr. Goldstein did. At least I can say the prayers the best I can. I think God will understand the Irish-Catholic accent to my Hebrew. It is my way of keeping the light burning for Mr. Goldstein while he's away.

~~~

Following in last year's tradition, the good sisters prepare to stage a Christmas pageant with the Spirit of Hope families as the stars. Sister Veronica sings Christmas carols loudly wherever she goes. Her voice echos down the corridors of the convent, spilling out into the homeless center. This year we won't have a newborn to play Baby Jesus, and we are missing Monica's contribution, but we will make do.

The pageant is again a success. Linda and Todd bring the governor and Angela with them. Karen brings Keith with her. Easily, I notice that Mother Elizabeth takes approving note of Keith's attentiveness toward her baby sister. Some gifts don't need wrapping. Karen's happiness is one of them. It pleases all of us who care deeply for her to see them together.

~~~

Cutting out the middleman, Grandfather invites me to spend Christmas with him. Maybe I should. I have no one to spend Christmas with, and neither does he—unless the cousins are there again.

However, I admit to myself that I am perfectly happy to spend the day on the beach. Maybe Livingston will be there for a nice Christmas walk. I'll take my headset and play Christmas music. That will be nice too. Yes, I am considering the beach over spending time with my new cousins.

Since Christmas Eve is on Tuesday, Mother Elizabeth tells the staff to take off the whole week and not come back until January 2nd. Very willing to have the time off, everyone is thrilled with the announcement.
~~~

With excess holiday time available, I call Grandfather and tell him that I would like to drop by early Christmas Eve afternoon.

Grandfather eagerly agrees, and makes no attempt to hide his pleasure about my visit plans. Since we have missed so many Christmas celebrations together, I want to do something special for our first Christmas.

The question is, What do you give a man like Grandfather McKenzie? The man has his own helicopter and mansion filled with staff. What else could he possibly need? What could he need that I can afford? Tough question.

While running on the beach, I think of the prefect gift from me. When I return home, I sort through recent photos and select one that I think captures my personality. I will give him the one thing money can't buy, a framed photo of me. As a matter of fact, it's the picture that Mr. Goldstein took. The rest of the evening I look through photo albums. There are so many good times in these photos. I am certain that my parents would have loved sharing those times with him. Poor old rich man, poor Grandfather.

I copy the best snapshots, the ones most representative of our past. One of my favorites has always been the photo of me with Santa Claus the first Christmas after my father was killed in the wreck. I arrange the photos in a nice photo album for him.

I wonder if Grandfather knew when Father died? Did he come to Dad's funeral? I have so many questions. I decide to give him the Santa photo framed rather than the more recent one, which I add to the photo album instead.

~~~

I drive my car this time. Grandfather and I spend Christmas Eve afternoon together. He gives me a diamond bracelet.

He cries, unashamed, when he opens my gift. It is a tender moment that I tuck away in my memory to save for later. I don't mention it was the first Christmas without my dad.

Grandfather wants to go to the garden. James and Stanley are gone, Conner is in the shower. Eleanor, the housekeeper, produces Grandfather's coat, hat, scarf, and gloves.

Lovingly, I wrap his scarf around his neck and tuck it inside his coat lapel. We go to the garden, leaving Eleanor inside the door watching after us.

A few winter flowers are blooming. I wheel him through the garden pathways. We talk some. Mostly, we inspect the plants and shrubs. I don't think he has been out here for quite a while. He doesn't seem to tire or be in much of a hurry. The weather, true to California tradition, is beautiful. I wear only a light jacket, but Grandfather is getting a chill.
~~~

When we get back to the house, and I use that term "house" loosely, I offer to make him some hot tea or cocoa. He smiles adoringly, and I am delighted.

When we arrive in the kitchen, I am impressed. It is a kitchen that any chef would envy. It is larger than my whole apartment.

"Do you suppose you could make something a little more powerful than hot cocoa?" He grins.

"I'm sure we can think of something interesting," I respond, enjoying the bond developing between us. I bet he isn't supposed to be drinking. He reminds me of a child sneaking a cookie when no one is looking.

"How about a hot buttered rum?"

That's not what I expected him to request, but maybe he was thinking of something I might like. Looking in one cupboard after another I say, "Let's see if we have everything we need first. We're in luck, two cinnamon sticks left." I hold up the spice jar.

Grandfather seems slightly surprised that I know what goes into hot buttered rum. I decide there is no particular reason to tell him about my life as a bartender in Nebraska.

"Look in there," he points to the pantry door. The place is stocked to the nines. He wheels himself out and returns with the rum, a very good rum. I didn't know he was mobile. Well, that old coot! We both have secrets.

We sip our drinks, mine has only a dash of rum since I have to drive home later. He has two drinks while he can get away with it. Maybe he can drink, but being sneaky is more fun.

~~~

On the freeway, I look at the sparkle of my new bracelet in the city lights. It seems that jewelry is the gift of choice with the McKenzie family. I could learn to love this custom.

My little beach community church still has Midnight Mass on Christmas Eve. I never figured out how they changed Midnight Mass to 10:00 p.m. at some parishes.

I like my parish. As Father Al says, "It is a poor parish." We really aren't so poor here in Orange County. Our church clothes don't compare with Beverly Hills, but we dress nicely. We sing with all our hearts, not always well, but happily. However, we do sing particularly well at Midnight Mass.

~~~

Early Christmas morning Mr. Goldstein calls from Austria. He is coming home. Would I be able to pick him up at LAX?

"Most certainly!" is the obvious answer.

He arrives early on the 27th. He looks fabulous. Immediately, we resume our daily walks along the beach. He tells me all about his visit with his niece and her family. Tears run down his face when he talks about the reunion with his sister-in-law.

He is particularly intrigued by the story of how she escaped the war dressed as a nun. He says that nuns had seen the Nazis come into their neighborhood and knew it meant trouble. The nuns caught her on her way home from the market and hid her. Two of the nuns went to the house the next day when things had quieted down on the streets. Someone told them that her family were taken.

They trained her to act like a nun and snuck her out of the country dressed in a habit, which hid her pregnancy. She stayed at another monastery until after the war. Then she and her son returned to search for Mr. and Mrs. Goldstein. They must have missed her by days. He looks sad at the thought that his wife had not seen her sister or nephew and didn't know they were safe and alive.

It comes as no surprise when he tells me he is moving to Austria. I expected it. I am surprised he came back at all. He plans to move mid-spring. I agree to help him sort through his things, so that the movers can pack what's left. I expect that it will result in a copious amount of quality time, enough to last us for the rest of our lives.

I do my best to act as my usual self while Mr. Goldstein and I walk the beach. There is no fooling him, he sees right through me.

"What's wrong, Katerina?"

I stop walking and look at him. I could say it was Monica, and that would be partly true. I could ask what he meant, as if I had no idea what he was talking about, but that would not be true. I could tell him how much I am going to miss him, but I don't have the words for it right now.

"I am happy for you," I say fondly.

"Where's your boyfriend? You have not mentioned him. I thought you would have a ring on your finger." He continues the conversation as if it is natural to be so raw with each other.

"He isn't coming back."

"Dah, he's no good for you. I know this the first time I see him," he answers with passion. I could hug him.

Mr. Goldstein is right, of course, Joseph is not good for me. I wonder what Mr. Goldstein saw in Joseph to give him such insight. I tilt my head asking for clarification.

"He is too much about him; no one else, just him. Am I correct?"

"Yes, you are 100 percent correct," I admit and leave it at that.

I must have finished my grieving. There isn't much emotion left. Instead, I move back to the moment with Mr. Goldstein.

A beautiful shell washes up in the morning surf. I give it to him as another memento of our time together. He will have no beach in Vienna. But we will always have our memories.

We set about the task of sorting through his things. He finds things he wants to give to various friends at the Senior Center. We make several trips to deliver them and stay for lunch sometimes. Other things he asks me to donate, including the furniture. Some things Dana might want. We're still waiting for her HUD voucher.

We accomplish a great deal during my holiday from work. We look through his photographs, all of them post-war. We study them just as we had studied my photos when I unpacked.

I love the stories Mr. Goldstein tells as we sort through the memories of his life. He gives me the pot Mrs. Goldstein used to make potato pancakes and promises to teach me to make them before he leaves. I like being adopted by him, but it makes me miss Mrs. Goldstein. It would have been fun to get to know her like I know him.

"Katerina, I didn't give you a Christmas present. Would you take this?" he asks, holding his menorah toward me.

"Oh! I couldn't."

He looks disappointed.

"Yes, yes, I would love to have it."

I reach for him. When I hug him, I begin to cry. I am going to miss him so much. I don't know if I should, but I am going to keep the menorah sitting out with candles in it all year long. I can't put it away and only bring it out for Hanukkah. Eight days a year is not enough to have Mr. Goldstein's gift sitting where I can see and touch it.

I will have to take lots of pictures of Mr. Goldstein before he leaves. Pictures on the beach in his sweat suit and street shoes. Pictures of us together. Pictures of him doing "Mr. Goldstein things." His eyes, I have to get a clear picture of his eyes. I don't want to forget anything about him. And pictures of him teaching me to make bagels and potato pancakes.

~~~

Well, it is another New Year's Eve; my second one since coming home. The novice drunks will be out. Staying home is a sensible alternative to driving tonight, the beach is a better idea than a commercial party somewhere.

Mr. Goldstein is going to the New Year's Eve party at the Senior Center. He is taking a nap now, so that he can stay up late. We had his suit cleaned and bought a carnation for his lapel on the way back from the cleaners this morning. He says they always have a grand time at the Senior Center New Year's Eve party, but that the bus will probably have him home at 12:01. He laughs about how those "old people" act at the Senior Center.

~~~

Karen called earlier to say she might make it over tonight for our traditional New Year celebration. Her children are going out to celebrate with friends.

I ask about Keith.

She was quiet for a long time, then said he was with his children this year. It is obvious how much they love each other. Little do I know now, it will always be like that with them.

Karen is such a good person. Spending her life standing as a sentinel to protect society from the plague of child abuse is a difficult and lonely job, especially for the Director of Children's Services. Karen deserves to have someone adore her. In thinking about it, she is the true enigma. Now, I am getting sentimental, but I want to embrace the richness of those in my life. It is all too apparent how fleeting our time together can be.

~~~

The afternoon sun warms me through my jacket. The Pacific is turbulent, but not in an enraged way. It is as if the ocean is full of excitement about the possibilities of the coming new year.

Last week's winter storm is gone. The novelty shells have been collected from the beach each morning by the resident beach people. I collected a few more for Mr. Goldstein to take to his family. Since then the sand has been raked with the machine the beach-keepers use to manicure the beach. It does feel like a new beginning. Life is settling into a comfortable rhythm again.

Last year coming home, I found a sense of belonging, friendship, and even love along the way. But this year has been tormented with losses, confusion, and a sense that, at times, I thought I would be swallowed up by the high tide of life.

Life found resolution, and so did I. I cannot explain any of the transformations and I don't feel the need to understand.

The moments of life seem so fleeting, so temporary. I want to capture them in my memory for when they are gone.

Dearest Maggie, Finally, I have found a sense of hope. It sustains me, underlying even the worst of days. I have learned the importance of living-really living, not just going through the routine. With the strongest conviction, I plan to make every effort to chase after life with the drive of an eight-year-old chasing an ice cream truck.

I passionately believe there is a spark of genius; a timid song sung strongly; a joyous dance; a dream of hope for the future; a moment of courage; a passion for life and a lifetime of love in each of us. Happy New Year, my dear friend.

~~~

Christmas without Father

Father's Beach

Storm Surge

You are the person
you are when
you think no one is watching.

~ CHAPTER 1 ~

Anonymity

"How was your trip?" Karen asks of my month-long vacation, as she looks over the back of the sofa into the kitchen where the most wonderful smell of brewing coffee permeates the air around me.

"Great! Austria was great!" I turn to watch the final drip of coffee land into the pot.

"And Mr. Goldstein?" She inquires about my old friend, now living in Austria.

"Mr. Goldstein is absolutely wonderful!" I inhale the rich coffee-scented steam rising from the cups as I fill them. "He is—"

"Katey! Listen to this!" Karen interrupts.

Karen points the remote toward the television—rapidly increasing the volume.

Karen is the calmest "calm-under-fire" person I know. The sound of danger in her voice sets off alarms in me. My pulse races in response.

Bringing our coffee to the sofa, I hand Karen her cup and stand, inquisitively watching the screen for what piqued her attention. The image immediately catches my eye. My cup halts midway to my lips. My attention is glued to the special news report:

> ...just minutes ago at a scheduled press conference, Alistair McKenzie announced his retirement and that his granddaughter, Kathryn McKenzie, will assume control and management of his multibillion-dollar empire beginning immediately...
>
> No, we don't know anything about her. There wasn't a bio on her in the media packet...

The reporter's voice trails off in the distance of my mind while I study the old man leaving the press conference in the wheelchair. The camera perfectly captures my grandfather's compelling nature. He is in control and he knows it.

The reporters don't push, shove, or shout questions at him. No one would dare show disrespect to the wealthiest man in California—nor, tempt the scope of his anger. Even the cub reporters seem to know, if they are reckless, he will have them for lunch with a glance. It is no secret he is ruthless—and that is exactly how he wants it.

The station returns to the news studio where the anchorwoman reads a litany of the McKenzie holdings while each company logo appears on the inset in the corner of the screen. The list is impressive.

I had no idea the McKenzie family, my family, controlled so many companies.

My gaze remains fixed to the TV as I move to the edge of the sofa to join Karen. Still in a daze, I lean forward to set down my cup, nearly missing the coffee table.

Karen intervenes, guiding my hand to avoid the impending mishap.

"Beginning immediately?" I gasp, then breathe out the words stuck in my throat, releasing the others lodged behind them. "Life as I know it just ceased to exist." The whispering echo of my words haunt me with their truth.

Fiddling with the heart-shaped locket around my neck I seek strength from the people in the photos inside it. But my dead parents cannot rescue me from Alistair Winston McKenzie.

I feel the weight of great wealth laid upon my shoulders. Tears well in my eyes in response to what Grandfather has done to me. He should have been grooming me for this. The way he did this, my God, that was so cruel to announce it publicly before telling me.

Not once in the past four years has he hinted at his intentions to involve me in the family empire. I was perfectly happy thinking I had been disinherited by default, since he disinherited his son, my father, for marrying a Catholic.

The ringing phone jolts me back to the present. Pushing my hand against the sofa cushions, I fumble to get up.

Karen puts her hand on mine and applies slight pressure. "Don't answer that."

Her instincts are correct about the phone. The answering machine picks up the call, allowing us to listen while a reporter leaves a message requesting an interview with "Miss McKenzie."

I sigh in frustration. "I need to get an unlisted number first thing tomorrow."

The truth is, I don't want the spotlight. The thought of it makes me feel ill. I resent the intrusion into the privacy of my life. His world was never a world I wanted.

Karen moves to the answering machine that has suddenly been transformed from "secretary" to "shield" against the advancing army of reporters. She presses the record button and lowers her face toward the machine:

> *"Miss McKenzie is not accepting appointments for interviews at this time. A statement will be released at a later date. Thank you."*

When Karen finishes recording, she smiles smugly and pushes the reset button. She takes the coffee cup from my hand before my lips can take a first sip of the steaming, life-sustaining liquid.

"What?" I hear her dump the coffee down the sink and set both cups in it.

"Get your purse and jacket. We're getting out of here." Karen proceeds to go through the apartment shutting off lights.

I grab my purse and Dodgers jacket. Karen takes the keys from my trembling hand and locks the dead bolt after us.

She keeps looking toward the street as we hurry down the stairs. We start for my car, but see a van from a local TV station rush into the driveway and stop abruptly in the fire lane of the parking lot.

Karen changes direction away from my car, pushing me around the corner of the building, toward the courtyard.

"This way. I parked on the side street."

We walk, slightly hurried, through the dimly lit courtyard toward the side entrance and her waiting car.

"Where are we going?"

"You're staying with me."

"But I need my car for work," I mumble in protest, looking back over my shoulder in the direction we had come.

My cell phone rings, startling me. My adrenalin spikes as I dig through my purse, fumbling to silence it before it calls attention to us.

We hear the thundering footsteps of someone running up the stairs. "Here it is! Over here," the voice shouts as pounding begins on a door: my door? We increase our stride and rush to the exterior of the complex.

When we reach the sidewalk, we slow to a hurried walk to be less obvious. Just as we are nearing Karen's car, someone hollers, "Do you know which apartment is Kathryn McKenzie's?"

"I don't live here, just visiting." Karen is deceptively truthful.

I keep my head down to avoid the streetlight, trying to act as composed as Karen. My heart is hammering in my chest. I feel dizzy from the adrenalin rush and steady myself against the car as I reach for the door handle and slide inside.

Karen clicks the door lock while shutting the door and sliding behind the steering wheel—all in one smooth move. I sink low in the seat, still trying to fasten my seat belt, as the car begins to move. A nervous laugh slips out as I continue to fidget with the seat belt latch. Karen is occupied with getting out of the parking space since the cars ahead and behind parked close, making it nearly impossible for her to maneuver away from the curb.

Another news van rushes past us and turns in to the apartment complex across the street from mine. We giggle at the van driving intently—in the wrong direction. Misguided, but determined, they are driven to scoop their competitors for the first photos and interview with Miss McKenzie. If they only knew how close they were.

Around the corner, Karen slows to view the activity in front of my apartment. Two more news trucks have arrived. People are tramping the landscape with cavalier disregard for the other tenants and the property. Men carrying cameras, following reporters with trailing microphone cables, hurry to get the first words with the new “matriarch of money.”

This whole thing is silly. I understand why Grandfather keeps them reined in. He masterfully manipulates them. Good for him.

But not so good for me. With the power of a few words, Grandfather turned our relaxing evening into chaos, and my life is permanently altered. It’s his style to do this from time to time. He enjoys the attention he gets by keeping the media stirred up, to appear in the headlines with precise timing to accommodate his business agenda. What was it this time, a hostile take-over, a buyout? What?

Karen drives past the freeway entrance ramp. Instead, she pulls into a fast food drive-through and orders two coffees. When the drinks are in hand, she says, “To your new life, Kathryn McKenzie!”

Ordinarily, I might have laughed. Tonight is far from ordinary. She’s right, it is a new life: full of protocol and spin doctors. I rise to the occasion and graciously accept the gesture. “And to old and dear friends.”

Karen stays on the surface streets rather than the freeway. I need every extra minute the longer route affords. A new life has been set in motion for me—there will be no going back. I can no longer keep secret who I am. Whether I want it or not, my face will be as well known as his. The marker dye has been cast into the ocean. But the Coast Guard can’t rescue me.

“He could have warned me. I need clothes for work tomorrow.” I plead disconnected thoughts.

“Are you planning to work tomorrow?”

“Well—” I realize how ridiculous I sound. “I should at least go in and give notice, don’t you think? It’s the right thing to do. Isn’t it?” I’m struggling to hold on to my life before every bit of it slips away.

“I should say goodbye to everyone at St. Mark’s—and Shasta. I must talk to Shasta!”

Shasta may be in the fifth grade, but she is as definite about how life works as when she was a first grader. She still greets me at the door every morning, though now not so much, to make sure I am coming back, as it is our routine.

~~~
~~~

My mind is racing with memories. I long to get lost in them, to pretend the present doesn't exist, certainly not this present.

Karen is on point with the current situation.

"You can wear my robe while I wash what you have on."

"Mother Elizabeth doesn't allow jeans."

"I think she will make an exception this time."

Of course, Karen should understand her sister-turned-Franciscan-nun better than me.

My mind circles in amazed disbelief. Grandfather gave no indication of his plans, even as recently as last month when I visited him before my trip to Austria.

I was perfectly happy with things the way they are between us. Besides, I have my own money. I have worked for years, saved, and invested, except for the five years I lived in Nebraska and worked in a bar. I live within my means and have managed my money wisely. Even in Nebraska, my expenses were much less than my income. Plus, there is the trust my parents set up for me. Granted, none of this is like Grandfather's money, but certainly ample for me.

I don't want the McKenzie money, not one penny. I didn't expect anything from him, nothing monetary anyway. All I wanted was to get to know him. I know too well, there are no guarantees of the time we have to be together. His age and wheelchair remind me that we have lost too much time already.

"How could Grandfather do this to me?"

Ignoring my tone, Karen speaks to the issue, "Who else is he going to leave in charge?"

"In charge?"

"He isn't a young man—" Karen's voice trails off, then returns echoing my own thoughts, "You know your McKenzie cousins."

The recognition of the truth spoken aloud washes over me. Hurt enters my voice.

"Oh God! Is that why he found me? Was that the only reason that he wanted to connect with his long-lost granddaughter?"

When he arranged for us to meet, I thought he wanted to atone for the way he treated my parents, or maybe to make up for lost time with me, his first grandchild. Now, it seems it was all a business tactic, nothing personal. He wasn't looking for his lost granddaughter, only for a successor, his heir apparent. Hurt doesn't begin to describe my feelings. I feel used. Because he's family, it feels even worse. It's all that I can do not to scream or maybe simply cry, grieving the loss of my life.

The confusion in my mind overwhelms me. The city lights blur past as Karen makes her way to her home in the foothills. I'm unable to take advantage of this last opportunity to be a commoner. Streetlights and confused thoughts, that's all there is; I have lost everything I had an hour ago.

It's a relief to arrive at Karen's house, secure from the media. My mind is unfocused for a sustained conversation. We talk intermittently and drink good coffee while my clothes launder. She was right about not waiting to pack a few things, even though it is inconvenient now. The media would have caught us if we had delayed even a moment longer.

She gives me a new toothbrush and toothpaste from the stockpile she keeps for when her daughters visit. Not having my own things only accents what has transpired this evening.

There is so much to think about. No doubt Grandfather expects me to move into Pacific Estate. I already spend a weekend a month at the mansion. But that isn't the same as being there full-time.

I certainly had not intended to "take on" my cousins who live with Grandfather. As a matter of fact, I have been careful not to play up the preferential treatment he gives me, or even acknowledge its existence.

Maybe it's because, out of the four grandchildren, I look the most like our grandmother. As a matter of fact, I look almost identical to the portrait of her hanging in the mansion's library.

I suppose it will be easier to learn the business if I lived with Grandfather for a few months. I hope this isn't his way to make me another possession, like my three cousins. I'd better keep a place of my own, so that he understands staying with him is temporary. Having my own apartment might be complicated, but it's worth having somewhere I can get away from the money-madness and go to the beach.

My thoughts are interrupted when Karen returns from the laundry room.

"Who called you?"

"What?"

"When we were leaving your apartment, didn't your cell phone ring?"

"I don't know. I shut it off so it wouldn't give us away."

She pauses, waiting for me to get the hint. When I don't seem to understand, she says, "Why don't you see who called?"

"Oh! Right. You don't think it was a reporter, do you?" I ask, half afraid to turn the phone on again. It is a relief to see the call is from my cousin Nick. I play back the message and roll my eyes, then grin at Karen. I play it again, this time with the speaker turned on.

"Katey, it's Nick. How 'bout a loan, Moneybags?" Followed by a devilish laugh. "No really, I'm just checking on you. If you need me, call. Love ya, Cuz."

"He's my cousin."

"Yes, I got that. Go ahead, call him back. I'll make sure your room is ready."

"Thanks. I'm fine. Really, I'm fine." I smile to make my point. We both know I'm not fine. I'm nowhere near fine.

It's good Karen was visiting when the announcement came on the TV. Imagine what would have happened if I hadn't known about it and reporters started banging on my door.

My cell phone rings. This time it is my cousin Ilene.

"Kate, I saw the news. Are you okay?"

"Yes, I'm at Karen's house for the night."

"You're welcome to stay with me, if you want."

"Thanks, I'm fine. Really," I lie.

"Did you know he was going to do that?"

"No, it was totally unexpected."

"Are you going to do it?"

"Do it?"

"You don't have to do what he says, you know."

"I haven't really had time to think about it yet."

Her point made, she changes the subject. "Aunt Grace is here. She says to make sure you are okay. She's heading home now, unless you want her to stop by tonight."

"No, I'm fine. Give her a hug for me. I'll call you in a few days—when I come up for air."

"I love you, Cuz. You know that."

"Yeah, I know. I love you too, Ilene."

My mother's family has gone into their rally-the-troops mode. God love them. I do need them. I can't think clearly. Never in my wildest dreams did I expect this from Grandfather McKenzie. I still can't believe it. This has to be a bad dream and I'll wake up any minute now.

I'm trying to be a good guest, but I'm squirrelly-restless.

Karen seems to understand this is not the time to push me. She foregoes wearing her therapist's hat and gives me a break.

I go to bed. Just before I turn out the light, I think of my diary. The missing diary is just one more reminder of my abrupt, forced exile. Damn him.

Emotions and thoughts are bursting for expression, but I don't have the energy to speak them. My heart aches. I lie in the darkness thinking what I would write, if I had my diary.

I can only hope that life progresses at a sane pace, so that I can handle this gracefully.

~~~
~~~

~ CHAPTER 2 ~

The Morning After

Sleep is restless. I finally settle into REM sleep when Karen wakes me. She has breakfast ready, but I'm interested in the coffee she hands me.

"Good morning," I lie. I pretend to be a morning person because it fits into society's expectations better than being a night owl.

"Good morning, Kathryn. How are you?" She sounds honestly concerned.

"Better. I am better today," I lie some more. I will have to go to confession if I keep this up.

"What's the plan for today?" Karen asks, as she leans against the kitchen counter, sipping her coffee, watching me search for words.

Quickly, I collect the random thoughts I tossed and turned with during the night.

"I could," I take a careful sip of coffee to buy me another minute, "go to work. I need to tell Mother Elizabeth I'm resigning. And the clients, I want to tell them goodbye before I leave."

Karen nods affirmatively, but not necessarily inferring agreement.

"Have you called your grandfather?"

"No, I'm not at all happy with him at the moment. It's best I don't phone him. He hasn't called me either. He may think I'm still in Austria, for all I know."

We haven't watched the television again. Who knows what the reporters said when they found no one home last night.

"I need to arrange to move to the Estate. There's the press release," I continue, as my thoughts begin to find some semblance of order.

"Eventually, you're going to need to plan beyond the next few days, but you'll know the answers when you need them. This is a lot right now. Give yourself time. Be patient. You can do this, I know you can." Karen uses her seldom-used motherly tone.

"I hope you're right," I whisper, assuming she means this new duty, and manage to fake a reassuring smile.

We look at each other. It's awkward. Her eyes don't reveal her thoughts. I can only hope my eyes do likewise.

~~~

Karen picks up where I left off with the more immediate needs. "I'll drop you at work on my way to the office. Check the girls' bathroom for makeup, maybe there is something there you can use."
~~~

I check the bathroom and find a supply of unopened cosmetics. I settle for mascara and lip gloss. That should do for today. I'll figure out the next step shortly.

~~~

The morning traffic is light. We find a media-swarm in a tight knot outside the front of St. Mark's convent when we arrive. Karen calls Mother Elizabeth.

"Okay, that works."

She drives past the mob and turns the corner. I think she is leaving until she drives through the alley. The garage door opens, and Karen pulls in next to one of the convent vans.

Mother Elizabeth is waiting with her hand poised at the door button on the wall. She doesn't speak. She simply puts the door down once we are parked. We follow her directly into the back door of her office.

Mother Elizabeth sits behind her desk, we sit in front of it. I'm waiting for her to say something, anything. I'm waiting for her to say I betrayed her by not telling her I was *that* McKenzie. I'm waiting for her to tell me that I could have trusted her with my real identity.

Alistair McKenzie is my grandfather, nothing more. The fact that he lives in a mansion overlooking the Pacific Ocean is no more out of the ordinary than people who live in convents and wear traditional habits.

It's a long silence. Sister Theresa brings a tray of cups and a pot of coffee. She sets down the tray, and grins a Cheshire cat grin at me when she hands me a cup. My love of coffee is famous. Sister Theresa gives Karen a cup, but Mother Elizabeth waves off one for herself. Sister Theresa leaves the tray on Mother Elizabeth's desk and backs out of the office in the strangest fashion, even for her. I don't think I will ever figure out that nun.

Mother Elizabeth's eyes are dancing, yet she's still not smiling. After all of this time, I should be able to read her, but the only thing I really know is that the nuns have heard the news that I am related to Alistair McKenzie.

Little Shasta appears at the door and invites herself into Mother's office. She announces my obvious indiscretions with her fists firmly on her waist.

"You came in the wrong door—AND, you didn't sign in!"

When she comes near, I push a curly wisp of blonde hair out of her eyes and ask, "Would you like to sign in for me?"

She still has her hands on her waist, sizing me up in a way that only an eleven-year-old can. To her, I am still plain old Kathryn. There seems to be no excuse for failing to follow the sign-in rule. It reassures me that being a McKenzie doesn't make any difference to her.
~~~

"Okay, this time."

"Thank you. Then, off to school. Sister will be looking for you."

Since she lived at Spirit of Hope for nearly two years, Shasta thinks she owns the place. She is the only non-resident student who freely comes and goes between the school and convent—as if anyone could stop her.

"Well, Kathryn?" Mother begins after Shasta leaves.

I wait for her to finish her sentence, but apparently she intends it as a prompt for me to begin. Begin what?

"Mother," I take a deep breath. This is awkward. "I don't know where to begin."

Karen comes to my rescue, intervening with her Sister-sister.

"Elizabeth, Kathryn feels she must resign her position. After the announcement last night, nothing is the same."

Nothing is the same, I repeat her words in my mind.

"I see."

Everything is in turmoil; perhaps Mother Elizabeth has decided it isn't worth discussing, since things will change from minute-to-minute until it reaches its equilibrium. Without a doubt, she is not silent because she doesn't have an opinion.

I take a sip of coffee and clear my throat. "Thank you, Mother, for everything. Being here has been absolutely wonderful."

Words are inadequate to convey my appreciation that she hired me for this marvelous job. I'm willing to be totally exposed in the expression of my feeling of fondness for the experience, if I can find the right words.

How does one sum up the experiences of Monica, Race, Shasta, the nuns, driving lessons, Paul's taunting me from the pitcher's mound, secret passages, and seem-to-be miracles on St. Francis' feast?

"You're welcome, Kathryn. We have enjoyed having you," Mother answers with the standard remark, then corrects, "I have enjoyed having you with us." Her admission would have been awkward under normal circumstances, considering she is Mother Superior and all. But nothing is normal now.

My emotions are jumping around like the balls inside a bingo spinner.

"I, I should make the rounds and tell everyone 'goodbye'—not that leaving will be easy."

"Yes." Mother Elizabeth finally smiles.

She pours a cup of coffee. "I suppose we could disguise you two as Franciscans and send Sister Theresa out as a decoy."

A slow grin comes over both Karen and Mother Elizabeth when their eyes meet.

I feel on the outside of an inside joke between them. Her remark about a decoy nun surprises me. I've never heard her joke about anything religious. I meant it would be emotionally difficult to leave. Surely she knew what I meant. Perhaps it was too awkward, thus the joke.

"Let's have a going-away party for you. We'll invite all the past clients, too. Make an evening of it." She makes a note and circles it.

I don't mention it, but immediately think about how she can't invite Monica. Despite all the miracles that happen here, saving Monica was not one to be had.

I would rather tell everyone goodbye individually, but telling them as a group may have to suffice. I hear myself agreeing with Mother Elizabeth's suggestion. Thank God that she didn't call it a retirement party, that would have been too final, even if it is probably the truth.

"I'll have Sister Theresa set the date with you. For now, we should get you out of here—if we can."

Whether or not the reporters know what I look like, they know where I work. I don't know how they know. Maybe someone should tell them I don't work here, now that it's true. I don't like being held captive by their presence. Strangely, Mother Elizabeth's idea of a Franciscan disguise is revisited and begins to make sense.

"Come with me and we'll disguise both of you."

Oh lord! I wasn't sure her offer of disguise was serious, but I guess it is. Maybe she knows best. Surely, this isn't another of those glimpses of convent life meant as a recruitment tactic. Can I make all of this go away if I join the convent? If only things were that simple.

We follow Mother Elizabeth farther into the interior of the living quarters of the convent than I have been before. There is a distinct rustic feel to this area of the building. The doorways are smaller than the semi-public portion of the convent or the modern mid-century schools between the convent and parish church. The original building can't possibly meet code. Parts of it must be from the Franciscan padres who came with the conquistadores.

The hallway is narrower and darker. There is a communal dining room, a parlor for family visits, and another hall of tiny rooms each with a bed, chair, and desk. Mother Elizabeth calls the bedrooms "cells." Hers looks no different than the others, with the exception of a phone on her desk. This one room has been her home for thirty-five years, except her time as a novice. That concept seems inexplicably odd.

At the end of the hall is a dormitory with a few beds lined perpendicular to the wall. There are forty or so beds missing, probably commissioned to furnish Spirit of Hope's former homeless families.

I won't call it a homeless shelter because it is so much more than a homeless shelter. It is a home. It is what each of us should do to ease the pain of our fellow man.

Mother Elizabeth opens a built-in cabinet with habits hanging in the left portion. The right side has shelves with drawers. There are neatly folded veils and other habit parts on the shelves. Mother opens a drawer with Rosaries, Profession Crosses, and a smaller box with a half dozen gold wedding bands. None of them look new.

Mother Elizabeth and Karen select pieces of the habit, periodically holding them up to me for sizing. In a bit of a daze, I stand there and let them proceed.

It is interesting to see how the habit works. I hadn't really thought about it, but I notice they are each handsewn. The headpiece is a little odd. Maybe, my hair is too long to fit under it correctly.

It's fun to try to pull off an escape from the reporters. I think we should drive past the building in our costumes just to have one more look at them. I'd like to honk the horn, but that would be over the top, wouldn't it?

Mother Elizabeth turns to Karen for her turn to don a habit, but Karen waves her off.

"No thanks, Elizabeth. I am not the nun-type. I'll be fine as myself." She smiles, set in her decision.

No fair. "I'm not the 'nun-type' either." I'm only doing what Mother said to do. They don't listen that I'm not the nun-type.

Just as Karen clips a rosary to my belt, Sister Bridget comes in and interrupts in an un-nun-like panic.

"Mother, Sister Theresa needs help at the front door!"

I've never seen her like this. She didn't even acknowledge my costume, and there is nothing normal about me in a habit.

Mother Elizabeth turns for the door. Karen is at her heels. I hurry after them. I feel terrible about what Grandfather set in motion.

Change of plans. "I'll go talk with them," I interrupt, knowing full well this is my responsibility, whether I like it or not.

The fun of the idea of sneaking out the back door is gone. This isn't a childish game. We walk past the statues of saints in the alcoves with their hand-painted angelic faces, past the chapel where Mother Elizabeth and Sister genuflect on the run, while Karen and I only make a Sign of the Cross, and pass the reception area.

Mother Elizabeth is first to reach the door.

A wave of profound sadness rushes over me as I realize my time at St. Mark's is coming full circle from the first day when I walked through this door. I pull myself together mentally, not sure if it's the calm faces of the statutes, wearing the habit, or that I find the strength within me to go through that door and face the media. Maybe it is because Karen, Mother Elizabeth, and Sister Bridget are with me, like brown-robed reinforcements of Marines. I pause to straighten my veil and follow them outside.

The reporters become animated when the four of us arrive to join Sister Theresa. Several cameras flash in our faces. They don't know who we are, but they're afraid they might miss a photo op if they don't shoot us. They might think Karen is me since she's the one in civilian clothes. Microphones move back and forth in front of us like a snake's head zeroing in on a target.

I step one step forward of my friends. We stand silently, while the reporters shout questions with micro-tape recorders, cell phones, and real microphones thrust at us.

We wait silently for the reporters to settle down. One man, seemingly unaware of the protocol, pushes forward through the group and to the side to get closer to us. He's standing in the flower bed near the steps.

I look him straight in the eyes, then at his feet, then back to his eyes again.

He gets the message and steps back to the sidewalk.

Is this power because I am dressed as a nun, or is it because he thinks I am "Miss McKenzie," a female offshoot of the old man who keeps strict order at his press conferences?

"Ladies and gentlemen," I begin, "this place is people's home." There is an awkward look on their collective faces as they shuffle to attention. It is so quiet, one could hear a pin drop.

"I am Kathryn McKenzie. I will announce a press conference in a more appropriate location. Your press desks will be notified of the details."

Cameras flash. The microphones have moved slightly closer—almost in unison. Enjoying the power I hold over them, I add, "You have behaved badly today. There will be no more of this. My friends are off-limits. I expect each of you will apologize to Mother Elizabeth in writing." I gesture toward Mother.

I look intensely at each of them. They are wide-eyed silent.

"Is that clear?" I expect only one answer.

They nod understanding combined with murmured, "Yes. Yes, ma'am," and one, "Yes, Sister." Then, several others thinking that they should have said, "Yes, Sister," change their reply. It's all corny, but I might as well lay down the ground rules from the start. After all, I am Grandfather's heir.

For added flair, I raise my right hand, make the Sign of the Cross over the group, and dismiss them. Let them wonder whether I am a nun or not. Serves them right. A couple of them hasten to make the Sign of the Cross, just in case they should.

Won't that give Grandfather a jolt to see the newspapers' photos of me in a habit? It doesn't top what he did to me, but considering his feelings about Catholics, it is probably the wildest thing I can do.

Once we're inside the convent door, we burst into laughter.

"Katey, you are awful!" Sister Theresa reports.

"I know!" I say proudly, then laugh.

"You enjoyed that too much!" Karen says.

"Yes. I have no remorse!"

I continue laughing until I realize what I have done, and look cautiously at Mother Elizabeth to see if I am going directly to hell for mocking Religious Life. It wasn't my intention to be disrespectful. I was caught up in the moment. Maybe the blessing at the end was over the top, but I don't think the Pope is the only one allowed to do the Sign of the Cross over a group, is he?

Mother doesn't appear disturbed with the incident, nor is she overly amused. As I remember, she started this charade, then it took on a life of its own.

"You know, you have to become a nun after that, don't you?" Mother pauses, then loses her poker face and laughs.

With the reporters gone, I change back to civilian clothes. With the full veil on, they probably didn't get a good photo of my face. At the very least, I am a free person until they get the photos publicized.

"This is great fun, but I have to get to work." Karen brings us back to reality. She looks at Mother Elizabeth. "Call me if you need to, I should be in the office all day."

"Yes, me too." Mother Elizabeth smiles and departs.

~~~

Karen leaves her car keys with me. "Go, buy some clothes and whatever else you need. I'll call if I'll be later than 4:00. Call my cell phone if you need anything, that way you won't have to go through the switchboard."

I'm grateful that Karen is thinking of the details. God knows I can't focus right now.

Sister Theresa, obviously eager for a reason to drive, offers Karen a ride to work, which leaves me a few more minutes at St. Mark's.

Now that the commotion is over and Karen leaves, I turn and walk down the hallway to Mother Elizabeth's office for the last time, ever. I hope desperately that she is available. There are so many things I want
~~~

to say to her, and this is my last chance to say them. I can't believe I will never practice social work again—especially, not at Spirit of Hope.

I knock gently on the open door. I feel as sad as when Maggie died. Maybe it's because my life is dying.

"Mother Elizabeth, may I come in?"

"Yes, Kathryn. Shut the door," she says, looking up from her work. Mother Elizabeth removes her half-glasses and squints a bit to adjust the focus of her eyes. It is an awkward silence. Even she seems to feel it and quickly offers me another cup of coffee.

Gratefully, I accept the warm cup into my hands. This is reminiscent of coffee with Maggie the day I returned from Nebraska after being "absent without leave" on a five-year, self-imposed exile.

Now, Mother Elizabeth and I are quietly having a cup of coffee before I go away again. Easily, I could cry without prompting. I suppose the only reason I don't cry is that I am numbed by the deep hurt of what Grandfather has done to my life—to me.

"Mother Elizabeth, I can't begin to tell you what Spirit of Hope has meant to me." I look into her beautiful, serene face as I speak, and feel the warmth of her spirit. "More than you know, you saved me by giving me this job. I have learned so much here. I have learned so much from you."

I stop speaking. The words are recalling moments of the past: Shasta and her secret passage; Monica preparing for her interview—wearing my scarf; playing baseball with the kids; Race's pronouncement of loyalty —unwavering loyalty—to Mother Elizabeth. I close my eyes and turn away, until she begins to speak.

"Kathryn, we needed you. You had the qualifications and the spirit I was looking for when I hired you. If you have ever thought that Karen pulled strings to get you hired, you were mistaken. We needed you and your social work skills, even more than I realized." Her voice gives way to a whisper.

Mother Elizabeth sips her coffee, then clears her throat. "Each person is a unique, irreplaceable representation of our Creator. We're each one ray of sunshine, one drop of rain, one song on the wind. All of us come together to make a symphony that brings joy to our Father."

She clasps her hands together on her desk, interlocking her fingers lightly, and leans forward ever so slightly. "Kathryn, you have been a gift, a gift sent by God. And now, He is sending you somewhere else."

She reaches for my hand curled around my coffee cup. I let go of the cup and respond to her reach. It is a little sad that we have never connected in this way before. I close my eyes to memorize this moment, knowing it will never come again. Tears well in my eyes.

Her hand is soft, yet strong. Holding hands lasts long enough that it might have been uncomfortable under any other circumstance. It wasn't an employer–employee exchange, it was a person-to-person moment. Maybe she is praying a blessing of some sort, but those are usually said aloud. At best, I can't describe this moment. It's awkward, but not.

~~~

After leaving Spirit of Hope, I head home to get my things. I know it is insane to go home, but it makes no sense to buy things I already have.

The sun flashes off something in a car parked directly across the street from my apartment complex. There is no traffic this time of day, so while stopped at the intersection, I watch the car a moment. It looks like a person with binoculars trained at my front door and window.

It was naive to think I could slip in and out of my place without someone noticing. This new status is a bigger deal than I thought. After I drive past, I look back at him in the rearview mirror. It doesn't seem there was any sign of recognition; he is still watching my apartment, not for me to drive by him.

It is too bad they found my address, probably from the phone book. Or did Grandfather give it out for dramatic effect? No, it had to be the phone book. Right? Grandfather wouldn't test my stamina under fire like this, would he? Maybe someone on his staff sold the information. No, then everyone wouldn't have it, only the buyer. Nah. That wouldn't make sense. But how did they know about St. Mark's?

I don't know the answers.

Slowly getting wiser, I stop at an ATM to get cash. I am not going shopping with a credit card with my name on it. Without my photo published yet, I should be able to go shopping, as long as it isn't my usual stores where they know my name and might put two and two together.

The first purchase is a pair of sunglasses. Karen will need hers for driving. Mine are in my car. I understand why people hate the paparazzi and wear sunglasses, at least as a symbolic shield from the intrusions.

After the incident at St. Mark's, I am gun-shy and stay put at Karen's house for the next two days. It is relaxing to lounge beside the pool and read, or nap. My concentration is sporadic, but it isn't like I am studying for an exam. I don't have to be sharp. Tuesday I slept quite a bit. Today is better, just a few cat naps. I still haven't checked in with Grandfather. He hasn't called me either.

An early dinner is on the stove. Karen announces Sister Theresa has scheduled the party for this evening. Despite my best effort to be
~~~

upbeat, I pick at my food listlessly. I had hoped for more time to prepare mentally and emotionally to say goodbye. I'd hoped to be more ready—to mysteriously rise to the McKenzie duty.

Karen keeps the dinner conversation simple.

I try to stay focused, but I stare across the table with little to say. Karen has kind eyes. That is all I can think of right now. I can't stay engaged in a conversation, but I look at her as if I am listening intently. I wouldn't have eaten at all, if I hadn't started feeling jittery from the coffee about midafternoon.

We store the leftovers and clear the dishes from the table. Karen leaves the television and radio off. It is a comfortable quiet, a soft quiet.

Our eyes meet briefly as we exchange food containers destined for the refrigerator.

"Well, we should get going," Karen says.

"Okay."

~~~

"Katey," she begins, as she moves her car into the traffic. "Let's talk while we can."

"All right."

"How are you doing with all of this?"

"I am still a little shaken, unsure of my instincts. All of this mania is leaving me unable to anticipate what will happen next."

"You don't have to concede to his announcement. He certainly didn't handle it well."

"I know, but if I don't do it now, it will be even more complicated later when he dies. I'll do it for my father."

"I think your grandfather sees in you the potential that the rest of us have seen all along. I know there have been hard times in the past, but you always rose to the occasion—and you will this time too."

I listen intently to every word. Karen doesn't seem to expect a response and I don't really know what to say. We both know I have to do this, at least for a while.

"I don't believe for one minute that he located you strictly for business purposes. I think he was reaching out to you because he knew his life wasn't complete without you in it. Finding you is as close as a man like Alistair McKenzie can come to admitting he was wrong about what he did to your parents. That admission, such as it is, doesn't come easy for him."

Karen is interrupted by the ringing of my cell phone. She nods for me to answer it.

"Kate, are you all right?" asks my aunt's gentle voice.

"Yes, Aunt Grace, I am fine."
~~~

“When you didn’t answer your phone at home, I had to get your cell phone number from Ilene.” She stops to take a breath. “Honey, I heard the news Sunday night. Is there anything I can do? Anything you need?” Her voice is maternal, as usual.

Aunt Grace is one of many of Mother’s sisters who came to my aid when Mother became sick and later died from breast cancer. She was always my favorite aunt, and she lived up to every reason for that to be true.

“I’m sorry I didn’t call. I left my apartment suddenly and just haven’t caught my breath. I am staying with a friend. I’m okay.”

“Does your friend work tomorrow? I don’t want you spending the day alone. Spend it with me.” She mothers me more than requests my presence.

“Yes, she does work. I’d like spending the day with you.” We conclude with making plans for her to pick me up at Karen’s house in the morning.

Karen resumes our conversation without missing a beat. “Katey, I think your grandfather sees what a capable woman you are, just like you saw the possibilities in Dana.”

“Dana is a talented fashion designer. I had nothing to do with her success. Besides, it didn’t hurt for Linda and Angela Whitmore to have her design their gowns. Once Angela wore one of Dana’s gowns to the Academy Awards, everyone in Hollywood wanted her to design their gowns.”

“True, but you did more than that. You helped her get off the street before you knew she was a fashion designer. You are the one who sent your friends to her for gowns. I think your grandfather can tell that you have the insight and intuition to make good business decisions for his companies.”

There is nothing more to say. I appreciate the vote of confidence.

~~~
~~~

~ CHAPTER 3 ~

Farewell

Sister Theresa orchestrated a nice party, especially on such short notice. I'm reflective. I memorize everyone's face and the feel of this place. I loved watching the disbelief in the eyes of the people as they came through the door the first time, then realize they are safe, warm, and fed. There is an honesty about them. I love them. And I love these nuns for opening their home to the homeless.

The farewell greetings are warm and heartfelt. Most hug me, even Race is tender as he bends down to my level and gently wraps his big arms around my shoulders. The clients give me a rosary as a going-away gift. Some of the children have drawn pictures for me. Sister Theresa pulls me aside and quietly gives me a key chain with Saint Christopher on it. I smile, thinking the Saint Christopher is a little late now that she has learned to drive. Her monthly stipend is ten dollars spending money, and it is touching she spent her money on me.

"Sister Theresa, it's perfect. Thank you." I hug her.

She responds with a tight embrace. Nearly too tight.

After the party, Karen and I help set the place right. Any excuse to stay longer is a good excuse. Finally, it's time to tell the nuns goodbye, one by one. It is even harder to do than I expected.

Mother Elizabeth's eyes water. She hands me a gift—a small statue of Saint Francis, complete with a gray seagull and tiny dried flower, which she attached to represent our time together in her garden. It is easy to see thought and time went into the gift.

"It's lovely, thank you. Thank you so much," I say as the tips of my fingers appreciate the coolness of the statue. My eyes burn. Dare I look up from the statue that is blurred by my tears?

"You're welcome, I just thought—" Her voice catches, causing me to look to her eyes.

"It's perfect," I whisper, feeling myself wanting to say, I love you, but I don't say anything more.

She draws me in for a lingering embrace. Her bulky habit becomes inconsequential. Mother whispers, "The will of God will never lead you where the grace of God cannot keep you."

The moment is powerful. Gone. But dwells on inside of me.

~~~

Aunt Grace arrives early, but I'm up and dressed, thanks to Karen's early routine. We hug.
~~~

"It's good to see you. How are you?" she asks.

"Good to see you, too. I'm fine," I say, happy to have her company for the day.

The three of us have coffee together before Karen leaves for work. Aunt Grace keeps glancing at me with concerned eyes. She is eager to entertain me, but calm with concern for the impact Grandfather's announcement must have made.

She knows me as well as anyone. I have to make this be okay, so everyone stops worrying. Grandfather's deed shouldn't give him access to make the other side of my family and friends worry about me. I smile reassuringly at her and sip my coffee. I will make everything all right.

Aunt Grace and I walked on the beach often while my mother was dying, so it seems only natural for us to go there now. It is funny how people gravitate to the familiar for safety when things are haywire.

It is a beautiful day. The sky is clear blue with a slight breeze coming inland. We went to Santa Monica, rather than to my beach, Seal Beach. We stroll along the water's edge, pausing from time to time to inspect seashells left behind by the early morning's receding high tide. Aunt Grace finds a shell she likes, and gives it to me. It is a dainty thing, but obviously strong enough to ride the tide without being broken. I slide it in my pocket, happy to have it—mellow with the gesture of the gift, and its representation of strength and perseverance.

We walk to the end of the pier and lean on the railing in silence, watching the waves come and go, and the people on the beach. The kite vendor has done well this morning. Several kites are in the air, tugging in the breeze. There are a few surfers sitting astride their boards patiently waiting for a ride to shore.

Seagulls are squawking at the pier fishermen standing near us, casting lines over the rail. One young gull stands on top of a piling watching a boy bait his hook. Father and son are craning their necks back and forth, intent on the bait sliding on just right. The gull watches two miscasts, then he lunges for the third while it's mid-air, which is a deadly practice if he gets hooked.

The boy laughs and shouts excitedly as the gull swoops toward the water in pursuit of the bait. The young gull returns to the piling after failing, to wait for the next opportunity.

The father shoos the seagull and scolds him to search elsewhere for his breakfast. The bird moves away, then back when the boy is distracted from the bait bucket. The behavior seems rather analytical for a bird. I didn't know birds had abstract reasoning. Maybe he is only opportunistic. Clearly I am searching the day for signs of how to solve my "McKenzie problem." I'll take anything, a seagull or an angel.

Aunt Grace smiles at me, fondly. She always knows when to appear on my horizon. This time is no different.

"How long have you known your McKenzie grandfather?"

"He looked me up about four years ago," I say.

"He looked you up?" She tilts her head, surprise that I hadn't mentioned it shows on her face.

"Yes. It went all right though," I add.

My parents were successful architects. There was never any indication that we were the rich McKenzies. Aunt Grace seems to have known about him. I suppose Mom talked to her about the man she was marrying and his father's excommunication that occurred because of it.

"Is he kind to you?" Her voice betrays her concern.

"Yes. He's always been kind." I turn to face her squarely.

"Your mother wondered if this day would come, and if it did, how it would play out." She offers a weak smile. She and Mom were extremely close. I wonder if Aunt Grace felt a specific responsibility to look out for me after Mom died.

"Oh! I wonder, too." I try to make light of my situation, but feel the weight of it.

"Give it a try. You have other options, if it doesn't suit you," she says.

"I'll do my best," I promise, not quite realizing what she is trying to tell me.

She gently sweeps a strand of hair from my eyes. "Katey, your grandfather has a strong personality. Keep the integrity of who you are. You'll be fine." She smiles fondly, then looks back at the waves below. "You are a bright, talented, classy lady. I am confident you will do well." She looks at me. "You come from strong stock," she quotes her mother, my maternal grandmother.

"Yes, I do," I say, leaning on the railing next to her. Our family has been through a lot of ups and downs, and always landed on our feet. We stick together. That is the secret of our strength. No matter what, we stick together.

Slowly, I am developing a sense of perspective about my situation. After spending the day with Aunt Grace, I feel better knowing that no matter what happens with the McKenzie family, Mom's family and the beach will always be as they have been. And I find that very reassuring.

I ask to go by my apartment for a few things. When we pull into the parking lot, the man with the binoculars' car is still parked in the same place as yesterday, but I don't see him. It's obvious I can't return home until this media curiosity is replaced with a more interesting news cycle. I tell Aunt Grace that I've changed my mind. We go to Karen's house.

Staying with Karen is fun, but we both need to get back to our normal routine. For Karen, that is relatively easy. As for me, normal might never be used to describe my life again. I'll tell Karen when she gets home that it's time for me to go.

~~~

Karen is already home when we return. She looks to Aunt Grace for an indication of how the day went. After all we've been through, she could have simply asked me.

With an ally present, Karen corners me. "Have you called your grandfather?"

"No, I haven't. I'll arrange to stay with him for a while."

I'm careful not to mention the man outside my apartment to either of them. I think it will be good to be away for a while and let all the media interest dissolve.

"You're taking this well." Karen is obviously more angry with Grandfather than I am at the moment.

The thought of staying at Pacific Estate is not appealing. Even in small doses, Brooke is obnoxious. Timmy follows her lead, but mostly he is a worthless playboy on the fast track to trouble. Danny is probably as trapped by Grandfather as I am. That summarizes my McKenzie cousins in a nutshell.

"No, not really. I'm angry, but the beach helped."

"You really don't *have* to do it." Aunt Grace solidifies her alliance with Karen.

I take a deep breath. "Don't worry. You taught me about family responsibility. The cousins are a mess. I've never met their parents. I'll do it until I come up with an alternative—hire someone, or something."

"Aren't you furious?" Karen is the psychologist again.

"I'm more than furious with him. The only way to win is to take control." The anger inside comes out in my tone, which is probably what she was after.

"It won't be easy," Aunt Grace says.

"You're going to have to set boundaries and not back down to him," Karen adds.

I don't feel that confident, but I nod and smile.

~~~

When I speak with Grandfather about staying with him, I put an emphasis on "short while," but there is no indication that he hears me.

Grandfather immediately says James will come and get me now. I ask to be picked up Saturday morning at the coffee shop down the street. Maybe it's selfish, but I want to spend one more day with Karen, and I don't want to risk the media coming to her house. Karen works a half day tomorrow. If I leave Saturday, we have tomorrow afternoon and evening together. Maybe we can get to the beach again before I leave.

I'm going to figure out a way to liberate my car, so I'm independently mobile again. The next thing on my agenda is to get a few clothes and my diary from my apartment.

"I should hire a look-alike and have her drive my car," I tell Karen. "With any luck, the media will follow her and I can get some things from home." The idea is amusing, but I need to settle down and devise a real plan. We both know I'm not serious about hiring a double. She buys that some media may still be at my place, watching for me.

Staying with Grandfather for a month or two is fine. It isn't what I want to do long-term. Besides, the thought of living with my McKenzie cousins full-time makes me shudder.

Karen refills my cup with coffee. "You know, you might learn media management from your grandfather. He has it mastered. Be firm with him on everything else, that might be hard at first." She takes a long sip of her coffee—leaving her words hanging.

That sounds good, but how exactly do I set boundaries with Alistair McKenzie? "Any specific suggestions?"

"Take charge. Start with the media. Have James come here. Don't sneak away." Karen looks like she is determining whether I understand, or if she needs to spell it out for me.

"What about you? What if the media follows James?"

She shrugs. "So what? They aren't interested in me. They won't hang around long." She rejects my concern. "I am sure James knows how to handle the media, don't worry about him either."

"That's probably true."

"Just be pleasant, not aloof, and go about your business. Don't give them control of the situation. Talk to them on your schedule and your terms. For now, just calmly get in the car, graciously."

"Charmingly unavailable?"

"Sure, why not?"

"If you are in the neighborhood, drop by," is all I manage to say, knowing the McKenzie mansion is not in anyone's neighborhood.

"I'll give you a couple of weeks. Get settled with your staff."

Staff? I hadn't thought about having staff of my own looking to me for direction.

Friday morning seems to last forever. Finally, Karen's home.

"It's nice to have someone here when I come home." Karen is happy to have a short day. Though, I never remember her working only a half day before. She drops her pager in the charger on the kitchen counter and looks toward the stove.

"Don't get used to having a personal chef."

Karen investigates what's for lunch. She lifts the lid of the pot, releasing a burst of steam from the soup. "Mmm, smells good."

We lean against the counter, looking at each other across the kitchen like we will never see each other again.

"You know, we are still going to be friends," I say.

It is easy to imagine the future to be exactly the way we want it to be. It is just as easy to fear the worst. I promise myself to make the effort to sustain my friendship with Karen, despite the McKenzie empire obligations.

~~~

James knocks at Karen's door. I'm not ready to go. We haven't eaten. Karen entices James into having a cup of coffee, but he declines the offer of lunch.

I'm tempted to send him away. This isn't the time we agreed to meet. He's a day early. But it isn't James' fault Grandfather ignored my wishes, so there is no reason to take my frustration out on him.

My appetite is gone. Might as well pack. "Ha! I am a bag lady," I say softly to myself as I fold the navy sweatshirt Karen gave me and put it into the shopping bag with my other things. Karen is a real trouper, but her eyes don't lie very well. We say goodbye to the past we shared.

~~~

The limo pulls smoothly from the curb. Karen stands at the sidewalk waving goodbye. James drives, silently. I don't have anything to say, either. What's there to say when someone has such ultimate power to change the course of my life?

After a while, I say. "James, let's take PCH."

"Yes, Miss McKenzie."

James moves the limousine effortlessly through the traffic toward Pacific Coast Highway. The limo wasn't necessary. I'm sure that Grandfather is trying to give me first-class treatment. I suppose he doesn't understand that I didn't know about the family fortune, so I grew up valuing other things, such as people, not money. Or maybe he does understand and thought, rightly so, that I would decline the succession to the throne if I had advance warning.

The road veers back along the ocean. In some places the elevation is ten to fifteen feet above sea level. The limousine rounds a curve in the road and I see the familiar sight I have been waiting for—Father's Beach.

"James, stop here for a minute, please."

"Yes, Miss McKenzie."

~~~
~~~

I expect James to stay with the car, like drivers do in movies, but he follows a few steps behind me.

Turning to face him, I say, "James, you don't need to walk behind me. Come," I stretch out my hand, "and walk with me."

He hesitates a slight moment, nods to himself, and joins me. "Yes, ma'am."

He is barely old enough to be my father and he calls me "ma'am." I don't like it, but I understand it's his job, so I let it be. However, there is no need for this large Black man to follow behind me. He doesn't have to behave like a subservient staff member with me. "McKenzie" is my name, not who I am. I have no intention of treating James as poorly as Grandfather does. Although, I really don't think it is personal with Grandfather. He sees all of us, including me, in a diminished light compared to himself.

We walk from the parking lot to the beach through the tunnel under the highway. James looks at the rock formations in the shallows, the seabirds perched on them, and the rising rock walls surrounding us. The waves are calm and the water is a deep blue.

"Isn't it beautiful here, James?" I ask as if he's a dear old friend.

We are standing side by side, looking straight out to the distant horizon. My arms are comfortably folded across the front of me. James has his hands casually in his pockets. It is as if the universe is standing still and we have this corner of it to ourselves. The sounds of the waves, the slight breeze, the clear water—everything is perfect.

"My mother always called this place 'Father's Beach,'" I say aloud to my newest friend.

James stirs and looks around with more interest.

It's not that I am disrespectful of Grandfather. I know we are going to be late arriving at the Estate, but I can't help taking these last few precious minutes, alive, free, and anonymous.

"James, I want to show you the next beach." I move to where the wall of rocks meets the water. I hold my hand parallel to my shoulder with the palm facing him, indicating for him to wait.

"When the wave goes out, follow me. Run. Run fast when I tell you."

Like waiting for a jump rope to swing out of the way, I gauge the motion of the waves. I wait for the biggest one in the series to pass, since it will recede the farthest and allow us more time to get around the rocks.

"Okay, get ready. Now! Go, now!" I run around the rocks through the temporary doorway the wave left behind when it went back to sea.

James clears the rocks just before the next wave comes in. We both turn to watch the passageway disappear underwater. The wave hits hard, then sprays into the air—majestically. James smiles a delighted smile, then we both laugh. His laugh is hearty and deep.

I show James the hidden entrance to the cave that leads to the next beach. He can touch the cave roof, if he stretches a bit. He is wearing dress shoes, so I advise caution on the wet sand and rock floor. I know we can only stay a short while because the tide is slowly coming in and will trap us here if we aren't alert, then we would have to mountain-goat our way back up to the road.

Besides, I remember that Grandfather is waiting for me. I just wanted one more visit to this place before I succumb to Grandfather's wishes, and I'm happy to have someone to share the experience with who knew Father.

~~~

Father's Beach

~~~

~ CHAPTER 4 ~

The Beginning of the End

On the way back to the car, we resume the roles defined by social obligation. Out of respect for James, I wait until he opens the limo door for me. We head north again. I no longer look at the ocean. This isn't the time to think about what's behind; what is ahead occupies my mind. I feel obligated to find out what is going on, not obligated to Grandfather, but to my father. The visit to Father's Beach was my way to confirm that I accept the proxy to stand in his place.

~~~

As we enter the gate of Pacific Estate, people scamper out the door and down the stairs. They look like actors hurrying for their mark before the curtain goes up.

By the time we reach the front of the mansion, everyone is standing properly—one person on each end of each step—like an honor guard. Stanley waits at the bottom of the stairs, ready to open the door and help me out of the limo with his white-gloved hand. I'm surprised there isn't a band—kidding.

I pause to acknowledge Stanley with a smile. "Thank you, Stanley."

I climb the steps beside him, acknowledging each person we meet with a nod and a smile. They are each dressed in costume-quality attire commensurate with their duties. Beginning today, I am the mistress of the manor—and that has changed everything.

Conner pushes Grandfather's wheelchair to the center of the porch. Grandfather sits there formally awaiting my ascent. It is as if this is an ancient, time-honored ceremony.

For an instant, I'm not sure if I should stoop and kiss him on the cheek, as I usually do when I arrive, or is something else the protocol?

I remind myself of Karen and Aunt Grace's advice: Be myself, or Grandfather truly owns me. I bend down and kiss his cheek in front of his staff. He responds in his usual fashion by reaching for my upper arm to hold me in place slightly—just long enough to stretch the moment.

Conner looks uncomfortable in hospital whites. Usually, he wears Hawaiian shirts with his white slacks. As a matter of fact, except for Stanley, most of the staff are usually dressed less formally.

Grandfather and Conner lead into the mansion. The staff file in behind us like a wedding procession. Grandfather instructs Eleanor, the woman in charge of all the household staff, to take me to my room. She nods, turns abruptly, and exits.
~~~

Obviously, I am expected to follow her. I enter the foyer and begin to ascend the stairs behind her. The feel of the mahogany banister is luxurious beneath my hand. Looking up the stairs at the back of Eleanor advancing ahead of me, she strikes me as the "little general" around here. The place runs like clockwork. Everything is in its place—perfectly.

Eleanor rarely works weekends. The few occasions we've been here at the same time, she has been strictly business and we have never really conversed. Today is no different.

She reaches the landing, turns the corner and continues up the next flight of stairs. She walks steadily, paced, measured.

I follow silently, looking around at my surroundings. Every piece of furniture, portrait on the wall, vase—everything speaks of money—a great deal of old wealth.

I've never been on the second or third floors of the mansion. Grandfather's room is on the first floor due to his wheelchair. Conner has an adjoining room, so he can attend to him during the night. I have always slept in the main floor guest room overlooking the east gardens at the rear of the house.

Eleanor stops, opens a door, and waits for me to enter. "Miss McKenzie, this is your room." She opens the drapes, then turns to face me. "Stanley will bring up your luggage."

I stand in the center of the room, while she moves around settling the room for habitation. It is obviously someone else's room. There are personal items and photos on the dresser, reading books on the night stand, and stationery on the desk.

"Miss McKenzie. Miss McKenzie?"

"Oh. Yes, Eleanor."

"Will there be anything else?"

"No, no. Thank you. Thank you very much."

"Dinner is at seven," she says, looking me up and down. "Be sure to dress for dinner."

She leaves, shutting the door behind her.

"Dress for dinner?" I mumble to myself. My "luggage" consists of a pink shopping bag containing jeans, pajamas, and sweats. What I am wearing is as good as it gets—white slacks and a light sage-colored sweater. "This will have to do," I tell the mirror as I fuss with my hair.

With my dinner attire settled, I snoop. This is an older woman's room, I'd guess by the look of things. Inside the closet is a large, richly decorated dressing room. I pick up a pretty bottle from the table, remove the stopper, smell the sweet aroma of perfume, then return it to its place. My fingertips brush across the crisp lace on the dressing table.

The dressing room progresses into a wardrobe full of clothes, rich old lady clothes. Some are elegant evening wear, timeless classic lines and fabrics—satin, taffeta, brocade. My fingers move over the fabrics, imagining the woman who wore them. Obviously, this must have been Grandmother's room. Seeing her belongings makes me wish I had known her.

In the main room of the suite, I study the framed photographs on the desk and dresser. There is a photo of a middle-aged, regal woman, not at all troubled with the worry of insecurities. The resemblance with the woman in the painting downstairs confirms she is my grandmother. I lift the picture closer and tilt it to the light for more study. The woman seems familiar, but I decide that it is probably wishful thinking, and I return it to its spot on the dresser.

There's a photo of a young man and woman, and three young children who must be the cousins who now live with our grandfather. I wonder how the cousins came to live here rather than with their parents? I study my McKenzie aunt in the same way I studied Grandmother's picture. She and I have a family resemblance.

There is a photo of my parents with me as a babe in arms. Only five years later, Father would be missing from our family photos. I wonder if she knew when her son died. I can't remember if I saw her at the funeral, there were so many people there. Surely she was there. It is curious that she has our photo.

It's also curious that Grandmother defied Grandfather and had a photo of her son, his Catholic wife, and the first grandchild, me. She must have been a headstrong woman to display a photo of the forbidden family. It looks like my parents made the effort to keep in touch with Grandmother. Good for them!

I love Grandfather, but he has a knack for destroying the people around him. I feel drained and frustrated. I back up, looking around the room, finally sitting on the bed. Good thing this is a temporary arrangement. As lovely as this is, my movie poster collection would be as out of place here, as I am.

Grandmother's picture strengthens me with her look of security with herself. Maybe Grandfather will consider someone else for this "honor" and let me quietly slip away. I'm realistic enough to know that's unlikely.

At least this room has a view of the Pacific. It is interesting that Grandmother had her bedroom suite face west. I see a resemblance with my apartment across from the beach. I inhale the moment.

~~~

The dining room is dark. Apparently I misunderstood Eleanor. Just as the door closes behind me, the light switches on. Stepping back to
~~~

investigate the unexpected activity, I hear the sound of talking and dishes being stacked. Opening the door slightly, I see the kitchen help in the butler's pantry. Maybe I have arrived early. I leave them to their duties.

I wait in the hallway, moving from one huge portrait to the next, examining the faces captured by the artists. Again, I study the one I most resemble.

"She is your grandmother," Grandfather says, as he approaches. "That was before we were married." He passes beside me. Conner wheels Grandfather directly into the dining room—promptly at seven-thirty.

I glance back one more time at the young, beautiful woman with chestnut-colored hair. I always wondered about the people in the paintings—especially her. I assumed that she was Grandmother, and am glad for the confirmation.

Did Eleanor lie about dinner time? It is probably simply protocol that I wait on Grandfather, rather than risk him waiting on me. It's obvious Eleanor attends to every detail, anticipating every contingency. I bet she intends for me to know my place, and to have me get in it—quickly!

~~~

The wine glasses sparkle in the candlelight. The air is filled with the smells of foods cooked to perfection. While Grandfather is settled at his place at the head of the table, I wait with my eyes closed, inhaling the warm bread and buttery spice smells of the Cornish hens, stuffing, snow peas, and all the rest.

Stanley seats me at Grandfather's left, which has always been my place when I visit. I glance at the other end of the table, the end where my McKenzie cousins sit, and am relieved there are no place settings. I'm not in the mood for Brooke's attitude after the week I have had.

Once the food is served, Grandfather says, "That will be all, Stanley." This is a bit unusual since the help always remains "at the ready" throughout the meal. After the door closes behind Stanley and his helpers, Grandfather pauses cutting his Cornish hen. "You haven't said 'thank you,' Kathryn."

"Thank you?" I repeat his words.

"Yes, for making you the most powerful woman in California." His tone seems to indicate that I have asked the obvious question.

"Grandfather, the only power I want—that I have ever wanted, is power over my own life. My apartment is like a crime scene—I can't get in. It might as well have yellow police tape keeping me out." My voice is a soft, unemotional tone, though I would have rather screamed the words.
~~~

“Bring more rice.” He looks at me and points to the side table with his fork. He is strictly business, but I can tell he is not pleased by my response.

“I’ll send for your things tomorrow.” He continues eating, undaunted.

“Grandfather, with all due respect, I would rather get my own things,” I say firmly, but as pleasantly as possible.

“We will discuss it later, your food is getting cold.”

Grandfather resumes cutting his meat. I wait for him to introduce the next topic of conversation, but he eats in silence. He doesn’t seem the least disturbed by my remarks, but I feel bad—no doubt I have disappointed him.

I revisit the beginning of the conversation. “Grandfather, I do appreciate your confidence in me. It was so unexpected that I was caught off guard. I’m sorry I don’t seem more appreciative.”

“Pass the vegetables, Kathryn,” he says as he looks up, again using his fork as a pointer.

I hand him the bowl of steamed snow peas. As he helps himself, he says, “That is how the world is, Kathryn. You are not going to be warned about the big things—only the insignificant things can be scheduled to your convenience.”

So, this is my first lesson. He was certainly dramatic in the delivery of this tidbit of wisdom. I know he is old, maybe he doesn’t feel like he has a lot of time for me to learn the workings of his empire. Maybe he doesn’t feel he owes anyone a warning.

After a final drink of his wine, Grandfather tosses his napkin in his plate, then pushes his chair back from the table.

“Stanley,” Grandfather calls toward the butler’s pantry door.

Stanley appears immediately. “Yes, sir.”

“I am ready for bed, call Conner.”

Conner doesn’t acknowledge my presence. He simply grips the handles of Grandfather’s wheelchair and pushes him out of the room while Stanley holds the door open.

Just before reaching the hall, Grandfather looks back over his shoulder and says warmly, “Goodnight, Kathryn.”

“Goodnight, Grandfather.” I start to get up to go to him with a hug, but Conner wheels him away without waiting, though I know he saw me.

I examine how Grandfather easily keeps business and personal separate, and smoothly switches between the two.

I turn back to finish my dinner, but the kitchen crew is clearing the dishes from the table. Now what?

I hear Eleanor tell Stanley she is going to her room, and asks him to finish supervising the kitchen staff. Most of the lights are already off in the mansion. Grandfather usually stays up later than this when I come for visits. Often, we are the ones shutting off the lights after everyone, except Conner, is in bed.

Fingering my locket, I start up the curved ornate stairway that was designed for grand entrances during social gatherings in times past.

Imagine this place in the forties. The McKenzie parties must have given the society column plenty of material. I imagine the young woman in the painting coming down the stairs to greet her guests. In the half-light, I can almost hear the music and see the expensive gowns. Now, the parties are quiet, and I feel the silence.

The staff quarters are located on the second floor. I don't know what else is there, but I don't snoop. I round the top of the stairs on the third floor and start for my room, but get drawn to the front windows to look toward the ocean. I throw open the drapery as Eleanor had in my room. The lawn is lit by the full moon. Farther away is the misty ocean. It seems surreal to be here—a little princess locked in the tower.

There is no possibility that I am going to bed by nine o'clock. In the medieval spirit of castles and princesses locked in towers, I explore my corner of the kingdom.

Past my room, I try the knob of the next door. It turns. I ease it open. It is dark inside the room compared to the moon-lit hallway. Rubbing my hand on the flocked wallpaper, I locate the light switch, go inside, shut the door, then turn on the light.

It's a bedroom, more masculine than mine. The furniture is heavy-looking even though it is draped with white sheets. The room is a mirror image of my room. When I open the closet door, there is a manly scent inside. More than half of the racks are empty. The remaining clothes are riding pants and boots, things Grandfather can't use now.

On a shelf is a silver chest that is monogrammed with Grandfather's initials. The chest is locked. I check under it and in several drawers for the key, but don't find it. There is drapery on the wall that is shared with my room. Behind the cloth is a door. Inside is a small, private sitting room and another door that opens into my room. Conjugal visits? How cute is that?

Back into the hall to the next room on my quest—the room across the hall from mine. It's locked. So are the next two down that side of the hall. Those three bedrooms must belong to my cousins—all of whom are apparently away from the estate tonight.

The fourth room on the other side of the stairs is unlocked. It is storage—a baby cradle, rocking horse, trunks, boxes, drafting table, and the like. Exploring this room is added to my mental "to-do" list for in the future.

Back across the hall to my side of the hall, there is a large parlor or sitting room. It's set up for entertaining a small informal group of household members—it's not designed to be seen by the public. Then, back toward Grandmother's suite, to the main stairs.

The stairs lead up to the next floor, but it is very dark up there. I haven't explored all I'd like for tonight, but the darkness above is unwelcoming. Besides, some exploring should be saved for the next boring evening.

In my room, I go through to the secluded parlor and lock the door to Grandfather's room. That allows me the use of both rooms with no unsecured entrances. Sitting in an overstuffed chair and putting my feet on the ottoman, I wish I had my diary and a cup of coffee.

As much as I would like to believe that I can return to my apartment in a few weeks, I am beginning to realize that isn't realistic. It's painfully obvious to me that I need to move into the mansion. It only makes sense. I need to be near Grandfather, not only for the little lessons he throws in my direction, but more importantly, to learn the art of managing the family businesses and make sure I'm not out of the loop —whatever the loop is.

The more time I spend with Grandfather, the more I can learn. With his health and age, time is a luxury I don't have. I do not like the idea, but feel more settled with the practical decision. My apartment can serve as a beach house for weekend retreats or when I need to stay in the city for business.

It's apparent this is to become my room. This whole arrangement is not going to be convenient, but I don't think convenience was a factor in Grandfather's decision to involve me in the empire.

Moving to the desk, I take a piece of stationery to make a list to organize my life again. I pause to touch the golden embossed letters, A-M-K, A. McKenzie. There's no name on the inside cover of the address book in the drawer, so I begin leafing through the pages. Under "Mc" is my parents' name and address. Birthdays have been added in the margin. Nothing in the drawer that reveals the meaning of "A."

Glancing at the photos on the dresser, I examine them again. Grandmother resembles Mother's "friend," Amelia. I tilt my head, remembering the times that Amelia came to our house for birthdays, holidays, and for no-particular-reason visits. Amelia came to see us often. The three of us would walk on the beach—me running ahead of them to collect shells, then run back to the women.

"Amelia, Mother's friend, was really my grandmother?" I whisper softly. I don't remember when she stopped visiting us—could it have been that she became ill and couldn't come again? It's funny how she came slumming in everyday clothes and an everyday car. I remember Amelia at Father's funeral now, but not at Mother's.

Tears fill my eyes and run down my face. I don't understand the secrecy about Grandmother's identity. There was no obvious point to sneaking around at our house. This makes no sense to me. I can only guess that it made sense to them. I try to remember every detail of Amelia's visits. She was very attentive and I loved her dearly. I'm glad for that.

I sit on the floor against the bed and lean forward to put my forehead down on my overlapping arms atop my bent knees. I'm tired of the deceit and frustrated with the games these people play with the lives around them, as if life is a plaything. How do I guard against Grandfather's knack for trumping my plans?

~~~

When I awaken the sun is nowhere in sight. Outside my window the moonlight is diminished and it's extremely dark in the predawn hours. Though it is early by anyone's standards, I am wide awake.

After a shower, I head for the kitchen in search of coffee.

Louise, Grandfather's cook, has always made it crystal clear the kitchen is her domain. No one is allowed to mess with her kitchen—that's final. However, she rarely works weekends. When I visited, Grandfather and I made ourselves lunch—as long as Louise or Eleanor wasn't around to catch us. I don't think for one minute that Grandfather is afraid of Louise. But, if he was afraid of someone, it would probably be her. Ah Louise, her black curly hair cropped close to her head, and her bosom as large as her laugh.

My desire for coffee is strong enough to spur my courage to make a pot of the dark brew. "Ah, coffee!" I say, leaning back in the chair, glancing out the window beside the kitchen's prep table, watching the early rays of morning on the dewy garden. The beauty invites me outdoors.

I take a full cup of coffee and my Dodgers jacket to protect me from the chill. The gardens are absolutely beautiful. It's calming to walk through the expansive grounds, free again.

As I follow the paths around the gardens, I walk a little more confidently. Grandfather was correct, there aren't going to be warnings, dress rehearsals, or places to hide. I'm not so naive to think that I'll always and immediately wear this role expertly. I have to figure this out and make it work.

~~~

At thirty-four, I am too old to run from this. It's time to accept the responsibility that came with my birthright as heir apparent. And, I will do my best to hold on to those moments when it didn't matter what my name was.

The sun has cleared the horizon. It began as pastel colors in the distant sky, now it's halfway above the edge of the dark Earth. The bright morning colors contrast against the Earth until the light washes over everything.

The fragrance of the flowers is particularly rich with the morning dew. I take a deep breath of the sweet-smelling air. More than any other time, I think I can master this new world.

In the distance, a dark figure is slowly moving across the landscape. The figure is tall, with spindly appendages that angle toward its back. As it advances, I see a small person with a rake and hoe over his shoulder. Methodically, the figure moves closer.

We rendezvous in the rose garden.

"Good morning, miss," the figure says and half-bows quickly three times.

"Good morning, I'm Kathryn," I answer, and offer a handshake.

The little Chinese man removes his gardening gloves and shuffles the weight of his hoe and rake, bringing them down to lean against his body.

Extending his hand, "Juan, I am Juan." He smiles.

"Huang. Mr. Huang, it is nice to meet you." We shake hands. "The gardens are beautiful." I gesture at the rose garden, figuring he is responsible for the beauty.

"I am Juan, no mister, just Juan."

"Yes, Huang like the Yellow River—Huang He. Right?"

"No, no. Juan Garcia Li." He smiles, revealing a missing tooth from his upper jaw.

"Juan Garcia?" I ask, trying to force my mind to make the connection with the Mexican name and the little Chinese man.

He grins again. "My mother gave me American name."

The connection is not as clear to me as it seems to be to him. I nod in agreement, returning his smile.

He smiles again, then starts raking around the base of a rose bush.

By the time I am back to the mansion and open the door, Louise looks up. She can't be that bad, or she would be in prison, right?

"Good morning, Louise."

"Did you make this coffee, Kathryn?" she asks, looking into the cup in her hand.

"Yes, ma'am," I admit as confidently as possible, knowing the rumors of what happens when her territory is breached. It's Saturday, I didn't expect to see her.

"It's good. What's your secret?" she says nicely.

Is this a bonding moment? "I use two filters. I think it gives a less bitter taste," I answer, ready to tell her anything she wants to know to avoid confrontation.

"I'll have to try that. What do you want for breakfast?" She moves smoothly to the next topic.

"I'll take the breakfast special."

She eyes me for a moment, then smiles.

Grandfather is slow getting around this morning. Usually, he is up and about by the time I am. Maybe he doesn't see any need to rush around on Saturday morning. After all, I will be staying here for a while, why rush? However, that doesn't explain why Louise is here on a weekend day. Even though I am curious, I ask no questions.

~~~

Karen calls to touch base. My plan is to go home and get some of my things, including my car. She offers to give me a ride. James doesn't live at Pacific Estate, so I wouldn't think of calling him to come and drive me on his day off. There isn't anyone here who I feel comfortable to ask to drive me.

"That would be great, if you don't mind the drive," I say.

~~~

Back in my room at Grandmother's desk, I finish the list of things to pick up at home. In preparation for moving my things in, I look in the closet again. I have to show this closet to Karen. She's fashion conscious—she will get a kick out of this. Wonder why everything was left in its place after she died?

I check on Grandfather. He's back to his sweet, doting self. When I tell him Karen is picking me up to get my things, he genuinely seems interested in meeting my friend. He suggests I have the gate open, so she can get right to the house.

From the vantage of the higher elevation at the mansion, I see Karen pull through the gate toward the circular drive. She pulls ahead enough not to block the steps to the front door. I meet her at the bottom step, as Stanley always meets me.

"I see you are still alive," she says. She looks up at the mansion, taking in the full view, but says nothing about it.

"Yes, I am doing well." I reassure her. After all, everyone knows that dread is much worse than facing the things we fear.

~~~

Karen is an immediate hit with Grandfather. He likes people with grace and intelligence. After years of working in the political arena, she can work any room with ease.
~~~

While I watch Grandfather and Karen interact, I realize she is just as curious about my mysterious grandfather as he is about my friends. The difference is she is more relaxed. He seems to be desperately making an effort to make a winning impression on her. More than any other time since I met him, he seems to realize that he knows little about me and the people in my life. It's as if it hadn't occurred to him before now that I lived in a world outside of his domain.

I tell him we are going to have a girls-only day and hang out, moving some of my things.

"You ladies will have to move Grandmother's things."

"Is there anywhere in particular you want them moved?" I ask, careful about disturbing the shrine that has been carefully maintained.

"No, she doesn't need them—do what you want to with them," he answers pragmatically.

It surprises me a little that Grandfather gave us carte blanche. It appears there was simply no particular reason to move her things, so no one did.

~~~

Karen's reaction walking up the stairs is like mine was. "Oh, this is a step back in time!" she says with wonderment.

"Yes, it is like walking into a movie; imagine the music."

"What is on this floor?" She looks around as we hit the landing of the second floor.

"Live-in staff. I don't know if there is anything else."

She looks down the hall as we round the steps to ascend to the next level. We see no one.

Again, on the third floor she looks around. "What a marvelous wall of windows," she comments on the windows that look out upon the ocean. She moves closer for a bird's-eye view of the dark blue Pacific.

"Yes, it is beautiful. You can see for miles from here."

We turn away, toward my room. She follows slowly, continuing to absorb the ambiance of the place. Her curiosity gets the best of her.

"What else is up here?"

"I'm not sure. I think these three rooms" pointing across the hall "belong to my cousins. That room was Grandfather's when he was able to take the stairs, and at the end of the hall is storage there and a sitting room across from it."

Karen tilts her head to look up the stairs to the next floor.

"What's up there?" she asks, moving toward the flight of stairs to the floor above.

"I don't know. Let's look." We pause, exchange glances, then nod in agreement.
~~~

Karen takes the lead. We move up the stairs quickly and quietly. It is dark and the air is stuffy as we reach the landing.

"Feel along the wall for a light switch."

Karen checks the wall to our right. I go to the left. In the dim light I get a sense there is a hallway running perpendicular to the stairs. There should be a light switch somewhere near the stairs—it only makes sense. Karen misses the corner of the hallway and works herself along the wall parallel to the stairs until she is opposite the landing.

Suddenly, sunlight floods the area. She found the window directly above the window on my floor and opened the drapery. Dust floats in the air on the beams of sunlight. There are two sets of French doors facing the stairs, opposite the window.

"Well, now we can find the light switch!" I tease about her ingenuity.

Once we have the light on, we open the French doors. The light from the windows and the hall shines through the opening. It doesn't shed light to the back of the room, but it is enough for us to see into the first few yards.

We look at each other in astonishment and slowly walk into the semi-dark room together. Around the perimeter of the room are tables with chairs turned upside down on them.

"Lights, Katey. Let's find the lights!"

"I'm on it. Is this what I think it is?" I ask excitedly as I walk across the room in search of the light panel.

"It's a ballroom," she half-whispers with excitement. "Katey, it's a ballroom!"

This is well worth all of the frustration of last week. "It's like an old black-and-white movie!" I echo her excitement.

I love the romance of the old movies and the lifestyle that went with them. It's as if we walked back in time and all of my little-girl dreams are reality.

Karen finds the light switch. A massive chandelier in the center of the room comes to life. I'm frozen in awe of my surroundings. This place is absolutely amazing. My eyes drink in every inch. The deep mint-green walls are stenciled with gold designs that were typical in the 1940s. The lower portion of the wall is painted burgundy. Despite the years of dust on it, the wooden floor feels smooth as glass under my feet.

I turn to look at Karen. She is dancing across the floor—she and her imaginary prince charming. I had forgotten that she loves to dance. What a magical place this is! Her face looks serene in a way that I have never seen before.

Breathless, Karen dances toward me. "I love your new house!" she laughs and dances away.

"I'll get this place cleaned up. Then, we'll have a party!" I encourage her excitement, as well as my own.

"Great! Come on—let's get you moved in, so we can get started."

~~~

"This isn't quite as grand as the ballroom, but look at this closet," I say as I open the doors to Grandmother's closet. We enter and finger all of the garments on the racks. "Isn't this something?" I remark, brushing my hand across the rack of ball gowns.

"Look at this one." Karen pulls out one of Grandmother's gowns and holds it up against her body.

"You look loverly, my dear."

"Thank you, Miss McKenzie."

We both laugh. Karen takes one last look at the dress and starts to return it to its place. "Let's move all of these to that rack. There, that should be enough space for my clothes until I have time to sort through these." I start to move the clothes.

"You're right, we have to get moving, but I will help you sort through these—how about next weekend?"

"Sounds great. Let's make a day of it. Champagne brunch on the patio—the whole deal! Shall I see if Dana wants to join the party?" My mind is racing with ideas.

"Oooh, she would love this! Yes, invite her!"

We relocate the clothes, tell Grandfather "Goodbye," and head south. Regardless of where the conversation veers, Karen always comes back to the ballroom.

What a discovery. I can't believe it. How could I have visited Grandfather so many times and never learned about the ballroom? Granted, I slept in the first floor guest room, and never snooped around the mansion before now. It seems that it might have been mentioned by someone in a passing comment or something.

~~~

~ CHAPTER 5 ~

Home, Sweet Home

We pass a man reading a newspaper in a car parked across from my apartment. It doesn't look like the same car, but the man looks like the guy with the binoculars. My anxiety rises.

Lots of people come to the beach to read. If they aren't on the beach with a paperback, they are usually on a bench under a tree on the green near the pier. I suppose there is no hard, fast rule he can't read in his car. I'm being paranoid.

When we drive into the parking lot, a sigh of relief slips loose. No reporters are in sight. It's good to be home. It may not have a ballroom, but it does have a beach.

I don't know what I expect to find when I open my door, but I open it slower than usual and look carefully inside. Once we're inside, I quickly lock the door. Everything is just as we left it. It takes a minute for the unfounded, spooked feeling to pass.

We pack the clothes on my list, while a pot of coffee brews. Until Grandmother's things are sorted, there isn't room for all of my clothes. I leave things here for when I need a weekend at the beach.

I slip my diary into my purse, look around, and move the last suitcase near the door. "Well, I think that's about it."

We have time for a walk on the beach. The man in the car is just that, a man in a car reading a newspaper. He doesn't appear to take notice of us crossing the street to the beach.

This time of year it's anyone's guess what the weather will be, but today is a nice spring afternoon. Low tide was a couple of hours ago. There is a slight breeze. A jacket might be nice, but not absolutely necessary.

"This beach has shared many life experiences with us," Karen says.

"Yes, it has witnessed the best and worst times of our lives."

"Have you ever heard from Joseph?" she asks, knowing he is mentioned somewhere in my previous answer.

"No. No, I haven't heard from him since he returned to Ireland—other than the roses on Thanksgiving every year, since—" I still don't mention Maggie's death out loud very easily. "Why do you ask?"

"He wrote and—"

I interrupt. "Joseph wrote? He never wrote to me, even when he should have written to save me the trip to Ireland. Maybe he's heard that I'm *that* McKenzie."

"I'll give you that one. Do you want to know the rest?"

"Sorry, I guess he is still a sore spot. But no, I really don't want to know the rest. Sorry." I soften my tone.

She studies me a moment. "No. I am the one who should apologize. I'm sorry. I shouldn't have mentioned him." She looks at me a bit more intensely than I like.

The seagull sounds come into my awareness, waking me from thoughts of my former lover. "I forgive you," I whisper. "Want to get a drink at Ruby's on the pier?" I deliberately move the conversation in a different direction.

Karen looks like she is going to say something more, but seems to think better of it. I don't press her. I will trust her judgment to leave it unsaid.

After a lengthy pause, I suggest, "Let's call Dana and invite her to join us Saturday and go through Grandmother's closet. We can play 'dress-up' all afternoon."

Dress-up? That's out of character. I was a serious child. I never, ever played dress-up, except to be a nun. When Father was killed, I went from shy to serious at the ripe old age of six.

"Dana would love it," she says.

"Can you imagine her eyes when she sees the vintage gowns?"

"Maybe she can alter some of them to fit you."

"Hmm, I hadn't thought of that, but it would be fun to wear one of Grandmother's dresses."

"This has been a good day. I still can't believe that ballroom," Karen signals she is ready to leave.

I pick up the tab.

"No, I'll get this. I missed your birthday while you were in Vienna." She smiles with a I-bet-you-thought-I-forgot look.

"All right, thank you."

As we walk back down the pier toward my apartment she asks, "Are you heading north now?"

"I think I will stay here tonight. I can go to Mass without making an issue of it with Grandfather."

"He knows you are Catholic. He must know you attend Mass." There is her logic again.

"I want to go to my parish this time."

~~~

After Karen leaves, I brew a pot of coffee, and put on music. The rich musical scores from my collection of movie music plays in the background of my thoughts. I look around the room at my movie posters, studying them, memorizing them. They are as different as night
~~~

and day from Grandfather's expensive art and commissioned portraits. We really do come from two different worlds.

The whole idea of being an heiress is an uneasy fit. But when I consider his alternatives in the family, I understand his choice. In my heart, I know it had to fall to me. Brooke is a selfish, spoiled brat. Tim is a worthless, wild drunk. Danny doesn't have the self-confidence to take on something like this. With his stammering, he would be eaten alive by the media, like he is by his brother and sister.

I'm the heir apparent, the eldest heir of my generation. I am the only one who bears the family name, my cousins' last name is Anderson.

Sigh. He didn't choose me; destiny chose me. As ridiculous as it sounds, I have to do this. The dye has been cast on the water. All of this is just a chess game. What's your next move, Katey? Swim for shore?

~~~

That's it. I'm out of here. I grab my keys and walk the six blocks to my parish church. With a profound sense of clarity, I know exactly what to do: Get a fresh start. It is time to say goodbye to the past and look to the future.

I bless myself with the Holy Water from the font just inside the door. The church is empty; it's a typical Saturday afternoon. There are a few votive lights burning by Our Lady's statue. The afternoon sun is bathing the walls with yellow-and-rose-colored light from the stained glass windows.

I walk down the center aisle, genuflect, and select a seat. I slip into the pew, bend to lower the kneeler, and slide to my knees.

"In the name of the Father, Son, and Holy Spirit," I whisper, as I make the Sign of the Cross and look into the face of the sculpture on the cross above the altar. I close my eyes and pour out my heart.

I'm ready now. The door to the confessional shuts. The light switches off when my weight settles on the kneeler. The window's door slides open in the wall in front of me. He is silent, but I know he is there because of the smell of his aftershave. Old Spice? Perhaps.

"Bless me, Father, for I have sinned. It has been awhile since my last confession." I speak into the dark, through the black screen between us.

"Proceed," says the pragmatic male voice from the other side of the darkened screen.

I thought I was ready, but the words stick in my throat. I clear my throat and try again. "Father, I—I love a married man." I bow my head in shame even though no one sees me. Why has it taken me so long to admit that I still feel love for Joseph?

"Are you having an affair?"
~~~

"No, Father."

"Are you interfering in his marriage in any way?"

"I don't think so."

"Is he in love with you?"

"No, Father, I don't believe that he is—maybe he never was." It is painful to admit, but it's true. I tell Father everything; I admit it all.

"Have you considered there is a difference between loving someone and being in love with them?" He talks me through the confusion of the remnants of feelings for Joseph.

I listen beyond the soothing sound of his voice, to the wisdom of his words. His counsel comforts my hurting spirit and untangles my confused emotions.

"Is there anything else?" Father asks in the darkness.

"There is one other thing, a duty that I must do. The person who gave me the task had no other choice, but still, I am angry with him because of it. I am selfishly thinking of myself and my feelings, rather than my duty."

Again, Father counsels.

After saying the Act of Contrition and receiving my absolution, Father says, "Katey, go and sin no more."

I take a quick breath at the loss of anonymity. Even in the dark, I cannot hide.

After finishing my penance, I stay in the church a long while. The quiet feels good after all of the noise in my thoughts lately. People begin to file into the church for Mass. We stand for the processional song.

~~~

The silent apartment is satisfyingly peaceful. With my feet on the coffee table, I am comfortably sinking into the back of the sofa. My empty coffee cup has been replaced by a glass of wine. I am glad to be home alone and have the outside world come to a halt for one evening.

Early Sunday morning, the hungry sandpipers search for breakfast while chasing the waves. The seagulls are noisily flocking on the deserted beach. Even though I haven't seen Livingston for a couple of years, I still watch for him when a flock of seagulls gather. Livingston isn't here. I suspect he is dead, but what a spirit for life he once had.

The morning slips away. Before I know it, it's time to return to the mansion. Tomorrow I start my new job. I'll put my things away and relax one more night. I might even get to bed early. My plan is to hit the floor running in the morning. I take a deep breath. I can do this.

~~~

Louise has breakfast ready when I come inside from my morning garden-walk. I am not anxious about the unknown expectations of the day. The McKenzie companies have been around for a long time. I am sure things are in place to run smoothly, and I can ease into my new duties.

After breakfast, Grandfather and I visit in the library while we wait for his secretary to arrive. She walks into the library exactly at 8:59 a.m. sharp, duty ready.

"Kathryn, I would like you to meet Mrs. Bailey.

"Mrs. Bailey, I'd like you to meet my granddaughter, Kathryn McKenzie. Get her settled."

He hasn't allowed the usual pause for the exchange of pleasantries between us.

"Yes, Mr. McKenzie." Mrs. Bailey excuses herself, turning to leave without looking in my direction or saying a word directly to me. Grandfather nods for me to follow her. She walks into a room down the hall that is obviously her office.

"These files are the companies you'll visit." She points with her ballpoint pen to a stack of files on a side table. She sits behind her desk and begins working as if I am not in the room.

When I turn away from her to see where Mrs. Bailey pointed, I mouth the word, "Visit?" The stack of files is actually two stacks of thick manila files, the shorter one hidden by the taller stack in front.

"Your schedule is in the top file," she adds.

There doesn't seem to be anywhere in this room for me to look through the files. Just as I am about to ask where I work, she looks up. "Are you still here?"

"No, ma'am!" I answer, stack all the files together, and leave with the combined stack bulging in my arms.

Clearly she enjoyed the fact that she has tossed her new boss out of her office. It seems to me that she runs her schedule with only a token gesture to Grandfather that he is in charge.

I wish I had thought to ask Grandfather where my office is. Unfortunately, there is only one solution. I return to the library with the unpleasant duty of admitting that I don't know where to go. Grandfather looks up when I enter, then goes back to reading his newspaper.

"Grandfather, where should I work?"

"Use my office. It's through that door." He nods toward the door. "Here's the key." He shifts in his wheelchair, struggles to reach into his sweater pocket and produces a key chain with a gold McKenzie medallion bobble.

"Thank you," I give him a kiss on the cheek and take the key chain. I collect the files from the nearby table.

"You'll do fine."

"Thanks," I say over my shoulder, hoping he is right.

The office is masculine, with large, heavy, dark furniture. I put the files on the empty desktop and pull the chair over from the work table since there isn't a desk chair—obviously because he is in a wheelchair. The straight-back chair isn't the right height for working comfortably at the desk, but it will do until I have a space of my own. In the event that Mrs. Bailey comes in unexpectedly, I want to be sitting behind the desk —not at the work table.

The stack of files is mountainous. I let out a deep sigh while unlocking the desk to locate a pen and a pad for taking notes.

Opening the top manila file, I am amazed to see Mrs. Bailey has scheduled me to start by traveling to two cities this week, Chicago and Memphis, and three cities next week, Hoboken, St. Paul, and Tulsa. The pen drops from my hand. The real surprise is that I am to be on Grandfather's private jet at 4:00 p.m. this afternoon!

I need coffee—lots of coffee! Louise reads minds. I smell a pot of coffee brewing long before I enter the kitchen.

Settling in with my coffee, I tackle the files again. They range in thickness from one to two inches. I flip through the next file in the stack. It contains business reports. Determined, I sort through the stack of files to locate the companies I am scheduled to visit this week and next. The files are neither in alphabetical or geographic order, making it more difficult to locate the ones I need. The annual reports are bound, but not with the files. Is Mrs. Bailey a bit passive-aggressive?

The rest of the files get squeezed into the file cabinet for later review. I lock the cabinet and take the key. I haven't owned a briefcase for ten years. Borrowing the briefcase from the closet, I shove the files into it to take with me.

I come out of the office and lock the door behind me. I leave my annoyance inside the office. It's typical to be out of step with things in a new job. It will get better, it always does. I have to get my head clear. I have to quit burning daylight and take control of this situation.

Grandfather is still in the library reading a book. He waves off my offer to return the office key and agrees to the use of his briefcase.

"I'll be gone the rest of the week, so I need to pack and go by my apartment to pick up a few things."

Without knowing exactly what to expect when I get to the companies, I will have to pack a wider variety of clothes than I brought to the mansion. Memphis can be cool, even in April. And most certainly, Chicago can be unexpectedly cold well into late spring.

"Have James take you, then you won't have to park at the airport."

~~~
~~~

James waits patiently while I pack a few cool weather clothes. Since I haven't been on the jet, I don't know what to expect, so I fill a thermos of coffee to take with me.

James delivers me to the airport, gets my luggage and me to the jet. He tells me he will send the helicopter for me Friday night, but I decline. "I'll take a cab to my apartment and ride to the mansion with Karen on Saturday."

~~~

There is a staff of three on the plane: pilot, co-pilot, and one crew person. Not only is the McKenzie logo on the side of the plane, it's on the back of the seats, cups, and everything imaginable. It's clearly a reminder of my duty—and wealth.

Once we are airborne, I settle back and begin studying the files. The itinerary for my trip is thin. It lists where I am to be and when, but not who to meet, or what I am to do once I get there.

By the state of the company files it's apparent Mrs. Bailey went to a great deal of trouble to give me files of disorganized non-information. It looks like the pages have been deliberately disordered. I had been mistaken to assume the volume of paper was equal to the amount of information contained on them.

At least I have my laptop. When I purchased it, I was thinking only of using it on the beach. In my wildest dreams, I would have never thought I would need it in a private jet to research Alistair McKenzie's companies. The internet yields useful information, though nothing confidential. Mrs. Bailey has tripped me up this time, but she won't have power over me in the future.

For the duration of the flight, I study the information from the internet and anything I can glean from the paper files. My eyes are tired, but I am better informed.

We land at Chicago's Midway Airport on the downtown side of Lake Michigan. The crew has better information than I do. We take a cab to the hotel. The flight crew has a McKenzie credit card to take care of our rooms. I put my expenses on my personal credit card, and will get reimbursed later. Mrs. Bailey "forgot" a company credit card for me.

A fax of my schedule is waiting at the concierge's desk when I check in. I don't have a meeting today after all. My meeting is at 10:00 a.m. tomorrow. Mrs. Bailey's behavior is definitely passive-aggressive. Now that I realize what she is doing, I'll just stay on top of the crucial matters. I'll get control of my schedule. I won't play her game, and I won't deliberately engage her.

After getting dressed for bed, I pull out a new diary to match my new job. I refer to my diaries "Maggie," after my best friend. It helps me to
~~~

feel like I am talking things over with her by doing it this way. I could tell her anything, not that I always did—but I could have. I'll stick with what works. There will be plenty of other changes for now.

Maggie, Amid the confusion that is churning in me comes the realization that this isn't any more difficult than many other things I have done. I can do this. I would have thought by now there wasn't much that could cause me to question my ability or stamina, but this perpendicular change has done just that. Maybe if I had more desire for wealth, I would gulp in this experience. I don't want to become as harsh as Grandfather is with everyone, everyone except me. Who would guess that self-confidence is so pliable? I simply have to find the delicate balance in this and make it me, rather than make me fit it.

~~~

It's a short cab ride to the company office. They're all dusted and polished to make a good first impression. I hadn't thought about it before, but it makes sense to curry my favor. At my age, they could be stuck with me for a long time.

The meeting begins promptly, the presentation folders are well prepared and impressive. From the jet, I'd checked the stock prices for the last eighteen months. It feels like a good investment. I'm expected to speak. Without experience in manufacturing, I speak of the future and the integrity of the McKenzie name brand—the usual pep talk melded with kudos for a job well done. They're polite, apparently genuinely so. I'm on the low end of a huge learning curve.

The crew and I catch a Cubs game, then head for Memphis where Southern hospitality comes with an easy smile. There are two McKenzie companies in Memphis, one bio-tech and the other manufacturing of technology components. Both tap into the presence of the artesian well water. The white-lab-coat-wearing scientists from the bio-tech company, younger than I'd expect, insist on Friday night out at Hollywood Disco. How retro!

Finally, it's time for the flight home. It would have been nice to know beforehand that I was scheduled to go dancing in Memphis. Oh, well. I have a new dress out of the deal. Overall, things went well. I collected information that will be useful in the future, both from my observations of the physical management of the plants and from the board of directors' meetings.

This blind date won't be repeated next week. I'll spend Sunday researching next week's companies. Mrs. Bailey won't get the best of me again.
~~~

It was great to sleep in my own bed the little bit that was left of last night. I take my coffee to the beach until Karen and Dana arrive for the trip to the mansion.

It's cool at the beach this morning. The sunrise is bright. The birds are busy competing with each other for breakfast tidbits in the morning surf. The steaming coffee tastes absolutely wonderful.

Karen and Dana arrive around 9:30 a.m. We sit on the patio while I give them the gifts I purchased on the trip. I didn't have time to shop for anything in Memphis, but I did get to the Navy Pier shops in Chicago. They both loved their silk scarves, red for Dana, and blue paisley for Karen.

I bought each of the household staff something small with "Navy Pier" written on it. I'll hand them out on Monday before I fly out for my next whirlwind week. For Grandfather, I bought a cashmere winter scarf to keep his neck warm when I wheel him around the garden.

~~~

Karen tells Dana about the mansion. They tease me that they knew me when I was a mere mortal. Very funny. I listen to Karen describe the ballroom.

Dana looks at me, astonished. "Maybe I need to find a gentleman friend and get married again, so I can dance in your ballroom."

"You are welcome to dance in the ballroom anytime, with anyone, and without something as drastic as marriage."

Married again? I repeat to myself. I didn't know Dana was married. It stands to reason, I guess. She is a beautiful, talented, intelligent woman. Her time as a bag lady, when I met her, was only a short down-on-her-luck time.

Recessions are hard on fashion designers. The fickle fashion trends here in L.A. make fashion design a volatile business. Hollywood keeps the fashion machine changing faster than the industry can keep up. But she isn't down on her luck any longer.

~~~

The drive to the mansion helps me make the transition between my two worlds. The sound of my friends laughing and talking lulls me into a satisfying calmness.

The closer we get to the mansion, the more excited Karen gets. She can hardly wait to show Dana the ballroom. I hadn't known Dana likes ballroom dancing too. Those two women are a mess, for sure!

Grandfather is gracious to my guests. He says it's nice to have young people visit. He is so cute. I'm thirty-four. Karen is about fifteen years older. I'm not sure how old Dana is. She looked older when she was a bag lady than she looks now.

The odd thing about his comment is my cousins have lived here for years. Did their friends not visit?

In anticipation of our arrival, Grandfather asked Louise to come in on Saturday and prepare lunch for us on the patio. I wonder what she thinks of working all of these Saturdays, now that I'm around. I'm sure the pay is comparable, so she won't fuss enough to go elsewhere.

I wheel him outside. He fits right in and jokes about living in the city when there is all of this space here. Maybe if Karen could stay in the ballroom, she would take him up on the offer—though they were just joking around. I can't imagine how Karen and Dana are able to wait through lunch before running up the stairs to dance in the ballroom. Somehow they do wait—not rushing Grandfather's hospitality. The idea of my friends at ease at the mansion pleases me.

As soon as Grandfather leaves for his afternoon rest, Karen is ready for the stairs. She has to see Dana's face when the ballroom lights come on. It might have been more of a surprise if Karen hadn't told Dana about it in the first place. Karen is so funny. Miss Calm, Cool, and Collected can't keep secrets very secret. Karen takes the lead up the stairs, hardly giving Dana a chance to look around as we ascend.

At the fourth-floor landing Karen grabs Dana's hand, instructs her to shut her eyes, and leads her to the French doors. I move into position on the other side of Dana. Karen and I swing open the ballroom doors. They wait at the threshold while I turn on the main chandelier and leave the sconces around the room turned off. Karen instructs Dana to wait to open her eyes until I rejoin them.

"Now, open your eyes!" Karen lets out an excited giggle.

Dana opens her eyes mysteriously. Her gaze goes to the chandelier in the center of the ballroom.

Her mouth drops open, "Oooh, my God! Oh, MY God! How beautiful! Oh, MY GOD! Katey! Is all of this yours?"

Her eyes scan the room, taking in every detail. Her hand is on her breast as if she is certain her heart will jump out of her chest. Pointing excitedly, Dana utters "Look!" and "Oh, my God," in amazement. "Look, at the wall. Look at the place for a band. Look—"

We exchange imaginings of the parties that must have been held here. "One of the three of us has to get married and have the wedding dance here," Dana says.

"One wedding? Make that three weddings!" Karen says.

They both look at me and grin.

"We could have a dance without a wedding!" I say.

In reality, Karen is the only one dating at the moment. She and Keith are more likely to marry before Dana or me; definitely not me.

Finally Karen says, “Okay, let’s see this closet of yours,” ending all talk of marriages. Thank God.

We start with the gowns. Karen holds one up to me. It is a dark, royal purple. Both Karen and Dana think it is a good color for me. Dana says it needs a little altering to fit perfectly.

“Let’s start a dry cleaning pile here,” I say, laying the gown on the bed.

Dana holds up a red taffeta gown in front of me. “No, I think this one would look good on you, Dana,” I say, taking the gown from her hand and turning it toward her. I know red is her favorite color.

Dana’s expression shows she is thinking about the offer. I turn her toward the mirror. She takes the gown and holds it against her body. It is the perfect red for her ebony skin.

Karen agrees and we convince Dana to accept the gift.

“Now, Karen, you need to pick out a dress,” I say.

“Take that one and try it.” Dana points at a dress.

“Turquoise? Really?” Karen asks.

I have never seen Karen wear turquoise, but I think Dana is correct. It’s the gown she first noticed last week when we were in the closet. The turquoise does look good next to her skin when Karen holds it up.

“Who wants the white sequined one?” I ask.

They hesitate.

“White looks horrible on me—someone speak up,” I say.

So go the rest of the gowns. Next, we go through the rest of the clothes.

The shoes are to die for, but none fit us. The vintage ones would have been fun to wear with the vintage outfits, but we put them in a box to give to the nuns at St. Mark’s for the homeless women. Won’t they be stepping out in style! That should be good for their self-esteem, wearing Mrs. McKenzie’s expensive shoes. Or maybe a benefit auction? I’ll let Mother Elizabeth decide that question.

The afternoon drifts away. Karen and Dana decline a dinner invitation and leave. Karen takes the gowns we have selected to keep, to drop them at the cleaners. She will have them delivered to Dana, who has measured both of us in every possible way one can be measured —no wonder her gowns fit perfectly and are so popular.

~~~

Grandfather went to his room early again tonight. The cousins are still away. I don’t know where they are or when they will return.

Frankly, I am relieved that they aren’t here, and it would be fine with me if they didn’t return for a few weeks, enough time for me to get settled before dealing with Brooke’s sarcasm.
~~~

The live-in staff are in their rooms or out for the evening—I don't know which. As best as I can tell, I have the house to myself, if you can call this a house. Might as well start working on next week's files since there isn't really anything else to do after I finish putting away my things.

By the time I finish unpacking, I rethink my earlier decision to work awhile. I'm too tired to work. In addition to setting boundaries with the staff, I need to set them for myself. I'll work tomorrow, but not tonight. It is too bad I can't go to the beach for a walk. A walk in Juan's garden with a fresh cup of coffee will have to do.

The roses are beautiful in the moonlight. Juan really has a way with them. I am not sure what all of the other flowers are. I recognize some of them. There are blue campanula, my mother's favorite. How funny. The man who kept my mother out of his life has her favorite flower in his garden. We are all connected to one another, more than we know.

There is a brisk breeze coming off of the ocean from below the cliffs on the other side of the highway. I snap my Dodgers jacket closed and wrap my fingers around my hot cup to warm my hands.

I love Grandfather dearly, but I don't want to become like him. I don't want to become cruel with a stony heart just because I have power and wealth. It will take constant vigilance to make sure I don't slip down that road—down Grandfather's road.

~~~

Morning comes too early. I follow my emerging routine: a cup of coffee and a walk in the garden before breakfast. It is still cool out, but the rising sun is promising a warm spring day. If I am going to maintain my identity, then I can't alter my religious practices just because Grandfather has no use for "heathen" Catholics. He has never said anything to me about religion, and I don't plan to wave my faith in his face, but I am going to Mass in town this morning.

When I return, Grandfather is reading the Sunday paper in the library.

"Good morning, Grandfather," I say, as I move behind him and reach around the side of his wheelchair to give him a kiss on the cheek and a hug around the neck.

"Good morning, Kathryn." He lays the paper in his lap. "How was your week?"

"It was good. Hectic. I learned a lot, though." I still haven't figured out if Mrs. Bailey's sabotage was part of his lessons or if he even knows what she is really like. I don't mention her influence in my experience. Most certainly, I am not going to whine about her treatment of me, but I am going to figure out if Grandfather had a role in this.

"What do you have planned for today, Kathryn?"
~~~

"I am reviewing the files of the companies I am visiting this week."

"Sometimes you have to put in the hours on weekends. I can't tell you it will ever get easier."

Maybe so, but this job does not warrant my weekend attention in the way that emergency child abuse investigations did. Grandfather probably won't understand, and I don't care to attempt to explain it.

"Do you mind if I work in here with you?"

"No, work where you like." He appears uninterested and goes back to reading his paper.

"I'm going to get a cup of coffee, do you want one?"

"No, thank you." He doesn't look away from his paper, as if I am a pesky intrusion. His loss.

After a couple of hours reading the files, I can't focus any longer. I lay down my pen and rub my eyes. This is tedious work. I need to think a minute.

Grandfather likes trial by fire. Is that what Mrs. Bailey's game is? Is she acting on his instructions to test me or my stamina, or is she just an old witch? Is he aware of what is going on? I have no idea, and this guessing game is pointless. It takes too much energy to be reactive. I need to stay sharp and be proactive.

"Grandfather, I need your help."

He lays down his paper, his eyes twinkle."I wondered when you would ask." He wheels himself to the table. "Let me see what you have there."

Sheesh, why didn't I think of this before? I tell him what I've done and where I've been, my flight schedule for this week, which companies I am visiting, and which files I have studied thus far.

"Who set this up?" He sounds annoyed.

"I thought you did."

"No, this is an inefficient use of your time. You can tour the facilities later." He controls his anger quite well. He clears his throat. "Get your tablet, take notes."

I feel relieved to have his help. I'm thankful I spoke up rather than operate on assumptions of his involvement in Mrs. Bailey's mischief—an assumption that was 100 percent wrong.

"These are our manufacturing holdings..." He lists the companies from memory. "These are banking and finance..."

For nearly an hour he lists categories and the companies within each category. I start to take a drink of my coffee, but my cup is empty. He notices the depleted coffee and suggests we take a break.

When we come back to work, our break is definitely over. Grandfather turns to me squarely.

"Tomorrow, tell Mrs. Bailey to cancel all of your appointments until further notice, and to give you a list of all companies who are bidding government contracts this quarter, and all companies who currently have government contracts. And tell her to have them on your desk by noon. When she gives the lists to you, tell her you want this year's budget and current stock prices for the public companies. And, Kathryn, never let an employee run your agenda again—make it perfectly clear you are in charge."

I don't want to miss a word. I stop taking notes and listen intensely, studying his face, while he gives me a well-deserved management lesson. When he stops, I take a quick drink of coffee.

"Tell her to have the budgets by two o'clock. When she brings them, tell her that you want a list of the CEOs as well as the members of the board of directors for each company in these files by noon on Tuesday." He smiles. "Let her know who is in charge." He winks.

"Thank you for your help," I say tenderly.

"Don't wait so long to ask next time," he grumps the words. This man has a reputation for ruthlessness, and it is well deserved, but he isn't comfortable when I get sappy-sentimental with him. He has no idea of the depth of my appreciation.

~~~
~~~

~ CHAPTER 6 ~

Moving Up to the Major Leagues

As usual, I follow my morning routine in the gardens, complete with a cup of coffee and my Dodgers jacket. When I come into the house, Mrs. Bailey is in the kitchen with Louise, Eleanor, and James. Usually, I'm getting dressed by now and miss the meeting in the kitchen, but today I arrive during their morning briefing.

The conversation stops abruptly when I enter. That can mean only one of two things: either they were talking about me or they were saying something they didn't want me to hear. I feel their eyes follow me across the room for a refill of coffee.

As I walk up the back stairs, the servant's stairs, I hear them resume the conversation. If they were talking about me, I'm not going to assume that it was bad.

Once the day officially begins, I approach Mrs. Bailey pleasantly, but firmly (if not confidently), with the directives Grandfather outlined yesterday. I had rehearsed with my notes before facing her, and execute the directives flawlessly.

Mrs. Bailey is not receptive to my requests. She doesn't say anything directly to me, but if looks could kill—I'd be dead. I know change is difficult at her age. I leave her to slam her file cabinet drawers in private. She'd better enjoy it, she isn't always going to get this luxury.

This only serves to further accent the contrast with this place and Spirit of Hope. Sister Theresa would never treat Mother Elizabeth the way Mrs. Bailey treats me.

~~~

A quick call to Mother Elizabeth is the perfect remedy for my homesickness. It hasn't been that long, but I am suffering from withdrawal symptoms, separation anxiety. It seems much longer; maybe, a lifetime.

Mother Elizabeth doesn't hide her delight in hearing from me. I'm shamelessly pleased to feel loved. I think about the antics with the Spirit of Hope kids on the playground and anything that has to do with little Shasta; the client's triumphs, large and small; and the nuns—they were much different from how I viewed them as a child in school. What an enjoyable place to work, a perfect example for me to follow.

Now I can return to reviewing the information I collected from Grandfather's mentoring yesterday. My eyes are tired from the excessive reading lately. I guess I'll have to bite the bullet and get an
~~~

eye exam for reading glasses. I make the call. The receptionist has a cancellation for tomorrow morning, so I take it. The sooner I get glasses, the better.

~~~

Mrs. Bailey delivers the first set of reports an hour earlier than the deadline. I praise her, then request the next items on the list. She is almost timid, like she doesn't seem sure how to take this upheaval in her domain, but she probably will be way ahead of me again before long. Although, she might feel the familiarity of Grandfather in the background coaching me.

By midafternoon, I conclude that reading reports is terribly boring, not to mention my brain has turned to mush. I'm well aware that at seventy-four, Grandfather has me beat, but I'll get up to speed as soon as I get my glasses. Just watch me.

While it is unlikely that one week of intense reading caused enough eyestrain to require reading glasses, it brought it to my attention. Now, I will be able to look over my glasses at people, like Mother Elizabeth does with her half-glasses, but my glasses will be cooler than hers.

After my eye appointment, I stop by Mr. Bradford's office. Obviously, I run to him because he is a connection, albeit a loose one, to my parents. Perhaps a third-party opinion to this situation is a good idea.

"I heard the announcement. How's that working out?"

"Truthfully, I don't know. I feel like a rookie."

"Are you the CEO of any of the companies?" He asks a point I haven't considered.

"Oh God! I hope not!" I gasp. "I'm in over my head as it is. I need help sorting out all of these companies. I can't even begin to formulate the legal questions that are sure to come. My schedule is out of control. I inherited the secretary from hell!" I blurt out an immense amount of frustration.

"Kathryn, I don't have the time to help you with a project like this," he says bluntly.

And truly, I have known all along that Mr. Bradford is swamped with his work and continues to manage my trust accounts only because of a long-ago friendship with my parents. Still, I am disappointed.

"I need someone I can trust."

"There is a young lawyer who works for me part-time. I'd highly recommend him."

I study Mr. Bradford for a moment. "You really trust him, don't you?"

He nods, "Yes, I think he has promise, quite sharp."

"Then, that's good enough for me," I agree, sure that Mr. Bradford would never steer me wrong.
~~~

The lawyer is Sam Jackson. I remember the name from when I was looking for Judge Jones' law clerk on the quest to find his daughter. Mr. Bradford calls Sam and passes the phone to me after a brief conversation.

It sounds like Sam is interested in talking about working for me. We arrange for a meeting at the mansion tomorrow morning. Apparently, he doesn't have much of a practice or he wouldn't have the time to do the things I outlined, especially on such short notice.

After the phone call, I get advice on the fee to expect from Sam. Until I feel it is a good working situation, I'll give Mr. Jackson one project at his hourly rate, which is considerably less than Mr. Bradford's rate. If it works out for both of us, I will offer him a permanent retainer.

~~~

It is midafternoon, so I spend the night at my apartment again. I talk Karen into coming over for dinner, Chinese takeout, but late, to accommodate her schedule. I have plenty of time for a stop by St. Mark's on the way home, and still have a solitary walk on the beach before Karen arrives.

I am reminded of the first time I stood at St. Mark's door. This time, I walk in rather than knock. When Sister Theresa sees me, she rushes to give me a quick hug, which is quite different from our first meeting.

It is painfully obvious, I have moved to visitor status now. I am treated to warm cookies fresh from the oven with my coffee. I feel a tearful fondness toward these people, but I don't cry.

Soon the nuns prepare for Evening Prayers, leaving me alone. Mother Elizabeth comes from her meeting. She invites me to Evening Prayers. This time isn't as awkward as the first time. I enjoy the singing and the prayers. Mother and I visit for a short while before she leaves for mealtime. I've waved off the invitation, but imagine it to be much like it was for Whoopi Goldberg in *Sister Act*.

At least it was a momentary diversion. Evening Prayers gave me a curiously delightful mood to take to the beach. Little does Mother Elizabeth know—or maybe she does know—I needed this today.

~~~

The man in his car reading his newspaper is here again. He is almost a regular now. Wonder what his story is? He looks up as I cross the street, so I wave, "Hello."

He nods and almost smiles. His presence is certainly curious.

The water is rough. The spring storm off the coast of Baja California is violently churning north, which is unusual. It is easy for me to identify with the ocean's restlessness. The two weeks since Grandfather made his announcement have been a churning mass of emotions for me.

Nearly everyone is off the beach. As I walk to the estuary with the sound of the sisters' voices playing through my mind, it isn't long before my steps are into the rhythm of the waves. The breakers are running high up the beach. The heavily misted air feels good on my face. The wind tugs on my jacket. In the strangest way it is almost as if the beach has missed me as much as I've missed her.

Since it is Karen's turn to bring the food, I have lingered on the beach long enough to walk off my uncertainty. The days of walking the beach with Mr. Goldstein are in my thoughts as I walk home. I miss walking with him. I miss our conversations and his counsel. But he is happy in Austria, and I have made peace with his relocation.

Karen arrives as I cross the street back to my apartment. We walk together from the parking lot. The aroma from the packages make me hungry. The wind has turned colder and it's good to get back inside. I start the coffee and get out the dishes while Karen unpacks the wire-handled cartons.

"I didn't get a chance to ask, how did last week go?"

"I was completely out of my element. It would have been easier if Grandfather's secretary had been helpful. It might be a little strong, but the word 'sabotage' comes to mind." I smile, but there isn't anything humorous about Mrs. Bailey.

Karen squints, seeing through the smile. "Okay, what did she do?"

"It wasn't so much what she did, as what she didn't do. I had enough information to barely get by, but getting by isn't enough in my position." I attempt to explain the problem, but now it sounds a little lame saying it out loud.

"You want someone who plays on your team. None of the passive-aggressive nonsense, right?"

"Yes! Exactly. I want useful information and I don't want to wonder what has been withheld. I don't have time for power games."

"I have just the person you are looking for—Zoe."

"Zoe?"

"Yes, Zoe. She is my right arm."

"Then, why don't you keep her?"

"She is perfect—young, energetic, takes direction well, smart."

"Karen," I stop her glowing endorsement. "Why aren't you keeping her?"

"I'm not letting her go. She's the best secretary I've ever had, but she is looking for another job. Our reports are too graphic. She can't take typing them." Karen stops for a bite of her food. "She can type like the wind." She takes another bite. "I lean against her desk and dictate letters. In a day she can crank out a week's worth of correspondence."

Karen looks squarely at me, "Katey, you won't be sorry if you hire her."

There seems to be a pattern in Karen's unofficial job placement service. Karen must have talked to Mother Elizabeth, despite what Mother said. Nonetheless, I'm sure that Mother Elizabeth made the final decision.

I agree with Karen's assessment. "Have her call me, if she's interested."

"There is one catch. Her anniversary is a month away. If she stays until then, she will accrue another week of vacation."

"Okay. I can live with that."

~~~

I deliberately get up early to have a sunrise walk on the beach before I head to the mansion. The storm is gone. There are glimpses of daylight peeking through the clearing cloud cover. The tide has crested and is beginning to move out to some other beach.

I hardly notice the trip back to the mansion. I am looking forward to meeting with Mr. Jackson. Maybe we can figure out a way to help me "step up to the plate." My mind is busy defining exactly what I need him to do. What task would be the best test of his skills and our ability to work together?

~~~

The scene at the mansion is just as though I never left. God bless Louise, she keeps fresh coffee brewing all day long.

Grandfather is reading by the window in the library. I didn't know Grandfather McKenzie when I was young, but my other grandfather would sit in his big burgundy chair by his window and read the Sunday comics aloud, complete with different voices for each character. He was a man who made each of his twenty-seven grandchildren feel special.

On the other hand, Grandfather McKenzie has only four grandchildren and has known me for less than five years—by his own choice. And where are his other grandchildren? I have been here two weeks and no one has mentioned them.

Mrs. Bailey announces, "There is a Mr. Jackson here to see you."

"Thank you, Mrs. Bailey."

"You know, he doesn't have an appointment," she quips.

He does have an appointment, but I don't bother to tell her.

"Hello, Mr. Jackson. Let's go in my office."

"Thank you, Miss McKenzie."

"Tell me a little about yourself, Mr. Jackson."

"I have an MBA in addition to my JD." He smiles. We both know he has this job pegged.

I like his succinct answer. He's right. An MBA is more useful to me at the moment than his law degree. Still, it's good to have an in-house lawyer. Maybe Grandfather has a firm of lawyers. I don't know. I do know that I want one of my own on *my* team.

I hire him on the spot. Negotiating the terms is quick. I give him the stack of files Mrs. Bailey gave me. Just to find out how he thinks, I don't give him specific directions—only that we will meet tomorrow afternoon to discuss his impressions.

With Mr. Jackson using the office, I go to check my messages. Mrs. Bailey is on the phone. There is a pink envelope with my name on it in her trash basket. She eyes me when I lift the envelope out of the trash. There is a wadded piece of pink paper under the envelope. I deliberately straighten the paper on the corner of her desk. Mrs. Bailey stops talking and the phone drops from her mouth.

I read the note as I walk out of the room.

Dear Katey:

I don't know if you remember me. You traded airline tickets with me, so I could stay longer in Ireland.

I had a wonderful time, but I didn't know how to reach you to tell you, "thank you" for your kindness until I saw your name in the newspaper.

Enclosed is a photo of us in Ireland, along with a small token of my appreciation.

Sincerely ~
Gwen

Oh yes, I remember Gwen, the ultimate tourist. I double-check the envelope—no photo. Wonder what else she sent? I can't believe Mrs. Bailey opened my personal mail. I'll put a stop to this. Homicide comes to mind.

When I reenter her office, Mrs. Bailey is off the phone. She jumps into action shuffling the papers on her desk. Oh, really? Nervous? Who would have guessed?

"Mrs. Bailey, where are the things that came with this letter?" I ask as calmly as if I was asking for the phone book.

She fusses with the papers on her desk, then reaches in the bottom drawer and hands me a photo, a business card, and a beautiful silk scarf.

"Mrs. Bailey, starting now, I will open all of the mail: personal, and otherwise." I look her in the eye. "Understand?"

"Yes, Miss McKenzie," she says with a tone that poorly hides the indignation in her voice.

I hang the scarf around my neck and put the photo and business card along with the note inside the envelope. Ah, coffee.

While I am pouring a cup of brew, my cell phone rings.

"Katey, are you sitting down?"

"No, not really. What's up, Karen?"

"Keith just brought me a copy of one of the tabloids from the grocery checkout counter. I think you need to see this!"

"Why do I need to see it?" I never read that stuff.

"Your picture is on the cover: 'NUN has alien baby' is the headline!"

"What! You're kidding. This is a joke, isn't it?"

"No, really. Go get a copy. The picture of you isn't all that bad." Clearly at my expense, she laughs devilishly.

Oh, great! She has to be kidding. "Okay, I'll get a copy. I need a break anyway."

~~~
~~~

~ CHAPTER 7 ~

Aliens and Yachts—I Need More Coffee!

The lady in front of me in the checkout line picks up a supermarket rag. I peer over her shoulder at the front page. It is definitely a photo of me in the habit. The woman says, “Kathryn McKenzie probably isn’t having an affair with an extraterrestrial.”

The other people in line laugh. The conversation becomes a group project.

Another lady says, “I have no sympathy for that spoiled little rich girl.”

My cheeks suddenly feel hot.

The checker notices the resemblance between the photo and me. Of course, I deny everything.“Do I look like a nun?” I ask and top it off with cheesy smile.

“You could be the model they used for the picture.”

I soften my tone. “Thanks, but I’m not a model.” I laugh again and pick up a couple of packs of gum. I’ve seen what I came to see, no need to purchase the paper. They will have to do without my money.

~~~

Mrs. Bailey flags me down as I come in the kitchen door. Looks like the whole staff has been watching for me to return. She has an urgent phone message. I really hope this isn’t about the photo.

No, it’s an international number. “Please, make the call. I’ll take it in the office.” I grab a cup of coffee to take with me.

Within minutes, she comes into the office and shuts the door behind her. Her face is pale. She discovered something more than my latest encounter with extraterrestrials.

“Frank, the McKenzie media manager, says that he found a Mediterranean newspaper headline that reads: ‘Kathryn Headed for Disaster!’”

First of all, I didn’t know there was a McKenzie media manager. Secondly, this seems a bit over the top about extraterrestrials.

“I’m afraid I don’t understand.” Acting like Mother Elizabeth, I look over my glasses to encourage her to elaborate.

Reading from her notes she says, with desperation in her voice, “The newspaper reported—on a path to destruction.”

“Mrs. Bailey, I’m not following you.” I try my best not to dismiss this entire conversation as ridiculous and give her one more chance to make her point.
~~~

"Brooke and Tim are on the yacht. The article is about their behaviors on the *Kathryn!*" There is heightened panic in her voice the minute she mentions Brooke and Tim.

"There is a boat named *Kathryn* and the cousins are on it?" The picture is beginning to emerge. "This is probably something you should tell Grandfather."

"No, ma'am," she says emphatically. "I'm not telling Mr. McKenzie about this! And, it isn't a 'boat,' it's a 268-foot yacht off the west coast of Africa!"

She is in a full-bloom panic, wanting me to fix it, and fix it fast before Grandfather finds out about it.

"Okay, I will take care of it. Thank you." I come to her side, gently take the note from her hand, and open the office door for her exit. I thought about touching her shoulder as I showed her out, to comfort or calm her. I refrained, deciding that it was too soon to soften after setting boundaries.

I don't blame her for not wanting to tell Grandfather. No sane person would want to tell him. Damn, those cousins. What have they gotten themselves into now? What about Danny? Is he with them?

This sounds like a good job for Mr. Jackson's counsel. I open the door and walk into the library as if I am passing through. Grandfather has his wheelchair moved closer to the window.

Mr. Jackson doesn't look up from his work. I had hoped to catch his eye and motion for him to join me.

"I'm going for coffee, do you need a break?"

He mumbles a distracted, "No thanks," and scribbles a note.

Damn! Changing course slightly, I pass close to his table and tap it quietly. "Sure?"

He looks up, then lays down his pen.

I give a "look," hoping he gets that I want him to come with me.

He hesitates enough that I'm sure I am going to have to be more verbal. Damn! We need a code word for the times I don't want to say much in front of Grandfather.

Mr. Jackson finally gets the hint and gets up. "Yeah, I think I do need a break." He stretches as he says it. Not an award-winning performance, but he joins me.

We step into the hallway where I tell him what I know. I give him Frank's phone number and ask him to figure out what is going on. I'd like to make a suggestion about the solution, maybe excommunication? After he gets back to me, I'll decide whether or what to tell Grandfather.

Mrs. Bailey is watching from her desk. She motions us to the door when I notice her. She whispers, "You can use this phone."

She drives me nuts, but she seems so vulnerable at this moment that I smile at her. “Come take a break with me, Mrs. Bailey. Let’s let the gentleman have the room to himself.”

She practically leaps up and is gone, beating me to the kitchen in record time.

Aliens and yachts—just what I need.

It isn’t exactly the sinking of the *Titanic*, but I have no desire to go down with the ship or, ah, the yacht. A yacht? For God’s sake, what are we doing with a yacht?

This sounds like a typical Brooke escapade. She is about thirty-two; it’s time she grows up. I don’t even know what to do with Tim. I think he has a bigger problem than his drinking. Again, where is Daniel?

Mrs. Bailey pulls up a chair at the kitchen table where the staff holds court. She and Eleanor exchange looks. Louise looks up from her food prep work and joins the two at the table.

I pour a cup of coffee and join the staff. Another round of wordless glances ensues. My engagement efforts are met with one word terminal answers.

I’m about to pour my second cup when Mr. Jackson comes into the kitchen.

“Coffee?” I hoist the pot in his direction.

He’s getting wise that the question is more than about coffee.

“Yes, thanks.”

“Let’s take our coffee outside.”

He nods.

Once the door is closed and we have cleared the patio, a good bit away from the house, I ask, “What do we have going on?”

“The yacht’s home port is on the French Riviera. The captain filed that they’d be out for a couple of months with no specific destination. They’ve been out for three weeks, wreaking havoc everywhere they go, especially in the Mediterranean port cities.”

“Havoc? Do I want to know the details?”

“No, ma’am. You don’t want the details,” he says. “Remember the Reagan years?”

“No.”

He grins, “Deny-ability!”

“They partied around the Med until they were run off by one government after another. Now, an island government is threatening to seize the yacht.” He turns his tablet around, so I can read his notes, and points to their location.

“Okay. Do I have the authority to intervene, or do I have to take this to Grandfather?”

"I want to call Mr. Bradford. I think if you can handle it, you should. It is a real mess. Mr. McKenzie won't be happy."

"And, neither am I. Go ahead; call Mr. Bradford. I'll call—who is it that I need to speak with on the island?" I look at his notes again and pull out my cell phone.

~~~

"Hello, this is Miss Kathryn McKenzie. I understand we have a common problem with the McKenzie yacht. Yes, I'll wait." I sip my coffee, poised for a response from someone in charge on the other end of the phone.

Mr. Jackson finishes his call to Mr. Bradford and writes a note on his tablet, then turns it my direction so I can read it right-side up.

I set my coffee on the sundial and write back, "the McKenzie family—not the business?"

He whispers, "No, YOU—Kathryn McKenzie—NOT the family, and not McKenzie Enterprises!"

Our eyes meet. I stare at him in amazement. It's my boat? That certainly simplifies things. I can do what I want and don't have to ask Grandfather's permission.

"Please hold for the Prince," a voice says on my phone.

"Your Highness, I'm Kathryn McKenzie. Thank you for speaking with me. How can I help with this problem my cousins are causing?"

The voice on the phone is very polite and formal. A soft and gentle voice, but sure of itself.

"I see. Very well. I am sure the captain and crew had no culpability in the matter. I will guarantee the payment of fines for the captain and crew, if you will let them take the boat back to its home port. As for the others on board, they are yours. They can answer to your laws, then find their own way home." Let's just say, I'm steamed. They better take the slow route home.

"Yes, I understand. Yes, your Navy has my permission to board the boat, um, the vessel. We have been unable to reach the captain, could you have him contact me as soon as your people are on board? I'll be at this number until I hear from you." I conclude the conversation by giving him my cell phone number. I don't want these calls going through Mrs. Bailey. He was very polite, but we both know he didn't need my permission to do anything.

Mr. Jackson looks at me, wanting information, but he doesn't ask for it. I have something more important to do than have a discussion with him. I turn toward the house in search of Mrs. Bailey. She's still in the kitchen with the breakfast meeting group. She makes clear her loyalties to Brooke. I know she has no loyalty to me, not even now.
~~~

I interrupt quietly. "Brooke and Tim have gotten into trouble. I want no one, absolutely no one, to mention it to Grandfather. Keep the televisions off the news stations. Mrs. Bailey, check the morning paper before you give it to him tomorrow, and bring Conner up to speed."

They stare at me as if they are about to fall asleep from boredom.

"The paper isn't my job," Mrs. Bailey informs me.

"It is now. Mr. McKenzie is to know nothing about this. Nothing, THAT is your job—protect Mr. McKenzie." I correct her publically because she questioned me publically, then I make eye contact with each of them. Mr. Jackson is somewhere behind me. But I don't look to him on this matter. They are my staff, whether they like it or not.

I hear a weak, "Yes, ma'am," just as I walk out.

I go to Mrs. Bailey's office and look through the file cabinets for anything about this yacht. Her files are nicely organized, but I don't find anything. I'll have to get the info from Mr. Bradford. I head to my office, where Mr. Jackson is scribbling quick notes on a legal pad.

"Mr. Jackson, how about another walk in the garden?" I ask, expecting he understands now this isn't really a question requiring an answer.

He takes the hint. "Please, call me Sam. I'll pass on the coffee this time, but the walk sounds good."

I pick up my cell phone and take it with me. I have lots of questions for Sam.

"How bad is my liability, Sam?" How did the boat get put in my name? How long have I owned it? What's Brooke and Tim doing partying around the Mediterranean with a boatload of— who are those people?

"You have the liability of owning the yacht, but I think we can prove you didn't give them permission to use it or had any knowledge of ownership." He checks his notes. "They were on board before the announcement. As your trustee, Mr. Bradford should have been notified, but wasn't. I think Mr. McKenzie is clever enough to claim deniability. I think we're all okay on this"... his voice trails off.

It is obvious the lawyer wheels are turning in his head, but he doesn't elaborate.

"I see." I look up at him. He's going to be worth every penny.

The phone rings, startling me by vibrating in my hand. "Hello, this is Kathryn McKenzie."

I can hear someone speaking French.

"Parlez-vous anglais?" I ask the voice on the phone. Apparently not. I turn to Sam, "Mr. Jackson, Sam, do you speak French?"

"I am rusty, but I'll give it a try." He takes the phone.

"Ask if any of the crew speaks English," I suggest.

He is right. His French is rudimentary—about as good as my Spanish. We're doomed if none of the crew speaks English.

"The navigator speaks some English," Sam says as he hands me the phone.

"This is Kathryn McKenzie. Hello? Yes." A pause. "I am Kathryn McKenzie. No, I am her granddaughter. Yes, I own the ship. You have been boarded by the local authorities? Navy? All right. Cooperate with them. Right. Yes. Please, tell the captain I have arranged for his and the crew's release." I hear muffled French as he speaks to someone there. "Take the boat back to its berth. Notify me when you arrive." More muffled speaking as he translates my words to the captain. "Thank you, and tell the captain, 'Thank you' for me."

Turning to Sam, "I want Brooke, Tim, and their friends to find their own way home. If they have a McKenzie Enterprise credit card, I want it canceled immediately. And, anything in my name, cancel it. I am not condoning their behavior, and I am not bailing them out of this mess." My tone is more revealing than I'd like, but this really takes the cake.

Sam nods understanding.

"Do we know where Danny is?" I move to the next item on my mental list.

"No, I haven't found anything on him yet." He surprises me that he was one step ahead of me.

~~~

When we return to the house, I fill my coffee cup and go check for messages. Mrs. Bailey doesn't see me at first. She's on the phone.

"Brooke, dear. We'll get you out of this." Mrs. Bailey looks uneasy when she sees me. I reach for the phone. She hesitantly gives it to me.

"Brooke, this is Kathryn. No, no, I am not going to bail you out of jail. Go ahead, ask Grandfather if you want. No, I'm sending the ship home." She hangs up on me after describing me with a string of hyphenated "colorful adjectives."

There is no point in telling Mrs. Bailey not to accept calls from Brooke or Tim. I can tell by the tone she was using with Brooke that she is fond of her. I might be out of a job when Grandfather finds what I have done, but I am going to do what I think is right. Besides, I wouldn't mind being fired. I bet Mother Elizabeth will hire me.

Sam is talking to the island authorities again. When he ends the conversation, I tell him, "We'll pay the crew severance pay when they get the ship back to port, no doubt they put up with plenty. Make arrangements to sell the yacht to pay the fines and the crew. Don't spend a dime on Brooke, Tim, or their friends."
~~~

"They found drugs on board. Brooke and Tim are facing up to fifteen years in prison."

"Oh crap! I bet they did. Any chance they were in international waters?"

"I'll find someone who can talk with the captain."

"Let Brooke and Tim stay in jail until we sort this out. At least we'll know where they are."

"Tim has already assaulted one of the officers."

"Oh, great! Do you want to work tomorrow?"

Sam nods.

"Would you take my cell phone home with you tonight? Just add it to your bill."

I haven't had much time to spend with Grandfather. I ask him about getting two cell phones for work; one for Mr. Jackson, and the other for me. I'll keep my personal phone for personal calls.

Grandfather says to call the finance office and arrange for a credit card, cell phones, a voucher to reimburse my travel expenses from last week, and some petty cash.

I ask Sam to pick up the phones on his way to work in the morning. I'll get reimbursed later. So far, this new job is costing me nothing but headaches and money. Damn, speaking of headaches. I need to take something for my headache.

Before bed, I write in my diary to help clear my mind and organize my thoughts. The only good thing about Maggie's death is she isn't here to torment me about my current circumstance. She would have enjoyed teasing me about owning a yacht.

Maggie, I'm exhausted. I feel the sobering effect of responsibility descending upon me. I must find the strength to hold on to who I am, and to wear the title, 'Kathryn the Great.' There are so many things I need to set straight. Where do I begin?

~~~

When I come from my morning walk, Conner is wheeling Grandfather to the dining room for breakfast. He invites me to join him and I accept. After we're settled and the food has been served, I turn to say, "Good morning, Grandfather," but he speaks over me.

"Brooke and Tim are on their way home."

Well, what can I say? He knows, but how much does he know? Who told him? Did he bail them out? I just look at him and smile sweetly. I am keeping my mouth shut.

He eyes my Dodgers jacket hanging on the back of my chair. He takes another bite of scrambled eggs, then wipes his mouth with his linen napkin.
~~~

"Baseball fan?"

"Yes, the Dodgers are playing Friday night, do you want to go with me?"

"No, I'm an Angels fan." He resumes eating.

That explains why everyone stopped talking when I came in the room wearing a Dodgers jacket. It's humorous how the staff worry about my jacket. I don't think Grandfather is going to fire me for not being an Angels fan, but the Brooke and Tim issue might just do the trick. Shall I pack?

"I'm giving you James as your driver."

I know he means he is assigning James to drive for me, but I don't like his choice of words. He makes it sound like he owns James. Maybe I am just being sensitive because James is Black. Would I find his words as offensive if James was White? I think it over. Yeah, I would find it offensive, but I don't think he understands the implications, or maybe he simply thinks he is superior to all of us.

"Where's Danny?" I ask, risking a mention of the yacht.

"He is visiting his parents at that damn commune they live in. His mother had surgery, and he is helping with her care." He says it as if I knew about the "damn" commune.

~~~

Waiting for my turn at the coffee pot, I think about Danny with his parents while his mother has surgery and the other two off raising hell halfway around the world. The surgery must have been serious for Danny to be gone so long. I wonder if they need anything—any help from us?

Sam comes in, picks up a cup, and gets in line behind me. I fill his cup while I have the pot in my hand, then introduce him to the breakfast crowd. He smiles at James.

"Hello, son," James says to Sam.

"Son? Why didn't you tell me James is your father?" I ask Sam, amazed by this well-kept secret.

"James? His name is Garrett." He seems surprised.

"Garrett?"

"Mr. McKenzie liked to say, 'Home, James,' and it stuck. My name is Garrett. I'm named after Garrett Morgan, the Black man who invented traffic signals in 1923."

I didn't know who invented traffic lights. I wonder if there is a familial relationship, but I don't ask.

"Then, I will call you 'Garrett' and so will everyone else."

I look at the breakfast-board-meeting group.

"Me, too," says Louise, followed with a stout laugh.
~~~

"Anyone else have an alias?"

"Honey, you wouldn't want to call me my other name." Louise grins widely.

Okay, I'll bite, "Louise, what is your other name?"

"Honey Bum, my Edgar calls me, Honey Bum." Louise laughs. "He's a Black Brit, you know."

Well no, I didn't know she was married to a Brit. I smile while the others laugh at my expense. No, I am not touching that one. She has a very ornery side to her. Besides, Sam and I need to get to work and discuss the yacht incident.

~~~

Sam had received a call in the middle of the night. Brooke's friend's parents sprang for everyone's bail and purchased their airline tickets. At least, Grandfather didn't bail them out. That is certainly interesting.

"The yacht is in your name, because it was purchased with your money."

"My money? Are you sure?" I don't understand how a yacht was purchased with my money. I have a headache. Literally, I have a headache. It has to be stress or the new glasses.

"It's complicated. Let me get a report written with the details for you."

~~~

Sam goes to work. I talk to Eleanor about an office for Sam. I know I can do what I want, but I think for now it is a good strategy to let her keep her place as the Mistress of the Manor.

Eleanor shows me three rooms, each perfect for offices, two on the second floor and one on the main floor. I select the main floor office for Sam because we are going to be running back and forth from each other's office until we get things figured out and settled down. Maybe eventually Sam will work downtown and not have to make the daily commute to the mansion. Maybe someday I can do the same and move back to my beach.

Sam tells me he has an idea. His plan involves hiring a computer whiz. A "geek named Chico" to get all of the McKenzie Enterprises information on a database and organized in a usable format for me—not at all like the files Mrs. Bailey set up. I agree about Mrs. Bailey's files, but Chico?

Let's review this: There is a Chinese gardener named Juan Garcia Li, because his non-English speaking, emigrant parents wanted their son to have an American name; a driver not named James; and I am not even going to ask about Honey Bum! Chico? This place is like a very bad, B-rated movie. And Mrs. Bailey is the innocent-seeming star.

Brooke and Tim are on their way home. I have another headache. Nothing over the counter seems to work on my head. How long did they say it would take to adjust to these glasses?

"Miss McKenzie, the press is ready in the library," Mrs. Bailey announces.

"What! Who scheduled that?"

"Frank. He thought you should answer questions about the yacht." She doesn't seem to think that anything is wrong with Frank's action.

Grandfather is nowhere in sight. I catch Sam's eye as he is coming out of the office and tilt my head for him to follow me.

~~~

This place is out of control. I straighten my skirt, button my jacket, and take a deep breath before entering the library—confidently, with a camera-ready smile.

I quickly move near the podium that has been set up. Sam takes up a position at the back of the room, directly in front of me. Good move, Sam! Cameras begin to flash in my eyes.

"Ladies and Gentlemen. As you know by now, I am Kathryn McKenzie. First, let me clear up the rumors. I have never had an alien boyfriend!"

Subdued laughter comes from a few of the reporters who get what I'm talking about.

"I have begun to tour the McKenzie holdings. In the coming weeks, I will continue to familiarize myself with the family business." I continue with the usual stuff about McKenzie Enterprises and feel pretty good about what I've pulled together off the top of my head.

One reporter takes advantage of the pause in my statement. "Is it true you own a 200-foot yacht, Miss McKenzie?"

I look at Sam who shakes his head negatively.

"No, it is not true. That is all for today. Thank you for coming."

I conclude my first press conference and manage to elude a barrage of questions about the yacht incident.

Apparently, not all of the reporters understand that we are done here. They remain in their seats. I don't want to get caught with questions about Brooke and Tim, and the yacht.

Sam comes to the front of the room and says, "Thank you for coming. Mrs. Bailey will show you out." He puts his hand on my elbow and escorts me out of the library.

Mrs. Bailey is standing outside the room. "They're all yours, Mrs. Bailey. Show them out, but don't answer any questions," Sam says.

She squints at him a moment with a defiant look in her eyes, then she goes into the library.
~~~

"Thanks for rescuing me," I whisper to Sam as we walk down the hall toward the kitchen—the opposite direction the reporters will be going.

"You're welcome. Coffee?"

"Yes, please."

I take a sip of the fresh brew while he fills his cup. Then I move slightly toward the back door. He gets the message and follows. It is risky to go outside while reporters are on the grounds, but I don't plan to venture off the patio. I want privacy to touch base with Sam.

He follows me out the door and stands beside me on the patio. We look straight ahead and talk, like we are in a spy movie and are pretending we don't know each other.

"Why did you tell me to answer 'no' to that reporter?"

"Two things: One is he had the length incorrect. You have never owned a 200-foot yacht." He grins at the technicality. "And, second, I have the yacht sold—so you don't own a yacht."

"You *are* clever," I compliment his legal mind. "You sold the boat. Good. Now what?"

"I might have been able to get another half million, but I didn't think you wanted to delay the deal, did you?"

I shake my head in agreement with his decision. "Do we know what the damage is for this joyride? Will the yacht price cover the crew and damage expenses?"

"I think there will be some money left over. Most of the offended countries were happy to settle for a promise the yacht gets sold. It was the prince you spoke with who wanted to purchase the boat. The Paris office is making arrangements for the money transfer. Everything will be ready by the time they reach port." His tone reassures me.

It amuses me that I have him calling it a boat too. "The prince could have impounded the boat, but it's nice that he bought it."

Sam raises his eyebrows and tilts his head like he is confirming that I'm right about his ability to impound the boat.

"Good. Now, how do I fire Frank? I am not happy. I don't want any more unauthorized press conferences." Maybe firing Frank will put Mrs. Bailey on notice.

"I'll find out if he works for the family or the Enterprise. He may not be an employee—we might be contracting with an agency."

I notice he said, "We," which means he is bonding with his new client—me.

"Get control of him. You can always fire him later," he says.

"You have a point. The person who really needs to go is Mrs. Bailey. She isn't making the transition. I don't have time to wait for her."

"Yes, she's going to cost you, if you keep her."

"There is someone who can start next month."

"That is a good idea; build your own staff," he says.

"Sam, would you consider working for me—exclusively?"

"What! Close my booming practice?" He feigns shock, then laughs.

"I know it will be a sacrifice, but let me know as soon as you decide."

I turn away enough so he doesn't see me smile. He seems to take everything in stride. I like that about him. I need someone who can keep pace with me. He has already saved me money for the daily cost of owning a yacht. If Frank hadn't tattled on Brooke and Tim, I don't know when I would have found out about the yacht. Maybe Frank can be salvaged.

"What did you decide about Chico?"

"Write up what he'll cost me and how much I can save by hiring him." Then, I think a minute. "I would like to meet with him and see his résumé. You're all the reference he needs."

"I'll tell him. When do you want to see him?"

"Let's look at my calendar." I turn back to the house.

Mrs. Bailey hesitantly gives me my appointment calendar. It's comical and a little sad to see her struggling to hand it over. We select a time on Monday. She stresses when I write on "her" appointment book. She reminds me of a mother cat who has to wash her kittens every time someone touches them. It's really not my intention to cause her anxiety.

Sam follows me out of Mrs. Bailey's office. I motion him to follow me up the stairs to the second floor. I show him both of the offices Eleanor showed me earlier.

"We'll put Chico up here—at least in the beginning. I need a price list of the hardware and software he will need, and—" Sam's wide smile interrupts my words.

"Thank you, Miss McKenzie."

"Look, Sam, as long as you advise me well, your opinion will carry a lot of weight with me. Understand?"

"Yes, ma'am. I understand perfectly."

"All right then, let's get back to work."

When he leaves the room, I pop a couple of pills to dull my headache. What a day. Is it noon yet?

This has been a lovely twenty-four hours. As a matter of fact, this has been a lovely week, and it's only Thursday. To top everything, Booke and Tim will be home for dinner tonight.

~~~
~~~

There is a commotion in the foyer. I had gone upstairs to get something for my headache, giving me a vantage point from the landing for the cousins' return.

Tim was flippant at first and laughed off the whole ordeal with the yacht, planting a kiss on Eleanor when she came to investigate the noise as they arrived home.

Brooke came with an attitude of vengeance. She rightly accused me of helping remove her from the yacht. She stopped short when she said I acted like I owned the ship, and Stanley—who had joined the group —gives her a silencing look from the doorway.

Did Brooke know who owned the yacht? Or is she just lashing out at me, the newest addition to the family? Did she go quiet only because no one wants Grandfather to hear her?

From my vantage point, I have assessed Brooke's mood. I brace for more of the same, and descend the stairs into the midst of the group. Surprisingly, Brooke quietly says hello as she passes me to acquire the stairs.

It's not that I think Grandfather needs my company, but I decide to come to dinner with him rather than make a quick sandwich and head for bed early.

The mood at the table is thicker than the gravy. The conversation is primarily brazenly formed, halted retorts. They are cruelly frank with each other. I observe their interaction in amazement. They aren't enjoying the meal or each other's presence. Grandfather remains silent, but not sullen.

~~~

I excuse myself as soon as I finish eating and go to my room. I'm tired. This allows them to have a private conversation, not that any of them worry about privacy.

It isn't nice of me, but I'm glad when I hear Brooke and Tim come upstairs, then leave again. I hope they can stay out of trouble, but they need to blow off some steam before they come home. They are disruptive to the household.

With my last cup of coffee for the day, I sit back in the chair and pick up a book from the stack of three books on the side table. Robert Frost. I am not a fan of his poetry. The only poem of his I like is *The Road Not Taken*.

I flip through the book to confirm I don't like his work. An envelope addressed to me falls out of the book. Addressed to me? I put the book down and open the envelope. Inside is a note that is handwritten. It's very curious that a note would be written to me years ago, and hidden in such a place as Robert Frost's collective works.
~~~

Dear Katey:

It was a privilege to get to know you when you were young. You are everything I hoped my namesake would be. I am confident you are worthy of the duties that will befall you. I send you all of my love.

Your grandmother,

Amelia Kathryn McKenzie

"Amelia KATHRYN McKenzie?"

Oh, I forgot that the last initial goes in the middle of monograms. Wrongly, I thought the "K" was the "Kenzie" part of McKenzie.

"Then the yacht is named after Grandmother," I whisper in amazement. I rub my finger across the embossed monogram, thinking of the woman who wrote the note.

It's time for a talk with Mr. Bradford again. He has a wealth of information that is pertinent to my life, but makes me stumble across it before he divulges anything. Then he gives me the least required information. It's time for him to come clean with everything he knows about me, my parents, and the McKenzie family.

I need to know everything he knows about the McKenzie machine. Surprise jewelry is one thing, but if I'm going to manage my family's assets, I need to know everything. I have neither the patience nor the time to eke out information in bits and pieces. This is the big league. I am writing the play book, and it's my "at bat." No yachts or press conferences without my approval.

God help us all, if this household is any indication of the status of things in the company. Grandfather must have let things run on autopilot as he aged. Everything is a mess.

There are so many elements to develop among the staff: loyalty, efficiency, teamwork... I will cut some players, and draft replacements. This is spring training.

Most important, I need to prioritize how we review this enterprise. An independent analysis of every company in the McKenzie Enterprise is warranted. It all seems overwhelming, unless I look at the trees more than the forest for a while. There is so much to do, just thinking about it gives me a headache.

Tomorrow night the Dodgers have a home game. After I meet with Mr. Bradford, I'll stay at the beach and take in the game—maybe I will spend the entire weekend at the beach. The game is the perfect excuse to spend time with someone from the other side of my family—the sane side.

~~~

I beat Mr. Li to the garden again. I like smelling each variety of roses in the rose garden. It is peaceful out here. No one interrupts me during my walks.

Sam has Chico waiting when I come to work. Chico is a bright kid. I can tell by his bright eyes and easy smile. As Sam said, Chico's résumé is impressive. Chico indicates he is ready to begin work today. I wonder what Sam told him?

Chico's first task is to make a list of the equipment he must have, and a wish list of what else he would like to have—then he can leave for the day. He pulls both lists out of his laptop case.

Okay, I'm impressed.

Sam smiles with delight.

"Mr. Jackson will coordinate your duties, but you answer to me. Any problem with that?"

"No, ma'am. No problem." He grins excitedly, followed by a pleasant shiver of energy running the length of his slim body.

I nod approval to Sam of his selection of Chico. Sam takes Chico to see his office, then to Mrs. Bailey to fill out his employment forms, tax withholding and such.

Sam returns and asks to meet with me. He has decided to be in-house counsel. He accepts the salary I offer him, and negotiates for insurance coverage. Since I don't know anything about the benefit package McKenzie Enterprises offers, I tell him to make an appointment for himself and Chico with the human resources director at the home office in L.A.

A courier arrives. Mrs. Bailey hands me an envelope from the pouch. It is our paychecks. I completely forgot about being paid. When I get out of her view, I peek into the envelope to see what my value translates to in dollars and cents. I nearly fall through the floor, even though there is no basement below. Fifty thousand dollars for two weeks' work! This is insane! I need a cup of coffee.

When I return to the office, Sam says he has the information I requested on Mrs. Bailey.
~~~

"That was quick!" I had forgotten I'd asked for it, and I'm not sure I was dead serious at the time. Besides, we've decided she is leaving.

"Not really. I asked my dad." He smiles. "He said that Mrs. Bailey's husband was injured in a mining accident. Your grandmother had bought the mine days before. The day after the accident, she sold the mine. She paid all of Mr. Bailey's medical bills. He died six months later. His wife had no marketable skills and four children to feed, so Mrs. McKenzie hired his widow, put the kids through college, helped out where she saw a need."

"I see." That's more insight into Grandmother than into Mrs. Bailey.

"Now you know what I know." He grins again.

"Thank you." She isn't making the transition, not only to me, but to the technology that I'm going to bring. The issue is whether I structure her job to fit her abilities and ignore her opinion of me. I think it is better to offer early retirement. If she has to work with me, she may become accustomed to me or she may end her career miserably. Considering how close she and Brooke are, it is unlikely she will ever accept me. I'll stick with the Zoe plan.

Before I leave for L.A., I write in my diary.

My Dearest Maggie, Everywhere I am reminded in a new way of the great responsibility of wealth. I want to understand what is required, what I can do that would most make a difference. "Even God would not appear to a hungry man in any form except bread." ~ M. Gandhi. What form do I take since I am not a god?

~~~

The cousins went out last night and aren't home yet. Guess we'll miss each other until next week. Too bad.

I need to get moving to be on time for my appointment with Mr. Bradford. My car is waiting, as usual, in the front of the house. Since there are plenty of clothes at my apartment, I don't have to pack to spend the night at home—my real home.

I toss Grandfather's briefcase on the floor behind the driver's seat, and begin to pull around the circle and down the drive. I slide on my sunglasses and lay my reading glasses on the dashboard. It's a beautiful day for a drive, but I am busy thinking about my appointment and formulating last-minute questions for Mr. Bradford. I want to guarantee I actually get information from him this time.

Suddenly, something hard smacks into the windshield.

"What the hell?"

In a moment another hole blasts through the glass and my reading glasses fly to the floor. In that split second everything seems in slow motion, and I see a hole rip into the headrest of the passenger seat. At
~~~

the same time—I don't know how that is possible—but at the same time I see the hole in the windshield is a bullet hole.

Immediately, I dive down in the passenger seat. When I duck, my foot comes off the clutch causing the engine to lurch and die. My mind begins to move in normal speed. I realize someone is shooting at me. But why? Why would anyone do that?

~~~
~~~

~ CHAPTER 8 ~

The Bevy

Another rifle retort sounds, but it doesn't hit the windshield. There is a thud, but I don't know where it hit this time. Another shot fires, and seems to miss my car entirely. Everything is a blur. I'm scared out of my wits: too scared to think or cry.

My cell phone begins ringing. I struggle to fish the phone from my pocket, while still lying low across the car seats. The shifter knob finds a soft spot above my hip and digs into my side. I wrench with the unexpected pain.

"Hello?" My voice is shaky. I clear my throat. "Yes, I'm all right." A big fat lie. "What's going on?" I ask, pretending to be calm as possible. Am I convincing? I don't know.

"There is someone behind the front gate with a rifle, firing at you." Sam's voice is rapid, hushed, distressed. His breath is hurried, not at all reassuring.

"Why would someone do that? Are they trying to kill me?" I beg for a reasonable answer, one I can comprehend.

"I don't know. Stay put. I've called the police." There is a long pause. "And, Kathryn," he says kindly, "I'll stay on the phone with you until this is over."

"Thank you. I'm all right, Sam. You don't have to stay on the phone. Keep everyone away from the windows. Check on Grandfather. I am worried about where the shot went that didn't hit my car. Make sure he is away from the front windows. Sam, please." I don't try to hide my concern for the final mark of the missing bullet.

Two more shots hit the windshield. The last one shatters the glass, spewing glass bits on me. I cover my mouth to muffle a scream, and quickly turn my head down into the seat cushion to keep the glass off of my face and away from my eyes.

Sirens come out of the distance. It seems like hours. Finally, someone opens the passenger door and reaches in to touch my hand that is contorted to shield my head from the glass. I hear soft voices, Garrett, then Sam, then Stanley, who turns toward the group of worried household staff congregated on the front stairs, and he reports that I am alive.

When I sit up, glass falls inside the back of my blouse.

Paramedics are beside the open door. I tell them I am fine and I can get out of the car from the driver's side. They insist on the passenger side because it's facing away from the gate, but I point to the gearshift obstructing my movement in their direction and they finally get the picture.

Garrett stands guard as close as he can without being shooed out of the way.

"Garrett, have Eleanor come to the car," I request, then smile reassuringly.

Eleanor arrives almost instantly. I ask her to go to the driver's door. Garrett is at her side and opens the door. This time the paramedics have to stand back.

I reach my left hand in his direction. "Just steady me, let me pull myself up." As I inch myself out of the car, the glass finds the small of my back, pricking my flesh. I stop dead. My eyes close and my back arches with the pain.

Garrett freezes.

Catching my breath, I begin to inch again. There is no avoiding the glass, all I can do is to continue to steadily pull myself toward Garrett. Eleanor is beside Garrett. She reaches for my right hand before my feet hit the ground.

I lean in close to Eleanor as I stand. She steps back a half step, then forward again when she understands I want to whisper to her.

"I have glass inside my blouse. Pull the back of my blouse out of my waistband so the glass will fall out rather than lodge and cut me with every move."

She is very gentle, and even picks a few dime-size pieces of glass from my hair to protect against them falling in my face and eyes.

"Be careful, don't cut yourself," I warn.

She whispers, as she leans close, "Your grandfather is terribly worried. Wave to him."

"Thanks. I will. Would you get me a robe? I need to get out of these clothes—they're full of glass."

Eleanor moves toward the house, stops to say something to Grandfather, pats his shoulder, and disappears through the door.

The paramedics want me to sit on the back of their truck. I decline because of the glass, some now inside my waistband. I can't sit down for fear of driving glass into my skin. There are a few scratches on my hands and a small one on the back of my neck—all from the glass that fell on me. Otherwise, I am fine—and I tell them so.

They insist on irrigating my hands, inspecting them now that the blood is washed away, and dressing the wound on my neck. They would have had my blouse off in front of all my staff, if I hadn't protested.

~~~
~~~

Everyone is talking at me at the same time. The sheriff wants my car for evidence, which is fine with me since it has to be towed anyway to get the windshield replaced, and to repair the radiator where one of the "missing" bullets landed. I ask for my purse and briefcase. For a minute I think he's going to claim that it's evidence. I'm ready to inform him otherwise. He sends someone to get my stuff. Smart man. Today is not the day to argue with me.

The sheriff says they caught the shooter. The man just stood there looking confused when the officers drove up with sirens blaring. No one seems to know why he was shooting at me, or if he was specifically aiming for me—though it does look like I was the target.

For a brief moment I think about Brooke. She is probably furious with me, but I don't think even she would hire someone to shoot me. Besides, I believe some part of her enjoys having me here to fling her anger toward.

The officers take statements from Mrs. Bailey, Mr. Li who was working in the front garden, Grandfather, and Sam—everyone else saw nothing—the witnesses only saw the man from a distance after the shooting began. Mr. Li had seen movement by the gate, but dropped to the ground like a rock when the first shot was fired. He had grown up in a rough neighborhood in San Francisco and knew quite well the meaning of the sound he heard.

Sam promises that I will give a statement later, after I remove the glass from my clothes and hair.

Garrett comes around the corner with the golf cart to give me a ride to the back so I don't have to take the steps and dig the glass in farther with each step. He eases me on the back where I stand, holding tight. I see Grandfather looking out of the window and wave to let him know that I'm fine. Garrett drives slowly, but each bump feels like a boulder-laden trail.

My knuckles are white. My breath is caught in my ribs. The thought of stepping down horrifies me. I whisper to undo my slacks fastener. Garrett hesitates. Eleanor is at his side, so she does the duty. The glass slips, but the pressure driving them into my skin is released enough that I move my hand to Garrett's, ease to the ground, and inch to the patio door.

Louise spreads plastic trash bags on the laundry room floor, hands me the robe Eleanor brought, and tells me to undress. I stand for a moment, alone. I take a deep breath, hesitant to move and give liberty to the glass' torture.

Alone, tears pour down my face as I ease off my clothes. I feel dizzy, probably more from emotional shock than from the minor injures.

I don't dare sit. I'd rather be anywhere but here, and have any name but McKenzie.

When I have the robe on, Eleanor is followed by Louise who has a damp cloth and tells me to wipe the bottom of my feet to make sure that there aren't glass slivers on them before I put on my slippers. Eleanor offers her hand to steady me as I balance to follow Louise's directive. Mrs. Bailey joins Louise and Eleanor—making the bevy of household women complete.

Eleanor put Mrs. Bailey in charge of shooing the men from the kitchen before Louise will let me out of the laundry room, even though I have on a robe. Nothing like a good shooting spree to bring all of us together. Despite my tongue-in-cheek thoughts, I am glad for their company. I feel shaky, but try to appear as calm as possible.

Louise sends Eleanor upstairs for my shampoo and cream rinse. In the meantime, she carefully inspects my wounds in the event the paramedics didn't do a thorough job. When she finishes with my hands, she gives me a cup of coffee.

My hand shakes, requiring both hands to hold the cup. She carefully cups her hands around mine so I can take a sip. Aaah. I admit, the coffee tastes marvelous. Louise is a saint.

Outside, there is the sound of a helicopter overhead. Stanley reports through the door that the helicopter belongs to a news station. Mrs. Bailey pulls down the shades and turns on the kitchen television. We watch a live bird's-eye picture of the activity in our front yard. It is eerie to see that what happened is real.

Eleanor returns breathless—apparently, she did not take the stairs in her usual measured fashion. Louise places a large pot in the sink and instructs me to put my head down over it. She pours diluted cream rinse over my hair and turns the water spray as low as possible and still be able to spray. Her theory is the cream rinse will make the glass slide out of my hair. She repeats the process three times, being very careful not to squirt water in my face or down the back of my neck where the bandage is. I limply comply with her instructions while I wait for the caffeine to enter my system.

Louise isn't satisfied that all the glass has been removed. She asks Eleanor to get her cream rinse, since mine is depleted.

"Wait, wait. This is good enough. I'll take a shower."

As Louise drapes a towel over my hair I add, "Thank you, thank you all for your help. I really appreciate it."

I start to leave without letting on how frightened I am.

Eleanor insists on helping me up the stairs, though she doesn't know where to safely touch me. She carefully removes the bandages since the bleeding has stopped and they are going to get wet in the shower anyway. Then she waits in my room, feeling, no doubt, that being on the main floor is too far away if I need assistance. I'm secretly relieved she stays nearby.

~~~

The warm water feels good on my increasingly tensing back muscles. I know it's just nerves. I put shampoo in my hands and make a rich lather that I dab on my shoulders, hoping that the foam washes down and takes away any remaining glass particles on my back. The shampoo stings in the cuts on my hands and back. Slowly, carefully, I begin to wash my body. The stream of water runs through my hair until I am convinced that there are no pieces of glass missed by Louise's cream rinse treatment. Then, I dab shampoo lather on my hair.

All of the emotions of being shot at well up inside of me. With crossed arms I hold my sides as I begin to cry nearly hysterically—gasping—while the water pours over me. I bend over as if I have stomach cramps. The last three weeks have been a nightmare. My left hand comes up to my forehead to cover my eyes—I bow my head crying, sobbing, lost. It's as if I will never stop pouring out the sadness, fear, and frustration that is inside of me.

Over the sound of the water, I hear knocking on the door. I try to regain my composure. The door opens slightly and Eleanor is standing in the door, looking awkwardly away from me in the shower.

"Kathryn? Kathryn?"

I take a sobbing breath, "Yes, I'm all right."

"The sheriff's ready for your statement," she says gently.

"I'll be down in a minute."

What can I tell him that someone else hasn't? I consider pulling on sweats and leaving my hair damp, but I pull it together enough to put on slacks and a blouse, fix my hair and makeup.

My position requires a public presence, regardless of my personal situation. I'll entertain my fear and frailty later.

It's too early to know anything concrete about the shooter. So far they haven't found a connection with him and McKenzie Enterprises, or any discernable connection to me. I don't remember him from any of my old cases. One of the officers calls Karen to run the name through her department's database, since she would have cases that didn't go to court that the law enforcement computer wouldn't have. When they finish, Karen asks to speak with me.

"What's going on?"

"I'll have to get back to you, okay?" I hope she catches the implication that our conversation isn't private.
~~~

"Katey?" she asks, insistently. Then, she relinquishes, "All right, call me. Please, call me back."

"Yes, I'll call, I promise."

The sheriff has an impatient tone. "Miss McKenzie, can we finish this?"

"Yes, of course. Honestly, I can't think of anything that connects this man to me." I'm not going to implicate my cousins without facts. If there is evidence of Brooke's involvement, they will have to find it on their own.

"Miss McKenzie, if you are holding back any information—" His threat is interrupted by another officer who tells him they have located the shooter's wife.

He just as much called me a liar to my face, the jerk, but I smile the McKenzie gracious-dame smile.

He looks back at me with an untrusting glance, hesitates, then follows the other officer out of the room. He turns back at the door and gives me a look to indicate that he isn't finished with me yet—and wants me to know it.

"We'll post an officer outside," is all he says before he is gone.

~~~

As soon as he leaves the property, I call the posted officer inside. "I am going to let the staff leave early. Would you drive down to the gate and make sure it is clear? I'm sure that it is—but just as a precaution."

"Yes, I will. Have the last one out to flash their headlights at me."

"Thank you. Oh, my cousins might be back tonight. I don't know for sure. I'll see if someone can give you identifying information." They've been gone since after dinner last night.

"I'll take care of it, Miss McKenzie." He puts on his hat as he opens the door, stops and turns back. "And, ignore Schmidty. He's harmless."

Until we find out why that guy was shooting at me, we don't know if there are other shooters out there, somewhere, or who the target is for certain—though it seems to be me. The rule will be "caution" until we know more.

"Mrs. Bailey, please tell everyone to put their work away and go home immediately. Do you know if Brooke, or Tim, or Dan are coming back tonight? The officer should be told how to identify them. Oh, find Sam, I need to speak with him."

It occurs to me that I haven't talked to Grandfather since the shooting. After checking the library for him, I go to his bedroom door and knock softly. Conner comes to the door ready to "shush" the person knocking on the door until he sees it is me. He opens the door wider and whispers for me to come in.
~~~

"How is he?" I whisper, looking at the frail old man lying on the bed with a blanket tucked over his shoulders. He looks small and defenseless lying there.

"He is terribly shaken," he whispers back.

"You two are making enough noise to wake the—" he stops before saying the word "dead."

I smile a reassurance to Conner.

"Hello, Grandfather," I move to his side. "It's Kathryn."

"I know who you are! I'm not senile, you know."

He doesn't fool me for one minute. He can be as grumpy as he wants, but I know he was shaken by the shooting. We all were scared —and still are.

"I just wanted to let you know I am all right. I'm sending the staff home early. I'll be back after I'm sure everyone has left," I excuse myself and nod at Conner with a smile on my way out.

Sam and Mr. Li are in the kitchen with the breakfast board: Mrs. Bailey, Garrett, Stanley, Eleanor, and Louise.

"Everyone needs to go home. Call Monday before you come in and we'll see where we are with things."

I turn to Mrs. Bailey. "Have you reached the cousins?"

I just guessed that she called them. It stands to reason that she would at least call Brooke. It's Friday night, maybe they won't come home until midafternoon tomorrow.

Mrs. Bailey doesn't answer me, so I continue. "When you drive out, give the officers at the gate the information about the cousins, so they can identify them and let them in."

I hope Mrs. Bailey gets the hint that the cousins shouldn't come home tonight and passes the message on to them.

Louise protests leaving early because she has dinner to prepare.

"No, go. We can manage."

Eleanor agrees with me that we can handle dinner. And we can, but Louise gives instructions to Eleanor anyway.

Mr. Li stands to leave. I ask Sam to bring up the rear of the caravan and flash his lights at the officer when he goes out to indicate he is the last to leave.

Unexpectedly, Brooke and Tim make their usual dramatic entrance. Tim grabs for Eleanor. She jumps back, so he misses.

We are all still jumpy. Clearly, Eleanor didn't care for the familiarity from a boy young enough to be her son, but she says nothing about it. The cousins seem unaware of the shooting, at least they don't mention it. They are aware something is up and ask suspiciously about the cop outside.

Mrs. Bailey moves near Brooke in a protective manner.

Perhaps she, like I, had a fleeting thought that Brooke might be somehow involved in the shooting.

Brooke and Tim disappear up the stairs, Mrs. Bailey leaves with the other staff. Stanley, Eleanor, and I are left. It's an awkward silence.

Someone has to move. I go to the kitchen and the waiting coffee. The others follow me to the table.

After a cup of coffee, Eleanor gets up and looks in the refrigerator. Stanley moves to the patio door and locks it, then to the back door to lock it. Lastly, he heads for the front door.

I slip away to call Karen and tell her the latest activity at the mansion before she hears it on the news, but I'm too late. Karen wants to come. I convince her we are fine and not to make the trip. She offers to bring Keith for added protection.

It's not safe for anyone to come right now. We need answers, such as, was it a lone shooter or are there others to take his place? And motive, what was the motive?

"Check with me tomorrow. Tonight I need to be available for Grandfather."

She says she understands, then falls silent. I wonder if she is worried she will lose me, like she lost Maggie. She rarely mentions it, but I know Maggie's death was hard on her.

"Karen, you won't lose me, I promise."

She gasps. "Katey, don't say that!" Her voice trembles.

It's obvious that she needs to see me to know that I am fine. She won't say it, but I know it's true.

"I'll send the helicopter for you and Keith at one o'clock tomorrow. You won't have to drive. Besides, it's fun to fly in it."

"We would love it. I'll tell Keith." She sounds relieved.

We make the arrangements for tomorrow and say goodnight. I call and tell the pilot tomorrow's flight schedule.

When I return to the kitchen, Conner is telling Eleanor that he and Grandfather will eat in the bedroom suite tonight. Eleanor hesitates when I offer to help prepare their dinner. I haven't always had a private chef—I can cook.

Her silence speaks volumes, so I don't comment further. All right then, I'll find something else to do.

The sheriff's Blazer is at the gate.

I walk out on the front steps. It isn't that I want to die, but I am not going to be a captive of fear.

The Blazer begins to back around and turn toward the front of the house. I stand and watch it approach.

The officer who climbs out of the vehicle looks as if he is considering scolding me for being on the porch. I beat him to the punch.

"Can I offer you coffee or dinner—or both?"

He is distracted from his duty long enough to smile. "No, ma'am," he answers immediately.

"Did you bring dinner with you? We're a long way from town." I watch the other officer scanning the fence line and the gate with binoculars.

The first officer returns to the vehicle, says something to the officer behind the wheel, and brings a thermos with him.

They will eat in shifts, for now he takes the coffee. Stanley and Eleanor observe my conversation with the officer. They seem more settled now that they know another shift of officers will come tonight.

Conner comes and makes a sandwich for himself. He says Grandfather isn't hungry and is going to bed. I tell him to come get me if Grandfather wakes up, and he agrees to do so.

There is a short clip about the incident on the six o'clock news. They don't know anything, but the overhead view of the house and grounds flash on the screen. They show a file photo of Grandfather and one of me taken at the press conference in the library. Both are pretty decent pictures.

Stanley and Eleanor aren't used to having a McKenzie spend off-duty time with them. I go upstairs and get one of Grandmother's three books from my room—not Robert Frost. The choices are Marco Polo's *Travels*, or *American Women of the Twentieth Century*. I'll take the women over Frost or Marco.

On the way down the stairs, I consider whether to remain in the kitchen or go to the library to read. I want to be a presence of strength for the staff, but I don't want to intrude on their space when they should be off-duty. To the library it is. They can find me if they need me. There are more comfortable chairs in there anyway. I pull up an ottoman and put my feet up, carefully.

The book is laid out with a chapter for each woman, and is about an event in their life that is the most memorable to them, not necessarily the famous event. They are social reformers, political activists, scientific pioneers, aviators and astronauts, Nobel Prize winners, philanthropists, and female greats in male-dominated fields—even the Unsinkable Molly Brown, someone I have always admired.

Reaching for my glasses and not having them reminds me again of being shot at—the very thing I am trying to escape. I don't know how long I will be able to read without them, but select Eleanor Roosevelt's chapter. She writes about her work with the United Nations on the U.N.

Children's Bill of Rights. One quote catches my attention: "*I think somehow, we learn who we really are and then live with that decision.*"

I skim through the book, reading bits and pieces of several stories. The women rarely write about the thing that made them famous. Their opinion of what was important differed from history's public opinion. My eyes are tired.

I know why Grandmother kept this book in her room. It inspires greatness. In comparison to these women, I have had a fairly easy life. The book will be an excellent training manual.

The officers take turns coming inside for dinner. I join them in the kitchen while they eat. There is no threatening activity on the grounds. The report is that the shooter laid down in his cell and went to sleep after he was processed into the system. When they woke him, he seemed to have no memory of the incident, then went back to sleep. His wife had no answers to why he was shooting at me. She didn't even know he had purchased a rifle.

After all of us have eaten, I help clean the kitchen. When Eleanor and I finish putting away the food, I say with a smile, "I guess I will read a little longer." My eyes should be rested now, besides, I crave the inspiration I found in Grandmother's book. I'm not ready to sleep.

"Miss McKenzie, sleep in the guest room or with us on the second floor." Eleanor and Stanley have separate quarters—both on the second floor. She is a widow. I don't know Stanley's story.

Did she notice that I was crying in the shower?

She seems a little less detached from me than she has in the past. I consider her suggestion, but finally decide to stay in my own room. Other than my furious cousins, the third floor is safe.

"I am fine, thank you. Do you think we should give the officers a key to the front door, or maybe have the night shift stay inside?" I ask both Eleanor and Stanley. I want them to have a voice in the decision so they feel a sense of control.

"I can take a nap, then stay up," Stanley offers.

"You probably don't have to do that, but I'll leave the decision to you." He knows his duties better than I.

At about ten o'clock, Eleanor comes to the library. I close my book when she enters, but keep my fingers in the page as a bookmark. She tells me she woke Stanley, and she is going to bed. She stands there for an awkward moment.

I wait to see what she wants to say. Finally, I decide maybe she is waiting for me to say something, but I don't know what.

"I'll go to bed shortly."

"How do you McKenzie women do it?"

"Do it?" I question, unclear what she means.

"Someone tried to kill you, and you are sitting there reading a book." She becomes emotionally animated.

"Eleanor, have a seat," I say and motion to a chair near me.

She sits across from me, but scoots the chair a few inches closer. I know it is just a gesture to feel close.

"They caught the man at the gate and he won't be back." I speak softly and calmly.

"When I first saw you, I knew you were just like your grandmother. That Brooke is nothing like Mrs. McKenzie." She takes a deep breath.

"Brooke has problems. I'm not sure what to do to help her." I look directly at her. "I am fine," I nod my head and smile slightly. "We'll get through this. I promise, Eleanor."

"Aren't you afraid?" Her eyes water.

"Yes, of course I am. But I think clearer when I keep my wits about me."

"How do you do that?" she asks—desperately.

I look at the book in my hands. "Here, this is Grandmother's book. Sometimes we have to look to our sisters to know what to do." I hand the book toward her. "We are all going to get through this—and anything else that comes." I say it with strength and calmness—for Eleanor, and for myself.

She rubs her fingers over the book jacket. It is something of Grandmother's that she can touch. I hope it helps. Reading it might make her feel the strength of sisterhood among women—something I think we all seek, even if we don't recognize it.

Dearest Maggie, I have run the gauntlet of emotions. I'm exhausted. Past disappointments have been hard, but I have learned lessons I would not have learned another way. I have to appear strong, even when I don't feel it. That is what is expected of me. That is what I expect of myself.

~~~

The morning shift of officers won't let me venture beyond the patio with my breakfast coffee. These two officers are less personable than the night shift were; arrogant better describes them. Both claim there is no new information about the shooter. I find that hard to believe.

They mock me, "It's Saturday, the sheriff's off for the weekend. Call him Monday."

My second cup of coffee will be taken upstairs to my room. I want some distance from all of this madness. Little people with a gun, amazing.
~~~

Since I gave the book I was reading to Eleanor, I add another entry to my diary.

Dearest Maggie, Yesterday is among the worst days of my life. A stranger tried to kill me. All of the days that rival the experience have the common thread of death and dying—my parents' deaths, the little girl in our case, you and Dave, Monica, and now me. The violence of the stranger's act is the most difficult to understand.

Your words resound in my thoughts, "It isn't how long one lives, it's how wide that matters." I am not sure my life has, to this point, been adequately wide. I look to the women I know and to those who went before for example. I look within myself for strength and wisdom. I look to you.

~~~

Grandfather has decided to spend the day in his room. He wants no company, not even me. Stanley is as steady as any English butler, though he's not English. Eleanor seems in better spirits today.

I'll busy myself attending to business calls, trying to appear "business as usual" for everyone's benefit. Mr. Bradford often works on Saturday. I'll start with him and apologize for missing my appointment. We reschedule for Monday.

Next, the staff. Mrs. Bailey is easy to convince to stay home from work on Monday, with pay. She sounds jumpy. She asks about Grandfather and Brooke, but not about me.

Louise insists on coming in on Monday. Maybe she is correct. Grandfather needs to get back into his regular routine. Louise's meals are a good anchor for him to get back on track. Mr. Li isn't home and doesn't have an answering machine. I'll try him again later. Sam plans on coming to work on Monday, but I tell him I will meet him at Mr. Bradford's office. That saves him a trip to the mansion. I tell him to have Chico wait a couple of days before starting work. Sam can get a purchase order for him and he can hand-pick his equipment; I'll sign it at Mr. Bradford's office when we meet.

Who am I forgetting? Garrett! He'll have to drive me to L.A. since I am without a car. Besides, I doubt I can get a "pass" to leave without him, otherwise I could take the helicopter. All of this would be comical if that guy with the gun hadn't scared me out of my wits.

~~~

When the helicopter arrives with Karen and Keith, I am at the pad to meet them. I didn't ask the officers' permission to leave the house.

Surely there was only one shooter and he is in jail. There is no reason to think there is some sort of hit ordered.

We hug and get into the golf cart. Karen is wired with excitement about the helicopter ride. It's a blast. I understand how exciting the first ride can be.

"He'll have to take you along the coast on the way home. You've never seen anything that compares!"

The sheriff's officers saw the helicopter land and make a beeline to intercept the golf cart with their Chevy K-5 Blazer. Obviously, it's no contest between our vehicles. A chubby officer gets out, hikes his pants up, and struts to the front of the golf cart. He stands there as a roadblock with his hand on his holster and demands to know what I'm doing. He scolds me about the dangers of being out of the house as if I'm a three-year-old playing with matches, and asks if I think my "friend" can protect me—meaning Keith.

Keith has silently watched the exchange. Once the officer stops chastising me, Keith asks the officer to step aside. The officer takes a defensive stance, showing no intention to yield his authority to a visitor. Keith shows his detective shield and tells the officer to step aside again. The officer opens his mouth to say something, but Keith repeats his request more firmly, "Step aside."

There is no way for the officer to move and save face, but he does move, and we drive past him.

We take our coffee to the library to visit privately. Karen is relieved to see me. Keith is surprised that I know nothing more about the incident. Granted, the sheriff's department shouldn't or wouldn't tell me everything they know. But Keith thinks I should at least know what danger remains, if any. He asks to use a landline phone.

As soon as Keith leaves the room, Karen moves forward in her chair. She wants me to stay with her awhile, but I can't. I need to stay with Grandfather and to be a physical presence for the staff. I tell her about coming to L.A. on Monday to get new glasses, see Mr. Bradford, and go to the bank. She welcomes a lunch invitation, but wants to know if my bodyguard, "Bubba" from the sheriff's office, will be joining us.

"You are absolutely awful!"

"I know," she says proudly.

We are still laughing when Keith returns. The officers will be replaced. Keith will register a formal complaint regarding the officer's behavior toward me. I am more relieved than I expected to be.

Keith has more information about the shooter. "The man thinks God told him to kill the nun who is having the alien baby. He had a letter to the Pope in his pocket. He 'flipped out' in his jail cell this morning. They transferred him to the psych unit—under guard and sedated." Keith looks at Karen for her reaction.

"The guy needs serious help. This also means that there isn't someone else out there waiting to shoot me, if he failed. That's good news, right?"

I won't say it out loud that I had wondered if Brooke was involved. She's absolutely livid about the yacht incident. Besides, she has never been fond of me. I always sleep with my bedroom door locked when Brooke and Tim are home.

"Good, then it's not Brooke," Karen remarks.

"Why do you say that?" I ask, surprised that she shared my concern.

"To begin with she doesn't like you, but then she lost the drugs on the yacht—that has to be a major problem for her."

"Money is nothing to her," I answer back. "I'm not sure what gives meaning to her life."

"Do you have security?" Keith asks.

"The gate isn't monitored, if that is what you mean," I answer, knowing it isn't what he means.

"I would like to have a friend of mine call you. You need to secure the mansion, and a bodyguard for you wouldn't hurt." He starts to say more, then changes his mind.

"I agree, Katey, you are doing things differently than they were done before, and that will threaten some people. Sooner or later you will need a bodyguard. Now is a good time to start."

"Jim knows what he is doing," Keith adds.

"All right, then. Have him call me," I agree, at least to a meeting. "Now, how about seeing the ballroom—I'm sure Karen told you about it."

Keith doesn't react to the trip back in time as we climb the stairs to the ballroom. I wonder if Karen is disappointed.

He walks around the center of the floor, checks out the chandelier overhead, scuffs at the floor with his shoe. He turns to Karen, smiles, and dramatically takes her into his arms—beginning to dance.

I ponder the scene. This is not the Detective Knight I knew. I stand back, observing Keith and Karen glide across the floor. They move as one person, in perfect unison with each other.

I look around the room, considering restoring, repairing, and basically renovating it. What if I have the skylight above the chandelier reopened—that would be pretty. Besides, it is time to open the light into this room—and into this house.

~~~
~~~

Grandfather is convinced to come out of his room briefly to say hello to Karen and to meet Keith. Karen charms him for over an hour. I ask Stanley to take Karen and Keith back to the helicopter pad for their trip home. I need to attend to Grandfather.

"Grandfather, come on the patio with me." I encourage him, happy that he has finally emerged from his room.

He sighs. But he doesn't protest.

Softly I say, "Come, it will be good to get some fresh air."

He moves his hands to his lap, where he always places them while his chair is being pushed. I take this movement as consent.

It is a pretty spring afternoon. At least, the change in scenery will be good for him. He stares straight ahead, "What have I done to you?"

"You haven't done anything to me. Nothing you did has anything to do with the shooter."

I move closer and unfold the newspaper with the picture of me dressed as a nun that Karen brought for giggles.

He takes the paper and studies it in silence, urgently scanning the photo.

"Don't worry. I'm not a nun. And, I don't have an alien boyfriend."

He smiles slightly at the photo. "Have you told his parents about the baby?" he asks with a straight face.

He's doing better. He just needed to get out of that room.

"The man who shot at me is very ill. He thought God told him to kill me because I was a nun who broke the vow of celibacy."

Grandfather turns to look directly at me. Religion is a delicate subject between us, and we have never admitted its existence in relationship to ours.

"He wrote to the Pope that he had been sent by God to purge the Church from evil nuns and priests. It had nothing to do with either of us. You did nothing to me," I say again.

"He's Catholic?" Grandfather turns to look at me with his loaded question.

"No, actually he isn't."

He has a curious expression that I can't decipher.

We move back to the kitchen where I invite him to stay while we prepare dinner. To the staff's surprise, he agrees.

"Would you like a drink—ice water, tea?"

He decidedly answers, "Something stronger."

While I fix Grandfather's highball, he asks Stanley to join him. At first Stanley hesitates, but I fix him one anyway. They both look adoringly at their glass after the first taste. I'm glad they appreciate the drink; however, I am still not mentioning where I learned to tend bar so exquisitely. The men nurse their drinks. They have never had such a perfect beverage.

Eleanor stops preparing dinner to watch the uncommon activity at the table.

"May I fix you a drink, Eleanor?"

She declines unconvincingly. Clearly, drinking with Mr. McKenzie is not done.

But these are not ordinary times. I pour two glasses of wine, and hand one to Eleanor. If nothing else, it may improve our cooking, I tell her. We touch our glasses together. I join Eleanor cleaning and cutting vegetables for our salad, this time without asking if she wants help. We're no real threat to Louise's job, though our meals have been edible.

Grandfather pulls the paper out and shows the photo of his granddaughter, the nun, to Stanley. Then he asks, "Have you seen this, Eleanor?"

She has a questioning look after seeing the photo.

"I can explain, honest! I picked up the alien at a bar, ah, when I was in Chicago visiting the factory there." Of course, my explanation doesn't fit the time line when the photo was taken.

Her eyes widen. She pauses a dramatic beat. "We'll have to set up a nursery."

Grandfather smiles, Stanley snickers nervously, and I laugh. The tension of yesterday's shooting is finally broken.

~~~

Rather than change the sheriff's officers as Keith had said, they remove them altogether. The unexpected abruptness of their withdrawal makes me feel uneasy again, but I mention it to no one. It is an irrational fear. I should be back in my proper place working at Spirit of Hope, and none of this should have happened. "Beam me up, Scotty."

After dinner, the cousins disappear again. Grandfather and I move to the library and talk at length about the shooting incident. We openly discuss our concerns, pragmatically. I tell him about Keith's security suggestion. Considering the unlikeliness of another person being "told by God" to shoot me, we decide to have the gate regulated and a monitored alarm system installed. Beyond that, neither of us want full-time bodyguards—perhaps only for special, high-profile occasions.

~~~

Tim is still gone. During the night, Brooke came home. Brooke is in rare form at the breakfast table—almost makes me wish I hadn't waited to eat with the family.

When she says it's too bad the shooter wasn't a better shot, Grandfather tells her that's enough and to apologize to me.

Rather than apologize, she says, "You just don't get it, old man—the only reason she looked you up was for your money!"

She shoots a glaring glance at me as she storms out of the dining room. Garrett came into the room just in time to hear Brooke's comment before she pushed past him. He looks at Grandfather, then at me, but says nothing about Brooke.

"Mr. McKenzie, if I am not needed tomorrow, I would like the day off. Yvonne's mother fell this morning and broke her hip. We need to go to Las Vegas to be with her during surgery. I'll come back tomorrow night," he gets right to the point.

"Kathryn?" Grandfather puts the ball in my court.

"That would be fine. Do you need more time?"

"That should be enough."

"No, on second thought, don't come back tomorrow. Stay a few days."

"Thank you, I will," he agrees easily and is gone.

"You handled that like your grandmother would have." Grandfather smiles.

"Thank you." I'm happy for the approval. I get up from the table, then give him a peck on the forehead. I appreciate his compliment, but more than that, I appreciate that he finally said something to Brooke, even though she didn't listen to him.

Both of us know what Brooke said was untrue. I don't know if Garrett is aware that Grandfather found me, not the other way around, but he probably is. He drove Grandfather to the park to meet me. He doesn't seem to miss much that goes on around here—neither does the rest of the breakfast group. I don't think Garrett believes for one minute that I'm after the money. All that matters is that Grandfather knows the truth. There is no point bothering with trying to straighten out Brooke on the matter.

~~~

Eleanor and Stanley are at the kitchen table sharing the Sunday paper. Two papers are delivered: Grandfather has one and the staff has the other one. While pouring another cup of coffee, I ask, "Is there a car I can use to go to town?"

Eleanor nudges Stanley. "Miss McKenzie wants a ride to town. Didn't you say you were going to town?"

He has no independent recollection of the conversation she is referencing.

She nudges him again, only harder this time. "Stanley, didn't you say you were going to town today?" She is obviously putting words in his mouth.
~~~

"Oh, sure. Sure, I'm going to town." He looks at Eleanor, who nods approval.

They might as well be married. Sheesh.

~~~

"So, where are we going, Miss McKenzie?" Stanley asks as soon as we clear the front gate.

"I just wanted to go for a short drive," I lie. I had other plans, if I had a car and no chaperone. I lean back and relax into my seat while Stanley drives south along the coast. When we get to town, he pulls into the market. He says he is going to get some, ah, something, and asks if I want anything. Very funny, he couldn't think of what he came to purchase. He is a terrible liar.

I wait, curious to see what he decided to buy once he was in the store. In a few minutes, couldn't have been more than ten, Stanley comes out with a six-pack of root beer, and we go home. A six-pack of root beer? That certainly warranted a trip to town. We are a pitiful bunch when it comes to deceit.

~~~

Night comes, then morning again. It feels good to be free to go outside again for my morning walk. It pales in comparison to the beach, but a person has to make the best of what is available. Today's plan is damage control from the shooting. I just want to make a few mental notes before I go back inside.

Tim and Dan haven't come home. Danny isn't expected back yet. I suspect Tim isn't coming back until Brooke gives him the "all clear" signal—either about the cops or me, I don't know which.

Brooke has steered clear of me. She isn't subtle, though. She slams her bedroom door or the refrigerator door if I'm nearby. Last night, she played her stereo loudly in her bedroom, the one across from mine. It wasn't worth engaging her wrath to get to sleep before she gave up and shut it off on her own.

As requested, Mrs. Bailey calls to inquire about work. She still sounds shook up about the shooting on Friday. I arrange to drop by her house later in the week, but for now she should take the week off. She eagerly agrees, seeming to be relieved not to come to work.

Sam and I confirm our plan to meet at Mr. Bradford's office. Sam in on his way to pick up Chico's purchase order from the corporate office downtown and bring it for my signature. I should visit the corporate office sometime, but frankly I need to take things in measurable steps, I will get to it in its own time.

Without my car or Garrett to drive the limo, I take the helicopter to L.A. It is faster, and parking is easier—but getting around on the surface streets is a problem when I fly. Sam offers to meet me and give me a ride to Mr. Bradford's office for our appointment. I agree.

Mr. Bradford is undeniably happy to see me alive and kicking. The shooting was a bonding of sorts, at least for those who like me and the neutral parties, like Eleanor, Stanley, and Louise. As for those who aren't all that crazy about me, they were rooting for the shooter. Maybe someday they will get their wish, who knows?

I know Mr. Bradford isn't comfortable with sentimental exchanges, so we get right down to business. As far as I am concerned, Sam should sit in on the whole meeting—he is part of the inner circle now.

Mr. Bradford produces a document for Sam to sign that prohibits him from ever divulging any information he learns about Kathryn McKenzie, the McKenzie family specifically named, and about any business involvements of myself or McKenzie Enterprises. We might as well ask for his first-born child too. All of this legal mumbo jumbo—I hate it, but I appreciate its purpose.

Sam and Mr. Bradford exchange documents. "Here, I know you will have to read it before Ms. McKenzie signs it." They both read the documents, while I soak in the oddness of my new world. Sam signs his papers and hands them to me.

His contract looks a little thick, if you ask me. Mr. Bradford laughs at the bundle of papers. "That's right, Sam. The large print giveth and the small print taketh away!" They both laugh.

Finally, they finish their legal jousting and are ready to work. "Mr. Bradford, I need to know everything you know related to the McKenzie family—or me." That should be specific enough to actually get answers from him.

He leans back in his chair and clears his throat. He looks like he's going to tip over, if he isn't careful. "Where would you like me to start?"

"At the beginning."

Mr. Bradford smiles.

Sam pulls out a legal pad and makes a desk out of his leg. Since I can get a copy of his notes, I am free to listen without distraction.

"Sam's father, your father, and I were friends at USC." He nods at each of us as he mentions our fathers. "I think your two parents were friends in high school. I didn't meet them until later our freshman year." He nods toward Sam. "Garrett had a football scholarship to play for the Trojans." Then, he nods toward me. "Your grandfather is a USC alumni and expected his only son to attend his alma mater—so your fathers roomed together in college. Kathryn, your mother and my wife were roommates, so it worked out that we did things together." Thus, he begins his story.

I wonder if it's strange to have the grown children of his two best friends sitting across the desk from him. He doesn't get sentimental, but to me it's interesting to hear about my parents from someone who knew them when they were young.

"Mr. McKenzie threw a fit when he found out his heir apparent was going to marry a "heathen" Catholic. He opposed the marriage. Kate, Mrs. McKenzie, didn't care, she loved your mother."

Mr. Bradford chuckles under his breath about her independence from Grandfather's opinions.

"When Mr. McKenzie was in Europe, they had a private wedding and party in the estate ballroom. He was furious when he found out, but Kate stood her ground."

Sam looks a little surprised. He probably didn't know about the ballroom.

"Kate?" I haven't heard Grandmother called Kate.

"Your grandmother. She was named after her mother, Amelia, so they called her by her middle name, Kathryn—Kate." He smiles that he is revealing a secret that I didn't know. "You're named after her. She really liked that." He laughs. "She protested, saying it was confusing, but everyone knew she was proud to have a namesake. She was some lady, that Kate!"

"When she was young, your grandmother was in love with an artist. Her father disapproved—he had someone else in mind to marry his only child. Kate struck a deal with her father, your great-grandfather. Both of the men were given a thousand dollars to invest any way they wanted. In a year's time, Kate would marry the one who made the most money.

I can feel my eyes open wide. "Grandfather is an artist?" I nearly whisper in amazement. I wonder if he painted the portrait of Grandmother.

"No, no, the artist lost. But Kate did well with the family fortune. She had a sixth sense about business."

"The artist lost?" That's sad.

"That was probably why she supported your parents' marriage. I think she regretted the bargain with her father."

"Grandmother ran the businesses?"

"They kept their money separate. They had a friendly competition to see who could make the most money—that Kate was one smart lady. Your grandfather lost most of his money in the first ten years they were married. After that, she just let the world think it was his money." He stops to think about her again.

"Hopefully, I inherited some of her business savvy," I joke. I wonder if that is why Grandfather is the way he is.

"I hope so, too. She left her entire family fortune to you—the only heir. Most of the businesses were hers, the house, yacht, nearly everything." He sits up and looks serious.

What does one say to that? I am speechless. Managing the corporations for Grandfather is one thing. I thought the cousins and I would divide things someday, and I wouldn't have to live this life. I don't see that the money has done anyone a favor in this family. It is a good thing Sam is taking notes. I don't really understand the implications of the legalese Mr. Bradford lapses into now.

"How much are we talking about?" Sam asks without looking up from his notes.

Mr. Bradford smiles wryly. "Let's just say Kathryn is a multi-billionaire in her own right. I'd have to check the latest quarterly reports —it might be another billion this quarter."

A what? At the moment I can't even think how many zeros that is. I can't imagine anyone with that much money. My breath is shallow. I don't know what to say.

"Kathryn, you didn't know it was your money?" Mr. Bradford asks.

I shake my head from side to side. "No, Mr. Bradford, I didn't know." I take a deep breath.

"Anything else you want to know, Kathryn?"

"I was going to talk to you about my salary. In a month's time, I will make more than all last year. I suppose this changes even that."

"Yes. There are some complications. You were to inherit next year. Your Grandfather stepped down early."

"Complications, what complications?" I think "oh crap" fits in here someplace.

"You are going to have terrible tax consequences unless you set up a charitable foundation."

"A trust?"

"Not a trust. A charitable foundation has fewer limitations than a trust."

Sam nods agreement.

"You are going to have to give away more money than you already do, now that your wealth has gone through the roof. I've started the papers, you need to decide on a name for the foundation."

"Do you need the name today?" I'm relieved that the complications aren't serious. I expected something worse than naming a foundation and giving away money.

"You have a week or two; we can add it into the document when you decide on something. You'll have to live with the name. Pick a good one. We'll get a logo trademarked."

The meeting with Mr. Bradford was overwhelming. Sam drops me off at Karen's office. I'm glad we are having lunch together. Then she's loaning me her car to run my errands. I'm getting a headache from all of the stress; besides, I am really hungry.

"Hi, how's your day?" I ask.

"Actually, quiet for us." Karen smiles. "How are things with you?"

"Things are good. Lunch is on me! Today and every other day."

Karen watches the traffic as she drives to the restaurant, but I can see she is pondering what I just said.

"Remember Grandfather's big announcement?" I ask, watching her think about that night. "It didn't matter. I was going to inherit it all next year anyway. My grandmother left everything she had to me. It was all hers, not his."

That got her. The look on her face is priceless.

She pulls to a stop at the light, and turns toward me. "What? You were getting this anyway and no one told you?"

"I know. Not to mention the questions I have about Grandfather. I had hoped he found me, I don't know—to get to know me. Maybe to atone for his decisions before he died. To atone for wiping me out of his life, sight unseen." I shrug. "I think he just did this to protect his image." I snicker. "I'm sorry, I shouldn't laugh, but this is too funny. I think he didn't want anyone to know that he is only a figurehead."

"Whatever his motive, you love him and have enjoyed getting to know him."

"Yes, I love him. I'm not sure of his motivation. I really wanted it to be me. I wanted him to want to find me—not the family heir."

"What about your cousins?"

"If they ever learn the truth, they are really going to be angry." With a huge grin I add, "I would like to kick them out of the house."

"Really! You wouldn't—would you?" She is amazed at the idea because it doesn't seem like I'd become so power hungry.

"No, not really. I have more options now. The house is mine —the art, statues, grounds—everything."

"And, the ballroom!"

"Yes, and the ballroom. Quit grinning. You know we can't talk about any of this once we get inside. Take a deep breath. Ready?" I ask as we open the door to the restaurant.

~~~

After the bank cashes my paycheck, and I pick up my replacement glasses, I'm on the way to return Karen's car when I drive past a Ford dealership. I pull in to look at the new cars. I really don't want my Mustang back. I don't believe they can get all of the glass fragments
~~~

removed from it. Besides, I don't want to wait for the repaire and have to bum a ride when I want to go somewhere. It might be time for a new Mustang.

At the dealership, the salesman catches me at the first car I stop to peek into. We go through the usual are-you-looking-for-a-car routine, and no, that's not my trade-in. While we play car-buying twenty questions, I move from car to car looking through the window for a five-speed. I'm focused on my search. Clearly, he is going through a script. I like the Thunderbird, but it's a five-speed automatic and the color is all wrong. We reach the Mustang section.

"Do you have authority to sell a car, or do you have to talk with 'someone' else to wear me down?" I ask, deliberately throwing off the rhythm of his script.

"Why, ah, yes. Sure, I can sell you a car."

I write a number on a paper and hand it to him. "I'll give you this amount in cash for this black, convertible Mustang, if you can agree to it now—on the spot. Ten seconds."

He looks at the amount, then the car, then the figure again and hesitates. Take it or get approval? Take it or get approval?

Maybe I shouldn't have put him on the spot, but I don't want to take all day. There are plenty of other dealerships.

Finally, he agrees to the purchase.

He should. It was a fair amount, but not the full sticker price. I've shot myself in the foot if there is a rebate on it.

We go inside. I lay out the cash in stacks of ten one-hundred dollar bills across his desk. The look on his face is priceless. He calls the cashier to come count it. I can tell by his side of the conversation that she doesn't want to be bothered.

"I have $20,000 cash on my desk! I don't want to move it until you count it!"

She's at his desk in seconds, and very pleasant to me.

We have a done deal, I fill out the paperwork, including my name. The salesman doesn't know who I am, but the cashier saw my alien baby photo and mentions it—that figures. After we joke about the alien, I sign on the dotted line. They'll have the car prepared and ready to go by the time I take Karen's car back and return in a taxi.

~~~

On the way home, I call Sam. He's stuck in traffic. I have a captive audience.

"Sam, I just want to make sure I heard correctly. Did Mr. Bradford say that my inheritance from Grandmother is in a trust, or whatever he is managing for me—along with the one from my parents?"
~~~

"That's right, why?"

"I'll talk with you about it tomorrow, not on the phone," I say.

Next call. "Crystal, is Mr. Bradford available? This is Kathryn."

"Sorry, Miss McKenzie, he is in a pre-trial meeting. I can have him call you when he is finished."

"That's fine, thank you." The conversation concludes as I approach the town south of the mansion.

I locate the hospital parking lot. No, I don't want to see the shooter. There is no point for me to try to talk with someone who is hallucinating, even if the officers would let me see him, which they won't. I am hoping to catch his wife. Rather than ask at the visitors desk, I find the psych unit and see if the shooter's wife is there.

The psych unit is a locked unit, as it should be. I find a seat in the waiting area outside the unit, facing the double doors. I can see through the windows in the doors there is an officer standing outside one room. In about fifteen minutes a woman exits the guarded door. She looks like the weight of the world is on her shoulders. I guess she is the shooter's wife. Laying down my magazine, I join her at the elevator. The door opens and we both enter. We utter token hellos.

"You look like you could use a cup of coffee."

"I don't know what I need," she replies.

I tilt my head slightly and tempt, "Coffee?"

She lets out a deep, weary breath. "All right, thanks."

Her hand shakes uncontrollably, nearly spilling her coffee.

"Let me help you with that." I reach for her cup.

She tries to smile.

We find a table away from the staff on their break. "I am Kathryn McKenzie."

She is surprised and uneasy with the news. "What do you want?" she whispers defensively.

"I know this is hard for you. How can I help?"

"You just want your name in the paper," she says.

"No, actually I'd rather you tell no one."

"So, what do you want?" She can't figure it out.

"I want to know how can I help."

I expect a flippant comment about curing her husband or something as ridiculous.

"Billy lost his job a couple of months ago. We're behind in our utilities and house payment. It was like something snapped in him. I'm really sorry he shot at you." She stops talking and looks down at her cup. "I don't know how I'm going to manage."

"I'd like to help with your expenses until you get back on your feet." I guessed about the children, when she mentioned daycare.

"I—I don't know what else to do. A few months ago, I was planning to go back to school this fall, so I could get a better job. Things were finally working out for us." She forces a smile. "He just wasn't the same after his deployment to the Middle East. He can't seem to keep a job, he's restless, irritable. I hardly recognize him." She looks up with all of the pain she feels visible on her face.

Her despair moves me. I can see she is destined to be homeless if something isn't done. "Let me help, so you can still go to school this fall, as a gift—just between us."

She pulls a tissue out of her pocket and wipes a tear. "I just don't know what happened to Billy. Things were going good. We bought a house last year, and, and—" She begins to cry.

"The doctors will figure out what to do for your husband. In the meantime, let me help, okay?" I take out my card and write my cell number on the back. I get her phone and address.

"I'll repay every penny—I promise."

"That's not necessary. Help someone else, sometime."

"I will, but I'll pay you back too. I'm so sorry that Billy tried to kill you, he isn't like that. I don't know what happened to him."

"It's all right. He just needs help right now. And you need to focus on taking care of your family. Here is my number, call me and we will work it out."

~~~

Calling me for help is probably too hard. I decide to take care of it myself. Tuesday morning, I research who holds the mortgage on the shooter's house and pay twelve month's worth of utilities, in person with cash to hope to be anonymous. I meet with the president of the little bank who holds the deed. I prove my identity to his satisfaction and swear him to secrecy. I know any small bank would be glad for the infusion of cash. I tell him if it leaks out that I've paid off the house, I'll own his bank before sundown the same day. He believes me.

It cost the Foundation less than $186,000 for both transactions. It is a bargain for a mother and children to have a life—it's definitely a bargain.

~~~

~ CHAPTER 9 ~

The Stuff Tabloids Are Made Of

Things settle down to normal again. Well, if anything is normal in my world. Mr. Bradford finishes the documents to create a foundation. All that remains is a name. Naming the Foundation is more difficult than I expected. I wonder if Mother Elizabeth had as much trouble naming Spirit of Hope. I tried a variety of practical and boring name ideas. I settle on Amelia Kathryn McKenzie Foundation. Boring, I know. It's a tribute to my grandmother, it's her money.

Mrs. Bailey is thrilled with my offer of an early retirement package, including a retirement party at the mansion—a place usually closed to outsiders. She is thrilled to show her friends where she worked.

I am equally happy that she won't be at the mansion longer. Frankly, I'm surprised by the number of her friends attending her party. The really interesting thing is how easily she laughs as she opens her gifts—that isn't the Mrs. Bailey I know.

Grandfather gives her and three friends a cruise to Alaska. All of the women are woozy at the thought of such a gift. He almost looks embarrassed by the fuss his gift causes. I give her a camera for her trip. We conspired on the gifts, but the cruise was Grandfather's idea. It is a classy gift. Good job, Grandfather McKenzie.

Chico starts to produce reports and financial analyses that make sense to me—a great improvement over Mrs. Bailey's reports. When Chico needs help to manage all of the data entry, I offer the position to Race. We'll put that computer training to good use.

It's good to see Race again and hear of his progress since he left Spirit of Hope. He wears his confidence well and is a semester away from a bachelor's degree in computer science. He plans to move his family to town, so that he can shorten the commute. I offer to pay him the industry standard and he thinks he is rich.

Later, I learn he and Lana plan to purchase a house next year, the first home they have ever owned—a far cry from the day they came to Spirit of Hope with only a trash bag of belongings for the entire family.

Grandfather comes out of his room and stays out longer each day. He is his old self again, possibly even more engaged with those around him than before. There is no hiding from Grandfather what we are doing, so we enlist his help. Sometimes it's only advice, other times he helps Sam and me analyze the businesses. We develop a plan to efficiently conduct site visits of each company. Grandfather is a wealth of information on the histories of the businesses and the reasons for their location. I don't think that he knows that I am aware that the businesses belonged to Grandmother all along.

As for the reports, I begin to understand the dynamics of the reports I read. The learning curve is incredible. Sam and I commence with my privately owned companies, saving the public companies for after I get up-to-speed in this new world of mine. We ease into the flow and take Grandfather's counsel by starting with the companies who bid government contracts. That is both interesting and mind-boggling.

~~~

Danny comes home. His mother is doing fine after her surgery. He doesn't volunteer what kind of surgery she had and I don't ask, it's none of my business. He missed all of our recent excitement.

Danny and I need to have a private conversation—sans his brother and sister. Luckily, Tim and Brooke are often away partying somewhere.

In the morning we are the only two in the kitchen, so I seize the opportunity at hand. "Dan, let's take a walk."

He shrugs. "Why not?"

"Bring your coffee."

When we are away from the house so not to be accidentally overheard, I begin.

"Dan, if you could do absolutely anything you wanted, what would you do?"

He stops and looks at me like he is considering whether it's a loaded question.

"You have to want more out of life than passing your days hanging around here."

"Are you kicking me out?"

"No, of course not. It is a simple question. Don't complicate it."

He takes a measured breath as he looks away, across the manicured gardens. Then he looks back.

"If you really want to know, I want to have my own architect firm."

"What's stopping you?"

He looks down. "Grandfather. I can't leave him alone with Brooke and Tim."

"I'll look out for Grandfather. Go have a life. Dan, live your dreams—life is too short not to live it well."

We have come full circle on the garden path. "Think about where you want your firm. Stay here as long as you like, but don't stay because you feel a sense of obligation. It's my responsibility now. I'll take care of Grandfather." I make my final point before we reach the patio and go inside.
~~~

Dan doesn't think I am after the family money. I genuinely want him to be happy and to have a life—something I want for myself, as well.

Besides, I have already had the opportunity to live as I chose. I have had successes and failures, made good decisions and bad, but I experienced my choices and their ramifications. Dan hasn't had that freedom because of his sense of duty to the family—it is time for that to change.

The next time I go to my beach apartment, I bring back the blueprints and design-idea notebooks that I have from my parents' architectural firm, McKenzie & McKenzie. I offer them to Dan, if he wants them. I want to help him set up his own firm any way that I can. He doesn't have to stay at the mansion any longer to secure his inheritance, or watch over Grandfather's welfare.

~~~

When Sam and I met with Mr. Bradford I learned that Grandfather gives each of his four grandchildren an annual allowance of $100,000. Mine was automatically deposited into Grandmother's trust for me—and I was blissfully unaware of its existence. If I had been Dan, I would have taken the allowance as soon as it was deposited and started my business without regard for the bulk inheritance, which doesn't exist anyway. No one should have to put their dreams on hold for such nonsense.

When I talk to Dan about his plans, he tells me he is just waiting until he is old enough to access his trust account. I offer him the assurance of five years operating capital—the minimum needed to start a business—if he really wants to start his own firm. If he's half as good as my parents were, he isn't going to need the money for five years. It seems like it had never occurred to him to just go get a job at a firm and work his way to the top, or get a business loan at a bank. He hesitates, then agrees with the promise to pay me back from his trust. I don't tell him that there is no trust for him and his siblings. They will get the annual allowance until they are thirty-five, plenty of time for anyone to get situated in life.

Almost immediately, as he begins to create the life of his dreams, his stuttering stops. He has a new bounce in his step and stands taller now that he is moving out on his own. I feel proud that I set him free. He only needed the encouragement to go.

Tim gets another driving while intoxicated ticket and loses his license. I warn the staff not to tell Grandfather about it. One morning the police are at the front door. They found Tim's car, wrecked. It smells of liquor and they find some drugs. The passenger is severely injured, but expected to live. As far as I know, Tim hasn't come home. I don't ask.
~~~

I suspect Brooke is hiding him somewhere. She left early this morning, which is an unusual time of day for her to get up.

As for Brooke, she usually steers clear of me, but I can't imagine that lasting forever. It is a pleasant reprieve from her hateful comments. I haven't come up with a foolproof strategy for the next time she lashes out at me. Detox comes to mind.

~~~

Zoe has smoothly made the transition to working for me. She is obviously loyal and has the energy to keep up with the pace we are setting. She handles my calendar like a pro, when it comes to giving me a manageable schedule. Zoe understands the importance of things like Shasta's dance recital, and doesn't overbook my trips to tour the companies. Finally, I feel like I can catch my breath. I feel secure that an in-house conspiracy isn't waging while I am away and unable to monitor my affairs.

Sam and I take a day to visit the plants near L.A. and Long Beach, and the second day to take the helicopter to Lancaster to tour that plant. We are beginning to put together what we are seeing on paper with what is at the plants—and faces to the names.

~~~

The next morning, I overhear Zoe on the phone as I approach her office. She is turned with her back to the door and doesn't notice me standing in the doorway.

She whispers desperately, "No! I can't. She would never agree! I can't ask her to do that!" There is silence as she listens to the person on the phone. "Yes, I understand, you know I would help, if I could."

"Agree to what?" I whisper from over her shoulder, startling Zoe who hangs up the phone without saying another word. Containing a grin, I ask again, "I would never agree to what, Zoe?"

"Well, you see, my boyfriend works for someone who wants to meet you."

I tilt my head in a questioning glance.

"He, he wants me to get you to agree to a blind date."

"A blind date? Oh, no, probably not," I agree with Zoe on that.

"My boyfriend's boss likes you. He wants to go to dinner with you," Zoe continues, then hesitates.

This seems a little junior high to me. After the Joseph incident I don't really think much of blind dates. I look at Zoe fidgeting with her pen. There is no reason to say no just because one blind date didn't work out well in the end. Besides, it doesn't require a second date.

"Is this a double date?" I query, watching her eyes grow wide with disbelief, and she nods and smiles big.

"I'll consider it. Let's get back to work—after you call your boyfriend back."

She jumps up and hugs my neck.

"I only said I would consider it." I caution her optimism. I smile at her zest for life as I return to my office. Oh, gee. A blind date? I hope I don't live to regret this.

~~~

The shooter's court date arrives. It has been a long time since I have been in court. Even though I never saw the shooter, I am on the State's witness list. I have been a witness hundreds of times, but I really don't want to do this. No one is served by putting this mentally ill guy in prison. He needs long-term treatment, and prison isn't where he will get it. Neither do I want him free on bail where he may decide to come after me again. In an ideal world he would be locked up while he receives treatment.

Trusting Keith's advice, I hire his bodyguard friend for the day. If, for some strange reason, the shooter is released after court on a technicality, I'll be ready.

It turned out to be a short hearing. The defense attorney filed a plea of not guilty by reason of insanity. So, now we wait while the shooter is evaluated by both the prosecution and defense psychiatrists.

The thing I tell no one is, the shooter is the guy who sat in his car and watched my apartment with binoculars. This wasn't a sudden onset of craziness. He'd planned this for a while. He had a better shot at me walking the beach, than at the estate. I wonder why he waited? There is something that doesn't ring true about this. There must have been some significance to the date or the location. Otherwise, why wait?

The shooter's wife leaves court alone. I deliberately miss the elevator she takes and take the next one to spare her from the media frenzy that will catch me.

The media catches me and my entourage outside the courthouse. I watch the shooter's wife slowly walk down the front steps—ignored, dejected, and relieved that she is invisible.

"My people" push me through the reporters until one asks if I am encouraging the prosecutor's office to go for the death penalty. My entourage nearly runs into me when I stop suddenly to respond.

I think persons preying upon others and robbing them of life should be permanently removed from society. No one should be condemned to live in fear because known murderers are released among us.

As perverse as their crimes are, I am not prepared to become like them by advocating their murder as recompense. I am not ready to become a poster child in the death penalty debate. I skirt the question.
~~~

"What are my thoughts regarding the death penalty?" I tolerate the question and the photos. "Let me remind everyone that the death penalty doesn't apply to this case. Now, no more questions. Thank you."

~~~

In the vacuum of reality, it is apparent the shooter needs long-term treatment in an environment that protects the safety of society; Brooke and Tim seriously need detox, and to learn the responsibilities that accompany their age and social position; and, as for myself, the media needs to find some other socially redeeming topic to report, not whether I attend baseball games, and with whom. I am out of sorts today.

Overall, there seems to be a waste of the human spirit in our society. It seems too important to play political games, flex perceived power, and to exploit the poor for the benefit of a select few wealthy scum.

Ugh, being in court again has tainted my mood. I need to get out of here and clear my head, and I don't really feel like having Garrett or my bodyguard's company.

"Zoe, I'm going for a drive for a couple of hours."

"Anyone going with you?"

I grimace, because I want to be alone. "I'm only going to Saint Leo's beach. I have my phone." I give more specifics to satisfy her, then take my leave before she can tattle on me.

As I slide behind the wheel, I toss my purse into the passenger seat. It feels good to be out, free, shifting through the gears. I think everyone has their own means to recalibrate their soul. For me it is always the beach, it's naturally honest.

Standing at the water's edge, I look at the piles of rocks with birds perched on them. Before long, the mood of the waves awakens the emotions I have hidden or ignored.

The sounds of the repetitive advance and retreat slowly strip away the noise in my brain clamoring to be foremost. The artificial world of commerce where I live seems very far away as I sit on Father's Beach. It is only the beginning, yet I am tired of being Kathryn the Great and crave a few moments as Katey the Ordinary.

After an hour of lounging in the warm sand, I feel ready to return to the mansion. I sit up a little too fast and make myself dizzy.

Within minutes, I am slipping through the gears into fifth, and on the way home. I have gone back to my own beach less and less often since the shooting.

Zoe reports my blind date is set for Friday night. Friday night seems soon. The last I knew, I said I would think about it.
~~~

Zoe and "friend" will join us for drinks, then we will be on our own for dinner, if I give her the signal that things are okay for her to leave.

"So, do I get to know his name?"

"Mark."

"Mark? Does Mark have a last name?"

"Well, yes. But, he doesn't want me to tell you." She smiles, making me all the more curious.

"Okay, then what does Mark do?"

"He is a musician." The phone rings and saves her from additional inquiry.

Garrett has agreed to work Friday night to drive me to Beverly Hills in the limo for my date. I haven't been on a blind date for more than six years, and I feel better having Garrett around, since Zoe and her date won't be staying for the entire evening.

~~~

I look in the mirror one last time at my black cocktail dress. My hair and dress look fine. Surprisingly, I am more excited than nervous. I am fully aware that this is a stupid idea.

We arrive prior to Mark. Garrett sits at a table where he can comfortably observe while he eats his dinner. Zoe looks lovely in a very young-styled cocktail dress. Her date admits he won lots of points for making the arrangements for the date. What can I say? We aim to please.

Mark arrives. He is quietly handsome in his charcoal suit with a burgundy shirt—no tie. His manners are impeccable. To my surprise, the conversation between the four of us is easy.

Garrett and I exchange glances. He nods his approval of Mark. Smoothly, Zoe and her date leave. Mark and I begin our dinner. He invites me to attend the preview of a movie for which he wrote the musical score, plus two additional songs. He says it's Oscar-bound. I'm a pushover for movies. I don't have to think twice about accepting. He does warn me that he has to appear in his public persona—Scourge.

Scourge? I can't believe it! Mark is the bad boy of rock? He is so engaging and polite. This can't be.

On the trip home, Garrett admits that first impressions are good. He thinks I should go out with him again. He can't believe Mark is Scourge. Frankly, neither can I. He asks if I have heard Scourge's music, it's loud. Unfortunately, I have heard a couple of his songs, parts of them. Garrett thinks I should still go out with Mark.

~~~

The two weeks since the date with Mark passed quickly. I have thought of him more often than I would like—definitely more than I will admit. Mark is unlike Joseph, who fell into periods of silence while his life carried on without notice of how much I loved him. Mark calls, sends flowers and chocolates—not all at once, but scattered throughout the fourteen days. He makes me smile. I don't feel those giddy feelings about him that I did toward Joseph. I think it is a good thing this is different.

~~~

Dana came last weekend to fit the gown she is making for me to wear to the premiere with Mark. We are scheming—I am going to wear something from her holiday line. It is, after all, a Hollywood affair and I am glad to debut one of her designs. The media is sure to be there. If they take my picture, I am hoping for something better than what the tabloids have run so far. ValDana's fashions never suffer when the rich and famous wear them—neither do the rich and famous.

She is cutting it close in delivering the "dress of my dreams"—as she calls all of her gowns. I do like it. It is hunter green—she also offered cranberry—made out of a shimmery blend of silk and something else. I forget what she said.

Dana and I run upstairs to put on the dress. Ooh, it is beautiful! The fabric is supple, but not limp. Dana wanted to address the alien baby issue by cutting the dress low in the front. It isn't in bad taste, but I hadn't thought of cutting it quite so low. I have to agree, the design works.

We look through Grandmother's jewelry case in the closet. Dana advises me on which to wear. She selects a ruby and diamond necklace and earrings—screw-back earrings. Dana says I need to have them converted to pierced before my date. We locate the matching ring, it is too large. I'll have it sized when I have the earrings done. Dana's keen eye appraises my hair and makeup. She adjusts the necklace to hang perfectly.

I feel beautiful!

Luckily, Mark warned me that he would be in his public persona. When he gets out of his limo with his leather "Bad Boy" outfit, I study the transformed Mark. Frankly, I am not sure anything I own would go with the chains and black leather. What a sight he is! A distasteful sight.

If I don't look at him, it seems like I am with the same man who took me to dinner two weeks ago. His Rod McKuen voice tells me I look lovely. He has a dozen roses in the limo for me. When I look at Mark and see his yellow and red-tipped spiked hair and black eyeliner, I don't know whether to gasp or laugh.

Struggling with his transformation, I try to make casual conversation about the evening without looking at him more than is necessary.
~~~

“Tell me about the premiere,” I begin, trying desperately not to stare.

He takes my hand in his, looks into my eyes and says, “Go ahead, laugh and get it over, so you can make it through the evening.” He opens his eyes and mouth wide and sticks out his tongue, then throws back his head and laughs ferociously.

I laugh nervously at first, then openly. It works. I feel more relaxed. He has champagne chilling in the limo bar.

“Tell me about tonight,” I prod again.

“I’m invited because I did the feature song for the movie.” He smiles proudly, lifts his glass high, and laughs again.

“That’s marvelous.”

“Here, listen to this.” He slides a CD into the stereo beside the bar.

Music, or rather, loud, obnoxious sounds and screaming lyrics blare harshly from the speakers. The suddenness of the sound causes me to jump.

“Should I assume this is not going to be a chick flick?” I ask loudly.

He turns down the volume of the music. “Actually, it is a touching story. That was my new CD, not the song from the movie,” he answers softly. He glides smoothly back and forth between his two personas.

“This one is from the movie.”

It is difficult for me to keep up with him. “How many personalities do you have?”

“Just one, Scourge is my manager’s creation.” He winks.

There were new expectations since Grandfather’s announcement, but no one expects me to take on an alternate persona. I am glad I don’t have to live like that. All I have had to do is learn new protocols.

We arrive at the theater and wait in the limo line for our turn for the grand entrance. There are fans for the various stars standing behind a barricade. The media is present. This is the first time I have attended a Hollywood affair. The whole scene is overwhelmingly fabulous. Even if Mark is in costume and has this bizarre personality, I am thankful that he is experienced in these matters and I am not making my debut solo.

Mark looks like an actor getting in character before he enters the stage. He says, “We’re next. Ready? I’ll get out first, then I’ll help you out. Take my arm. We will pause for a minute for photos, then walk toward the door. Smile like you just won an Oscar. Try not to get cornered with personal questions from the reporters. Sound bites, you know. I’ll keep us moving.”

This is it. Mark gets out of the limo, raises his arms in the air like a presidential candidate who just won the Iowa primary, then offers his hand. I place my gloved hand in his, and slide out of the limo.

The cameras flash. An official reporter, invited to cover the premiere, kisses Scourge and asks who is his date. He smiles and gestures toward me. "CeCe, may I introduce Kathryn McKenzie."

Her face lights up. It is entertaining to see her awestruck. She quickly regains her wits, "Miss McKenzie, your gown is beautiful! Which designer made it?"

My cheeks are hot. I feel like I'm blushing. These Hollywood extravaganzas are fun. "It's a ValDana design." I say with pride that Dana is my friend, and turn a bit to show it off.

"You are beautiful! Enjoy the premiere, dears." She moves down the line to the next waiting couple.

This is the ultimate movie experience. All of the cast and principals are present. The producer makes a few remarks. The director thanks everyone he has ever known, or might know in the future. The movie begins. Mark's title song is tame for him. I am a little surprised, as are others who haven't heard it yet.

At the reception, Hollywood stars are mingling. Some are watching the room to see who notices them, most are not concerned with such things. Mark is more popular than I thought he would be since his standard music isn't what I imagine most of these people would listen to regularly. Several people tell him that he should expect an Academy nomination for the song. He seems to take it in stride—no ego problem for him. Everyone he introduces me to is gracious. Some are not quite sober, but still they are gracious.

~~~

Mark sends a dozen roses and a personally written note thanking me for attending the premiere with him. This is much better treatment than I ever had from Joseph.

Monday, the tabloids hit the stands. The most noteworthy is the cover story of "ex-nun dates devil," complete with a photo of Mark and me. At least the picture is better than the last one. The other tabloids are not as rich as the first's headline. I hope this headline is not another invitation to get me shot at, or killed by another mentally ill person.

~~~

I show Grandfather the paper before he sees it some other way. He asks questions about my intentions with Scourge. Of course, I have no intentions with "Scourge," but Mark is nice. I explain Mark's two personalities to Grandfather. In some ways it's convenient that he is unrecognizable as Mark. However, it won't be long before I am readily recognized by the public at large as Kathryn McKenzie.

Grandfather cautions, "Have him checked out. You'll be sorry if you don't."

I promise Grandfather that I will run a check on Mark. I will be alert regarding him and everyone else I meet. It doesn't take a rocket scientist to know that questions must be asked about anyone who makes the extra effort to get near me now that I have become "Miss McKenzie." No worries, I am not a lonely, rich old maid blinded by the attention of every gold digger that comes my way. Joseph taught me to guard my heart.

Brooke comes into the library with a smug look on her face. She is armed with the tabloids. It was a good decision to show the them to Grandfather before Brooke had the chance to cause agitation between us. She masterfully plays the concerned cousin and feigns outrage. Grandfather laughs and shows his stack of them.

"Kathryn was about to autograph these for me. Would you like yours signed, too, Brooke?" He smiles innocently.

She disappears as quickly as she arrived. When she is gone, he offers a chuckle regarding our alliance in warding off Brooke's advance.

I don't see Brooke again for a week, but there are indications that she is in and out of the residence.

~~~

Officers are once more at the door looking for Tim. They won't be specific about why they want him. I convince them to allow me to ask Grandfather about Tim, rather than trust the task to them.

I introduce the officers to Grandfather. "These officers are looking for Tim. Have you seen him?"

"I haven't seen Timmy since he came back from Europe," Grandfather says gruffly.

I don't know whether to believe him or not. Brooke is not likely to give me a straight answer, or a civil one for that matter. There is a slight chance that Mrs. Bailey might know some of Tim's friends; she is obviously fond of Tim and Brooke.

I apologize that I do not know my jet-setting cousins very well. The look on their faces indicates the officers are hesitant to believe me, but it's the truth, whether they believe me or not. I give them the phone number for Mrs. Bailey, and send Zoe upstairs to find Brooke.

I go about my own business. Brooke takes the officers outside the front door. Before long the officers are gone.

Mark calls again for a quiet dinner, but I decline. At the moment I don't have time for a relationship. I need to slow this down a little until I get acclimated to this new job. Of course, it is an excuse and I am simply being cautious. We agree to have dinner in the next week or two instead.

~~~

To further complicate my organizing efforts, Chico found unusual bookkeeping practices in the Seattle company. All we have to go by is the final numbers on the quarterly reports. Chico needs raw numbers to really determine what is happening and hopefully who is responsible. He wants to go to Seattle and infiltrate the company. He starts to explain how he'll do it, but I don't speak "geek" so we bypass that process.

I am not sure about the idea, but Sam thinks it's good. I arrange to send Chico to apply for the mailroom job that is open in the company. Grandfather loves the sleuth idea of spying on the company to determine the extent of the creative accounting. He wishes he had thought of it.

Race is left to hold down the fort while Chico is away. Everyone working at the mansion is told Chico is returning to New Mexico to attend to family matters. We arrange for Chico to move to Seattle and apply for the position. Sam will be Chico's reference, so that we can control the information given out about him. Chico doesn't think his previous boss knows he came to work for me, so we are safe listing him on the application.

As a mailroom worker, Chico will be able to move freely around the office complex delivering the mail and perhaps collect information necessary to determine the nature of the problem and hopefully the person responsible.

Sam wants to contact the Feds. I think it's premature. Grandfather agrees with Sam since the company has a lucrative government contract. It takes my best effort to present my case to wait to have something more concrete. They could barge in and tip off the guilty, if there is anyone guilty.

In the end, they both acquiesce to my decision to wait. When Chico is hired, he tells them the reason for moving to Seattle is to attend college in the fall. Just to be safe, he enrolls in photo journalism classes, something he has always wanted to do anyway.

In the meantime, I ask Sam to put together a list of items we need to find before notifying the authorities. When we get hard copies of the information, we can determine if there is a problem requiring reporting to the security regulators. I hate to fuel a witch hunt if there isn't really embezzlement, just sloppy practices. The Chico operation is in place.

~~~

After Chico leaves for the great northwest, Race finds two more companies with similar accounting practices. These people should be artists with all their creative talent. It isn't likely this is a random occurrence or a coincidence. Race is looking for any connections between the three companies. One company is manufacturing, one is
~~~

an intellectual properties company, and the third is a holding company for four overseas firms.

Even though the companies are outwardly unrelated, if their products interface, then perhaps they intersect somewhere else. Race is also looking for bookkeeping, marketing, auditing firm connections, any connection on a subsurface level. The last thing I can think of is a connection between key personnel in the three companies: relatives, college friends, prior common employment, anything that ties them together. What a task.

I remain hesitant to infiltrate the other two companies, one in Tennessee and the other in Texas, until we have something from Chico about Seattle. It's a tough decision whether to wait to get definitive information from Chico or go into all three companies simultaneously. If there is a connection between the three companies, I don't want to tip off the remaining two. It is difficult to decide whether to keep the bird in the hand before going after the two in the bush.

Grandfather is shaken by the possibility that there is corruption in the corporation. He misunderstood what I said, but when he mentions his concerns to me, it makes me think we should look closer to home—the McKenzie Enterprises corporate office. Our investigation widens. The added stress is fueling my headaches. I am sure that the anxiety, fatigue, and eyestrain contribute to both the stress and headaches. I need a vacation—and I have only yet to begin my new reign.

~~~

Government probes, tabloids, bad legitimate press, alien babies—my headaches increase exponentially. I have trouble focusing, mentally and visually, on the reams of paper Race is generating. Another visit to the eye doctor reveals that the eyestrain has rewarded me with stronger reading glasses and the promise of full-time bifocals in the near future.

In the meantime, reviewing corporate expenses reveals there is an inordinate number of trips taken on the two company jets. I realize that the jets might be in the company as a tax deductible business expense. However, some of the trips are to locations where we have no holdings.

Until I know who to trust to provide accurate information in the company outside my closest circle, I contact the airport where the jets are hangared. It takes speaking with several people before I find someone at the airport who can provide me with a list of the flight plans filed by the McKenzie jets and helicopter. The catch is that I will have to come, show identification, and sign for the information personally.

~~~

Since I am going to the airport, I arrange for a meeting with all of the pilots and flight staff. Zoe is able to set the meeting for tomorrow. She has spoken with each flight crew member and scheduled a conference room at the hotel across the street from the airport.

The catch is that the meeting will have to be held at noon. Zoe suggests arranging for a light lunch to be served. I only anticipate the meeting lasting a half hour, but I think protocol expects a meal. Until we know where the problems lie, I put the room and the meal on my personal credit card so it doesn't have a corporate record. I'll get reimbursed for the expenses once the corruption question is answered.

~~~

Grandfather and Sam agree with my idea for Sam to attend the meeting with me. I suggest that Sam comes casually dressed, rather than in a lawyer-looking suit. Since it is getting late, I ride to the city with Sam so we can discuss key issues for tomorrow's meeting. I will spend the night at my apartment. Sam can pick me up in the morning. My mind is racing. The plan is to designate a senior pilot and crew member. It is a perfect excuse to get copies of their résumés and begin to know who these people are flying the McKenzie skies.

LAX is on the way to my apartment, so we stop for the flight records. I'll partially review them tonight and brief Sam before the meeting tomorrow. Hopefully, the records will provide enough insight to get the flight costs under control. Maybe it will reveal a pattern of activity that will lead to answers about who is going where and for what reason, particularly who is jetting between the three companies in question.

~~~

I head for a walk on the beach. It seems like I have been away for months rather than weeks. First thing I do when I reach the beach is draw a deep breath. Then, savor it as it escapes. The ocean smell is rich in memories. It feels good to be home again. The sand, spray of the waves breaking, and the sounds of seagulls intermingled with it all—it is rich.

Summer-people populate the beach. Lifeguard stations are in position to watch over the activities. Children are playing. Sandcastles have sprung up like tulips in spring.

My thoughts are deeply focused on the problems of the Enterprise. This is bigger than me. What if corruption does exist? What if it is not isolated in Seattle, or even three companies? What if there are similar problems in the public companies? All of these are legitimate questions. The hard questions must be asked. And they must be asked now.

I hate corruption. It is nothing more than greed. Sharing, taking turns, using manners is all preschool stuff. But there are people who think they are above the basics. In the final analysis, corruption cannot be tolerated in civilized society.

I devise a chart for the flights and begin plugging in data: Who went where, and when. I look for anything that correlates in a less-than-natural manner, including flight crews. Dates are the first element that line up suspiciously.

I run a probability formula and find that it isn't a natural coincidence. There is a destination that keeps coming up oddly. I think we are in big trouble. I am concerned that we have sent Chico into a dangerous situation.

It is time for a meeting with people I trust. I leave Grandfather out of the loop for the moment—deniability. I call Sam and see if he is available for a meeting. Then, I'll call Karen and Keith and see if they are available. That should do it—a lawyer, a politically savvy friend, and a detective. Between the three of them, someone must know someone we can trust not to leak this to the media. The media is watching to see how the first one hundred days go. I don't want to cause an unwarranted hiccup in the public companies' stock prices.

Sam is sitting down to dinner with his family when I call. He agrees to come to my apartment tomorrow evening for a short meeting. Karen will check with Keith, and bring him with her, if he is available. Mostly Karen is moral support.

Sam calls back. Chico caught something that points to a cluster of short selling in another group of our companies. Now we have another problem, or is it a related problem?

Even though I am feeling my way through uncharted territory, I feel more settled about tomorrow now. With a fresh cup of coffee, I sit down to write in my diary.

> *Dearest Maggie, the older I get, the more circumspect I become about petty people. I do not believe that we are outnumbered, but I think we can be outsmarted, if we don't learn to understand how greed works in the mind of men. I intend to become cunning and braver than they are. I may not have been able to make the Judicial system work for my dead little client, but I can make my empire work as it should. I may not have chosen this path, but I will landscape it! When I'm finished, everyone will know I have arrived.*

~~~
~~~

~ CHAPTER 10 ~

Camelot

Before Sam arrives to go to our lunchtime meeting, I take a morning walk on the beach. The fresh ocean air clears my mind. I have a hunch the flight information will be useful even if we don't detect a connection involving the cooked books theory and the corporate office. Regardless of the data, I want control of the spending on the McKenzie airline, whether or not the people abusing the use of the planes are involved in the creative bookkeeping.

Beginning on Monday, all flights will be cleared by me. It is micro-managing, but I can ease back later. In this age of technology, I can't imagine anyone in McKenzie Enterprises needing to fly around the country as much as our jets are in the air. All flights will be reimbursed from department budgets, so there is accountability for usage.

Personal use will require advance out-of-pocket payment, or better yet, not allowed at all. Foundation use will be paid by the Foundation. It's that simple.

The flight service won't make money, but at least it won't run at a complete loss. Primarily, I will be the only person using the planes and helicopter from now on—but I am not telling them that yet.

Sam agrees with my idea, at least in theory. I see no reason not to trim the fat out of McKenzie Enterprises. Personal use of the air fleet is not a perk that I am willing to offer. With Grandfather aging, everyone has had too much freedom to dictate the operations of the Enterprise, as well as the private companies and corporations.

We probe the flight records with a cup of coffee in hand. Brooke and Tim use the jets as their personal vehicles for their jet-setting. That will stop today. There are several names from the Seattle company that keep appearing. There are a few flights to Tennessee and Texas to pick up passengers at the other two companies in question. They rendevous in the Caribbean. We have no companies in the Caribbean. Didn't they think anyone would notice? Maybe they thought they had one more year—providing they were aware of the trust-vesting age. They were probably not aware, since it is a "secret."

Tomorrow, when I return to the mansion, I'll have Race database the flight information. It will be easier to see patterns in dates, destinations, and passengers. Maybe we will see the less obvious too.

We arrive at the hotel meeting room early enough that Sam can sit next to me. He can write notes to me, if needed.

After everyone arrives, I begin introductions around the table to my right, so that Sam will be the last one introduced. I won't mention that Sam is a lawyer. As each person introduces themselves, I write their name in the margin of my tablet.

Sam introduces himself as my assistant, which is actually true.

"I am Kathryn McKenzie. I have met a few of you, but I wanted to put faces with your names and get input from you. All of you fly for McKenzie Enterprises; you must have opinions about improvements in our flight division."

Most of the staff come prepared with paper and pen. I take note of the ones who do not by placing a small mark by their names on my notes. Their coworkers give them paper.

After they write their name at the top of the page, I ask the flight team for two nominations each of pilots and flight crew they would like to see as senior pilot and senior flight staff for the jets, and a senior helicopter pilot.

"Also, write suggestions you have regarding operations. Speak now or forever hold your peace, as the saying goes."

A few people laugh. I make note of that, too. They get points for laughing at my jokes. I want staff who are engaged in the process, and with me.

"The last item is, which is the best aircraft and why is it best?"

While the staff write their assignments, the hotel staff indicates lunch is ready to serve.

"Now, ladies and gentlemen, on with the feast!"

I excuse myself to make a phone call, leaving Sam in the room as my eyes and ears. Rather than make a call, I use the time to find something for my headache.

After the meeting, Sam heads to the corporate office and I take a taxi home to the beach. Finally, I feel like I am making progress in rounding up this stampeding herd.

In the afternoon I read through the comments from the lunch meeting. They offer several good suggestions about staffing and fiscal management. One idea that has merit is static teams. That is, the same people work together as a team, so they are a finely tuned crew. Also, they suggest that those who speak foreign languages be divided among the teams. They request more emergency training. I hadn't realized they didn't have CPR training, unless they did it on their own. They will be happy to hear I have decided to keep both jets. They probably don't have a good resale value anyway. A cross-reference of the notes of who was prepared for the meeting with the suggestions of senior pilot and flight staff suggests the staff is accurate in their nominations.

I designate senior staff for each aircraft, complete with an increase in pay.

Again I visit the beach before my guests arrive. I won't have time for a walk, but I can go to the beach and stand watching the waves for a few minutes to soak in strength from the energy of the ocean.

The evening breeze is beginning to blow inland. It is still hot out, a July hot. The sand is radiating the heat it accumulated from the day. The breeze is slight and gentle against my cheeks. I almost feel like my parents are here. There are plenty of good people in my life, but I still miss them.

My cell phone rings. Dan is excited about his new office. He wants me to come see it. I explain that I have a meeting in an hour and that I don't have a car in town.

"I don't care, Katey. I'll come get you when your meeting is over. Just call me when you finish."

"It's a deal. I'm at my apartment. I'll give you directions when I call you. And, thanks. Thanks for the invitation, Dan." I respond to his excitement as I begin to walk home, happy to have a developing connection with Dan.

Coffee is brewing and everything looks fine for company. Sam arrives first. He looks around while I pour him a cup. He comments about my movie posters. "I see you are a movie fan."

"My friends would say 'possessed by old movies,' if you asked them." I laugh.

"Really? Calm-under-fire Kathryn—is possessed?" He adds comments about the tabloids of the premiere with Scourge.

"Yes, really. My friend, Maggie, always said that I saw life as one movie after another. Sometimes a romance, sometimes a musical—"

Sam interrupts, "Sometimes a tragedy?"

"Yes. Or a horror!" I add a fake monster laugh.

"You handle them well. I'll have to meet Maggie sometime."

I smile. Sam doesn't need to know Maggie is dead. I appreciate his compliment, though.

Karen and Keith arrive together. They are openly seeing each other now. I think they are in love. She has never said so, and I am certainly not an expert on such things. They come bearing Chinese takeout. I hadn't realized I was hungry until I smelled the wonderful aroma.

We laugh and relax during dinner. Keith, Karen, and I teach Sam to use chopsticks. He is really funny to watch. I have never seen anyone have such trouble learning to use chopsticks before now.

"I'm Black, you know." He plays the ethnic card to justify his difficulty.

"What does that have to do with anything? We're White, but we can use chopsticks. You know, there isn't a chopstick gene that only Asians have," I say.

I don't let him make race excuses, but I offer him a fork. That's all it takes to get him determined to master the chopsticks or starve trying.

Sam gives Karen and Keith an overview of our suspicions. We caution that it is only that, suspicion, at this point. Keith agrees that it would be a federal issue, since we cross state lines conducting business.

Sam says, "It might be a gray area since the companies are all free-standing, but McKenzie Enterprises or Kathryn owns these companies—either way, Kathryn, you are the principal at risk here."

Both men exchange nods of agreement.

Keith has a friend who is a federal marshall in Chicago. He'll ask who we should contact out here. Karen agrees that we are way out of our league with this, especially if it isn't contained in Seattle, but links to other companies or the corporate office.

If everything goes well with Keith's friend, we should be talking with the local Feds by this time next week. We'll let them figure out what is going on. That's a relief. Conducting internal investigations always makes the findings suspect.

Soon we can bring Chico home and put his talents to better use. Good thing my companies aren't publically traded. But not so good for the other companies' stockholders.

Karen and I lag behind the guys as we walk out. I can tell she has something on her mind.

"Keith asked me to marry him." She grins a schoolgirl grin.

I reach for her hand to see her ring. It is beautiful. I can't believe I didn't notice it.

I whisper "Congratulations!" when I hug her.

"Katey, I need to get an annulment in the Church first. Will you be a witness for the Church tribunal?"

"Yes, of course I will. Just tell me where and when."

I love the way he treats her. They deserve each other and all the happiness they can catch. Wonder how non-Catholic Keith likes the idea of the tribunal?

~~~

As soon as they leave, I call Dan, as arranged. He is as excited as a kid with a pony when he arrives. He looks around at my humble surroundings. "You live here?"

I'm not sure of the implication of his question. "Yes, this is 'Home Sweet Home.' So, tell me about your new office."
~~~

"You'll have to see it for yourself," he answers proudly as he puts his hand on the doorknob, encouraging me to hurry.

Dan has a nice office and a good location. I compliment both.

"Thanks for the push," he says, as I look around the reception area. "I needed a push to get out of Pacific Estates. That place was killing me."

"I know what you mean." I laugh, but it isn't funny.

He uncovers a paper on his drafting table. "I wanted to show you what I'm going to paint on my door. "McKenzie, McKenzie & Anderson Architects" is drafted on the paper.

I am taken back. He included my parents. They would have been proud to work with him.

"I thought your parents would like it. I just added my name to theirs," he says proudly looking at the paper, then to me. "This is your dad's old drafting table from high school. I found it in the storeroom upstairs—the one down the hall from our rooms."

"Yes, they would be very proud." Not for one minute do I think he is using the McKenzie name for anything other than a tribute to my parents, his uncle and aunt. He is different from his brother and sister. It is almost as if they aren't related, but all three look like McKenzie descendants, even if they don't bear the name.

"I can never thank you properly."

I am not used to such sentimentality from the McKenzie side of the family. It is an awkward moment of silence. Then, he hugs me. Finally, there is a connection with one of my McKenzie cousins. My eyes mist. Maybe I will invite him to Thanksgiving in the park and show him how family can be. I'll think about it.

"Do good with what you have, be happy, that's thanks enough."

~~~

This week seems to go on forever. I'd like to say today is Friday, but it is only Thursday. Keith calls, as Sam and I are on our way north to the mansion. His friend is on vacation, but Keith thinks the FBI might be a better choice than the Justice Department and its federal marshals.

As soon as Keith says it, it rings true. Sam and I agree with his advice. The one thing for sure is, if there is a problem, I don't know its size or its form. I hope that the probe doesn't make things worse.

"There has to be a way to investigate the three companies without tipping our hand and allowing the evidence to be hidden, or worse—destroyed," I confide to Sam.

Another question I have is, "Can the government handle this without making it worse?" I've outgrown my belief that systems work as they should. I know a little dead girl who is proof of that.
~~~

Zoe calls. The officers are at the mansion and looking for Tim. "Is he home?" *What's next*, I whisper. "Zoe, keep them away from Grandfather. See if Brooke is home, and have them talk with her."

"She's not going to like that," Zoe says.

"Yes, I agree, but she will simply have to do it, if she is there. Tell them I am about thirty minutes away. Call me if there is a problem. And, thanks for keeping me informed." I band-aid the situation for thirty minutes.

Sam and I discuss Chico. The first piece of confirmable information Chico finds, he is out of there. Desperate people can be ruthless. At the moment, Chico is my major concern.

Just as we are about to call Chico's cell and see how he is, my cell rings again. This time it is Mark, a pleasant diversion. He wants to get together tomorrow night. I can't make any promises yet—it's too early in the day. However, Mark is willing to be flexible. What a great guy.

"Let's get to the mansion before anything else happens," Sam says.

"No kidding!" I agree.

"Seriously, I think your Grandfather has to be told when we go to the FBI. Don't you?"

"I agree, we need to tell him. We don't have anything more than suspicions. I am not ready to act on the FBI." I look at him squarely. "I'll tell you when the time is right."

"Are you worried about his reaction?" He won't let it go.

"I have no idea how Grandfather will react. He almost always responds differently than I expect. Oh! I forgot about calling Chico!"

While I dial Chico's number, Sam has an afterthought. "You don't think your Grandfather is involved, do you?"

That possibility hadn't even crossed my mind. Damn.

"He is definitely ruthless. I can't predict what he is going to do next. He is a 'rule' man. He likes to set the rules, but I can't imagine him cheating. No, I don't think he is involved. He would be stealing from himself." I answer without conviction in my voice. Now I have a new worry. How much information should I trust to Grandfather?

Chico doesn't answer his phone, so I leave a message for him to call me. It will probably be best for him to pick the time and place to make the call.

At the gate to the mansion, a sheriff vehicle meets us. They left a subpoena for me to appear at the next hearing for the shooter. "Oh great! One more thing to juggle."

Sam laughs.

Does he want to trade places with me? Then, we'll see how much he laughs.

Race is excited about putting the info into the computer. He thinks he'll have it by the end of tomorrow. He has come a long way since his days at Spirit of Hope.

Zoe arranges my schedule for court and the next flight meeting. Grandfather is in the library. I join him and work at the library table, so we will be in proximity to each other.

Race has done a great job mimicking the report on the other two suspect companies like Chico generated on Seattle. The information certainly looks similar to the Seattle information. I take a thoughtful sip of my coffee, and massage the back of my neck—damn headaches. If Chico finds a specific red flag in Seattle, then I think we'll proceed in investigating the other two. Maybe even send him in there under another name. Wonder if we can do that. I mean, legally change his identity temporarily.

~~~

Brooke storms into the library like a whirlwind. "What do you think you're doing, helping the police find Timmy, you gold-digging bitc—" her admonishment is cut short by Grandfather.

"That is enough, Brooke," Grandfather says forcefully as he lowers his newspaper to his lap.

Brooke stops short. "But, Grandfather—"

"Where is Timmy, and what has he done this time?" He coldly looks at Brooke, and I wouldn't want to mess with him in the mood he's in.

"I'm not telling you, old man!"

"If you can't be civil, pack your things and get out." He settles the matter without so much as batting an eye.

"Well, maybe I will."

"Yes. You will. And, you will today."

It's clear she pushed him as far as he is going to let her push. Grandfather looks directly at her.

Brooke looks at me with a hateful glare, questions my parentage again, then leaves angrily—not saying another word to Grandfather.

I let out a deep breath. I can tell she is as hurt as angry. She doesn't really hate me, just the threat she perceives. I had hoped to show her that I wasn't a threat, and also trim her jet-setting life of drugs and lack of direction. She needs a role model, but now I won't have the opportunity to reach her.

"Kathryn, she has no right to talk to you like she does."

"I understand. She's just afraid that I'm going to disrupt her world."

"She is out of line. I thought you would put her in her place the first time, but you didn't. Now, I have had enough." He opens his paper again, obviously finished with the conversation.
~~~

I'm not finished yet. "I was hoping to reach her. She's scared." I talk to the back of the newspaper—since I can only see the top of his head.

He lowers the paper enough to look directly at me.

"Tell Eleanor to have the locks changed today and change the code on the gate." He is obviously finished with the discussion and not willing to give Brooke another chance.

"All right." I leave to follow his wishes.

~~~

Eleanor understands the situation. She says that is what happened with his daughter, Brooke's mother. I tuck away the new information on my aunt. We decide that only the house staff, Eleanor, James, and Louise need keys—and me of course. There is always someone in the mansion to let everyone else in. Grandfather is never left alone.

Since Eleanor is in the mood to provide family history, I ask about Grandfather's confinement to the wheelchair.

"Eleanor, did Grandfather have a stroke?"

"When your grandmother died, he stopped making an effort to walk. Before that he used the wheelchair only when out of the house, as necessary. Why do you ask?"

"Just curious."

~~~

Grandfather may be ready to shut the door on Brooke, but I'm not. He should learn that his way of excommunicating his family doesn't work very well. It's what he did with my father too.

I climb the stairs to the third floor and knock on Brooke's door.

"Go away!" she screams.

"Brooke, I want to talk to you." The door isn't locked. I doubt she really wants to be left alone. I open her door partway.

"I don't want to talk to you."

"Then listen—I'll talk," I say, entering the room.

It's obvious she has been crying. She isn't as hardcore as she would like everyone to think. She drops the clothes she is packing, and looks submissive—something I hadn't expected.

"Brooke, let's not burn bridges between us. You know what happened to our parents. We don't have to continue that tradition. Like it or not, we're family. We just need time to get to know each other."

She sniffs and wipes her nose. She's embarrassed, but she says nothing.

"You deserve a life better than this." I pull a Maggie-trick and get right to the heart of the matter. "When the party ends, it feels empty, doesn't it? What do you really want to do with your life?" The question is more for her to consider than to be answered.

Brooke lets out a whimpering breath. “I don’t know,” she says in a frustrated tone.

“If you like the beach, we can see if there is an apartment near mine. You can sort out what you want from life. It’s peaceful, healthy. You don’t have to stay there permanently. Just a thought.”

“I’d like that.” She smiles slightly and wipes her eyes.

“You can stay at my apartment a day or two while you get your own apartment. There are several complexes in the same neighborhood. Pack your stuff. Put some of it in my car. After work, I’ll help you move and show you my neighborhood, okay?”

“Okay.”

She responds to me better than she ever has. Brooke just needs a big sister right now. This is my chance to show her what family is supposed to be. And, I’m not going to let Grandfather continue to wipe out all the members of his family, one by one, except Dan and me.

“I need to get back to work. Catch me later, okay?” I want to pat her shoulder. I have pushed my luck enough, so I restrain the urge of further connect. I know that we will still have ups and downs. I just caught her with her defenses down. I know we’ll have a big issue when I broach her drug problem. As matriarch of the family, I want to fulfill my duties well.

I turn back to say something about Tim, but think better of it. She’s right. I did give the police Mrs. Bailey’s contact information. How was I to know he was staying with her?

~~~

“Grandfather, I’m going to stay at the beach tonight and this weekend.”

He tips his paper slightly, then goes back to reading. He still pours over the financial pages, and watches the hard news for coming trends that will benefit him financially. He has his investments and two companies of his own, but the bulk of the McKenzie empire is mine. I can’t understand why Grandmother left everything to me, and nothing to her daughter or other grandchildren. My maternal Grandmother would have never behaved that way. With her, it is share and share alike. One for all and all that.

~~~

I’ll see if dinner tomorrow night will work for Mark. Since I am going to be at the beach it is much easier for us to go out, than when I am at Pacific Estates. I am relieved he is available. In light of everything else, Mark seems to be rather tame—even with his alternate persona. I wonder if Brooke would like to meet Scourge.

~~~
~~~

There are apartments available in my complex. I don't have the numbers to the complexes in the neighborhood. Brooke might not want to be my immediate neighbor. I hope she will make friends with the beach and somehow find herself there. We can have dinner at the pier tonight. In the morning, I'll teach her to walk the beach. I hope the beach and the ocean become her new drug of choice.

~~~

The day with Brooke has gone surprisingly well. She decides to get an apartment at the complex one street away, rather than where I live—lived. Dan comes and helps move her things to her apartment. They decide to go shopping for furniture for her new beginning. She hasn't squandered all of her allowance, since the planes and the yacht were on my tab.

It was a surprise that Brooke seems to enjoy the beach this morning. She looks around with an abandon that I had not expected from her. She collects a pocketful of shells. I risk discussing her new beginning and suggesting new friends that aren't rich brats idling away their life with drugs and parties. Of course, I said it better than that. She denies a drug problem, which is a typical response.

Brooke confides she has always wanted to be a grade school teacher, like her mother. Both items are news to me. I would like to meet her parents sometime. I suppose that, too, will come. It almost seems my larger duty as heir is to bring the family back together. Could Grandmother McKenzie had hoped for this, or had she only desired managing the money?

With an allowance of one hundred thousand dollars a year, Brooke doesn't have to work. In theory, she could go to school full-time and live comfortably. Dan encourages his sister to have a worthwhile life.

Dan and Brooke go out to dinner, while Mark and I go elsewhere. Mark really is a nice person. When I get through the initial crisis period of the first couple of quarterly reports, I will spend more energy getting to know him.

We go to a little out-of-the-way restaurant. It is nice and quiet. Mark talks about taking his music in another direction—thank God. The hard part is to ditch the Scourge persona. Scourge is extremely popular and the music, such as it is, has been lucrative.

Someone, a tourist, I think, takes our snapshot. Mark leans over to smile for the camera. The lady is delighted that we allow the photo. She asks for an autograph. I decline, but allow a photo of her with me. It's strange that anyone would want a photo with me.

"How do you like being a celebrity?"

"Oh, Mark! It's a thrill a minute, an absolute thrill!"
~~~

"It is harder than it looks, isn't it?" His voice becomes consoling.

"How do you manage it so well?" I ask, truly hoping for a clue to survival.

He smiles a cheesy grin. "For a musician, it's a dream come true. It sells CDs!" He leans forward. "Without fans, there is no one to hear the music. I might as well sit in my room and play to the walls."

"That's true for you, but I don't need fans."

"It is part of the responsibility of being who you are. They need to have people to dream about, to reach for, to make sense of things that life is—that it can be better than it is now." He trumps me.

"Isn't that sad? Living vicariously, I mean?"

"Support charities that make life better for people. You'll feel better. A person really doesn't need the kind of money we have. It only makes sense out of things, if you use it to help others."

"I agree. I've been so busy, that I haven't had the time to do more than I was doing before the big announcement." I say it as if it is the black plague—"big announcement."

"It will come. You'll get things under control, soon. Be patient with yourself and the new world you're in."

We talk nothing more about the duty of being rich. I can't believe I confided in him. Even more so, I am surprised he understood what I am going through.

The food is good. I decline the wine, since I have taken so much medication for my nagging headache. When we get up to leave, I am a little dizzy. Mark grabs me to keep me from going to the floor. The dizziness passes quickly. I just needed some air.

"Okay, what was that about?" he asks when we get to his car.

"I don't know, low blood sugar or something."

"Right. You just ate. It isn't low blood sugar."

"Practicing medicine now, are you?"

"Yes," he says.

He drives away from the direction of my apartment.

"Where are you going?"

"To my parents' house. My dad is a doctor."

I set him straight. "I don't need a doctor. A good night's sleep and a few days at the beach is what I need."

"Don't bother to argue. We're going—that's all there is to it."

~~~

Oh cute. Mark's dad, Dr. Armstrong, has a happy face sticker on his stethoscope. Good Lord, he's a pediatrician. All that aside, he thinks my blood pressure may have dropped suddenly, but it's temporary. It's still slightly low, but nothing to worry about for now. Mark tells him that I've
~~~

been having headaches—the big blabbermouth. Dr. Armstrong's brow furrows. He tells me to see my physician as soon as possible. I promise that I will.

Mark takes me to my apartment. He makes me promise again to call my doctor on Monday. The timing isn't good, but the advice probably is. Mark insists he should stay with me for a while. I am worn out—he has to leave—I'm going to bed.

Brooke calls and says she is staying with Dan tonight. I get the rest of the evening in peace. I take a deep breath and enjoy the quiet. I consider shutting off my cell phone. I'll do it when I get up. It feels good to sit here with my feet resting on the coffee table, sipping coffee. My main thought is on walking the beach in the morning. Ah, this is restful.

~~~

Sunday morning on the beach is unusually chilly. A summer rain comes early, before daybreak. I welcome the fresh, new-earth smell after a rain. When I was growing up, the air was choked with smog; we call it haze now, and rain clears the air. The memories are a pleasant escape from the present.

In many ways, I am standing on the threshold of a new beginning—not only for me, but for the McKenzie legacy. An added bonus is that two of my three cousins are embarking on a new life—I guess Tim is, too, in his own way. What is ahead, I can't imagine. Maggie says I interpret life as a movie; always wanting a knight in shining armor to gallop in and save the day, for good to triumph over the bad guys. Sometimes I do think it would be easier if the good guys wore white hats, so I can tell who they are.

As I walk back to my apartment, it begins to sprinkle again. Life is good, not always easy, but life is very good. Before I head north to the other side of my life, I stop to attend Mass in our neighborhood church.

~~~

Monday reminds me of the stunt where the actor is dancing and runs up the wall and does a back flip, and keeps dancing as if any of us could do the same without missing a beat. I set the beat at the mansion. And, if necessary, I will run up the wall, flip, and land on my feet.

Chico finally returns my call while I am in the garden with my coffee. He thinks he can infiltrate the mailroom computer for remote access, and carve a backdoor into the server from his wireless laptop. He has created a specific program that will activate tonight when the Seattle company uploads their end-of-the-month reports to the corporate office computer system.

If I understand him, the backdoor program will go into the corporate system along with the Seattle reports. Basically, it acts like very specific spyware. From his laptop, Chico will be able to monitor the Seattle computer system. From within the corporate office system, he can send the same program to any of our companies as they link with corporate.

The backdoor can give Chico access to anywhere in the McKenzie Enterprises computers. As soon as he knows it works, he'll be on a plane for home. Good work, Chico. Hurry home!

He can get through the firewall, but cautions if the in-house security tech notices it, it'll be short-lived. We'll have to download as much as possible tonight and get the less important files second. I don't know how long it will take to dissect the information, but I am hoping to know soon whether to turn over the info to higher powers or institute new accounting protocols.

We definitely need to hire a new auditing firm. Once it's determined which computer in the L.A. office is exchanging cooked books for the real ones, Chico will link to that computer and monitor all information exchanges from it. If there are no automatic triggers, then we'll begin with the companies with government contracts.

Let's see, there was Mrs. Bailey, the press, the yacht, Mark, the cousins, the shooting, the conspiracy: I'd say that was a full test. It seems I pass my ninety-day probation in this new life, figuratively speaking.

No contact from Brooke today, but that isn't uncommon for her. At least she is doing something besides getting into trouble. Dan makes me the most proud. I think the only two things unfinished are the shooter's trial and Tim. Maybe things will settle down to a normal roar.

~~~

Karen calls. "Karen, I'm sorry. I haven't written your reference yet. Oh, okay. I'll wait to hear from the tribunal first."

"Actually, I called to remind you of Linda and Todd's Halloween party. I thought you might want to get started now, if you wanted Dana to make something."

"I totally forgot, thanks for reminding me."

"You're going, aren't you?" She catches on quickly.

"I haven't given it any thought. What's the theme?" I ask.

"You'll love this—favorite movie character!"

"That is a very good theme! Who are you going as?"

"There are so many great choices, I don't know yet. What about you, any ideas off the top of your head?"

"Ah, maybe Katharine Hepburn or I might take a trip to Casablanca —I'm not sure."

"You do a good Katharine Hepburn impression. Dana won't tell me who she is going to be." Karen laughs. "Are you going with Scourge?"
~~~

"No, I'll go solo." I can't believe she asked that. We are definitely not an item.

"Good. Andy will be there." She tries to be coy, but isn't.

"I know—'he's dreamy.' That is probably why he was married last Valentine's Day. You are too much, I need to get back to work before you start trouble," I say to end this matchmaking discussion.

"Oh, all right. See you later."

Every time I think things are perfect, something happens. I do my best to mind my own business, and here comes trouble.

Karen has been as giddy as a schoolgirl since she and Keith became engaged. She wears love well, but some of us have work to do. I don't need her help to get into trouble.

~~~

My phone rings again. Now what is Karen up to? It's Mark wanting to know if I have called my doctor. Mark is an annoying mother hen.

"Sorry, I forgot, but I will do it as soon as we hang up," I promise.

True to my word, I call my doctor and tell the nurse the reason for the appointment. If there's a cancellation, I'll take it. Otherwise, it will be three weeks before they can get me in to see the doctor. Fine with me.

~~~

For the last three days, Chico has been generating reams of raw data. His little virus, mole, or whatever it is, is working perfectly and he is downloading the accounting department's records. The firewall hasn't stopped the intrusion. That's certainly something we'll have to fix in all our computer systems.

I'm not sure there is enough coffee on the planet for this job, but Louise is keeping up with the demand for the steamy brew. I review this year's numbers from Seattle. Sam has last year's, and Grandfather is going over the year before that.

Grandfather seems to enjoy being in the thick of things. His suggestions of what line items to cross-reference first is extremely helpful. He has cut at least a week off of the process already. He loves it too. He has a sparkle in his eyes, and if he could walk, I bet he would have a bounce in his step. He remarks he feels ten years younger. He looks it too.

The only two correlations Chico finds in the companies Race red-flagged are they both have government contracts for the same project and are owned by McKenzie Enterprises. One manufactures microchip components, the other has a secretive military contract.

There's nothing suspicious on the third company. We are unable to find connections among senior staff. There isn't obviously questionable email among the companies. Chico thinks they must use an encrypted tag file piggybacked onto innocent-looking email. It sounds mysteriously sophisticated for a gang of thieves.

When a fourth company, one in Kentucky, shows the same financial problems with cost overruns and bookkeeping practices, we begin to look more intensely toward the corporate office. Chico gets Race independent on running the downloads. Sam focuses on the Texas plant, while Chico takes Tennessee and Kentucky. We test our new phone system and pull Zoe from her desk to help Chico.

~~~

Eleanor catches me on the way to the patio for fresh air and a cup of coffee. She starts with returning the book I loaned her. She knows something is "afoot" and wants to know if we need her help. I hesitate for a moment under the guise of thoughtfully sipping my coffee, not sure what to say.

She points to the book and says Grandmother has written a note to me inside.

I look inside the first few pages. Nothing is there, so I hand the book to Eleanor to find the page.

She quickly flips through the pages and easily finds it. We put our heads together and read:

> "Kathryn, the key to your question is in this book."
> She signs the note with her initials.

I look at Eleanor. She shrugs and shakes her head.

"Kathryn, your grandmother confided in me that she was putting everything in your name—the mansion, everything. If something happened to Mr. McKenzie, I was to contact an attorney, B-something, Branson, Bradley—I have his name in my room. I can show you her note, if you like." She pleads the case of her trustworthiness.

"Mr. Bradford?"

"Yes, that sounds right."

I know she is telling the truth, because I have told no one that I own Pacific Estates. It is unlikely Grandfather would have told anyone that all of this is not his.

"We could use the help. Let me finish this coffee. What about Stanley?"

"Stanley is as good as gold, miss." She vouches for the butler with a calm, but proud stance. I know she loves to read mysteries, so vouching for the butler is saying a lot. I am sure she hopes to see herself as a female Dr. Watson in what is occurring in the library. We need a Dr. Watson.
~~~

"Good. I need Stanley and Garrett to cover the windows in the library. Chico has some kind of film that is difficult to detect, but no one can electronically eavesdrop through the glass. I have something you can help with, too." I want to confirm her usefulness. She beams with excited loyalty.

"You can trust all the house staff; Mrs. McKenzie hired us."

"What about Conner?"

"He isn't very bright, but he is good with Mr. McKenzie."

"All right, then. Thank you."

Garrett passed inspection the first time I met him. So, we have our knights of the McKenzie round table—or library tables. These are "Kathryn the Great's knights," no Lancelot among them. Grandfather beams approval of my realm.

Stanley and Garrett cover the library windows with Chico's special film. Then they cover the lower half of the library windows with butcher paper donated by Louise. The thick, waxy paper is perfect. It's opaque, but the white color still lets in light. I'm guessing the point of the butcher paper is to make it harder for a sharpshooter. I don't ask.

Eleanor supervises Garrett and Stanley as they set up the easels and place the huge tablets on them. The two whiteboards are hung where priceless art hung only an hour ago. We'll rehang the art after each meeting and lock everything in my office at all times, when we aren't using it.

After lunch we have a meeting in the library where Chico outlines assignments. Only Chico, Sam, Grandfather, and I know the purpose behind our activity.

Eleanor has the neatest handwriting, so she is designated the official scribe. Grandfather watches Eleanor organize her markers, and all of the other activity in the room. It obviously energizes him.

Garrett was a business major in college, until his football injury his senior year ended his education a semester short of graduation. He becomes my designated hitter, and takes my place with the Seattle data once Sam gets him orientated. Zoe gets Stanley, "her apprentice," settled with the new phone system, and he is temporarily in charge of the house.

Eleanor doesn't seem to mind Stanley in her domain, now that she is involved in something mysterious. As for me, I free myself to oversee the process, check on Race, and eventually substitute for Grandfather if he tires—not to mention, my eyes could use the break.

By the time of our afternoon break, we have gathered enough information for Sam and me to see a pattern emerging in the administration of the government contracts in the Seattle company.

Chico focuses on a couple of glaring line items found in the other three companies. We direct the focus exclusively on the administration of government contracts with the four companies.

We continue to collect information from other McKenzie Enterprise companies and Kathryn McKenzie companies. Chico spends time with Race to re-adjust his computer searches, but we will hold that information until we complete the in-house, informal audits on the four companies we have started. Zoe checks on Stanley, who is proudly sitting at her desk, then helps Eleanor set up for what's next, after we all have a break and some of Louise's hot apple crisp, fresh from the oven.

The sinfully delicious aroma is probably what encouraged us to find a stopping place. Congregated around the kitchen table and the kitchen island, my knights are all beaming with pride of purpose. Even though most of my knights have no idea what we are doing, they are eager to be engaged in the process. This activity, even more than the shooting incident, has forged us into a single-minded unit.

~~~

Mark calls. I go out to the patio with my coffee and cell phone for a bit of privacy and sunshine. His youngest brother is in a theatre group, and the dinner theatre is hosting a fund-raising dinner on Sunday evening.

"We can take him to dress rehearsal Saturday afternoon, then find something to do that evening. You could spend the weekend at the beach." Mark, the tempter, doesn't ask about the doctor.

With the week I foresee, he wouldn't have had to go to such dramatics to convince me to take the weekend off and away from the mansion. I accept his offer of a diversion.

"Sounds great, but I won't get down there until late Friday night. I have a full week ahead of me."

"Did you call your doctor?"

Ah, I knew it was too good to be true that he wouldn't pester me.

"Yes sir, I did. Three weeks at the latest, sooner if there is a cancellation."

"Okay, okay. You win," he says.

"Sorry, I didn't mean to be so abrupt."

"You sound stressed."

"I am, a little. But—"

"Do you want me to come and take you to dinner?" Mark interrupts.

"Thanks, you're sweet. I'm going to bed early tonight."

"Sure?"

"Yes, I'm sure. Thanks though."
~~~

After dinner, I return to the library. My mind is too tired to work, but I sit with a cup of coffee looking over the fruits of our labors. My eyes move from one easel to the next, hoping I will see something we missed before. God bless Eleanor, she has everything color coded and very neat. She was a perfect choice for scribe.

~~~

Tuesday and Wednesday are carbon copies of Monday. We make great progress. We are organized and engaged in our tasks. Thursday, I have Eleanor use the whiteboards to create graphs of the boiled-down data. We graph the materials cost and overruns, delivery deadlines and tardiness of the companies in question. She catches on quickly. We could have used the software to do the graphs, but walking though it is better, less likely to miss something by manually creating them.

I begin to list the people at each of the four companies whose names appear on the email address lists at any other of the four companies. The first and second list have one name in common, simple enough if the pattern is consistent throughout the sample. The third company shares one name with each of the first two lists, but they are different names. If I am correct, the fourth will have a name in common with each of the other companies, but again there will be no duplication.

My hypothesis is correct. There are three people at one company, each communicating with one person at one of the other companies.

I remove all the names and start a Venn diagram with the Seattle name that communicates to Texas, the second who communicates with Kentucky, and the third Seattle person who communicates with Tennessee. I do the same with the other three companies. I am left with three names in each company.

The McKenzie employee list on the laptop is by department. I sort them alphabetically. There are no matching names to whom "the twelve" send emails.

I'm disappointed. I thought we were onto something. That's enough for today. We are all tired and stop an hour early.

Grandfather asks me to stay after the others leave the library. We look at the charts and lists posted around the room.

"Kathryn, what do you see?"

"I see patterns, but I can't put together the centralized element."

"Do you think it is a random pattern?" he asks.

"No, I think there is some connection—I just don't know what it is."

"Then, let's call the FBI, the Justice Department, whoever Sam and Keith say we should call. We know enough to know that there is a problem. Let them take it from there. Otherwise, someone will pitch a fit because we waited to call them."
~~~

"Yes, you're right. I'll call them tomorrow," I say.

"You did a good job on this project. I'm proud of you."

"Thanks, Grandfather." I turn his wheelchair toward the door.

After dinner, I return to the locked library. I lean back in the leather chair and sip my coffee—looking at the schematics on the walls and thinking about the activity of the week.

With my cup drained, I replace the whiteboards with the art that had been temporarily removed—erasing any sign of the week's activities. I stash all our evidence in the office and lock the door. I think we have all earned a short day tomorrow. And, I am spending the weekend at the beach.

This alleged corruption in the companies has taught me that I don't want my life full of complications. This has not been enjoyable. The only good from it is that the household staff are now my staff. Since I am paying the expenses of the house and the staff, it is nice to know that they are loyal to me.

Zoe makes copies of the materials to give the FBI. Chico moves his operation upstairs to his office. Since we still have the backdoor open, he and Race will continue compiling information on all of the McKenzie properties, manufacturing and intellectual. We don't mention that we haven't removed our hidden portal. I don't want any more surprises, I have to get control of this conglomeration—it has been on autopilot far too long.

~~~

While I'm walking in the garden with my morning coffee, I visit Garrett in the garage. He is hand-washing my limo. Garrett always brings my Mustang to the front when I'm going out. I've never been to the garage, and this seems like the prefect time to check out the place.

He proudly gives me the nickel tour. It is no surprise that everything is in its place and orderly. Garrett utilizes his business sense to manage his corner of the realm.

"Wow, what are all of these cars?" I ask in amazement at the fleet as I survey the lot of them.

"This one was your grandmother's car." He points to a Bentley relic. "This was your grandfather's until he bought the new limo," he points to it. "That is, of course, your limo. But, this is the prize."

He removes the cover from a cream-colored Jag with crimson and biscuit interior.

"What is this?" I ask looking at the gleaming chrome of the beautiful two-seat convertible.

"This," he extends his hand proudly, "this, is a '53 Jaguar roadster XK," he says as if he is speaking of his first love.
~~~

He walks around the car, touching it as if it is a beautiful goddess, opening the engine compartment, the trunk complete with the stock toolbox from the factory, and finally the driver's door. "Try her out."

I slide behind the large steering wheel, rubbing my hand across the leather seat beside me. It truly is a marvelous vehicle. I can't reach the clutch when I sit back in the seat, and the seat isn't adjustable. I guess, one size fits all.

"Your father drove this in college." He beams, gently touching it on the door he opened for me.

"Really!" I look at the car again with more admiration.

He grins widely. "We had a lot of fun with this car."

Opening the door and sliding out, I ask, "Does she run?"

"Oh yes, I keep her in perfect shape."

"Then, let's take her for a spin," I say needlessly, since he already has slid into the driver seat and has her fired up the minute I got out.

I set my coffee on the workbench and call the house to report to Zoe our impending disappearance.

The passenger seat is surprisingly roomy for a sports car. The gauges in the wooden dashboard are streamlined and sleek, with overstated chrome typical for the '50s. Exempt from the seat belt laws, it is strange to sit without a lap and shoulder belt.

Garrett proceeds down the drive, turns right to head north up the hill, across the WPA bridge, and along winding Highway One, with the Pacific Ocean dropping below to our left. Garrett doesn't seem to notice the lack of power steering as we take the narrow curves on the two-lane PCH in considerable excess of the speed limit. There is only one way to drive this car on this road, and that is fast. If I had a scarf over my hair, trailing behind me and rhinestone sunglasses, we could be out of an old movie.

I don't ask, but I can imagine Father walked away from this car that he loved when Grandfather disapproved of Mother. I imagine them in this car. I try not to think about the fun Dad and Garrett had with it before their wives arrived on the scene. But I see those two cruising Sunset Strip in style, slow enough to catch the girls' attention.

When we return to the garage, I look over the fleet again. "Who owns all of these vehicles?"

"You do," he answers and pulls out the registration. It reads, "A. Kathryn McKenzie and/or Kathryn McKenzie Trust."

"All of them? Are you serious?"

My eyes widen and my jaw drops. It makes sense, but I still can't quite grasp all this wealth is mine. "Wow."

"Yes, ma'am."

"We don't need all of these cars. We'll keep Grandfather's limo, my Mustang and limo, and the Jag. I do like Grandmother's Bentley, maybe we'll keep it too. Garrett, I need advice on selling everything else."

"There's Barrett-Jackson auction in Phoenix or there are companies that purchase cars to lease to movie companies."

"I like the possibilities of the cars being in a movie. Let's take that route. And, thanks for the drive. It was fun! We will definitely do that again." I recover my abandoned coffee.

Today seems like a good day to deliberately begin to simplify the excess that started with the sale of the yacht.

Liquidating a few companies isn't going to happen over night, more like five to ten years. We'll have to consider tax consequences, sale prices, and what to do with the cash. Most of the money will go into my Foundation, but I have to consider the operating cost of the mansion. It's much too large for me, not to mention it is too far from my beach, but I will keep it as long as Grandfather is alive. It isn't an immediate problem, but I need to be apprised on the household expenses.

The alleged conspiracy theory in the companies still entices me to want to sell my stock in the public companies where things are even more out of control, but I'll wait, the timing is off for that. I'm sure it would make the news if I did anything to my stock portfolio right now. We don't need that kind of press.

~~~
~~~

~ CHAPTER 11 ~

Bellwether

Things are back to normal at the mansion, if normal is an adjective that should be used in the same sentence as anything "McKenzie." Rather, I should say that everything is back in the comfort zone for those of us who are connected to the mansion.

I'm happy to take time to go home to the beach. As the mansion disappears from my rearview mirror and the miles between me and the beach decrease, I think about what I leave behind me: the McKenzie money curse. Grandmother wasn't able to marry her artist lover because he was from a lesser social class. Who knows what the story is about my aunt and uncle who live in a commune—one way or another, it suggests an abandonment of the family money.

Dan, though educated, was trapped in the mansion like he had an albatross around his neck. The limitless wealth hasn't served Brooke or Tim well. Drugs, booze, and who knows what else as they jet-set around the world robbed them of purpose, direction, and meaning to their lives.

Grandfather has no intimate relationships with his family. I am the closest to him, yet he keeps me at arm's length. As for me, the family money took my life away, and I terribly miss the simplicity it had.

~~~

The weekend with Mark goes well. We have a casual dress rehearsal. Of course, the actual production is adorable, and Scourge is nowhere to be seen. Being with Mark is less complicated, since he isn't switching between both personalities.

Mark gives me a signed copy of his new CD. How sweet is that? Not only is the cover art in questionable taste, I hope I'm not struck deaf by the content of the lyrics.

~~~

The Monday morning meeting with the FBI agent is less intimidating than I expected. Agent Dexter is a young, clean-cut, bright-looking kid —probably only one year out of law school. He listens carefully as I explain my purpose for contacting the agency. He seems clueless until I point out that each of the companies are having "trouble" with creative bookkeeping when it comes to their government contracts. He brings in his supervisor, Agent Davies.

Agent Davies is a woman a litter older than I am. She is wearing a government-issue-looking black suit. Instantly she bristles and takes command. Her primary interest is questioning why I have brought this problem to them. She is skeptical of my motives and doesn't bother to hide her skepticism. I guess I should have taken this to the securities people. It figures. Oh well.

I say, "Thank you for your time." I stand and extend my hand to Agent Davies, then to Agent Dexter, and gather my stuff.

"What are you trying to pull here?" Agent Davies asks in a condescending tone.

"I am not '*pulling*' anything. Now, if you'll excuse me, I have another meeting." Sam opens the door, into a big room where we walk between the row of cubicles. An older, balding man is approaching in the narrow walkway. He hesitates when he sees me, seemingly recognizing my now-public face. After we pass each other, I overhear him ask Agent Davies what "Miss McKenzie wanted?"

As the elevator doors close, Agent Davies is hurriedly walking toward us. The look on her face is priceless when the doors close before she reaches them. I was not going to push the button to hold the door for her. It was hard not to smile until we started down.

During the descent to the lobby, we discuss the need to document our attempt to solicit their help to figure out what to do about the apparent embezzlement of government funds. Sam is sure this is going to blow up and get ugly before it's done. I just expected more fiscal responsibility for tax dollars. I thought the FBI would want to be involved in the process. At least she didn't scold me for our rudimentary in-house investigation.

Two men in black suits approach Sam and me as we leave the building. "Miss McKenzie?" the shorter man asks.

"Yes."

"Come with us."

I think of a quip remark about being kidnaped, but neither man strikes me as having a sense of humor. While we are waved through the security screening, Agent Davies walks out of the elevator.

She apologizes for her disregard as if she has been told to make reparations, and invites us back upstairs.

"I'm sorry, I really must go. Here is the information I brought. Call if you have questions."

I smile and hand her the file folder. She had her chance to pay attention the first time I presented the information, but oh no, she wasn't going to give us the time of day. There is no apparent reason for me to sit through another meeting. I had expected to be asked to leave the file anyway, so it's no great loss. The original is under lock and key at the mansion, she is welcome to the copy I brought.

On the trip back to the mansion, I try to listen to Mark's new CD. It is a good thing Sam is in his own car. The first song is crude and rather loud, even at the volume level still set for the previous CD. I skip forward to the second song and decrease the volume. The song is heavy metal, revisited. I skip to the next song. I grimace. It is the worst song yet. I can't hear myself think. That's enough for now.

The silence is a welcome relief. I wonder if the FBI is going to assign much priority to the information we compiled. Perhaps we should continue to figure out what is going on with the creative bookkeeping for ourselves.

Damn! I had hoped to give this problem to someone with the experience and resources to get to the bottom of what is going on in the four companies in question, and possibly the corporate office. One would think there would be more interest in how the government money is spent. I'll figure this problem out, but I am not spending the rest of my life babysitting these companies—or the FBI.

My doctor's office calls, they have a cancellation for today. I look at the clock on the stereo. I suppose I can make it on time if I turn back to the city now and don't run into any freeway snags. I call Zoe and Sam about the change in my plan, without being clear it is a doctor.

~~~

"Hello, Doc!" I hide my dislike for doctor appointments, although I do like my doctor.

"Katey, I ran into Dr. Armstrong at the hospital this morning. I hear you are having headaches—" his voice trails off as he palpates my neck below my ears, looks into my eyes, then pulls a penlight out of his pocket to check my pupillary reaction.

"Yes. Headaches, dizziness, and my visual acuity is diminishing." Might as well put all my cards on the table and figure out what we can do about these headaches.

"Open, say 'Ah.' Any trouble swallowing?" He continues his rudimentary examination.

When he finishes poking and palpating to his satisfaction, he excuses himself and leaves the room. He returns with a list of tests he wants done as soon as possible. He is referring me to a neurologist, and these are the tests they have agreed are necessary.

I call and check in with Zoe and Sam. With the fasting lab work early tomorrow, I'll stay at the beach tonight rather than at the mansion. Everything seems under control there. I tell them it is personal business and I will be back on Wednesday afternoon. There is no need to mention the word "doctor" yet.

~~~

Spending the afternoon on the beach will clear my mind from this morning's meeting and the problems behind it. It will help keep my mind off of the lab work and the MRI of my brain. Wednesday promises to be equally entertaining with a trip to the nuclear medicine department for more brain-investigating tests.

Thursday offers the shooter's court date. The prosecution hasn't had time to go through a witness prep with me. But I'm not worried about the witness stand—I have been on the stand a million times. The only questions that he can ask are relatively clear cut. I didn't see anything since I was lying across the front seat while bullets broke the windshield.

That leaves Friday to catch any urgent business I've missed this week. Grandfather will be due for some extra attention by then. He would never admit the need for family, but I can tell he enjoys the attention I give him. Maybe we will have time for a game of chess. He is a shrewd opponent. It's been a long while since our last game.

~~~

The September beach is lovely. The weather is warm. With school's resumption, the tourists are few. The sky is clear and a crisp, rich blue. There are no clouds or smog today. The warm sand feels good on my feet as I carry my shoes. After a while, I turn and walk back in the direction I've come—this time at the water's edge.

There are three people in the water wind sailing. They glide effortlessly over the water's surface. I imagine that I am gliding over the water, free of worry. The truth is that in addition to everything else, and as dismissive as I act, I am concerned about my headaches now that the doctors are alert about the situation. Their concern seems honest. I don't think it has anything to do with special treatment because of who I am.

~~~

After two days of tests, court is a welcomed change. Due to the media interest in the case—I suspect because of my involvement—Grandfather wants James to drive me to court. He still calls Garrett, "James." The darkened limo windows provide added privacy.

Neither the prosecution nor defense attorneys represent the interest of the witness, so Sam accompanies me to court. Lastly, Jim, my part-time bodyguard, rides in front with Garrett.

My cell phone rings as we are leaving the Pacific Estate driveway. It is the neurologist's office, they want me to come in today. Because I have court, the office staff settles for an appointment on Monday. She won't tell me the nature of the urgency, other than it's to go over my test results.

The phone call certainly upstages the court appearance. I hardly notice the swarming reporters who meet my limo at the courthouse steps. Jim moves them back while Sam guides me safely through without letting the media push me to answer their questions. I struggle to refocus my thoughts to the trial.

An Asian woman, in her mid-fifties, stops the prosecutor just before he enters the courtroom. She is speaking earnestly in a quiet voice. The prosecutor looks surprised, rubs his beard a minute, then asks her something. The scene holds my attention. The prosecutor seems troubled, but grateful for the information. The woman nods her head in agreement, then leaves hastily.

I have a feeling that was bad news. For a brief moment—I'm not sure why—I fear the shooter is going to get released today.

Inside the courtroom, the sketch artist is quickly catching the defendant and the Judge. Watching the sure, quick strokes distracts me from my concerns. The shooter has shed his disheveled appearance, but has a dull look of pharmaceutical influence on his demeanor. We are told to rise, court is in session.

After the docket is read and the preliminary statements are made by the Judge, she tells the court that the shooter was found competent to stand trial.

Sam filed a notice of appearance. The Judge remarks though it is unusual for a witness to be represented by an attorney, it will be allowed if there are no objections. Neither the prosecution or defense object. I feel better with Sam officially involved.

The State puts on its case, calling the officers and myself as witnesses. None of the State's witnesses are qualified to clearly address the insanity defense. To me, it seems like a gap in the prosecutor's case. Maybe it was covered adequately in the competency hearing, or some agreement was struck to stipulate to his mental health status. Clearly, I am more familiar with Juvenile Court. The only criminal cases I have experience with were putting away the worst child abusers.

The defense attorney cunningly cross-examines each witness, careful not to appear to attack me, the victim. It seems that he is still pursuing an insanity defense and doing a fairly decent job. I think he has won the jury's sympathy.

Since depositions weren't taken, Sam listens carefully to both sides to learn what would have been revealed during discovery.

The prosecution looks around the gallery, hesitates, then rests his case.

The defense makes a half-hearted motion for a directed verdict, citing the prosecution failed to make a prima facie case.

The Judge denies his motion to dismiss, thus requiring the defense to proceed. Their case is largely a parade of doctors explaining the shooter's mental illness and how he is no longer a threat, since he is on psychotropic medication and is stable. I have a different definition of "stable." But there is no hint of a technical error or mistrial to set him free today.

Just to be sure, I write a note to Sam that many mentally ill patients respond well to medication, so well, in fact, that they often stop taking their medication, thinking they no longer need it. Then, they are prone to another episode of their illness, and this guy is a threat to society when he is psychotic, especially when his auditory hallucinations tell him God says to kill me.

The prosecution's cross-examination is feeble attempts to discredit the defense witnesses, rather than to question the extent of the illness on the afternoon the shots were fired, or highlight that the shooter wasn't out-of-control crazy until the day after the shooting, or even that he has the real potential to be a threat again. Apparently, the young prosecutor was unaware of the propensity to stop taking psych drugs by psych patients.

Just as the defense rests, the Asian woman appears and quietly takes a seat on the prosecution side of the gallery.

The prosecutor sees her entrance, rises from his seat, then asks to re-cross the defense witness who administered the psychological tests.

"Now, Doctor—that's a Ph.D., isn't it?"

The witness answers "affirmative."

"Refresh my memory. The tests revealed the responses of someone with schizophrenia, is that correct?"

"Yes, there's no doubt he has schizophrenia."

"No doubt? No doubt whatsoever?"

"Absolutely none."

"Would it be accurate to say that there were no test answers that indicated anything, but schizophrenia?"

"Every answer pointed to schizophrenia, as I have already said." The witness' voice rises.

I know from experience, the witness is close to being designated as hostile, if he doesn't watch his tone with the prosecutor. That is not something he wants to do. The questions can become more pressing and harsh after that. Even though the witness is in his late thirties, he should know to be careful. He should be more experienced than to fall into the prosecutor's trap. Didn't the defense prep their witnesses?

A strange look comes over the witness' face. He must have realized how close to the line he was.

"Would it be correct to say that, in fact, the test answers were letter perfect? Even the questions built-in to weed out false test results?" The prosecutor shows where his questions are going.

The witness hesitates, ponders, his eyes open wide before he replies, "Why, yes. Yes, all the answers were perfect!"

The prosecutor has managed to get the psychologist to repeat his words. Well done. The witness is putty in his hands now. He is acting like a novice on the stand.

"Isn't that unusual? What conclusion would you draw from that?" The prosecutor is on a roll.

"Um, I would say that the test was invalidated," the doctor answers, his cheeks turn beet red.

"Invalidated by false answers, deliberate, planned answers?"

"I would venture that he studied the test and memorized the answers to look schizophrenic." He fidgets in his seat. "I should have noticed that he answered all the questions to look schizophrenic, paranoid schizophrenia." The witness foolishly volunteers information.

The prosecutor says, "That's it for this witness, Your Honor."

So, he faked schizophrenia? Why would anyone do that? I don't understand what just happened. I understand that the shooter is not really mentally ill—I don't understand why he would fake schizophrenia, or why he shot at me.

The shooter's wife's expression changes from concern to confusion. I watch as she looks toward her husband with questioning eyes, even though he is facing away from her.

The Judge is obviously pondering this new information. Her expression is neutral, but her eyes reveal she is thinking seriously about this new development.

Based on their expressions, most of the jury realize something just happened. Several have the look that "something isn't right here," but I am not sure they have moved beyond the schizophrenia question to the shooting question. I'm not sure what lies behind all of this information, but I hope the jury gets that things have drastically changed, that this was a deliberate shooting. The Church, the Pope, all of it was a ruse. I wish at least one of the jurors would have a spark of understanding on their faces. But they don't. They hardly look like they were paying attention.

At least the shooter is not going anywhere today. The Judge won't let him loose with this new information in evidence. It suits me fine, because I know he is the guy who was watching me and it makes a bit more sense that he faked mental illness than that he is mentally ill. The question remains: Why?

Court adjourns for the day. We'll be back tomorrow. The prisoner is ordered returned to his cell. The gavel falls. We rise. The Judge leaves. They remove the jury as we walk out in the other direction.

~~~

The sky has become overcast while we were in court. Sam and I walk down the stairs together. Jim is on the alert, walking slightly ahead of us. He keeps the journalists at bay, but they still shout questions at me until the prosecutor appears at the top of the stairs behind us. Then they go after him.

My thoughts land on the question of the shooter's fake mental illness. Then, on my health. This has been a draining week. During the ride back to the mansion, I should ask Sam for an update on the corporate conspiracy we have going on, but I'm too tired. It can wait.

~~~

Jim stays at the mansion. He has taken up residence in the guest room that I used before I came to live here. He seems calm and deliberate. He is cunning. I can almost see his mind working as he secures the house for the night.

Eleanor made it a point of privately mentioning to me how thorough Jim is. I think she is attracted to him. They are polite and businesslike toward each other, but their mutual attraction is apparent to anyone paying attention. He is younger than Eleanor, but I don't think she should let that get in the way.

~~~

Court starts with the prosecution calling a rebuttal witness, the Asian lady from the hallway yesterday. Basically, she is covering for the person who did the psychological testing for the State. The original tester is on their honeymoon. When reviewing the file for court prep, she noticed the test oddity. That's what sent the prosecution down the road that his cross-examination took yesterday.

There is no explanation for the shooting, which I find glaring—and unsettling. The one thing that is apparent is that it was not borne out of a hallucinogenic episode. Both sides deliver their closing statements, and we are done. But it doesn't feel finished.

The Judge instructs the jury and recesses for the weekend. In my opinion, the State didn't do an extraordinary job of addressing the motive for the shooting. We will have to wait and see how it turns out.

Of course, I am afraid that he may actually shoot me next time he gets the chance. In open spaces around the house, it would be hard to protect me from someone with a rifle. Almost all of his shots hit my car. Without the car for protection, I could have been killed. I turn to whisper to Jim, who keeps watching everyone rather than look at me. He agrees
~~~

to work for me exclusively until I stop listening to him. Then he will be gone. Fair enough.

It's not necessary that I'm in court when the verdict is read. I'll tell Jim I have an important meeting on Monday. I'll keep my doctor's appointment with the neurologist, instead of waiting for the jury at the courthouse. There is no guarantee that the jury will finish deliberating on Monday. I don't think they got whether or not this guy is guilty of attempted murder. Perry Mason could have done better and he isn't real. God, this is frustrating.

Again, we descend the stairs outside the courthouse. Jim takes the point. Garrett has the limo waiting. Sam walks beside me. None of us speak.

I watch the shooter's wife leave ahead of us. This time she is not able to escape the press. She desperately tries to move forward and ignore their hounding. Her husband has set her life in turmoil. Her sadness shows on her face and in the weight her body seems to carry from this place.

Suddenly, we hear a gunshot. Sam and Jim have me to the ground instantly—Jim covering me with his body. Everyone is down flat or crouched behind a car. A second, then a third shot echoes off the buildings. Officers are alert, scanning the crowd for a shooter. Quickly, someone is at the side of the shooter's wife, helping her up. It looks as if one of the reporters had pulled her down, then dropped to her side when the shots continued. An officer rushes to her. She looks shaken. Sam and Jim rush me to the limo where Garrett has left the door open and is back in the driver's seat for a quick escape.

I think about the shooter's wife. I remember how shaken I was when I heard the shots being fired at me by her husband. Was someone now shooting at her?

~~~

As soon as we return to the mansion, I tell Grandfather about hiring Jim full-time. He seems relieved.

However, Grandfather is disappointed the jury didn't finish what he considers a clear-cut decision. Either way, it's up to the jury now, and that's plenty reason for celebration. Grandfather agrees and has Sam mix highballs for them, while I mix myself a Cuba Libre, rum and Coke with lime. Libre, liberation! I wish.

I know Jim will be hard-pressed to protect me if the shooter is set free and proceeds to gun me down. He can fortify our defenses and educate us how to be more careful. There's not a lot more he can do. Our only hope is to catch the shooter before he gets to me. But I don't mention this. This shooter isn't the only nut in this fruitcake world. If he
~~~

can come this close to killing me, then someone else may do the same—or worse. Remove one and there will always be another to take his place.

~~~

It has been a hectic week and I feel the need for another weekend at the beach. I feel safe there, though it is wide open for a sniper, and the other guy was there watching me. Jim pitches a fit and gets to come with me.

Saturday morning early, I forgo the walk in the garden and drive directly home. I arrive in plenty of time to prepare Chicken Kiev with steamed fresh vegetables. Mark is visibly impressed with lunch. I remind him that I have not always been rich, and I have many useful skills. It is a harmless dig at his silver-spoon existence. He grins a sheepish little boy grin. He doesn't get any mileage out of the grin, but he is cute.

The afternoon is another clear-sky day. The water is enticing on this summer-warm fall afternoon. We walk close enough to the water's edge to feel the waves' spray. It is too much like a romantic movie to take off my shoes and walk in the water. I don't want to hint at romance, since Mark is becoming a comfortable friend. Besides, Jim is following us.

One minute we are walking and the next I feel dizzy. Not exactly dizzy, I feel hot and motion-sick. My face must have turned white or flushed, there is something about the way I look that prompts Mark to stop his story and ask if I am all right.

"I'm fine, just a little dizzy." I stop walking.

He turns squarely toward me. "Are you sure? This is the second or third time you have been dizzy lately."

With a forced smile I say, "I'm all right, really, I'm just a little tired. It was a long week."

~~~

The next thing I know, I feel hands on me, laying me flat on my back on a gurney of some sort. I want to tell them that my left ankle is turned funny and is hurting, but I can't speak. I can see them and myself in a detached third-person sort of way. I remember it being dark. My eyes are shut and I can't open them. I think, this must be what dying is like, then I hear Mark talking, muffled. My whole body and soul is straining to focus on his voice.

"Doctor, how is she? Is she all right?"

"She is resting now, Mr. McKenzie," another voice says.

"Mark, call me Mark, and this is her mother, Karen."

He is lying, that little sneak, I think inside my misty head.

"What can you tell us about her condition?" Karen asks.

I struggle to force open my eyes. I'm frightened and I want to see Karen. If I can see her, maybe I can focus on her calmness. I must be in a coma. My mind screams, I'm here, Karen, I'm here—I just can't open my eyes.

The conversation catches my attention again. "I want to keep her tonight, then rest at home for a week. We'll run some tests after she is rested," says an unfamiliar voice.

I feel like I am eavesdropping. "Home," I whisper inside myself. If I will go home, then I must be going to be all right.

In the background, I hear the rhythmic beep-beep-beep of a medical machine somewhere above my head. It slows to a calmer pace. It is kind of weird being so acute to the sounds around me. I feel someone let go of my hand. I wasn't even aware anyone had been holding it. I contract my fingers, but I can't tell if they respond. There is a kiss on my forehead just as I drift off to sleep.

When I wake up, Karen is sitting by my bed. "Hey, sleepy-head, you gave us a scare." She tells me that Mark took the night shift, and now it's her turn. She also tells me that my physician came in this morning. He's going to tell the neurologist where I am. "What is this about a neurologist?" she asks.

I ask about Grandfather. I am relieved to hear he hasn't been called. The last thing I want is a McKenzie entourage descending upon the hospital—then the media is sure to follow.

"The neurologist?" Karen presses.

"Oh, just tests because of my headaches." I brush past an answer.

"Headaches?" Karen questions, but seems to decide not to push for an answer right now.

I know Karen, like Maggie, does not let go of anything so easily. I predict she will bring the conversation back to the neurologist before she leaves.

"Do you want to call your family, maybe Aunt Grace?"

"No, we don't parade our illnesses in front of each other, we show off our children." I attempt to change the conversation into a joking mood. "Seriously, it will probably be cured with a good dose of rest. I'll be fine by Thanksgiving, and no one will have to know about this little dizzy spell."

Karen's face shows that she doesn't like my answers, but she will have to live with them for the time being.

~~~

The doctor dismisses me from the hospital during his early-morning rounds. I have time to go home to my apartment, clean up, and make it to my original doctor appointment to get the results of my tests.
~~~

I call a taxi and slip out while Jim isn't here to say otherwise.

I'm surprised to see Karen enter the doctor's waiting room. I called her from my apartment to tell her I had been discharged from the hospital and would catch up with her later in the week.

"Hello?" I greet her.

"Hello. I came to be with you," she says softly. "Don't look so worried, someone accidentally called my number when they were trying to reach you. They think I am your mother," she whispers, then grins, probably with the thought of the deception—the deception she doesn't know that I overheard.

"My mother?" I look quizzingly. "You aren't old enough."

"As far as they are concerned, I am."

"I don't suppose you would settle for waiting out here, would you?" I ask, already knowing the answer. I'm relieved that she is here with me, though I would have never asked her to come.

In my heart, I know I am ill. I have never admitted it out loud, nor how worried I am becoming. I just don't feel well. I have headaches, eye problems, dizziness, and memory problems. I know it is more than fatigue. I had things to accomplish before I could take time to be ill. But, the illness seems unwilling to wait.

"If you really want me to leave, I will." She jumps to the extreme to force me to admit that I want her to stay with me.

"No, it's all right. Come in with me," I whisper with a forced grin on my lips that feel as if they are trembling like I am inside. That is as close as I can come to admitting that I don't want to go through this appointment alone.

Inside the doctor's office, he has my brain scans on the x-ray film light board. The look on his face makes it obvious that he doesn't like what he sees. He points at various films, making circular motions with the end of his ink pen as he explains generalities about the films.

He asks, "How many headaches?"

"I've had quite a few. Almost constant now." I might as well tell him everything. "Lately it's not only an ache, it is more of a stabbing pain—like a sharp letter opener stabbed swiftly in my head, then pulled out. It is a strong pain, but it only lasts seconds."

At first, he has his back to me, looking at the back-lit films. He turns partially as he listens to my symptoms. Now he is looking directly at me.

"It disables me for a moment, but it passes quickly. And, I have vision problems, stronger glasses—actually bifocals, but I thought that was eyestrain from the increase in reading I've been doing the last couple of months." I pause, reconstructing other symptoms from my recent past. "I've had some memory problems too."

"Short-term or long-term memory?" He asks a clarifying question as he studies me for a moment, then turns back to the cross-section scans of my brain.

"Nothing out of the ordinary—it's just fatigue. I have been pushing myself lately."

"That might be a factor, but it's more serious than that."

"The memory loss is more of a loss for words. I can't think of the name of common things like 'glass of water'—but it isn't that often. It may happen several times in one day, then not again for days."

"The headaches and vision problems are likely to increase," he speaks softly, as he looks at both Karen and me. He begins to rub his forehead, while he searches for the words to explain the situation.

"What is it, Dr. Billingsworth?" Karen asks when the pause seems to linger too long.

"See this area here?" He points to a specific spot on the film that he has moved to the center of the screen. "This mass is the problem." He pauses again, but only slightly.

"Mass?" Karen and I say nearly in unison.

He faces us. "It looks to be a tumor, astrocytoma. It's growing, causing more and more pressure on these areas." He points on the film with his pen. "That is why you are having headaches. That pressure is the problem. I just don't like the kind of pain you describe."

"Tumor? Is it cancer?" Karen whispers the word "cancer."

I feel disoriented the minute the word leaves her lips. Mother died of breast cancer. It can't be cancer. I listen numbly as he speaks, unable to ask questions of my own. I am intent on his words, but hear none of them.

"It may or may not be malignant. It's hard to tell from a scan, but it is definitely there, and it is definitely a problem."

"So, so, what happens next?" I rejoin the conversation. "A biopsy?"

"That would be the usual option," he says.

"But?" Karen encourages.

"But, the position of the mass is the problem. I don't like where it is. It is dangerous to probe in this location." He points to the location on the film, like seeing it would mean something to us. "I can't recommend going in there. If the surgery doesn't kill you, it's very likely to leave you in a vegetative state."

"Can you treat the mass as if it is cancer with chemo or radiation, shrink it somehow or even kill it?" Karen asks.

"Either of those would only be marginally successful."

"What would you do, if it were you?" Karen isn't leaving without a treatment plan better than nothing can be done.

"It needs to be removed. The surgery isn't usually successful. It's not even done in the U.S." He raises one eyebrow.

"Where is it done?" Karen asks.

He explains a new procedure being tested in Sweden. He's been following the study with a great deal of interest.

"The study is in its fifth year. Early results are promising. It is several years away from FDA approval. I think you are a pretty good match for the profile, but you can't wait long. The surgery is showing good results on young, otherwise healthy patients."

Clearly there is only one cure, regardless how risky, it's my only choice, my only hope is experimental surgery.

Dr. Billingsworth wants to refer me to the medical team in Sweden as soon as possible. He'll make the contacts and get back to me. They might be pleased to have such a prominent patient in their test group.

"It will likely take months to get in, but I think surgery is your best choice. Considering that you wouldn't be a charity case, they might be more willing to consider you for a test subject and streamline getting on the list." Finally, being Kathryn McKenzie is a good thing.

"So, what do we do first?" I ask.

"Let me get you into the study group. We can do the preliminary lab tests here and send them with the referral. You must be ready to go at a moment's notice." He tries to smile, but looks grim.

"I see. Then, let's do it." I nod agreement.

"I'll call Dr. Klienfelter and get back to you."

"Thank you, Doctor," Karen is saying as she puts her hand on my wrist.

"Yes, thank you." I get to my feet, feeling wobbly.

"Make sure we have your cell phone number," he adds, as I sling my purse strap to my shoulder.

My hand shakes. It takes two attempts for the strap to stay in position. By then, Karen is handing him her business card. "We'll be there—just say when and where," she confirms.

I feel numb. "Cancer" I repeat over in my head. I can't breathe.

Karen's hand is on my elbow. She moves me through the waiting room and outside. I fumble in my purse for my keys.

Gently, she places her hand on mine and pushes the keys back toward my purse. "You look pale. I'll drive," she says. It isn't a request or an inquiry, it is final. In no uncertain terms, she is driving. Keith can help her get my car later.

Vanity can't force me to protest. I feel faint and can't wait for the elevator to reach the ground, so I can get into the fresh air. Once we are in the car, Karen starts the engine, runs the power windows down, and starts the A/C on full for more air. “Lean forward, put your head down,” she instructs as she puts her hand on my shoulder.

I begin to gulp in the cool air. She brushes the hair out of my face and makes an audible, “Shuu-u, shu-u-u” sound.

“Katey, don’t hyperventilate. We’ll get through this one step at a time.” She continues to stroke my hair away from my face.

Slowly the blood returns to my head and I don’t feel so lightheaded. Karen’s hand is on my upper arm. When I open my eyes, I can see she is leaning forward to look in my face. I take a deep breath and begin to sit up. Her hand slips away, but not her gaze.

“I know you are frightened, but we will do this together, understand? I better not find out that you have gone to any appointments without me or that you didn’t call me when you needed to talk.”

I intend to answer affirmatively, but whisper, “Cancer.”

“I know,” she says softly.

Tears run shamelessly down my cheeks. “My mother died of cancer,” I whisper.

“We are not going to let you die. We are going to tackle this.” She takes a breath. “Katey, I know you’re frightened. I would be. But you aren’t alone. Don’t ever think you’re alone.” She looks intensely at me to make sure I understand.

“I know,” I whisper and grasp the back of her hand.

“Stay with me tonight,” she says as she begins to back out of the clinic parking garage.

“All right,” I agree—relieved.

After we clear the parking garage, I phone the mansion and tell them I am staying in L.A. for the night. By now, no one thinks much about me staying in the city. Things at the mansion are in the hands of the capable staff. If it takes too long to get into the Sweden program, I may have to rely on them more in the future.

~~~

Karen fixes a pot of coffee, then wonders if I am allowed to have coffee. I assure her that, of course, I can have coffee. I’m not giving up coffee at this stage of the game—after everything else I have given up these last six months. It would be horrible to spend my last months without coffee or the beach. I hope that I am not disabled and have to spend all of my time at the mansion. No coffee, no beach, that would be a horrible death.

We sit, talk, and have coffee. Karen has taken the day off from work. We finally decide my situation is better than an incurable malignant cancer that would course throughout my body and eat away
~~~

at me from the inside out. This, in time, will kill me by crowding my brain, but there is one possible cure.

"Please, don't tell anyone about this," I ask.

"Why the secrecy?"

I turn to make sure she understands that I do not want her sneaking around behind my back on this one. "The media. I don't want pity. I want everyone to behave normally. If they are angry with me, I want them to tell me, to yell at me, if that is what they need to do." I searched for words to express my thoughts. "Karen, if this surgery doesn't work—I, I want the time I have to be real," I say softly, raising my glance to meet her eyes. "Including coffee," I add for good measure.

She shifts in her chair, a little uneasy. "Tell Mark, and I promise not to tell anyone, except in a medical emergency."

That compromise is probably the best I am going to get. I agree. We lean in for a hug. No tears, just a hug. I hope I am accepted into the test group, so that I can live many more of these moments with my friends.

I prepare her for what might happen."Karen, I am going to designate you as my Power of Attorney and Executor of my estate."

"We'll get through this. You're going to be fine." Karen attempts to reassure me of the future.

"Still, will you do it?" I face her squarely.

~~~

In the morning, Karen drops me at my car. I feel fine now. I just want a few minutes at the beach that I don't have to be the heiress McKenzie before I get back to work.

The sun is beginning to turn the sky into sunrise colors. The beach is waking. The waves seem fresh. The birds, seagulls and sandpipers, are busily going about their morning routine. There are two men running side by side along the beach. Otherwise, the beach is deserted. The beach patrol drives by as I walk past the pier. I am trying to memorize all of the sights and smells of the beach, and the feel of the water on my bare feet.

I brought my camera to take photos of everything I love about the beach, the waves, the pier, the seagulls in hovering flight, all of it. I fill a small California wine bottle with sand. I know it is childish. I know sand in a bottle cannot replace the feel of the sand on my feet or the spray on my face or the sounds and smells, but I have to take a bit of the beach with me as long as my heart cannot leave this place.

I would rather stay here and concentrate on getting well—or preparing to die. But I feel a sense of duty to my father's place in his family.
~~~

His face and the soothing sound of his voice comes into the forefront of my memories. It doesn't take long to feel ready to face the uncertain future.

There are business matters that need set to autopilot for the near future. There are arrangements to make for my private and public lives. I need to call Mr. Bradford and tell him I am having surgery, and, as always with surgery, something could go wrong. He'll need to prepare a will naming Karen as the executor of my estate, and Power of Attorney. There is no heir. I trust her judgment. The bulk of the estate will go to the Foundation, and I want it set up in a way that the McKenzie cousins and possibly their parents will not contest my will. Obviously, they would have no claim to the money my parents left me in the trusts, or that I have made from my investments. Mr. Bradford will be creative in figuring out a way to set up a trust for Spirit of Hope, so that the Church can't get their hands on that money.

I had hoped to establish a place similar to Spirit of Hope for families with a family member with AIDS. I planned to call it "Monica's House." I had so many ideas, hopes, and dreams. I wonder how many of them I can accomplish in the time I have left. And I want to establish a college scholarship fund for the children who go through the Spirit of Hope doors.

Sam will have to have a Power of Attorney to run the business aspects of the McKenzie Enterprise while I have surgery. If I die, it will all revert to Karen in six months. I need to tell him of my plan to trim the fat through attrition at the corporate office. And I want to give Father's Jag to Garrett. He looked perfect behind the wheel. Zoe can have my Mustang—her car is a piece of junk. I wonder if she can drive a stick shift? I don't have the time or stamina to teach her to drive it. Wouldn't it be funny if Sister Theresa taught her. Paybacks! No, I'm sure Garrett will help her.

Mr. Bradford promises to get started on the documents this afternoon. He doesn't press for details about the surgery. Maybe he thinks it's something female and asks no questions. He does seem to understand the sense of urgency to get this done now.

~~~
~~~

~ CHAPTER 12 ~

The Verdict

By the time I arrive at the mansion I have told my face not to reveal my worries. There is a lot to put in place before my surgery, and no time for further self-pity. I'll either live through this or I won't.

As soon as I hit the door, Sam warns me:"Kathryn, Jim is looking for you. He is furious you didn't check in with him after the shooting!"

"The shooting?" I'm clueless. The last that I saw Jim we were on the beach.

"The shots when we left the courthouse on Friday. Didn't you hear what happened?" He sounds surprised as I turn and see Sam standing in the doorway.

"What happened?"

"Your shooter was killed by a sniper as they were exiting the side door to go back to jail! He's gone. It's over!" Sam says, happily relieved.

"I haven't listened to the news since then. But it leaves a lot of questions about why he faked schizophrenia. What about his wife? How is she?" How did I escape the media?

~~~

"Jim, good morning. I hear it's over." I'm trying to get him past the part about not checking in with him before he scolds me. I should tell him about the medical stuff, but I'm not ready to discuss it with anyone.

"Good morning. It isn't over yet, Miss McKenzie."

"Oh, I must have misunderstood."

"The shooter is dead, but who shot the shooter? And the bigger question—WHY? No offense, but I don't think you have a loyal fan out there revenging you."

His words make me uneasy."What do you think?"

"There are many aspects to consider. I think there is a correlation to the testimony that he faked his illness and the shooting. Before that, he was not much of a threat. But who is he a threat to?" He looks questioningly at me.

"Me?"

"Yes, he was a threat to you, but you were not a threat to him. You wouldn't retaliate for what he did. Although, I bet you are a suspect. Is there anything you need to tell me?" he asks suspiciously, looking between Sam and me, and back again.

"I haven't hired a mercenary, if that is what you mean. I don't want to be shot at, but I would never kill anyone," I add softly.
~~~

"If you think of anything let me know. I'll keep checking. Someone wanted him dead before he could talk."

Maggie, The jury may not have decided the fate of the shooter, but the verdict is in for me. I am dying at a more rapid rate than the general population. I knew the McKenzie money carried a curse! Not literally in a spiritual sense — bad luck certainly follows the money in this family. I have a tumor.

There's a lot to do in an unarguably short amount of time. Surprisingly, I have been thinking clearly about my personal business, and even about some of my McKenzie duties. There is nothing like adversity to make one rise to the occasion. This is the greatest test of my character to date. I can only imagine what lies ahead. I hope I'm ready for it.

Tuesday always seems an odd day to start the work week, especially when everyone else worked Monday. I'm already a day behind. I hadn't realized how upset the staff was with the shooting. There is a noticeable relief now that he is gone. There's no point in telling them that Jim is staying on the payroll because he still has an uneasiness about the shooter's death. Maybe I'll hint to Eleanor that I am keeping Jim around so she can spend more time with him.

I begin to join Jim's uneasiness about the shooter's death. I don't think his wife was involved. Clearly, she wasn't expecting the shots. I truly doubt it has anything to do with her. So, who does that leave? Not me, not her. Another crazy person? Honestly, that seems unlikely.

So who wanted the shooter dead? Who can hire a sniper? Who would my shooter be a risk to, if he lived and spilled his guts to someone, and it leaked to the media? Is that person going to come after me and finish what the shooter didn't?

I can't worry about another threat. It is possible I am not going to live anyway. I need to advise Sam of the Power of Attorney. There is no reason to give him the specifics behind my decision. He doesn't usually question my business decisions. I am sure I can waltz past this one without missing a beat.

I have to make every minute count. After the safeguards are in place in my official life, I can take a breath while I wait for the call to fly to Sweden. This isn't a good time for regrets, but I wish I had made time to attend more Dodgers games this summer. I don't even know who won the World Series this year. That is most unusual for me. The funny thing is that I could have afforded box seats at the games and gone to all seven of them.

One thing I can't put off is to tell Grandfather that I am planning to have surgery. There is no need to give him every detail, but I do need to be candid about the big picture. I'll start with generalities, then go from there. That way, he will understand when I suddenly fly off without advance notice.

While we finish the bottle of wine from dinner, I decide this is as good of a time as any to talk with Grandfather. Unless he insists, I have no plans to relinquish my position as Kathryn the Great. He made his decision to step down. When the need arises, he is welcome to advise Sam, but after my recovery I am going to fulfill my duty—if I recover. Besides, that is what Grandmother set in motion all these years ago, and he is well aware of that.

"Grandfather, I'm going to have surgery and I wanted to tell you about it now, since I don't know when it will be. The procedure isn't available here, so I have to go to Europe." I dive right in. After all, he did the same to me with his retirement announcement, I think he expects things to be done in that fashion.

He takes another drink. "I suppose it is not a routine matter, since you can't have the procedure done here."

"No, it isn't routine. I don't have the information about what to expect yet, but I have to be ready to go at a moment's notice."

Grandfather tilts his head to ponder my answer.

"I've asked Mr. Bradford to make a Power of Attorney for Sam to handle anything that can't wait for my return. The FBI is taking the point on the corruption enquiry. Still, Chico, Race, and Sam are going to continue with our in-house investigation."

He nods approval, while I tick through the items on my list of McKenzie duties. He is a patient listener.

"A friend is having a Halloween Masquerade party in San Francisco, but before that I am thinking about taking one of the McKenzie jets to visit a friend in Austria. I need the jet so that I can go to Sweden, if I am called for the surgery while I am in Vienna." I smile and squeeze his hand.

"Are you all right?" he asks softly, reaching his other hand out to touch mine.

"It's pretty serious, but I'll be all right. I'm a McKenzie."

"Yes, yes, you are. Your grandmother would be proud of you." He smiles, but his eyes are unaware of the smile and have filled with tears. I can only imagine what he must be thinking, but I don't dare minimize the situation too much.

I stand to bend over him with an affectionate hug. That went well, but I think he will need a little more attention from me than usual for the next few days. As far as my McKenzie cousins, I have neither the time or the energy to worry about telling them. That would leave the door open for trouble—trouble that I don't have time to squash.

Grandfather's approval of what I have done, and more so that Grandmother McKenzie would be proud of me touches me. More than I realized, I needed his and Grandmother's approval.

~~~

The only way I can think of to tell the staff to call Karen in a medical emergency is to have Zoe make up an emergency call list for all of the people who live and work at the mansion. That way Karen's phone number can be listed for me.

Zoe loves to make documents. She takes on the task with youthful enthusiasm, and has the list completed in no time. She gives a copy of the emergency phone list to everyone and places one in her master notebook in her office. If she gets any more organized I will have to move her to the corporate office and unleash her on that mess.

~~~

Mr. Bradford's secretary, Crystal, calls to say the first wave of documents are ready for my signature. The documents will have to wait a day or two, I have work to do here. Monthly reports are coming in, and the third-quarter reports should come on their heels.

I'm not cleared to run around and get fatigued. Sam will have to attend the board of directors' meeting in Chicago next month. It's getting cool in Chicago this time of year, but Sam is welcome to take his wife with him for a mini vacation. Chicago is a marvelous city anytime.

Sam has been putting in long hours since he came to work for me. They are probably due for time away, together. The board meeting won't take much time. The only downside to the trip is that it isn't baseball season. With the Cubs and the White Sox in town, it could have been fun to send them to a game at each field. I am sure they will find other ways to be entertained in a city as grand as Chicago.

Thursday evening, I head to the city after work. First thing in the morning I have tests to add to my surgery profile.

~~~

"The latest news is the surgery is past test status in Europe," I tell Karen. I look from my coffee cup to Karen's concerned eyes.

It takes a moment before Karen responds, but she understood immediately.

"That opens up the surgery for you without being accepted in the test group." Her eyes water and her voice softens to a whisper.

"Finally, a break my direction," I admit, also in a whisper. I am relieved and feel exhausted.
~~~

We wait outside for the tests to be printed, so they can be added to the medical file I have to keep in my briefcase, so that I can be ready to go at a moment's notice. Karen breaks into tears. That is all it takes for me to burst into tears of relief too.

I am a million miles away, thinking about living and dying. I certainly have a new perspective on my life now that I am ill.

Karen is quiet, obviously lost in thought. She startles me when she suddenly speaks.

"Katey!" she reaches for my hand. "Katey, you don't have to be on-call. You can schedule your surgery. You can choose the time. Why don't you call your doctor and get your surgery scheduled as soon as possible?"

Karen catches me off guard. Wow! She is absolutely correct. Her words are liberating. This illness, this tumor, has been outside my control. However, the thought that I can select a date for the surgery gives me a piece of control over this thing that otherwise scares the beejeebies out of me.

I look up to meet her eyes. "You're right! Thank you. I can't tell you how relieved I feel with the idea of having a little control in this, this situation. I'll call the neurologist in the morning and let you know when it's scheduled. Do you want to fly on my personal jet?" We both laugh, finally.

~~~

The tests, except those of my head, are normal. My doctor sent the results and interpretation files via email to Sweden. They have requested the films, but have made a tentative appointment for early December. That gives me slightly less than two months to get everything ready for my absence. I still don't know how long it will take to be back to normal. There is much to do. Regardless of what happens to me, the businesses will continue on with their own momentum.

What worries me is time for seeing everyone again if something goes wrong with this risky procedure. Mr. Goldstein is covered. We have the arrangements made for my visit to Austria next weekend.

Signing the documents with Mr. Bradford makes it crystal clear in my mind that this health problem is a problem. I call it many things just to avoid saying tumor or cancer. I don't want to face it, but I cannot not face it. Quickly, I make a mental list of the people I want to see this weekend before I return to the mansion on Sunday evening.

"Thank you, Mr. Bradford, for doing all of this extra work on such short notice."

"Kathryn, I am happy to do it. I know your father would look after my family if the situation had been reversed."
~~~

"I just want to make sure you know I appreciate what you do for me—what you have always done for me."

Mr. Bradford never seems to pay full attention to what is going on. He is always shuffling papers or reading a document. But this time he isn't multitasking. He is listening completely without distraction. His eyes narrow and his brow wrinkles.

"Is everything all right, Kathryn?"

"As right as rain."

Mr. Bradford nods in acknowledgment—relieved to hear the answer he was hoping for.

~~~

I go to see Mother Elizabeth and everyone at Spirit of Hope —Mother, the nuns, the clients, and that place were pivotal in my recovery of self after returning from Nebraska, not to mention a change of professional direction.

Standing before the heavy-weathered door, looking at the metal door-knocker brings a myriad of memories of my first impression of Sister Theresa. The image of her speeding through the hallway brings a smile. I should have known she had a lead foot when driving, but I never figured it out until she was behind the wheel. I smile.

Inside the convent doors, the cool air is noticeably cooler than the fall weather outside. Sister Theresa is wearing a sweater, something I have never seen her do before. The older sisters sometimes wore sweaters over their habits, but Sister Theresa never did.

After our greetings, I ask Sister Theresa, "What's going on?" I look around and notice everyone is wearing a sweater or jacket, and I am beginning to get a chill.

"The boiler went out last week. We are trying to get it repaired. Every company that looked at it has a different opinion about what is wrong with it."

I touch her wrist. "Where is Mother Elizabeth?" Obviously, Karen doesn't know about the boiler or she would have mentioned it.

"She's looking at the boiler with another contractor. You can wait in her office."

We walk down the hall, past the statues in their alcoves, and into the waiting area outside Mother's office. This time, when we pass the chapel doors, we both genuflect.

While I wait alone for Mother Elizabeth, I call one of my cousins. He is from my "real" family, the one I grew up with, attended family dinners with, and watched his children learn to walk. He is a builder—multi-million-dollar homes. Possibly he will know someone in the boiler business even though his homes don't have boilers.
~~~

Luckily, I reach him on his cell phone. "Mike, this is Katey. I need your expertise."

I laugh at his comment about my questionable mental health and his doubt there is a cure. "I am certainly glad that you aren't a shrink. Seriously, the boiler is out at Spirit of Hope. I need someone I can trust to look at it. Got any contacts in that area?"

"I don't put boilers in my houses."

His heating and air conditioning contractor might know someone who specializes in boilers. I just have to wait for him to call me back.

Mother Elizabeth comes into the room. She looks tired and frustrated, until she sees me sitting on the sofa, then she greets me with a cheery smile, as if she hasn't a care in the world.

"Hello, Mother Elizabeth. What's this about your boiler?"

"I think it is shot—or should be shot."

"It's that bad?"

"Unfortunately, I think it is. Everyone who has looked at it has found something else wrong with it." She pauses for a long, deep breath. "We used up most of our reserves with Spirit of Hope. We are a Diocesan Community. The Bishop is in Rome for a month, and the bank won't give us a loan." She humbles herself to explain her situation. She is a formidable, independent person. She prefers to be self-reliant. I'm sure it was difficult to tell me her problem.

"It is supposed to dip down into the forties tonight, and it's already cold in here." I state the obvious. "How long have you been without heat?"

"It is almost a week now." She looks away as she speaks.

My cousin calls back with a phone number of a boiler expert. I excuse myself to make the call in the adjacent conference room. He tells me that he is booked. There is no way he can look at the boiler before next Tuesday.

That won't do. I tell him there are women and children, and elderly nuns here. They can't go without heat that long. Apparently, my cousin didn't tell him that I am Kathryn McKenzie.

To my mother's family, being a McKenzie is not a big deal. My aunts and uncles knew of the connection with the McKenzie fortune, but no one ever hinted that it made any difference, and so it never did. To them, I am Katey.

However, I am not above playing the McKenzie card if it will get heat for these people. I ask who he would use, if he couldn't use his own company. He hesitates to give me his competitor's name.

"All right then, how much do you want for your company?" I ask, quite annoyed with him.

"What?"

"How much will it take to get you here, or to buy your company?"

"What are you talking about?" He is sounding angry.

"Look, my cousin says you are the best. If you won't tell me the name of your biggest competitor, and you won't come, then, I will buy your company or whatever it takes to get heat for these people—it is that simple."

"Is this a joke?" he snaps back at me.

"No. No joke. I'm Kathryn McKenzie and quite willing to pay you full market value of your company, if that's what it takes."

"McKenzie Enterprises—that McKenzie? I have a bid in on the new plant you are planning for Long Beach—" his voice trails off into silence.

He probably thinks I already knew that, but I didn't. His humanitarian side is certainly not making a good impression.

"Where can I reach you? I have to call you back with the number." He seems more interested now that he hopes to influence the bid letting for Long Beach.

I give him my phone number. Though I know better than to burn bridges, I certainly am angry with his attitude.

Mother Elizabeth is sitting at her desk when I tap on the open door to her office. She looks like she has the weight of the world on her shoulders.

"Mother, do you have someone who can replace the boiler right away, if you had the money?"

Her eyes light up. It seems that she forgot that money is not an issue for me. She still sees me as a former staff person, not Kathryn the Great—ruler of an empire.

"The last fellow thought that he could get the boiler in the Spirit of Hope center running tonight with a patch job. The two systems are linked, but he thinks he can isolate the shelter's system and get it going. It doesn't seem to be in as bad of shape as the convent boiler."

"Do you think you can have him come back and talk with both of us?"

"Sure, why not?" she beams.

The boiler man and his father return to the convent within thirty minutes. They meet with Mother Elizabeth and me. The father looks at the system with his son and they come up with a plan to get the heat on, and hopes it will last until they can correctly fix the boiler by replacing it. The father is retired, but he started the company forty years ago. He is the expert on these ancient boilers.

I ask about switching the system to heat pumps and duct it for heat and air conditioning, something they don't presently have. It gets hot in in here during the hottest months of the summer. The problem is that running that kind of system without an in-house generator would be astronomical. Solar panels can't carry the load. The best we can do is to replace the boilers. The major catch is that a hazmat company will have to come and remove the asbestos covering the pipes and boilers, before they can be replaced. Currently, the covering poses no threat. Once the coating is disturbed, the asbestos will become airborne, and that's a problem.

The old man says there is room in the old high school, currently Spirit of Hope, to set the new boiler beside the old one. That way as soon as the asbestos is peeled off, bagged, and the air exchange has been completed, the new system can be hooked up. The old boiler can be removed later.

The convent boiler is an entirely different story. The current boiler is a monstrosity. There isn't room to set a new one beside it and make the switch. The old boiler has to be removed before the new boiler can be installed. The only catch is, it has to be cut into pieces to get it out of the building.

That is the best we can do. Hopefully the boiler will run until the new one arrives. I guarantee payment and write him a deposit check from the Foundation for twenty thousand dollars to get the new boilers ordered and shipped in the most expedient fashion. The men proceed to the Spirit of Hope boiler room to get the old boiler to fire up and run.

The whole system will have to be flushed and all of the radiators checked, something that can be done while the hazmat team works in the boiler room. I ask Mother if she needs cots to move the nuns into the auditorium until the convent system is repaired, but she says they will manage in their cells.

I write another check, this time for fifty thousand dollars and warn her that the Diocese is not to get a penny of the money, if it exceeds the boiler expenses. I know that I won't be here next week, so I am hoping the check will cover all of her expenses and purchase the extra blankets they need in the meantime.

With the situation at Spirit of Hope on the mend, I leave without addressing my desire for one last personal moment with Mother Elizabeth. The opportunity for a heart-to-heart did not present itself. It is probably better that things worked out this way. Besides, I think she knows my feelings toward her.

We hug goodbye. It is a hug that lingers a moment longer than usual. I suppose for her it is gratitude for the boiler, but for me, it very well may be a final goodbye.

~~~
~~~

~ CHAPTER 13 ~

Life in Review

Threatening to purchase the boiler company to get what I want embarrasses me. That's something Grandfather would do. My behavior surprises me. I have to take a long hard look at how I behaved. The question is, "Am I less constrained now that I am dying?" Am I really a rich spoiled brat when I need to be? Or am I in such a hurry to pack as many accomplishments in the time I have, that I abandon who I am?

The concept of dying is new to me only in the sense of perspective. I remember Mother's approach to both, living and dying. I was sixteen toward the end of her life. She shared some of her thoughts about life with me. However, considering my desire to keep this illness to myself, I am now questioning how many of her thoughts she kept to herself.

On the way back to the beach, I call Dana to see if there is a time in her weekend when we can get together. She opts to come over tonight for a nightcap and a walk on the beach. I am not sure how to go about saying what I would like to say to her, and allowing her the opportunity to say what she would say if she knew I was dying.

I don't want her to thank me. The thought of her gratitude embarrasses me. However, I realize she may need to express her appreciation for getting her off of the street and in a position to reclaim her life as a fashion designer.

Yet, I'm not ready to say aloud that I might be dying. It is a choreographed dance to not leave anyone with the regret of unspoken words, like I was left when Maggie died.

"So, what is the reason for this sudden get-together?" Dana asks as the evening gets underway.

She's intuitive. It must be the artistic spirit in her.

"I didn't know we needed a reason!" I smile sheepishly. "Seriously, I am losing touch with everyone. I decided this is the week to start catching up—so, here we are!" I smile and squint at her.

She laughs a vigorous laugh that is reserved for special occasions —occasions outside the fashion arena. Dana seems to accept my explanation.

We catch up quickly as if we'd seen each other regularly over the past months.

"Oh, before I forget, I am going to Austria and will miss Linda and Todd's big Halloween party—" I begin, but Dana interrupts.

"Don't even think I am going to tell you what character I'm going to be. If you want to know, you have to show up!" Dana laughs again.

"Artists!" I feign dismay.

Dana tells me she has her spring collection finished and is nearly finished with her summer line. She exaggerates her words and hand motions—making fun of me. What she doesn't realize is how I appreciate her skill. She is so ahead of the game that she is beginning to work on her fall line for next year. Dana laughs again and says she isn't organized—she is driven.

She stops walking and looks into the distance. "Shh, listen to the waves!" Our conversation falls dead silent. Then, just as suddenly she throws back her head and laughs.

I don't know what that was all about, but the laughter is nice. It is another facet to add to my experience of the beach with friends. I stow images of Dana into my memory for later.

"I have the perfect holiday collection just for you." Dana grins as she draws me back into a conversation.

I catch myself from saying my thought aloud—I may not be here for the holidays this year, or any other year.

"Really? I'll have to stop by," I say.

Maggie, I am pragmatic about my life now. I have moments of regret that life could be so short. There are also times when I feel absolutely certain that the surgery will be successful and this will all seem like a bad dream. However, all of the time I feel driven to get everything to a place that it can continue on without me. Now, if I can only allow everyone a chance to say goodbye without knowing this might be the end.

Saturday morning, I drive to my aunt and uncle's house. We reminisce about family experiences. My aunt starts telling stories about my childhood, including the home perm one of my older cousins gave me, without adult supervision or permission.

It didn't take long for the smell of the mix to make the perm obvious to the adults who had been visiting on the patio. It was disastrous. There wasn't any fix for the tight frizzy curls. Unfortunately for me, the next week was school photos and mine was unusually bad that year. That was first grade.

In third grade I had a black eye for my school photo because my older cousins let me play baseball with them. We all were in trouble when I walked into the bat during a practice swing. I don't remember them trying to run me off, that wasn't the way things were done in this family—everyone is included in everything. And I had a black eye to prove it! I do hope they have better memories of me than those.

~~~

For lunch, I go back to the beach and rest before my next visit. I have been trying to pace myself. It is unnerving to know that at any minute, it could be my last. I try not to become too pensive. Hasn't it always been—no guarantees of tomorrow? The only difference is that, because of the headaches, I am acutely aware of it now. "It isn't how long one lives, it's how wide."

~~~

I visit another aunt and uncle. He is such a ham that he keeps us laughing so much that my sides begin to hurt. It is a nice hurt, though. He is full of family stories of things he and his siblings did growing up. Some of them can't possibly be true. He has a full dose of blarney. Luckily, most of them are not about embarrassing things that I did.

When the laughter dies, my aunt asks how I am since Grandfather McKenzie's announcement. I confide to her that being wealthy is greatly overrated.

She smiles. She agrees that there are other kinds of wealth—the kind I already had. I almost tell her about the surgery, but at the last minute I change my mind. It just doesn't fit into the conversation.

On the way back to the beach a headache starts. This time it's a dull headache, not the shooting pain headache. It is probably an ordinary headache, the kind everyone gets from time to time, but it reminds me of my situation. Those thoughts are never far away.

After not finding my camera, I walk to the store two blocks away and purchase a disposable one. I am sappy-sentimental as I walk through Main Street of my hometown toward the beach to take photos.

The waves seem exceptionally dramatic today, full of white foam that rushes toward the beach with an uncommonly loud roar. I think of Dana and how she laughed at the waves last night. I never did see what made her laugh, but I do have the memory of the laugh to savor.

The sun sets early since it is late fall, so I cut short my walk and head home. About the time I am at the place where I turn away from the ocean to go home, the sun breaks through the clouds and bathes the beach in magnificent colors.

The sunset is absolutely beautiful. Turning to the west, I notice the birds have begun to congregate on the beach behind me. When a wave recedes, the birds are silhouetted on the mirror image of the sunset. I have never seen anything like this sunset in all of my years on the beach. I shoot the rest of the roll of film as the sunset changes from minute to minute.

Just as I finish dinner, Mark calls to tell me he is going to London this week for a recording session. He invites me to join him. Mark has everything figured out: We'll fly together Wednesday, spend the night in Paris, he'll go to London while I go to Vienna. We will meet in Paris a week later, after his recording set. The only "catch" is that it will take several days for him to show me his favorite spots in Paris. He rattles off the list of places he wants to take me, enticing me into agreeing with his scheme.

"Katey, think of it, Le Quartier Latin, Centre Georges Pompidou, Les Halles, Galleries Layfayette—"

I interrupt his litany with a laugh. "Okay, okay! I give in. It sounds wonderful—I get my own room."

"Ah." He pretends to pout. "If you insist."

"I do." I like our relationship just fine. Besides, I note, he didn't protest strongly.

It's worth having the extra time and a traveling companion. I don't mind running around L.A. alone. I'd rather not travel to Europe alone with a ticking bomb in my head.

~~~

Sunday morning is the last of the time I can devote to visiting family. Everyone else will have to wait until Thanksgiving dinner. Catching three sets of aunts and uncles, Mother Elizabeth, Dana, and Karen is a lot to accomplish in such short time. Even Mr. Bradford can technically be added to the list.

The morning traffic is light, and I arrive before my uncle returns with fresh pastries. Aunt Grace, the one who came to pick me up at Karen's house so we could go to the beach, takes one look at me and asks, "What's wrong, Katey?"

"I just haven't seen you for a while."

"That is the official story. What's the truth?"

My eyes water. She holds my hands in hers and looks straight at me. I hug her and she holds me tightly.

"I have a brain tumor."

She tilts her head lovingly.

"I have to go to Europe for surgery after Thanksgiving, and I wanted to thank you for everything you have done for me, for all of the times you made time to help me, for—" my voice gives under the great well of emotion I feel.

Aunt Grace holds me again in a motherly hug. She has always understood me, especially when words fail. We move to the sofa and sit in soft silence. When my uncle returns, he is surprised to see two teary-eyed women in the living room.
~~~

Aunt Grace tells him the news of my surgery. The three of us have a long talk. I feel almost as if my parents are here. We drink coffee and eat the light, flaky pastry that melts when it touches my tongue.

~~~

On the way home, I drive through Forest Lawn Cemetery where the McKenzie family is buried. Impressive copies of statues by Renaissance masters are sentinels throughout the grounds. Most, I recognize—Michelangelo's David and Pieta (from Latin for "dutifulness").

Gently, I pull to a stop and walk for a while. "Dutifulness," I whisper the name. It saddens me. Not so much for the dead Christ across His mother's lap, but for Mary. Dying is really hard for the people left living. I feel gravely sad about all of the things I haven't accomplished, and I may not to be able to accomplish now. There are so many humanitarian projects that I haven't had time to begin. I feel cheated.

Maggie's words come to mind, but I haven't lived nearly wide enough yet. I need reassurance that all of my projects will continue. At least Grandmother had that hope in knowing I existed and the child she watched grow for a while.

When I reach the McKenzie section of the cemetery, I sit at the foot of Grandmother's grave. I wonder if I should plan my Requiem Mass? I want my parish priest to have my Mass, as he had each of my parents' Masses. He was the one who gave me the Sacrament of the Sick—Last Rites—as a precautionary measure. My Dear Father Confessor, I will miss you.

Silently, my body shakes with tears of grief. I don't try to bargain with God, there are still five weeks for bargaining. Today, I am sad. Tomorrow, who knows?

The one consolation is this will be the last funeral I attend. I do hate funerals. That's when it struck me. "Oh, God! They aren't Catholic!" My hand covers my gasping mouth. "Will Grandfather allow me a Catholic burial? Does it matter what I plan or he will turn this into one of his political media events?

My posture slumps with the weight of silently deep-into-the-soul sobbing. This ground hasn't been disturbed for a long time. It feels hard and unyielding, even though the lawn is hardy. The grass should be cushioning, but it's not.

Self-pity, Katey? There isn't time for that. Wiping my eyes, I get up and walk to my car.

Pulling away from the curb, I catch a glimpse of myself in the rearview mirror. My face is red. The mascara held up, but I must not have put on waterproof eyeliner. Now I have puffy, raccoon-looking eyes. I can't go home looking like this. Where can I go?
~~~

Ignoring the occasional glances of other drivers, glances caused by my red face and black-smudged eyes, I move north toward the mansion. When I reach Father's Beach, I know one more place I must go.

Almost as if a second Baptism, I reach my cupped hands into the Pacific. Over and over again, I fill my hands with the icy water and put it to my face. The heat in my skin is subsiding, and maybe even some of the puffiness around my eyes too.

~~~

When I return to the mansion, Grandfather and I spend the evening together. He's glad that Mark is accompanying me to Europe. I take advantage of the opportunity to tell him of the legal arrangements I've made. It surprises me that he approves of my decisions. He tells me how proud he is of me and the decisions I have made since I became "Miss McKenzie"—my words, not his. He talks of his disappointment with his other three grandchildren. I remind him how well Dan is doing and suggests he visit Dan's new office and look at his drawings.

Grandfather promises to pay Dan a visit. He says the police found Tim in a L.A. bar last night. It seems one of his friends set him up to be at the bar, so the police could pick him up there—in front of people he knows. The police found a kilo of cocaine in his car the night of the wreck. Grandfather is convinced that Tim is the one who got Brooke addicted to drugs. He plans to not intervene in the natural unfolding of Tim's case.

Even though Grandfather is ruthless, he never drinks to excess and has no tolerance for drugs. He has, as is his custom, cut off all ties with Brooke and Tim. Another generation (except me) is cut out of his life. I hope he seeks a relationship with Dan. And so the family legacy continues.

~~~

~ CHAPTER 14 ~

Bon Voyage

It is funny how the important things become little, and the little things are important to me now. I have started walking in the garden more often. I don't think about anything in particular, certainly nothing enlightened enough to bring about world peace. Mostly, my mind is busy making memories of the dew on the flowers, and recalling the ocean spray at the beach during a winter storm.

In two days I'm off across the Atlantic. All I can think of during today's morning walk in the rose garden is about seeing Mr. Goldstein again. I love that old man. The memories come over me with the warmth of a blanket: his first attempt to walk the beach, Hanukkah, unsolicited decorating advice, stories about the women at the Senior Center, the internet experience—every memory brings a fond smile.

I return to the patio to sit mindlessly watching the sun come up. The purple, pink, and finally the first glimpse of yellow appear on the horizon. With the sunrise, regret creeps into my mood. My emotions run the gamut with absolutely no warning of their changing.

My coffee has grown cold. Tears well up in my eyes. It is almost as if I am physically reliving the events of yesterday as I think about them. Louise comes to the patio to refill my cup—awakening me from the memories. She joins me for a few moments in the fresh morning air. The sun has finished its birthing and has fully cleared the horizon.

"Miss McKenzie, there is a gentleman here to see you," she says as she hands me his business card.

I stare at the card. Eleanor is awaiting instructions per Louise. We never have guests arrive before the office staff. "Thank you. I will see him in the library."

I take a minute to finish my coffee and collect my thoughts. I wonder what he wants?

I would like to refill my coffee again, but I set it down and walk to the library. No coffee, this is not a casual visit by my definition, no coffee cups in hand for this one.

"Hello, Joseph," I say.

Joseph turns away from the window when I speak. He looks older than the years since I have seen him. I can see he is fumbling for words—oh, how the mighty fall. Ordinarily, I would help smooth an awkward moment, but I haven't quite figured out the purpose of his visit. He stutters a hello.

I move to one of the chairs and motion for him to have a seat across from me. I briefly study him. His behavior is self-consciousness.

Strangely, seeing Joseph doesn't rekindle any of the emotions I once had for him. I had wondered what I would feel if I saw him again. Confession worked. I realize the silence and remember my role as hostess. "How have you been?"

Joseph smiles warily. "Divorced." There is a slight hint of sadness combined with bitterness in his tone. The divorce is either recent or was brutal.

"Sorry to hear that," I say softly, genuinely.

"If that is true, will you have dinner with me tonight?" He reverts back to his former self-absorbed style.

"No, but thank you," I say, remembering how he treated me.

He looks annoyed, but it passes quickly.

"Come with me, let's go for a walk in the garden." I rise from my chair, so that there is no misunderstanding that this is not a negotiable request. No one could have overheard us in the library, but I wanted the feel of privacy.

Joseph looks out across the garden, then remarks that it is a far cry from a walk on the beach that I loved so much. His tone verges on sarcasm.

"Yes, it is a different world, in a different time." I turn to face him. "Joseph, what are you doing here?"

"I can explain." He takes a defensive step backward.

Explain? Explain what? Explain why I didn't deserve to be told you were married, and not to come to Ireland? Explain why you think you can waltz back into my life now and expect me to clear my schedule to have dinner with you without a moment's notice? I maintain my best witness-stand poker face.

"Just give me a chance to explain." He continues, though I have said nothing.

That is enough of this nonsense. The only thing that has changed is that I am unavailable. If he is more interested in the McKenzie money than me, I hope he is smart enough to keep his cards close to his chest. I have work to do and two days to get it done. He is not going to disrupt my life for one minute more.

"Joseph, this is life, not a baseball game. There is no three-strike rule. I don't know how many 'chances' you think you get." I move the conversation to a swift conclusion.

"Katey," he pleads.

"Sorry, Joseph. It was over between us a long time ago." I have timed my final comment to coincide with our return to the house.

Joseph almost looks as if he is weighing the option of kissing me goodbye.

"Goodbye, Joseph," I say in a formal tone.

He nods and softly says, "Goodbye, Kathryn."

Joseph's unexpected visit is only a momentary distraction from work. I'm pleased he didn't stir romantic emotions when I saw him. It is finally finished, and I'm glad for the confirmation that there is nothing there to return to. I appreciate having that conclusion, especially now.

I have a lot to do. First, is to write a letter to Linda and Todd with my regrets about bowing out of their par— Oh, what bad timing for a headache to strike! I shut my eyes and lean over my desk, breathing slow, shallow breaths until the shooting pain subsides. I think my headaches are getting worse. Only a few more weeks until my surgery. I can endure them that long. Either way, live or die, the headaches will end soon.

My staff thinks that my illness is exhaustion. They are a little more pampering than when I first came to live at the mansion, but most of that comes from the shooting incident. I do like the calmer and kinder environment since Mrs. Bailey left. I'd rather have it this way. I can live with mild pampering, but not morbid sympathy.

I'm glad Karen told me to tell Mark about my brain tumor. He took it well, as far as I know. At least, he never mentioned it again. I saw very little change in his behavior, other than he was careful to keep our outings to a reasonable length. As I hoped, he behaved as if I had fatigue and needed to slow down—that was all.

I think preparing to die is very private. Up until the end, I want everyone to behave naturally. After I return from Austria, I'll make contact one more time with the people who are most important to me, the people who have contributed to the richness of my life.

Being sick, incurably sick is a bit like going crazy. I can rationalize anything I want to simply by twirling it around in my mind enough times. The world of dying is a fantasy world that allows me the liberty of any thought I want to have. There is a sane logic to this insanity. I feel like I am living a double life, but I want the luxury of privacy in dying.

~~~

Grandfather goes to bed early, I finish packing, then sit in the chair by the window. Across the room, in the place on the dresser where Grandmother's photos once stood, are photos of my friends. Surveying the lot of them is a reminder of how rich my life has been. There is little Shasta in her tutu, Karen with Mother Elizabeth, Sister Theresa in her habit holding up her new driver's license, and one of the beach photos of Mr. Goldstein. The tabloid photo of Scourge and me is oddly one of
~~~

my favorites. We had fun toying with the media that night. Mark is such a nut, it will be fun to run around Paris with him.

~~~

Tuesday morning, I feel much better. Not only has my headache not been back, I have more energy and a much more upbeat attitude. Zoe and I have been on a roll cranking out documents and letters for two hours.

I look up from my desk to see Zoe and Mother Elizabeth standing in the doorway. Quickly, I shut the file and set it aside.

"Hello, Mother Elizabeth!" I nod to Zoe, as I get up to greet Mother Elizabeth.

"Hello, Kathryn," she replies softly.

"We will be more comfortable in here, Mother." I gesture toward the library.

"How have you been, Kathryn?" Mother Elizabeth asks in a gentle tone.

"Fine, Mother, and yourself?"

We approach the library door. I am becoming more and more comfortable in being the "Mother Superior" of the mansion. She looks good, but worried.

"Mother, may I offer you a cold drink?" I ask as I go to the wet bar and she seats herself in the rich leather chair.

"Yes, that would be nice—tea, if you have it."

"That sounds good," I say and get two glasses.

She looks around at her surroundings as I prepare our drinks. My house is as rich as hers is poor. I am sure she knows that in actuality, she is the rich one between the two of us.

"I know that you couldn't possibly have been in the neighborhood. What brings you all the way out here?"

Mother shifts slightly in her chair. She takes a drink and sets down her glass. She takes a breath.

"What is it, Mother?" I ask softly, concerned.

She looks down to her hands in her lap, then straight at me in her Mother Superior style. "I came to tell you thank you for the new boilers." It's obvious she has something else on her mind.

"Mother?" I try to encourage her without making her uncomfortable. The woman goes to confession weekly—something I could never do—yet, she finds talking to me difficult.

"Do you have heat? Do you have everything you need?"

Sitting in my house, she has to realize that helping her was no sacrifice for me, and certainly not the slightest hardship. Her presence, full traditional habit embarrasses me to be surrounded by such wealth.
~~~

“Yes, yes. Thank you. We have everything we need—thanks to your generosity.” She sounds like a nun again.

I smile. “Anytime you need something—great or small—call me. I have more than enough, and it is a pleasure to help you any way I can.”

She thanks me again and moves forward in her chair, as if she is preparing to leave. She hesitates, then sits up straight at the edge of her chair. Her soft blue eyes begin to fill with tears.

“Kathryn, Karen and I were talking about you. I told her what you did about our heat problem. Then, we talked about different things you did, the baseball game with the kids, Shasta, and sneaking around with Sister Theresa, so she could learn to drive. Karen started to cry. Don’t be angry with her. I made her tell me why she was crying.” She hesitates, choosing and timing her words. “Kathryn, I am so sorry about your brain tumor. I prayed all night before the Blessed Sacrament for you and your health—” Her voice breaks.

It is all I can do not to cry with her. Watching her, I am reminded how she took the news of Monica’s illness. I can see her in the garden, praying her rosary and Karen coming to her, holding her Sister-sister in her arms as she cried.

“Mother Elizabeth, there is a very promising surgery for this type of tumor. It’s not at all like with Monica.”

When tears run down her face, I move closer to her to comfort her.

“And there is such a thing as miracles,” I add.

~~~

After a while, Mother Elizabeth and I walk out the front door together. I’m surprised to see Sister Theresa sitting in the driver’s seat. She could have come inside, but the way she is smiling and holding on the steering wheel it looks like she is guarding her position as driver. Now that she has her license, I doubt anyone would challenge her right to the wheel.

As soon as Mother Elizabeth shuts the car door, they are off in a flash heading for the gate. I doubt Mother has her seat belt on yet. It almost looked like she had a whiplash when Sister took off. I would never ride with that nun after all the driving lessons I sat through with her.

Ordinarily, it is a two-hour drive back to the convent. The way Sister Theresa barely stops at the gate before she pulls onto the Coast Highway, I doubt it will take them that long to get home. I created a monster when I taught her to drive! Maybe not. As I recall, Sister Theresa drove that way from the beginning.

~~~

~ CHAPTER 15 ~

Flight to Paris

Flying has become such a large part of my life that I rarely notice the whine of the engines preparing to thrust us into the atmosphere. Turbulence is insignificant. In a way, it's sad I have forgotten the thrill.

Mark looks up from his guitar and smiles. I put down Grandmother's book, sit back on the sofa and look out the window at the sun shining up through holes in the clouds as it sets on the Earth far below. My martini tastes better than usual with nothing competing with it for my attention. Mark continues to pick out a rhythm on his twelve-string Fender.

"Is that one of the songs for your new album?" I ask, actually liking the melody.

"Yes, do you like it?"

"I do. It seems different from your last album."

"It is—very different. I like the softer sounds. This will be on the new album I'm putting together in London." He begins to play slightly louder and adds the lyrics.

When he finishes I comment, "That's nice. It almost has a Rod McKuen sound to it."

"Rod McKuen? You know Rod McKuen?"

"My mother wore out one of his albums. She loved him!"

"My mother does too!"

"How are you going to sneak that on Scourge's album?"

"Scourge was my last manager's idea. I'm going to record this album under my own name." He beams sheepishly.

I sit up, interested. "Really?"

"Yes. Scourge might have to retire, if this CD sells!"

I study him in surprise. "Let me hear your other songs."

The pilot says we are in French airspace.

Without warning, a sharp pain shoots through my head. My eyes hurt. I close them, but it doesn't help. I feel myself begin to slump off the sofa in slow motion.

Mark moves my body back onto the sofa, then touches my cheeks. He is speaking loudly in a panicked tone to the cabin page.

"Put the pilot on the intercom! Quick! Do it!"

"Yes, sir?" I hear the pilot's voice.

Everything swirls around me like a Van Gogh painting. Through my blurry vision things seem to be in a third-person view. I can see and hear everything, but not quite.

"Miss McKenzie needs a doctor, IMMEDIATELY! Where is the nearest airport?"

~~~

Everything is quiet, dark. Funny, so this is dying? Not that I'm complaining, but I thought dying should be catastrophic, spiritual, musical, maybe in someway a movie-moment. I've had an interesting life, I can't complain about dying. I drift in and out of consciousness.

I hear voices that are human-sounding, no angels. I feel hands lifting and moving me. I smell hospital smells. There is an annoying buzzing sound. Oh, I get it, someone is shaving my head. Hey! Careful, I'm not dead yet! The inside of my head is pounding to burst through my confining skull. It is hot, burning my brain. Dark again, then nothing.

~~~

I can hear muffled voices. I reach up to feel my eyes to see why they aren't opening, but my arms don't move. There is a steady whooshing sound and clicking commingled with beeping sounds. I'm cold. I ask for a blanket, but no words come out.

Concentrating, I make out the sound of Karen's voice. "Mark, you've been here for a week. I'll stay with Katey—go get some rest." She is using her motherly tone—which is legitimate now that they had lied about their identity the first time I passed out.

Karen's voice talks to me about the beach, Livingston, Mr. Goldstein, Maggie, the sunsets, the mist from the waves. I drift off to sleep.

~~~

The days that follow are painful days. It's hard to think with the throbbing in my brain. Finally, it's quiet on the day the respirator is permanently disconnected, and wheeled out of my room. The dainty beeping machine is removed the next day.

When I finally am able to force my eyelids to respond to my wishes, I see a blurry light. There is a stir in the room. Mark notices my eyes are open. He wakes Karen. When they lean over me just right to block the bright light, I can make out the fuzzy outline of their silhouettes.

It's hard to grasp the passage of time. What day is it? What time is it? How'd the surgery go? I had surgery, didn't I? I can't speak, so my questions are left unasked. I can't tell for certain which things I remember and which I remember because I was told about them.

Even though I am awake, the staff talk around me as if I am not in the room. They tell Mark that nothing is wrong with my vocal chords or my trachea from the respirator tube. They think my aphasia is a result of the swelling in my brain and it will pass. I know what is wrong. It is a deep black void between my brain and my lips.
~~~

Karen has to return to the States. There is so much I want to tell her. It will have to wait. Before she leaves, she takes my motionless hand gently in her hand. With all of my might, I will a finger to move. When I lightly squeeze her hand, tears run down her cheeks. She tries to hide them at first, but once tears spilled out the corner of my eye, she releases hers too.

We both know that I will be okay.

~~~
~~~

~ CHAPTER 16 ~

Do You Wanna Dance?

Mark is at my side every time I open my eyes. For me, time passes in disjointed intervals while I am in the hospital. Mark struggles through my breathing treatments, physical therapy, and painful tests. I think it's worse that I am not able to speak, than unable to move—from his prospective and mine. I would like to complain. I think that would ease my frustration.

~~~

When I can speak again, I don't feel like complaining, rather, I squeak Mark's name. He is delighted. Eventually, my speech begins to return. Sometimes I am aphasic. Sometimes I misuse words. But in time, sentences begin to form more often than not. And more often than not, I say what I meant to say.

One Thursday morning during physical therapy, tingling begins in my left shoulder. In a few days the tingling travels down my arm. I am able to clumsily move my arm to a more comfortable position with several flailing attempts. No one knows, or at least admits to knowing, why my recovery has been slower than anticipated.

I surmise it is because the physicians familiar with the surgery did not preform it. Mark says the expert had to advise a local neurosurgeon, Dr. Nidhi, via video conferencing during the surgery. No one hinted that the surgery team had to improvise with neuro-clamps and retractors, rather than the instruments developed for the new procedure.

My recuperation has been slower than anyone else's recovery. My right arm and leg are still numb and move only when it is their choice. For reasons no one seems to understand, my right side resists the passive physical therapy. I wish for anything encouraging from my right side—even pain. It looks like I'll have to learn to write with my left hand. Well, it could be worse in many ways.

Before occupational therapy begins to work on my fine motor skills, I need to get reliable gross motor responses from my left side. Progress is slow and discouraging. Mark and I fake that we aren't concerned.

~~~

The McKenzie jet brings Karen to visit again. Not only have I missed the Halloween party as expected, Thanksgiving has passed, and Christmas is threatening. Karen says she copied names and phone numbers from the address book in my purse, and made the necessary calls after her last visit.

"What calls?—Sorry. Thank you. Who were you able to reach?" I rephrase my question.

"I called your Aunt Grace, because she is the only one of your family I know. I told her your basic situation, and we discussed what she would tell everyone else at Thanksgiving. We have spoken often since then. She loves you a great deal." Karen takes a minute to check her mental list. I don't interrupt.

"I called Zoe and told her you were detained in Europe. She had me speak with Sam. He wasn't aware of your condition—I don't know how you hid it. I thought it would be better for him to tell your grandfather about the emergency surgery."

I nod agreement with her triage of the situation. By now, "detained" in Europe probably doesn't work. That would have been only a temporary bluff.

"I forgot to tell you that I brought someone with me." She smiles mischievously, as she gets up from the chair.

"Wait! Who is it? How do I look?" I ask as I run my hand across the inch-long stubble on my head.

Karen leans over me with a comb and careful not to injure the tender incision line with the teeth, she combs my hair into fluff. She re-combs it again, apparently unsatisfied with the first outcome. It is uncertain how truthful Karen is when she says my hair is "fine."

"Fine?" I ask under my breath as she goes out the door.

"Oh, my God! Mr. Goldstein!" I whisper in awe when Karen opens the door and Mr. Goldstein steps into the open doorway.

Mr. Goldstein's expression explodes, his eyes twinkle, his grin is full and continues to widen—hiding any concern he has.

Karen has kept him informed, but I think he is relieved to see me for himself.

Mark and Karen excuse themselves under the guise of needing coffee, leaving Mr. Goldstein and me alone to visit privately.

"How are you, Katerina?" he asks softly, patting my hand.

"I am getting better. I can't walk yet, but I will."

"Goodt, goodt," he says and pats my hand again.

"I am so happy to see you! Sorry I missed our visit, but I will come in the spring."

~~~

When the time arrives for my discharge from the hospital, Mark makes arrangements to move me to a house in Scotland. The seacoast house belongs to his friend, Jake.

I am excited to be leaving the hospital, though I had hoped to be recovered enough to go home. I never mention to Mark my concern that
~~~

I might live the rest of my life like this—unable to move on my own, a future that discourages me. I tell him, "It is all bridge under the water now."

He looks at me strangely as he lifts me from the wheelchair to the bed that has been placed in the living room. The bed was moved out of the bedroom, because the seizures continue, though they are more infrequent as time passes. I think the idea is that I'll be less discouraged not cooped up in the bedroom.

I grin to turn my remark into a joke. In a way it is true my bridge is underwater. But at the time, I misspoke.

Mark has been nice to coordinate the "spin" on my disappearance from the public eye with Zoe and Frank, my public relations person. No, I never got around to firing Frank.

The stories are varied with conflicting accounts of my whereabouts. The (planted) leaks work to our benefit, as they had planned. Mark has a copy of the tabloid photo of us, framed and by the bed. It is obvious that he tries to keep my spirits up, so I don't want to disappoint him by telling him how discouraged I am. I remind myself that I could be dead if I hadn't had the surgery. I long for an explanation for the seizures and the paralysis, so we can find a remedy.

Mark waits on me and anticipates my needs. He sleeps beside me, so he will awaken if I have a seizure. He makes jokes about my (loss of) weight when he lifts me in and out of the bed. I am sure taking care of me is impeding his new CD promotion tours, but he never mentions it.

~~~

In a week, Jake joins us at the cottage. He's a songwriter by trade, sometimes he's Mark's songwriter. He's going to help Mark nursemaid me while working on a new project. This should be interesting, a romantic setting, two men pampering me, and I can barely move.

I didn't make it to Sweden for the new surgery, but the doctor thought it had gone well. My hair is about two and a half inches long, but it has grown back in blotches. I am assured that it would eventually all come back, but for now, I look like a dog with mange.

The second day after Jake's arrival, a Kawai baby grand piano arrives for the guys and a hot tub for my rehabilitation. Jake appears to be able to compose music in his sleep. The house is filled with nearly constant music. The piano seems to sense what Jake's mind hears and his fingers dance across the keys at all hours of the day and night. He has the recorder going nonstop, burning CD after CD of perfect songs on the first take.

When Jake takes a walk above the rocky shoreline, Mark picks out tunes in his mind as he puts on his "ballad" persona. Just imagine if it
~~~

was Scourge's music! I'd lose what I have left of my mind. I like his softer side of music far better than his Scourge music. His new music reflects the romantic, gentle person that every woman longs to fall in love with. When I listen, becoming lost in his words—half sung, half spoken—I almost forget that I am not my old self. He sings of Camelot and princes and queens in Scotland, loves not lost, chivalry, steeds, and royal banquets. My mind drifts into the fictitious romantic past. I remember Mother's Rod McKuen songs, and can almost hear her sing along.

When the physical therapy hurts, Mark makes up ditties to entertain me. I never complain, but I easily could have in other circumstances. I'm not used to being dependent. It is humbling. In a way, it is probably good for me. Slowly, I ease into wellness.

~~~

February. One day after a discouraging failed attempt to stand, the guys decide to polish my toenails to cheer me. I can't feel them rubbing lotion on my feet, but I imagine the feel of it. They enter into a disagreement about the correct way to apply the polish, which, by the way, is bright red. Whose idea was that? I would never wear red polish. Besides, they really are clueless about this process.

"You two sound like an old married couple!"

They are surprised by my comment and quit fighting immediately. That's not what I meant, and I feel bad for saying anything.

Mark decides to let Jake polish my toenails, because he is going to give me a facial. Great! Where am I going with four-inch-long hair that I'll need a facial? Nevertheless, he massages cream into my face with the confidence of a baker kneading bread dough. Strangely, it feels good. I lean deeper in my pillow. Life is good, definitely not easy, but good.

Sam, Zoe, and Frank keep busy lying to the press. Who knows what they tell Grandfather. Karen keeps my family, Mr. Goldstein, and the nuns informed of my status. I'm bored, discouraged, and restless. I have trouble imagining the future in worse shape than Grandfather. I am in desperate need to get outside and away from this bed and all the rehab paraphernalia.

~~~

In April, the guys use fishing line to hang various shapes of crystals in the windows. The breeze moves them gently, causing flashes of rainbows to dance across the walls and ceilings. They add to the mood of Mark's new music. The days blend easily from one to another.

The facials are now as much of the routine as the range-of-motion exercises. One rainy afternoon, Jake decides they should apply makeup and, yes, I am the practice dummy. My aim is improving, but they both jump out of my reach.

"Wait until I get my hands on you two crazed musicians!"

There is a method to their madness. They are trying to make me presentable for a visit from Karen without spoiling the surprise arrival.

When I see Karen, I forget my threat. Mark has a concert engagement in London, and Karen is the relief nurse. She says she is assigned to keep an eye on Jake.

These are nice people, but they are terrible liars. I know that my care is a burden, one they appear to accept willing, but still more than enough for one person. My right side begins to recover faster than my left. Still, I can't hold a pen if my life depended on it.

My ego is adjusting to being dependent on my friends. However, sometimes at night, I can't help crying quietly about how good they are to me. I always took care of everyone else; this was a hard lesson for me. Mark and Jake do their best not to make it obvious they have put their careers in a holding pattern to help me recover. Jake keeps saying he might have to do all his projects here, since he gets more done than when in his London studio. I don't believe him, but don't mention it.

Someone always sleeps beside me. I haven't had a seizure in months, but they still wake easily if I move abruptly in my sleep. Then they wake me to make sure I'm okay.

Like a child, eventually I learned to sit up on my own. I am beginning to have deliberate movement in my arms. The guys put disposable gloves on me, tape a spoon to my gloved hand and make me feed myself. It is a messy endeavor.

My sense of humor slowly returns with the constant bombardment of their antics. Mark tapes the spoon to my gloved hand with white medical tape as usual. There's a slight problem. I don't say anything. Finally, Jake tells him that I am right-handed.

He lifts his right hand and says, "This is the right hand." He mocks Jake's ignorance.

"Yes, that is YOUR right hand, but THAT is Katey's left hand!" Jake wins.

"Oh, Katey, why didn't you tell me?" Mark looks like there has been a mutiny.

I laugh as he cuts the tape and glove off my left hand. He hadn't realized that the way we were sitting, we were opposite of each other. What a dope!

~~~

Things continue on as usual. Well, usual for us. The day I announced that my legs are beginning to tingle was nothing short of a
~~~

miracle in their eyes. Mark lifts me to a standing position beside him and tries to talk my feet into walking. We have been through this a million times at the parallel bars as I work thought my therapy routine. It still doesn't work.

Not to be disappointed, he enlists Jake to stand on the other side of me and they drag me around the room and say I am walking. They walk me right out of my slipper. From then on, when I need to move, they walk (drag) me around the room—even to move to the chair near the bed. Eventually, their efforts pay off. I begin a stuttered step, as long as one of them steadies me.

As I become stronger, Mark pulls me around in front of him. "Stand on my feet, Katey," he instructs as he moves my arm around his neck. I move the other one around his neck, while he holds me at my waist. Swaying slightly, he begins singing a love song he says he wrote for me. Slowly, he begins to dance with me like an adult dances with a child standing on their shoes. Jake plays the music to the song Mark is singing. It is a nice slow-dance song. I can almost feel the beat in my feet. More than dancing, I like the words to the song.

Jake turns on the stereo and comes to cut in. He is stronger than Mark and lifts me at the waist, relieving some of my weight from my feet. I never imagined that I would ever dance again.

Mark cuts in, but Jake wouldn't bow out. I have an arm on each of their shoulders and the three of us dance together. Life is good. It is certainly not what I expected, but it is good.

~~~

I begin to make phone calls to the mansion. Grandfather is glad to hear from me, so I call him daily. During this time, Sam and Zoe hold down the fort at home, under the careful watch of the house women. I'm getting simplified reports about our internal investigation. Danny and Susan, his love interest, are setting up housekeeping.

By the time my hair is nearly touching my shoulders, I can walk tentatively on my own. I work at it every chance I get. Winter and spring are gone and summer has arrived. I am able to walk outside, but never alone. Often Mark and I sit in the garden listening to the new CD of his authentic persona. It is good. Much richer than Scourge's. It's more hopeful, more loving. This is the Mark I know and love. Jake approves.

One afternoon while we are walking outside, I watch my shadow's gait. I hadn't realized how crippled I walk. It seemed like such an improvement from being paralyzed, that I hadn't noticed and no one mentioned it.

"Mark!" I gasp as I grab his arm.

"What!" I startled him and it showed in his voice.
~~~

"Did I have a stroke? I walk like I had a stroke!" My voice reflects the tears inside my heart. I know I should be happy that I am still alive —and I am. I really am happy to be alive. I just hadn't realized how I looked when I walked.

"Not exactly a stroke, you'll be fine."

I leave it at that. Either it is an unknown or no one wants to say what happened. I guess it doesn't matter what it is called or what happened. I have to keep going.

Later that evening, Frank faxes the latest headlines. The media has been silent about Kathryn McKenzie for months. Zoe fed them a steady diet of tidbits about my donations while I was ill. She failed to mention my illness. Finally, someone in the media noticed that no one had actually seen me for a while. One of the scandal sheets asked in big bold letters, "WHERE IS KATHRYN McKENZIE???"

Because of my obvious limp, Mark and I agree with Frank to leak that I had been in an auto accident and "was recovering nicely."

The wire services pick up the story and run with it as if it were true. Apparently, I had a car accident in a remote (unspecified) location in Europe, and "Miss McKenzie expressed gratitude to her well-wishers for the flowers and gifts that were showered on her."

"Really? And they believed that?" I ask, surprised at the details that have been added to our press release.

Mark shrugs his shoulders and smiles as he reads further. "Scourge was driving and was killed instantly in the accident." No one ever mentioned that he had been giving concerts on and off all the time I was recovering from "the accident." That was Scourge's last concert. That worked out well.

~~~
~~~

~ CHAPTER 17 ~

The Journey Home

Now that Mark is free of Scourge, he cuts his hair and lets it return to its natural blond color. Without the greasepaint, no one recognizes his former identity. I can't say that I miss Scourge, but the media is sure to miss his staged antics.

One morning, Mark and Jake decide—without consulting me—that a walk to the ocean is in order. As in the days when we sit in the garden, the sunscreen is generously applied, as well as my floppy hat to keep from sunburning the incision scar on my head. Even though the guys are wearing short sleeves, I must wear a jacket. Still frail in comparison to my former self, I tend to easily get a chill.

The beach is rocky. I can only imagine a sure-footed goat walking to the water's edge with ease. Mark and Jake tightly hold my arms. There is zero possibility I will fall, even if I trip over a rock. I feel like an old woman being helped to the car for a trip to the local care home. I struggle with the terrain and my concept of self. When I sit in the sun with the guys, I can delude myself that I am the same as I was.

Walking to the beach is an entirely different story—a difficult story. But the smell of the water is a refreshing coming-home smell that I have missed tremendously these last eight months. I love the sound of the water crashing on the rocky shore and the waterfowl squawking at each other. I haven't seen much of Scotland, since I am sequestered on Jake's property, but I am in love with Scotland now.

When I'm totally recovered and have everything that requires my attention at home caught up, I am hopping on the McKenzie jet and coming back to Scotland. I am going to visit the highlands, castles, and the people. I love the feel of this place. Of course, I'm drunk with the ocean today, but I don't care. I might even visit Wales—where Grandmother McKenzie's family once lived generations ago.

There is a sense of coming home and being in the land of my ancestors. I knew that I was Welsh-Irish, but adding Grandmother's Scots to the mix seems to complete me. I can feel it now, standing here on this rocky beach. And now, I am ready to go home to my beach.

The next afternoon, I am reading near the window, comfortable to be alone with my thoughts. It is peaceful. I could stay here forever, but I know that I have to go home and take care of business sometime soon. As humble as it makes me feel, I am going to fully embrace being "Kathryn the Great" when I get home. Finally I understand my purpose on Earth.

Jake is off to London for a recording session with one of his clients. Mark is out for a walk along the bluff above the ocean. He says it gives him inspiration. And I am here quietly redefining my self-image.

I practically have Grandmother's book memorized. I could read others, but I'm still in pursuit of the key she mentioned. Certainly there is a lot of wisdom and encouragement within these pages, but I don't know the question or the answer. As I straighten the cover jacket of the book to lay it down, I feel something in the spine. I remove the jacket completely, but see nothing. Closing my eyes and running my fingers slowly up and down the spine, I feel something under the cloth backing.

Mark bursts in the house breathless. "Katey! I have an idea!" He takes the book and helps me out of the chair.

"What?" I have learned to expect wild ideas from this man. Ask first, always ask before trying any of Mark's ideas—that is the number one rule when dealing with him!

"Come walk the beach with me. The tide is out. I think the sand will help strengthen your lower legs and feet, so you will walk normally again!" He is delighted with his idea.

So am I.

Quickly, I go along with his scheme. I bet it will work—the sand will provide gentle resistance, passive resistance, the physical therapist used to say. I would beat him to the beach, but I am not that steady on my own over open ground. He holds my hand with the other arm around my back.

We have to walk inside the water's edge to get to the sandy area. The waves splash up our legs—more on Mark than me, because he is deeper in the water than I. As we walk in the sand, I can feel the back of my heel and my calf pull. My stamina for walking is shot from months of inactivity. It makes me think of the first time I took Mr. Goldstein for a walk on a faraway and very different beach from this. If nothing else, being in the water is fueling my soul.

~~~

When we return to the house, I am tired and cold, but happy. After I change into dry clothes, Mark helps me pull my feet under the covers and I begin to drift off to sleep.

Mark insists on a full week of walking on the beach before he pronounces me ready to return to the States. Little does he know, that I have all ready decided it is time for me to go home.

Besides, Dan is engaged to Susan and I have offered them the mansion for their wedding and reception. He teased that he would have used the yacht for a honeymoon on the Mediterranean, if I hadn't sold it. I'll rent a yacht for him, if that is the wedding gift they would like.

~~~

When we arrive on the tarmac, the reporters are waiting inside. I suspect that Frank tipped them off that I was returning. I won't ask. That way he won't have to tell me, or lie.

"Miss McKenzie! Miss McKenzie! Welcome home, Miss McKenzie!" reporters shout.

"Miss McKenzie, how are you?" asks another.

"I'm fine, Sheila, thank you. Thank you all. It is good to get home again." I stretch out my arm and wave.

The cameras flash in my face. Defensively, my hand goes up to shield my eyes from the light. That is one thing no one had thought about. The light hurt my eyes with a sharp pain.

Mark quickly pulls my face to his chest and holds up his hand to halt the reporters.

"Please, please, no flashes, PLEASE!" Everyone falls silent and stands still—an eerie still.

When they lower their cameras, Mark releases his hold on my head.

I turn around. No more media games. I am going to tell the truth. They can spin it as they will. I am not my grandfather, and I no longer admire the sport of spinning the media.

"Thank you for coming to greet me. I am recovering from brain surgery. I had a brain tumor." I drop my eyes to the floor for a second to think of what to say.

There is a shuffling sound while the reporters wait respectfully.

"I am fine. I had a stroke during the surgery and have had seizures —that is why your flash hurt my eyes. I am fine, but we will have to take it slow at first." I turn to leave, then turn back. "If I may, I would like to offer my condolences to all of Scourge's fans. We will miss him." I take Mark's arm and he helps me off the small step that I had been speaking from.

Garrett is standing beside the limousine in his chauffeur's uniform that Grandfather made him wear after he decided to call him "James." Garrett looks very proper standing at the ready, except for when his large lips burst apart into a wide, toothy grin. The contrast between his white teeth and dark skin accent the size of his smile all the more.

Garrett opens the limo door for me, vying with Mark for his rightful position as my attendant.

As I lean down to enter the limo, my attention is moved from the chivalrous men in my life to a pair of legs with black high heels attached to the feet. Moving into the vehicle more, I see a gray suit skirt, and quickly look up to see Karen's grinning smile.

"Katey, welcome home!" She warmly reaches to help me inside.

"Oh, Karen!" I reach to hug her.

Mark moves a newspaper and slides to the seat facing us.

"Where to, ma'am?" Garrett looks back over his shoulder with a grin.

"Home, let's go home." I feign seriousness.

"The Coast Highway, ma'am?"

"Yes, absolutely—the Coast Highway."

The newspaper headline catches my attention, though I make no move to retrieve the paper. It reads that one of the McKenzie company's CEOs is being indicted for embezzlement of the pension fund, and something about government contracts that I can't make out because it is at the fold of the front page.

Karen squeezes my hand in excitement. The paper can wait until I get home and Sam fills in the details. For now, I am going to enjoy the ride up the coast with my friends. I smile at Karen and squeeze her hand in response.

"Katey, we decided to wait until you were home to tell you—" She pauses long enough for me to glance at the headline again in anticipation.

"Your grandfather is not well," she says softly.

Dazed by the unexpected news, I ask, "What?" in confusion.

"He took to his bed three months ago. Brooke was picked up on drug charges on New Year's Eve. She gave up Tim to deal her own release and lured him into a trap. Then, while Tim was in jail awaiting his bail appearance, he was stabbed and died. After Brooke heard what happened, she took an overdose." Karen pauses.

"I'm so sorry, Katey. Your grandfather took the funerals hard. Eventually, he just stayed in bed." She looks at me, then at Mark. Then, she says softly, "I think he was afraid he had lost you, too."

"They are both—" I pause before saying the word, "they are dead?" I ask, then look at Mark who is stirring in his seat.

It is obvious Mark was aware of the situation and the decision had been made not to tell me about it. There is no point in accusing him, for I am, after all, Kathryn the Great again.

"How is Grandfather now? Does he know I am returning?"

"Zoe told him you were coming today, but she doesn't know if he understood. He's depressed and refuses to take medication for the depression because of how it makes him feel. She showed him the video of your birthday that Jake and Mark shot, and he seemed to do a little better."

I look in Mark's direction. I had forgotten about that silly movie. We were being giddy. We danced, laughed and horsed around with party hats on our heads. A deep fondness for my friends comes over me.

Mark and Jake are sweet. And Karen has gone beyond the call of duty keeping my aunt and Mr. Goldstein apprised of my condition.

Garrett looks over his shoulder at me. "Missy, I told Mr. McKenzie he had to get himself out of that bed today for your homecoming. I told him you would be disappointed if he wasn't in that chair of his and on the front porch where he belongs."

We all laugh at Garrett's sincerity and enthusiasm—and daring. We will know if his lecture worked as soon as we drive into the gate. I would ordinarily ask to stop at Father's Beach, but considering Grandfather's condition, I say nothing about stopping. Garrett looks in the rearview mirror and catches my attention as we approach the turnoff. I shake my head slightly. He gets the message, and nods his head to acknowledge.

~~~

As we move up the drive and the front of the mansion comes into full view, I can see the staff assembling on the front steps. Everyone is there. Zoe is wearing a young person's business suit. Sam has on a suit and tie. Chico has on black slacks and black shirt—open partway down his chest—and his hair is pulled back into a ponytail. Both flight crews and the helicopter pilots are to the right of the stairs in their uniforms. Louise is wearing her white jacket and chef's hat that she wears only for formal occasions. Danny and a woman, who must be Susan, are there on the top step. Race, his wife, and their children—all cleaned and polished—are standing opposite of Dan and Susan. Juan is at the bottom of the steps with a bouquet of roses in hand. Stanley, always dressed as a butler, is standing in the forefront of everyone, white-gloved hands ready to assist me out of the car.

Eleanor is wearing a pretty dress that distinguishes her as the head of the house. She stops in the center of the porch. Everyone stands at a civilian version of attention.

The flight personnel salute as the limo pulls slowly past them. That's pretty slick that they got here ahead of me. Good thing I have a helicopter, isn't it?

Grandfather is missing, but he likes to make an entrance.

I reserve comment.

Garrett pulls the limo to a gentle, perfectly executed stop in front of Stanley, then gets out and goes around the front of the car to open my door. Stanley reaches in his white-gloved hand to assist me. When I am fully standing, he hands me a cane. As I take it in my hand, I notice it feels as if it were made especially for me. It is a beautifully balanced cane. As Garrett assists Karen and Mark out of the vehicle, I wait, using my new cane to steady myself.

Karen and Mark stand on either side of me to help me up the stairs. Stanley walks one step ahead of us and Garrett one step behind. I smile
~~~

warmly at each member of the welcoming committee that has gathered. At the top step, Karen moves to the side to stand with Keith.

As if on cue, Conner—dressed in his white orderly uniform, rather than his standard beach-boy look—wheels Grandfather out the door. He parks the chair beside and a little forward of Eleanor. We are, after all, very particular about rank at these welcoming ceremonies.

Grandfather beams at the sight of me. I love that old man. I swoop down to hug him and kiss his cheek.

"Kathryn, I have missed you," he whispers.

"I love you very much, Grandfather," I whisper.

I stand beside him, holding his hand, facing the welcoming party. Stanley, Garrett, and the flight people have moved in along the bottom step. Juan ascends the steps and sheepishly hands me the roses, tips his hat and blends into the crowd on the sidelines, collecting their approving giggle at his sense of style.

I smell the roses and say to all, "Thank you. Thank you so much. It is very good to be home."

Eleanor whispers from her side of Grandfather's chair that there are cookies and punch on the patio.

"I am told there are cookies and punch awaiting us." I motion for everyone to join in the fun.

The party doesn't last long. Slowly everyone has said "welcome back" and left to enjoy their weekend. Karen says that the doctor has prescribed rest after the party. Grandfather nods and agrees that it is what he is going to do. Eleanor says she'll turn down my bed and tells Stanley to bring my luggage up to my room. Mark and Karen can walk me up the stairs.

Keith says that he will give Mark a ride home when I'm settled.

Mark nods his head in agreement.

"Thank you for everything you have done," I say and give each of them a sentimental hug, and Mark a kiss on the cheek.

I am tired. A nap before dinner sounds good. I stand at the bottom of the stairs and look up. I know that I can take it slow and get to my room, but coming back down alone might be an entirely different story. I have grown accustomed to having Mark and Jake at my side all these months. I feel a little wobbly at the thought of Mark leaving, but I don't mention it.

Slowly, we embark on the assent of the stairs. Because of my "gimp" leg, we have to step on each tread with both feet, rather than alternating as most people climb stairs. The cane slows the process, so Karen carries it and Mark and Keith promise to carry me, if necessary.

Eleanor is coming out of my room as we reach the third and last landing of the stairs.

"Kathryn, we put in the skylight in the ballroom that you talked about wanting. Would you like to see it?"

"Oh, yes!" answers Karen before I can speak.

I say nothing about having to manage another set of stairs to see the skylight. Eleanor opens the ballroom's double doors.

"Oh, it is already dark! Let me get the lights. Wait right there," she says as she walks to the light panel for the switch.

Eleanor has barely had time to reach the light switch when the chandelier comes on.

"Surprise!!!" yells everyone who is hiding in the room.

One by one, they must have slipped up the back servant stairs after they left the cookie reception. Such is the richness of my life! Most of them laugh with nervous excitement. The hand-carved Italian crystals of the palace-size chandelier have been cleaned. There are thousands of twinkling rainbows on every surface of the room. I thought artificial light didn't refract into a rainbow. Ah, who cares? It is beautiful! I am touched by all of this. Words can't describe how I feel.

Standing around the room, and beginning to congregate behind Grandfather's wheelchair is everyone from the original welcoming committee. They must have carried his wheelchair up the back stairs. They were quick!

In addition, Dana, Sister Theresa, Mother Elizabeth, some of the original Spirit of Hope staff and clients, Danny and Susan, Jake, Aunt Grace and most of my uncles, aunts, and cousins are there as I look from face-to-face, and back again.

"I can't believe it!" I keep repeating, tears streaming down my face. I'm no longer thinking about a nap.

From the back of the crowd someone is moving forward. People move aside until I can see Shasta. She is leading Mr. Goldstein to me.

"Katerina! Katerina!" he shouts. Everyone laughs again. We hug, and I kiss him on the cheek.

Shasta gives a full body, tight hug.

My face hurts from smiling so hard. Louise and her crew have set up a buffet table. The ballroom is decorated for a party to rival any other party ever held in it.

It takes a few minutes to greet everyone. Each person comes to me with a hug and well wishes. Karen even flew in Dr. Nidhi and some of my therapists in the McKenzie jets. Karen stands near me in the reception line, hand on my arm to help steady me. I reach for her hand and give it a squeeze.

We turn around when music starts. Jake is conducting an eight-piece band. Race has his sax and begins to move in front of the other band members. I recognize the sweet, sweet sounds of New Orleans.

A trumpet player begins to echo Race's notes. They get into a musical dialogue playing off of each other in the most magnificent rendition of the song as I have ever heard. I wish we were taping this!

The eager applause is well-deserved. Jake announces that I have missed a very special Christmas recital. The music starts. Shasta comes out dressed as the Fairy Queen and dances the ballet beautifully—to the delight of her audience.

Mark leads me to the dance floor, directly under the center chandelier. The perimeter lights dim when the music begins.

Jake, with his husky, sexy voice, begins to sing Mark's latest love song. Mark and I dance. No longer standing on his shoes, I close my eyes and enjoy being alive.

Toward the end of the song, the lights come up. Taking the cue, I motion everyone to join us on the dance floor. I sit out the next couple of dances. Shasta dances with Mother Elizabeth, then Mr. Goldstein, then Stanley. She loves to dance and is "in her element" in the ballroom.

Grandfather seems to be enjoying the party he arranged for me. As friends and family come to our table, I introduce them to him. He is a little overwhelmed with the variety of people in my life at the party.

He is in awe at meeting my mother's family. It wasn't the response I had expected. I thought, at best, he would be properly polite. Instead, he seemed to be longing to be part of a family. I think I will include him in some of my family outings in the future.

Mr. Goldstein is staying for two weeks, and he is in the downstairs guest room until he goes to visit Karl. Karen and I meet eyes and I nod approval of her scheme to bring him to the States. It is a good thing that I own two jets to bring all of my distant friends and family together.

What a day this has been. I am looking forward to spending time with everyone.

I'm tired, a good tired.

~~~
~~~

~ CHAPTER 18 ~

Phoenix Rises

Karen and Keith stayed in the room that connects with mine, with the door ajar—just in case I called for her to help me. Dan and Susan stayed in Dan's old room. Jake gave Mark a ride home. They had everything planed down to the minute details. I suspect Zoe was the mastermind behind the logistics.

~~~

Eleanor comes upstairs to see if I need any assistance this morning and was surprised to find me showered and dressed. I did allow her to help me down the stairs, since this was the first time I faced descending three flights of stairs.

Louise has a fabulous breakfast prepared for her houseful of people. If she had her way, the house would always be full of guests. I propose we eat in the kitchen or even the patio to ease her work, but she will have none of my idea. We will eat in the dining room. And that is that.

Grandfather, who hasn't eaten in the dining room for months, sits at the head of the table surveying his guests: Dan and Susan, Karen and Keith, Mr. Goldstein, and me.

We visit intermittently while Grandfather drinks in every bit of our being together. Grandfather loves Dan's girlfriend, Susan. Maybe he is finally learning a bit about family and acceptance.

Susan is a recent transplant to L.A. from Denver, they knew each other at the university and reconnected on Facebook. Dan promises to be back in a couple of days after visiting Disneyland, the Huntington Library, and the beach. He wants to take Susan to San Francisco and ride a cable car. I offer the use of the McKenzie jet and he accepts, then thinks better of it and decides to drive, since PCH gives such a splendid view of the ocean.

As for Mr. Goldstein, Garrett and I are taking him to the city to visit his Senior Center friends for a few days. Then, I will be back to give Grandfather my undivided attention. Mr. Goldstein and I can resume our beach walks, at least for a week.

~~~

We finish our breakfast and everyone else takes off, seeming to suspect Grandfather, Dan, and I need a moment alone.

When they are gone, I offer Grandfather and Dan my condolences for Brooke and Tim.

Grandfather wipes his mouth with his napkin and stirs in his chair.

Dan interrupts whatever Grandfather was preparing to say. "Thank you. I miss them, but they chose the direction for their lives and no one could stop them," he says quite calmly.

Grandfather clears his throat, and looks at Dan. "Yes. I thought I could do something that your parents couldn't when I brought you here, but I may have made things worse."

I start to respond, but Dan beats me to it. "Grandfather, it wasn't anyone's fault. They had choices and kept making the easy ones—the wrong ones. The only thing either of them wanted was to live in the fast lane. I guess they just got to the end of the road," he says, then smiles.

Grandfather grunts a slight response and drinks the rest of his coffee.

"Grandfather, your children and grandchildren are our own people. Even you cannot control our destiny, it's in our hands, and we do make our own choices." I look directly at him.

And it is true. Dan and I are proof the money and power cannot change who people are—it might only accent our flaws.

~~~

I kiss Grandfather on the forehead and tell him that I will be back for dinner—Mr. Goldstein and I have a date with the beach before he goes to his friend's house for a few days.

Mr. Goldstein and I are quite a pair. Both of us walk with a cane now. He has had more practice, but I am not going to let him get the best of me.

"Katerina, do you remember the first time we did this?" he asks as we walk across the sand, leaving Garrett and the limo behind in the parking lot. He keeps an eye on us, just in case...

Not sure if he means the first attempt or when we walked along the beach, I simply answer, "Yes. Yes, I do."

Remembering what Mark said about walking in the sand being therapeutic, I reach down and pull off my shoes and carry them in my free hand.

"Yest, I do, too." His English isn't as American as it once was. "You are strong. I know it has been hard. You were afraid, yes? I know you. You will be okay. Don't ever forget what I tell you." He stops walking to look at me.

"I will remember." I stuff my shoes under my elbow and squeeze his hand. We are pretty hopeless with only one free hand apiece.

We walk along our beach—the place where we came to know each other and to find ourselves.

~~~

After my outing with Mr. Goldstein, Garrett and I take him to Karl's house. Garrett takes me back to the beach, then heads home. I have not been alone in forever. It kind of feels good to be trusted to be alone. I take a nap, then fix dinner, then go straight to bed. It's a good tired. I'm taking Mr. Goldstein at his word that I will be fine. I will get out more than before. Sure, I'll pace myself. But I don't plan to waste a day. The doctors think they got all of the tumor, but maybe there's one cell left that will awaken someday. I am going to stay ahead of the game and get my strength back and live a rich, full life while I can.

~~~

Karen and I are having lunch today.

"Sorry, sorry I'm late," Karen says when I open the door.

"Come in, I wasn't worried. I knew you weren't lost." We leave to walk to the end of the pier for lunch.

After lunch, I'm tired, but say nothing about it as I look along the seemingly endless pier back to the sidewalk. We stop midway and stand at the railing, watching the kids on boogie boards ride to shore. I welcome the rest stop.

"How are you doing?" she asks without looking at me.

"Fine. And you?"

"The letter came from the Church this morning."

"Really? What letter?" I ask, obviously clueless.

"They denied my request for an annulment." She turns to me and fakes a smile.

"What! Wasn't that a hasty decision?" I ask, forgetting about the time I lost after my surgery.

"It's been a year. They're trying to move cases along, so they don't get a backlog again."

"Well, still—"

"I haven't told Keith yet."

"Excuse me for saying so, but considering the sex thing with all of those priests, aren't they being a bit judgmental that you married someone who cheated on you and his vows?"

"Two wrongs don't make a right." She defends their decision.

"That's nonsense! Isn't there something about checking your own eyesight before removing a splinter from someone else's eye?" I misquote the Bible, but that isn't the point. "You can't tell me that God would rather that you and Keith stay alone for the rest of your lives, because your spouses left you? I don't think so. I think the Church is wrong."

"I have to sort it out and to figure out how to tell Keith. He isn't Catholic. This is my religion, this is what I believe—what I have always believed."

"I know," I say softly, "it is my religion too. But I can't imagine God withholding happiness for you and Keith. The Church is wrong." I dare
~~~

to toe right to the edge of the line that a tribunal of nuns and priests have a clue about marriage. Don't get me started on the child-raping scandal cover-up.

"I don't think God would have decided as the tribunal did. Keith and I have a difficult decision to make. The one thing that keeps coming to mind is that no one has treated me like Keith does. He is respectful and loving in the most tender way—the way women hope a man will treat them. I have never met such a thoughtful person." She smiles as she speaks about Keith.

I say no more before I get excommunicated, but in my heart I know that the Church is wrong—maybe not in matters of doctrine, but they are terribly wrong about Karen and Keith.

~~~

Mark leaves on his new album tour. I don't know what Jake is doing. I feel surrounded by couples in love: Karen and Keith, and Dan and Susan. Not that I would consider contact with Joseph, but I miss being in love.

I listen to Ann Zimmerman's song, "Kiss on the Mouth," while I write in my journal for the first time in months. The song seems to fit me—unfortunately. Ann's voice tells of my longing.

> ♪♪ It's winter to spring and summer to fall,
> I've seen the years pass and I've seen the stars fall,
> I've watched in the flood and I've watched in the drought
> But I've watched without you and your kiss on the mouth...
> If I had a grand share of all the world's wealth,
> Still a pauper I'd be with no kiss on the mouth.♪♪

©Ann Zimmerman

I'm tired and a little melancholy tonight. I am sure it will pass. Besides, I need to focus my energy on getting stronger. Mark will be back soon and we can spend time together. I miss him.

My Dearest Maggie, It seems that I should make the most of my wealth by aiding sojourners along life's journey. There is much I want to do and now is the time to begin.

When I finish writing, I'll look for Gwen's business card. As a registered physical therapist, maybe she can recommend a local therapist. Grandfather and I need to gain more strength, even though he will never walk again. I still need to do strengthening exercises. It will be fun to call her and visit for a few minutes, she is so energetic.
~~~

On Monday, I begin half days at work. Gradually, they are full days. Gwen talked to her partners and took a leave of absence to come provide physical therapy to Grandfather and me. Gwen will train Conner to take over Grandfather's treatment when she leaves.

Around the house, with Gwen's skillful therapy, I become able to leave my cane in the umbrella stand. Walking in the garden, I still use it. Gwen is often at my side in addition to two scheduled sessions a day for each of us.

Life seems the same to an onlooker, but I know that it is different. I am different. More determined, perhaps. If McKenzie Enterprises wasn't sure who was in charge before, they know now. The operation is more efficient, and definitely less corrupt. I learn Grandfather had torn down the apartment building Dana lived in and built a parking garage and luxury condos. It was our fault Dana became homeless. I take all the profits from that property and funnel it into the homeless shelters that serve the people Grandfather displaced. We locate the former tenants and find housing for those still homeless.

Zoe becomes my personal assistant more than ever before. She thrives on all of the projects I give her, like finding the displaced tenants. Dana provided some names. Zoe likes having her own secretary.

After cleaning out the graft in my companies, Sam makes the unions happy when he negotiates benefit packages that are real benefits for the remaining employees. Chico has a little army of techy weirdos. He and Race have divided the work. My dear Race manages the household accounting data and keeps our computers and servers running tip-top. Chico freely visits all the companies. No one has dared to complain about Chico, at least, not so that I hear about it.

Jim has a security detail in place, and I think I might have more security gadgets than most federal buildings. Keith retired from the police force, his time in the department completed. He and Jim formed a partnership. They consult on security matters for the McKenzie Enterprise, the estate, and my personal safety.

I still haven't told anyone the shooter was watching me at the beach for weeks before he came to the mansion to shoot me. I haven't put the pieces together, but shooting me at the beach would have been much easier. Something still doesn't make sense about this. They never did discover who shot him. So that person is still at large. Figures.

~~~

The first three months after my return there isn't much time to spend at my beach. To relax, I begin writing a novel. It's a legitimate escape from Miss McKenzie, Kathryn the Great.

Life is good. I *will* it to be that way. No longer am I taking what comes. To Mr. Bradford's amazement, I have developed a keen sense
~~~

for investing. I invest some in the usual money-generating fashion, but more importantly, I invest in the human factor. The human investments are paying well.

Monica's House for families with AIDS is up and running, following Mother Elizabeth's model. McKenzie Grants for arts and sciences in inner-city schools are second to none anywhere. Only when strategically necessary is my name attached to my projects. Unfortunately, far too often the name is needed, but that brings more money from people who are hoping to get a contract bid or something else from me.

Zoe, Garrett, or Sam, and sometimes Grandfather go with me to visit the people in the shelter, so we can assess the needs firsthand. Because of the weakness still in my left leg, operating the clutch tires me, though I do like driving standard transmission vehicles. I usually find someone to drive me to these outings. However, I think any one of them would go even if they didn't have to chauffeur me.

Simply for the thrill of it, I ask Garrett to take me for a ride in Father's Jag once a week. He loves that car. It is easy to get him talking about him and Dad running around town in it when they were at the university.

Without saying anything, I sign the '53 Jaguar title over to Garrett. The day after the new title arrives in his mail, Garrett comes excitedly into my office holding the paper. He puts it on the desk and keeps poking at it with his finger as he talks.

"Miss McKenzie, I, I don't know how this happened," he stutters in a panic.

"Garrett, it's a gift," I answer as I look up from my work, struggling to keep a straight face.

"I assure you, I had no part in this."

"It's a gift," I say again.

"I'll get to the bottom of—" He finally realizes what I said. "Miss McKenzie! I can't accept this." He is awed.

"Father would be pleased. Now, get your car out of my garage. Scoot. Take the day off. Give your wife a ride in your new car."

I pull the keys out of my desk drawer and hand them to him.

"I noticed the keys were gone from the garage. I should a known you were up to no good." Garrett fingers the Jaguar key chain.

"Ah, thank you, Missy," he says and hugs me until it hurts.

"You're welcome. Now, go on. Get out of here. I have work to do." I shoo him out of my office.

As he leaves, I smile to myself. I bet Dad is smiling too.

As the fog continues to clear from my brain, I remember the key in Grandmother's book. I think I found it, just need to see how to get it out of the spine of the book. I wonder how she got it in there?

With the door to the office locked, I remove the book jacket. I can't see anything unusual about the bare spine, until I turn on the desk lamp. I tilt the book and run my finger over it, looking for the area to concentrate my interest. There is a spot, nearly undetectable, where I feel something inside. I don't see any place that looks like the spine was split on the side and repaired. I'm guessing it was slid in from the top when the book was open wide.

I hold the book fully open, lifting the spine opening eye level, with the other end toward the lamp. I'm not sure I see anything, but I tell myself that "possibly" I do. It is smack-dab in the center, so it isn't easier to reach from one end or the other. I rifle through the desk drawers, looking for something to poke down the tube-like opening.

I grab a pencil and try to thrust it inside the spine. I can't angle it so the lead tip scrapes along the cloth side. I throw the pencil back into the drawer. Pens aren't of any use. Way back in the center drawer is an old-style letter opener. It seems perfect, but slides right over the spot I've deemed "of interest."

I leave the letter opener in partway and close the book slowly, testing periodically. Finally, I have things just right so the letter opener finds the edge of something, and by the slight "clink" I'd say it was metal on metal. I push harder, and push the tip of the letter opener through the cloth. Damn.

That wasn't the plan, but I decide, what difference does it make if I cut the spine, I can have it repaired. I remove the letter opener and insert the tip through the rip from the outside, making a flap to pry open. There is a small key. Grandmother had meant a physical key, not something philosophical to learn from the book. I feel a bit the village idiot. I don't know how much clearer she could have been. I had the message wrong. She said the key was in the book, well, yes, it was. Goodness! Where did she get that idea?

The silver box in Grandfather's upstairs bedroom comes to mind as soon as I see the key. I bet it's a perfect fit. Extra trips up the stairs are something I've avoided. I consider asking Zoe or Eleanor to fetch the box for me, but I think it is best no one knows I have an interest in it. Or in Zoe's case, she doesn't know the box exists. It is slow progress, but not impossible to go upstairs alone. I'll have an excuse ready if anyone comments about me going up now. "Off to take a nap," that should do.

I'm not winded when I reach the top step at the third floor, but it was a slow labor and I've broken a sweat. That's a good reason not to do this in the middle of the day, next time. I go into my room, then enter Grandfather's old room through the adjoining doorway. I don't think anyone is up here to see me, but it is certainly normal for me to go to my room. Nothing suspicious.

My hands jitter with excitement as I lift the silver chest from the shelf. The little chest is heavy. I set it back on the shelf, take my cane into my room, then come back for the silver box. I stay close to the wall so I can lean against it, if I lose my balance. I have to use both hands to carry the chest since I still have residual weakness on my left side.

Breathlessly, I get to my bed and set the chest on it. I locked my door when I came in, now I return to lock the door between the two bedrooms. I don't think anyone will come in, but an ounce of prevention is worth a pound of cure.

I inspect the chest. It needs a good polishing. I fish the key from my pocket, get settled on the bed—pulling my legs up, since I'm not allowed to let them dangle when I sit. I settle the box facing me, kiss the key, and turn the lock. When I lift the lid, papers spring up. They had been packed down tight so the lid would shut. I start removing them, keeping them in their order, in case that was planned. There is a note from Grandmother to me, a letter to her that is very thick, a newspaper clipping, some photos, and bits of paper with notes, numbers, dates—various things, in Grandmother's writing.

Grandmother says she is happy to see that her curious granddaughter is still curious, or I wouldn't have found the box and the key. Happy Birthday, since I must have turned of age to get the trust. *I wish she could see me now.* She hints at the questions again, but writes there are two main questions to be asked about McKenzie Enterprise. She says the letter from Eli Reed will answer most of them and send me in the right direction for the rest.

The letter is ten or twelve pages, written in longhand. The writing is hard to read since the ink is faded. Mr. Reed is writing to Grandmother because he is dying. He has cancer. I look for a date, but find none. He seems pretty certain he won't live, since the cobalt treatment didn't work. I date the letter to be prior to the development of chemotherapy.

Mr. Reed starts with information of how Grandfather won the bet to marry her. Basically, Mr. Reed told Grandfather information from a friend about a government contract the friend's company was getting, and when it would be announced. Al [Grandfather] bought stock in the company prior to the announcement of the contract. It seems funny to hear Grandfather referred to as Al rather than Alistair.

I'm three pages into the letter when the writing changes to a neater, more feminine hand. "I am writing for my father, as he is too weak to finish, but he feels he must tell you the rest before he dies."

There's a knock at my door and Eleanor's voice calling my name, asking if I'm okay.

"Yes, Eleanor. Just a minute."

I hurry to return everything to the box and lock it. I can't return it to the shelf, so I put it under my pillow and fluff both pillows against the headboard. Quickly, I lay down to mess the bed as if I had been resting.

I answer Eleanor that I am getting up now, and would she wait to help me down the stairs. I look back at my pillows, wishing to finish what I started; but I understand that I'm missed if I disappear, after being gone for nearly a year.

Eleanor eases me down the stairs and I join the household activities. Race brings reports and I give him the time to explain them to me, though I don't need the explanation. They all want to "be by me," and I do my best to accommodate their need.

After the staff leaves, dinner is finished, and Grandfather has had his share of attention, I inch up the stairs, aware that Stanley is watching to make sure I do okay.

Once I'm ready for bed, I get the small silver chest again. Mr. Reed's letter is incredible. He gives names, companies, and more specifics than I would have expected. I'll have to read it again, but the big question is what to do with the information.

I put the box in my closet for the night. I've been a pack rat with the things I've found in the two rooms, so I don't think anyone will think anything about it if they see it there.

The key is a different matter. Grandmother was right to hide it well. I pull back the covers and lift the mattress by the hand strap, just enough to be able to slip the key under the box spring, onto the bed frame. It won't be quite as easy to retrieve it. I'll have to lift the mattress, wedge something between it and the frame to hold the mattress and springs up while I get on my knees and get the key out. I'll use a book to hold the mattresses up, maybe the Frost book. Finally, it is good for something.

My sleep is tormented and I wake late. I don't dare break with my morning routine and arouse concern by indulging my interest in the silver box contents. I'll have to save reading the letter until bedtime.

~~~

This time, as I read, I make notes. There are so many questions about all of this. I wonder whether I need to notify the Securities and Exchange Commission about the alleged insider trading Grandfather did many decades ago, and probably is unable to recall? This is something to ask Mr. Bradford to advise me regarding, since he knew Grandmother. Maybe she told him about this. Maybe not.

What about the government contract information? I suppose that isn't as important as some of the other information in the letter. The fact that Mr. Reed wrote that Grandfather later rewarded him and his friend with key positions in his companies is worrisome. Of course, he is dead
~~~

and the other guy is either dead or old like Grandfather. Jim can get that information.

I guess that's my starting place. I'll give the name to Jim and see what he comes up with, then go from there. I wonder if Grandfather remembers any of this? I wonder if he suspected any residual effect from our investigation last year. Damn, this is still a mess.

Sam briefs me on the investigation details I missed while I was recovering. He kept a file of the letters from the FBI and newspaper clippings, as well as printed anything he found on the internet during that time. I know about the outcome. Some guy got indicted, then committed suicide before he went to trial.

"Great, Sam. I'm glad we have that sorted. If you think of anything else, let me know."

It sounds like it was a superficial investigation resulting in a sacrificial lamb. From what I know now and what I suspect, there is something much more corrupt below this iceberg. Whatever they were, Grandmother had her reasons for hiding this information. I think she hoped I would investigate. I'm not going to let her down.

I ring Chico and arrange for a meeting between the two of us tomorrow at Father's Beach. I ask him to mention it to no one. That beach is used more by L.A. film crews than beach bathers; it's likely it will be vacant.

~~~
~~~

~ CHAPTER 19 ~

The Plot Thickens

Chico is at St. Leo's beach by the time I arrive. This time I leave Garrett at home. I'm not ready for anyone, except Chico, to know what I'm doing.

We sit in the sand. I have a sketch pad and attempt rough sketches of the rock-lined beach while we talk, just in case anyone walks up and sees us.

I brief Chico on the names I learned from the letter, but don't tell where I got the information. I want him to trace those people and see if they are in any way connected to anyone who works anywhere in the McKenzie companies—mine included.

He takes the folded list I palm to him and tucks it in his shirt pocket as he retrieves a pack of smokes. Very smooth. I like his style, even if he does light up.

I continue sketching as we talk. He agrees that they probably think it's pretty safe now, since they skated through the FBI investigation. Maybe they'll relax their guard and get sloppy, or cocky, as he put it. He suggests we look at the major traders of McKenzie company stock, the individual companies, the board of director members, everyone, even the document courier companies. Checking SEC staffers, if warranted, will be a bit more tricky. And we have to look at all "fingerprints" on the government contracts. We'll start with the current contracts and hope to get lucky. Then we can follow the chain backwards and see where it leads us.

"There is another problem, Chico." The way I say the words has Chico's attention more astute. "Remember the guy who shot at me? He spent weeks watching my apartment, missing a lot of opportunities for an easy shot."

Chico says nothing.

"The question is, why wait until I'm at the mansion to take a shot? Had he intended to miss? Was it more of a warning to Grandfather, if he had knowledge of the corrupt activities? The guy who shot the shooter had to be a sniper, not someone off the street with a gun. They never found him, so he must have shot from a safe distance. There would be security cameras on the courthouse entrances. I think this is something else.

"Chico, you can walk away from this, if you want to. I won't think twice about it. You'll still have my trust, and your job is secure. We would say this conversation never happened."

"No, I'm okay to do this. I'll be careful. They won't even know I've been in the system. I can make it look like routine server maintenance, if they do notice."

He needs help, and wants Race onboard. I know we can trust Race, but this could be dangerous. Race has a family. It isn't like I think Chico is expendable, but he's single and has no kids. Me, I'm expendable.

"I trust Race. But he has little kids. Tell him as little as you can about my sniper theory, but make sure he understands that this might be very dangerous. If he has any hesitation, let him back out."

"I will. If there is something else, something that was missed by those piss-ant Feds, we'll get it."

"Be sure to keep the usual reports coming, so Sam—or anyone else—won't suspect we are doing this."

"Of course."

"Thanks. Keep your eyes open. Watch your back. Do you want Jim to assign someone to you, as a 'roommate' or on your staff, or something?"

"Nah. I'll be careful. My grandma lives in the barrio. I can disappear there and no outsider can get to me. My uncles and cousins are tougher than anyone Jim has."

"Sounds like my kind of family."

He takes my tablet and helps me up, since I'm not good at getting up (gracefully) from the ground with my gimp leg. I see a gang tat on his outstretched forearm. Bet he was inducted as a little tyke. Figures. Bet his grandmother made him stay in school too.

"Hey boss, you draw pretty good."

"Buttering up the boss won't get you anywhere that your skills haven't gotten you already." I chuckle. "Seriously, thanks for doing this. Be careful."

We walk back through the tunnel under the highway to our cars.

"I'll keep Race safe. But I'll keep him busy."

"Okay. Chico, let me know as soon as you find things."

"Hey, are you supposed to be driving?"

"I'm good. Just want to keep this between us for now, okay?"

~~~

When I return to the mansion, Zoe gives me a look like she is going to say something about me going out alone. I shake my head to tell her not to ask—and she doesn't. We go to my office and get to work. There are letters she needs me to sign. She updates me on appointment changes. It's mindless activities, which works fine, since I'm still thinking about Chico and the letter, not about working.

I want answers and I want them now. Waiting is going to be the hard part for me. I know it will take months to flesh out the information,
~~~

so I might as well settle down and accept that I can't have the answers immediately. I'll play my cards close to my chest for now, not to tip any suspicion that I'm a threat. With God as my witness, they'll rue the day when I learn what is going on.

If Grandfather is involved, he will have to take his lumps too. I love the old guy and honestly don't think he remembers much these days. My illness and the cousins' deaths have taken their toll on him. They aren't going to do anything to him now.

~~~

Mark and Jake are headed back to California, and we made arrangements for a dinner date.

We give each other kisses on the cheek and tight hugs. Mark gives me a dozen red roses. I've missed them. I'm glad it worked for Mark to change identities. He seems much happier now that he can be himself. Scourge made more money, but I like the new music better. His fan base will grow. He still gets royalties.

"Wow, guys! The limo treatment, eh?"

"Yes, nothing too good for 'our' girl," Mark says. Jake nods agreement.

"So, where are we headed?"

"Anywhere you like, Kathryn," Mark says.

"I want a big juicy steak," says Jake.

"I thought you were a veg—" I say.

Jake laughs. Those goofs. Still at it, I see.

Mark and I schedule a day for just the two of us. Jake smiles like he's playing matchmaker. Mark and I are happy to accommodate him.

Needless to say, we have a great evening and I'm not near as serious when I get home.

~~~

~ CHAPTER 20 ~

Kathryn's Beach
(Two Years Later)

Quietly entering my room after another of the many humanitarian award banquets on my calendar, I set down the crystal award on the table near the door. It feels good to kick off my shoes.

"Ah, what a grand gala." I drop my wrap on the bed, look in the mirror, and begin to remove my diamond earrings. "Kate, it's never a good sign when you begin talking to yourself. It always preludes trouble, big trouble!" I say aloud.

I smile, as I think of the various decisions over the years that have complicated my life and how ridiculous they seem now. Turning around, my gaze is caught by the gleaming shine of the crystal award. Lifting the cool, heavy award, I study the sparkle of the object, its form, and its weight.

It isn't that I don't appreciate the gesture. Certainly, I have earned it with my generous philanthropic works. It is just one more of many "trophies" to add to my undesired collection of awards.

In the beginning, I felt awkward with the recognition. Now, I understand why none of Karen's awards are on display; that's not why we do the things we do. Of course, I understand the need to give awards, the vicarious emotions and excitement the award-givers receive, and need, for a variety of reasons.

Setting the beautiful award on the table, I remove my necklace and place it in its jewelry case, studying its sparkling beauty in the dim light.

"Funny, this necklace is worth more than I would have earned in ten years of social work."

Gently closing the case, I return all of Grandmother's jewels to the hidden safe in my closet. I change into pajamas, then pull the pins from my hair and shake my head to ease the hair out of place, and shake off the formality of the evening. There is something about these events that leaves me fatigued. Sometimes following afternoon society events, I come home, unable to function until I have had a nap.

Tonight, I am refreshed with thoughts of sitting and writing, undisturbed by the world. I crave the quiet moments when I am not required to meet the demands of my social position. I rely less on my diary to release my pent-up emotions and thoughts. As the days passed, I turned to a new method of release, fiction writing, and found it strangely healing and relaxing. It is freeing in an unexpected way that I never expected.

Years of typing reports taught my fingers to fly over the keyboard. I'm slower now with my gimp left hand. I can't keep pace with my thoughts as they unfold into the story of my return to California, now nearly ten years ago.

The interpretation of my memory is questionable. I was careful to make the events in the story pure fiction; they are designed to remind me of something not to be made public. It is the essence of those days that I seek to capture. I'm not worried about the details.

Like a protective mother I have nurtured my manuscript, and my quiet time spent with it. Last night, with a mixture of emotion, I had the distinct sense that the last chapter of the story would be finally written.

With a satisfied sigh, I print the completed manuscript, my first and only work of fiction. The laser printer devours the paper from its generous tray. I lean back in my chair and feel the emptiness I had only a few hours ago melt into a satisfied sense of fulfillment.

Removing the warm, first few printed pages from the tray, I hold them to my chest. I can feel their warmth dissolve my required persona. Lifting the first page, I begin to read. The last page prints and the machine falls silent. It is finished.

While reading, I hadn't noticed the night was gone. Without a hint of egotism, I have an intense sense of satisfaction that I have something that is mine alone. This stack of paper isn't the result of being a quintessential social worker or a McKenzie. It is the product of a human heart, nothing more—nothing less.

I reach for the phone and dial Karen's number. Briefly, I glance at the clock as the phone begins to ring. I grimace. It is only a quarter to six, a bit early to call anyone—even Karen—on a Saturday morning.

"Hello?" Karen's voice reveals that I have awakened her.

I hesitate, then softly say, "Karen, it's Katey."

I hear the sounds of her becoming awake and struggling to sit up in her bed. Quietly, she speaks, "Katey, what's wrong?"

"Oh Karen, nothing is wrong. I, I was wondering if we could meet later today, or maybe, maybe tomorrow?" I am embarrassed that I called so early. As a token restitution for the inconvenience, I offer, "I can send a car for you." Damn! That sounded like a rich spoiled brat, a label that I ordinarily avoid like the plague.

"Keith is leaving in a couple of hours. I have a few things to do this morning. We could meet after lunch, if you like."

"Yes, thank you. I have something to share with you," I say.

~~~

As I hang up, Chico calls. He has the final piece of the "conspiracy theory," as we have come to call our project.
~~~

He must have called from his car because he is at the door by the time I'm showered and dressed. The minute I reach the bottom of the steps, he takes my arm, then leans toward me and whispers.

"Let's take a drive."

"Okay."

He has obviously found something big. We have been playing cloak-and-dagger with our out-of-the-way meetings for two years. Is this the end of the hunt?

Once we are on the road, he calls me "Miss McKenzie."

This is it. I brace for what he is about to say.

"I found the sniper."

"What! You found the what?" That isn't what I expected.

"It was buried pretty good, but I found the payments."

"Payments?"

"Yes, they paid $50,000 to the guy who shot at you from the gate. Looks like he was to get the other half when he killed you, but he missed."

"Wow. That really isn't much money."

"They paid the second sniper five million to kill him."

"What? That doesn't make sense."

"Just wait. I'll give you the overview, but I have all the details." He pats his pants pocket. "I've everything on everyone."

I want to say, "everyone?" but got the cue to let him talk and quit interrupting with questions.

He takes a deep breath and checks the rearview mirror for anyone following us up the Coast Highway. Smart of him to go north where there is less traffic. People do take this road, so someone behind us is likely following us because there isn't anywhere else to go but up the road. But I get his point. Occasionally he slows to see if the car behind him will pass, and they always do.

"I don't know how some of this was missed by the FBI, but I suspect there is some CIA involvement in here. Someone in the government is laundering money through your companies. It's going into offshore accounts at about the time 'things' happen in 'certain' countries."

He takes a breath and so do I. What in heaven's name is all this about?

"There's some skimming from the guys in there who blackmailed your grandfather into this arrangement. I can't find what they had on him, but it must be big."

I know what it is—cheating to win his bet with Grandmother.

"Anyway, these guys are bidding certain jobs they are told to bid, they win the contract, take a cut for themselves, launder some for the 'group,' and still supply the goods."

"Oh crap! This scares me."

"It should. This is bad shit. But as long as they think you are satisfied with the FBI investigation, you're probably safe. You can't do anything about this. They'll get you. And next time, they will hire a better shot."

"Thanks, Chico. You did a fantastic job. I've got to think. This is so—oh, wow, I can't believe this. Oh wow!"

"Don't do anything. I was careful. I don't think they noticed I was there. But God—if they ever find out—"

"Okay, we tell no one. I mean no one, not ever. Where's the info?"

"I brought a copy of everything for you. I've got mine stashed 'someplace' safe."

"Good. Don't tell me where you put yours, and I won't tell you where I put mine," I say.

"If anything odd happens to either of us, the other one goes to the media with all of it. Deal? I can make it look like a media feed from Langley. I just have to—"

"Shhh, jeeze, don't tell me. Let's hope they get me, not you."

"They probably aren't ever going to know."

"Probably not. Let's go back to the house now, Chico."

Chico helps me up the steps to the door, then leaves. Inside, I retrieve my cane from the umbrella stand and head upstairs. I'll put the micro drive Chico gave me in the silver chest with the other information. The key goes back on the mattress frame. I still haven't thought of a better place for it.

~~~

When I arrive, Karen opens the door with a cup of coffee in her hand, and holds it toward me with a knowing grin.

I take the contraband drink. Karen turns back to retrieve her cup and lock her house. Within moments, the limousine is on the freeway heading toward the beach, our beach.

I smile, thinking back at the time when I thought Karen was my worst nightmare. Now I recognize how blessed I was to have met her, and become friends.

"So, what is it that has us out and about today?" Karen interrupts my thoughts, knowing that something is up, since I called her early in the morning.

Before I can speak, my face is consumed by a self-conscious smile. I exhale a breathless confession.

"I have written a manuscript, Karen, a novel!"

She tilts her head. "A novel?" She has a curiously excited, hushed tone.
~~~

"It nearly wrote itself," I confide the ease of the feat. "I know that you love to read. I'd like you to be the first to read it."

"What's it about?"

"A young, well-meaning but misguided social worker who is trying to find her way home again."

"Who is this?" she asks, pointing to the name on the front sheet of the stack of manuscript papers on my lap.

"It's a pen name. I want to see if the story gets published on its own merit—not on the McKenzie name."

After a pause, Karen says, "It sounds interesting. Is the social worker anyone we know?" She has a smirking grin.

"No, it's fiction—lies, all lies."

"Really? You'll have to read it to me. How about it?"

"I'd love to read to you."

"Good, I'd love it, too," she says.

After Garrett and our bodyguard check my condo for intruders, and are content that we are secure, they find the TV remote and begin preparing for the Dodgers game.

Garrett comes from the kitchen and promises to have snacks ready for us before the game starts. The coffee machine is already hissing and dripping the rich brew into the pot. It is obvious that Garrett senses —or hopes—that we will be at the condo all day.

I offer Karen coffee and request juice for myself—my permitted drink. We move to the patio. With the ocean sounds in the background, I begin to read aloud.

"*'And you,' he asks, 'what about you?'*"

Karen says nothing as I read. Occasionally, I glance at her for a reaction, but her dark glasses hide the comments of her eyes. The waves break on the nearby beach in a constant rhythm to my words as I read on through the afternoon and into the early evening.

As I lay down the final page, Karen speaks: "Katey, I had forgotten some of the essence of those years."

"It's pure fiction." I hand her the portfolio containing the story. Karen rubs her fingertips over the luxurious leather case.

She opens the cover and tilts the page into the light.

"I never told you, but I was afraid that you were going to die," Karen admits.

"I know," I say softly. "So was I. Thanks for helping me through that. I wouldn't have made it without you."

"Now, look at you."

Karen squints as she studies my face. It's a long moment of silence. Finally, she looks away and says, "After Maggie—" her voice trails off before she finishes her words.

I reach to touch her hand, then put my arm around her shoulder and tilt my head against hers. I don't feel awkward about telling her I love her and knowing she understands. I know I don't have to say a word, and she understands that too.

"Karen, it's all right. It's not how long we live, it's how wide that really matters."

She looks out at the changing tide. "What did you call your book?" she asks after a moment.

She looks back at me.

I smile widely.

"What? Tell me."

"It's title is, *Kathryn's Beach*."

~~~
~~~

~ CHAPTER 21 ~

Enigma
(Eighteen Months Later)

Grandfather is very ill and it is clear he is dying. I ask Conner to give us the room. Alone, I hold Grandfather's hand and talk to him. I tell him I love him. I tell him I know about the bet and the blackmail.

He becomes restless. He doesn't open his eyes. He hasn't spoken in weeks.

I kiss his cheek and say, "I forgive you, Grandfather. And I love you very much."

He takes an odd breath. It is his last.

~~~

Alistair Winston McKenzie's funeral is a well-covered media event. There is a huge crowd to send him off. Off to where, I do not know. He knows I love him, and that is all that matters to me.

Karen and I rode in the limo to the funeral. When we drop her at her house, I give her a book, *Kathryn's Beach*. It got published. In the book's spine, I hid the key to the silver chest and all the McKenzie family secrets.

~~~

~ Acknowledgments ~

My family, aunts and uncles, twenty-seven first cousins, their spouses, children, grandchildren, and great grandchildren who really do gather for Thanksgiving dinner at a park in Southern California;

To the spirit of our grandfather, Arthur Thomas Stewart, and our grandmother, the love of his life, Minerva Jane Evans Stewart. She was matriarch of our clan, the goddess of wisdom, an example of inner strength, and more importantly the one who taught me to laugh in the face of adversity. Graciously, she left her family a rich legacy;

For research assistance, Chief Warrant Officer 3, Michael L. Tibbs, Sr., USCG, Baltimore, MD; Janice Laman Zitek, my sister-in-law; and David Shrimplin, my cousin.

Special thanks to Terrie Berg, my friend, who started this project when we were snowed in during an ice storm. She called and said she had nothing to read, so I wrote. Terri asked, "Then what happened?" wrote a chapter every night after the kids were in bed and emailed it to her. Without Terrie, there would be no Kathryn. My deepest gratitude is to Terri.

Special thanks to Nidhi Dhawan, M.D., India, for consultation on the medical issues in this book.

Special thanks to Nancy Ross Milner, Ph.D. for fashion design assistance.

Special thanks to Joyce at Design by Joyce for support, advice, and a fantastic website at www.NadineLamanBooks.com.

Special thanks to Ilene Shrimplin Wood for unwavering support and assistance throughout this project.

Thanks for the comments, advice, and commitment:
Elynor Breiding; Tom Brown; Elda Clyma; Judy Craig; Ray Derby; Mary Ann Gabel, Sister Ann Cecile Guame, C.S.J; Father Alvin Herber, C.PP.S.; Asmaa Kadry; Keri Kahle; Karen LaMunyon; Shawn McKee; Beverly Post; Sister Rosemary Rader, O.S.B; Charlotte Stewart Saben; Judge Pauline Schwarm, Retired; Ruth Stewart Selee; Carlene Stewart Smith, and Neil Burton.

~~~
~~~

Made in the USA
Monee, IL
09 February 2025

11714400R00299